SUPERSIZED BLUES

by

Roger St. John

Published by
Corker, LLC
Post Office Box 1544
Grants Pass, Oregon 97528

"Supersized Blues" is a work of fiction. The names, characters, locations, and incidents are the product of the author's imagination, or are used fictitiously. Any resemblance to actual events, locales, or persons, living or dead, is coincidental. The viewpoints and attitudes of the characters are expressed in order to develop the storyline and are not necessarily those of the author.

DISCLAIMER

"Supersized Blues" is a work of fiction meant solely for the purpose of entertainment. It is not intended to be used as an authority on any of the subjects contained therein. Places described are based on the facts of how they used to exist, and still live on in the author's memory, but may have changed in the intervening years. The chapter pertaining to the L. A. Archives is based on personal experience. The Archives used to be accessible to the public, however, it is my understanding that since 9/11 the underground tunnels have been closed to the public, and, as I have been informed, any interloper will be escorted out by bad-ass guards.

We do not recommend this as a "how to" primer on illegal activity. The conditions described pertaining to unlawful gunrunning, have significantly changed where the Federal Government has cracked down, foreclosing the described avenues of such pursuits, and/or have drastically increased the penalties. The same applies to stock manipulation and insider trading. Nor is this book intended to impart medical advice of any sort. The depiction of problems with medical devices is based on lawsuits regarding past conditions that, presumably, no longer exist and should be approached with the advice and assistance of your doctor. The subjects of diamorphine and SV-40 are fundamentally factual but are very controversial and the author does not vouch for the veracity of the claims regarding them. For more information on the carcinogen, SV-40, read "Dr. Mary's Monkey" by Edward T. Haslam, which alleges on page 300 that a genetically altered compound bio-weapon of SV-40 was tested on a prisoner who died within 28 days.

Diamorphine is a combination of heroin and morphine. It is illegal in the United States but is used as a painkiller in Britain. Believe it or not, heroin addicts have a blog wherein a contributor stated that a combination of heroin and morphine would obliterate the pain of even a gunshot. Being an addict does not necessarily make him a liar, so I ran with it. More information is available through Wikipedia. Again, the purpose of the description of these two substances is solely to advance the plot of the book.

"Happiness always looks
small while you hold it
in your hands, but let it
go, and you learn at once
how big and precious it is."

—Maxim Gorky

IT'S HER
2004

A Mercedes S430 screeched to a halt in the drive of a mini mansion in the heart of Beverly Hills. It disgorged three men who walked with a purpose, their heads down. Silently, the door swung open and, with just a nod to acknowledge her, they swept past the maid into the marbled halls of Hal's new digs. "He's expecting us." One of them said in passing.

Hal, a man in his early thirties, approached. He was tall, slightly overweight, with a beefy build. A broken nose, deep brown eyes, and dark, close-cropped hair gave him an aura of determination that was the hallmark of his character. His eyes mirrored concern as he searched the faces of his friends. "Are you sure it's her?"

The shorter, older man and the burly black man answered in unison. "It's her." The third man, a detective, who made a successful living by fading into the background, just nodded in agreement.

"Come on back..." Hal spoke just above a whisper. They all retired to his office where he took a seat behind a large oak desk. Deuce, the large black man, complained, "Why did you have to move to Beverly Hills? Do you know how hard it is to drive from anywhere to get to Beverly fucking Hills?"

It was just a rhetorical question, but it reminded Hal of the remorse he felt ever since he moved in. As small as his house was, by Beverly Hills standards, it far exceeded his needs and he felt like a lonely pinball bouncing from room to room. "Where's the file?"

The older man, called Big by his friends, smacked the file down in front of Hal, and took the only seat on the opposite side of the desk; the other two men stood behind him.

Hal stared at the file, rubbed his face with both hands, and then stared at it again. His stomach did a flip-flop as he turned over the cover to find her face looking up at him. He removed the picture from the paper clip and tried to keep his expression from reflecting the pain he felt. "Four years, four damned long years..." He whispered.

Ray, the detective, made his presence felt in an unobtrusive voice as he softly droned on with the facts. "She lives in Sonoma County...and she's married to a..." He flipped a page in the notepad he held. "...Ed Baker...their address is in the file..."

"Married." Hal spoke the word as if it was the only thing he heard.

1

Big scrutinized him with sympathetic eyes magnified by horn-rimmed glasses into large, dark pools. His thin face sported a mixed gray, well-trimmed, beard and his hands danced with each word to accentuate and give fullness to their meaning. His high pitched, raspy voice waxed philosophical. "Son...though you are not the fruit of my loins...you are the progeny of my creation...an adoption of the heart, if you will...and I feel it is incumbent upon me...more of a demand of the soul to share the mysteries of the universe to enlighten you upon the vagaries...nay...the perversities of life. Whatever your expectations may be...the fantasies of your mind and heart...your plans, your will, your most precious desires...life will not only disappoint...but it will bugger you!" His gesturing hands finished choreographing his speech by pointing a bony finger at Hal.

"My advice to you...mind you, just a strong suggestion, proposal...counseling...perhaps more of an admonition...a plea to your better senses...do not charge like the proverbial bull in the china shop into whatever the situation may be...pushing your way amongst the bric-a-brac...overturning porcelain art...creating shards in your path." He leaned back and turned his head as though he envisioned the wreckage. He quickly turned back again. "Create a plan...plan 'A'...plan 'B' and 'C, D, E, and F' if need be for every contingency...every possibility...every eventuality...and even...I know you don't want to hear this...a viable picture of correctness...an exit plan if things do not pan out your way. Life...being the perversity that it is...the ugly, wretched, deviant thorn in man's soul...it is more likely than not that life will not hand you what you want...so you must acquit yourself with all due propriety, alacrity, and propinquity to the approximation of your goal. In other words; to put it in what I would call a legal term of art...DON'T FUCK UP!"

***

PART ONE

STILL GOT THE BLUES

"Still Got the Blues for You," blared out of the car speakers from a CD he usually played when he was alone, as the night crushed in on him, burying him in reminiscences and regret. The guitar solo struck every nerve, reverberating in the depth of his emotions. It had been so many years—four and a half to be exact—since he had seen her face. The lyrics picked at his wounds. He wondered if she still remembered, or cared, how it used to be between them, or if she only remembered the last, vile things he said to her. The thought could still make him cringe with self-loathing.

He opted to take Highway 101 instead of I-5. With I-5, once he was past the Grapevine, he knew he could stomp on the pedal and fly at 100 miles per hour to eat up the distance between them. But he needed to slow everything down, slow his excitement, his rampant anticipation, and his racing imagination. Deliberately, he took his time. He had mapped out a plan and it was already in play to make sure he could see her alone. Tomorrow, her husband was to keep a business appointment, to review a deal Hal had furtively arranged through one of his front companies. It was an offer he was prepared to finance if it was accepted, but one that would have served its purpose, even if it was rejected.

Rehearsing different scenarios in his head, the thought occurred to him, *Dear God...what will I do if she won't see me...if she slams the door in my face?* It was a real possibility and he couldn't blame her, but the very idea made his heart hurt and he dismissed it. He fixed his attention on her as though his mind could will the outcome of his intended supplications. He envisioned her smiling, running to him, and wrapping her arms around him. *Reality check...that's not going to happen...you had better get down on your knees and beg forgiveness. Married. What did you expect? Of course, she would be married.* His brain paced back and forth like a caged animal and he hit the steering wheel with his fist in frustration, causing his car to swerve to the right. He almost overcorrected as he maneuvered out of a fishtail. He cautioned himself; *Stay focused or you will instantly solve your problem...the hard way.* Then he settled in for the long trip ahead.

His hand involuntarily moved to almost touch the right side of his head as his recollections invoked the feel of her. Visions played back in his mind as if on a looped tape. Every morsel of memory had to be chewed and digested before he started again from the beginning....

***

THE NEW GIRL
1997

Angel City Magazine's headquarters occupied the sixth and seventh floors of the Salter Building skyscraper in downtown L.A. The gossip mill was always grinding at Angel City, since news, trends, and opinions were what they did, but it was not limited to the production of their magazine. Hal Golan, at twenty-eight years old, was the youngest and most able contributing editor at the magazine. However, being well respected did not keep the flotsam and jetsam of office tittle-tattle from washing up at his door.

Martin stuck his head inside Hal's office, "Man oh man...did you see the new girl?" He shook his hand up and down. "Smokin' hot!!" He had the face and personality of a demented court jester, with his lively eyes a bit off kilter, his mouth slightly askew.

Hal looked up, annoyed at the interruption, "Yeah...yeah...yeah. You guys are always going on about some chick and they turn out to be nothing special."

"Not this one. Come on...she's in the lunchroom. Go take a gander." Martin cupped both hands to his chest and slightly bounced them. "I said smokin'..."

"What are you...a tenth grader? I'm busy. I'm sure I will run into her eventually and I'll try not to act like a letch when I do." He turned back to his work. "Calm down or you'll be accused of sexual harassment."

"OK...it's your loss, buddy. I just wanted to be there when your tongue hits the floor."

"Too bad you won't be there to see it."

Later that day Hal passed what could only be the new girl in the hall. *Goddamn, Martin was right!* He thought. Her white suit, with a fitted blazer, perfectly set off her figure. Under masses of long, pale yellow curls, she had a face that was the envy of angels. Her bosom was full, but not grotesquely so, which in L.A. was often seen as the mark of a boob job. With a tiny waist and delicate ankles, she had been superbly sculpted from top to bottom. She smiled and said "Hello." Her voice was as soft as a kitten's. He nodded and averted his eyes as she passed him. A light floral scent emanated from her and he feigned going into the lunchroom to get a glimpse of her behind. His eyebrows went up. *Nice...really nice!* She walked without affectation, but with the sweet undulation of a choice little ass. *I'll be damned if she doesn't look like she just stepped off the silver screen*! Hal laughed at himself. *As if it matters to you...you'll never get near that!* He instantly felt sorry for her. *Too bad the women in this place will tear her apart.* He decided to pour himself some coffee, since he was there anyway, and forgot all about her.

***

The hierarchy at Angel City was clear-cut. The patricians' executive offices and reception were housed on the seventh floor along with the secretarial pool. The executive editor had a separate suite and conference room. The rest of the editors' offices were strung along the edge of the hallway.

The sixth floor held the plebeians, with numerous desks in the open space of a common area. One step above in the pecking order were the research analysts who were afforded cubicles. The managers of each department had separate offices. The rest of the drones that keep an office running, such as those in the mail room, were kept out of sight. Hal, being one of the patricians, only had to pick up the phone to summon his research analyst to his office. "Cora, please come up here. I need to run something past you. I think there may be a mistake." Hal replaced the phone on its cradle and continued to read.

A few minutes later Cora strolled in. She was a round faced brunette with aspirations of being pretty. "What's up, Hal?"

"This has got to be wrong."

Cora glanced at the paper. "Oh that...that's Mari's work." She shifted the blame.

"What's a Mari?"

"Oh...that's the new girl. Her name is actually Marie, but she spells her name with an 'iiiii' instead of an 'iiiii-eeeee'..." She dragged out the vowels valley girl style. "...pretty corny if you ask me...kind of pretentious..." She rolled her eyes. "That is why I call her Maaar-i...to kind of annoy her."

"OK...I just want to know who did the work. Isn't she assigned to Dirk?"

"Yes...but for some reason she gave it to me...to give to you..."

"Please send her up so I can talk to her."

Hal reviewed the Mitchem file that had just landed on his desk. The facts and conclusions were off the mark from what he understood about the recent, sensational, murder case. *What am I supposed to do with this mess? It is total speculation all the way down the line. Vee would fry my ass in boiling oil if I gave him a piece based on this crap.* He referred to Mr. Vougiouklakis, or Vee, as he was called, who was the Executive Editor. *This new girl has made a mess of this thing. I hate to take her down a peg when she is just starting, but she can't get away with submitting sub-par work! No wonder Dirk turned it down...even he wouldn't run with this shit.*

"Cora said you wanted to see me." Mari Carlson walked into his office but left the door open.

"Please close the door." Hal did not like to reprimand an employee where others could hear. "About this Mitchem case...where did you get this information? It is completely contrary to the police report and the prosecution's case."

"Yes, I know. Through a friend of a friend I was able to get copies of the witnesses' depositions. I went through each and every one of them and they tell a different story. It looks as though Mitchem could be innocent. You see right here?" She leaned over to show him the point she was trying to make. The faint floral scent drifted to him and he turned in her direction and got a face full of her hair. "Oh...I'm sorry." She flipped her hair out of the way, over her other shoulder, and continued. "I cross-referenced witnesses' statements that contradict some pretty important evidence..." Abruptly, she stopped and walked over to close the blinds of the glass partition that looked out on the rest of the office. "Dirk will have a hissy-fit if he sees me talking to you."

"If you are right about this...it could be a bombshell." He gave her a quizzical look. "Why didn't you give this to Dirk?"

"I did. But he didn't want it. So, I thought I would do Cora favor and give it to her."

"You were doing Cora a favor...?"

Mari shrugged. "It wasn't doing anybody any good sitting on my desk..."

"I want to see more of this. What do you have?"

"Just the depositions...and that's it. But Mr. Golan...I can't be seen talking to you. I'll get fired..."

"It's OK to call me Hal."

"Alright."

"Can you meet me...at a coffee shop or something...say around sevenish tonight and bring those depositions?"

"I guess so. Where?"

Hal grabbed a slip of paper, wrote down the address and handed it to her. "Is that anywhere near you?"

She looked at the paper and nodded. "I'll be there."

"By the way...I hope you don't mind my asking you this...that perfume you wear...it's quite nice. I can't quite figure out what it is."

"Oh, that's not perfume. I make my own shampoo and conditioner..." She smiled. "The scent is plumeria. Perhaps you know it as frangipani."

"I don't know it as anything. It's new to me."

"Have you ever been to Hawaii where they put fresh flower leis around your neck?"

"No."

She laughed. "Neither have I...but I heard they are made with plumeria. Do you have a special lady?"

"Not at the moment."

"Aw...I was going to give you a set from the batch I made to give to your girl..."

"My mother might like it..." He felt like a dork a soon as he said it.

She seemed pleased. "That's sweet. Then I'll bring some for your mother. I hope she likes it. See you tonight." She opened the door and gave him a tiny conspiratorial wave as she left.

***

Hal was no sooner handed the menu when Mari breezed in carrying a large, green tote bag and a smaller black shoulder bag. Wearing casual jeans, a bulky knit sweater, and a floppy hat, she looked like she was ready to knuckle down to the job at hand. He walked over to her and carried the oversized bag the rest of the way to the table. "Thank you so much for coming. Have you had dinner yet?"

"No. I only had time to grab a muffin on the way out..."

"Well, we'd better order something or they'll kick us out of here." He waved for the waitress to bring another menu. When she did, she fairly sniffed at Mari and tossed the menu on the table. Hal was taken aback. "What got into her?"

"She's probably just having a bad day." Mari studied the menu.

"What...in the last five minutes? She was all smiles just a while ago." He considered broaching a subject about women that made him curious. At first, he decided against it, and then changed his mind. "Mari...women don't like you very much, do they."

She looked up, met his eyes, and then looked back down at the menu. "I don't know. Some do...some don't, I guess. I can't be everybody's flavor of the month."

"Well, I just wondered. I mean, like our waitress...some of the girls in the office seem to be a little catty when it comes to you. I don't mean to talk out of school...but does it seem like that to you?"

She put the menu down and made a little grimace. "Mr. Golan..."

"Call me Hal."

"Hal...they haven't had a chance to get to know me...but when they do..." She thought for a bit. "...they'll still hate me." She laughed and then sighed. "I'm just there to earn a living...not to win a popularity contest...but thank you so much for thinking of me. No one else ever seemed to notice, or care."

"Tell me something else...if you don't mind my asking...your eyes are such an unusual shade of blue...sort of a richer, darker blue. Are you wearing contacts?"

"Contacts?" Her hand flew to her mouth to stifle a snicker. "Mr. Golan..."

"Hal."

"Hal. Are you having fun at my expense?" She chirped. "No...I'm not wearing contacts. Yes...most women hate me. And you, my dear sir, are snapping my panty-girdle...aren't you?!"

"Snapping your what?"

"Panty-girdle...that's something my grandma used to say."

"No...no..." He tried to refute it but succumbed to laughter as they both got a case of the giggles.

They tried to settle down when the waitress came for their order. Hal got it together long enough to order. "The lady...my friend and esteemed colleague...not to mention comedienne ...will have the

10

corned beef on rye with a side of coleslaw. I will have the same along with a well-deserved smack on head." He rapped the side of his head for emphasis.

By the time the food arrived they had the contents of the tote bag spread across the table. She brought three depositions, which were Xeroxed copies, and a legal pad. The pièce de résistance was a new laptop she removed from the black bag. She set it out on the table and flipped it open. Hal watched with fascination. "That's really cool."

"It's the latest model...just released...and it has a lot of innovations. Windows 95 is preinstalled on it, so you don't have to go through that dreaded installation process. Are you familiar with Windows 95?"

"Yes. But I never used a laptop before. How does it work without a mouse?"

"By touch...watch." Mari turned it on, waited for it to boot up, typed in her password, and then lightly dragged her fingers over the touch pad to direct the cursor. "Here...I'll show you. She reached over to take Hal's hand and placed his index finger on the pad. Gently holding his finger, she slid it over the surface of the pad. "The right and left click are below the pad."

Her fingers were gentle on his, almost like a caress. He felt a slight tremor in his hand and withdrew it. "Before we get started, let's eat."

"Good idea...I'm starving."

Mari took a hungry bite out of her sandwich and studied Hal while he ate. He was casually dressed in a pullover shirt, but still had on the slacks from the suit he wore earlier in the day. With his earnest dark eyes, and compelling smile, she thought he had a pleasant face. Curiously, she did not feel wary around him as she did with most men. He seemed direct, unassuming, and honest. Moreover, he listened. *I hope my intuition is right about the Mitchem case. I think he can do the story justice and show up that no talent stinker, Dirk.* She laughed to herself. *It would also go a long way to expose what a fraud Dirk is and that he had his head way up his ass when he asked me, "What kind of dumb blonde bullshit is this?"*

Hal focused on his sandwich as he tried to get the soft feel of her fingers out of his head. *That's not what she's here for and she will*

11

flounce right out of here at the slightest hint of what you are thinking. Bad Hal! Corned beef...yes...bad thoughts...no...corned beef...yes...bad thoughts...no...

Mari's soft voice interrupted his self-condemnation. "As soon as we are through, I want to show you my method of cataloging the contents of the depositions according to relevance. My summaries are quicker and easier to use, but I still think you should read the actual depositions for yourself in order to catch something I may have missed."

After their meal, Mari turned the computer screen to face Hal and went into the Mitchem file. "You see...I have listed the volume, page numbers, paragraph numbers, and a brief summary of each statement. I have also cross-referenced the pertaining statements of the other witnesses." She looked up, searching Hal's eyes. "When you put it all together, you will see that the police report and the prosecutor's version of the case do not exactly fit what the witnesses said. The witnesses do not necessarily disagree with the prosecutor's conclusion...but some very salient points of their testimony do."

"This is a lot of work you did." He scrolled through the pages.

For the next hour Mari walked Hal through the anomalies and conflicting evidence. Three different witness statements agreed on a timeline that differed from that of the prosecution. Moreover, it appeared as though there were other witnesses that were never engaged or questioned to any degree. "Hal, do you think that things were overlooked on purpose? I mean...to the casual observer it looks like Mitchem is guilty...but the prosecution is not a casual observer...at least they shouldn't be. If I could ferret out these inconsistencies...you would think that the prosecution would have done so, too."

"Or, Mitchem's attorney." Hal observed. "Believe me...it is not that unusual for this type of thing to happen...unfortunately."

"Not unusual? But this is a man's life..."

"Tell me about it. There is one thing we must not do when we write about this...and that is to publicly accuse the powers that be of malice in this 'oversight' because we will really have a fight on our hands...and it will be daunting enough as it is to point out these 'glitches' in the case."

"But...these are more than 'glitches.'"

"You know it...and I know it...but we must write it as though they were 'understandable errors' so that we will be listened to. No one wants to think that a governmental entity, especially one that is supposedly meting out justice, would intentionally draw the wrong conclusions or chalk up a case as solved to rack up brownie points."

"Brownie points?"

"Yeah...their 'win-loss' score. Prosecutors' careers are made on wins...not losses...and the defendant be damned."

"That's a scary thought...please tell me you're being cynical..."

Hal's dark eyes grew somber. "I wish I could. I have a friend from college who went on to law school and became a prosecutor. It was a revelation to him how many things determine the outcome of a case that could result in a wrongful conviction. He categorized wrongful convictions in three ways. The first is an honest mistake, where all the available evidence points to one person. The case has been efficiently investigated...honest and straightforward in its prosecution...and in spite of best efforts...the wrong guy was nailed.

"The second is hunch prosecutions. That is where the investigators have a strong sense of the suspect being the perpetrator...and there is some evidence pointing in that direction...but not enough. Depending on the suspect...they can let him go or prosecute. If he's rich he will walk until there is more or better evidence. If he's poor or a minority...they may help the evidence along, with a gut hunch that they have the right guy. If they are wrong...and they have been habituated by innocent people going to jail behind an honest mistake...they tell themselves it was only slightly less than honest...and they really believed the suspect was guilty. Or they can rationalize that the suspect was a bad guy and would have ended up in jail in any event."

Mari was confused. "How can they 'help the evidence along'?"

"By drawing an inference or conclusion that is different from what the evidence suggests. For example, testimony of friends and family might be ignored, while tentative facts are favored. Or, like in the Mitchem case, where they assume the witnesses' time frames are mistaken because they do not comport with the prosecution's theory of the case."

"Oh...how awful."

"The last is truly frightening...the intentional framing of a suspect. Where there is public clamor to solve a case...or a conflict of interest...or a vendetta...where the evidence is phonied up. It can include pressuring the suspect into a false confession...pressuring witnesses into changing their testimony...planting evidence...changing the characterization of evidence in what it is purported to prove and ignoring or concealing exculpatory evidence."

Mari sat open mouthed at the idea that such things could happen, and yet she had before her in the Mitchem case, the strong argument that it did. "Unbelievable..."

"Getting back to my point...this is going to be a tough slog. In the Mitchem case...I think what we have is a 'hunch' situation...but we are going to treat it as though it was an 'honest mistake' in order to have a prayer. From what you have here...it may be a case of the cops were lazy and that Mitchem was convenient...so they ignored the discrepancies."

Mari was hopeful. "So, you are going to take it on?"

"Yes...I think so. I think you have something here. It will take a lot more work...but it's worth it because this is a huge story. Dirk is really missing the boat on this one."

"Dirk the jerk."

"Awww...Mari...that was too easy..." He chided her but his eyes crinkled with humor.

"That's what everyone in the office calls him."

"What if his name was Harry?"

"What if he wasn't such a jerk?" She countered.

"Good point." He looked back at the screen. "This is really impressive. I would like to read it in detail."

"Oh, you can take my laptop home with you. The password is taped to the bottom...you can take it off once you know it. Be sure to plug it in...the battery is pretty low..." She wrinkled her brow "...and, please...please...please...don't go into my picture file..."

Hal squinted and stroked his chin. "Well, I wasn't planning to...until now..."

She leaned her head into her palm. "My boyfriend took a picture of me that's not so nice. It's of me getting into the shower..."

"...and you think I'm not going to look at it? Why didn't you delete it?"

"I didn't think I would be lending my computer to anyone. It's not a bad picture if it's just between me and my boyfriend. But I wouldn't want to go showing it around to other people..." She sighed. "I just thought that this case was more important."

"OK...OK...I won't look at it."

"Liar." She half smiled. "Just don't tell anybody...OK?"

Hal leaned forward not quite suppressing his merriment at her discomfort. "What if Dirk had taken you up on this story angle. Would you have loaned him your computer?"

Her mouth flew open. "Not just 'no'...but 'hell no'." She screwed up her face. "Besides...if that were the case, I could have just used the computer at work. But even if I couldn't...like now...I wouldn't have that jackass touch anything of mine...and the thought of him seeing that picture gives me the creeps..."

Hal's eyebrows raised and he chuckled. "...and the thought of my seeing it doesn't?"

"Well...no...sort of...not exactly. I don't see you as being a cretin...you know...going berserk at the sight of a bare butt. I mean you've seen butts before...and if you see mine, I don't think you're going to go all wacky doodle..."

Hal held up his hands and laughed out loud. "Don't count on it!"

She put her head down on her arm and laughed as hard as he did. "Well, at least you're not Dirk."

"He thinks he can score with you...you know..."

She looked up. "What an arrogant putz!"

"I'll tell him you said so..." Hal teased.

"Swell...pick a fight with my boss for me."

"Nooo...I wouldn't do that. But I have to admit I would love for him to know what you think of him."

"Before I forget..." Mari handed him a gift box. "...this is for your mother."

"Thanks." He looked at the box that was decorated with ribbons and tiny silk flowers. A small card was attached. He smiled. "This is really sweet of you. I'm sure she will love your gift. You know, you're not at all like I expected you to be."

"What did you expect?"

"I don't know. Sort of wrapped up in yourself...superior...looking down at us mere mortals..."

"You've got to be kidding me. Do I come off like that?"

"No...not when I talk to you. I think you are down to earth and rather nice. It's just that you are such a drop-dead looker. Most people who are extremely attractive act as though they are God's gift..." She looked away and didn't seem to take the reference to her looks as a compliment. "I'm sorry. I didn't mean to offend you..."

"No offense...I just thought you liked me as a person." Her blithe mood had changed.

"I do...I really do." Hal hoped he could restore her lighthearted spirit, but as time passed, they both became engrossed in the research. By ten o'clock it was closing time and Hal was ready to call it a day. He helped her pack everything back into the bag and then he reached across the table and took both of her hands in his. "I must tell you two things." His dark eyes studied hers. "First, I want to apologize. People are always labeling and stereotyping other people...and I hate that. Labels allow them to put others into a mental cubbyhole where they don't have to think...or do the work of learning about a person's character. If it had been race or religion...I would never do such a thing...but I labeled you for your looks and it was unthinking and unkind. I am truly sorry..."

She shrugged it off. "I don't think you really meant it that way..."

"The other thing is...I want to thank you for the work you did and entrusting it to me. You've shown a lot of gumption...intelligence...and you did a lot to clarify the issues. I couldn't have done as good a job. You may have saved a man's life." He put her hands back down on the table and grinned at her, "And I am honored that you trust me with your picture...now I am not saying that trust is deserved..."

She blushed. "Oh my God...I've created a monster."

"You know, Mari, this has actually been fun. One of the best evenings I have had in a while. I hope you will continue to work on this project with me...I will pay you extra."

"No you won't. We're in this together...and I won't take a dime. I just hope we can save this guy."

***

Hal checked the messages on his voice mail. His mother had called, but he would see her this weekend and it was too late to call her back. He took the tote and the computer bag to the spare room that served as his office and off loaded them onto his worktable. His desk, on the other side of the room was sacrosanct. It held the novel he was writing, related notes, and was used exclusively for that purpose. He was bushed. All he could think of was to fall into bed. Then he looked back at Mari's computer. He scrunched up his face. *Yeah...I want to take a look.*

He peeled off the password, memorized it, walked over to the desk, and stuck it to the bottom of his top drawer. When he got into her computer he went into "Documents" and briefly perused the names of the files. Her files were clues to who she was, and he made a mental note to look at them later. Then he went to "Easy Photo" and into the stored photos it contained. What he saw was breathtaking. While there were photos of a good-looking guy, who looked like he considered himself a stud and used any excuse to pose without a shirt, most of the pictures were of Mari. Mari at the beach, stunning in a bikini; Mari at home working at her computer; Mari in the kitchen cooking, Mari looking adorable in a robe and slippers, eating popcorn, Mari, Mari, Mari, and yes, Mari entering the shower. Her full, naked back was toward the camera and she was looking over her shoulder, smiling at the fortunate photographer. He felt a tremor run through him. *She was wrong...I have seen butts before...but none quite so splendid...so beautiful. It should be on canvas...framed. Her body is pure poetry...and it does make a man go 'wacky doodle.'* When he finally went to sleep, the delectable image drifted in his dreams.

***

Benny's was a neighborhood bar that, unlike most things in L.A., had existed for years. It had a long bar with a mirror and the ubiquitous televisions strategically placed. In an attempt to become more than it was, it had a pool table in the back room, a bowling machine, and a jukebox that all went unused. Those that went to Benny's did not want to play the golden oldies on the jukebox that made them remember times they were drinking to forget. Those seeking music went to other places where they created memories and could dance to the music that would become the soundtrack of

17

their regrets. Most of the customers were regulars, each with a claim to the seat they inhabited at the bar. The tables, of which there were many, were generally eschewed until Hal and Deuce made Benny's their habitual meeting place at a window table, opposite the middle of the bar.

Even though Monday Night Football would not commence until the end of August, Hal and Deuce continued their habit of meeting on Mondays to have few beers and chew over the past week's events. Deuce was a big man in both height and weight and his dark eyes looked at you in a steady non-evasive gaze that said, "I don't take or give bullshit." His brown face was half covered with a beard that was a little more than a five o'clock shadow. A thin mustache lined the edge of his upper lip. The ever-present skinny brimmed hat covered his shaven head, and his broad, toothy grin was reserved for his friends.

Out of desperation, as a young man, he started a plumbing business that mushroomed into a thriving success but had consumed most of his life. "There are times when I think I am getting too old for the plumbing game." Deuce grumbled. "I put in two weeks straight, including weekends, and now I am going to take off for the next couple of days and do nothing!"

"Quit your bitchin'...you make more money than God."

"That's 'cause He ain't into money...it's not His thing. He's into helping the poor...helping those that help themselves...taking care of fools and babies...listening to all those prayers...you know...all that God type stuff."

"Yeah." Hal sipped his beer. "He really should start charging for it!"

"What you been up to?"

"I think I'm on to something special. There's this girl at work..."

"Oh...you got a new girl."

"No. Nothing like that..." He chuckled. "...I only wished it was like that..." He thought of her picture.

"Yeeaahh?" Deuce eyed Hal. "What does she look like?"

Hal nodded his head up and down. "Oh...she's a knockout alright...but that's not it."

"A knockout huh?" Deuce held out his hand and rocked it. "Where is she on the scale of one to ten?"

18

Hal snorted. "A fifteen."

"Wha...wha...wha...! What you doin' with a fifteen, man? You have to stand on your tippy toes to be considered a five...and you want to go after a fifteen? You gotta be shittin' me..."

"I'm trying to tell you...it's not like that..." Hal paused. "...and I'm at least a seven..."

"I hate to break it to you man...but you a five..."

"The point is that she works in research and she came across some interesting stuff that could blow the lid off a murder case. She's assigned to Dirk the jerk and he nixed it...so she gave it to me. I took a look at what she had, and I think she's right. For the past couple of days, we've been working on it in our spare time." Hal held up his hands. "But really...that's not even it. She did something so...I don't even know what to call it..." A look of puzzlement crossed his face. "...thoughtful...kind...unusual..."

"Well?"

"She gave me a gift for my mother..."

"Your mother?" Deuce made a face.

"It's a long story. Anyway, she put a card on it and you'll never guess what it said."

"OK. See this face..." Deuce drew an air circle around his face with his finger. "This is me not guessing."

"It said, Dear Hal's Mom...da-da-da-da-da...about how she hopes she likes the shampoo...etc....and then it went on to say...'Everyone thinks that Hal is the nicest man in the office. That speaks well of you. You must be very proud. Best wishes, Mari.' Who does that sort of thing out of the blue?"

"Nobody I know." Deuce was puzzled. "Shampoo...?"

"Another long story. I mean it was very sweet of her to do something like that... but she hardly knew me when she wrote it." Hal shook his head with incredulity. "It's kinda weird..."

Deuce scratched his forehead. "You know what's peculiar is that we live in a world where a random act of kindness is considered weird." He shrugged. "Well, at least you know she likes you."

Hal drained his beer mug and held it up to order another and then took a sip out of Deuce's mug while he waited. "I like her too...she's a good kid." He sat Deuce's drink down between them to share. "You're right though. She wouldn't look twice at me. But I'll have you know…I'm a seven…"

"Dream on Bro'…dream on. What does she look like?"

"A walking dream. She has this mass of crazy blonde hair…long…real long…all curlicues and ringlets. On her it looks fantastic! On anyone else…not so much. Her eyes are the most beautiful shade of blue I've ever seen…and when she looks at you…you feel like an ice cream cone that has been dropped on a hot Sunday sidewalk…all melting with nothing left but your hard sugar cone…"

Deuce pointed at Hal with his pinkie finger, waving it back and forth, signaling he sensed bullshit. "I see…it ain't like that…she means nothing to you…not the least bit interested." Giving him a knowing smile, he reached over and cuffed him on the shoulder. Hal cuffed him back. In unison they both exclaimed, "BITCH FIGHT!" and started air-slapping at each other and then fell back laughing.

"Look man, I'd be lying if I said I didn't want her…but like you said…I'm a five…"

"No…I was just shuckin' with you. You're a straight up seven."

***

YOU'RE ON CANDID CAMERA

Hal frantically searched for his file. He was sure he had laid it on his desk and now it was gone. GONE! But how? He felt like he was losing his mind. He double-checked his briefcase and his desk drawers, as well as the trash can. Even so, he knew he couldn't have absentmindedly placed it somewhere else. It was too important.

For weeks he and Mari had worked on the Mitchem case. They had moved from the coffee shop to Hal's place, spreading the paperwork over his living room floor. When they had put together a comprehensive argument that Mitchem was innocent; Hal wrote the proposed article.

When the project was finished, they allowed themselves a little celebration. When Mari stood at the door to leave, she looked at Hal with admiration. "Your facility with words is amazing."

He took both her hands. "This, my little one, is yours. You saw it...you put it together...and you kept me going. If anything comes of this...it is all your doing." He kissed her upturned face on the forehead. "Scoot along home and I'll see you tomorrow."

Now when everything was set for Hal to make his presentation, the file was missing, and the pit of his stomach was up in his throat.

Mari knocked on his office door, "Hal...follow me to the elevator." She said in a hoarse whisper.

"I can't right now. I can't find our file..."

"I knew he was up to something! Follow me now!"

Hal looked both ways out of his office door and then followed Mari into the elevator. While they were collaborating on the Mitchem case, they had taken to using the elevator to communicate at work. As soon as the doors closed Mari started talking animatedly. "I was in the supply room when I saw Dirk coming down the hall. I've been avoiding him ever since you said he had a thing for me...and I certainly did not want him to catch me alone in the supply room so I hid behind a stack of cartons...you know those big cartons of copy paper...and you'll never guess what I saw him do. He climbed up on a chair and put a file on top of that huge cabinet...you know the one that holds toner, paperclips, and stuff and such."

"That's got to be our file. That rat bastard!" Hal punched his fist into his hand. "I just stepped out of the office for a minute. He must have taken it then. You know the editor's meeting is right after lunch.

He wanted to steal our stuff and leave me flatfooted in front of Vee...and probably present it as his own work."

"He can't do that..."

"Sure he can. He can say I stole it from him..."

"No he can't. I'll tell Vee it was your project..."

"And you work for Dirk. He can say you were the one who took it and passed it on to me. Now that we know where it is...let's go get it. But don't let on that we have it. I'll just keep on acting like I'm going nuts looking for it until I spring it on him by presenting it at the meeting."

"Can he still claim it is his...?"

"Maybe...but I don't think so. Without the file he has nothing else...no notes...nothing in his computer...to back it up. If he doesn't present it...it's not his. You said the supply room on top of that cabinet?"

"Yes. I'll go with you."

"No. You keep Dirk distracted. Tell him you've got a problem with something but keep him busy."

"Yuk!" She twisted her face. "The things I do for you!"

***

Mari softly knocked, "Dirk...may I see you for a moment?"

"Yes...what is it?" He was annoyed that she had interrupted his contemplation of flushing Hal down the porcelain fixture. It was all too easy. *Let Hal do the work and I'll will take the credit.* For weeks now he had suspected something was up and he wheedled it out of Cora that she thought Hal was looking into the Mitchem case.

Mari strolled into the room and, instead of taking the chair, she sat on the corner of his desk, crossed her legs, and handed him a paper.

Is she trying to sucker me into a sexual harassment suit? Flashed through Dirk's mind. It had finally dawned on him that Mari could barely tolerate him. That didn't deter him, but just made annoying her all the more amusing. His gaze shifted from the paper to her legs. "Well...well...what's all this?"

Mari leaned over and drew his short attention span back to the paper. "It's the eminent domain scandal." She gently removed the paper from his hand, put it on his desk, and gazed into his eyes. "For a pittance the state took more property than necessary to build a

22

freeway. You know about this...right?" She wanted to drag out her explanation as long as possible.

"Well of course...some of it. But you tell me what you have."

She got up and paced slowly around his office, mainly because she couldn't stand sitting that close to him and because she knew he would watch her walk. *Hal owes me big time for this.* She thought. "You see the state...you know put all those families out of their homes..." She put one hand on her hip and faced him. "...practically on the street. I mean all those little children. The story practically writes itself!" She sank into the chair with her face in her hands. "I'm sorry whenever I think of the children I just tear up." She took a breath. "After taking their homes...and for years..." She put her head in her hands again. *Hurry up Hal!* When it looked like Dirk might get up, she started to walk around the room again. "...for years those homes sat empty. The state didn't need them...and the children suffered..."

There was a knock at the door and Hal stuck his head in. "Have you guys seen a file lying around anywhere?"

"No." Dirk could barely contain a grin.

"Me neither." Mari feigned.

"OK...just thought I'd check on the outside chance." Hal was out the door and down the hall, biting his lip with a worried look on his face for all to see.

Dirk turned back to Mari. "Go on."

"Well...now that I think of it...the story sort of sucks. The children are all grown now, and they probably give less than a fig. Not that the state didn't make out like a bandit...because now it is selling those houses at today's prices. What do you think?"

"No."

"OK...that's all I needed to hear." She fairly skipped out the door and down the hall when a perverse idea occurred to her. *Oh...this will make Hal's day.*

***

When the meeting commenced Hal sat at the conference table with a concerned look on his face. He had asked Vee if he could make his presentation last. *I'll stick it to Dirk when he realizes that he's got nothing and his asshole puckers. It wouldn't be the first time he's come up empty handed, and Vee is getting impatient with him.*

Hal looked around the table. You could sniff out those who had something and those who did not. Dirk looked supremely smug. *He looks like he has it dicked. He hasn't gone to get it yet.* Hal bit his lip to keep from grinning.

After the first two presentations, Dirk excused himself to go to the men's room. When he was gone for quite an interval, Hal gained Vee's attention. "While we're waiting...I may as well make my presentation. It seems that Mr. Nelson is going to need more time."

Someone muttered under his breath. "I hope he didn't fall in."

Martin quipped, "I do."

When Dirk returned to the conference room, Hal had just come to the end of his proposed article. "We do not impugn the prosecutors, or investigators, of the Paul Mitchem case with purposeful, or even negligent, conduct. Even with the best of intentions and diligence; human error, misconceptions, misinterpretation of the evidence, and false impressions, can come into play to distort the conclusions and the outcome of a prosecution. We believe that is the circumstance in the instant case. As a result, justice has been perverted. Paul Mitchem's life will be wrongly confiscated; his wife will be left without a husband, and his children without a father, all to the detriment of justice." Hal paused for affect. "From the Magna Carta to the Bill of Rights, the goal of mankind, and the promise of America, is justice. When we have justice for the least of us, we have justice for all." He closed the folder and his colleagues started to applaud.

"Great work, Hal. That is the best I've heard in quite some time." Vee beamed, "I can tell you right now, that is a winner and we're going with it just the way you wrote it...no changes. I want to review everything you have on it in my office tomorrow."

"Yeah...you've got some great big brass ones to take a slap at the county like that!" Martin said, while still clapping.

Dirk looked flattened and forlorn. With his brow furrowed, he crept to his seat, his face was flushed, and his jacket was ripped. Having no mercy, Martin jibed, "Tough ride on the toilet, Dirk?"

Vee turned his attention to Dirk. "Are you ready to go?"

"I'm a little rattled. I just slipped and tore my jacket."

Vee's raspy voice took on a high-pitched tone of faux commiseration. "Aw, gosh...we're sorry. We've all had bad experiences. But you said you had something big. Let's hear it."

Dirk stood up. "Back in...well. When the state built the freeway...the poor little children suffered. The state took away their homes through eminent domain and threw the children out on the street. Now they are selling those homes for a lot of money..."

Vee screwed up his face, "Am I missing something here? What freeway...whose homes?" Vee looked around the room. "Wasn't that thirty...forty years ago?"

"I think we did that story back in....ummm...the early seventies...or so. In any event the 'poor little children' are all grown up by now." McMurray idly tapped his pencil on the table.

Vee clasped his hands together. "I know you have had a bad day, Dirk, or this would have been unforgivable. You can't tell me you have something big and then come up with this drivel. It would have been better if you had nothing at all." He looked around the table. "Well I guess that's it. Great work Hal. See you tomorrow."

Briskly walking back to his office, he passed Mari in the hallway and gave her a barely perceptible nod to let her know the project was on. To his surprise she quickly slipped a note into his breast pocket and kept moving down the hall. Back in his office, he locked the door and read her note. *I'll drop by your place at seven. Please, please, please be there. I have something to show you.* There was a knock at his door, and someone tried the door handle. Martin yelled through the door. "Open up Golan...I know you're in there. What are you doing? Whacking off?"

Hal opened the door. "You could have at least waited until I came. Have you no decency, sir?"

Martin gave Hal a sly look. "Come on Golan...give it up. What went on in there...?" He gestured back at the conference room. "...you ripped Nelson a new one and he won't be able to sit down for a week! What did you do...and how did you do it?"

"No...you got it all wrong. Nelson fucked himself...as usual."

"OK...then tell me what's going on between you and the Carlson girl?"

Hal puffed up his chest. "You think there is something going on between me and that gorgeous girl? Thank you!" He laughed, "What makes you think there is something going on?"

"Just about every time she gets on the elevator...you dart in right behind her."

"So, I'm a pervert...I like to look at her ass...so sue me."

"Oh...OK. I can understand that." Martin shrugged, and then turned back to Hal. "Then why do you look like the cat that swallowed the canary?"

Hal leaned forward and grinned. "One of these days I will tell you a little fairytale that will get you all a twitter. But for now...get out of here, Martin."

Martin pointed his finger at Hal on his way out. "I know you are up to something..."

***

Mari showed up in western garb. She wore a black fitted blouse with mother of pearl, snap closures and tight, black jeans with studs down the side. Her high-heeled boots and a velvet ribbon around her neck, to which was pinned a red rose, completed the outfit. She carried a camera bag and an evening purse. Hal regarded her with open arms. "And you are dressed for...?"

"I'm supposed to meet Zack at the Country Barn. We're going line dancing. Isn't that swell?" She rolled her eyes. "But before I go anywhere, or do anything, I have to give you this." Mari handed him an envelope. "It is the name and address of Mitchem's attorney. You have an appointment with him on Monday...I also had copies of everything we have couriered to them...so they will have it all when you get there."

"Good work, kiddo!"

"That's not all." She broke into a broad smile. "I had to show you this! Let's go into the kitchen so I can put this on the table." She slung the camera bag from her shoulders and marched to the kitchen. Once there she saw two New York steaks on the counter and two place settings on the table. "Oh...am I interrupting something?" She looked nonplussed. "You were expecting someone?"

"Of course. I was expecting you. Whenever you come over...you never get a chance to eat...so instead of ordering Chinese I thought I would try my hand at cooking something for you."

"Awwww...Hal, that is so sweet. You did all this for me." She walked over and hugged him and that was enough to make it worth it to him. She backed away and stared at him. You could see her mind weighing her choices; she could leave early to meet Zack for an evening of line dancing or stay here with Hal to share the satisfaction of their success. She pursed her lips, "You know what Mr. Golan...?"

"Hal."

"Hal. I'd rather spend my evening with you. I'd rather eat your lovely dinner...show you what's in this bag...and gloat over our success. Trust me...Zack will find some chick to dance with and he will be just fine. Besides, I'm sick of country. I used to like it, but that is all Zack plays and I have country overload. I mean what about opera...jazz...blues...or even rock? Sometimes I think if I hear one more twang, I'll scream. So being able to spend a scintillating evening schmoozing with you is a godsend." Her beautiful eyes sparkled, and he was beginning to get that ice cream cone feeling again.

"Wow...I beat out Zack, country music, and line dancing? Let's hope I don't burn dinner!"

"Do you want to see what I have for you in this bag now...or later?"

"I guess now!"

"Bring the other chair around and sit next to me." She cleared one place setting from the small table and stacked it on the other. Taking the camcorder out of the bag, she flipped open the screen, sat down, and motioned for Hal to sit next to her. They both hunched over the tiny screen and watched as the camera whirred.

Within a few seconds Dirk came into view. He took a chair from one of the worktables, dragged it to the cabinet, and climbed up on it. Reaching over the top he felt around for the file. Not finding it, he felt around again. He paused in confusion and then tried again. Frantically, his hand jumped all over the top as far as he could reach. He stopped, got down, and moved the chair to the front, climbed up again and, started feeling around once more. The chair was not quite high enough for him to see the cabinet top, so, in desperation, he tried to both leap and pull himself up to see where the file was. The chair toppled beneath him and he fell, ripping his jacket on the handle on the way down, landing hard on the floor. He laid there for a moment staring up at the ceiling and then slowly got up, righted the chair, and sat down. You could see the realization creep across his face that someone found that file and probably gave it to Hal. But who—how did they know?? He got up and slammed his fist into the cabinet and shoved the chair across the room. Defeat cowed his head and shoulders as he brushed off his suit and surveyed the rip. Realizing there was nothing he could do about it now; he slinked from the supply room.

Throughout the video they both watched intently. When it was through, Hal howled, "Oh God...play it again!" Now there were shrieks of laughter and they both whooped it up and repeated the playback again and again.

"Mari, how did you get that?"

"Well, I figured he had to go back for the file...so I sort of set up a nest by rearranging the cartons of paper. I stacked them so I couldn't be seen and opened up enough space between two boxes for my camcorder to get a view of the cabinet. Then I turned on a fan to cover the camera sound and voilà! Once it was set up, it didn't take too long before he came into the supply room and I nailed him."

"How is it that you had a camcorder at work?"

Her brow furrowed. "I'd rather not talk about that now. We are having too much fun. Maybe I'll tell you later before I go home...it's probably nothing."

"OK...but you will tell me?"

"Sure." Her mood brightened. "So, tell me what happened in the meeting!"

"We got it...we got the project."

"Yes...I know. I picked up on your little signal."

"It looks like they may want to turn it into a series...like a campaign to free Mitchem."

"Really!?!"

As he cooked dinner, Hal related to her the events of the day. Soon they were laughing again. When he finished, he added, "If it's alright with you...I'm going to ask Vee to trade Cora for you so that you will be working with me. I plan to let him know that the Mitchem project was your baby and that you helped to develop it. It is all the more reason for you to continue with me."

Her mouth dropped open. "If it's alright with ME!?!" She threw her arms around his neck almost knocking him over. "Oh, thank you, thank you, thank you for getting me out of Hell."

"My pleasure. Now sit and eat."

The hour was late and as she turned to go; she became somber. "Hal...?"

"Mr. Golan," He teased.

She laughed and wrinkled her nose at him. "Hal. Would you mind keeping my camcorder for me?"

"What...the fastest camcorder in the west? I already have your computer. Why do you want me to keep your camcorder too?"

"That's what you wanted me to tell you." She took a deep breath. "I'm not sure and perhaps I'm wrong...so please don't say anything...but I think Zack may be stealing from me."

"Come on back and sit down." He sat with her on the couch and took both her hands and looked directly into her eyes. "Tell me why you think so."

"I had a small TV...you know the kind you put on the kitchen counter? One day I came home and went to turn it on while I cooked...and it was gone. I asked Zack what happened to it and he said he accidentally knocked it over and it fell on the floor and broke...and he threw it in the trash. I figured...oh well...and didn't think anything more about it. Then my digital camera goes missing. He said I must have misplaced it...but that camera was expensive, and I am meticulous about putting it away...but it is not as though I couldn't have forgotten where I put it. Then one day I caught him going through my purse...and he said he thought he saw me put his lighter in there. I don't smoke...and I don't do hoot. Why would I want a lighter?" Her eyes started to tear up. "My camcorder and my computer are the most expensive things I own...and I just want to keep them safe until I can find a place and move out."

"Do you think that you are safe with this Zack fellow until you move? Are you sure he will just let you go peacefully?"

"I think so. He's never been violent with me...or anything like that. You know he used to be the picture of respectability. He had a good job at a brokerage firm, nice car, good manners, his own place...and then everything went downhill for him. That's why I let him move in with me...to help him get back on his feet. I don't believe in leaving someone for a run of bad luck...but now I am thinking that it is more than just bad luck. I think he is on something or why else would he steal? If that's the case...I don't want to be anywhere around him. That's something I can't fix in him...and I am thinking at this point...why should I try?"

"Do you love him?"

"No...not now." She shook her head. "I'm not sure if I ever did. I thought I did at one time...but it could be that I just liked him a lot. You know being lonely is a terrible thing and it sometimes makes you accept people into your life without giving it the critical consideration you should. He was sort of witty...he was smart enough...but now...we hardly talk."

"Does he love you?"

She quickly shook her head, "No. I don't think so. There may have been a time when he was infatuated with me...but I think that is a different thing from love. A friend once told me that he wanted me as a trophy on his arm. I didn't believe her at the time...but now I do." She lowered her head. "Now I feel like I am just one more girl...just another notch..." Her voice took on an edge and she didn't finish the thought.

"I find it hard to imagine that he has you right there in the palm of his hand...and he doesn't love you to pieces." Hal sighed. "I can't stop you from going back home...I would if I could because..." Hal felt desperate, but he had no right to control her life. "Look Mari...you know you can stay here. I'll sleep on the couch...I would never ever bother you. I have such a bad feeling about your going back."

"Hal, I'll be fine. I'm probably overreacting anyway. I just think it's time to move on with my life...because I feel I'm going nowhere." She slipped her hands from his and her face brightened. "I really had a wonderful time, Mr. Golan."

"Hal."

As she got up to leave, she handed him the camera bag and kissed him on the cheek. "Hal."

***

30

For several days Hal was at loose ends. At the office, Mari only passed him in the hallway with a tiny, furtive wave. The transition to being reassigned to Hal was a slow process, made more so by Dirk holding things up. With the project on hold, Mari had no reason to come to his house and he sorely missed her. He returned again and again to her pictures and, yes, he went "all wacky doodle." Picking up his desk phone he started to call downstairs to her cubicle and then put the receiver down again. He wanted to ask her to dinner but had no excuse to do so. He picked up the phone again. "Hey kiddo...you want to go to lunch and chew the fat?"

"Yeah. Things are crazy here and I could use a break."

"OK...meet me at Waldo's"

"Where is Waldo's"

"It's at..."

"Silly...I know where it is. It was a joke."

"OK...smarty. See you there at one." He put down the phone and breathed a sigh of relief. *"Now that wasn't so hard...."* He told himself.

***

Mari was already waiting at one of the outdoor tables when Hal arrived. "Hope I didn't keep you waiting too long."

"No."

Her usual smile at seeing him was absent so he asked her, "Is something wrong?"

"No...just everything..."

He took both her hands, "OK, little one, tell me what's wrong..."

"At work or at home...where shall I start?"

He wanted to find out about what concerned him most. "At home..."

She slowly shook her head back and forth. "Zack crashed my car...totaled it."

"When?"

"Last night. I gave him the keys so he could go visit his...'mother'..." She made air quotes. "He wasn't hurt or anything..."

"How did it happen?"

"He said he hit a big rain puddle in the middle of the street, hydroplaned, went into a skid, and hit a tree."

"Do you have insurance?"

"Not for the car. You know it was just an old beater...but it was paid for. I didn't think it was worth the extra premiums..."

"Is there a police report?"

"It usually takes a few days before they are available...but there should be. He said the cops had the wreck towed. I'll go get the report next week."

"How did you get to work?"

"I did something nobody ever does. I...took...the...bus!" She looked heavenward. Bus transportation in Los Angeles is notoriously slow, even during rush hours, and the passengers were sometimes questionable.

"Oh...how horrifying for you." Hal sympathized. "Perhaps there is something I can do to help. You're dead meat in L.A. without wheels. I'll see if I can arrange to get a company car for you. Meanwhile, I'll give you a lift home after work."

"You don't have to do that." She changed the subject. "Now let me tell you what is going on in research. Cora is purposely being a slow learner because she doesn't want to work for Dirk...and he is throwing a monkey wrench into the whole transition process by insisting that we trade the projects we started, rather than carry them to our new assignment."

"He's not trying to get the Mitchem project...?"

"No...that is a lock for you...but with everything else he is insisting that we walk each other through it so that he keeps the projects I started working on and you keep Cora's. It would be a lot faster if I just brought my work to you...instead of trying to bring Cora up to speed on what I'm doing...and vice-versa."

"How do you feel about chucking it all? Cora can work on what she has in the pipeline while she is figuring out what you were doing. Maybe Vee can kick some ass and speed things up."

"I don't know. There are a couple of juicy stories..." She squinted in thought. "...but Dirk doesn't know about them..." She smiled. "...I'll take them with me."

"What's for lunch? Hamburgers...chili dogs...burritos...?"

"I'll have a chili cheese dog...and a Coke."

They ate in silence, without etiquette, wolfing down their hotdogs and licking the dripping chili off their fingers. Mari paused, wiping her mouth with an overused napkin, "You know...I really miss you. You're so easy to be around and talk to...about anything."

Hal found it hard to swallow his food past the lump in his throat. After a pause he said, "I miss you too."

At the end of the day he looked for Mari to drive her home, but she had already left.

***

A woman boarded the bus late at night. There were only three passengers on board. She limped and her face had been battered. "I can't pay." She whispered with an unspoken plea in her voice.

The driver's jaw tightened as he looked away. "How far you goin'?" He spoke softly.

"I want to go to Silverlake."

He reached over and took a transfer, punched it, and handed it to her. "You gonna need this. Now, you sit right there where I can look out for you."

"Thank you."

***

When the door buzzer sounded, Hal was waiting for the start of the "Tonight Show." He was going to watch the monologue and then go to bed. He looked at his clock. It was almost half-past eleven. *That can only be Deuce. His wife probably locked him out...again.*

As he approached the door, he heard a soft mewing interspersed with sobs. "Hal...Hal..."

"Mari?" He yanked the door open to find Mari bracing herself against the door jam. Her head was down and her hair covered her face. The sleeve on her blouse was torn and she was holding her right foot slightly off the ground. "MY GOD WHAT HAPPENED!?!" He went to her and she slumped in on his chest. He lifted her up and her hair fell back revealing her face. He heard himself cry out between his teeth as his heart exploded. Carrying her inside, he gently laid her on the couch. "Did he do this to you?" Tears were now openly running down his face.

Every bit of her physical resources had been used up trying to get to Hal. Now that she was there, she was exhausted and on the verge of passing out. "The pink slip was gone. I looked for the pink slip and it was gone. He sold...my car. I told him I knew what he had done, and I was going to call the police. He...he...pinned me down and I couldn't

33

move…and he kept hitting me." She broke down sobbing. "He threw me out of my house with nothing…no money…no place to go. I didn't know what to do. I thought if only I could get to you…you would know what to do." She started to cry again.

He moved onto the couch with her, lifting her onto his lap he held her to his chest and rocked her back and forth. "You did the right thing. I'll look after you. You're safe here. Shhh…don't cry…I'm here."

After a while she fell asleep with only spasms of sobs between breaths. He carried her to his bedroom and tucked her into his bed. He looked at what Zack had done to her beautiful face and for the first time in his life, he wanted to kill.

***

Hal called Deuce in the middle of the night. When he arrived, Hal checked on Mari to see that she was soundly sleeping and then signaled to Deuce to follow him outside. They went into the garage where they could talk in private. "I want to kill that motherfucker…I want to tear his cock out by the roots and make him suck it! I'm going to stomp that piece of pig shit into a grease stain…I want to shoot him full of holes…I need a gun…I really need a gun!" Hal paced up and down in the garage while his friend interspersed his pronouncements with, "Naw, man…no you don't…that's not the way…you ain't supposed to touch pork…I ain't getting' you no gun…forget that."

Deuce could see that Hal was not going to calm down, but he tried to talk sense to him. "Look…by everything you say…she ain't even your woman…!"

"She came to me, Deuce…she came to me! Are you going to help me or not?"

"Of course I'm going to help you. I've been sitting here for half the night watching you walk in circles talking like a crazy man. All I'm saying is we can't go throwing our weight around like some two-bit mafia. We have to work out what we're going to do…make a plan and stick to it. Now, she has to get her stuff out of her apartment…right?"

"I haven't discussed any of this with her…but yeah…she's moving in here." Hal pointed to the ground to indicate that he had made up his mind that's how it's going to be. "If she wants to leave later…that's up to her. But until then…I'm looking after her."

Deuce raised his eyebrows and stared at him. "OK. What you said. Now, when we go to get her things, you can take care of some business there...and tune him up...but you ain't goin' to kill nobody. Are we straight on that?"

"Yeah."

"Promise?"

"Yeah...yeah...I promise..."

"Good! Now, here's how we're going to go about it."

***

A week later the Two-Bit Mafia got rolling in Deuce's van. Deuce and Hal sat in the two front seats and were dressed in coveralls to appear like hired movers. Mari sat on the bench seat behind them. At the hospital it was discovered that she had a lateral malleolus fracture and wore a walking cast on her right leg. Dressed in cut-offs, a sweater, and one sandal she was only there to identify her property. Since she had rented a reasonably priced, furnished apartment in Hollywood, with no furniture to move, all they had to do was to collect her clothing and other belongings. Around ten in the morning they pulled up to the Rosewood, a California modern apartment building, with a pool as its central feature. It was painted a light gray with Sago palms decorating the front. "Is there an alley to the back of the building?" Deuce turned to Mari.

"No...there is only the one driveway."

"Well, that's it...we're parking out front. Let's go."

Armed with tape guns, flattened cardboard boxes, and a dolly, they proceeded up the stairs. Hal assisted Mari as she gripped the wrought iron railing while slowly making her way along the second story walkway that overlooked the pool. Approximately halfway down the passageway, she approached a door and knocked. "Zack...it's me. Please let me in."

They heard movement inside the apartment, and they helped Mari to move to one side of the door. When the door opened, Hal and Deuce rushed Zack, bowling him over. "This is your surprise party...motherfucker." Hal had his fists up and danced like a boxer while waiting for Zack to get up. "You like beating up on women...huh? Come on...come on you pussy!" Zack scrambled to his feet, swung and missed. Hal's fists were a blur as he put him down again. That wasn't enough for Hal. He half lifted him by his shirt and whaled on him some more.

"Whoa...whoa...come on man...you promised..." Deuce intervened.

Hal backed off. "Ok...bring Mari in and let's get this show on the road."

As Mari walked into the room, Zack moaned, turned over, and cleared his head enough to glare up at her. Now that the tables were turned, he could not intimidate her. "How does it feel, Zack?"

"You bitch." Zack spat out the invective, along with a tooth, as blood streamed from his mouth and nose.

"What did you expect...for me to be a good sport about your stealing my stuff and beating the shit out of me?"

Zack made a move toward her and Hal had him down in an instant with a knee on his chest. The man couldn't move or breathe. "Calm down, cowboy, or I'll put your lights out for good." He lifted Zack by the hair, like a rag doll, and threw him in a chair. "You stay right there and don't make a move until we're gone."

The first thing Mari did was to look for her purse. Just as she thought, her credit card and cash were missing from her wallet. *Thank God Hal had me cancel my card.* She was also glad that he had her give notice that she had moved. Hal cautioned her that Zack was probably into drugs and she should take her name off the apartment immediately. She decided not to mention the missing money with Hal on the rampage. *If I can get out of here with my things...I'm good.*

From the bedroom the sound of Mari taping boxes, and of Deuce dumping the contents of drawers into them, could be heard. Next came the rattle of kitchenware. Before long Deuce had the dolly loaded with several boxes and made the first of several trips downstairs. Then came her clothes, unboxed and still on hangers. When all was packed in the van, Deuce came up and said, "That's all of it...we're ready to go."

"Take Mari down and get her in the van. I'll wait here and give you ten minutes, and then I'll be right down."

Hal checked the clock. It was almost time to leave, and then looked back at Zack. He saw a tight little smile cross his face. It annoyed him that this little shit had the nerve to be arrogant about his situation.

36

As Hal went outside the door he turned. "Look you fucking prick...if you ever come near Mari again...I will kill you. That's a promise."

"You think she's worth all this? I'll have you know that for the last month that little whore has been fucking her boss...and she will play around on you too."

"She's been fucking her boss, huh? I'll bet you'd like to have a piece of him."

"Yeah...and I'll kick his ass into next week!"

Hal laughed and gave him a broad grin. "Yeah...well come on..." Hal motioned for him to come over. "...the man she's been fucking is me!"

A look of uncontrolled rage crossed Zack's face. "YOU!" He jumped up and charged full speed at Hal to tackle him. As he came flying through the door, at the last split second, Hal sidestepped him. Zack went sailing, headlong, over the railing, landing splat on the poolside cement below.

Hal's eyes went wide with shock. He quickly looked around and then it took him two seconds to realize he needed to get out of there fast. *Oh shit, oh shit, oh shit! Don't run...don't run. Try to look normal.* He walked briskly to the van and once inside he started yelling at Deuce. "GET US OUT OF HERE NOW!! GO...GO...GO!"

Deuce started the engine and stepped on the gas. "What's going on? Are you nuts?"

"Not too fast...not too fast...don't draw attention." Hal tried not to look back.

"What do you mean?" Deuce's eyes darted back and forth at Hal.

"Something happened back there. Something so wild and crazy I can't believe it. I was getting ready to leave...and I said a few things...you know like leave Mari alone...and he came at me. You know...hard charging...and when I realized what was happening...in the very last moment I stepped to one side...and he went flying over the railing!"

"You...you...you...threw that man over the railing?" Deuce screwed up his face.

"I DIDN'T THROW HIM...HE JUST WHIPPED PAST ME AND OVER THE SIDE HE WENT!!"

Mari looked back in the direction of the apartment. "Zack fell over the railing!?! Maybe we should go back!"

"NO! We're NOT going back! We don't want to have to answer any questions!"

Deuce shot Hal a look. "WE?! What do you mean WE! I ain't answering no questions...I WASN'T THERE!! I KNEW YOU WERE GOING TO KILL THAT MAN...I JUST KNEW IT!"

"I DIDN'T KILL HIM!"

"Deuce...if Hal said he didn't kill him...I think we should believe him. Besides...we don't know he's dead."

"That's right...that's right. Very good point, Mari."

"Hal you said you were going to kill him...and now look what you did. I didn't sign up for this..." Deuce squinted at Hal.

"It was just a figure of speech! I didn't mean *kill*...kill!"

"Did anybody see you?" Mari whimpered.

"I looked around and I didn't see anyone. You know I think Zack was just as shocked as I was when he went over that railing...because all the way down he didn't make a sound!" Hal made a downward motion with his hand.

"I think we should all calm down right now and just go home." Mari nervously nodded her head up and down. "Yes...that's it. We...we will just all go home like this never happened."

The Two-Bit Mafia made their escape.

***

JUST THE FACTS MA'AM

Two men in suits stepped off the elevator on Angel City's seventh floor and went directly to reception. What differentiated them from the rest of the suits in the office was the holster bulge in their jackets, their coiled-spring demeanor, and the unmistakable L.A.P.D. swagger.

Hal started down the hallway and immediately spotted them and knew in an instant exactly why they were there. He turned, went back to his office, and picked up the phone. "Mari, you know what we talked about? They're here. I'll be right down to wait for them to buzz you." He grabbed some papers to look as though he was taking them to Mari.

She was surprisingly calm and in control when he got there. She spoke sotto voce. "Hal, let me handle this. I know exactly what to say. You're just with me to help me walk…and you know nothing, and you say nothing. Agreed?" She was adamant. "Besides, it was my name on the rental agreement…they will only want to talk to me. No matter what happens…don't say anything." Her phone rang. It was Vee. "I'll be right up."

The two detectives were standing next to Vee's desk, when Hal assisted Mari into the office. Vee rushed to her other side to help steady her. As he did, he explained why he sent for her. "Mari…these gentlemen are from the police department and they would like a little of your time to answer some questions."

Mari looked bewildered. "Ask me questions?" She gazed in the officers' direction and then fidgeted against the attempts to seat her in a chair. "It's easier for me to sort of lean against the desk." Vee and Hal accommodated her, and she half sat on the desk, leaning back on both arms. To be as inconspicuous as possible, Hal retreated to the chair at the far end of the office. Her eyes fixed on the officers once more. "In what way may I help you?"

The older one asked the questions, while the younger one regarded Mari as a hungry man regarded a pork chop. "We found your name on the rental agreement of apartment fifteen of the Rosewood Apartments."

"Yes?"

"How long did you live there?"

Mari looked as though she was searching her memory, "For about ten months or so."

"Do you know a man by the name of Zachary Allen?"

"Mari's face turned dark in a perfect combination of angst, anger, and embarrassment. "I am ashamed to say that I do. He was my boyfriend." She looked at Vee. "I know I said that I fell...because I was too ashamed to say what happened..." She turned back to the officers, "...because Zack did this to me..." She made a sweeping gesture with her hand to indicate the vestiges of injuries to her face and the cast on her leg. Although her face was still marked by some bruising and a cut, it was on the mend and she had the look of a battered angel. It tugged at the heartstrings. "...needless to say, I left him. Is he in some kind of trouble?"

"When did you leave him, ma'am?"

"About three weeks ago." She lied, but they were satisfied with her answer because it confirmed the date that the apartment manager had given them.

"Was he living at your apartment?"

She bowed her head. "I am mortified that I was ever mixed up with the man Zack is now...but he wasn't always that way. He used to be what mothers refer to as marriage material. I don't know what changed in him." She looked up at the younger officer. "Yes. We were living together...but I caught him stealing from me and we had an argument about it...and he..." She put her hand over her mouth and her eyes became moist; she looked away. Gathering her composure, she looked back at the officers. "What has he done now?"

The young officer visibly swallowed and looked down at his feet. The older one quietly said. "We are investigating his death..."

Mari's face crumbled, she slightly bent over, and her hand went to her stomach. Hot tears sprung into her eyes. This time, as the demise of Zack was confirmed, she was not acting. She truly felt sorrow for someone she once cared for. "H-h-his death?" She stammered "How?"

"We're not sure...but the door to the apartment was open...and his...he was found by the pool. We believe it was probably the result of an accident...that he fell over the railing. But we have to investigate these things."

"God...his poor mother. When did it happen?"

"A couple of weeks ago."

"Mari's eyes opened wide as though a thought occurred to her. "You don't think he committed..." Her mouth flew open and she started sobbing. "Oh my God...it can't be my fault...could it?"

"No...no...it wasn't a suicide..." The younger officer went to her and put an arm around her shoulders to comfort her. "...they found cocaine in his system. He probably went outside and just fell." After seeing Mari, and now knowing that the DB had recently lost her, the officer did think that suicide was a distinct possibility, but he did not want to burden her with that thought.

Vee offered Mari a Kleenex. She gratefully took it. "This is very difficult for her. Are you almost finished?"

The officer stepped back. "Just one last thing...can you give us the name and address of his mother and tell us the names of any of his friends.

"Yes. I'll write it down for you." She held out her hand for the officer's pen and notepad and wrote out Zack's mother's information. "He did have some friends where he used to work. But after he was let go...they all disappeared. I really don't know his recent friends...or if he had any for that matter. For a long time now...Zack would come and go as he pleased. We weren't that close anymore, and I focused on my job." Mari sighed. "He was on cocaine..." she whispered. "It was all so hopeless then...." She trailed off.

"If you will...write down the name of the company where he worked, as well, and we will be on our way."

When they left, the older one said, "I think it was an accident. He was higher than hell and just stumbled over the side."

"That's what I thought until I got a look at his girlfriend. Now, suicide is a front-runner in my mind. Can you imagine what he felt like knowing that he fucked up with a dame like that? I would croak myself too!"

"Like you don't have enough women problems as it is...."

***

"My God, Mari...you were Meryl Streep in there! Real tears and all! You had those officers eating right out of your hand!" Hal finally had Mari in the privacy of his car, where he could praise her performance, as he drove them home. "Pass the envelope please...and the best actress award goes to...Mari Carlson!"

"Most of it was an act...there are times when life forces you to do what you have to do...but the tears were real." She shook her head. "Looking back, I could probably tell exactly when he started using cocaine. You know...right up until the officer said he had died...I hoped he was alive. There again...he would have been severely messed up." She looked out the window. "Zack asked for everything that happened to him...but it is still tragic..."

"After what he did to you...you can still feel sorry for him?"

"Hal...he was a lost human being. I know he was the architect of his own fate. But that does not make it any the less sad. Besides, I didn't want the officers to think you did it and the thought of that scared me more than anything."

"Mari...I didn't do it..."

"I know...I already said I believe you..."

In a way, Hal was miffed that she thought he didn't have the chutzpah to kill. "What? You believe that I couldn't have killed him for what he did to you?"

"Oh, for Christ's sake!"

***

"What's all that?" Hal wandered into the kitchen in search of something that would pass for lunch and found Mari at the kitchen table with what looked like surgical instruments, laid out on a towel, and an artist's selection of colors.

"I finally found my manicure stuff..." She fanned out her fingers. "...and boy am I overdue."

"Your nails look fine to me..."

"Far from it...wait until you see them when I'm finished. Would you mind getting me a small bowl of warm water...?"

"Sure...how small?"

"Large enough to soak my hand..."

He came back with the bowl and sat down. "Do you mind if I watch?"

"No...in fact...let me see your hands. Just as I thought...you could use one too."

She put a few drops of liquid soap into the bowl, agitated it with her fingers, and then let her hand soak in the water.

"Me? I don't know how to do that..."

"Don't worry...I do. When I'm through...I'll give you a manicure too...if you want..."

"Sure...I'll give it a try." He smiled. He watched with fascination as she went through nipping, pushing, and filing until her nails were perfect ovals. "What color are you going to paint them?"

"Until I finish doing your manicure...I'm not painting them. But I was thinking that since I am relegated to home and office...I'll probably go with a nice shade of pink. We'll need fresh water for you."

"Why pink for home and office?" He rinsed the bowl and filled it again.

"Because it's demure...in good taste..."

"What about those browns, greens, blues, and reds?" He returned to the table.

"The browns, greens, and blues are for fashion statements...the reds are flirtatious...and the tiny jewels, flowers, and doodads...are for both..."

"Amazing...it's another whole world of art...and sending subtle signals."

43

"Do you have a TV tray or something...it would be easier to work on..."

He went to his office, returned with the small table, and set it up between them. Then he shifted his chair while she laid out the instruments. She took his hand and looked at it. "Good to see you're not a nail biter...but they could use more care..." She added soap to the water bowl, put his hand in it, and pushed it down until it was submerged, with the water rising to the very top. "We could have used a larger bowl..."

After a while she took his hand out and laid it on the towel, patting it dry. Shifting the bowl to the other side she placed his other hand in it and then started to work on the first, cutting his nails to a uniform length. Her touch was light, as she held each finger in turn, and it sent a little zing of pleasure coursing through him. She brought out the nippers and went in search of hangnails. "This one looks like it must hurt."

"Yeah...it does a little..."

"Let me know if I hurt you when I go to cut it...I can file it if you want."

"Naw...go ahead."

Because she was doing it, the little jab of pain felt good. She ran her finger over where the excised hangnail used to be. "How's that? It shouldn't hurt now..."

"That feels great..."

She smiled and went to work on the rest. Arming herself with an orange stick, she tenderly pushed back his cuticles. "I may have to go over these a second time...with some cuticle remover..." She thought she sensed a slight tremor in his index finger, and passed it off as nervousness, but by the time she got to his little finger it was apparent his hand was shaking. "Are you OK?"

He pulled his hand back a bit. "I've never had this done before..."

She took his hand again. "It's OK...I'll only be a little bit longer." Applying cuticle remover to each finger, she let his hand rest. Lifting his other hand out of the water, she dried it, started cutting his nails, and then noticed that there was trembling in that hand, as well. She looked up to find him shyly looking down. His gaze was soft when he lifted his eyes to hers, but he pulled his hand away.

"I normally live here alone, Mari…I'm not used to this much attention…your hands are very gentle…and the touch of them…"

"I understand…it's OK." She said softly and then took his hand in hers and began to work on it again. Keeping her eyes down she asked, "Why don't you have a girlfriend, Hal?"

"I did until four…no…five…six months ago…"

"What happened?"

"I was putting in so much time on a story…Cora was never that great…I was doing her work as well…that my lady friend just got tired of waiting around for me all the time…I guess…and she found someone else…"

"You're a decent looking guy…I would think that some girl would have swooped down on you in six months' time…"

"Oh…I've had some swoopers…but no takers…"

Mari laughed. "What does that mean…one-night stands?"

He laughed and shrugged. "No comment."

She looked at the clock. "We have to get this hand into the water now and rinse off the cuticle remover…" She switched the water bowl to the other side and dunked his hand in.

"Mari, you said I was a decent looking guy…as an objective opinion…what do you think of my looks?"

"In one word…masculine."

"Don't all guys look 'masculine'?"

"Oh, no…most guys don't…they look male…but not masculine." She looked at him with a tight little smile. "It's a quality…not all guys have it…but if they do and have other good features with it…it can be quite attractive…and even downright devastating…and with your hair close cropped the way it is…it only magnifies the effect."

"Do I have good features?"

"Yeah."

"Well?"

She looked up from the finger she was working on and squinted at his face. "Your best feature…is your eyes…they're so dark and expressive…penetrating." Her face turned serious as though she was looking at his eyes for the first time, with more than a little surprise. "…your eyes are sort of compelling…" Her gaze moved over his face. "…your next best feature is your mouth…especially your smile…it's very charming. After that…you have a wonderful nose…and I think

45

that is what gives you your masculine quality...because it's different...rugged...like it's been broken right here..." She started to ask how his nose was broken but changed her mind. *If he wanted me to know he would have told me.* She placed her finger on the bridge of his nose and drew it down as she described it. "It starts off as a Roman nose...but right about here...just as you are about to get to the tip...it looks like it changed its mind and wanted to do something else...and at the very tip here you have a slight cleft. All in all...you have a very pleasant face." She went back to work on his finger.

"But not handsome...?"

"No...you are what girls would call...masculine...it definitely puts you in the running in any girl's book. Besides...you have big guns..."

"Big guns...what's that?"

"Your arms...you've got big arms...and you're a big guy...that counts for a lot too." She stopped as a thought occurred to her. "If my being here gets in the way of your being swooped..."

"No...if I'm going to get swooped, I'd rather take it to a motel anyway...not where I live."

She finished his nails and to complete the manicure she warmed hand cream in her hands and started massaging his hand and forearm. "This is unscented lotion...so you're not going to reek like a petunia..."

"Oh, God, Mari...that is too sensual..." He closed his eyes. "...you're giving me a chubby..." She went on and massaged his other hand and arm as he enjoyed the onslaught. When she was through, he laughed, "Well aren't you going to finish me off?"

With a smirk, she handed him the lotion. "Go finish yourself off!"

***

DOMESTICATION

As the time grew near for Mari's cast to come off, Hal became morose at the thought of her being self-sufficient and moving out. When the doctor said that she should take her time getting back into the swing of things, and that she needed to rebuild the strength in her leg by doing daily exercises, Hal felt like he had a reprieve from being sentenced to being alone again. In a desperate move, he took off from work, cleaned out his spare room, and then awaited delivery of the bedroom furniture he ordered. His inviolable desk found a new home at the window end of the living room.

All during the drive to pick Mari up from work, he was assailed by doubtful butterflies beating their wings against the wall of his stomach. *She is going to think it is presumptuous of me.* Then he bolstered his courage. *No...she will be delighted because she has no place to go right now. It will be a way of letting her know she is welcome to stay.*

On the drive home Hal was unusually quiet. Mari tried to engage him in conversation, but he would abruptly end the flow of banter with short answers. "Where were you today? I rang you for lunch..."

"I had some things to look into..." He didn't expand on the subject.

"There's been some interesting goings on..." She looked forward to sharing the gossip with him.

"Right now I'm trying to think. You can tell me about it later."

"OK." Mari took a sideways glance at him. He was definitely preoccupied with something.

***

"Close your eyes and follow me." Nervously, Hal walked into the house, but Mari didn't follow.

"Hal...do you want me to close my eyes...or follow you. I can't do both!" Mari laughed.

He smacked his forehead and laughed with her. "Come on." He went back and took her by the shoulders to guide her forward. He stopped at the spare room door that was now her bedroom. "OK...open your eyes." He held his breath.

Mari opened her eyes. "What is all this?"

"It's your bedroom...I fixed it all up today."

"But Hal...that's a lot of money..."

"It's mine to spend..." He shrugged. "...and now I can get off the couch." He looked for any sign of approval. "I got it in white because I thought that was a color a woman would choose."

Walking inside the room, she surveyed the double bed, nightstand, dressing table with attached mirror, a chest of drawers, and a full-length mirror. Running her finger over the smooth white finish of the dressing table, she sat down on the matching chair. "I love it." She whispered. "But I don't understand...you want me to live here...with you?"

"Come here Mari...let me explain something to you." He walked into the living room and she followed. He took both of her hands. "See that desk?" She nodded. "That is the only limitation for you in this house. You must never touch my desk. Other than that you have the run of the place to your heart's content. This is your home."

"But Hal, you've done so much for me already...I can't expect for you to do more...it's too much. I feel like you're letting me take advantage of you."

"Do you want to get your own place?" His heart throbbed and he feared Mari would feel it in his hands.

"No...that's not it." The thought of moving out, paying first and last and a security deposit did not appeal to her. But, more than that, she enjoyed Hal's company.

"What then..."

"You've been so open hearted, and you have given so much of yourself to me...and I have nothing to give you in return..." Tears welled in her eyes.

"Have you heard me ask for anything?"

"No. That's just it...you are so unselfish...you have not thought of yourself...not once." She placed both of his hands to her chin and slightly rocked against them thinking. "I will stay here on one condition...that I pay half your rent...and I make the payments on the bedroom set."

"The bedroom set is already paid for..."

"Ah...ah...ah..." She cajoled, "You're not getting away with that...then I will make payments to you. How much is half the rent?"

"Three hundred..."

"You expect me to believe that you're only paying six hundred a month for a two-bedroom one bath place in Silverlake?"

"OK...four hundred...but that's my last offer!" He smiled. "And, if you do the cooking...I'll pay the utilities."

She smiled and wrinkled her nose at him. "Done!"

He picked her up and swung her around. "Welcome home, Mari Carlson!"

"Oh...and one last condition." She stopped laughing and he put her down. "Yes?"

"About the toilet paper...."

***

The next few weeks were like a revelation to Hal. He thought his place was just fine the way it was. But he found out that when he told Mari she could have full run of the place, she turned into a dynamo. With her arsenal of Playtex Gloves, scrub brushes and sponges of every size, a kneepad, Comet Cleanser, Lysol, TSP, and drain cleaner, she launched a major offensive against the offensive bathroom. "Hal, do you have a ladder?"

He walked to the bathroom door to see her on her hands and knees scrubbing the bathroom floor, with her derrière in the air. Her back and forth movement sent him into a daydream from which he was rudely awakened.

Without turning to him she chided, "You really should step a little closer to the toilet."

"You want a ladder?"

"Yes...the whole ceiling needs to be scrubbed."

"The ceiling...?"

"See those brown spots up there...that's from steam...and I really need to scrub it with TSP before I paint..."

"Paint...?"

"Oh my God, yes...does it need it...and the light fixture needs to be changed to both vent and heat all in one. The old heater you have is dangerous."

"The light, vent, and heater..."

"Uh-huh...and what color do you want the bathroom?"

"Whatever color you want, Mari."

He trundled off to get the ladder. "I had no idea I was living in such a shit-hole!"

***

"She's gone crazy, Deuce! She is scrubbing every inch of the place...painting every room...except mine...that's where I draw the line. When I told her that she could do anything she wanted...I didn't know I was going to get a remodel..."

"No...that ain't no remodel, man...you haven't seen a remodel! I once told my wife she could do whatever she wanted to do...and eighty thousand dollars later...she finally finished what she wanted to do...knocked out walls...put in 'mood lights'...which is apropos because she's always got a moody thing goin' on. You just thank God there's no landscapin' involved. What's that on your head?"

Hal felt around to the back of his head and felt a dried splotch of paint. "I must have missed that spot." He turned to show the color to Deuce. "See that...that's the color we painted the living room..."

Deuce squinted. "I'd say it is pale beige...almost white...like coffee with a lot of cream..."

"She says it's restful..." Hal shrugged. "I got to give it to her though...she has radar for dirt. When she cleaned the kitchen...the gunk she got out of the range hood...ugh...I never saw it...I never knew it was there. No wonder the damned thing never worked right. But I hardly used the kitchen before now...or I should say she's using it."

"You never cooked?"

"Just once...for Mari..."

"HOW DOES IT LOOK?" A high pitched, raspy voice came from the vicinity of the bar.

Hal and Deuce looked to where the voice came from and just saw the usual people sitting there. HOW DOES YOUR PLACE LOOK NOW? The same voice queried, but this time an older gentleman turned on the bar stool to face them. "I couldn't help but overhear your conversation...and it reminded me so much of my Lily." A man of average height, with narrow shoulders, and slight build climbed off the stool and ambled toward their table. His hair was dark with a gray streak running through, complementing his mixed gray beard. He wore horned rimmed glasses that enlarged his dark eyes. "My name is Biggerston, but my friends call me Big. He pulled up a chair, sat down, and then went back to the subject. His eyes and face were animated, and his hands gestured to dramatize his words. With wiggling fingers drifting down to indicate falling feathers, he

50

pronounced, "Your wife is feathering, my friend...she is gathering unto herself all the accoutrements...the finery...the silly little doodads...the esoteric...the exotic...and indeed the necessary doohickeys and thingumajigs that go into the décor...the style...the scheme..." He held his hands out to encompass the subject. "...all the whimsical, magical, hoo-hah...that goes into a woman feathering her nest. And my question to you is..." He leaned in with his eyes focused on Hal. "...how does it look...what was the end result...was it a hit or a miss...does it please your sensibilities?"

Hal and Deuce looked at each other and, as the older man continued, found themselves leaning back under the barrage of words. Then Deuce turned his head toward Hal. "Well?"

"You know I never thought of it before...but the place looks great...really great!"

Big leaned back with his face indicating puzzlement. "For some...inexplicable...enigmatic...mystifying...perplexing reason...the fair sex...the distaff...the feminine gender...whether she be womanly or girlish...all have this desire...no...need...an innate...inherent...distinctive...characteristic...known only to females...and gays...but I digress...to improve...and even glorify their surroundings." He then leaned back again facing his amused audience. "Why they do it...I don't know...men would be happy with orange crates...a beer...a color TV...and a toilet. If they ever...whoever 'they' are...find a way...a means...within the acceptable parameters of society...of combining all four...a man could be extremely happy. But not a woman! You were wise...even sagacious...and astoundingly astute...to give your Missus free reign."

"She said she does it because that is where she lives..." Hal swallowed. "...and she's not my Missus."

"Oh...my apologies. Your girl..." Hal shook his head. "Your significant other..." Hal shook his head. "Your squeeze..." When Hal shook his head again, Big looked back and forth between Hal and Deuce. "Gentlemen...I may not be up on all the latest terms for things...perhaps you can enlighten me."

"She is a dear, beautiful, lady who works with me...who, due to no fault of her own, found herself in an extreme circumstance...and I offered her a place to stay...with me. She is a wonderful person and..." Hal chuckled softly at himself. "...I would give her everything I have."

51

"Well...that type of relationship defies...scorns...stumps...constrains...and confounds...definition. Platonic will not do." His eyes opened even wider than their magnified appearance. "Ah-hah! That is because we are attempting to define a relationship where there is none. What we have here is a case of unrequited love!" Big's hand went to his heart.

Both Hal and Deuce leaned on their elbows and looked at Big. "Go on..." Deuce bade. "I want to hear this." Hal shot him a look.

"It sounds to me as though your friend here has taken pains...action...extreme measures..." Big tapped his index finger on the table to bring his point home. "...over and above...beyond...far out of the realm...of normal friendship. Being a friend would be to give her succor...perhaps money...moral support...but not to let her turn his house topsy-turvy! Perhaps I overstep..."

"Naw...go on...overstep..." Deuce goaded.

"Young man...what is your name?"

"Hal."

"Hal...you are either a man deeply in love...or a fool...and you don't look like a fool to me."

Deuce leaned back laughing and pointed at Big. "What he said...man oh man...what he said!"

"So what...even if everything he said is true...Mari doesn't feel the same about me...so that still puts me back at square one. She's never going to look at me like that." Hal leaned his forehead in his hand. "She's always doing these little precious things...I mean the simplest of things...mixing her shampoo and hair stuff...she makes a killer meatloaf...but the other day I had to tell her she can't hang her underwear in the bathroom...I bought her a drying rack for her room...God...I felt like a perve every time I went into the bathroom..."

Deuce smirked. "I'll bet you did...whackin' off to that girl's panties...shame on you..."

"Oh...like you'd never!"

"Gentlemen...I've pondered the facts...given it some thought...contemplated the state of affairs...and all things considered...the situation is not as bleak as one might think. You are not at square one...you are more accurately at square five." Big counted on his fingers. "She seems to trust you...she seems to like you...she seems to like the smell of you..."

"Smell?" They both said in unison.

"Oh...that's a very important thing...smell. If she doesn't like your smell...it's a deal breaker. But, to go on...she is in your house...and she is feathering her nest...you are almost there, son!"

"Almost where?"

"Mark my words...she will be in your bed by the first of the year."

"From your mouth to God's ear..."

"You shouldn't make the man dream like that...hold out false hope..." Deuce chided Big. "...this girl is really somethin'...and I met her on her worst day..."

"No...no...no...I would not offer false hope...insincere flattery...obtuse optimism. I invite you to look at me...a shamble of bones...a physique of a whippet...the visage of the proverbial nerd...bespectacled and half-blind...and yet I won the heart of my Lily...the fairest of the fair...the most beauteous damsel to grace the earth! How did I do it? I wooed her...I mean I wooooed her. I pulled out all stops...all tricks fair and unfair..." His hands gave further interpretation to his words. "I sent her flowers...I wrote poetry..."

Both Deuce and Hal made a face. "Poetry?"

"Don't knock it until you've tried it!" He wagged a finger at them. "I pursued her until she was smitten...until she was besotted with me..."

"Sounds like stalking to me." Deuce sniffed.

"As my wife would say...I chased her until she caught me!"

"I guess I could try my hand at poetry...what if it's no good...what if it creeps her out?"

"Believe me...it does not have to be good...it has to be romantic. Have you told her that you love her?"

"No. I think *that* would creep her out even more...and I'm afraid she'll leave."

"Then woo her...do little things..."

"He's already done some damned BIG things..." Deuce commented under his breath.

"No...little things like letting her know you think of her...let her know you appreciate her..."

Deuce nodded in agreement. "Yeah...yeah...I can see that! And, it would not hurt for you to lose a few pounds..."

"Look who's talking...you could use a membership to a gym."

Deuce leaned forward. "Hal...I'm married...I'm already riding in the bus...I don't have to chase it!"

***

THE BLIND DATE

Tying up his running shoes, Hal stood up, lightly jogged in place, and, without further ado, he started jogging. He had measured the distance by driving it and he was sure a five K run was about right for him. It was a sunny, California, Saturday afternoon and, with the words of encouragement from his buddies, he was feeling better about his chances. *Deuce was right...I need to drop a few pounds and get in shape. That Zack guy was buff...not that he could've taken me on his best day.* He threw a couple of air punches. *Yeah...I feel pretty good. I can do this.*

After the first kilometer he wasn't quite so spirited. Completing the second he began to flag. During the third he interspersed his jogging with walking. Determined to see the full five kilometers through, he pressed on.

Staggering up to his door he let himself in. His breath came in ragged gasps that ended in wheezes. He fell on the living room floor and lay there. Mari came up the hallway and spotted him. "Hal? HAL! Oh my God...what happened to you?"

Running to him she knelt beside him. He had the telltale redness of face that showed he was overheated. Running to the linen cabinet she grabbed a handful of towels, wet them, and ran back to put cold compresses on him. She felt his heart. It was pumping fast, but evenly. His breathing slowed enough for him to talk. "I went running...I did the whole five K..."

"Oh, Hal...five kilometers...are you crazy?"

As his breathing returned to normal, she helped him to his bed and took off his shirt and shoes. "There must be an easier way to get you to take my clothes off." Even as wrecked as he felt, he still teased her. "What! No mouth to mouth?"

"You're incorrigible!"

"I speak well of you..."

She cooled down the towels and returned to apply them again. "I'm going to make you a banana shake to help put you back on your feet...and then you have some 'splaining to do..." She kissed him lightly on the lips, "...and there's your mouth to mouth."

"Hey...nurse...you can do better than that!"

When she went to the kitchen her heart was pounding. Seeing Hal like that shook her to her core. She knew that he was teasing her as he always did, but something had snapped in her when she realized that she wanted to go back into his room, throw her arms around him, just climb into bed with him, and hold him. She shook her head. *No...that can't be...me and Hal?* She threw the thought from her mind and went back with his shake. "Here...drink this. Bananas are rich in potassium and the natural fruit sugar will help revive you."

"This tastes really good."

"What on earth were you doing trying to run five kilometers?"

"It didn't look so far when I drove it. Deuce said I looked out of shape and I need to drop a few pounds...so I thought I would start jogging."

"First of all, Hal, you have to consider your body type. You have a beefy build...you are never going to be skinny..." She patted him on his tummy, "...and having a little happy fat has its own charm...so you look fine. Tell Deuce to mind his own business. Secondly, if you want to exercise just to stay healthy...you can't start way up here..." She held her right hand up to indicate an advanced level. "...you have to start way down here and take baby steps to get up here." She placed her left hand low and then let her fingers air-walk up to her right one. "You should have started out walking a mile a day and work your way up to five kilometers...and then start all over again jogging." She saw his dark eyes watching her above the rim of his glass, so boyish as she lectured him. She started to look away, but she looked back again as something stirred in her. "You know you made my heart stop when I saw you lying there...you scared me half to death. What were you thinking?" She wanted to throw herself on his chest and she might have done it, had it not been for the drink he was holding. *Mari...back away from him before you make a fool of yourself. He will think you're crazy.*

That night she lay awake trying to sort out the inexplicable emotions that had blindsided her. *You've fixated on Hal because he has been so very good to you. He doesn't love you, or else he would have said something by now...and he is NOT the type of man to take advantage of you. What are you fretting about? Just go to sleep and forget it.* But she couldn't forget it. The match had been struck and the fuse was burning.

***

Lather foamed up in Hal's hand and as he went to put the aerosol can down, it tipped and fell to the floor. *What the fuck!* He picked it up and looked at the sink to see what caused it to fall. A flat, pink dial partially filled with tiny pills, that he had not noticed, was sitting on the sink to the right of the faucet. It gave him pause, because he knew immediately what they were. *Why is she still on the pill? Who is she with?* His heart took a nosedive. *Who is she screwing...or planning to screw?* He finished shaving and put on his robe.

Mari was frantically searching her tote when he knocked on her open door. "I found these on the bathroom sink...I think they're yours..."

"Oh...thank God! I've been looking for them everywhere." She dropped her bag and went to retrieve her pills. Looking up at his face, with dots of white toilet paper on it, she showed concern. "Boy! You cut yourself up pretty bad..." She reached up to touch his face, but he pulled back a bit. "You should have your license to carry a razor revoked." She quipped.

"Is it alright if I ask you a question?"

"Sure."

"Why are you still on the pill...do you have a new boyfriend...are you looking around?"

"No...and no..." Her eyes met his. "Well...maybe...but no..." At his puzzled look she added, "You don't just go on and off the pill...you just stay on it unless you join a nunnery...and even that's not a sure bet...or you and your husband decide to have a kid...but that's not going to happen any time soon..."

"So, once you start taking it you stay on it?"

"Yep...pretty much...why do you ask?"

"No reason...just curious."

She laughed and half-jokingly wisecracked, "Well...if you ever want to make my day, Mr. Golan..."

He blushed. "Yeah...this is Hal here...and like that is ever going to happen..." Retreating to his bedroom, he tossed over his shoulder, "I know...I know...only in my dreams..."

***

Mari strode into the living room and swirled like a runway model. "How do I look?" She showed off a dress of pale blue sateen. It had a loose-fitting blouson bodice and long sleeves that had slits to reveal

57

her arms. The skirt was slightly clingy in the hip but flared at the hem. A matching pale blue, velvet ribbon was around her neck with a pink rose attached. The strappy heels she wore matched the dress color.

"Like you always look...on a scale of great to great...you look great. What are you all gussied up for?" Hal tried not to sound worried.

"I have a blind date..." She screwed on pink, faux pearl earrings while she talked to him. "...with Vee's son Steven...if you can imagine. Vee asked me himself...I could hardly say no..."

"Steven...eh?"

"Yes." She started putting on the other earing. "This dress isn't too 'come hither' is it? I want to wear something nice...something that says I'm a girl...but I don't want to encourage ungentlemanly attention. Lord knows I just came off of one disastrous relationship and if Vee hadn't asked me, I wouldn't be going out on this date."

"Everything you wear says 'come hither.' Try wearing a burlap sack."

"If I didn't know better...you almost sound..." Mari bit her tongue.

"Jealous? I don't know...maybe I am. Why haven't you ever gone out on a date with me?"

Mari stopped fiddling with her earing and blinked a couple of times before answering. "Because, you never asked me."

"Are you saying that if I asked you...you would go out with me?"

"Of course." She shrugged and waited a decent interval for him to ask her out. Yet, when the interval became an awkward overtime of silence, she turned away. "But we occasionally have breakfast and dinner together and it is so very interesting talking with you...that it almost feels like a date." She kicked herself for letting him off the hook. *Why hasn't he asked me out? According to him, I'm not exactly chopped liver...so why not?* "Should I wear my hair up or down?" She took them both out of an uncomfortable subject.

He loved her hair down, so he gave her the opposite advice. "Try it up for a change." When she lifted her hair and started arranging it in an up-do, he instantly regretted his suggestion. Her hair looked stunning either way. He anguished, *I don't know where she is going...and I don't know this Steven guy...I don't care if he is Vee's son.* "Is he picking you up?"

"No...remember, we agreed that we wouldn't tell anyone at work that we are living together...I mean roommates. So, I'm taking a cab."

"Why don't you let me drop you off?"

"I don't know...what if he should see us?"

"So? Where are you going, anyway?"

"The Mirabeau Restaurant..."

Hal sat up. "That's at a hotel!"

"So? You act as though he is going to club me over the head in front of the Maître d' and drag me off to his lair. The Mirabeau is a highly respectable, famous restaurant...I hear it has a fabulous nighttime view of the city. I'll be in the public eye the whole time."

"I'm still driving you."

"OK...I could do with saving the cab fare."

"I can pick you up as well..."

"Oh, for Christ's sake!"

***

"I'm Mari Carlson. A Mr. Steven Vougiouklakis is expecting me." She smiled. "I hope I didn't mangle his name too much. Please show me to his table."

The Maître d' was good-natured. "I was hoping that myself when I first read it. Please step this way." He led her through the semi-lit, perfectly appointed restaurant. The crisp, white linen tablecloths shone brightly under each table's lamp. The expansive windows gave a panoramic view of the multicolored lights of L.A. It was definitely a setting to impress for a romantic dinner.

She was taken to one of the better tables by the window. As she approached, a man who appeared to be in his mid-to-late-twenties stood to greet her. He was tall with the dark good looks of his Greek heritage. The term Adonis could be freely applied to him. "My father described you perfectly."

"He didn't describe you at all. I guess that is because no description could adequately do you justice. I am sure he is very proud of you."

"I am honored to have you as my guest for the evening." He assisted her with her chair. "Mari is an interesting name...where did it come from?"

"It is an old-fashioned Scandinavian name. I was named after my grandmother. It is the same as Marie, except that it is spelled without the 'e' and that makes it a little awkward for most people. Instead of saying Marie...everyone pronounces it Maaar-ri...so I'm stuck with it."

He gave her a charming smile. "Would you enjoy an aperitif?"

"I don't do well with alcohol...but I would love a cup of tea."

"How did my father convince you to have dinner with me?"

"To be perfectly honest he is my boss...so when he asked me if I would consider going on a blind date with his son..." She held up both of her hands. "I said...sure! But I don't know why he would want to foist me on you...you must have your pick of an array of beautiful girls."

"Like everything else...he likes to choose for me." Steven said softly. "But tonight...I do not resent his choice...you are charming and most welcome company." His mouth spoke the words, but his eyes reflected preoccupation. "I hear they have an unusual appetizer of chilled cream of avocado soup...I should like to try this...would you as well?"

"I am adventurous when it comes to food...yes I would."

As the evening wore on, Mari felt no magnetic vibes from Steven, no spark. Even men she had no interest in had a certain "charge" to them. For as handsome as Steven was, she sensed a dead battery.

"Tell me about what you are interested in outside of your job." Steven searched for a common activity to enliven the conversation.

Mari could only think to say "Hal" as she found that he was taking up more and more space in her head, but she desisted. "I have this hobby that I was...in a way...forced to take up out of self-preservation. I got a terrible rash on my face from using a commercial cosmetic. Now I make my own cosmetics...hair...makeup...skin. It's time consuming...but I know what goes into it...and I haven't had a problem since."

"Your own cosmetics...that is fabulous! Tell me more about it." Steven's face lit up and for the rest of the evening they were like magpies, discussing makeup techniques, moving on to fashion and hairstyles.

As the evening came to a close, Steven remarked, "I wish you could meet my friend Brian and see his fashion debut. He is so well versed in all things aesthetic."

"I would love to. I am enjoying your company so much I was about to suggest we should do this again." When Steven looked pleased,

Mari knew why he had no girlfriends. She took his hand. "Steven, I don't want to pry...but I am sure there is more to you than just an evening's worth of chit-chat. I would love to meet your Brian and I am not judgmental. So, if you ever want to get together for lunch...or just to shoot the breeze..." She smiled. "...give me a call." She wrote out her number for him. "...and if you don't invite me to Brian's fashion show...I will be crushed."

Steven realized that she had guessed. "What will you tell my father about this evening?"

"I will tell him the truth...that you are handsome as all get out...that I had the most scintillating evening that I have had in a long time...and that I would love to see you again."

***

"She went on a blind date! Can you believe that? She went on a blind date." Hal griped to Deuce and Big. "I've never been so insulted..."

"After all you've done for her...lettin' her live with you...not to mention redecorate your cave. That's some cold shit!"

"Well she thinks she's paying half the rent...but that's beside the point..."

"She's paying half the rent? That's not beside the point at all...that is very germane to the point...that makes her a free agent." Big interjected. "Have you told her you love her...?"

"No."

"Have you ever given her any indication that you love her?" "Sure...lots..." Hal frowned. "I got her out of an abusive situation and moved her into my home..."

"That makes you 'Sir Galahad'...not a potential suitor. If he needed it...you would do the same thing for Deuce. You work with her...she helped you...you helped her...that does not amount to L-O-V-E. What did she say about this date?"

"The date was arranged by our boss. When she came home, she said he was very handsome...very nice...and she gave him our phone number...and if he calls she said she would go out with him again...I mean what kind of shit is that?"

"I admit it sounds very bleak...and you have to go into crisis mode. Forget what I said about doing little things...you have major competition...so now you have to do something BIG! Something so spectacular it will take her breath away…and then declare your love for her…and your intentions…"

"My intentions?"

"Yes…that you want her to be your girlfriend…that you want a relationship…that you want her to marry you…whatever it is that you want from this girl…"

"Yeah, man. You never even told me what you want from Mari…you only said that you would like to go to bed with her…and you haven't even made that clear to her…maybe she is looking for more than just that out of a man…something substantial…secure…of some permanence…" Deuce jabbed his finger in Hal's direction. "…and with this new guy…you may have taken yourself out of the picture."

Big waxed profane and then poetic. "You had better shit or get off the pot…because living with regret is a motherfucker. 'Of all sad words of tongue or pen, the saddest are these, it might have been.' So, if you love this girl…take it from John Greenleaf Whittier…DO something about it…and soon!"

***

Vee called his editors to his office. "We have to do a tasteful piece on the passing of Princess Diana. Who thinks they can do it justice?"

Hal looked up and volunteered an idea. "We were watching the outpouring of grief on TV in the lunchroom…and Mari made a comment that I think we can use as the theme. She said, 'Now the fairytale…turned nightmare…is over.' She was young, beautiful, brave, and naïve. She had no idea what she was getting herself into."

"She tried to fight back." Martin quietly observed.

"And, she lost." McMurray whispered.

***

AN ADORABLE KITTEN

Hal gazed at Mari across the breakfast table. Seeing her with no makeup, and in her house robe, he often thought that he liked this version of her better; it was private, more intimate, a side of her she didn't share with anyone else and, to him, she was just as beautiful. He took a deep breath. He couldn't have loved her more. *Deuce and Big are right. Because I never thought she would look at me...I never thought of what my intentions were...nothing much beyond wanting her. If I don't lay it all on the line...I could lose what little chance I have with her.*

Taking his friends' advice, he spent all of the next day with Claude, the entertainment editor, cajoling his opera tickets out of him and bribing him by paying twice their exorbitant price for the best seats in the house. He spent even more time asking Claude for his guidance as to what constituted a gala evening at the opera and then scoping out the terrain at the Music Center. Once he had the evening set, he planned how to tell Mari what was in his heart.

"Mari, I was able to wrangle two tickets to the opera. Would you like to go out with me...on a date?"

Her mouth dropped open. "The opera...with you? I can't think of anything I would love to do more!"

"Yeah?"

"Yeah." She sparkled in her excitement. "When? Oh...what should I wear?"

"Next week...because of the location of the seats...in the rows of the front section...it's formal...so you're expected to wear a gown...and I have to wear a tux...but it is supposed to be something really grand. Do you know 'La Bohème'?"

"Oh yes...I love Puccini!" Mari wrinkled her nose, scrunched up her shoulders with delight, and clasped her hands together. "Oh Hal, I feel like Cinderella..."

"OKaaay...that's good, right?"

"Yes...yes...yes...that's very good!"

***

Mari seemed to float in a dream as she walked into the living room. A smooth, upswept, Grecian hairstyle, decorated with pearls, replaced her curls. Elegant simplicity denoted the white column gown. It was cut to one side, leaving one shoulder bare, with a side slit that showed a flash of leg as she walked. The soft crêpe de chine lightly caressed her bosom and hips, but only suggested the rest of her form. The entire affect was sophisticated, chic, and classy. Hal caught his breath as she approached. From the expression on his face, Mari did not have to ask if he approved. "You look like a movie star...no...better. I'd pinch you to see if you were real...but you'd probably slap me!" He laughed and offered her his arm. "Our limo awaits..."

"A limo!?!" She threw a wispy, lace shawl over her arm and grabbed her evening clutch.

"Tonight...nothing but the best for you."

The chauffeur held open the door like a footman to a magical carriage. Driving in the opposite direction of rush hour traffic, the limousine breezed over the freeway to the Dorothy Chandler Pavilion at the Music Center. Several decanters with an assortment of spirits were stored inside a compartment. "Would you like to have a drink?"

"No thank you." Mari's gaze swept over Hal. "You look scrumptious in a tux!"

"Scrumptious?" Smiling, he gave a slight bob of his head. "OKaaay...I'm good with scrumptious..."

She moved closer to him and put her arm in his. "I hope I don't wake up."

Pulling up to a rather discrete doorway, they took an elevator up to the fifth floor to the posh eatery, Impresarios, located above the opera house. Crystal chandeliers festooned the wide expanse of the room lending it a well-lit, but subdued atmosphere. A pastel mauve color scheme, set off with a light green carpet, dotted with pale pink, linen covered tables, completed the setting. A harpist filled the air with delicate notes to please the senses.

As they were led to their table, a hush rippled over the room as diners looked their way and then the hum of conversation resumed. Hal noted that ever since they emerged from the limo all eyes went directly to Mari, as expected, but then they went to him with a regard he had never experienced before, spontaneous respect.

An unctuous waiter presented the menus with a flourish and then prepared to take the order for their drinks. "May I suggest cocktails?"

Hal reached across the table to take her hand. "What are you having, my dear?"

"I'll have Schweppes Tonic Water with three dashes of Angostura Bitters...a squeeze of lime...over ice in a chimney glass."

A baffled expression passed over Hal's face. "Does that have a name?"

"Oh...madam was quite succinct..." The waiter tapped his head with his pen. "I have it all right here...and the gentleman will have?"

"I'll just have a Heineken."

"Excellent choice, sir." He made a quick bow of the head and then retreated.

"What was that you ordered?" Hal looked bewildered.

"Oh...it is something that a friend suggested that I drink whenever I'm at a social gathering where alcohol is being served. You have what looks like a drink in your hand...so they will stop insisting that they get a drink for you...and I have developed a taste for it."

"You don't drink?"

"Not very often..." She leaned forward to whisper a confidence. "It doesn't take that much to get me potted."

"Oh" He nodded his understanding. *Had I taken her out before...I would have known that. No wonder she never touched my beer.*

All through dinner, his eyes caressed her face, her bare shoulder, and her bosom that defied gravity. Discerning a slight jiggle, he surmised that she was braless, a thought he had to drive from his mind. *Don't stare...don't stare...look at her eyes...concentrate on what she is saying...oh, her skin!* He looked down at his plate and focused on his steak.

"...I know I don't understand the language...but the beauty of his voice and the music is so incredibly moving it gives me chills..."

"Whose voice?"

"Pavarotti's." She seemed a bit puzzled but went on. "Like I said...I have a CD by him that I love."

"Oh...that's right...you were just saying that you did." He dodged. *Pay attention... she is going to quiz you!*

"I must be going on like a little chatterbox..."

"Not at all." He lied.

"What made you think of an evening at the opera?"

Hal shrugged. "You said you liked opera...so I went to Claude and begged him for his tickets...and when they weren't forthcoming, I threatened to beat them out of him." He laughed. "Actually, he was happy to sell them to me...for double the price."

"Double the price?"

"Yeah...he knew they were sold out and that he was the only game in town...so he scalped them to me."

With no idea of the cost, she made light of it. "Pooh on Claude! See if I will ever ask him if he wants me to get a sandwich for him again."

"You get sandwiches for Claude?"

"Sometimes...you know he's sort of an old guy...so when I go to lunch...if he's stuck in the office, I ask him if he wants me to get something for him. He has always been very nice to me."

"I am sure if he knew the tickets were for you, he would have given them to me...so keep buying his sandwiches..."

"Oh...I don't buy them. I just deliver them. I'm not Fort Knox."

"You could be."

"What do you mean?"

"Fort Knox." He became serious. "Mari, I look at you and what I see is that...you could be a model...a movie star...and sometimes I wonder what are you doing working with me. What brought you to L.A....the old lure of Hollywood?"

"No...I was getting away from my family. I was raised by wolves, you know." She raised an eyebrow. "I did a short stint in show biz as a dancer...but it was just a job that would take me nowhere...and not one I could likely do in my forties...it wasn't for me." Her eyes softened. "There's nothing I would rather be doing than working with you...I've learned so much."

"Yep...and soon you will know as much as I do, and you will want to move on to bigger and better things...and more money."

An involuntary pout came over her lips. "I don't think so. There are a lot of things more important than money..."

"Like what?"

"Happiness...I'm happy where I am."

"As long as you're happy...I'm good."

Gripped in the throes of both torment and exhilaration, Hal finished his meal and waited for Mari to pick through her plate.

"We'd better get going…I don't want to be in a rush to find our seats." He motioned to the waiter for the check.

When the waiter presented the check, Mari asked him, "What is your name?"

"My name is Godfrey, Madam."

"Godfrey…I want to thank you for helping to make our evening very enjoyable."

He managed a tug at the corner of his mouth to indicate his pleasure. "Madam is most welcome." He took Hal's card and sauntered off.

"That was nice of you."

"Not really." She whispered. "I just wanted to get his name…because he had such a stick up his ass. Now…when I make fun of him…" She made a face, imitating Godfrey's staid demeanor. "…I'll know what to call him!"

With its clean lines, white marble, grand staircase, and chandeliers, the Dorothy Chandler Pavilion is a masterpiece of simplicity. It gives the full elegant expression of an opera house, without the fussiness of traditional design. Strolling into the Grand Entry Hall with Mari on his arm was a thrill for Hal. With no effort, they were the most important people there. Heads turned, conversations stopped, and the whispered, "Who is she?" could be heard as they passed by. "You are causing quite a stir."

"Maybe I am…or perhaps it's you."

"Me?"

"Yes. Is your fly open?" In his first reaction, he almost looked down to check and then realized she was having him on.

"That's right…I'm snapping your panty girdle." She laughed.

"You bad girl…you're having way too much fun."

"Yes, I am." She paused and reached up to needlessly straighten his bow tie, and then gestured for him to bend down and kissed him on the cheek.

"What was that for?"

"Putting up with me." She took his arm again and they found their way to their seats.

When the house lights lowered the conductor took the stand to thunderous applause. "That's Placido Domingo…what a thrill. He is the best tenor in the world...unless you belong to the Pavarotti faction like me. The debate rages on as to who is number one. He is conducting tonight to showcase his protégés...so this should be interesting."

"How do you know all that?"

"It's in the program."

"Oh."

Act I opened on a scene in a Paris garret where young men struggled against poverty for the sake of their art. Rodolfo, the writer, Marcello, the painter, are the main protagonists. Colline, the philosopher, and Schaunard, the musician are the supporting characters. Into this world stumbles Mimi who falls in love with Rodolfo. The translation was projected above the stage and Hal watched with some amusement, but he was more intrigued with Mari's reaction. During the first aria, *Che gelida manina*, sung by the tenor Rodolfo, Mari's hand went to her breast and she seemed gripped with emotion. As the tenor's voice swelled, she held her breath. At the end of the piece the audience erupted in applause as the singers froze in place until the clapping subsided before continuing the scene. By the time Mimi sang her aria, *Si, mi chiamano Mimi*, Hal thought he detected a tear. *Is she crying? Why is she crying?* At the end of Act I, Mari was dabbing at her eyes with a Kleenex. "Are you OK?" Hal asked.

"Oh...yes. The music is so beautiful...such voices. It takes my breath away."

Hal took her hand. He didn't know if he should comfort her, but he thought it was the gallant thing to do.

Act II was a humorous street scene that featured the character of Musetta, Marcello's former lover. Tiring of her rich, but old, devotee, Musetta tries to rekindle her romance with Marcello. To entice him she sings *Quando me'n vo'*. He resists but cannot withstand her charms and the act ends with the two lovers reconciled. The soprano, Inva Mula, was sensational as was the ovation she received. Hal was relieved by Mari's amused expression and the intermission. He could use a break from all the dramatics. Mari whispered, "I need to go to the little girl's room. Could you escort me there?"

While he waited, Hal tried to absorb and analyze the evening. *She certainly enjoyed the evening so far...but how am I going to bring her around to the subject of how I feel about her? Perhaps if I can get her talking about how she feels about me I can get a clue of how to begin.* His brow furrowed. *What if she thinks that my loving her is abhorrent and she decides to move out? Is that a gamble you're willing to take? If you don't take that gamble...what then?* His insides began to squirm as he started to rehearse and then reject what he was going to say later that night.

"What's the matter, Hal? You look so serious."

"I was going to ask you if you wanted anything...but the refreshment bar is so crowded that I doubt we will be able to get back in time."

"Maybe after the opera."

They returned to their seats just in time to see the curtain go up on Act III. As the gate to the city is open to workers and peddlers, Mimi can be seen lurking in the shadows racked with a coughing spell. She seeks Marcello who is living at an inn where he now works. Musetta lives with him. Mimi reveals to Marcello how Rodolfo has fits of jealousy and has mistreated and deserted her. At this turn of the plot, Mari's eyebrows knitted. But the news becomes worse as Rodolfo approaches. Mimi hides, but overhears him tell Marcello in *Marcello, finalmente* that he fears Mimi is dying, that he is too poor to help her, and that he is pushing her away so that she may find another man who is wealthy and can care for her. Rodolfo learns of Mimi's presence when he hears her weeping, and coughing, and then Mimi sings *Donde lieta usci* where Mimi tells Rodolfo that she is leaving him, but because they are still in love, they agree to part in the spring. During Rodolfo and Mimi's reconciliation, Marcello and Musetta have an argument and decide to part. As the curtain came down on Act III, Mari leaned over to Hal and whispered, "That Rodolfo is a dick!" Hal shook his head and grinned at her pronouncement.

In Act IV both Rodolfo and Marcello, back in their garret and still dabbling in their respective arts, find out that their former sweethearts have found wealthy suitors and Musetta has been seen in an elegant carriage and Mimi dressed in finery. Both men regret the loss of their loves and Rodolfo's regret is expressed in *O Mimi, tu piu non torni*. Abruptly, Musetta appears and has brought Mimi with her. Mimi had left her wealthy, viscount suitor and Musetta found her, gravely ill, wandering the streets. Mimi begged Musetta to take her to Rodolfo. As everyone leaves to seek help for Mimi, Rodolfo and Mimi sing a duet *Sono andati?* At the end of the act, Mimi dies, and Rodolfo is left crying out her name. As the curtain descends Mari whispers to Hal, "Now I am sure of it...Rodolfo is an idiot!"

The audience erupted with a standing ovation, and, as the players reappeared, one by one, their performance was rated by the length and volume of the applause. Bouquets were tossed and the lead singers were handsomely rewarded with cries of bravo and brava! Placido Domingo, beloved in L.A., evoked the loudest response of all. As the din subsided, and the audience began to file out of the opera house, Hal and Mari remained seated until the crowd thinned. "What do you think of your evening at the opera?"

"I think it was sumptuous...lush...divine!" Mari cooed. "What about you?"

"I could use a drink! There is a place downstairs where we can decompress. How about an après opera nosh and something to drink?"

"You've certainly earned it!"

The night was still warm and all aglitter with tiny lights as they emerged from the opera house out to the plaza. It was a brisk walk to the Brasserie and soon they were seated at a table inside the bar.

Hal asked Mari, "Do you want to share a drink with me?"

"We're not going anywhere else this evening...are we?"

"Nope...this is the last stop."

She held up one finger, "Then I will have a Champagne Cocktail."

"It's an Old Fashioned for me."

Mari quipped, "The opera was that hard on you...was it?"

Hal took a breath. "It was...different."

The waiter took their order and returned with their drinks. Hal took a sip and leaned back in his seat. "So...you didn't like Rodolfo...why not?"

"Well, he could sing a good game...and made Mimi believe that he loved her...but, he did nothing to keep her. He just kept hanging with his buddies in the same cold garret...following a failed pursuit. He would rather push her toward another man than to get off his duff and work to keep her. He abdicated his responsibility to her...if he really loved her. For all the romantic folderol...I don't think he was serious about Mimi...or else he would have fought for her. As usual, I think he was just another dick who wanted to go to bed with her."

"Is that how you view men?" His expression was guarded.

She nodded her head as though it was an accepted fact. "Well, yeah...just about all men."

"Is that how you view me?"

"Oh...no, Hal...not you. I always thought you were very sweet from the moment I met you. It's not that I saw you as any less of a man...quite the opposite...but I never felt wary or under attack from you. I always thought that you considered how I felt...and that you would never hurt me."

"You're right...I never would." He paused looking at his drink. "What about Mimi...how do you think she felt about Rodolfo?"

"Oh...she loved Rodolfo. She would rather die than be with someone else. There are all kinds of deaths, you know. Even if she lived with someone else, it would have killed her...spiritually." Her eyes grew dark. "There are some women who go back to men...again and again...who are no good for them. My mother was like that." She jerked her mouth to one side. "Not that she was any prize either."

"What type of man are you looking for, Mari?" He studied her.

She started to answer with a joke, but his dark eyes told her he was at least semi-serious. She blinked and took another sip of her drink. *Is this just casual conversation...or is he putting me on the spot? If I tell him how I feel about him first...he'll think I'm too aggressive...too forward. The man always tells a woman how he feels first. Why is that? I have to tell him something.* "Oh...no...you go first, what are you looking for in a woman." She leaned forward on her elbows.

Hal had no other choice but to tell Mari something. "OK...first and foremost, I want her to love me...she would have to...to put up with me. She should be intelligent...wise...witty...so I don't end up talking to myself."

"Children?"

"Sure. I'd like to have a couple of rug-rats...you know...who love their daddy...the picket fence...the whole nine yards. I would like for her to be pretty...but a guy like me..." He shrugged and held out his hands. "I can't expect too much in that department..."

"Why not?"

"Mari…look at me. I'm not exactly Brad Pitt."

She screwed up her face. "Brad Pitt? Why would you want to look like Brad Pitt? I mean he's probably a very nice person…but he looks rather vapid to me…he doesn't hold a candle to you. If you ask me…Brad Pitt had better watch his back for the 'Golan' rivalry!" She laughed.

"You're just saying that because I suffered through an opera for you…"

"Oh…no…no…well…yeah. I mean that's a part of it because that is who you are, Hal. You are good…kind…hard working…strong…highly intelligent…you can sit through two and a half hours of opera…and you look great in a tux. What more could a woman ask for?"

"OK…now it's your turn."

"My turn? I just gave you a litany of what I'm looking for!" She hid behind her glass as she drank its contents. "Hal? May I ask you something personal?"

"Sure."

"Why haven't you married? You look as though you would be happy in a marriage."

"It just never worked out for me. I wasn't interested in a long-term relationship with the girls that were interested in me…and they soon lost interest. As it turns out the one person I do love…"

"Yes."

"She wouldn't have me."

Mari's heart sank to the ground and she agonized. *No wonder he never approached me…he's in love with someone else. Oh fuck, fuck, fuck!* "She's a foolish girl." She said calmly.

"Not really. I don't think she knows."

"You haven't told her?" Mari's heart got off the ground. "You must tell her…believe me…she would want to know. May I have one more drink?"

Hal signaled the waiter indicating another round. "OK, kiddo…why haven't you married?"

She nodded to him. "With the exception of present company…just about every man I ever met turned out to be a putz on some level. Don't get me wrong. I am still holding out hope…because the picket fence and the whole nine yards sound pretty good to me too."

72

The drinks were served and they both quietly took a sip and then both broke the silence at the same time."

"Mari?"

"Hal?"

"Yes?" They both said in unison.

"Ladies first."

"I just wanted to tell you what a magical night you gave to me. Each moment I felt as though I was walking through a dream."

"Me too."

She was beginning to get a little tipsy. "Can I tell you another thing, Mr. Golan..." She said softly.

"Hal" He whispered.

"When I think of you...and how good you are to me...it just makes me go all ooey-gooey inside and tears come to my eyes and I just want to cry..."

Hal squinted at her. "I make you want to cry?"

"...I can't talk about it...or I'll start crying...but you mean that much to me." She fluttered both hands at herself to try to settle her emotions, blinked back tears, and then looked around. "I believe I'm getting a little potted." She giggled. "I think you'd better call for the pumpkin."

Hal put his arm around Mari's shoulder and walked her to the waiting limousine. Once inside, his arms went up in surprise as she crawled onto his lap like an adorable kitten, put her head on his chest, and in under a minute she was asleep. *What just happened?!* He was totally baffled. Nevertheless, he enfolded her in his arms and looked into the face he cherished. "I love you, Mari." He whispered, gently kissed her on the lips, and held her all the way home.

***

"You did what? Oh man...tell me you didn't do that! I thought you knew better than that!" Deuce screwed up his face in disappointment.

"What are you talking about? All I did was take her to the opera..."

"No...what you did was to create a need in that girl that she didn't know she had. Now you've corrupted her, and she will never...ever be the same."

Big stared hard at Hal and held up both hands as though fending off the horror of what he had done. "You have set a terrible precedent...a precursor of things to come...a model of an unspeakable commitment. You have shown her the woman's Shangri-La of the entertainment world where romance and drama...are surrounded by fashion and society...conducted in an edifice of such proportions as to rival the Taj Mahal. It is catnip to all women...and at the same time you handed her the key to male misery and suffering...to your private hell..."

"It was just the Music Center..."

"And oh...how deceptive it is to the uninitiated! It is her training wheels...nay...her training bra...her first taste of power...her first dose of smack!"

"What Big is trying to say is that you screwed up!"

"You guys told me to do something big!"

"Yeah...but we didn't tell you to trip over your own dick! From now on you are going to be obligated to take her to the opera EVERY YEAR!! That's right...I said every year...and you only have yourself to blame. And, if that isn't bad enough...after she gets home...you have to listen to opera for an entire week!"

"Oh...I didn't know..." Hal put his hand to his face. He could see Mari...his intended future Mrs. Golan...dragging him out of the house every year like some modern-day Dagwood. "You mean it's like a recurring nightmare?" Deuce and Big both nodded.

"At least tell us that your evening was otherwise a success...a veritable triumph...that your damsel has been told of your love for her and is now enthralled." Big hoped Hal took away a measure of success.

"Not exactly..."

Deuce looked sideways at Hal. "How much did you spend?"

Hal flinched. "Well with the limo...the tickets...dinner...drinks after...tips...a tad over a grand..."

"Oh, fuck me! You had better sit there and tell me that you got laid!" Deuce pointed a finger at Hal. "You did get laid didn't you...you got laid!?!"

"Uh...no..."

Both Deuce and Big dropped their heads to the table. Deuce softly muttered, "And Jesus wept."

"Look it was an unforgettable night...but things did not go exactly as planned. She told me she goes all ooey-gooey...and that I make her want to cry...and then in the limo she sat in my lap and went to sleep! I don't even know what ooey-gooey means!"

"It is not in my lexicon..." Big looked around.

"Hal...I think you'd better start from the beginning...and...because you didn't get laid...don't you leave anything out!"

After Hal related the events of his date with Mari, Deuce and Big were more impressed. "That was really nice..." Deuce puckered his lips in thought. "...classy...you got closer to her...and she was affectionate..."

"But not overly so..." Big chimed in.

Deuce deliberated. "...and it was your first date. If you ask me...I think ooey-gooey means she loves you...or likes you one hell of a lot..."

"Or it could mean that she still sees you as her Sir Galahad..." Big surmised. "...why don't you just ask her when you get home?"

"Because...she's not speaking to me..." Hal murmured.

"WHAT!!!"

"Well...we had this difference of opinion. What happened is she....."

Pavarotti's powerful voice could be heard throughout the house as Mari, still in a trance, went about putting dinner together. Hal got a respite from his chore of vacuuming, so that the music would not be drowned out. Mari called him into the kitchen to get his opinion of the sauce she was making. "How's this?" She held a spoonful for him to taste.

"That's really good."

"It doesn't need more salt?"

"No…it's perfect the way it is."

"Good."

"How much longer are you going to listen to opera?"

"Oh…do you have a game or something you want to watch?"

"No…I've just never seen you so carried away…"

"I guess you can call it an afterglow or something." Mari dreamily looked at him. "I can't wait to tell Steven about what an enchanting evening we had."

Hal took a step back. "You can't wait to tell Steven?"

"Oh, yes…he is going to absolutely die!"

"What are you trying to tell me, Mari? I just spent a mint on you and now you want to tell Vee's son everything that happened?"

"Of course…why not?"

Hal narrowed his eyes. "Are you kidding me? Why are you telling this guy about what we do? Why is it any of his business?"

Mari put the lid back on the pot and turned to face him. "What are you implying, Hal?"

"I don't think I am implying anything…if you are seeing this guy, I think I should know about it…"

"Why?"

He threw his hands up and walked out of the kitchen into the living room and Mari followed him. "I want an answer…if I'm not free to choose my own friends then I want to know why."

"What's going on between you and Steven?"

"You think there is something going on between me and Steven?"

"I don't know."

"We're just friends…we talk…that's all there is to it."

"Mari…are you trying to make this Steven guy jealous…is that it?"

"WHAT?!"

"I demand that you tell me what's between you and Steven!" Hal's finger jabbed the air.

Mustering her courage, she stood up to him. "Alright, Hal, I will tell you everything, right after you tell me why it's so damned important to you!" She stormed off.

Down the hall he could hear her door slam and a "For Christ's sake" while Pavarotti sang *Vesti la giubba*.

Deuce couldn't believe his ears. "After you give her the date of a lifetime...you get into a jealous rant with Mari? Oh...really smooth move, Hal! Couldn't you have just told her you would like to meet Steven and then get to see for yourself if there was any hankying with the pankying? I mean this Steven guy obviously knows about you..."

"What's there to know? What is she doing with me that is so hankying-pankying? NADA! Nothing! Bupkes!" He sat quietly for a moment with his head in his hand. "If it hadn't been for you guys, I wouldn't have gone after her in the first place...she's out of my league. I don't even know what I was thinking...and for you guys...my friends...to tell me that I fucked up. What was I supposed to do...let her play me while she's playing the field?"

"You still don't know what ooey-gooey means." Big thought out loud.

"Oh, fuck it...I'm out of here!" Hal got up, threw his jacket over his shoulder, and left.

Deuce's eyes followed him. "Don't worry...he'll be alright. He'll go home and fume...maybe even cry a little...but he can't help but get back in the chase...'cause she's right there in front of his face every day."

"Well let's hope that ooey-gooey means she loves him because that boy needs to get laid."

***

For the next two days Hal lived in despair. Mari would just mutter a few words to him as needed. It was total silence in the car. At this, the worst of times, the company car request that Hal put in for Mari, came through. It made it appear as though he was totally rejecting her. The utter desolation in her eyes, when he handed her the keys and parking pass, was only exceeded by the sadness of her voice. "I won't be riding in with you anymore?"

"No." He blurted. As she walked from his office, Hal started to go after her, but decided against it. He didn't want to cause a scene.

Mari met with her friend, Loretta, the fabulous Lo-Lo, at her apartment in Hollywood. An exotic beauty, with ebony skin as smooth as velvet, Lo-Lo had the refined features typical of Ethiopians. She was a daughter in the tradition of the queen of the kingdom of Sheba, who entranced Solomon. With her hair in a multitude of braids drawn up and banded at the top of her head and then cascading down in bead-decorated plaits, in a modernized African motif, her style was stunning. Wise in the ways of the world, Lo-Lo always had advice, according to her philosophy. There was no situation so dire that you couldn't ride it out by looking like a movie star. Why reinvent the wheel when the studios worked out the formula decades ago? Image is everything. If worse comes to worst, turn to your recipe book, whereby cooking in the bedroom surpasses cooking in the kitchen. That was the code she lived by. She found Mari's naiveté charming and reminiscent of the girl she once was. She took her under her wing, because she considered Mari the only genuine person in Tinsel Town.

Mari was in tears. "He's not speaking to me...he doesn't even want me riding with him anymore. I can't believe he thinks I'm having an affair...I'm always with *him.*"

Lo-Lo's face was unruffled. Her level gaze told Mari there was nothing to worry about. "Men never make no sense, sugar...especially when they're crazy about you...and he's definitely crazy about you..."

"Are you sure? I'm not so sure..."

"Aw...look at you...like he couldn't love that." She turned Mari's face to a mirrored wall. "From what you told me...he's going nuts right about now. So, you need to give him some more incentive, honey...and I know just the thing. I just bought a 'Jean Harlow' nightgown...never took it out of the box. It will look marvelous on you. All you have to do is let him get a glimpse of you in it...and this gown will explain it all! He'll come around...guaranteed! Now stop crying...you'll make your pretty eyes all red and puffy. Let me fix your face...I'll put green tea bags on your eyes." She headed to the kitchen. "I keep them chilled in the refrigerator for emergencies...you could use a facial too..." She stopped and turned. "I hope he's worth all this bother...and he better not be a musician..." She wagged a knowing finger at Mari. "...don't have no trek with a musician."

When Mari got home, she was surprised to find Hal there, as well. "I thought tonight was 'football night' with the guys."

"It was."

"Sorry I'm late...I'll rustle up something to eat. You'll have to settle for some leftovers..." She changed into shorts and a sweater and was back in the kitchen rummaging through the refrigerator to find something quick to fix. "Is meatloaf OK?"

"Sure...why not."

Within twenty minutes all was ready. "Come...sit down."

She set a plate in front of him on the table and he grasped her hand and held it. He was in a downcast mood. "Mari...what I said to you the other day...I knew I was wrong when I said it. I just want to say I'm sorry."

"Me too." She said in a soft voice.

"I had no right..."

"Yes...you did...you have every right." He looked up at her, and she continued, "I wanted to tell Steven and Brian...because they helped me get ready for the opera. Brian did my hair and makeup and he picked the gown for me. He was going to loan it to me...but he said no one else could wear it like I did...so he gave it to me. They were so excited for me...so I wanted to tell them how wonderful my evening was."

"So, Steven is...gay?" The irony of it all struck him.

She put her fingertips to his lips. "Shhhh. Vee is in denial about his son...he doesn't know. I promised to keep their secret if they kept mine."

"Yours?"

"Yes...that we're living together...roommates."

"Now I really feel like a shit. Why didn't you tell me this the other night?"

"Because you kept acting like I was up to something...like you didn't trust me...and that really hurt. I wanted you to see that I was telling you the truth...and then you sort of...well...pissed me off." She pouted. "But that's not all of it...it was also because, it wasn't my secret to tell. Please don't tell another living soul...I think Steven wants to come out in his own time...and in his own way. Vee mustn't know."

"Be sure to tell this Brian something for me...he did a fantastic job!"

***

"Hal?" Mari poured herself a cup of coffee.

"Uhmm." He grunted from behind the newspaper.

"Would you like to come to see me dance?"

"What?"

"Do you think you would like to see me dance?"

"What are you talking about? Dancing? When did this happen?"

"Salsa dancing...I entered a contest with Raul Torres from marketing...he's quite good you know."

Hal lowered his paper to focus on what she was saying. "No...I didn't know. When were you going to tell me this?"

"After we knew for sure that we were going to go for it. I wanted to surprise you."

"OK...I'm surprised. Tell me all about this Raul guy...and how all this happened."

"There was talk around the office about Raul...in marketing...and how he was this really great dancer...you know Latin jazz...salsa...and you know I used to dance...so I got to talking with him about it..."

"How did it happen that you were just talking to him about it?"

"Marketing is just down the hall...and I ran into him...so I asked him about it..."

"You just ran into him..."

"Yeah...and I asked him to show me a few steps...and I showed him a few...and as it turned out we danced well together."

Hal folded the paper and set it aside. "OK...go on."

"Well...we...he thought that if we were good enough we could enter the salsa contest at the Montezuma...and as it turns out we are very good...so I agreed. We've been rehearsing on Mondays while you were watching the game..."

"And 'as it turns out' I suppose this guy is gay as well?"

"Oh no...not at all."

"And has he come on to you?"

"Of course...but only in the mildest way possible...and I made it clear to him...strictly hands off."

"And you think that will stop him?"

"It has so far...and if he breaks my rules...I'll just drop out. He really wants to win...so I don't think there will be a problem. Do you want to come and see us?"

"I wouldn't miss it for the world."

***

The Montezuma Nightclub was packed. There were more people standing around the edge of the dance floor than at the tables. Hal, along with Steven and Brian, was seated at a table on a different level with a better view. After watching a few contestants dance, Hal was not sure he liked where this contest was going. Salsa dancing seemed to be overly sensual, depending on the dancers, some more so than others. The girls' costumes ranged from much abbreviated cocktail dresses to being almost nonexistent in the form of the briefest of festooned bikinis. Other than her hair and makeup, Mari did not give the slightest hint of what she would be doing or wearing.

Hal had taken the time to track down Raul at the office but could not locate him within the building. He did not want to appear anxious by asking everyone about him. Word drifted back about the contest, from the office scuttlebutt, and the girls' sighs and swoons over the elusive Raul had Hal concerned. *Who is this yo-yo?* Many in the office planned to be in attendance, nonetheless the whole affair rankled Hal. Now he was more irritated than ever. *Why did she have to get involved?*

When the announcer introduced Raul Torres and Mari Carlson, Mari walked out to the center of the dance floor followed by a man of perfect proportions and Latin good looks. Her skimpy costume left nothing to the imagination. It was a French cut bikini with beaded fringe on the back that could not be properly called a modesty cover. Her perfect ass was barely concealed by the fringe of dark blue and silver beads that swayed with each step, giving a peek at what was underneath. The front was all silver sparkle. The top that was decorated with the same type of beaded fringe and silver sparkle, revealed cleavage, and was fastened with what looked like little more than a string across her back. Her superbly shaped, bare legs tapered down to a pair of silver-strapped high-heels.

Hal's expression of surprise darkened into consternation. My God...she looks like she's naked. *What is she...some kind of exhibitionist?*

Raul stepped some feet away from her and was simply dressed in black pants with a dark blue vest that showed his well-muscled arms; his physique was cut with broad shoulders accenting narrow hips and long legs. He had black curly hair and was of a cinnamon brown hue, and his features were typical of a cover model on a romance novel. Hal sat ramrod straight in his chair as his eyes narrowed on the scene before him.

Brian was the first to comment. "Mari just rocks that outfit. I knew she would...and look at that guy...oh, honey...he has dancer's buns..."

Steven watched intently. "Wait until you see him move...oh, divine...and Mari is his perfect equal..." He caught Hal's stare. "...in dancing that is."

The music started slowly with a distinctive beat. As Raul approaches Mari, she turns and walks the other way, and he follows. Moving close behind her he puts his hand on her waist and, stepping in time with the music, they undulate in unison. Then she turned toward him and they both danced with their hips swaying to the beat. "This part is called the bachata sensual." Steven whispered to Hal. With each step Mari's long hair was tossed and the beaded fringe flipped. Raul took both of her hands and put her through a set of intricate turns in and out of his arms and then leaned her back over his leg with his hand on her stomach and she undulated in a wave under his touch. Someone in the audience yelled, "Aaahhhooooooah!" while the rest oooohhh'd their appreciation. As he brought her back up, they moved together and then apart, each swaying slowly to the rhythm. Then Raul moved closer, holding her to him with one leg between hers, with their bodies rolling in unison as he seemingly caressed her. Then she moved from him again and turned away. The crowd reacted to the move with a whoop. Raul followed her, put his arm around her waist, pulled her back close to him, and they moved as one again. As the dance continued it seemed to Hal that it was essentially a mating rite.

Both dancers were marvelous, but Mari's form was graceful and fluid, adding a higher level of volupté to the interpretation of what was already a suggestive art. The visual was amazing, but that did not mollify Hal. *He's pawing her on the fucking dance floor!*

Suddenly the tempo changed, and Mari ripped off Raul's breakaway vest and now he was dancing bare chested. Brian squealed, "Oh...rip the shirt!"

"Calm down sweetie..." Steven pursed his lips at Brian. "This part is Salsa dancing." He whispered to Hal.

Stepping much faster to the salsa rhythms, they faced each other and Raul did his signature hip roll to the sound of the Latin drumbeat and Mari did a vibration that started in her hips and went up through her body to end in a shimmy of her shoulders, much to the delight of the audience. Before they danced together, with hips swaying and bodies undulating, they went through a series of passionate moves before Raul spun Mari down to the ground where she stopped with a pose of a beauteous extended leg. By now the people were shrieking with glee. Pulling her back up, Raul danced apart from Mari, with each one showing unique steps until they dove toward each other in some precise acrobatics that made Hal's heart stop. *If he drops her...if he drops her...he's a dead man.*

Dancing close once more, Raul pulled her to his body and stepped in a circle, bending back and forth in what appeared to be simulated sex. "Oh, my God! He threw in a little Lambada!" Brian fanned himself with his hand. Oooohs and ahhhhs rippled through the spectators. Without missing a beat, Mari pushed him away and then bounced her stomach against his. As the music paused Mari froze with her hip out toward Raul and, as planned, he gave her a little smack on the ass. It was a crowd pleaser, but not a Hal pleaser. As the music resumed, at a furious pace, they both danced apart and then came together for the finale. Swirling Mari up to hold her high above his head, he suddenly dropped her into his arms and ended the dance with a kiss.

Hal ran his hand over his forehead and was surprised to find he had been sweating. Both mesmerized and outraged, he watched as Mari and Raul took their bows to thundering applause. Utterly confused and appalled by her participation in such a spectacle, he quietly fumed through the rest of the show.

***

Hal walked Mari to the car without a word. With a coat over her costume she briskly walked to keep up with him. Opening the door, he held it as she got inside. While he did not slam the door, he firmly closed it. He then strode to the other side, got in, and started the engine. Revving it a couple of times he peeled out of the parking lot and onto the street. After a mile in silence, Mari was perplexed by his obvious wrath. "Hal, what's the matter with you? You look like I did something to you. Aren't you happy we won?"

"You won...Mari? Just exactly what did you win? Dancing half naked with his hands all over you...what happened to that hands-off policy of yours?"

"His hands were where they should have been to properly execute the dance...and I was dressed the way at least half of the girls were dressed...it's called a costume."

"Did you have to dance with his leg in your...crotch?"

"His leg wasn't in my crotch...it was on a specific place on my thigh! I would not have been able to dance if it was in my...hoo-hah! It was just a part of the dance!"

"And you think it was just all about dancing for him?"

"There is nothing else it could be!"

"Yeah...then why does he look at you like you're a burrito with melting cheese?"

"Bad metaphor, Hal..."

"What?"

"Bad metaphor...in case you haven't noticed...I'm a girl...the metaphor should have been 'taco.'"

"What the fuck?" Hal spit out through tight lips. "So that's the type of sexual connotation you would have me apply to you?"

Mari's eyebrows went down. "Well, you started it...you picked the context. I only corrected the metaphor. Guys are burritos...or if their lucky...big chimichangas...girls are tacos."

"Will you shut up with the Mexican food metaphors...like I need those images in my head right now..."

"What is your bitch, Hal? I thought you would like to see me dance..."

"Dance...yes...but you were practically screwing that guy on the dance floor out there. What were you thinking?"

"Are you kidding me? Latin dance is an art form..."

"So is pornography, baby...but I wouldn't want you doing it!"

Mari's mouth flew open wide with disbelief. She couldn't utter a word as she stared at him. Finally, she took a couple of deep breaths. "OK...that's it! Stop this car right now!"

"What the fuck?"

"I said stop this car right now…I'm walking…" She pushed the "unlock" power button.

"Don't be crazy!" He pushed the "lock" button.

"You as much as called me a whore…and I'm not riding with you another minute." She hit "unlock" again.

He locked the car once more and reached over and grabbed her hand. "Look…if you get out of this car and start walking right now…at this time of the night…the way you are dressed…if a cop stops you…and gets a gander at what's under your coat…you will get arrested for solicitation. But, that's just my opinion." He put her hand down in her lap.

"That's what you really think of me?" Tears started streaming down her face.

"Oh…that's it! Really good, Mari…play the crying card…"

"It's just that I thought that you would see that I am talented…and that I looked graceful and pretty dancing. I never thought you would be angry with me."

"OK…you got it…I think you looked gorgeous…and the way you dance is nothing short of breathtaking…but that guy…did you have to have him all over you?"

"Well…yeah…that's a part of the dance…"

"Did he have to kiss you…?"

"Nope…that was not a part of it…we didn't rehearse that…and I am sort of pissed that he did it…but it worked. Look…if you're back to this…is there anything between him and me thing…forget it because there isn't. And if Raul has any kind of imaginings on that score…he can forget it too…because it ain't gonna happen. He was just a dance partner…a prop…nothing more."

"Oh…you mean like a brass pole?"

Her chest heaved a couple of times as she fought back tears and then she started sobbing. "I have nothing else to say to you…"

"Hey…hey…hey…kiddo…I didn't mean it…" He slammed his fist on the steering wheel. "Look…I'm pissed off at myself…I didn't mean it. Don't cry…please…don't cry."

By the time they got home she had stopped crying and was sitting in utter silence. Once inside, she took off her coat and hung it on the rack and walked to her bedroom door. She stood there for what seemed like a couple of heartbeats while staring back at Hal with a great deal of sadness in her eyes. Then she went into her room and closed the door behind her.

He was up and down all night. Walking in circles, he couldn't get the visions of her dancing out of his head. He thought that he should go to her and tell her he was at fault because he could not stand to see another man touch her, but then he would have to explain why. He went and tried her door. Finding it locked, he raised his fist to pound on it, but then dropped it by his side and leaned his head on the door. In turmoil, he walked in circles again to end up back in front of her locked door. Agony was his companion the rest of the night.

***

"Look...she made Salomé look like small potatoes...and made Madonna look like a church social! It was the sexiest shit I've ever seen...and here is the woman I love dancing practically naked with some latter-day Romeo. Before you say it...I know it is my fault...but goddamn it...what was she thinking?! How could I expect that she would do such a thing?! I'm going nuts...why would she do that?" Hal bit his lip. "And you know...I practically lost it. I tried her door...and I am not even sure I know why. I keep telling myself it was to tell her I was sorry...but I wanted to take her...I really wanted to take her so bad."

Deuce and Big looked at each other, smiling. "Are you thinking what I'm thinking?"

"I think so."

Deuce smiled at Hal. "There's some good news and some bad news to this shit. What do you want to hear first?"

"I could use some good news about now."

"Well the good news is that you've won!"

"I've won? What have I won?"

"She is making a last-ditch effort to make you get off the dime! She wants you man! She has managed to contrive...in a socially acceptable way...a means of showing you all her goodies...all her moves...what could be yours for the taking. You have won! All you have to do now is pick up your chips and go home...'cause she's yours..."

"You're crazy. You mean she did all that just for me to look at her?"

"She as much as told you so. She must have been thinking that she had to get your head in the right place as far as wanting her...you haven't shown her that is where your head has been at all along...so she was laying it all out there."

Hal sat rubbing his forehead for a while. "She did that for me...?"

"Who else did she do it for? She don't care about that Raul guy...she could have had him all along if she wanted...and she don't care about no contest...all she cares about is you..."

He looked up. "...and the bad news?"

"The bad news is that she's through...she has pulled out all stops...and your getting mad at her didn't help...and making her feel like you think she is some kind of whore...what were you thinking? She's hurting right now...because the only person that she cares about what they think of her is you...and you just said the worst things you could have said to her...especially when she doesn't know that you love her...if you don't say anything...to her now...she's done..."

"She's done...what do you mean?"

"She's run through all her bag of tricks for you. She's cooked for you...she's cleaned for you...she did over your cave and made it look like a home...she even told you that you made her feel ooey-gooey...and that could only be good. You two have been playing house in every other way...and she's just waiting for you to drop the 'L' word. Since you have not done so...she thinks you don't care for her in that way...and she is not going to stand by and have her soul crushed by you...she's ready to pack it in."

"I'm crushing her soul?"

"Look man...you've accused her of being interested in every Tom, Dick, and Harry that even looks at her...and you've got to stop that. The way she looks...that's all you'll be doing for the rest of your life. And yet...you never told her why you're so damned jealous of her...how you feel about her."

Big interjected, "I know it is too late to get flowers today...but you have got to work fast...with all due haste...alacrity and rapidity. If this lovely lady of yours is half of what the two of you say she is...she will not be on the showroom floor for very long...while you are wasting your time kicking the tires. You had better yell 'you've got a deal' right away and drive her off the showroom floor...before another buyer comes along.

***

I'M STAKING MY CLAIM

It was the first of November and the weather was still warm. Mari soaked in a tepid bath to cool down and refresh herself after day of running errands and grocery shopping. Then she dressed for comfort. With her hair pinned up off of her neck, she was dressed in shorts, a tied-up blouse, and wedge sandals. While constructing two "monster" dinner salads, her large blue eyes regarded Hal with sadness. He had been withdrawn and had hardly said two words to her since the salsa contest. It was obvious to her that he was still furious with her, keeping it all pent up inside. *I wonder if he really believes the things he said to me. He can't be serious! Please God...don't let him hate me. I just wanted him to look at me...I wanted him to see me. Maybe he regrets having me move in with him.* She wilted at the thought. *What will I do if he wants me to move?* She bolstered her courage. *If he doesn't want me here...if he wants me to move...I'll die...but I had better know that now.*

She carried the two huge salads to the table. "It's too hot to stand over a stove so I made my monster salads for dinner...there's tuna salad...egg salad...tomatoes, onions, olives, cheese, baby corn, and mushrooms...all on a bed of lettuce." She handed him a bottle of dressing. "I made a nice Italian dressing to go over it." He regarded it without interest, poured a measure of dressing on it, and dutifully ate it. Mari poured iced tea in his glass. "Is it OK?"

"Yeah...sure...it's fine."

Her brows knitted, she took her seat, and they ate in silence. While washing dishes, she felt his eyes on her. *He wants me to go...I can feel it.* "Come on...you're supposed to dry the dishes."

He went through the motions, put the dishware away, and then retired to the living room, but he did not turn on the TV. He sat there in introspection. Mari watched him from the kitchen and in fits and starts she tried to decide what to do or say. Finally, she went to him and knelt down on the floor in front of him. "Hal, do you have a minute to talk? I want to ask you something."

"Sure. What do you want to know?"

Her eyes did not meet his. "I know that there are times when I am...sort of...upsetting for you...or get under foot...and do things differently than how you would want. I honestly don't mean to be a pain..." She looked up at him. "...but I was just wondering if you ever regretted saying that I could live here with you."

He seemed stunned. "Oh...no...not for a minute."

She held both hands up to him like a plea for him to take them when he talked to her. "Are you sure you don't want me to go? We don't ride to work together anymore...we don't go to lunch...and at dinner you hardly say two words to me. You don't even joke with me anymore. I'm sorry about the contest...honest I am."

He took her hands. "No...no...no, Mari...you've done nothing wrong. You could do no wrong...it's all me. You see...I don't know what to do...and it is all about you...but it's nothing that you've done..." He took a deep breath. "...it is very hard for me to tell you...to be honest with you. It is just that there are times when I look at you and...and...I desire you more than life itself. It's a passion that I feel...that you don't share." The words he once found so hard to say came spilling out now that he knew she thought he didn't care, and it was the only hand he had left to play. "I keep asking myself if I should keep trying..."

Her eyes were wide. "Do you mean you want to fuck me?"

"Oh...no...no...well...yeah...but no."

"You don't want to fuck me?" She frowned.

"Well yeah...I kinda do...but not like that..."

"Well then what??"

"Shhhh. Listen." His dark eyes held hers. "Mari...you fill my heart...my head...my dreams. I can't think of anything else but you. My God, Mari...don't you know I love you? It makes me crazy sometimes..." His eyes turned darker with longing and he took her in his arms in a deep kiss that sent them both tumbling onto the floor. She met his kiss, snugging into his lips. Then her leg went under her and as she tried to move it, she caught it on the coffee table.

"Hal...wait...stop!"

He instantly let go of her and got up, mumbling, "Sorry." and left the room. Mari straightened out her leg and then sat up. *Where did he go?*

Hal went to his room and closed the door. Frustrated, he paced like an angry tiger, punching his hand with his fist. *Why did you climb all over her like that! She must think you're a maniac. She was already talking of leaving...now she will probably pack up*

90

and get out. The thought made him sick at heart. *After old Jolly Roger calms down...I had better make amends.*

Mari went to her room and pulled out her secret weapon. Slipping the "Jean Harlow" nightgown over her naked body, she looked in the mirror at how the charmeuse clung to her figure. She let down her hair. *He said he loved me...and then ran away. Why? Well he's not going to run this time.*

There was a soft knock on her door. "Come in." Mari did not attempt to conceal the revealing gown as she fiddled with her hair. Hal opened the door to the vision she created. She half turned toward him. "Yes?"

"I just wanted to apologize for..."

"Apologize for what? Kissing me? I was kissing you back...there's nothing to apologize for."

"So you're OK?"

"Quite OK." She strolled over to pick up her brush, her breasts jiggling with every step, and started brushing her hair. He stood in the doorway transfixed. "Is there anything else?"

"No...I guess not." He closed her door.

Fuck, fuck, fuck!!! At this point why does he have to be such a gentleman? She put her hand to her head and paced. *That's it...if he won't come to me, I'll just have to go to him. Before this night is through he is going to tell me he loves me again...over...and over...and over!*

Mari knocked on Hal's door. When he said to come in, she stepped into the half-lit room where he held a book under the lamplight. He looked up from his book. *Ja-heeez-sus! What is she doing? She has practically nothing on! Oh...she's beautiful!* He ached.

She smiled, set his book aside, and then in a soft voice that ran over him like a ripple, she uttered what he longed to hear, but thought he never would. "Hal, you just told me you loved me. I had almost given up hope that you could love me." She stammered, "B-Before I could tell you that I love you too...you went away." Tilting her head, she mustered her courage. "The way I figure it...is like this. You love me...you chose me to love. I love you...there is no one else in the world for me. So, I guess there is only one thing for me to do." She pointed to the far side of his bed. "I hereby stake my claim to that side of your bed...and woe unto any woman who tries to jump my claim! Now, you are bigger and stronger than I am...so if you don't want me there you can carry me back to my room. But, if you don't...that is where I'm going to sleep!" She sauntered to the other side of his bed, pulled back the covers, and slipped between the sheets.

As Hal stared in disbelief, his heart pounded and his breath quickened. *She just got into my bed...she said she loves me...and just got into my bed! Am I fuckin' dreaming!?!* He leaned over her, lightly caressed her hair, and then touched her face. "Mari...is this really happening...?"

She could feel his heart pounding. "Do you want it to happen?" Her eyes glowed with an emotive light as they met his and she lightly drew her fingers down the side of his face.

"Oh...God, yes!"

"Then it's happening." She held his face in both her hands and gently brushed her lips on his.

His fingers became lost in her silken curls as he closed his hand to hold the weight of her hair. Her eyes glowed with invitation to sink into those soft lips that had raced a thousand times through his dreams, her face, her skin, her body so near to him was no longer living only in his imagination but was a reality that surpassed his fantasies. He devoured her lips with his kiss and his desire left him breathless. "Dear God...I'm shaking."

"That's you? I thought it was me." Her breath was hot on his ear.

"Oh...Mari..." He enveloped her in powerful arms and lifted her to him. His kiss was urgent, hot, and intense and their tongues met in an electric flash. Pent up desire flooded through him as he was free to touch, to explore, and caress every inch of her body that he had yearned for; he took command of her. At first she was overwhelmed, but then her body came alive responding to his every move. The delicious thrill his hands evoked sent her spiraling and he felt her tremble as she moaned his name. His mouth moved down to her neck, her shoulders and then he insistently tugged at her nightgown. She slipped the top from her shoulders and he became lost in her luscious breasts, tipped with rose petal pink nipples. Lavishing his attention on them with such ardor he sent sensuous currents running through her, igniting an inferno inside her. Removing her gown, his hand slid downward over her satin smooth abdomen to lightly caress the gold, silken hair below. Where his hand explored, his tongue followed finding her landica pearl and lingered until evoking an earthquake of such exquisite pleasure that he heard her cry out his name. Now she hungered for him to penetrate her. "Do you want me, Baby? Do you want me right now?" His voice was hoarse and urgent.

"Yes...yes..." She whispered.

With one strong stroke he was inside her and then began moving slowly. As she rolled her hips to meet his thrusts, he sent her spinning even higher, on the brink in a world of molten intensity. As she moaned, her hands clutched at the sheets in paroxysms of pleasure. He struck a place deep inside her that demanded more, and he fulfilled her every need, sending her soaring higher than before. She felt the power of him and as the pleasure became too intense the explosion of spasms rose from the center of her being to envelope her and took control of her body. As he came with her, in long, hot streams, the ecstasy repeated over and over and over until, drenched with sweat, he fell into her arms.

He remained inside of her and felt the afterglow of her residual contractions. His senses were filled with her: her taste, her scent, her touch, her beauty, the feel of her soft, tight sex.

Dear God...she's perfect. "Oh, babe...there must be a word so much bigger than love to describe what I feel for you." Hal breathed in her ear.

"I'll research it for you on Monday...right now my head is still reeling." She gazed up at him. "I had no idea you packed such a wallop."

"Really? 'Wallop' is my middle name." He laughed. "Oh God...I'm dripping all over you."

"No...don't move...I love it. We're both wet."

"What did you imagine I would be like?"

"Oh...I don't know...maybe more tame. I had no idea when I fell in love with you that you came with a boatload of "E" tickets." She blushed and hid her face in his chest.

His eyebrows went up as he smiled. "OK...I guess that's good." He became serious. "Just when did you fall for me...I agonized for such a long time. I fell for you right away."

"Not me. I idolized you at first...sort of put you on a pedestal...like beyond my reach...sort of...too good to be true. But that day you came in from running and fainted...it hit me like a ton of bricks...I couldn't bear to be without you."

"Why didn't you say something?"

"I did! I just blurted it out...right after the opera. I know I had too much to drink...but I still meant it."

He pulled her closer to him. "I told you that night too...and kissed you...but you were asleep."

"Well...I'm glad you didn't tell me right away when we first met. It would have seriously creeped me out."

"Hey...hey...hey. Come here you." He went to kiss her, and she pulled back.

"Go wash your face first..." She wrinkled her nose.

He pointed at her. "Don't move...I'll be right back." As he got up to walk to the bathroom a thought occurred to him. "I suppose you're going to tell Steven about us..."

"Of course!" She laughed. "He's just going to absolutely die!"

***

Hal was subdued when he walked into Benny's. It was proven to him how right his friends were, by what he now knew, and how his life had been sent soaring. He had been in a trance all day, unable to focus on work, trying not to phone downstairs to Mari, and cherishing the images in his head from the weekend.

He knew his buds would want a full accounting that he was not prepared to give. It was too sacred, too private, and too emotional to divulge. Besides, he did not give a fat flying fig about the game between the Kansas City Chiefs and the Pittsburgh Steelers. After making love to Mari all weekend, he wanted more of her, just to be with her, and the constant reaffirmation that everything was real. He wanted to go home.

"Hi guys." He tried to sound casual. "Before I say anything, I want to apologize for all the times I was a dick. More than that, I want to tell you that I owe you a debt of gratitude. I was right about one thing that I said, and that was if you hadn't egged me on to go after the woman I love, I never would have taken a shot at it. I really...really want to thank you. You're the best.

"On Friday I told Mari that I love her...." He sighed. "...and she told me in no uncertain terms...in the strongest manner possible...with every fiber of her being...THAT SHE LOVES ME TOO!!"

"Ha-haaaaaahhh!! Goddamn! I thought you were going to say that she told you to go fuck off! Awwww man...that's the best." Deuce got up, smacked Hal on the back, and grabbed him by the shoulders. "Listen up everybody. SHE LOVES HIM!!" The bar exploded with applause and some groans.

"You told everybody?"

"They asked what was wrong with your ass...so I told them." Deuce shrugged.

"Geesh! What kind of mother confessor are you?"

"The second word is not 'confessor'." Deuce chuckled. "Oh...I couldn't be happier! Come on let's get you a drink."

Big waxed philosophical. "Of all the mysteries...the inscrutabilities...the vagaries...conundrums...and enigmas, the female mind...psyche...her mystique...is profound...unfathomable and remarkable in its ability to elude all sense of perception...insight...discernment...and we mere men can only stand in awe. For God's sake...did she tell you what ooey-gooey meant?!"

"Yes." Hal smiled and held out his hands. "That's what it meant...she was all ooey-gooey about me. How could I miss that?"

"OK...now let's get down to it...did you get laid?"

"Yeah."

"And?"

Hal took a deep breath. "I can't talk about it, man..." He touched his chest. "...it's just too sacred..." He closed his eyes. "I can't believe how beautiful she is...how she looks at me as though I am the only thing her world is about...there are no words." He stared down at the table with his head full of visions.

"Well...that is somethin'...I'm happy for you, Hal." Deuce backed off knowing that sooner or later it would all come out and he would be there to listen.

"Hey guys...I think I'll hit the road. I'll check in on you next week." Hal took an early leave.

"It ain't just the road you'll be hittin'." Deuce laughed.

***

THE POET

Hal passed Mari in the hallway. As she walked by, she wrinkled her nose at him and it had the effect of an arrow to his heart. Involuntarily, his hand went to his chest. Still, it was the better part of discretion not to reveal their living, and now loving, relationship to their coworkers.

As Hal sat at his desk, he daydreamed about the previous night. Never in his life had anyone so preoccupied his thoughts. He wanted to do something to please her, but there was no time to go to the jewelers and pick out something. *I don't even know what she would like.* He thought. *Big said women love poetry...even if it's bad.* He certainly did not want to come up with the "roses are red" schlock. He racked his brain and then reached for his yellow efficiency pad. He scribbled a few lines, crossed them out, and started over. For over two hours he wrestled with his emotions and tried to put them into rhyme. Then he came up with a method that worked for him. For each stanza he wrote his main thought and then tried to rhyme the rest. Surprising himself, he came up with two rather decent poems. Typing them up, he looked them over.

If I lived one thousand lifetimes,
And searched the length and breadth of all,
'Tis but one beautiful face that I'll e'er recall
'Tis but one who stirs my passion, and all I desire
And sets my heart yearning, sets my soul on fire.

Mari, Mari, I found you at last,
My journey across eons is now through
All my desperate dreams are fulfilled by you
After my ship was tossed on a stormy ocean
The treasure I seek is your love and devotion.

Mari, Mari you live in my dreams,
When I run my fingers through your hair
And feel the heat of the kiss we share
The words to speak of my love for you
Are written in the sky and the morning dew.

Mari, Mari always in my thoughts
The very thought of you gives me a rush
With visions of you that make me blush
The heat of your body melts my existence
Into one with yours without resistance.

Mari, Mari I'll love you forever
Our lives should be for always entwined.
If we live where benevolence has shined
With our love to shelter us from the cold
Together hand in hand I wish to grow old.

"It's not perfect...and I am saying an awful lot here." He said out loud. He read it again. *That last part almost sounds like a proposal of marriage!* His mind sat up at the thought. *Would that be so bad? I think I'll leave it in there...just to float the idea and see if she buys it.*

He shuffled the papers to read the other poem.

Mari's periwinkle eyes have strange powers
They fill your life with sun, or with showers
With a smile and a backward glance
Your heart will soar and it will dance
Like a kite to which she holds the string
Swirling in happiness only she can bring.

Mari's periwinkle eyes have strange powers
They fill your life with sun, or with showers
With one errant tear or a forlorn sigh
It rends your heart and you want to die
What have you done to bring on her blues?
To bring such sorrow I never would choose.

Mari's periwinkle eyes have strange powers
I could look into them for hours and hours
Lost in the depths of those beautiful pools
Sparkling and shining like precious jewels
When I hold her, and she looks at me,

In her eyes I am everything I hope to be.

It was shorter and rather sweet, but it didn't have the sentiments of the other. He decided to save the extra one for another day.

Signing it with a tiny heart that had "H+M" in it, he smacked himself on the head for being so juvenile. *I can't erase it now.* He looked for a file that had current business, slipped the poem under the first page, and then went downstairs to Mari's workstation. "Mari...I want you to look over these papers right away and pay special attention to the second page." Sounding and looking businesslike, he turned and went back upstairs.

He no sooner settled in his desk chair than his phone rang. "Hal...can you get down here? Mari's crying..."

"She's crying? Why?"

"How the hell should I know? It's probably one of those woman things...but I'm not going to go near her. I don't know what came over her. Could you get down here now?"

"I'll be right down..."

When Hal arrived at Mari's cubicle, she was clutching the poem to her breast, sobbing openly. Thinking fast on his feet, he shooed everyone back to their desks, went to her, and spoke loudly, "How did that notice get into the folder? I'm so sorry about your grandmother."

"Hal...I love you." She whispered.

"I know you loved her, but she has gone to a better place now..." He lifted her from her chair and put his arm around her to walk her from the room. "Come, come now...let me take you to my office where you can grieve in private."

As he walked her down the hall, she still held the poem to her chest with tears streaming. "What's wrong with Mari?" Martin stuck his head out of his office.

Hal mouthed the word "Grandmother" and drew his finger across his throat in the universal sign of "died."

"Oh." Martin bowed his head.

Hal took Mari into his office, locked the door, and drew the blinds. "Mari...what's wrong with you?" He spoke softly.

"Oh Hal...it is the most beautiful thing I ever read. Nothing...nothing ever written has touched me so deeply. I couldn't stop crying." She looked up at him with her eyes brimming with tears. "I love you so."

He took her in his arms and held her. *Shit...I didn't know it was all that! I should have given her the other one.* "Shhhhhh. Don't cry. I wouldn't have written it if I thought it would make you cry..."

"Oh no...I will cherish it for the rest of my life..."

He took the poem out of her hands and stuffed it into his suit pocket and then his lips brushed away her tears, tasting the salt of them. His mouth found its way to hers and she responded to him with fervor. He started to break their embrace, but she clung on to him wanting more. "Baby...you're getting me all stirred up here..."

"I love you, Hal." She murmured into his neck and continued to kiss him there. She took his hand and moved it under her sweater and moaned under his touch as he caressed her.

"You want me, baby...you want me right now?"

"Oh...yes...this is crazy..."

"Yeah, I know..." He lifted her skirt and slid down her panties and put them in his pocket alongside the poem.

"Oh God...if we get caught we'll both be fired."

"Ask me if I give a shit." He picked her up and sat her on the desk. "You have no idea how many times I fantasized about making love to you right here."

"I want you so..."

He quickly removed his slacks and started into her. "Put your arms around my neck," he whispered. Then he put his arms under her legs, locked his hands together behind her, and lifted her onto him. "Here comes you're 'E' ticket ride." Raising her off the desk, he made love to her in a crazy waltz, whirling around the room, that ended with him hammering into her against the wall.

As he made love to her, the small, muffled cries of "Oh my God!" and "Yes...yes!" could be heard through the door. Martin stood outside his office and, as people walked by with a questioning look, he would give them a sad nod and whisper, "Death in the family."

When Hal and Mari finally emerged, he said to Martin in passing. "I think I had better drive her home."

"Yeah...you do that, Hal. You do that..." He held out his fist in a sign of respect.

***

99

"Big...you're a genius! I had no idea that you were such a connoisseur of women!" Hal sat at their usual table. "Poetry! Who'd of thunk it!"

"It is like veritable catnip to the little darlings...in a word 'pheromone'...it is aphrodisiacal in nature. It does something extraordinaire to the core of their beings...they have no resistance to it."

"I wrote a poem and gave it to her at the office and she became so verklempt that I had to comfort her right there and take her home."

"You gave the poor girl a poem you wrote for her when you were at the office? How could you be so gauche? The girl has no defense for such a thing. She was all over you, wasn't she. She was in tears."

"Yes."

"Use poetry with finesse, son...at home...in the bedroom...in the bathroom...do not spring it on her in the kitchen...and never in public!"

"Why the bathroom?" Deuce was intrigued.

"Not all women will let you co-exist in the bathroom...even if there is only one...she will keep it to herself until she is ready to relinquish it to you. That is why two bathrooms are a must. That is where they perform their toilette...not to be confused with toilet...their ablutions...the grooming of their delicacies...and men have no place in the process. However, milady's bath may be a different question. She just might let you in...if you come up with a good reason...please her while you're there...and don't make a pest of yourself."

"I'm listening." Hal was now a devotee of his new guru.

If she is using shavers, curlers, clippers, files, rasps, anything to do with hair, power tools, or anything that hums...just keep going because you are not welcome. But if she is just taking a relaxing bath...the chances of her wanting you there increase tenfold...more so if she is playing music...and even more if she is burning scented candles or incense."

"What then?"

"If your Mari has lovely hair...tell her you want to wash it. Or, tell her you will wash her back. Once you are in...follow your imagination to pleasure her. But whatever you do...don't try to fuck her in the bathroom! It's cold...it's uncomfortable...and it's not very sanitary. Carry her to the bedroom."

100

"No wonder your Lily is a happy wife!"

"I never did that with Lily…"

***

The sound of soothing notes emanated from the bathroom and Hal could smell the perfume of a candle burning inside. A piano solo of Moonlight Sonata was playing on repeat on Mari's cube CD player, as she pampered herself by soaking in her bath. He stared at the door and then, bolstered by previous success, decided to enter milady's inner sanctum. *Whatever I do I've got to keep it low key. I don't want to ruffle her feathers.* He took a bath sheet from the linen closet and hoped he would be welcome. Softly knocking, he waited for her voice to bid him to come in. The sonata started again.

As he approached, she looked at him with languid eyes. Her slick wet hair hung down her back into the water. Islands of foam floated on the water's surface and she slightly turned toward him with a questioning gaze. "I want to wash your hair." He whispered, but his expression suggested more. She started to speak, but he gently put his fingers to his lips and with a "Shhhh" he quieted her. She lay back in the bathwater. He placed the towel on the counter and went to the side of the tub. Kneeling, he placed his right arm around her shoulders and gently pulled her to him and she placed her head on his shoulder. He gently kissed her and nestled his head on top of hers. Slowly he swirled his left hand in the water and lifted it to drizzle water over her shoulders, her arms, and her breasts. To soothe her, all the while, his whispered "Shhhh" was barely audible. Dipping more water, he smoothed it over her body as she luxuriated to his touch.

The sonata started over. Continuing to wash her with his hand, he gently kissed her and quieted her; as he drew lazy circles, her breath came quicker. His right hand lightly caressed her shoulder as the other moved with more purpose. His "Shhhh" was so light now it sounded like a gentle breeze, but her breath was faster, and she was in a trance. Totally under his spell, the beauty of the music, and the splendor of his touch, Mari drifted to the edge, the very edge and tumbled over, tumbling, tumbling in his rhapsody.

Lifting her from the tub, he wrapped her in the bath sheet and carried her to bed. The sonata started over.

***

101

WHAT IS KOSHER?

Hal's Camaro Z28 SS sped up the coast as he and Mari got an early start on Thanksgiving weekend. Taking the Wednesday before and the Monday after the holiday, they looked forward to six days of bliss. Following the signs in San Luis Obispo, they turned onto Highway 1 to take the world-class scenic drive to Monterey. Giddy with excitement, Mari took the new digital camera that Hal had given her out of the straw tote she carried and took a picture of him behind the wheel.

He flashed a smile at her. "Don't waste anymore pictures on me...save it for the scenery..."

"It's not wasted. I want pictures of you everywhere in the house."

"Did anybody ever tell you...you're strange?" He laughed.

"I'm not strange...I just love you!"

"Yep...you're strange."

***

The fire ate at the paper that wrapped the compressed wood log, igniting it in colorful flames. "This is the only kind of log they allow you to burn in their fireplace. The fire is not going to be very large, but it will be pretty to watch..." Hal shut the glass screen to the fireplace and returned to the couch to sit with Mari. "Because they only give you one log per day with the room...I bought more of them, so we won't run out. This place is perfect since it's central to everything we want to do. I looked for a hotel with both an ocean view and a fireplace and couldn't find one...but I figure we will be at the beach all day tomorrow...."

"I love this room." She patted her lap indicating for him to lay his head there. "The drive here was nothing short of spectacular...who did you used to come here with?" She felt a slight pang of jealousy.

"My parents." He missed her reason for the query.

Her finger wandered over his ear, explored his face and then down his nose and felt the small knot on the side of the bridge. "What happened here?"

"Before Deuce taught me how to fight...I got beat up by this kid in school..."

"That's terrible! How did that happen...?"

"Oh he was jumping around...making fun of my name...until I finally ran at him...right into his fist. It hurt like a mofo..."

"What's wrong with your name? Why would anyone make fun of it?"

"My first name…"

"Harold? What's wrong with Harold?"

"My first name isn't Harold…"

"But isn't 'Hal' short for Harold…?"

"Not in this case…Deuce gave me the nickname of 'Hal' to keep me out of fights…"

"Well what's your first name?"

"Promise me you won't laugh…"

"How terrible could it be? Of course I won't laugh…"

He paused as his mouth twisted to one side. "OK…it's 'Hillel'…an honorable Jewish name according to my mother…"

"Hillel…Hillel…" Mari repeated to herself and then she covered her mouth and started to snicker and then her tummy rolled with laughter.

"Come on…you said you wouldn't laugh…"

"But it's so funny…"

"My name is that funny to you…?"

"No…not your name…I love your name. It's kind of…romantic…"

"Then what's so funny?"

"Me! Here I have been living with you for almost three months…we've been fucking our brains out for I don't know how many days…and I'm madly in love with you…and I didn't even know your name!" She broke out laughing again.

"Yeah…that is kind of funny." He chuckled and then broke out laughing with her.

"Hillel…wow…I really like that. I have to agree with your mother. What does it mean?

"I don't know…I always resented it…" He paused in thought. "If I recall…I think my mother named me after my great grandfather."

"Ohhhhh…what was he like?"

"Well that's a long sad story…and I don't know all of it…you know how you are when you're a kid…I was a kid when I heard it and I don't know much about it…"

"Tell me about him…"

"All I know is that my great grandparents, who lived in France, were running from the Nazis as they were closing in. He put my great

103

grandmother and my grandmother...who was just a girl then...into coffins that were going to be shipped somewhere to safety in order to escape. The ship went to Lisbon. They never saw him again. My great grandmother searched for him the rest of her life...but never found him...he was probably killed. They eventually made their way to the states...where my great grandmother had some relatives...and that's all I know." By now he could sense when Mari was about to cry. "Hey...don't cry...it happened a long time ago...fifty-five years ago..."

"It is a good thing your great grandmother had a child...she had to live for her child...or else it would have killed her. I don't know what I would do if I was ever parted from you like that...it would tear my heart out..." Her tears started to stream. "...I would die..."

"You don't have to worry...I'm not going anywhere." He sat up and pulled her to his chest. "I guess that is why I think my great grandfather was killed...because that's the only way they could have kept him from finding his wife again."

"It's so frightening how things beyond their control tore them apart like that." They both lay down together and he spooned her in his arms while the fireplace flames reflected on their faces.

***

"Steinbeck would spin in his grave if he could see this." Hal stood at one end of Cannery Row and surveyed the tourist trap it had become. "Did you ever read 'Cannery Row'?"

"No."

What have you read of Steinbeck?"

They both said it together, "'Grapes of Wrath'."

They started walking toward the enclave of shops, restaurants, and boutique hotels. "You know 'East of Eden' was written about the families that lived in this region. I would say it was his second-best work. Steinbeck told their secrets and he was ostracized for it...now he is celebrated in the gaudiest way...I think he would have preferred their snubbing him."

Soon they were in the center of it all and taken in by the lure of everything from the kitsch to the sublime. Hal stopped in front of a shop that had a mannequin with an aqua colored Polynesian type bikini top with a sarong skirt. The floral pattern looked like stylized white hibiscuses. "Let's look in here."

Mari wandered through the door. "What's in here?"

"I don't know...just look around and see if there is anything you like." Hal got the clerk's attention. "That outfit in the window...do you have it in her size?"

"The one in the window is the last one we have...but I think it will fit her because it is somewhat adjustable..."

"Get it out of the window then because we're taking it if it fits her."

While Mari obliged Hal by trying on the outfit, Hal learned to stand with her tote and wait like a dutiful husband.

Her hand stuck out of the curtain. "I need my bag."

Hal handed it to her and then did another little walk around the shop and waited.

She called for the salesclerk and they conferred while he waited.

When Mari finally stepped from the dressing cubicle, he turned to find her transformed. She had brushed her curls into big, wild billows that cascaded over her shoulders. The clerk had given her a flower for her hair. The bikini she wore was covered from the waist down by the sarong that exposed one leg. "Yabba... dabba...doo!" Was all he could say.

The clerk exclaimed, "Oh...I have never seen anyone look so exquisite! Will that be cash or charge?"

Back on the street again they poked their noses into one shop after another until Mari spied something she could not resist. "Hal...please don't buy me another thing on this trip...except for that..." She pointed to a shop that sold kites that had spinners and streamers decorating the outside. "I've always wanted to fly a kite! Please can we get one...?"

"Sure...whatever you want, Babe."

"Tomorrow can we go on a picnic and fly it?"

"Do you want to go whale watching in the morning...and fly a kite afterwards?"

"That sounds wonderful!"

"OK...let's go for it."

***

Lying on a semi-deserted beach the two of them watched the kite soar higher as they let out more string. "Hal...what is Kosher?" Mari asked out of the blue. "What does it mean and how important is it to you?"

"Not very...it used to be when I was a kid...you know...my mother cared about it a lot more than I did...but now keeping up with all the do's and don'ts gets to be too much of a hassle. Why do you ask?"

"Because I cook for you and I never took any of that into consideration."

"Well...right there...according to some...because you're not Jewish, your cooking for me is against Jewish dietary laws. I couldn't be that strict."

"Do you follow any of the dietary laws?"

"Some...if they make sense to me. Like I don't eat pork..."

Mari winced. "Hal...I have a terrible confession to make to you. You see...I never thought of you as being Jewish...or anything else for that matter. You're just unique and wonderful and it doesn't occur to me to apply labels to you...I just think of you as Hal..." She gave him a look. "...and mine!"

"That's not so terrible..."

"Well, it can be if I'm not using my head. It's not that I don't respect others' religious beliefs...because I do...but I sort of made an awful mistake. Promise you won't get mad at me..."

"What could I possibly get mad at you for?"

She hunched her shoulders. "You know the meatloaf I make that you like so much?"

"Yeah..."

"I put three kinds of meat in it...beef...veal...and I'm so sorry...pork."

"What? I've been eating pork...?"

"Only in the meatloaf...I won't make it anymore..."

"Oh, Mari." He started laughing. "It's damned delicious...you keep making it...and don't tell my mother...or my Rabbi!"

"You don't mind?"

He grew philosophical. "You know...sometimes the weight of history...the weight of tradition...the weight of an inherited ethnicity and religion...being one of the 'chosen people'...doing what is expected of you...it all gets too heavy to bear. What is even more ironic is that those who suffered the least...demand the most. My father...whose family has lived in America for generations...and did not lose one family member to the Holocaust...has the chutzpah to demand that I marry a Jewish girl for the sake of propagating the

Jewish ethnos...to replenish what was lost in the Holocaust. He sees it as my duty. I say bullshit. Why is it my responsibility to conform everything in my life to solve the world's fucked up problems?"

"You should honor your great grandfather...he was a hero..."

"He was desperate...so he did what he had to do to save his wife and kid...that was mostly scared...and I guess that was heroic...but he was probably rounded up like all the others and sent to a death camp." Hal saw the darkening clouds come over Mari's face and decided to change the subject. "Besides...I carry his name...and had to fight my way through school because of it. That boy I told you about...after Deuce showed me how to fight...I beat the dog shit out of him. Deuce had to pull me off of him...and now they call me 'Hal'...and that is about as much weight as I am willing to carry. To be sure...I am proud of my Jewish heritage...but that's it..."

"Do you think I should convert?"

"Mari...you believe what you want to believe...or not at all...it doesn't matter to me."

She shaded her eyes to watch the kite soar higher as Hal let out more string from the spindle. "Look at how neat the spinners are...do you think we should get more of them?"

"Yeah...why not? You know that poem I wrote for you about how pretty your eyes are...?"

"Yeah..."

"The feel of the kite's pull on the string...it's stronger than I imagined...I should have found a way to work it into that poem. The tugging is kind of like the pull you have on me...like an invisible force." She rolled over and cuddled into his chest, with her hair spilling over him. Happiness ran like a thrill through him. "Kite flying...who would ever guess."

***

107

Stepping into her gown, Mari shimmied into it as she pulled it up. She stood in front of the full-length mirror and inspected herself. "Hal...I need a zip." She called out. As he walked into the room, she cautioned him, "If you mess up my hair or makeup...I promise you we will be here for at least another hour..."

"I wouldn't dream of it...but when I get you back home tonight...all bets are off..." He found the zipper tab and pulled it up. "That dress fits you like a glove...it doesn't leave much to the imagination."

"Oh...really?! It was made for Dyan Cannon...you know...the movie star...but she chose another gown..."

"So, what did the other gown look like...?"

"Believe me...it was hot..." She rolled her eyes. "...but since I am a bit bustier than she is, Brian added this sheer top part of the bodice...to keep me from bouncing out...or this would have been even more revealing...that's why he made it somewhat modest for me..." She turned from the mirror to face him. "What do you think?"

She sparkled in a white, lace fitted gown sprinkled with iridescent sequins and beads. What would have been a strapless top was reconfigured with a sheer, long sleeved bodice appliqued with lace and scattered with beads and sequins. With her straightened hair swept up and decorated with iridescent pearls she looked like she stepped out of a Vogue Magazine.

Hal put his hand to his chest and gave her a low wolf whistle. "Every time I think you couldn't possibly look more beautiful...you turn around and outdo yourself. Tell Brian for me that he is a wizard."

"You can tell him yourself tonight. Steven is bringing him to the dance...as his plus one. I don't know if he told Vee or not...but I think he may be coming out..."

"That ought to be interesting...oh, the drama...the shit storm...the recriminations..."

"Oh, stop it, Hal...just wish them well...and hope that Vee understands." She checked his tie and cuff links and turned him around to survey his tux. "Do you have your speech ready for when you receive the 'Story of the Year' award?"

"There's no guarantee that I'm going to win it..."

"Oh, tosh and piffle...everyone agrees you have it in the bag...so you'd better be ready."

"By the way...I have something for you..." Hal reached into his pocket and pulled out a black lacquered box. "I picked up this little trinket for you...I thought it matched your eyes..." He took a necklace out of the box and held it up to place it around her neck. "It's your first Chanukah present."

"It's beautiful, Hal! It's amazing what they can do with rhinestones these days...they almost look like real diamonds...the centerpiece looks like a..."

"Sapphire..." He fastened it behind her neck and turned her around to the mirror. "That makes the picture perfect."

"Oooooh...I can't wait to get you home tonight!"

***

The Angel City Magazine Christmas gala, and annual awards, was a formal event. Christmas garlands, ornaments, and red velvet bows bedecked the ballroom. Golden wreaths, with gilded pinecones and candles, adorned the banquet tables and a dais of tables with a lectern in the center was set up on a stage. As Hal and Mari walked in, he whispered to her, "Try to look like we're not an item..."

"That's going to be hard for me...it's all I can do to keep my hands off of you...I'm tired of pretending." She stopped and straightened his tie. "Before the evening is through...I'm going to kiss you in the middle of the ballroom floor...in front of God...Vee...whichever comes first...and everyone!"

"Mari...don't do it...Vee still thinks that you and Steven are an item..."

"No he doesn't...and if he hasn't guessed that Steven and I are just friends...he will certainly find that out tonight."

"I think we are seated somewhere towards the front...we'd better find our table...I hope we like the other people seated with us..."

"It might be more fun if we didn't...especially when you win..."

"Don't jinx it..."

As soon as they were seated a waiter came by and filled their glasses with champagne.

Hal noticed that she moved her glass over to his. "I'll go to the bar and get you your drink."

The bartender was still setting up as Hal went to put in his request. "Have they given you your tickets yet?" He asked.

"Tickets? No."

"Nobody is ever ready on time...they should have handed them out at the door. Each person gets three tickets for drinks...after that it's pay as you go..." He held a finger up. "I'll go ahead and pour one for you...but be sure to get your tickets as soon as they start handing them out."

Hal ordered Mari's drink and then leaned against the bar while he waited. Out of the corner of his eye, he saw Martin approaching with a silly grin pasted on his face. *Don't make eye contact...maybe he'll keep going...turn your back and pretend he's not there...aw shit...he's coming over.* Hal put on an ambiguous smile and gave Martin a sloppy salute. "How's it going, Martin?"

"Hal...my hero! I swear, man...when I grow up I want to be just like you!"

"What...overweight and Jewish?"

"Stop the bullshit...you have got to be the luckiest mofo...or the smartest. I can't decide which. You're not only up for the best story of the year...but it's you and that Carlson girl...what a babe...!"

"I don't know what you're talking about...she's just my plus one for the evening. It was the least I could do...she was the one who handed me the story..."

"OK...if you want to play it like that...nudge...nudge...say no more..."

"Big Python fan...huh? I'm impressed...you have eclectic tastes."

The bartender set the drink on the bar and Hal thanked him and took it. "Got to go...the Carlson babe wants her drink..."

"Don't rub it in...you lucky bastard!"

Thanking the gods for a quick escape, Hal went back to his table. "Martin is on the rampage...he already thinks we're an item..."

Mari picked up her drink and held it up to Hal. "Before the evening is over...he will be sure of it..."

"Is this table six?" A tall gentleman with white hair was searching for his table.

"Yes it is..." Hal nodded.

"Come, dear...we found it." He held a chair for his plump wife to sit down and settled in next to her.

"I'm sorry...I don't recall seeing you at the office..." Hal held out his hand. "...I'm Hal Golan...and this is Mari Carlson..."

"Pleased to finally meet you Mr. Golan...Miss Carlson...I'm not with Angel City Magazine...my name is Vince Kinney and I'm with Peer Publishing. This is my wife Elizabeth. We're Vee's guests...and we were hoping to meet you. Vee is quite impressed with your writing and he thought I should meet you...he said you were working on a novel..."

Hal's eyebrows went up. "Yes...but it is not yet completed."

"I'm always looking for new talent...I think it would be advantageous for both of us to have an opportunity to discuss your work. I don't want to bore everyone here by talking shop the whole evening...so I will get right to the point. I would like to see the first three chapters...to get a feel for whether it is something we would be interested in. Let me just give you my card...and perhaps we can get together over lunch while I'm in town...shall we say next week?"

"That would be good. What days do you have open...?"

"The only day I have open is Wednesday..."

"That's Christmas Eve..."

"Business doesn't take a holiday...that's my philosophy..."

"And right you are. Where are you staying...?"

"The Biltmore..."

"We can have lunch there...say around noonish...?" Hal dug into the inside pocket of his tux, fished out his business card, and handed it to Kinney.

"That works out well for me..." Kinney sat back in his chair and tucked the card into his wallet. "Now that that's settled...we can relax and enjoy the rest of the evening."

Vee crossed the room and ambled over to the table. "I see you have all found each other...have I missed anything?"

"Young Mr. Golan here has agreed to meet with me next week..."

"That sounds great...do you mind if I join you for the meeting..."

"Not at all...I think you would be an asset to our discussion."

"I'll come back and sit with you later...but for now I must greet everyone." Vee cast his eyes on Mari. "Do you have a moment? I need to discuss a favor with you." He held out his hand to indicate he wanted to talk to her alone.

"Of course." Mari got up and followed Vee's lead.

Kinney's eyes fixed on Mari as she walked away. "That's a stunning looking woman...are you two...?" He drew a circle in the air to indicate a relationship.

"She does my research for me...we're colleagues. But to be honest...if she ever wanted to..." Hal drew an air circle. "...I would certainly be up for it."

"Up for it...up for it...that's a good one, son!" Kinney chuckled.

Hal realized how his words were taken and laughed. "Pun totally unintended..."

Mrs. Kinney sat there with a detached smile on her face and sipped her champagne. She had fortified herself before she arrived and would sit in a polite stupor for the entire evening.

Vee found a table in the back of the room that had no occupants and they both sat down. "Mari...I have to ask you why you are here with Hal instead of Steven...I thought you said you and Steven were seeing each other..."

"Vee...I absolutely adore Steven...I love him...and I am sure he loves me too...but he isn't in love with me...he doesn't feel that way about me. We are the closest of friends...and we see each other all the time...and I depend on him in so many ways...and he is good to me...but I think he asked someone new to the Christmas dance..."

"She really must be something else if he thinks she is better than you." He held out his hands in frustration. "Damn it...I like you a lot, Mari, and I was hoping the two of you would hit it off..."

"Maybe you'll like his choice better...at least I hope so...I would hate to have been dumped for nothing..." She gave him a touching look.

"Oh...my dear...I hope he didn't hurt you..."

Mari looked down and sighed. "He let me down as gently as possible..."

"What's going on between you and Hal?"

"I don't know...he asked me to be his plus one for the evening...so I said yes. He's the nicest guy in the office you know...all the girls think so...and I want to thank you for assigning me to him...he is great to work under..." Mari allowed herself a little private joke.

"Well if Steven doesn't have the good sense to sweep you down a church aisle...then you couldn't ask for a better catch than Hal...mark my words...he's going places."

"I'll keep that in mind...on the outside chance that he's interested..."

"My dear...I don't think there is a man in this room who wouldn't be interested...including me...but I'm shackled to the missus for life..." He patted her hand. "You're a good girl, Mari...I hope you find someone who will be good for you. I had better get to it...a lot of hands to shake." He got up, lifted Mari's chin, and studied her face. "My son's an idiot!" He kissed her on the forehead and strode off to greet incoming guests.

When Mari sat down next to Hal, she whispered in his ear, "He really...really likes you. Now that he knows Steven has 'dumped' me...he hopes I'll set my hat for you..."

"Steven dumped you?"

"Well...what else could I tell him? You have to leave people their pride..."

"Oh." Hal smiled. "I guess I'll just have to pick up the pieces..." Mari gave him a crestfallen look.

The hall filled up and the buzz of conversation grew louder with little clusters forming and regrouping. As people wended their way to the tables, conversations started over again as new arrivals sat down. Microphone squawk filled the air as the stage sound system was being set up. Finally, Vee stepped up to the podium, and a hush fell over the crowd. "Has everyone found their table? You out there...what table are you looking for?"

"Twelve." A voice yelled out.

"Will the people at table twelve please wave your hands...yeah...that's it...there you go...table twelve. Is there anyone else who's lost?" He looked around. "OK...it looks like the others found their way." Vee looked up to see Steven make his entrance with a decidedly pretty looking young man, blond with a slight build. They were dressed in matching tuxedos and sat at one of the front tables. He started to speak but left the podium and walked off stage. He went out on the balcony on the side of the ballroom and looked over the city. Suddenly, he hit a wall of realization. It was not as though the inkling of the idea had never occurred to him, but he was always able to dismiss it before. *My son is gay? Of course he is...he's thirty years old and hasn't had a serious relationship with a girl in all those years...it was right in front of me all along. That's why he had no*

113

natural inclinations toward a beautiful girl. What the fuck does this mean? No grand kids? What is he going to do in life? What did Mari mean when she said she loved him? Does she know? Of course she knows! He turned to watch through the glass doors and saw Mari go over to Steven's table. He got up and hugged her as did the other man. They talked for a while and then she indicated where Steven could find his father. *Shit...everyone knows except me.*

Steven walked out on the balcony. "It's a beautiful view." He took out a pack of cigarettes and offered one to his father. Vee took the proffered cigarette, although he had quit smoking. Steven placed a cigarette between his lips, flicked his lighter and held the flame to both.

Vee inhaled deeply, stared off in the distance, and quietly spoke. "Why didn't you tell me, son."

Steven was relieved that his father finally understood. "I was working on building up enough nerve...you're not always easy to talk to..."

"Do you fancy that you're in love with...?"

"Brian...yes...I am."

"Can you understand that I am deeply disappointed?"

"Yes...but it's not about you...or your life. I have wished a million times that I could be like other men...and I finally had to realize that I had to accept myself as I am. It is nothing that you or I could change."

"Mari said she loves you and that you 'dumped' her."

"Oh...my darling, darling Mari...I am so glad you sent her my way...yes we love each other madly...but not in the way you hoped. She's a dear person...and my best friend. She always says I dumped her...as an inside joke...and to make me look like I'm manly and rakish...but Brian and I adopted her."

"What about children...I'll never have grandchildren..."

"Why not? Both Brian and I can father children...we intend to have a family when the time is right..."

Vee turned to his son. "So this is how you intend to live your life?"

"Yes. I just want to know one thing...do I still have a father?" Steven's eyes misted.

Vee was stunned by the question. "How could you doubt it?" He ruffled Steven's hair. "You're still my sunny little boy." He put his hand to his face. "I don't know how to tell your mother."

"She already knows, dad...she has known since I was a child...she just didn't know how to tell you..."

Mari did not want Brian to sit alone while Steven talked to Vee. She stayed at his table and held his hand.

"Don't worry, dear heart...everything is going to work out just fine..."

"But what if his father rejects him? I can't stand for Steven to be unhappy...he doesn't deserve it."

"He loves you, Brian...and whatever he has to go through...it will be worth it to him."

"Are you sure..." He started to snuffle. "I'm just so..."

"Don't cry...you want to look good when you meet his father." She saw Steven and Vee coming through the balcony door. "Look! They're smiling!" She got up. "I've got to go back and leave all of you to get acquainted." She pecked him on the cheek. "Put on your happy face."

"I thought you deserted me for Steven..." Hal helped her with her chair.

"Nope...Brian. You may have to look out! A man who can make me look this good...is some major competition...gay or straight!"

"I can learn how to sew..." He pleaded.

Dinner was served and collected without a hitch. Company achievements were announced, and speeches were made. It was now time to announce the awards. Certificates were handed out for everything from attendance to employee of the year, culminating in the "Story of the Year" award. Vee read the nominations. "Those in contention for the award are...Dirk Nelson for 'The History of Freeways in Los Angeles'...Murray McMurray for 'The Gilded Age of Los Angeles'...and Hal Golan for 'The Case of Paul Mitchem: a Los Angeles Tragedy'. In relation to the last contender, 'The Case of Paul Mitchem'...we have an announcement to make. Part of the deciding factor...was the urgency and importance of the article...as is shown by the fact that the court has just ruled that Paul Mitchem will get a new trial! The award goes to Hal Golan!" The applause was thunderous as Hal was given a standing ovation.

"This is for you, baby." Hal whispered to Mari as she hugged him. He walked amid well-wishers to the center stage. He was handed the award, a bronze replica of the Los Angeles City Hall embedded on a teakwood base that had a small brass plate with his name and year engraved on it. "This award is exceedingly gratifying for me...received in all humility...and for someone else who deserves half the credit...and that person is Mari Carlson. She was the first one who noticed the discrepancies and inconsistencies of the case...and worked on it by my side...through to the very end. Mari...please stand up." She stood with her hand over her heart to receive the outpouring of the audience. "The cumblston...cumbertson...sorry folks...she's so lovely, I get tongue tied every time I look at her. She graciously agreed to be my plus-one tonight...and on the ride over here...her conversation was articulate...astute...and scintillating...while I sounded like Elmer Fudd!" Playing to the laughter, he put his hand over his eyes. "The cumbersome task..." He dropped his hand. "...of going through reams of material mostly fell on Mari's shoulders. She isolated the pertinent facts and summarized them in a coherent way to give me the depth of understanding it took to write the story. Thanks to her work...and my writing...a man will get another shot at life...and justice." He held the trophy up and put his hand to his chest. "Mari...I love you..." At a ripple of chatter through the audience, he added, "...yeah...yeah, as though I'm the only one...and all you guys out there don't!" He laughed. "Thank you...thank you all!"

He went back to the table to receive congratulations all around. Kinney shook his hand vigorously. "I'm very impressed...very impressed." He looked down at his wife who was glassy eyed. "I must get back to the hotel...but I am looking forward to meeting with you on Wednesday"

"It will be a pleasure."

The stage was cleared, a bandstand was set up, and the call for everyone to dance went out. Hal and Mari were one of the first couples on the dance floor and spontaneously everybody clapped. "Well it looks like we turned into an item after all..." She gazed at him.

"If you keep looking at me like that...I can't be held responsible."

"Well...I was ordered by our boss to go after you...and I think that's just what I'll do...I'm going to kiss you, Hal..."

"No..."

"Incoming..." She pulled him to her and kissed him full on the lips, much to the delight of onlookers who applauded their approval. "I'm so proud of you...and so in love with you..."

"That goes both ways."

Around midnight they left the dance and went downstairs for a quiet drink before leaving the hotel. "Why didn't we just go home?" Mari asked.

Hal tilted his head. "I wanted to show you off some more..."

She clasped both hands beside her cheek and mimed a kiss at him. As the waiter approached, she asked, "Do I dare have a Champagne Cocktail?"

Hal nodded. "Just one." And he ordered.

"Is that Dirk over there? He looks drunk as a skunk." Mari pointed with her nose toward the bar.

"Don't look...we don't want him to notice us and come over..."

"You know...your acceptance speech was so touching. You gave me practically all the credit when you were the one who wrote the article in a way that was so affecting...it grabbed the readers and broke their hearts. You hit it out of the ballpark!"

"We're a team...you and me, Babe."

The waiter served their drinks and Hal gave him his credit card. "I don't think we should stay too long and press our luck." He pointed his thumb in Dirk's direction. "You know...all in all...he pulled it together and ran with the freeway bug you put in his ear...only with a different take...it turned out to be an interesting story."

"He had to do something because Vee was on his ass...I just wonder who he stole it from." She took a sip of her drink.

"I love how champagne fizzes on your nose..." She wrinkled her nose at him.

"I love it when you do that..."

"What?"

"Wrinkle your nose."

"Weeell...it looks like we have a love fest all the way around here." Dirk, a little slur footed, walked over to their table. "A perfect world for Hal and Mari...Beauty and the Beast...." He sang the refrain.

"Dirk...do yourself a favor and take it back to where you were sitting."

"Oooohh...the great Hal Golan...you stole my girl...and you stole my story."

"I don't suppose it would do any good to tell you that's not true...arguing with a drunk is a waste of time. Go back to your seat and sit down...and we'll call it good." Hal was losing patience.

Weaving, Dirk leaned over Mari. "Why him...huh...honey...what's he got? Why him and not me?"

"That's it, pal." Hal grabbed him by the lapels and called to the bartender. "This gentleman is leaving...has he paid his tab?"

"No."

"Put it on my tab." Hal turned him around with a bouncer's grip and marched him through the lobby and out the door. He told the doorman, "This guy is too drunk to be served...or to drive. Call him a cab." He let Dirk go and he dropped to the ground.

"Don't think I'm going to forget this Golan..." Dirk struggled to get up.

"The hell if you do...you owe me for your drinks!" Hal dusted off his hands.

***

"Deuce…what's it like to be married? I'm really thinking of asking Mari to marry me…but…I don't know. You hear so many men gripe about it…I don't think I know what I'm getting into." Hal picked up the paper coaster that came with his beer, folded it in half and then into quarters.

"Don't ask me. I don't know if my marriage is typical or not. You know I had to marry Wanda…I thought I loved her…but then I was too young to know much about love or anything else." Deuce took a deep breath. "If you remember…I was all set to go to college…when she decides to finally give it up…and we started getting it on. The next thing I know…she's pregnant…and there went my college education. After I was older…I figured out she did it on purpose. I guess she thought I would go away to college and find somebody else…and I probably would have. It's good to have somebody who cares about you…and raise the kids…but if you think the passion is there…forget it. Maybe if I didn't have to get married…maybe if I found someone who I was crazy about…who knows? But don't go comparing you and Mari to me and Wanda. No two couples are alike."

"Aren't you and Wanda happy?"

"Oh…fuck no! We get along…that's all. What marriage does is to grind down your rough edges. It makes you smarter…in a lot of ways. One thing that being married and having kids did for me…though…was to get me motivated to make money…and lots of it…so there is an upside in that regard. But, if I had it to do all over again…I think I would have done it differently. I would have gone to college." He saw Hal's wary expression. "That doesn't mean that is how it would be with you and Mari…"

"That's why I want you to get to know her…when you met her she was still in pretty bad shape…it wasn't the best of circumstances to say the least…"

"Not with you killin' that guy…to say the least…"

"Look…I didn't…oh fuck it…"

"Alright…whatever you say…"

"All I want is for you to meet her now…get to know her…and tell me what you think."

"What do you want to involve me for in your love life? If you love her...what do I have to say about it? All I'm goin' to do is to tell you what you want to hear anyway."

"Shit...you never do that...you are the most contrary person I know."

"What do you want me to do...point out all of the girl's flaws so we can argue about it? No thank you! If you want to marry her...then marry her. The only involvement I want is to be your best man..."

"Well that's a given..."

"OK...then I'm done here."

"No you're not! You're going to get to know her and tell me your honest opinion...then you can be my best man..."

"Alright...I may as well meet her if you're going to marry her in any event."

"I want you to talk with her...without me being there...and find out what she really thinks about me."

"Aw man...that's fucked up! You want me to draw her out...to spy on her for you...why don't you just go ask her yourself..."

"I guess the thing I can't get over...is why should she love me? Every swinging dick in town would love to have her...why would she pick me...?"

"And any one of those swinging dicks she chooses...would be asking himself the same question. It just so happens you're the dick she chose...DICK!"

"I just want to know why."

***

Hal and Mari walked into Canter's Deli. Deuce was already seated at a booth and had been waiting for them. He watched the couple and what their body language told him. She wore a white parka with a blue fox trimmed hood. Clinging to his arm, her face was radiant as she looked up at Hal. She was noticeably taken with him. He was solicitous of her, but he was always a little offbeat when he knew he was being less than honest, and Deuce could spot it since they were kids. Casting an askance eye at his friend, he wished he had not agreed to the ruse.

He smiled as Hal waved and directed her toward the booth. "Sorry we're late...we left early but the traffic was atrocious."

Mari slid into the booth. "Hi, Deuce...it is so nice to see you again." She smiled.

Hal sat next to her. "What a day we had at work...of course it's always crazy just before we put the baby to bed...before we print..." He looked around for the waitress. "I'm starving!"

Deuce put on his affable face. "Well...Mari...don't you look pretty...your face all framed with fur...I'm glad to see you're all better now."

Her hands went to her face and her brow knitted. "Yes...I'm so fortunate that I don't have any permanent marks or scaring...at least not on the outside."

Both Hal and Deuce were surprised that she still harbored sentiments about their encounter with Zack. Once they were in the clear, the only feelings they had about it was that Zack deserved what he got. Other than Deuce holding a high degree of respect for Hal for doing what he had to do when the shit jumped up, they forgot about it. Deuce found the right thing to say. "Well...I hope those wounds will heal too, someday."

The waitress came over and took their orders. Mari mentally changed gears and her face brightened. "So you like my new coat..." She stroked the fur on the hood. "It is one of my Chanukah presents from Hal. For Christmas I got him tickets to the Rose Bowl game...which we really enjoyed. I figured it was the least I could do for him after he sat through an opera...and he said I would need this coat to keep from freezing my buns off at the game...I love it!" She looked at Hal. "But you buy me too many presents...I can't keep up with all of that..."

"Baby...you're keeping up just fine."

She did a double take at him when she realized what he meant. "Is that why you buy me so many presents? You don't have to you know..." The smile left her face.

"No...no...well sort of...you make me happy all the time...I just want to make you happy..."

She brightened. "I'm happy just to be with you..."

"OK...you two lovebirds can fight over who makes whom the happiest later on...what's going on...?" Deuce interjected.

"Like she said...we went to the Rose Bowl...she wrangled Martin's tickets out of him...and boy what a game...Michigan beat Washington State..."

"I know...I watched it on TV...and didn't freeze my buns off..."

"Yeah...but there's nothing like being there...the atmosphere and the excitement...no commercials..." He made a slight gesture toward Mari for Deuce not to let on that it was better to see the game at home. "I wouldn't have missed being there for anything...wrapped in a blanket with my sweetie...drinking hot cocoa out of a thermos..." He looked down at her. "...there's nothing better."

The hostess approached their table. "Are you Mr. Golan?"

"Yes."

"There is a call for you...they said it was important..."

"I wonder who knows I'm here...I better see who it is..." He followed the hostess back to her station, slipped her ten dollars, picked up the receiver, and talked to the dial tone. After an appropriate interval, he went back to the table. "That was Vee...like a dummy I mentioned that I was going to be here with a friend...he needs a major re-write...now...and he can't get ahold of McMurray. Shit...I'm stuck with it...and I've got to get over there right away." He turned to Deuce. "After dinner...can you drive Mari home...?"

"Sure...no problem."

"But what about your dinner? You haven't eaten anything." Mari implored.

"I'll grab a burger on the way..." He started to go.

"Hal!" He heard her voice like it was a wail, pleading for him to stay, adding to his guilt. Instead, when he turned, he saw her pointing to her lips for him to kiss her before leaving. He went back, nuzzled her nose, and gave her a smooch. He drove back to work in case she should call him there—and waited.

Deuce sympathized. "I hope I'm pleasant company for you...I would hate for your evening to be ruined."

Mari seemed to be resigned. "These things can come up...especially just before the magazine goes to press. Sometimes you think everything is perfect and ready to go...and then someone catches a screw up and it has to be dealt with. I just hope that Hal doesn't have to pull an all-nighter...he put in a lot of work today...and he hasn't eaten. I hope he stops and gets something to eat like he said he would...and doesn't drive when he's too tired."

"Don't worry...he's a big boy..."

"That's just it...because men are so strong...they always think they're invincible...and they don't take care of themselves..." She smiled. "And that's why women have to look after them."

"I guess you have your hands full then..."

"Yeah..." She nodded. "Do you mind if I ask you something?"

"Ask away..."

"What is your real name?"

"What...don't you like Deuce?"

She squinted at him. "You got that name in middle school or high school...right?"

"OK...yeah."

"It seems to me that you have an intellect and heart that your nickname doesn't measure up to...what does your mother call you?"

"My mother calls me Terry." Deuce looked puzzled.

"Terry...is that short for Terrence?"

"Junior...my son's the third..."

"Terry...I like Terry...do you mind if I call you Terry? I think it is more respectful."

Surprised, Deuce laughed and held up his hands. "Lady...you can call me Terry...but only you...and my mother can call me that."

She beamed. "That's a relief...I always thought that 'Deuce' was so out of character for you."

"I heard that you just found out Hal's name."

"Yeah...it threw me for a loop that I didn't know his name...but, I love his name...Hillel..."

"Shhhh...don't ever tell anyone..."

"Sorry..." She hunched her shoulders. "I can get carried away talking about him..."

"By the way...he said you once told him that he made you feel ooey-gooey...what does that mean?

"He told you that!" She giggled. "Have you ever felt so strongly about someone that it flattens you like a pancake with warm butter and syrup all over you?"

"I can't say that I have..."

"Neither did I until it hit me that I was in love with Hal...and then it hit me really hard...like a steamroller."

"Does he feel that way about you...steamrolled?"

She closed her eyes. "Oh dear God...if he didn't I would die...but he said he does, and I believe that he does. The only thing that worries me is that he is always buying me things...spending too much money. I think he's trying to impress me...and he has already impressed me...he doesn't have to try..."

"What if he was rich...?"

"I'm sure he will be one day...if that's what he wants...he's certainly talented and smart enough to be..." She put her hand to her chin in thought. "But I don't think that's his goal...this is just my opinion...but I think there are things he values more than money...like his integrity...societal justice is very important to him...if you read his article...no one could write like that if they didn't feel it. That is what struck me about him from the very start...that and the way he speaks to you...like his eyes could look into your heart..." She gave him an impish smile. "Did you know that he has a stray dimple right here?" She pointed to her cheek just to the right side of her mouth. "You can only see it when he talks."

Deuce scratched his head. "I don't think I ever watched him that closely."

The waitress served the orders. "Wasn't there a third party here?"

"Yes...he was called away on an emergency. Please pack his meal to go...he'll have it later tonight when he gets home." Mari requested, and the waitress whisked the plate away.

"While we're on our favorite subject...how would you rate Hal on a scale of one to ten?" Deuce wanted to keep her talking about Hal.

"Definitely a ten..."

"He rated you a fifteen...off the charts!"

"Awww...he rated me a fifteen?" She gushed. "I didn't know you could go higher than a ten...he's definitely a fifteen or more..."

He chuckled. "I only rated him a seven..."

"Only a seven...why so low?"

"Well...he's OK...but he's not that great looking..."

"Ohhhh...but you're not a woman..." She said coyly. "...and you've never been to bed with him..."

"Naw...I missed that part..."

"Your loss!" She laughed.

He sat back and grinned. "So he's good at what he's layin' dowwwn!"

"No...not just 'good' but great, excellent, marvelous, wonderful, divine...pick your adjective...and he exceeds it." She sighed. "Sometimes I feel like I can't keep up...I have to learn more."

"Is he...doin' it too often...does he need to back off?"

"Oh dear God...no!" She blushed. "I don't want you to think I'm a terrible person...but I can't get enough of him! I just want to know more about how to please him...because he certainly knows all he needs to know about pleasing me."

"Why don't you just ask him what he wants?"

"Oh...no...I couldn't do that...I could never say it...get the words out. Besides...I want to surprise him."

"And how are you going to do that?"

"I have this friend...she's a beautiful girl...and she knows things. She has what she calls her recipe book...only for cooking in the bedroom...not the kitchen...and I am going to ask her if I can read it..."

"Well...shit howdy...girl! Aren't you somethin'!"

"I hope so!"

"Where do you see you and Hal in...let's say five years?"

"Together...happy..."

"Married?"

"The thought of marriage actually frightens me...but I'm frightened even more of the thought of ever being without him...or even worse...that he wouldn't want to marry me."

"Why would you be frightened of marriage?"

"My parents' marriage...now there was a match made in Hell..."

"Do you think it would be like that for you and Hal?"

"No...not at all. He's wonderful...not at all like my father...and I'm nothing like my mother. He said he wants the house with the picket fence...children...and I think he could make it work."

"Tell me...how old were you when you came to L.A.?"

"Sixteen."

"Sixteen!?!" Deuce made a face. "You must have run away from home!"

"Yes…and no." She looked down at her plate. "Yes…I left without telling anybody I was leaving or where I was going…but…no…regarding anybody caring or bothering to look for me. There was never a 'missing person' bulletin put out on me…I checked…and I'm sure my family did not want me back."

"And how old are you now?"

"Twenty-three…almost twenty-four."

"You made your way in this world…all by yourself…for that long?"

"I put myself through college…and I have a bachelor's and a master's degree. I'm not saying that it wasn't rough…because it was…but I never dishonored myself…and I worked and paid for everything I got." She became morose. "Terry…please don't tell Hal anything about this. We're both so happy now…and I've never been this happy…I don't want to spoil it by telling him about the sad piece of shit my life has been up until now." She paused. "I will tell him one day…or if he asks me…just not now."

Deuce leaned forward. "Would you tell me?"

She studied his face. *We already share a huge secret, what's one more?* "Yeah…If you promise not to tell Hal…or anybody else."

"Alright."

"I don't want to spoil your dinner. Let's eat and talk about nice things…after dinner we can go for a walk and I'll tell you about a little girl who was raised by wolves."

***

Deuce rapped his knuckles on the table. "Marry her! If you have any goddamned sense at all you will marry her. That girl is so in love with you that she thinks that the sun rises and sets right in your ass. I didn't have the heart to tell her that the sun rises in the east and sets in the west…and has nothing to do with you!"

"Well tell me what she said." Hal sat forward in his seat.

"Word for word…or just to summarize in a nutshell…she thinks you're…great…wonderful…excellent…marvelous…and she rated you a fifteen!" Deuce twisted his face. "And here I work my butt off and my wife can't be bothered to get out of bed to fix me a hot breakfast…fuck!"

"A fifteen…you must be kidding."

"No I'm not…she took umbrage that I rated you a seven…told me I didn't know what I was talking about because I wasn't a woman…and a few other things." He shook his head. "Man...she even thinks that she is not good enough for you...and that she has to learn stuff to make you happy...that's the most precious shit I ever heard."

"What? You're making this stuff up."

Deuce held up his right hand. "If I'm lyin'...I'm dyin'. She even said she had to read up on stuff to make you happy. I'm telling you...you had better marry this girl before she finds out what a shit you can be...well...not a shit...but mediocre."

"What does she see in me, Deuce?"

"Fuck if I know...but just keep doing whatever you're doing because it works." He narrowed his eyes. "You goin' down on this girl?"

"Every chance I get!"

"Oh...no wonder she loves you...that would tend to elevate your repertoire..." He took a slug of his beer and set the mug down.

Hal drained his glass and signaled for another beer. "I wanted to do that for so long...and I did from the first time I made love to her. Everything about her is so beautiful and so damned delicious." He reached for Deuce's mug.

Deuce pulled his mug away. "You ain't drinking out of my glass now that I know where your mouth has been!"

Hal grabbed the mug back, took a deep drink from it, set it down, and grinned. "And that's as close as you're going to get to it!"

***

THE RECIPE BOOK

Mari knocked on Lo-Lo's door. A voice from inside asked, "Is that you?"

"Yes...it's me..." Mari answered. She heard the sound of deadbolts unlocking before the door opened.

"Girl...I am so glad you're here. I almost burned the place down." Lo-Lo's dark face still reflected her embarrassment. "I put on a pot of ham hocks and beans...and then I toked a hoot...and fell asleep. The next thing I know smoke was billowing out of the kitchen...and someone had called the fire department...I'm still shaking..."

"What did they do?"

"I just explained that I was cooking and things got out of hand...and there was this really fine brother...all in his fireman's hat and shit...ended up asking me for my phone number so he could check to see if I was alright." She smiled to herself. "I just might have him come over to put my fire out!"

"Oh, girl...you are so bad!" Mari laughed.

"So, what's going on with you and Hal...is the course of true love running smoothly?"

"Ooohh...yes! But I think I need to be more...more...you know..."

"Bring more to the table...or I should say bed?"

"Yes. I want to know how to do things...you know...from your recipe book..."

"You have to be careful with that book...you don't want to do everything in there." She pursed her lips.

"Are there some things you can teach me...?"

"Sure. The main thing you want to remember is that men are mostly visual...you want to give them a show along with sensation. You wouldn't believe how many women just lay there while their man does all the work...it does nothing to set the woman apart from other women...and it's not very satisfying for the man."

"Thank goodness...I don't just lay there with Hal. I can't help being enthusiastic. I sort of glom on to him and do what comes naturally until we're both happy." Mari grinned.

"That counts for a lot. Now, I think what you need is to get in the fast lane...but don't veer into anything weird...and you need props for the visual...lingerie that is either tasteful or trashy...music that is suggestive...and you already know how to dance...so you know how to move...oh...yes...and use your hair..."

"My hair?"

"Yeah...you've got long hair...throw it around when you're on top of him..."

"Oh...when I'm on top of him?"

"OK...let's take it from the top. Here...you can borrow my CD until you get your own...and you want to set the sixth cut...'I Want You'...to repeat. You start off by....."

***

Hal opened the door to find the kitchen table in the living room covered with a tablecloth and two place settings. A centerpiece with burning candles lit the darkened room. A bottle of champagne was on ice. Scented candles were placed around the room. Wafting from the kitchen was the smell of something mouth-watering. Bewildered, he stood in the middle of the room looking around.

Mari came into the room wearing an ivory peignoir of opaque silk that draped in gathers from her shoulders in a "V" neckline to a sheer lace band that went from under her bust to her waist. The long opaque skirt opened slightly in the front to reveal the bikini panties underneath.

Her hair was down and hung in her natural curls around her shoulders. She walked straight to Hal and pulled him down into a deep kiss and then breathed. "I fixed dinner for you."

He stared after her as he took off his coat, went to hang it on the coat rack, missed the hook, and the coat landed in a heap on the floor and remained there. She picked up the bottle of champagne and wrestled the cork free, as she was taught to do, by releasing the pressure slowly to avoid spilling the bubbly. Pouring a glass, she took it to Hal.

"What's all this?" He asked.

"I made something special for you tonight..."

His eyes glowed. "Yeah...what did I do to deserve all this?"

She gave him a dreamy look. "It's just 'happy I love you day'." She handed him the glass.

"Oh...I should have marked that on my calendar..."

"It's hard to keep track of…because it comes around several times a year…" She smiled. "Dinner is almost ready…go wash up and get ready to sit down."

When he returned, she had just placed the rosemary rack of lamb dinner on the table. He could not keep his eyes off her all during the meal. There was something different about how she ate, as though each bite was delectable and even sensuous. "So, this is what you were doing today?"

"Uh-huh…" She picked up a baby carrot with her fingers and held it in her lips for a moment before biting it.

"This is very nice…"

"It's just the start…I have plans for you…"

"Plans? What kind of plans…?"

"You'll see…it's sort of…a surprise…"

He tilted his head. "OKaaay…"

After dinner she took Hal by the hand and led him to the bedroom. Removing his clothes, she invited him to lie down on his stomach, and then proceeded to give him a back massage. After a while she turned him over on his back and started the music. Stripping off her peignoir she climbed on the bed and kissed him and continued to kiss him down his chest, his stomach, and down and down, she went down. He was enthralled. "Oh…baby…what are you doing…ooooohhhh…" She practiced her newly acquired art. When she was satisfied that he was ready for her next move, she climbed on top of him, and, moving her body to the music, she tossed her hair as she undulated in a dance, with her breasts jiggling in sync with the rotation of her hips. He grabbed her hips and moved with her. As the pleasure became more intense her rhythmic motion came faster until she could see he was in the grips of total ecstasy and, within a moment, she followed him.

Collapsing onto his chest she whispered. "Did I do it right?"

Bemused, he looked at her and smiled, "Oh baby…did you ever…you're damned straight…you did it right!"

***

"You look happier than a pig in shit…what's goin' on?" Deuce sat down.

Smiling, Hal shook his head. "I can't believe my life keeps getting better every day."

"OK...spill it."

Hal paused and then said, "You know how you said that Mari wanted to learn more ways to make me happy?"

"Why do I have the feeling I'm going to hate you?"

"Well the other day...she gave me a BJ like a pro...and then got on it and fucked me into a coma...and then asked me if she 'did it right.' Isn't that the most adorable thing you ever heard?"

"It's official...I hate you. The last time I got a BJ was on my birthday...and somehow Wanda worked it into her getting the present...not me!"

"She said she wanted to do something special for me for 'I love you day'...that is so sweet...I love her so much..."

"Oh...shut up! You guys make me sick...always so damned happy...I can't wait for you to get married...and you only get a BJ once a year..."

"What's wrong, Deuce? You used to be happy when things went well for me...now you're an old fussbudget!"

"Fussbudget? What gang you hang with...the West Side Mother Fakers?"

Hal laughed. "OK...OK...I'll get off your case...and stop teasing you before you kick my ass."

"Say that again..."

"What?"

"Repeat what you said."

"I'll get off your case..."

"Well I'll be damned...there it is..."

"There is what?"

"She said you had a stray dimple...I'll be goddamned if you don't have that dimple she talked about...shit...I never saw that before. That girl has your face...every last detail...committed to memory...I should say to her heart. You better marry that girl...marry her today...and no later than tomorrow. Don't you let her slip through your fingers...she belongs to you...so you had better make her yours...and do it now."

***

GODFREY

The table sat in the living room for a week. Every time Mari walked past it her heart skipped a beat as she remembered "I love you day" and she wasn't quite ready to put the table back into the kitchen. By Saturday she thought, *well the table is still out here...maybe I should make something else for a special dinner...he might enjoy it.* She went grocery shopping early and picked up a small standing rib roast. She justified the expense to herself, *there will be plenty of leftovers to make hot roast beef sandwiches during the week and I could freeze the rest for another dinner.* She ferreted out beef bacon to make bacon bundled string beans and horseradish to mix with whipped cream.

Hal started in on his assigned Saturday chores, dusting and vacuuming, when he noticed that Mari was cooking rather than cleaning in the kitchen. He took a peek inside the door and saw her preparing a rib roast. He frowned, searching his mind. *Oh, shit...is it Valentine's day?* He remembered seeing Valentine's cards and candy in the stores; he grabbed his jacket, and rushed out of the house, calling out to Mari, "I got to go out for a while. I won't be gone too long..."

Mari shrugged and went back to threading fresh thyme under the layer of fat on the roast.

***

Hal sat stuck in traffic. He had driven down to Tustin to see if his order had come in yet, or, if it hadn't, to buy something else. Now, things were stop and go on the way back up the Santa Ana Freeway and he needed to get to a florist and a department store and still get home in time for dinner. He berated himself for waiting until the last moment to get something special for Mari, but Valentine's Day had slipped his mind. As he finally passed the wreck that had held up traffic, in typical Angelino style he shook his fist and started yelling at the smashed up car, "There had better be some blood on the freeway for you schmucks holding me up and making me late..." He drove on. It wasn't that he was uncaring, but with the regularity of accidents causing long delays and traffic jams, he was desensitized through habituation, and all that was left was frustration. Picking up speed, he figured that if the traffic played along, he would be on time.

***

Creeping in through the back door, Hal stashed his presents in Mari's old bedroom and heard her shout out, "That had better be you!"

"Yeah, Babe...it's me."

"Thank God...dinner's ready in twenty..."

"I'll just pop in the shower and change..."

When he was dressed, he heard her busying herself with dinner and took the opportunity to set his Valentine presents up on the coffee table. Two dozen red roses, a box of Godiva Chocolates, a card, and a small gift-wrapped box were put out on display.

When she came out of the kitchen, carrying the rib roast to put on the table, he was somewhat disappointed to find she was not in a negligee, but was dressed in a simple black turtleneck sheath dress. Her hair was casually pinned up in the mode she usually wore to get it off the back of her neck, or out of her way when she was working. She looked as lovely as ever, but it did not portend what he thought she had in mind, or, what he had in mind. Placing the platter on the table, she turned, without seeing her presents, and went back to the kitchen for the side dishes. Returning, she sat down at the table. "Dinner is ready...come and eat. You're going to have to carve the roast...I'm not very good at it..."

She did not look up across the room. Without comment, Hal went to the table. "Well...that's the man's job anyway..."

"Where did you go today?"

"Shopping..."

"What...you...shopping?"

"Yes."

"What did you get?"

He went to her, lifted her out of her chair, and walked her over to the coffee table. "This is what I got...for you..."

Her hands went to her mouth with surprise. "Oh...they're beautiful!" He sat her down on the couch. "Roses...and candy...and what's in the box?"

"Open it..." He helped her struggle with the ribbon.

She opened the box to find a pair of earrings that matched the necklace he gave her. "My God! They're stunning!"

"I had to wait until they could match the color of the stones...they're close to the color of your eyes..."

"They look so real! But...why?"

"For Valentine's Day..."

"I love all of these beautiful things you gave me...and I love you so much...but it's not Valentine's Day..."

"It's not?"

"No...it's next week...on a three-day holiday..."

"Then why were you making a special dinner?"

She shrugged, "Because the table was still out in the living room...and I thought you would like it..."

He screwed up his face. "Well...shit! I busted my butt to get this stuff on time for you..."

"For sure it's on time." She saw it was of no comfort to him. "We can call it 'Happy Table Day.'" He still wasn't mollified. She got up and put her arms around his neck. He could smell the plumeria in her hair. "It's even more endearing to me that you sort of got it wrong...because you really got it so right. I love you more than ever for it." She kissed him and he melted into her lips. He tried to get his fingers in her hair but ran into the hardware she pinned it up with. She backed away, pulled out the bobby pins, and shook her hair down. Seeing the effect on him in his eyes, she turned around. "Unzip me." He did. She turned to him and let her dress drop to the floor, revealing a black lace teddy. "Here is your 'Happy Table Day' present." She smiled.

He grinned. "Oh...baby...let's celebrate the table!"

She backed away from him, put her little finger in her mouth, and tousled her hair with her other hand. "Tell me what you want! What do you want to do to me?" She taunted.

"Tell you? I'll show you all night!" He grabbed her and tossed her over his shoulder while she squealed with delight. Carrying her past the waiting table, he took her into the bedroom to celebrate Happy Table Day and the advent of Valentine's Day.

***

"God...I'm starving..."

"Me too..."

After an hour or so, they emerged from the bedroom and stood at the table looking at the cold, forlorn meal they had deserted. "I forgot all about dinner..."

"Me too." Mari echoed. "It just goes to show you...we can't be trusted...we're hopeless..."

"Yeah...goddamn you're hot, Mari...I look at you...and everything else just fades out of the picture..."

She smiled. "Yeah...I sort of couldn't wait to get my hands on you too..."

"Is there anything you can do to fix this stuff up?"

"Yeah...but it won't be as good as when I first put it on the table...I'll reheat everything..."

When they finally sat down to dinner, Hal dug into his meal. "This isn't half bad...it's really good..."

"I did the best I could to save it..."

After they ate, Hal sat back in his chair and chuckled. "It's a good thing I didn't make the mistake of booking reservations for dinner..."

Mari hunched her shoulders and laughed. "Like I said...we can't be trusted! We're demented...incorrigible! Can you imagine the look on Godfrey's face when he comes to our table to serve us?" She got up and struck a pose imitating the waiter, Godfrey. With her nose in the air and her eyes half closed she adopted a disdainful look. "I am ready to take your order sir..." She widened her eyes with alarm. "Will the gentleman please get his head out from under madam's skirt...and will madam..." She looked away with pursed lips. "...put her tit back into her dress..." She resumed her austere pose. "That's better. Now may I suggest oysters on the half shell for the gentleman...and a kosher salami for madam...madam...madam...there is nothing in the gentleman's pants that should interest you at the moment. Please...please have a modicum of decorum. Sir...sir...you must refrain from fucking in the booth!" Giving a distressed look and pantomiming tossing away the order pad she finished her act. "You are the most disgusting and vile people I have ever served...and I expect to get a huge tip for putting up with your disgraceful behavior. I'm so disturbed by your outrageous antics; I think I'll go and flail my fandango!"

Hal was howling with laughter. He let out a loud guffaw at each of her lines. "That's funnier than shit...Mari! We can't go anywhere!!"

Giggling, she sat down in his lap. "Can you just imagine poor Godfrey trying to maintain dignity and propriety around us when we can't keep our hands off of each other...long enough to order?"

He growled and buried his face in her neck. She pulled back with a serious expression. "Oh, my...what would Godfrey say...?"

"While Godfrey is jacking off...I'm taking you back to bed..."

***

"Babe...didn't you say that Valentine's Day landed on a three-day weekend?" Hal relaxed on his pillow.

"Yes...President's Day is Monday...so it's a long weekend." Mari snuggled under his arm.

"Do you want to go anywhere for the weekend?"

Mari thought for a moment. "No...we can't be trusted..."

***

THE SLUMS OF L. A.

Mari tapped on Hal's office door and stuck her head in. "Are you busy right now? I have an idea for a story...."

"Come on in...I have a moment..."

She came in, sat down, and resisted the urge to flirt with him. The story was a serious one that needed his full attention. "The last time I saw Lo-Lo, she told me something that was rather distressing. She said that the projects where she used to live as a little girl...and some of her family are still there...are so dilapidated and disgusting that they should be condemned. The conditions there are so horrifying that no human being should live there...and the property is owned by the City of Los Angeles. She said that the city was the biggest slumlord of all. I found that hard to believe...but I verified that the property of the projects is owned by the city...but I haven't been able to confirm that the conditions she described actually exist. That would require going out there with a photographer to document whatever we find. I know we would be stepping on some pretty big toes in City Hall...if the story is true...and we expose it...but I thought you may be interested."

"What kind of conditions did she talk about?"

Mari lowered her head and read from her note pad. "She said that there was frequently water damage from plumbing that never gets fixed...from pipes and toilets...that caused some of the ceilings to break and insulation to fall through...that the place is overrun with roaches so thick that their feces has turned the kitchen countertops brown...and rats...exposed electrical wires...do I really need to go on...?"

Hal's frown turned to outrage. "No...no you don't..."

"Do you want me to follow through?"

"I don't want you going out there...and I don't want to use a crew to investigate...that would tip our hand...and they would come down on us with both feet before we can find out what's happening...or write the article. Let me think on it...if it's true...it would be one hell of a story."

***

Hal came home to find a black woman sitting at the kitchen table crying. Mari's digital camera was sitting on the table beside her. "Who are you? Where is Mari?" He desperately looked around.

137

The woman reached for her hair, pulled it off, and golden curls spilled out. "It's me, Hal. Lo-Lo disguised me to look black..." She took out her brown colored contacts. "I got your pictures for you..."

"What the fuck! I told you not to go out there...it's too dangerous for you..."

"For me...yeah...but not for me looking like I'm black too...and Lo-Lo went with me."

"Why are you crying?"

"You can't see what I saw...and not cry..."

"Oh, baby...you shouldn't have gone there...and expose yourself to what's ugly in this world. Come on...let's get you cleaned up." He put his arm around her, took her to the bathroom, and helped her wash off the skin color. "You know...you looked surprisingly authentic...and not half bad as a black woman."

"Lo-Lo says that I must have been black in a previous life..." She looked at her white face and started to cry again. "Oh, Hal...all that separates us from them is this..." She rubbed the skin on her cheek. "...and an accident of birth."

She retrieved her camera and downloaded the pictures of the Nicholson Projects into Hal's computer. He reviewed each image as she described what was depicted. "This hole in the closet ceiling is caused by a broken pipe from the toilet in the upstairs apartment...the stench is unbearable. The woman who lives there can't use the closet and keeps it closed against the smell...she has reported it several times...but nothing has been done." She went to the next picture. "Here is the roach parade...they're everywhere...just that thick. Spraying does no good because the whole building is infested, and only fumigating the entire complex has a chance of getting rid of them...or at least abating the infestation..." She changed to the next picture. "...and that is not the color of the kitchen counter...the brown coating is roach feces...they come out at night...they come out in the day...you kill them, and it makes no difference..." She went on to the next. "The water pipes don't work in the bathroom...she runs water into that bucket from the kitchen to use to flush the toilet...and she has to bathe her children in the kitchen sink..." In the gloom of the darkened room, she went from each horrifying scene to the next until she came to the end of the compilation. "Don't worry...to make sure we did not carry

138

any beasties home...Lo-Lo and I inspected ourselves...and our bags...for any little passengers or hitchhikers that may have snuck in on us while we were there...."

Hal did not meet her eyes as he continued to study the pictures. "Did you get the affidavit of each person whose apartment you photographed?"

"Yes...and Lo-Lo's affidavit, too...and I had Lo-Lo take a picture of me as a black woman so that those I interviewed would recognize me. Everyone was hopeful that something would be done..."

"You have no idea how intransigent the 'powers that be' are...they will make every excuse...throw up every roadblock...and intimidate anyone where they think they can get away with it..."

"Does that mean you won't do the story?"

"No...that means I will..."

***

"Vee...this is going to be a tough one because it will cost the city millions to clean up their mess and make those projects habitable. You'll be getting calls from the mayor...threats..."

"No...you'll be getting the threats...the mayor will probably take me to lunch to ask me to be reasonable. How sure are you of your facts?"

"Damned sure. You saw the pictures...we have sworn statements...we have witnesses...and I am not going to divulge the names of the residents so they can't be intimidated...but it's all right there in the file. I don't even think we should ask the city fathers...or should I say mothers...their side of the story...I think we should just run with it..."

Vee sat in thought, rubbing his forehead. "OK...write the story...pick out the most egregious pictures to go with it...and I'll back you up. But don't let a word of this get out...or you had better start watching your back."

***

Mari paid the cab driver, ran into the building, and took the elevator to Angel City's floor. She ran down the hall to Hal's office. Bursting through the door, she wailed, "Someone followed me!" She was obviously shaken.

Hal got up, took her in his arms, and held her as she trembled. "Who followed you? What happened?"

139

"I was so frightened…" She cried. "I went to see Mrs. Cuthbert…you know one of the tenants in the projects. She called me and said she thought someone was watching her place. I assured her that no one knew that she had talked to us…but she sounded so rattled that I had Lo-Lo make me up and I went to her home to talk to her."

"Why did you do that? I told you to stay away from that place…you've got to promise me to stay far away from there…and this story…"

"I promise you…you will never have to worry about me ever going there again."

"Tell me what happened…"

"After I reassured her there was nothing to worry about…I left…and there was this white car that followed me…just a couple of cars behind me…all the way up the freeway. So I decided to get off the freeway and double back on the side streets…and the car followed me like they wanted me to know they were there. I got back on the freeway and kept going into downtown and they continued to follow me. I didn't know what to do…so I pulled into the Biltmore Hotel parking garage…and went to a restaurant there and used the bathroom to take off my wig, wash my face and hands, and stuff my coat into my tote. After that I went out to the front entrance to catch a cab…then I looked down the block…and I saw the car parked down the street in a loading zone…across from the parking entrance. I got a cab…and came straight here. I left my car in the parking garage."

"They're on to us…but how?" Hal seethed. "Come on…I want you to tell Vee everything. He picked up the phone and rang Vee. "We've got trouble…"

He walked Mari to Vee's office, and they related what happened while Vee listened intently. When they were through, he folded his hands on the desk. "OK…that's it…we're shutting the story down. We have a backstabbing rat in our midst…and until we find out who it is…we will never be able to publish another controversial story…without putting our people at risk."

"Are you sure we have to shut it down…a lot of people are in need…" Hal hated to back down.

"Hal…you know as well as I do that when you stand in the way of someone making millions…or are the catalyst for someone to lose millions…or lose a lucrative position where they can skim millions...you are likely to find yourself severely dead...or at minimum...hurt. We don't know how deep this scandal goes. If the city has delegated the job to a contractor...and it got ripped off somewhere in the middle...and the money was never spent on maintaining those apartments in good order...then we have no idea where the shit is coming from...or how rough the people doing it want to play. I don't want you or any of my people put at risk. Right now...my only concern is who put it out there...and that may lead us to their contact in City Hall. From now on...you walk on eggshells..." He turned to Mari. "Thank God they have no idea what you look like..." He wagged his finger at her. "...and you listen to Hal from now on..."

"Yes sir..." She muttered.

"How do we know that they will call off their dogs...and how do we get the car back when it is being watched?"

"I'll have it towed to a car dealer I know...who will sell it at auction." He turned to Mari. "Do you have anything of value in the car...?"

Mari rummaged through her tote. "No...I think I have it all here..."

"Is there anything with your name on it...?"

"No...it's just registered to the company...and my parking pass is in my bag."

"OK...the car is as good as gone. Hal...the word has to be out there that you are the one on the story...I'll see what I can do to get them to back off..."

***

"Babe...where do you think you're going?" Hal saw Mari getting dressed for work.

"To the office with you..."

"No way...no how...you're not going back in to work until I know it is safe for you to do so." He admonished.

"But you're going in..."

"That's different..."

"How?"

"If the shit goes down...I know how to handle it..."

"Hal...you're scaring me..."

"No...shhhh...don't be scared..." He touched the curls at the side of her face and then ran his fingers through her hair and bent down to embrace her.

She threw her arms around his neck. "Hal...hold me..." She tried desperately to entice him to stay. "Stay here with me." She lavished him with kisses.

"I can't...if I don't go in...it will eventually lead them back here...it would only be a matter of time before they find out where I live. If they want me...they will find me...if I don't find them first..."

Her eyes filled with tears and he frowned. "No...don't do that to me, Babe...don't cry." He took her arms from around his neck and held her to him for a moment to calm her, "I'll be back tonight," and then he left.

***

Martin stuck his head into Vee's office. "You got a minute, Vee?"

"There is a reason for a door, Martin...and that is to knock on it..."

"Yeah...yeah...I wouldn't bother you with this ordinarily...but there's something going down...and I don't know what it is. I think I am being followed...in fact I know I am...I just don't know why. It would be one thing if it were just me...but Stan and McMurray think they are being followed too. So, I am sure it has something to do with the magazine...because it wouldn't be my wife..."

"Is Dirk being followed too?"

"I don't know...we haven't asked him...do you want me to find out?"

"No...don't mention it to him at all...and tell the others not to say anything either..." Vee paused. "Have they followed you to your home...?"

"Jesus...I don't know...has someone lost their cheese? Do I need to be worried?"

"I'm not taking any chances...I'm putting you guys up at a motel...until we sort this out. Send Stan and McMurray in to see me." *So...they don't know that it is Hal...or they're not sure...maybe I can misdirect them...*

It wasn't long after Martin left, when Vee's phone rang. Hal's voice came through. "Vee...I'm being tailed."

"I thought you were in your office..."

"I was...but I left for lunch...and someone in a white car is on my tail..."

142

"If it is a white plain wrapper...that's the city alright...Martin, McMurray, and Stan are being followed as well...that means they either don't know it is you...or they're not sure. Come back to the office...we need to have a meeting. Oh...and whatever you do...don't tell Dirk...I want to find out if he is being followed too...to see if he tells me...because if he isn't being followed, he's the rat..."

"I'll be right in."

Hal hung up the pay phone, dropped more coins in, and made another call. "Deuce...I need a huge favor..."

"Oh, man...what's wrong with your love life now..."

"This is serious...I'll explain it all later...but I'm in trouble and I can't go back to my house...it could be dangerous...and Mari is there alone...I need for you to go get her and take her back to your place where she'll be safe..."

Deuce sat up and shut off the TV. "What's goin' down?"

"It has to do with a story I was working on that turned dark...really dark...Mari can tell you about it...but don't let her talk about it to anyone else but you...this has to stay under wraps. And whatever you do...make sure to make it look like you live there...go in the back door and don't let them see you take Mari out...and make sure they don't follow you."

"Is there a way I can call you after I get her?"

"I'll call you later tonight."

"I'm on my way!"

"Thanks, man...and tell Mari I'm OK."

Hal had gone to his favorite fish fry place that was an open-air restaurant, not much more than a shanty, just east of downtown. Still the food was excellent, and the patrons lined up. When he walked back to his car, he scanned the street and could see the white car was still parked on the opposite side, but no one was in it. He went to look around when a fist connected to his head and he saw stars. Blocking the next punch he was able to make out that he was up against two men, the smaller one was chicken shit and he knew that if he could land a solid blow that hurt him, he would be out of the fight, leaving only one for him to deal with. He danced away from the larger man and sensed the smaller one come up behind him. With a sudden turn he dropped the smaller one with a rock-hard jab to the nose and was able to duck the right from the larger man and come back at him with a body blow, doubling him over. Kneeing him in the face and taking both hands to slam the back of his head, Hal brought him down.

Grabbing the larger man up by the collar Hal asked him, "Why didn't you just ask me what you wanted to know? I may have told you. Now you're going to have to speculate." He shook the man. "Tell me what I want to know...who sent you?" He hit him again. "Who sent you?" Dropping the larger man, he went over to the smaller one whose nose was bleeding profusely. The little guy scrambled to his feet and ran. He went back to the larger man. "OK...tell me who sent you and I won't call the cops."

"McCredie...that's all I know..."

"How long have you been following me?"

"We picked you out this morning..."

"How do you know me...?"

"From this picture..." He reached into his shirt pocket and pulled out a snapshot of Hal.

"Do you know my name?"

"Yeah...Hal Golan."

"Why did you jump me?"

"We were told to teach you a lesson..."

Hal took the picture and wrote down the license number of the car. He frisked the man for a wallet to no avail. "What's your name?"

"Fuck you!"

"Your mother had a sense of humor." He could hear sirens off in the distance. "OK, Fuck You...it probably won't do any good to have you arrested...if you're the city's stooge you'll be out in an hour...but I think I will anyway."

"You said that if I told you what you wanted to know you wouldn't call the cops!"

"I didn't call them...but they're on their way anyway. Sorry, Fuck You, but it may be the only way I can find out what I want to know. They will have to make out a police report. It must be embarrassing to give them your name. But, that's the breaks."

***

"Sorry I'm late...but I had a little dustup." Hal strolled into Vee's office.

"Fuck...what happened to you!" Martin backed away as far as he could while sitting down.

144

"Two guys jumped me...one ran away...the other is being booked...but they will probably let him go since he was the city's goon. He said he was sent by someone called McCredie..." He slammed the picture down on Vee's desk. "He picked me out from this...and was tailing me since this morning."

"That looks like it was taken at the Christmas party...your collar is shiny like a tux..." Vee remarked. "But why follow all of you...?"

"And they obviously want us to know that we are being followed...they are not taking any pains to try to hide it..." McMurray added.

"It's an intimidation tactic..."

"They did more than intimidate Hal...which one of us is next?" Martin murmured.

They all sat in silence. The sight of Hal sent shivers down their backs and they could not help but think that the same would happen to them if they went out the door. Hal finally spoke. "There's only two places that file has been...my office and Vee's office. Because I had a bad experience...I lock my office at night...and I take the files I'm working on home with me...that doesn't mean that someone couldn't have riffled through my desk when I went to the restroom or something..." He looked at Vee. "How long did the file sit on your desk before we talked about it?"

Vee shrugged. "A couple of days..."

"Someone got a look at it...and it must have been while it was in your office...or else they would have known it was mine..."

"When you said you had a bad experience...what did you mean...?" Vee was curious.

"Dirk took a file off my desk and hid it...I think he was going to say the story was his..."

"When did this happen...why didn't you tell me...?"

"Just before the meeting where I submitted the Mitchem story...he was so humiliated I thought he realized that from then on...he shouldn't fuck around..."

"Can you prove any of this...?"

"As a matter of fact, I can...Mari videotaped him when he went back to retrieve the file from where he hid it..." Hal held up his hands. "That doesn't mean that he's the rat in this instance."

"No...but it doesn't look good..."

"Do you lock your office?"

"Not always..." Vee admitted and then sat back in thought. "I'm going to arrange for all of you to be smuggled out of the building and put up at a motel for a couple of days. I think it's a good idea for you to disappear until I can work something out. Don't use our phones to call your families...use the pay phones down the hall..."

McMurray reached in his pocket. "I've got something better...a cell phone...we can call from this..."

"I've got to get one of those..." Hal observed. "No more carrying around change. Where did you get it?"

"My wife got it for me...now she can keep track of me...call me to tell me what to pick up from the store on my way home...she loves it!"

There was a knock on the door. They all looked at each other as though they knew who it was. Vee held his finger to his lips to indicate that no one was to talk and then said. "Come in."

Dirk stuck his head in the door. "No one told me there was going to be a meeting..."

"Where were you...we looked for you. I assumed you went to lunch, so I sent someone to go look for you...you didn't happen to see someone looking for you...did you?"

"No."

"No one in a white car...?"

"No...they should have been able to find me...I went to my usual place..."

"Well...shit...they will probably be out there for a while..."

"What's the meeting about?"

"Why don't you guys get back to work...I'll fill Dirk in." As soon as all the others left, Vee invited Dirk to take a chair. He decided to set a trap. "There is a story we were working on about the projects...and we just decided to kill it...you know the story I'm talking about...right?"

"Of course...the Nicholson Projects...awful stuff..."

"Did you work on it?"

"No...I just heard scuttlebutt..."

"I see. Well...it probably would have been a good story...but it would take too long to develop...so we're killing it..."

***

146

Deuce was frustrated by the cross-town traffic. When Hal called him, it was already past late afternoon. He was an hour on the freeway and only halfway to Hal's place. Agonizing, he decided to get off at the next off-ramp and take the side streets. It would be faster.

Mari heard banging on the back door. She took a peek down the hallway and was relieved to see Deuce's face through the door window. "Terry!" She ran to let him in.

"Pack a bag...I got to get you out of here..."

"I can't go...Hal will be here later tonight..."

"No he won't...he called and told me to get you out of here and that is just what I am going to do...even if I have to carry you out. He said it was dangerous for you to stay here...and I was to sneak you out the back..."

"Hal...where's Hal?"

"He said to tell you he's OK and he is going to call us at my place tonight...so we had better get a move on...so pack..."

"I don't have a suitcase..."

"Get a trash bag...and throw everything in it...fast! I'm going out the front and turn the sprinklers on to show my face...like I'm the one who lives here...by the time I turn them off...I want you packed and in the back seat of the car layin' low..."

Mari ran to the kitchen and grabbed a plastic bag while Deuce sauntered out the front door and turned on the sprinklers on the small patch of lawn and flower bed. He looked around the little yard as if he was checking his garden, as he cast an eye along the street. He went back inside to help Mari pack. "Are you almost ready?"

"Yes..." She scraped the contents of her dressing table off the surface to drop into her plastic bag and tied it up. Putting the bag in with the one that held her clothes, she tucked her hair in a hat, and told Deuce, "I'm ready to go."

He went out, opened the rear door of his car and returned for her. "Now we gonna have to do some low runnin'..." He kept her low as they crept to the car and he put her on the floor in the back and covered her with the bags. "I'll be back." He went through the house, turned on the TV, and then went out to the front yard. He slowly turned off the sprinklers and, not seeing anything suspicious, went back through the house and out the back door. Jumping behind the wheel, he slowly drove out the driveway and down the street. He wasn't sure, but he thought he saw a car pull out without lights. He pulled into a convenience store lot and parked. "I'm going into the store to see if we are being tailed...I'll keep an eye on you while I'm in there." He went in and bought a six-pack watching for any cars that looked familiar. Not seeing any he paid for the beer and went back to the car. As he grabbed the handle, he thought he saw a car he had seen on Hal's street. *Oh...the shit's on now!* He got into the car and told Mari, "It looks like we might have company. We may have to make a run for it...don't worry honey...I got this..."

Deuce surmised that, by now, the freeway traffic should be free flowing, and he followed that hunch. He drove slowly down to the Hollywood Freeway, keeping his pursuer in the rearview mirror; he got on and headed east toward where the freeway splits between the San Bernardino and Santa Ana Freeways. Keeping in the lane that goes to San Bernardino, he saw the car keeping pace directly behind him. He made sure there was another vehicle to his right with cars behind it. As he approached the "V" where the two freeways split, he stayed in his lane until the last second and then gunned the car to swerve onto the Santa Ana, ahead of the car to his right, barely missing the barrier there. He got a glimpse of his pursuer behind him attempting to swerve out of his lane to follow. But, blocked by the vehicle on the right, the car went into a fishtail, and was forced to continue on the San Bernardino, missing the transition. He lost them.

Letting out a hearty laugh, Deuce told Mari, "We're in the clear. You can come on out now." Shaken, Mari climbed out from under the bags to sit in the back seat. "Hal said that you can tell me what's goin' down...but he said it was important not to tell anyone else..."

"Yes...oh, Terry...I'm afraid I started all of this." She poured out the whole story, "And now Hal's in danger..."

"Shit...that's a hell of a story...Hal's got some balls to take it on. I wish he would've come to me...I could've clued him in on a lot of stuff...especially not to fuck with it. Look...he's smart and he's going to be OK...he was just worried about you. You're safe now. Every guy that works for me is standing guard at my house."

***

Vee locked the Nicholson Projects file in his safe, gathered his people like a mother hen, and took them down the freight elevator to the building's loading docks. There he loaded them into a janitor's

148

van. Getting in and closing the door, he signaled for the driver to go to the designated motel. The rooms were booked under the magazine's parent corporation name and before he left, he cautioned, "Don't use the motel phones...there's a pay phone downstairs...and don't get into any car or van...unless I'm in it..." With that, he went back to the office to wait for the phone call he knew would come.

Martin picked up the motel writing pad that had its logo on it. "Jesus...isn't this the motel where Janis Joplin died?"

"Every motel on Sunset lays claim to that fame." Hal politely replied, wondering how he got stuck in a room with Martin. "I got to go make a phone call...do you want me to bring you a soda or something when I come back?" He thought it was best to try to make nice-nice under the circumstances.

"Yeah...a cola...whatever brand they have would be good. Thanks." Martin brightened at Hal's considerate attitude and wondered why he wasn't his surly old self.

Hal went to the soda machine and fed it a dollar and got a quarter change as a can dropped. *Seventy-five cents...are they kidding?* He put in another dollar and bought another soda to get more change. He went to the phone and dialed. "Deuce...it's me...did you get Mari alright?"

"Yeah...she's here. We had a little bit of excitement...someone tailed us...but I pulled an old drug dealer's trick on them..."

"Old drug dealer's trick? You never told me you dealt drugs!"

"That's because I never did...but I know some old drug dealers and they can teach you a thing or two."

"They must have your car's plate numbers..."

"Probably so...but the car is registered to my company...not my home. Anyway...we lost them, and I got a guard around the place...nobody is goin' to get to Mari...she's safe...how's things goin' for you?"

"I had a bit of trouble...I got jumped...but I took 'em down... got a bit of information out of them...but not enough...Vee's got all of us sequestered at a motel until this shit blows over."

"Do you need me to come over and back you up?"

"No...you stay with Mari and take care of her...I'm safe for the time being. Let me talk to her."

149

Deuce smiled. "Someone wants to talk to you."

"Hal...where are you? Are you OK?"

"I'm fine...Vee put Martin, Stan, McMurray and me up at a motel for a few days. You stay with Deuce until I come and get you. I love you, Babe..."

"I love you too...please don't take any chances...I'm so scared."

"Don't worry...Vee says he's going to take care of all this...he just needs a couple of days. I can't wait to get you home. I gotta go now."

"Be careful...I love you." She heard a click on the phone and then the dial tone.

***

Vee sat at Harry's Bar & Grill in Century City. He had a friend in the mayor's office that he knew would call for a meeting. When he did, Vee was ready and knew what he was going to do. As a silver haired gentleman crossed the dining room to the table where Vee sat, he got up and extended his hand. "Johnny...good to see you...it's been too long." Vee studied him. "I hope you've got something good for me...what does the mayor want the people to know?"

Johnny took a seat. "That's a good one. The tom-toms say that you've been holding out on us..."

"Tom-toms? They never could be trusted...what is it you want to know?"

The waiter came by the table, gave them the menu, mentioned the house specials, and prepared to take orders for drinks.

"I'll have a martini on the rocks." Johnny routinely ordered.

Vee ordered a bottle of Meursault wine and a carpaccio appetizer. "Johnny you will love their carpaccio...how about my ordering a plate for you too."

"Sure." Johnny eyed Vee. "I heard about this story..."

"Hey...I've got a big one for you that I have a guy working on about the projects."

"According to the tom-toms...you killed that story..."

Vee was now sure that Dirk was the rat. "Nope...it's very much alive...we just wanted to get the City Hall's take on it..."

"Our take on it is that we had no idea...we contract out the maintenance work... the money was paid..."

"Who has the contract?"

"You didn't hear it from me...but it's McCredie Enterprises...they got the contract on the down low...so somebody's making a bundle if they're not doing the work...now it's your turn to give...who's on this story..."

"You know I can't tell you that!"

"Why not? I stuck my neck out for you...big time."

Vee looked around. "You got a card?" Johnny passed him one of his business cards, and Vee wrote down a name and passed it back.

Johnny looked at it. "This can't be right..."

"What do you mean...?"

"This name can't be right..."

"Well that's who's on it...and he's running with it...he's one of the cleverest men I've got. He hasn't told me much about what he's uncovered...but he did tell me he's embedded with City Hall...like deep inside. If your tom-toms said the story was killed...it was probably to take you off your guard."

Johnny put the card in his pocket. "That's good to know..."

"You'll go easy on him...?"

"Yeah...sure...like cotton candy..."

***

Mari sat in front of the TV not watching the show. She was caught up in her own thoughts as she anguished about where Hal was and if he was safe. A news bulletin interrupted the show. The news anchor came on the air. "There has been an explosion in the Salter Building in downtown Los Angeles. It appears that a car bomb exploded in the underground parking garage there...with unconfirmed reports of one fatality." Mari got up and walked toward the TV and then, screaming, she fainted.

Deuce ran into the living room to see her on the floor. "What's going on...?" He saw the story unfolding on the screen. "An unidentified person was killed in a car bomb explosion that rocked downtown Los Angeles. Police are investigating what looks like a mob style hit that has been associated with Angel City Magazine. The car was parked in the area reserved for that magazine's employees...but there is no confirmation that it was one of the employees that was killed."

"Dear Jesus...that can't be Hal." Deuce went and lifted Mari off the floor and put her on the couch and watched as she came around.

"Mari…we don't know anything yet. The last I heard…he was at a motel…so it can't be him."

"I'll die if it's him…I don't want to live if it's him…I'll want to die…" She sobbed into Deuce's shoulder.

"I know…I pretty much feel the same way…but he was at a motel…it can't be him." He reassured her, but he wasn't so sure. He took her to her room and gave her a sleeping pill to help her calm down and sleep. Later, he checked on her and she was soundly sleeping.

When he came back into the living room, Wanda was waiting for him. "I want her out of this house!"

"What?"

"She's nothing but trouble…and I want her out of here."

"I hate to break it to you…woman…but I would sooner put you out of this house than her."

"Are you telling me that you would put her before your wife and children?"

"Maybe not my children…but definitely you! How could you be so cold and evil? That girl is Hal's life…she means everything to him…and you would turn her out just like that?!" He snapped his fingers. "If you want to take the kids and go to your mother's go right ahead…but she stays here until Hal comes for her…and if he never comes for her…" His face screwed up as he fought back tears. "…then I'll look after her for him…as long as it takes…" He wiped his face with his forearm. "…and that's the way it's gonna be…get to liking it…"

***

It was at the close of the day when a muffled explosion was heard, and fire alarms went off in the building. Anyone left in the office had to evacuate immediately. Vee herded everyone to the stairway to join the mass exodus from the other floors. He checked all the offices and went to the lower floor to check the cubicles before leaving. Standing outside on the sidewalk, he saw smoke billowing out of the garage area and fire trucks were on the scene; black and white patrol cars, with lights flashing, blocked the street while police redirected traffic. The siren of an ambulance approaching was heard. He got the attention of a reporter on the scene. "What happened?"

"Car bomb…looks like one person is dead."

"Does anyone know who it is?"

152

"Not yet...but it is in the area reserved for Angel City Magazine employees...so it may be one of theirs..."

Vee knew instinctively that it was Dirk. He went to the side of the building and threw up. *I thought they were going to just tune him up...nothing monstrous like this!* He located a telephone booth and called Johnny. "I got the message...is there anything else I have to worry about?"

"I don't know what you're talking about...but I would say no...we don't have a problem with you anymore now that the story is dead. I don't think anyone else would be interested in it...do you?"

"No...no one else would be interested...the story is dead."

"I'm glad we understand each other. Good to hear from you...let's do lunch soon." The line clicked off.

***

The next morning Deuce's telephone rang. "Deuce...it's over. Can you come and get me? Vee is arranging car rentals for all of us until our cars are released...but I can't wait...I need to see my two favorite people...especially the pretty one."

"I didn't know you were that anxious to see me!"

"Stop kidding around and bring Mari to me!"

"You got it!"

Mari...get dressed in something pretty...we're going to pick up Hal!"

They were in the car and on the road in twenty minutes. Mari turned down the visor mirror to check her make up. "Do I look alright, Terry?"

"Awww...girl he's just going to eat you up! You look great...and to him...you'll look like happiness..."

When they pulled up, Hal opened the door and Mari was in his arms in a flash. Locked in a kiss she held on to him. Hal looked out of one eye at Deuce and waved. Martin looked on with perplexed admiration. He said to Deuce, "Sometimes I think that Hal isn't even real...that he is a figment of my imagination. The guy is so fuckin' lucky...WHY?"

***

"The problem I have with Dirk being killed the way he was...is that it forces you to feel sorry for him and makes you forget what an unmitigated turd he was." Hal and Mari lay in bed and talked about the events surrounding Dirk's death.

"I don't feel sorry for him...he was putting your neck in a noose...that could have been you...I'm not saying that I wanted to see anybody killed...but I'm damned glad it was him and not you..." Mari turned on her side and propped herself up on one elbow. "...I think he suspected that it was your story all along...he was jealous of you...of your talent...of your intellect..."

"And of you..."

"Well that was a tragic waste of time out of his life...if he spent even five minutes thinking about me...because that never would have worked out for him."

"When you stop to think about it...nothing seemed to work out for him...and I wonder why that was...he was good looking, white, protestant, good education, came from a good family...and yet he could never quite pull it together."

"He was dishonest, sly, sleazy, arrogant, lazy, dimwitted, wanted things handed to him, and he thought he was God's gift to women...and I'll bet you dollars to donuts that he had a short dick he was trying to compensate for..."

"Talk about speaking ill of the dead...if I wasn't mistaken...I would think you didn't like the guy..." Hal chuckled.

"Remember...he did not die in a fit of good taste...he died trying to screw all of us over...especially you. Did you ever ask yourself why you were the only one who was attacked?"

"Everyone was followed..."

"Yeah...but you were the only one they tried to beat up...but you showed them that they fucked with the wrong guy!"

Hal squinted at her and half smiled. "You sound like you're proud of the fact that I tuned those goons up..."

"You're damned right I am...no one is going to mess with my guy..." She made a tough face.

"Oh look at you...what's next...throwing gang signs...are you going to jump me into the Mari Marauders...?"

"Yeeaaahh!" She balled up her fist and started to softly pummel him. "Take that...and that..." She shook her shoulders. "Are you going to join my gang now?"

"Ooohhh...I can't take any more...I'm yours!" He reached over and pulled her to him. "Oooohhh...stop making me kiss you...." He kissed her down her neck. "Oooohhh...stop making me play with your boobs...."

***

"Hey...Big...where you been?" Deuce got up to clasp Big's hand in an upward handshake.

"I took Mrs. Big to a play..."

"To a play...?" Deuce was taken aback. "...for two whole months?"

"Yes...indeed...I whisked her away...hopped the pond...absconded with my fair Lily...and took her to a play...in London...and then I took her shopping...window, clothes, bargain, grocery...every kind of shopping there is...in Paris...I just got back..."

"World traveler...huh?"

"Yeah. I heard there was a bit of excitement while I was gone..."

"What did you hear?"

"I still have friends in the D.A.'s office...they said there was a car bombing where Hal works..."

"Yeah...one of the contributing editors was working on a story that struck a nerve...and boom! When Mari heard about it on the news...they didn't know who was killed...and she went nuts thinking it was Hal...but it wasn't his story..." Deuce thought it was the better part of discretion to keep a lid on the facts.

"Someone said that Hal was assaulted..."

"Yeah...but he took them to school..." Deuce leaned back looking relaxed, but wondered how much Big knew, and if he was being pumped for information.

Big leaned over to tell Deuce in confidence, "At first they thought it was Hal...because the informant said he thought it was...but wasn't sure...and told them to tune him up anyway. Then they learned the truth...that it was the informant himself who was on the story...and was ingratiating himself to get deep inside City Hall...and so...they took him out! Now when I say 'they' it wasn't the city...it was the contractor who was skimming for decades...with some in City Hall paid to look the other way...be sure to tell Hal...but tell him to keep

far, far away from it...he doesn't want to fuck with those people..."
Big leaned back.

Deuce nodded. "Thanks, man...I'll be sure to let him know..." He was relieved to know they had a loyal friend in Big.

***

The funeral for Dirk was a sad affair. Very few people were in attendance. An ex-wife with two young daughters, the parents, his brother and sister with their families, and those colleagues from the magazine who deemed it their duty to attend, were scattered throughout the church pews. While Vee encouraged attendance, he did not make it mandatory and, except for himself, only Hal, Mari, and Cora were there.

The Lutheran church had token flowers and a wreath laid on the coffin. With questionable skill, the organist played and sang hymns. She seemed to favor "All the Way My Savior Leads Me," a hymn that seemed satirical, as it was the one hymn that she replayed amongst the others.

"All the way my Savior leads me;
What have I to ask beside?
Can I doubt His tender mercy,
Who through life has been my Guide?
Heav'nly peace, divinest comfort,
Here by faith in Him to dwell!
For I know, what'er befall me,
Jesus doeth all things well;
For I know what'er befall me,
Jesus doeth all things well."

"This is a rather poor showing..." Hal whispered to Mari. "...the man was bereft of friends."

"Don't try to make me feel sorry for him...if it wasn't for you...I wouldn't be here."

"I'm just sayin'."

"I feel sorry for his ex-wife. She probably got rooked into marrying him...found out what a jerk he was...she's divorced with two kids...not a good prospect for getting another husband...and now the

156

spousal and child support have come to an untimely end...for her sake I hope he had plenty of insurance..."

"Well Miss Pragmatic...aren't you a ray of sunshine..."

"I'm just sayin'...besides...it's a funeral...no sunshine allowed..."

The minister took to the pulpit and the prayers for Dirk's soul started in earnest. The strain of the pretext of bereavement showed on everyone's face, for there wasn't a wet eye in the church except for his mother's. The minister droned on and then his father, brother, and sister said a few words; the atmosphere of hypocrisy grew. It was with utter relief that the services came to a merciful end.

Hal and Mari got into his new '98 Camaro Z28 SS; his last car, having been parked near the blast, was totaled. Then they joined the funeral procession to the cemetery. "God that was awful. Mari...when I die...all I want there is you, Deuce, and my mother if she's still living...and all I want you to say is...he was mine and I loved him...no big ceremony...ritual...or other folderol..."

"I won't be there..."

"What...why not...?"

"If you die...I couldn't survive it for another day...I'll just take a fist full of pills and go with you. There would be nothing left for me to stick around this fucked up world for...so it would be a double funeral. Poor Terry...he would be the one to mumble a few words over us..." "

Yeah...and he would probably be so pissed off at me he would have a stroke and go too...and my mother would be so verklempt that she couldn't go on...and we would all be laying there in one big pile..."

"So...you're not allowed to die..."

"Still...that was the saddest funeral I ever went to...in that no one was sad...except his mother."

"And I was beginning to think that she was only unhappy out of a feeling of being obliged to cry..."

"Oh, how cynical we've become..."

"Yes...and I am beginning to agree with you that we all resent being forced to pity him...and I for one...do not feel obligated to feel..."

At graveside Mari stood next to Dirk's ex-wife. She reached out and took the woman's hand. "It must be a great loss for you and your children...I am so very sorry."

157

"How do you know my husband...ex-husband?" Her eyes reflected surprise. It was the first gesture of condolence she had received all day.

"I worked with him...I can't say that I knew him very well...but he was a colleague...and it was all so very tragic..."

When the pastor launched into more prayers, the youngest of Dirk's daughters wriggled out of her chair and ran off amongst the tombstones with her mother calling after her. "You stay here...I'll go get her." Mari quickly went after the child. Scanning the grounds, she saw the fabric of the child's dress showing from behind one of the gravestones. Looking behind the stone she saw the little girl rocking back and forth, repeating, "My daddy has gone to Heaven...my daddy has gone to Heaven."

Mari stooped down. "What is your name...little one?"

The girl looked up. "Carly. My daddy just died...and I miss him..." She looked back down and stuck out her lower lip. "He can't read to me anymore...or sing me a song..." Her face crumbled as she sobbed, "I love my daddy, and he went to Heaven and left me."

This was a side of Dirk that no one at the magazine had ever seen, and it touched Mari. She took the child into her arms and held her close. "You must remember that your daddy is still with you...watching over you...and whenever you miss him more than anything...sing this song... 'Daddy loves me this I know, for my mommy tells me so, to my heart he still belongs, that is why I sing this song, yes daddy loves me, yes daddy loves me, yes daddy loves me, my mommy tells me so.' ...now sing it with me." They sang the requiem together to the tune of "Yes Jesus Loves Me" while they both shed tears for Dirk.

**

SHE DID A THING

In complete darkness, the only sound in the room was that of gentle snoring. Hal stirred in his sleep and murmured, "Mari" and she snuggled closer to him and kissed him behind his ear. He leaned into her kiss. Half asleep, he felt an erotic sensation. "Babe...wha' ya doin'?"

"Shhhhhh..." She continued what she was doing.

"Oooohhhh...ooohhh...ooohhh!" He went limp in her arms and immediately felt awkward. "I spooged all over your nightgown." He whispered.

"That's what I bought it for." She softly reassured him. "Go back to sleep..."

***

At the breakfast table Hal watched Mari over his coffee cup as she busied herself with his breakfast. "Babe...last night...what was that thing you did?"

She looked back over her shoulder at him and beamed. "I don't know...did you like it?"

"Well...yeah...couldn't you tell?"

"Yeah...I think you liked it a lot..." She smiled and put his plate in front of him and sat down.

"But...what did you do...what do you call that?"

"I don't know." She shrugged. "I don't think it has a name...it was just something I did because you seemed to like it."

"But that was really something...different..." Hal's hand unconsciously went up to his right ear.

"I know." She shrugged. "It just happened...I was so into you...and you were soooooo into it...I just kept on doing it until you got off to it..."

"You mean it was not something you learned or planned..."

"No...I kissed you behind your ear and you liked it so I kissed you again...and you tasted salty on my lips...so I licked you there...and I felt you sort of...I don't know...react...so I licked you some more...and you reacted some more...and so I kept it up..." She blushed. "...and then I got into it because you got into it...and there you go!"

"Oh." He looked bewildered.

***

All week long Hal could not get that "thing" out of his head. Was it sex, and if it was, what kind of sex? If it wasn't sex, what was it? Was he weird, or was she? Several times a day his hand went up to his right ear as if the explanation could be found there.

After work he went to Benny's. Although football season was over, there was an unspoken agreement to continue meeting there on Mondays. As Hal walked up to the establishment, Deuce could see him through the window. "Uh-oh...our boy looks serious..." He remarked to Big. "...what's goin' on now?"

When Hal got to the table, he greeted them with a cheery "Hi, guys..." and ordered a beer. He took a slug out of Deuce's glass and looked from one face to the other. "What's goin' on?"

"We were about to ask you the same thing. When I saw you comin' up the sidewalk...you looked like you had the weight of the world on your shoulders...how are you doin'?"

"You know it's really annoying that you think you can read me all the time...that you can just look at me and then with such assurance ask me what's wrong..."

"OK...what's wrong then...?"

"Nothing's wrong...just confusing...I'm just trying to figure something out..." He shook his head. "It's not important..."

Deuce's eyebrows went up. "What's not important...?"

"It's just a thing..."

"A thing?"

"Yeah...it's something Mari did..."

"Now what did that little girl do to get you turned all inside out...?"

"That's just it...I don't know...she did a thing...she doesn't even know...I mean it was like a week ago and it's still stuck in my head..."

Big's large eyes fixed on him. "Then it is indubitably incumbent upon you...essential...obligatory...and necessary...for you to convey...express...communicate...and to tell us what transpired...occurred...took place...so that we may explain...elucidate...clarify...and expound on what happened."

"Yeah...what went down?" Deuce asked.

"Well it was the middle of the night...and I was asleep...and I woke up sort of...I can't say that I was fully awake...you know like when you are half awake?"

"Yeah." Deuce nodded.

"Well Mari kissed me right here...behind my ear...and then she licked me there...well it felt good so I guess I sort of...reacted in some way...anyway she said I did...and she licked me some more...and she said I seemed to like it so she kept on doing it. By this time...I was sort of...more awake...but not completely...and it felt really good what she was doing...and after a while I started to squirm...you know...she kept on doing it...and she pressed her body next to mine and sort of moved with me as she kept on doing it. God...I'm getting a chubby just talking about it. Anyway...after a while...it was so goddamned hot that I felt a thrill go up and down my spine...and then shaking...bam...bam...bam...I came all over her..." Hal seemed perplexed. "...I didn't know if I should apologize or what. She told me it was OK and to go back to sleep. Now...what was that?"

Deuce had a half smile on his face. "Damned if I know...but it sounds good and nasty!"

They both looked at Big whose eyes were wider than ever. "Big?"

"I got nothing!"

***

CINCO DE MAYO

Escaping downtown L.A. to Alhambra for lunch, Hal and Mari decided to try what was rumored to be the best pastrami sandwiches in SoCal, at The Hat. Pulling into the lot of an inconspicuous looking pastrami stand, that was unremarkable except for the line waiting to order, Mari staked out a place at the picnic tables while Hal got in line. Grinning, he placed a large bag on the table, "I think there is enough here for us to eat for dinner too...these pastramis are huge! I had them cut yours in half...so you can pick it up..."

Mari unwrapped hers, examined it, and decided that there was no dainty way to eat it, so she attacked it. "Vee is hosting a Cinco De Mayo party at the warehouse next Tuesday...we are all invited." Mari took a sip of her Coke. "It sounds like fun...do you want to go?"

"I pretty much have to go. He has hired a replacement for Dirk...and I have been assigned to babysit him...get him acclimated to the office...and if he needs help getting started...that is down to me too."

"Then I take it we're going to the party?"

"Yep."

"I hope this guy is nicer than Dirk...you know like a positive influence or something..."

"I don't care one way or another...he's just somebody I have to work with until I can scoot him out on his own...and you will have to work with him too if he needs the help...but I will try to minimize your involvement..."

"What about Cora...she's the one assigned to him..."

"Yeah...I know...and until he is in a position to crack the whip on her...he's not going to get much work out of her. Believe me...she's a slacker...and if it hadn't been for the fact that you were reassigned to me...I would have eventually dumped her off the magazine."

"That bad?"

"That bad."

"Okie-dokie...but if he turns out to be a dick...all bets are off."

***

"Maaar-eee...did you see my boss? I've been looking for him...everywhere." Cora swanned by Mari's cubicle.

"I don't even know who your boss is...and I wouldn't know him if I saw him." Mari turned over the paper she was working on and put it on her desk.

"Well...his name is Lance...can you believe it...Lance...how romantic..."

"Do you want to find this guy...or screw him...?"

"Oh, Mari...sometimes you are just awful..."

"Some people would call it honest...does this Lance have a last name...?"

"Berdeaux...if you see him...tell him I'm looking for him."

"Will do." Mari picked up the phone and called Hal. "Is there a Lance in the office with you?"

"Yeah...he's here..."

"Cora came by my desk looking for him...but I think it was more a case of bragging rights now that she has a new boss...and is in no danger of being cut..."

"That's not a sure thing...but why did she go to you?"

"Beats the hell out of me...but she said his name is romantic...so I think she is trying to impress me..."

"Why don't you come up and meet him..."

"Now?"

"It's as good a time as any..." Hal figured that she was going to meet Lance in any event and it may as well be sooner than later, and, in his office.

"I'll be right up." She locked her work in her desk and took the elevator up.

When she entered Hal's office, while he looked calm, she sensed he was somewhat uneasy. Then she saw the reason why. Seated by his desk was a man who would be a shoo-in as a male model. He was tall, more than just good looking, and he had an athletic build. *Oh...shit! Hal is going to go into one of his jealous tirades...sooner or later.*

"Lance...this is Mari Carlson...my research analyst..."

When he got up to greet her, he did an involuntary double take. He held out his hand and Mari held out hers to shake it; but instead he took her hand and bowed. "I am pleased to meet such a lovely lady..."

"Why thank you...we are pleased to welcome you here." He did not sit down but gestured for her to take his seat. "Do I detect a slight southern accent?" Mari guessed.

"I thought I had been in California long enough to lose it...but yes...I'm from Dixie..." He laughed. "I came out here when I was nineteen...eight years ago...and L.A. is a fascinating place. I may go back home to visit...but I'll never live there again."

Hal studied Lance's dynamics as he interacted with Mari. *OK...Elvis...you come near her...and you will definitely leave the building...you gave her your age...what else do you want her to know about you.* He thought.

"Did Hal tell you that we are having a Cinco De Mayo party at the warehouse next Tuesday?" Mari was careful not to cross her legs or she would hear about it from Hal all night.

"I didn't get around to that yet..." Hal interjected.

"Cinco De Mayo...I've heard of it. That's a Mexican celebration isn't it?"

"Yes...I guess you can say it is sort of like St. Patrick's Day...where everyone is Irish for a day. On Cinco De Mayo...everyone gets to be Mexican for a day...eat Mexican food...drink Margaritas and Mexican beer...and salsa dance..." She gave Hal a look. "...it is actually to celebrate the Mexican army's victory over the superior numbers of the French army at Puebla...when the French invaded Mexico...but nobody really cares about that...it's just an excuse to party!"

"Well I can't pass up an event like that! Where do I get my sombrero?"

"It starts midday on Tuesday...we'll be taking you...so look for us to come get you...and no sombrero needed. Oh...by the way...Cora...your research analyst has been looking for you."

"I just met her...I don't know why she would be looking for me."

"Somehow, I got the feeling it wasn't important...perhaps to tell you about the party." Mari took a look at Hal. *Crap! I know that look!* "Well I had better get back to work. Hal, may I see you for a minute?"

"Sure...I'll be back in five..." He waved to Lance.

Mari walked to the elevator. "Ride down with me..."

"What for?"

"You didn't used to ask..." The elevator door opened, and she pulled him inside. When the door closed, she threw her arms around him and kissed him. "...that's all I wanted."

"Mari...I don't have time for this..."

"Really? That's news to me. You used to have time for a little kissy-face to cheer me up."

"If you haven't noticed...I have my hands full today..." He softened. "I'll take care of you tonight."

"That had better be a promise." She stepped off the elevator.

***

Putting on her black leotard, Mari dressed for dance lessons. She had a slight skirmish with Hal the night before about her reference to salsa dancing. Hal wasn't angry, but he did seem annoyed.

"Did you have to bring up salsa dancing with Elvis?"

"Elvis?"

"Yeah...that cornpone...Lance. Jesus! Can you imagine naming your kid 'Lance'? What were his parents thinking?"

"Actually...I brought it up for your ears...not his. The subject of what is done on Cinco de Mayo came up...and I thought I would throw it out there. You know...you never apologized for what you said...and you hurt me more than you can imagine...I cried all night..."

"Why are you bringing that up now...?"

"Because you never let me prove to you that it wasn't what you thought it was..."

"I already told you I love you...that you didn't do anything wrong..."

"No...what you did was forgive me...and that is different...that is absolution for a wrong."

"Why are you splitting hairs?"

"For the same reason that you brought up that I mentioned it...to Elvis! I saw the look on your face when I said it. It still sticks in your craw. I just want you to give me a chance to show you the mechanics of how the dance is executed so that you will know...really know...that I did nothing to be ashamed of!"

"OK...OK...if it will get you to pipe down...you can show me..."

165

When Mari strolled into the kitchen in her leotard, Hal was reading the Saturday morning paper. "Time for your dance lessons...you're too big to hide behind the newspaper...I can actually see you..."

"What?"

"You promised that I could show you my dance moves...and that is what I am going to do."

"Come on, Mari...that's ridiculous...I...I..."

"You have nothing that you are doing at the moment...except filling your head with sports scores! You promised me...and now you are going to keep that promise...come on..."

"Fuck...a man can't have a Saturday morning in peace..." He got up and followed her into the living room.

"I heard that! No grumbling allowed!" She put a CD into the stereo, but she did not start it. "You're taller than Raul...so some of the moves might not work out right...but you can get the idea. Now...positioning is everything...and we both must know each move in sequence. When we dance together...you will hold my right hand...but my left will be in front of your shoulder...not on your shoulder...that way I can gauge the distance between us...so that we don't get too close and bump into each other. Next...when we do hip rolls together...the man moves forward...I move backward...we are not moving forward at the same time...or bumping uglies...that would throw everything off. Look at this spot on my thigh." She pointed to a place midway up her inner thigh. "While it isn't necessary...I like to have the man place his leg on a specific spot so I know where it is...that leaves me free to do a hip roll without making improper contact...it looks sensual...but it isn't."

"The hell it isn't...what about when he caresses you?"

"Give me your hand." She took his hand and ran it an inch or two away from touching her down the side of her body. "He never touches me...but it gives the illusion of a caress..." She backed away from him. "What you need to understand is the level of focus that is involved...the necessary precision...if we were to lose concentration on what we were doing...we could never execute the dance...and that could be dangerous if we missed our cues..."

"It could be dangerous for him..."

"Oh…stop it! Let's try out some moves…" She walked him through some steps.

"Now…move closer…and we will move in unison…" He grinned at her and grabbed her ass.

"Hal! That's not dancing…that's foreplay! Behave yourself and focus!"

She worked with him until he could handle himself fairly well through an unchallenging bachata. After she was satisfied that he understood that it was dancing and not fornication, she called it a day. But she had one more lesson to teach him. "Hal…I want to say something because I know you so well. About this guy…Elvis…I shouldn't call him that…but Lance is just as bad…I saw the look on your face that showed you are not comfortable with him around me…"

"I saw the way he looked at you…"

"Just like a thousand other men…and it means nothing. You are in charge of him for the time being…and it is up to you to give him a fair shake. I don't have any sense of him one way or the other…but until he shows himself to be otherwise…I guess he's a pretty decent guy. But before you go into one of your tirades because he looked at me…" She walked up to him, looked into his eyes, and placed her hand on his cheek. "…I want you to know…he doesn't have a prayer of a chance with me. Believe me you have nothing to worry about…I love you…I love you now…I'll love you a year from now…and I will love you when I'm old, gray, and toothless…and my tits sag down to here…" She put her hand down to her waist and laughed. Pulling her lips in over her teeth she said in a shaky voice, "Come here…let me gum you!"

Hal laughed. "That could be interesting!"

***

The front part of the warehouse had been cleared of boxes and forklifts were parked out of sight. It was transformed overnight into a banquet hall with a Cinco de Mayo theme. Lights and small piñatas had been strung overhead, while tables with floral arrangements had been set up around a dance floor. A bandstand was on one side, and a table groaning under the weight of food was behind the banquet tables on the other. An open bar was set up in the back with four blenders going full blast. Next to the bar were wash basins filled with

167

Mexican beer on ice. Surrounding all were latticework panels screening the workplace off from the party area. Hal, Mari, and Lance arrived just in time to snag a table at the edge of the dance floor. As the tables filled up, strolling mariachis, dressed in black with silver designs on their clothes and sombreros, began to serenade from table to table. Waiters from the bar fanned out and were soon delivering drinks.

Cora appeared at the table. "I guess this is where I should sit." She took the chair next to Lance. "Isn't it all so very...Mexican! Did you see the food? Some of it was catered...but most of it is potluck..."

"There's Steven and Brian...I didn't know they would be here...I'm bringing them over!" Mari crossed the room and was given a hug by Steven and an air kiss by Brian. "You must sit with us..."

"Oh darling...what are you wearing? It's not you at all...you should have come to me." Brian scolded.

Mari was attired in what passed for traditional Mexican garb. She wore a black peasant blouse with an elastic, ruffled neckline, worn low showing her shoulders. Completing the outfit was a black flared skirt, with brightly painted floral patterns, which she bought on Olvera Street. She wore her usual black velvet ribbon with a red rose around her neck. Her stylized, tousled hair fell over her shoulders and down her back. "I had to throw something together...I can't dress myself without you!" Mari confessed.

"Don't listen to him...you look lovely as ever...he's been bitchy all day." Steven clucked.

"Well come on over...there is someone you should meet..." Mari took them both by the hand, ushered them to the table, and sat them in the last two remaining seats. "Lance...this is Steven...Vee's son...and his friend Brian..." Lance stood and shook hands and Mari went back to her seat. "You know, Lance...we have nicknamed you 'Elvis' because you kind of...sort of look like him..."

Lance gave her his 'Elvis' face. "Thank you...thank you very much." The entire table erupted with laughter. "I used to make a lightweight living imitating him...I still do from time to time."

"You're kidding...I would love to see that!" Brian gushed. Steven gave him an aloof arching of his eyebrow.

Hal turned to him with a sarcastic edge. "Yeah...I'd love to see that too."

"Ya'll want to hear me sing like Elvis?" He looked around the table.

"Oh...yes...yes..." Cora practically swooned.

"Well...if those fellas with the sombreros know any Elvis tunes...you've got it."

Steven went to the Mariachi players and talked to them briefly and returned to the table. "They have one more request and then they will be right over. The song that they know is 'Can't Help Falling in Love' if that's alright with you..."

"Couldn't be better..." Lance nodded.

When the musicians came to the table Lance got up and talked to them for a couple of minutes and their hats bobbed "yes." The lead singer handed him his microphone. Lance turned back to the table, took a rose bud out of the floral arrangement, and handed it to Mari. "I want to dedicate this to Mari, the prettiest lady west of the Mississippi...and probably east of it too." He struck an Elvis pose and the musicians started to strum the melody. In a perfect imitation of Elvis' high baritone voice, he started to sing. "Wise men say only fools rush in, but I can't help falling in love with you..."

Mari took Hal's hand under the table and gave him what she hoped was a reassuring squeeze. Lance poured on the charm and gave emotional meaning to every word. She politely held the flower and pasted a pleasant smile on her face. Brian's eyes went, from Lance to Hal to Mari and back again, picking up on the subtext. Hal wasn't glowering, but he wasn't happy. Cora, feeling snubbed and overshadowed once more, sat in a blue funk and continued to drink.

Lance walked around the table to sing directly to Mari. "Like a river flows surely to the sea, darling so it goes, some things are meant to be..." She felt Hal flinch and she squeezed his hand tighter. As he continued, she found herself having to dig her nails into his hand to keep him in his chair. When he finished the last chorus, the mariachis started to sing it in Spanish. When they finished, he sang the last chorus again finishing with a flourish. It was a flawless performance. Everyone at the fiesta applauded and of course Lance responded with "Thank you...thank you very much."

Mari put the flower down on the table. "That was wonderful, Lance. Hal...wasn't that great..."

Hal shook his hand free from Mari's grasp. "Yeah...really great..."

The afternoon turned into night with dancing, drinking, and eating. While Cora kept trying to get Lance's attention, he kept trying to politely ignore her. Lance kept trying to catch Mari's eye, while Mari kept trying to mollify Hal, and Hal kept trying to keep a lid on his temper. Steven and Brian were entertained.

An attractive waitress came by to check on the drinks. Hal ordered another round for everyone. She put her hand on Hal's shoulder and let it slide to his back as she leaned into him with a hug. "Amorcito...could you repeat the order. I did not get it..."

Mari took immediate umbrage. "Excuse me...excuse me...I'm sitting right here!" The girl looked up. "I'll thank you to take your hands off of my boyfriend...!"

"Oh...I didn't know he was your boyfriend...I don't see no ring on your finger..."

"I don't see my foot up your ass either...but it is still a distinct possibility!" Mari leaned forward with her eyes blazing. "I suggest you take your flaca ass out of here."

Hal's eyebrows went up and his eyes widened with surprise as he looked at Mari. He turned back to the waitress. "Please send another waiter here."

Lance was befuddled. "Well ain't you the spitfire...I didn't know you two were that way about each other."

"We try to keep it low key at work..." Hal explained.

"I'm sorry if I stepped on your toes..." Lance felt confused.

"No harm...no foul..." Hal felt magnanimous.

"The nerve of that bitch...right in front of me..." Mari was still steamed.

"She was probably drinking on the job..." Hal eased back in his chair with his eyes half closed now that everyone knew that Mari wasn't going to take no shit—when it came to him.

***

Hal dialed downstairs to Mari's desk. "Hi kiddo..."

"Hi, sweet dick...what's up?"

"Mari...stop calling me that at work!" He blushed even though he was alone in his office. "When you are out in the field do you ever have the occasion to go to the Los Angeles County Archives? Do you know where the County Archives are?"

"Sure...that's the Hall of Records..."

"That's gotta be wrong because Elvis is at the Hall of Records right now...he's looking for an old court case file...and they told him to go to the Archives...and he can't find it. No one else seems to know what he is talking about."

"Oh...that! Yeah...I know it...and boy is it hard to find if you don't know where it is and what to look for. There is a door across the street..."

"He said the clerk told him that...but there is no building there...there is nothing..."

"There is no building...just a door...and if you have never been there before...you will never know what to look for..."

"How did you find out...?"

"I have my methods...Mr. Golan...which brings to mind a wonderful story you may want to do...it has to do with..."

"I have Elvis on hold...come up to my office so you can help him out..."

"OK, sweet dick..."

"Stop that!"

Mari breezed into Hal's office just in time to hear Hal say, "Where are you again? OK...I'll have Mari meet you there...she knows exactly where it is...yep...yep...about twenty minutes..." He looked at Mari for confirmation of the time and she nodded. "Meet her out on the steps at the front of the building...yep...OK...see ya." Hal hung up and gave Mari a slip of paper. "This is where he is..."

She looked at the paper. "He has no way of knowing it...but he's right across the street."

"You said something about a story...can you break it down in five?"

"Sure. George Cryer...Mayor of Los Angeles from 1921 to 1929...he did a lot of great things for the city...the Coliseum was built...and our

171

City Hall. Now most people do not know that under the city there is a labyrinth of underground tunnels...for miles...running from the Hall of Justice...to the Hall of Records...to the Court House...to City Hall...et cetera...and the County Archives are stored in just part of it.

"Now the kicker is that during prohibition...many saloons went underground into the tunnels...where they located their speakeasies, for which Mayor Cryer and his bootleg buddies supplied the booze. He was hooked up. I thought it would be a wonderful historical piece about the Roaring Twenties...when L.A. was fast and loose." She looked at her watch. "Four minutes left. Of course there is a lot more to the story...so I am able to help you embellish on it...but that's it in a nutshell."

"Sounds like it has possibilities...when you get back write up a short synopsis, locations, people, facts...and we'll see how it plays out. You better run now...Elvis is stuck in the building..."

"Cut the guy a break..."

"I am...I'm sending Wonder Woman to rescue him..."

***

Cruising by the Hall of Records, Mari saw Lance standing on the steps and she honked and came to a stop, holding up traffic, while he ran for her car. Hopping inside he looked relieved as she drove off again. "I sure am glad to see you little lady..."

"I thought I should pick you up first before finding parking...who knows how long that would take..."

"Before we go to the Archives...is there anywhere I can grab a bite to eat...I've been out here half the day...and I could eat the backside of a mule..."

"Sure...where do you want to go?"

"Somewhere that serves a lot of food for a little money...I'm on a budget right now."

"We can't go too far...we have to get back before the Archives close..."

"You've been there before to get a court file...?"

"Yep...something like that..."

"How long does it take?"

"Not too long...if you're not burned out on Mexican food...we can try Olvera Street"

"I love Mexican food..."

172

"OK…but it's my treat…because I want to pick the place."

"I couldn't let you pay…"

Mari glanced at him and smirked. "This is L.A.…you don't let me do anything…I do what I want…and I want to buy your lunch…because you suffered enough for one day…"

"Yes, Ma'am!"

Soon they were sitting in the outdoor section in front of La Golondrina Restaurant digging into a starter of nachos and then chicken mole burritos with rice, beans, salad, and a side order of chili rellenos. "I know there is way too much to eat here…but once I start ordering when I'm hungry…I don't know when I should stop…it all looks so good." Mari smiled.

"Where I come from you don't have the wide variety of food you see in L.A. They don't have a Mexican restaurant in the whole town…here they have food from all kinds of countries…that I never even heard of before. I fell in love with this city…that is why I want to write about it."

"Well here is a tidbit of a story I can throw you if you're interested…"

"Are you sure that Mr. Golan won't mind?"

"It's not really his kind of story…he mainly works on exposing corruption…I can't say this story has never been done before…but maybe you can put a new twist on it…give it a more historical context. Just a few yards from where we sit, at the end of the street, is a little shack of a café that was started by the last wife of Pancho Villa. How and why she was in L.A. at the time and why she opened that tiny eatery is anybody's guess…but the combination of cuisine…history…and local flavor should be interesting. As a matter of fact, that is where the taquito was born."

"That sounds like it would be fun to work on." He changed the subject. "Tell me…how did you and Hal get together?"

"We were working on a story together last July…and because I was assigned to someone else…we had to work on the story after hours and on weekends…and that is how I got to know him. Then I was reassigned to be his research analyst…replacing Cora…because I knew the story. He won the Story of the Year award for that article…you know. During that time…I fell pretty hard for him."

"I can see that by the way your eyes sparkle when you talk about him. What made him so special?"

"Everything! Funny...the first thing I thought of when you asked me that...was his smile. But he is so much more than that...he's smart...fun...hardworking...brave...strong...and he is so very good to me...he's the whole package."

"Sounds like he doesn't have any faults."

"Just one...he's kind of jealous...in fact he's very jealous...but who am I to talk...I practically bit that waitress's head off when she touched him...so I guess I have some of the green monster in me too!"

He laughed. "Yeah...that took me by surprise! But she did have a point. He hasn't put a ring on your finger. I had no idea you were taken...or I wouldn't have had Elvis sing a love song to you...although I did mean it...I was quite taken with you." He looked like he was going to say something but then shook his head and changed his mind.

"What were you going to say?"

"Miss Mari...I really shouldn't say this...because it sounds ungrateful for all he's done for me..." He frowned. "...but to my way of thinking...he should have put a ring on your finger a long time ago. If it had been me...I would have claimed you as mine with a ring the day I met you..."

"Oh dear God! Don't ever let Hal hear you say anything close to that...he will flip and really go berserk on you. As for me...I'm very happy as things are with him. If he decides to take it to the next level...then I'll go there with him."

"What about you...what about what you decide?"

"Lance...at this point I think I'll keep my thoughts to myself."

After lunch they carried their doggie bags back to Mari's car. "It would be faster to walk than it would be to try to find parking again." Mari suggested.

"Yeah...it didn't look too far." He held out his arm. "It looks like they didn't take high heels into consideration when they made these streets..."

She took his arm. "Or short people..."

As they arrived across the street from the Hall of Records, Mari pointed. "There it is..."

"There what is...?"

174

"Do you see that door all by itself?"

"Do you mean that blue door...in a block of cement?"

"That's it..."

"That's what?"

"That's where we're going..."

"I was right here all along...?"

"Yeah...you were looking for a building...right?"

"Or at least a sign...I saw this door...but I thought it was some kind of utility thing for the city works."

Mari turned the door handle. "Here we go...follow the yellow brick road..."

When they entered, there was an elevator door inside. She pushed the button and the elevator doors opened. They went down to the Archives level and the door opened to a cement hallway with a yellow line running down the middle. It led through double doors that opened into a vast concrete warehouse, which was filled with stacks of boxes. On the right side was a counter behind which sat a staid, light-skinned black man. "We're looking for a court file...do you have a form for us to fill out?" Mari took the lead.

"Yes...and I will need to see your driver's license." He handed her the paper and went about his business as they filled in the paperwork with the courthouse, the case name and number of the file to be pulled. When they were through, he placed a call, a forklift appeared, and he handed the operator their request as they sat down and waited.

Lance looked around the warehouse. "This is amazing...I never would have guessed that all of this was here."

Mari started to tell him that there were miles of tunnels, of which this was a small part; but until Hal told her that he was not interested in the underground story, she kept it to herself. "Yes...can you imagine the decades of cases here...it really is a treasure trove."

"Don't you want to know what I'm working on?"

"No...and you shouldn't tell me until after you present it."

"You already have the file name..."

"And that is where it will stay..." She motioned that her lips were zipped.

Lance studied her for a while and then folded his hands in front of him as they waited. After about twenty minutes the file was delivered to the counter and they were called. "This file will be delivered to the courthouse within three days...you can view it there and if you wish...have it copied. If you do not go to the court after it has been delivered there...within the time allotted; it will be returned here." He gave them a sheet of paper that spelled out the rules and other particulars.

"That's it?"

"That is all there is to it...be sure to go to the court clerk's office to view it and get a copy." She handed him the paper.

They walked back to the elevator. He stopped her outside the Archive's double doors. "Thank you for showing me the ropes." He looked down at her, wrestling with his thoughts. "Mari...if it doesn't work out between you and Hal...would you consider giving me a chance?"

The question gave her a cold chill. "That question scares me to death...the very thought that it might not work with Hal and me is devastating to me...and it leaves no room for thoughts of you. Lance...don't let your heart trip and stumble over me...I could never think of you in that way...and it could only hurt you." They rode the elevator back to daylight in silence.

***

"You've been quiet this evening...usually you're my pretty little chatterbox." Hal pushed his chair away from the table and leaned back. "...how did it go with numb-nuts this afternoon...?"

"Hal...don't call him that..."

"What...all of a sudden you're Miss Sensitive? I just want to know how he did today."

Mari was pensive. "Look Hal...I am trying to find a way to talk to you without your stomping around...and jumping to conclusions...because I want to discuss a point he made...that I would like the answer to as well. But unless you promise me that you won't get angry...or at least control that temper of yours...then I won't discuss it with you at all."

"What the fuck is it now?"

"You see...there you go! You're not able to listen and rationally discuss anything! I can't even talk to you." She put her fork down. "I want to share my thoughts and feelings with you without a big brouhaha...but instead...you force me to keep them locked up inside me…and then you have no idea what I am thinking…or why. I want to share with you what was said today…without you going nuts…now do you want to hear it or not?"

He leaned forward, his chin in one hand with his elbow resting on the table, squinting at her. "Yeah…I want to know what was said…every word."

"I promise you…that if you start yelling at me…or take out your anger on Lance…I will never tell you anything again…ever!"

"You got it, Babe…you tell me from start to finish…and I won't interrupt you…and I won't get angry…"

She spent the next half hour relating the events and the conversation of the afternoon. Then she concluded, "He really was a gentleman in every way…and he was honest…"

"That's it?"

"Yeah…that's it…"

"So, you let Elvis down easy…is that what you wanted to tell me?"

"Yes…and no…you're missing the point…"

"OK…what's the point?"

She knitted her brow and looked around like she was searching for an avenue of escape from having to explain the question to him. *How can he not get it? Is he pretending not to understand?* "Didn't you hear what I said? He told me that the reason he came on to me was that he thought I was…available…because he did not see a ring on my finger. I'm not fishing for a ring…let me be clear about that…but it does raise the question of why not."

Hal half smiled and looked away. "Can't you see that the guy is bird-dogging you?"

"What…what-ing?"

"Bird-dogging…he's pursuing you…trying to make you unhappy with me so he can step in and…"

"Step in…Hal…nobody's stepping in…"

"Is that why you took him to lunch?"

"He had a rough day…he was hungry…so was I for that matter…he was skint…so I paid…what's wrong with being considerate? Don't try to evade the issue…this has nothing to do with Lance…I just want to know why…"

"I think you gave him the best answer…"

"My answer to him has nothing to do with your answer to me…"

"As far as that goes...I just haven't..." He searched for the right word.

Her hand went to her mouth. "Made up your mind?"

"No...no...I don't know..."

She got up, left the remainder of her dinner on the table, and went to their bedroom. Sitting on the edge of the bed, she tried to grasp his reasoning. *He was the one who said he loved me...now he's not so sure?*

Hal came into the room. "Look, Babe...whatever that guy is telling you it's working overtime on you...why are you listening to him...?"

"I'm not...I'm listening to you."

"Then why are you so upset?"

"I'm upset because I love you...and I just wanted to know where you see us going...I wanted to know why you haven't openly declared that I am yours..."

"You're upset because you love me? That sounds like a contradiction in terms."

"Do you doubt that I love you?"

"When you are listening to this guy...I don't know..."

"YOU DON'T KNOW!?!"

"You tell me all this stuff about wonderful Lance..." He held out his hands. "I don't know..."

"You are so ready to talk yourself into believing that I think Lance is wonderful...and yet you cannot comprehend the simple fact that I love you? Really swell, Hal."

"I just said...I don't know."

"For Christ's flippin' sake...what do I have to do?" She started to cry. "Fuck you, Hal...I mean seriously...fuck you!" She ran to her old bedroom, slammed the door, and locked it.

***

Hiding in her cubicle for most of the day, Mari tried to keep busy to avoid the people around her. She had applied chilled, wet teabags to her eyes and gave herself a mint facial that had somewhat mitigated the ravages of crying. But, the pain in the pit of her stomach had no cure. She had stayed in her old bedroom all night, refusing to answer Hal's knocks at her door. She was up and out of the house before it was time for his alarm to go off. She drove until she found a twenty-four-hour coffee shop, ordered breakfast, and then picked at it. The blue cloud that settled on her didn't allow her to think, she only had strength enough to mope.

Her phone rang. She picked it up. "Mari Carlson..."

"Babe...it's me..." She hung up.

The phone rang again. She stared at it for a while and picked it up on the third ring.

"Hello?"

"Mari...listen to me..." She hung up again.

The third time it rang she picked it up and said, "Stop calling me!" and hung up.

Staff at the desks near Mari's cubicle picked up on some sort of predicament with her but had largely ignored it. But Lance drew attention wherever he went, and when he approached Mari's desk the eyes and ears of the office went with him. "Miss Mari...I just called...and I got the feeling someone has been annoying you...who's been calling you?" He got a glimpse of her forlorn expression. "Are you alright?"

"No...but I will be...what can I do for you, Lance."

"I just wanted to ask you more about that idea you gave me...you know...about Pancho Villa's wife. You said it's been done before...I wanted to see what we already had...it will give me something to work on while I wait for my file."

"Sure...I think those files are at the warehouse...Cora can go there and look under Pancho Villa...tell her to bring you everything we have on him...we may have something on all of his wives..." She held up her fingers in quote marks. "The Los Angeles wives of Pancho Villa!"

Suddenly, there was a stir as Hal came in. "OK...that's it...back off Colonel Sanders...this chick is taken..." Hal walked up with blood in his eyes. "You go bird-dog someone else's woman!" A communal gasp went up and the analysts came to watch from the entrance of their respective cubicles. The entire room was alerted to an impending fight.

"Oh, God Hal..." Mari hid her face in her hands.

Lance turned to face him. "I was just asking her a question...but now that you mention it...she ain't yours until you put a ring on her finger and say 'I do'...until then...she's fair game..." He turned and started walking away.

"Hey...you! I'm only going to tell you once. Stay away from her...if I catch you anywhere near her...I will rearrange that face of yours..." Hal glowered.

Lance turned around with his fists held at his sides. "You think that I can't take you!"

Hal beckoned with his hands. "Come on...would you like to try!"

Mari stepped in between them. "Stop it...stop it...you two gorillas act as though I have no say in this..."

Keeping his eye on Lance, Hal asked, "OK, Mari...what do you have to say about this?"

She pled her case to the one she concluded was the most reasonable. "Lance...you're as handsome as all get out...you have a wonderful voice...and you should stop imitating Elvis and do your own style...and you are a really nice guy...the only thing wrong with you as far as my caring for you goes...is that you are not Hal. Right now...I am so mad at him that I could spit nails...stomp my foot, yell, and throw things at him...but...I still love him from head to toe...he's mostly wonderful...but you caught him on a bad day. All I can say is that warts and all I love him...and I'm stuck with it...you're stuck with it...and he's stuck with it...and that is not going to change...so there is no need to fight over me. Sorry..." She turned and walked away.

As she walked by, Hal called out, "Mari..."

"I'm not speaking to you...asshole!" she brushed by him.

Hal leveled his gaze back at Lance. "Well she called it. She loves me...and I'm an asshole. That settles it as far as I'm concerned."

Lance nodded. "I suppose you're going to have me fired."

"Hell no...you're the only guy 'in the building' that I know I don't have to worry about! Ordinarily, I would buy you a drink to make amends...but I gotta go buy some flowers...and a ring!"

***

BABY, DON'T BE LIKE THAT

Mari walked down the hall from the bathroom toward her old bedroom clad only in a lace bra and panties. Hal came out of his room and blocked her way. She went to walk around him and when he reached for her; he got his hand smacked. "Did I say you could touch me? I don't remember saying you could touch me." She snapped.

"Baby, don't be like that...I've apologized a thousand times..."

"Yeah...and it's just talk with you...just like everything else you told me. You tell me you love me...and then you're not so sure...when I tell you I love you...you don't know if I really do...you act like an OG gangsta threatening a co-worker...you're acting so crazy, I can't figure out which way is up with you...and until I do, you are not touching me."

"OK...OK...I know I deserve that...but it's been almost a week now...how long are you going to keep me in purgatory?"

"I'm keeping *you* in purgatory? That, Mr. Golan, is where you put *me!*"

***

"Oh, God, Lo-Lo...he's gone nuts...I've never seen him act like this before." Mari went to consult her guru.

"No...he's fine...he's just fighting the hook." She languished on her couch toking a joint.

"The hook?"

"Yeah...he's just realized that you have the hook in his mouth and that he's being reeled in...and like those big fish you see jumping out of the water...trying to free themselves by fighting the hook...that's just what he's doing."

An incongruous expression passed over Mari's face. "But why? I never set out to hook him...he's the one who started it...he said he loved me first..."

"I know...they always do...and just when everything is working between you...and they know they don't want to lose you...they start feeling the hook in their mouth because they see their freedom fading fast...and there is something in their nature that makes them fight against that. I'm not saying it is a conscious thing...I don't think they even know they're doing it. All I know is that they start throwing out irrational shit...left and right...trying to fend off the inevitable.

When they see that you're tired of it...and about to walk...they come around real fast."

"I don't know what to do...I've stopped speaking to him...and cooking for him both in and out of the bedroom. I'm sleeping in my old room..."

"But you do parade it for him...in your frillies..."

"As a matter of habit I always walk around with not much on...so he's used to that..."

"No he's not, honey...especially when he's not gettin' any..."

"So I should just walk around in my skivvies...and then what?"

"You wait until you think he is contrite enough for you to give in...but you let him talk you into it..."

"How do I know he's really sorry? Sometimes I think it's only talk with him to try to get back into my panties...rather than my good graces...and God help me...part of me wants to let him..." She took a deep breath.

"How long have you been at this?"

"About a week."

Lo-Lo smiled. "Alright! Get ready for the best sex you ever had...because make-up sex is over the top!"

***

"...so after that...Mari refuses to speak to me...or anything else." Hal confessed all.

"Why are you treatin' that little girl like that?" Deuce didn't mince words.

"You're always taking her side..."

"That's 'cause you're always in the wrong!"

Big tried to interject a little sensitivity. "What you appear to...fail to grasp...entertain the concept...should I say, understand...is that your lovely Mari tried to confide in you...bare her soul...open up to you. Most women don't do that...finding their men to be too obtuse...dullards...simpletons...unreceptive...intolerant   or defensive. So they clam up and use manipulation...subterfuge...and deceit...to gain their ends. Your Mari wants to be honest with you...and open up to you...it is something that should be encouraged..."

Deuce looked askance. "I don't want Wanda opening up to me...I'm scared of what would come flying out of her. I think that woman is full of bats and shit..."

"But she was talking all this smack about another guy..." Hal lamented.

"What did I tell you about being jealous? You found out in the end that it didn't amount to nothin'..." Deuce admonished.

"If you want her to confide in you...to trust you with her secrets...to reveal her innermost thoughts...you have to stop jumping all over her...and slamming her when she does..." Big tapped his finger on the table.

"And what's all this about telling her you weren't sure she loved you? That was really a slap in the face! I already told you she loves you...and I wouldn't have said that if it wasn't the God's honest truth...you may as well have slapped me in the face too!" Deuce stared at him from under his hat.

"Whatcha gonna do...stop speaking to me and cut me off sexually too?"

Deuce frowned. "You see that's what's wrong with you...always the snappy comeback instead of listening to good advice. I told you a while back you should marry her...but, oh no...you know better..."

"I bought her a ring..."

"Well...what did she say?"

"I haven't given it to her yet...she's not speaking to me..."

Losing patience Deuce spelled out what Hal needed to do. "You better go home and beg that girl to forgive you...cry if you have to...but get her back into the fold before she wakes up and changes her mind about you...then you will play hell trying to get her back. You had better pull out all stops if she lets you back into her heart again...and learn to behave yourself."

Big added, "There are two words you need to rehearse...practice...utilize...and revere! 'Yes, dear.' Memorize those two words...use them often...and regularly...let it become second nature...and you will have a happy life.

***

Standing in front of the bathroom mirror, Hal lathered up to shave. The face that looked back at him was haggard from the strain of the past week. Loss of sleep, self-recrimination, and crummy food had

183

taken its toll. *I have got to put a stop to this standoff...but how? She won't accept my apologies...my gifts...she won't talk to me...and if she doesn't fuck me soon I'll explode! She doesn't cook anything...how is she eating?* Using short strokes, he shaved his sideburns and then he used long strokes on his face, running the water over the razor after each sortie and tapping the excess off in the sink.

Mari knocked at the door and then burst into the bathroom. "You're running late and hogging the bathroom...and I have to take a shower..." She turned the faucets on, stripped off her flimsies, and got into the shower. He tried not to stare, and failed, as his heart went up and down on Hell's trampoline. With shaving foam around his mouth, he turned back to the mirror to see the sad faced clown looking back at him. He finished shaving and then went to his room to get dressed.

He had just pulled on his pants when he heard the water turn off and he could see, in his mind's eye, how she looked emerging from the shower, smiling as she towel dried her hair, put a mysterious lotion in it, and brushed it in. He ached to dry her back and wrap her in a bath sheet. Right about now she would be applying her deodorant and then slathering her arms and legs with another mystery lotion. He loved that she allowed him in the bathroom with her.

The door handle turned and without thinking he dashed into the hallway to confront her. She appeared with her long, wet hair hanging down and only a towel wrapped around her; she looked past him and headed to her room. "Mari...we've got to talk...please..."

She flashed him a glance and kept on walking. When he wouldn't let her pass, she tried to push him away. "Let me by...I have to get dressed."

"I'm not going to let you by until you talk to me." He blocked her.

Frustrated at her inability to budge him, she started shoving and then slapping at his arms and chest. "Damn it, Hal...get out of my way!"

He grabbed both of her hands and forced them down behind her back and held them there. In the skirmish her towel slipped and fell to the floor. The sheer mass of him overwhelmed her, but she persisted to struggle against him. "Babe...stop it...please just give me five minutes, Mari…just five…" He pleaded. The feel of her warm breasts against the skin of his chest and her scented hair inundated his senses. He pulled her to him in an embrace and kissed her long and hard until she stopped struggling and melted in his arms. "Babe…oh God…you feel so good. I love you, Mari…and I will for all my life. Please believe me…"

She was breathless and trembling. Pulling her hands free she wrapped her arms around him and held him tight. Locked in an embrace they frantically kissed and whispered the words that each of them longed to hear.

Moving as if in a dream, he carried her to bed. Her eyes reflected the sparkle of a million diamonds as she gazed up at him while he undressed. Enclosing him in her arms she moaned under the weight of him. As he moved back and forth; she picked up his rhythm and each of his thrusts sent delicious waves of sensation through her. For a while her eyes held his, so dark with passion, and her hands felt the power coursing through him as she stroked his back. Enveloped in her, every move sent a thrill through him as she clasped onto him, complementing his motion inside of her with involuntary contractions. He held on and kept driving until he heard her familiar cry and felt the sweet sensation of the contractions of her orgasm. As he took her to climax, he finished with a guttural growl. She gathered him in her arms and caressed him. "Hal…oh…Hal…" She sighed. "You were so magnificent."

"You're damned magnificent yourself, Babe."

She bit her lip. "Oh, yeah…but that's not what I was talking about. I wanted to tell you before, but I didn't want to encourage…bad behavior…"

"Mari…I'll be goddamned if I know what you're talking about…but I never do…I thought you liked the walloping I just gave you…"

"Mmmmm…I loved it…" She breathed. "…that was heaven…and I needed that." She rolled her shoulder up and kissed him on the ear.

"What was it that I did that you thought was magnificent?"

"When you told Lance that you would kick his ass if he came near me again…you should have seen yourself…you had the look of eagles. Of course you were totally wrong and wholly inappropriate…but my God were you ballsy."

"Then why were you so mad at me?!"

"Hal…you can't go around like a loose cannon…telling me that you're not sure if you love me…when you do…or that you don't know if I love you…when you do." All the sadness she felt flickered over her face. "I wanted to die." She knitted her brow and continued her reprimand. "And you can't go around threatening people."

He stared at her for a moment trying to gather it all in. "But you liked the fact that I was ballsy?"

"Yeah…the more I thought about it…I had to say to myself…oh fuck yeah!"

He shook his head, took her in his arms, and said, "Yes dear!"

***

MARRY ME

Hal sat in his office staring at the big red X on his calendar. It was the day he had set for himself to propose to Mari, and the X loomed larger and more daunting each day. He thought of the ring he had sitting in his desk drawer at home, waiting for X day. *Once you put that ring on her finger...that's it...for life. There goes your independence...no more strange pussy...no more coming and going as you please.* Thinking of the limitations that marriage would impose on him, he realized that he had willingly accepted them long ago when Mari first moved in with him, and he had no regrets. Still, it was a lifetime commitment. *Will I feel the same five years from now...ten years from now...will I be happy...will she?*

Mari knocked and stuck her head in the door. "Hal...do you have a minute?"

"Yeah...sure..."

Beaming, she closed the door behind her, locked it, and closed the blinds. "Everyone knows you love me..." She sang and did a happy dance around his office. She stuck out her butt and pointed to her left cheek. "...see that...that's your brand on my ass!" She giggled. "Guys that used to try to chat me up...barely speak to me! If I say good morning...they give me a quick 'morning' and keep on walking..." She imitated their stiff walk and mumbling out of the side of their mouths. "They're all afraid that you'll kick their ass if you even catch them looking at me! I swear it's a scream..." she laughed.

"You're happy about that?" He calmly asked.

She quieted down at the serious look on his face. "Well...yeah...I am. It's a relief! Every time I turn around I don't have to worry about some guy coming on to me...it works for me." She tilted her head. "I thought you would think it was funny...did I catch you at a bad time?"

He sighed. "No. I just have a lot on my mind." He got up and prepared to leave. "I'm taking the rest of the day off...I'll see you at home..."

"Did I say something wrong?" She was nonplussed by his mood. "Will you be home for dinner?"

He walked over to her and fiddled with her hair. "No...you didn't say anything wrong...and yes...I'll be home for dinner." He pulled her to him, kissed her, and then he was gone.

***

Breakers turned over and crashed along the beach. In shirtsleeves and rolled up slacks, Hal strolled barefoot along the sand as the foam tinged water lapped over his feet. Even though it was mid-week, there were picnickers, kids playing hooky, and retirees dotting the shore. He watched the waves and, in his memory, could see himself and Deuce body surfing in the sunny days of his childhood. In the distance, in an unpopulated area, he could see an old man surf fishing. Incredibly, the geezer had enough strength to cast his line beyond the breaking waves. Dressed in a plaid shirt and khaki pants, he wore a crumpled hat, with a brim that was rippled with age. The old-timer seemed to have expertise and, walking toward him, Hal watched with interest. As he approached, he shouted over the noise of the surf. "What are you using for bait?"

The old guy nodded. "Sand crabs...the ones you dig up on the beach are larger than the ones they sell...they make good bait...and they're free."

"Do you come out here often?"

"About once a week or so...this spot is pretty good. I usually come here...or up that way about a mile..." he pointed north. He looked at Hal. "From the way you're dressed...I would say you're a refugee from some office..."

Hal raised his eyebrows and nodded. "Good guess...I just had to get out of the office to think things through."

"Well...whatever it is...don't overthink it...you can end up tripping yourself up. Never overthink it...break it down to simple terms...the basics...and then roll the dice..."

"What do you mean?"

"What are you grappling with?"

"I want to propose to my girl..." Hal confided. "...but that's a huge step."

The old man fixed his eyes on Hal and chuckled. "That's an easy one to figure out. I broke it down this way...before I asked my wife to marry me I asked myself two things...do I love her..." He sighed "Oh...I loved her with the deepest passion you could imagine."

Hal found it hard to imagine that this wrinkled, bent old guy was at one time capable of passion, but he went along with it. "Yeah...I feel the same about my girl."

"Then the only other thing you have to ask yourself is…can you stand the thought of seeing her in the arms of another man? If you cannot stand seeing her with someone else…then you have no other choice but to marry her. It's that simple!"

"Yeah…you're right…I couldn't stand to see her with anyone else." He thought to ask another question. "Did everything work out in your marriage the way you thought it would?"

"No…nothing in life runs smoothly…we had our ups and downs…but we loved each other…raised two kids…and I was happy with her for all my life…" The old guy swallowed hard. "She's gone now…died two years ago…and I miss her everyday…" The old-timer's eyes misted over. "You marry your girl…and whatever life throws your way…you make her happy. I was married to my wife for fifty-four years…at your age you cannot conceive how short a time that is…and you cannot regain any day that you lost…" He patted Hal on the shoulder. "I wish you the best of luck, son…" He reeled in his line and packed up his gear. "See you around." He trudged off down the beach.

Hal looked down and saw that the man had dropped one of his fishing weights. He picked it up and started to call after him, but the old guy was out of hearing range. Staring at the weight for a moment, he put it in his pocket as a memento.

***

Hal sped along the Santa Monica freeway trying to think of the fastest way to get home as traffic was beginning to fill up. *What was I thinking? Of course I want to marry her…I want to marry her now! Strange pussy? Shit…I've got the best I ever had in my life…I don't want any other. Freedom? Independence? Free from what? Her? I never want to be free from her! It would kill me to see her with anyone else. Fuck X day…I'm asking her tonight!*

After fighting his way through ungodly traffic, he was still ebullient at the thought of proposing. Arriving home, he went through the back door and, once inside, started taking off his sandy clothes.

"That better be you." Mari called from the kitchen.

"It's me…I can't come in until I take off my clothes…they're full of sand."

"Sand?"

"Yeah…I went to the beach…"

"In your suit?" She stepped into the hallway.

"No…well…yeah…just my slacks and shirt. I better get in the shower before I get sand all over the place." He looked up at the white lace peignoir she was wearing "Baby…you look gorgeous…"

"I'll shake your clothes out and put them in a bag to take to the cleaners. I thought you could use some cheering up…so I made something special…"

He bussed her on the lips as he scurried to the bathroom and into the shower. "I have something special for you too."

"Yeah? I can't wait!" She picked up his clothes and shook them out the back door. "What's this in your pocket?"

"You might say it's a good luck charm…put it on my nightstand."

When he got out of the shower he started to put on a pullover and changed his mind. He picked a suit and tie out of his closet and dressed for the occasion. As Mari puttered in the kitchen, he went to the living room and grinned at seeing the table set up there. Going to his desk, he retrieved a small box, and opened it. He stared at the dazzling object it held. *This is forever.* He closed the box and put it in his pocket.

Mari entered the room holding two plates. Puzzled at the way he was dressed she asked, "Are you going somewhere tonight…do I need to get dressed?"

"No…you're perfect the way you are."

"OKaaay…what's up?" She shrugged and put the plates on the table.

"You'll see." He sat down to a thick porterhouse steak. "Babe…this is just what I wanted and didn't even know it…I'm ravenous!"

She served herself a small New York strip and poured a glass of red wine for him. "I drove up to Pasadena to get the steaks…so they should be primo. I hope the wine is good…I really should learn more about wine…but I asked for a good one and the clerk suggested this Pinot Noir…I hope you like it. I also got champagne as a backup…"

He knife and forked his steak, putting a chunk in his mouth, and gazed at his beautiful fiancée to be. As he chewed, he thought, *how did I ever get so lucky?*

After dinner, he took her over to the couch and sat her down. "I thought of taking you somewhere special…but you already had a special dinner for me…and frankly…I couldn't wait any longer…" He got down on one knee, took the box out of his pocket, and opened it. "Mari Carlson…I love you and I can't live without you…please make me the happiest man in the world…will you please marry me?"

She gasped and her mouth fell open; she couldn't speak. When she found her voice, she spoke in a voice so low that it was almost a whisper. "Hal…we never took much time to talk about ourselves…there's really not a lot we know about each other…you really don't know much about me…"

"I love you and that's all I need to know…" He paused. "OK…have you ever committed a murder?"

"No!"

"Well, there you go…that's all I need to know…I'm good!" He gave her his most charming smile. "Marry me, Mari…you'll never regret it…"

"Yes." She whispered. Surprised at herself, her hands immediately went to her mouth. "Oh, my God…I said 'yes'…I said 'yes' didn't I!" She said out loud and then threw herself into his arms, toppling him over. "Yes…yes…yes!!!" He took her in his arms and rolled on top of her and she gazed into his eyes as she caressed his face. "I'll be the best wife to you that I know how to be…"

"You already are, Babe…I'm just making an honest woman out of you…" He beamed.

"An honest woman…what an old-fashioned notion…I have been honest all along. Wasn't I honestly making love to you? I would say that's pretty damned honest!" she laughed.

He looked around. "The ring…what happened to the ring? I'm supposed to put it on your finger…"

"I don't know…I didn't actually see the ring…all I saw was you…"

"It has to be here somewhere…" They both started frantically searching around the floor.

"What hand did you have it in?"

"My left…of course…"

"Why of course? Then it's probably in this direction…"

"It must have gone under the couch…"

"Oh…there it is…in the corner!" Mari retrieved it and handed it to Hal.

"Don't you want to look at it?" He asked.

"Not until you put it on my finger...and I know that this is not a dream..."

He lifted the ring with shaking hands and slipped it on her finger. "This is not a dream...I mean this with all my heart...and fifty or sixty years from now...you'll still be my beautiful Babe."

***

FOURTH OF JULY

Turning off of the Santa Monica freeway, Hal headed south on La Cienega towards Ladera Heights, the affluent black neighborhood where Deuce resided. His annual Fourth of July barbeque was legend, making attendance a tradition. Mari recalled the last time she was whisked down this street. "You know...it's all such a blur now...the last time I was here I was so afraid...I really don't remember much of anything. It seems forever ago."

"Don't dwell on it, Babe."

"I mostly recall how very nice everyone was to me. By the way...you never told me that Terry was rich..."

Hal shrugged. "He does alright...what makes you think he's rich?"

"I'm sure you've seen his home...it's exquisite...and it smacks of money..."

"Yeah...his home is alright..."

"I never would have guessed...because he doesn't act the least bit snobbish...he's down to earth...and I guess that's what I like about him..."

"That's because he didn't always have money. The way he puts it is that he woke up one day and found out that he was broke with a baby on the way...that's when he went from being a boy to a man...when he realized he had to do something about it! That was twelve years ago...he's a self-made man..."

She gazed at him. "Like you..."

"Well kind of...sort of..." He smirked. "I never really had to work that hard at it...but there again I didn't have that kind of incentive. But you might say I'm carving out my own path to where I want to go..."

"Don't worry...you'll get there..." She smiled.

"And if I don't get rich like Deuce?"

She turned to him. "Success means different things to different people, Hal. To many it means money...acquisition of things...to others it means becoming what they want to be...or doing what they want to do...reaching their personal goals in life...whether or not it brings them fame or fortune. Like you want to create a novel that will have a lasting impact on those who read it...whether it's a best seller or not. Money was never that important to me...but a worthwhile goal is." She sat back. "I'm just glad that you are taking me with you on your adventure...and I think it will be quite a ride!"

***

Cars were filling up parking space along the street, so Hal had to park a half block away. "How many people will be there? It looks like a lot..." Mari surveyed the cars lining the curb.

"His family...his employees...his friends...just about half of L.A...."

Bringing gifts for the hosts, they walked up the circular, herringbone, brick drive to the double doors of the pale yellow, sprawling, single story house. A green, velvety lawn with sculpted box hedges lined the side of the drive and a spectacular, specimen Adonidia palm majestically ruled over the meticulous landscape. A deep melodious chime responded to the push of the doorbell. As they entered, they received a warm welcome. "Hey...if it isn't the man of the hour...and his beautiful bride to be..." Deuce announced. "Come on through to the back...and get amongst it all..."

Mari handed him a box containing a bottle of Krug Gran Cuvee Champagne. "This is for Wanda...to thank her for being so kind to me..."

"And this is for you..." Hal took his fist and rapped himself on the chest and gave Deuce a bottle of Hennessy Paradis Extra, a rare, aged Cognac. "You're the best, man..."

Deuce took the gifts and put his fist to his chest and whispered, "Knight's honor..."

Hal repeated, "Knight's honor..." The two men clasped each other's hands in an upward shake. A meaningful moment passed between the two of them before Deuce broke the silence. "I better take you out back...before you start cryin'." He sniffed, blinking his eyes. Leading them through the house, Deuce yelled out, "Wanda...come here...look who's here..."

A pretty café au lait woman with medium length, black hair hurried out of the kitchen. Her body had remained slightly plump from her last pregnancy, five years ago. She reached out to Mari and gave her an air kiss. "You're looking much better from the last time I saw you..." She took Mari's left hand and gasped. "What is this?" She looked at the ring with the eye of an expert. "Oh honey...this is something...somebody call security! I hope you last longer than his last one."

194

Hal's eyebrows went down. "Who would that be...Wanda?"

"Oh...I don't remember her name...it's not important..."

"Look what Mari brought for you...for being so kind to her..." Deuce gave Wanda a pointed look.

"Well aren't you the sweetest thing...we'll have a glass together. Oh...that's right...you can't drink." She looked back at Deuce. "Just lock it up in the liquor cabinet for later..." Wanda sidled off toward the kitchen. "I had better finish the salad...good to see you again."

Deuce took them to the sports bar built around a flat screen TV in the family room, where he locked the bottles in the bar cabinet. "Let me fix you a drink..." He started mixing Mari's glass. "...I know what you're having, Mari. What are you drinking, Hal?"

"I'll just have a beer...whatever you have..." At the expression on Deuce's face, he added, "I've got to drive across town..."

"You can always stay the night..."

"Uh-uh...not with your ear glued to the door..." Hal grinned.

Deuce frowned. "Always depriving a man of good entertainment."

"Oh...the barbeque smells sooooo good..." Mari cooed.

"I've been cooking it over a slow fire since four this morning...I have a nice slab of beef ribs set aside for you, Hal..."

Hal laughed, "Mari's been feeding me pork...and I found out that I wasn't going to die...and God didn't strike me dead..."

"I didn't mean to..." She protested.

Deuce shrugged. "Well...I been tellin' you all along...I don't know if it's good for you...but it tastes like it is. My grandma used to tell me that at hog killin' time they would slaughter the hogs and eat everything but the squeal..."

Mari smiled, "Yes...we used to say that too!"

"That's right...you're a farm girl." Deuce handed Mari her drink.

"Yeah...Hal and I are going to Minnesota in a couple of weeks to meet my parents. I'm not looking forward to it..."

Hal laughed, "And then she gets to meet mine...my mother will love her...but other than that my family is no prize either..."

"Why are you two traipsing around meeting each other's families...?" He flickered a look at Mari and then focused on Hal. "Take my advice and just run off and get married by a judge...or go to Vegas...forget about this meeting the family shit."

Hal sighed. "You know I can't do that...it would break my mother's heart...and I should get to know Mari's family..."

"Alright...but families have a way of sticking their noses in where they're not wanted and spoiling things...just don't give anybody too much say so..."

Deuce's yard was scattered with tables and filled with clusters of people greeting each other and chatting before moving on to the next circle of friends. Mari thought she recognized a face. "Hal...there is a gentleman I would like for you to meet..." They walked toward an older brown-skinned man with gray, crinkled hair and a bulbous nose. His brown eyes revealed a gentle soul who, in spite of experience, retained his compassion. Hal and Mari sat across the table from him and Mari reached over to take his hands. The man looked up in surprise and then recognition crossed his face. "If it isn't my princess...how are you doing...did everything turn out alright for you?"

"Yes..." She smiled. "I don't even know your name...but I owe you such a debt of gratitude for helping me keep from going crazy when my world was falling apart..."

"You don't owe me nothin', darlin'...sometimes life gets too heavy to bear alone...and we all need a little lift from time to time. Is this your young man?"

"Yes...this is Hal...Hal Golan..." She scrunched up her shoulders. "...and we're engaged..."

"George Bixby..." He shook Hal's hand and turned back to Mari. "I told you your man would come back to you...yes, indeed...I knew he would move heaven and earth to get back to you..." He looked at Hal. "...am I right, son?"

Hal nodded. "Wild horses...and all that."

"What you been up to?"

"We're working on a story about Los Angeles in the 1920's...we're still doing the research..."

"Ooooooweeeh...my family goes way back in L.A....most everybody comes from somewhere else nowadays...but, I have an aunt that can tell you all about that. She was a wild thing...a pink toe...you know...pretty as they come back in the day...and she used to run with bootleggers. She's ninety-three now...and the stories she tells...my, my, my..."

"I would love to hear what she has to say. Do you think she would talk to me?"

"I don't know why not...she would love the attention."

"Does she know about the tunnels?"

"Honey...back in the day there was all sorts of tunnels...under the city...from the cliffs down to the beach...from the mortuary to the tearoom...this city is riddled with tunnels...and I'll bet it still is...for all sorts of reasons."

"Like what?" Hal's ears pricked up.

"Hal...we're sticking to the 1920's...we don't need to know about what's going on now." Mari cautioned.

"She's right...that shit can get too deep."

"OK...I'll take a pass on that." Hal feigned lack of interest but made a mental note for another day.

Mari took a notepad from her purse. "Let's exchange numbers...is it alright if I call you next week?"

"Sure...I'll go by her place tomorrow and arrange for her to see you...she'll like that..." He smiled and wrote down his number. "She has pictures she can show you, too...one is with Tony 'The Hat' Carnero who was a big time bootlegger and ran gambling ships off the coast back in the day...he died in '55...some say poisoned...and she just cried and cried when he passed away..."

Hal looked across the yard and saw Deuce throw open the customized steel drums he had fashioned into barbeques. "It looks like he's about to serve up." Hal went to secure a place in line while Mari walked behind him, hand in hand with George. The grizzled man murmured, "Don't you let him look into what is goin' on today in some of those tunnels...or you'll be right back here in tears again..."

As night fell, a deejay set up and a dance floor was put into place on the lawn. Deuce and Wanda were finally able to have a respite from their hosting and sat at a table to survey their guests stepping to the beat of the music. Deuce nodded toward Hal moving with Mari through a slow dance. "I never seen that boy so happy...look at him...just fillin' his eyes with her. I knew from the start that she was the one for him..."

"From the start? Just when did all this happen?"

"For him...about a year ago...from the first time he saw her..."

"Poor little skinny, washed out thing...it's a wonder he doesn't break her..."

Deuce gave her a look. "Why you gotta say stuff like that for...and why did you put it in her head that he had someone else? You know he didn't bring a date last year...or the year before that...and he never put a ring on another girl's finger...why do you want to start shit with her for? She likes you...she thinks you're just great!"

"I'm not starting anything...I'm just speaking my mind..."

"Are you opening up to me? I don't want you opening up to me..."

"What do you mean?"

"Talkin' about your feelings and shit..."

She gave him a deadpan stare and then looked away. At the end of the slow dance the tempo changed to a Latin beat. Hal started to walk to Deuce's table when Mari removed the scrunchie and pins holding up her hair, shook it down, and pulled him back on the dance floor. Executing the moves she taught him, he was able to pull off a credible salsa. "Well...won't you look at that!" Deuce laughed. "Oh...he's goin' to hear about this..." When the dance was through, Hal and Mari made their way to Deuce's table. "Well...ain't you the Mambo King..."

"Mambo is the granddaddy to the dance I was doing..." Hal held out his hands and smirked at Deuce. "I was salsa dancing...and if you don't watch out...I will dance a bachata!" He cut a move. "How do you like me now?!"

"Mari...look at what you unleashed on us!"

"He's actually quite good...the floor was too crowded to show all he can do..."

"Why did you let your hair down?" Wanda critiqued.

"Oh, that...it's a part of the image for some dances...when you are dancing professionally...I'm just used to doing it..."

"Ah...you're a bit of a diva..."

"Something like that." Mari looked at Wanda's hair. "Speaking of hair...I would love to style yours..."

"My hair...what's wrong with my hair...?" Wanda squinted. "...and what do you know about black hair...?"

"Nothing is wrong...your hair looks beautiful...but I thought you could carry off something a little more exotic...and I've styled black hair before...here, let me show you..." Mari dug into her tote and retrieved a wallet sized picture from an inside pocket. "...this is my friend Lo-Lo...I created this look for her and it took me three days to do it...I think she looks beautiful..." She handed the picture to Wanda.

Mari had no way of knowing that she had crossed several lines of biases held by Wanda. The skin tone of the woman in the picture was black...which in Wanda's hierarchy was several shades below her. The hairstyle was distinctly African...a look Wanda wanted no part of. The woman in the picture was extremely beautiful...something she instinctively resented...as she did with her not so well concealed resentment of Mari. She handed the picture back and gave Mari a cold stare. "No one but Mr. G does my hair...he knows what I like..." She got up, "Excuse me...I have to see to my guests..." and flounced off.

"Did I say something wrong...?"

"No...pay her no never mind...that's just her way..." Deuce knitted his brow. "Show me that picture..."

She handed it to him. He glanced at it and then looked back again, studying it. "That is somethin' alright..." He looked at the sloe-eyed girl staring back from the picture. "...and you did this hairstyle...what made you think of doing her hair like this?"

"I was studying African history and was struck by pictures of some of the hairstyles the women wore...and I thought that with some modernization...it would really look stunning on some women in general...but particularly African-American women who have the exotic features to carry it off...giving them a different brand of beauty all their own. Lo-Lo says it is a showstopper everywhere she goes."

"Yeah...she certainly is a showstopper...is this the one with the recipe...?" He pointed at the picture.

Mari cut him off with a, "Yes..."

Deuce smiled to himself. "I see..." He handed the picture back and chuckled. "There is no way Wanda could look that good...she has the features...but not the attitude. But it was nice of you to offer. So that's the Lo-Lo show...ummm...ummm...ummm!"

***

"Are you sure you've got it all? The kitchen sink is still in the house...are you sure you don't want to bring it along?" Hal teased Mari as he put his keys in the Camaro's ignition.

"My philosophy is that it is better to have it...and not need it...than it is to need it...and not have it..." She sniffed. "...besides, it's mostly clothing...and my hats...I want to look pretty for you..."

Hal smiled at her. "I guarantee you...you're not going to need all those clothes..."

"Do you have your cell phone?" She checked her purse for her own.

"Yes...and your cell number is in my wallet."

"Good...OK...let's go over the check list one last time." She called out each item on the checklist and he responded with "done." She heaved a big sigh. "Kiss me for luck...!"

He leaned over and checked her seatbelt and then gave her a smooch. "Don't worry so much, Babe. This is going to be fun..." He turned the key and the car sprang to life with a low throaty growl. The Cayenne Red Metallic Camaro Z28 SS looked like it was in flight while standing still and it restlessly idled in the driveway before he pulled out into the street.

As the car picked up speed, Mari looked back at their home, the only place she ever felt secure. She crossed her arms, holding herself, and wondered if she had made the right decision. She had been loath to discuss her family with Hal, and she deferred it to the point that she never broached the subject with him. Now, she was wondering if she should discuss them at all. *Perhaps I should just rely on their talent for being contemptible to show Hal who and what they are. Maybe it is better not to color his thinking and let him come to his own conclusions.*

During the early Saturday morning hours, the freeways were clear, and Hal was able to open up the Camaro. Soon L.A. was behind them as they barreled toward their first stop, Las Vegas.

***

Cigarette smoke hung thick in the air as the slot machines' lights flashed and emitted a staccato of notes that sounded like broken pieces of circus music. Fixated gamblers sat at the machines, reflexively sipping a cocktail or taking a drag from a cig and paying to see the wheels spin on the chance they might align in their favor. Hypnotically, they fed the slots with coins and the machines reciprocated with infrequent payoffs, rewards timed to sufficiently nurture fascination, without upsetting the balance that favored the house. The time of day was assiduously avoided, for in Las Vegas, inside the casino, time was always indeterminate.

With Mari on his arm, Hal strolled through the casino, observing the gamblers with mild curiosity. "Do you want to try your luck after dinner?"

"No...not really." Mari took a prudent view of the gamesters.

Avoiding the buffet, he guided her to the restaurant and was shown a table in the dimly lit surroundings. She sparkled in a silver cocktail dress with a scoop neckline and he was appropriate in a suit, but they were at a loss as to what they wanted to do. "After dinner do you want to see a show?" He perused the menu.

"I believe that Siegfried and Roy are sold out..." She advised. "...and so is Cirque du Soleil."

"Who else is playing in town?"

"I don't know...I really don't want to leave the hotel..."

"Come to think of it...neither do I..."

The waiter approached to take their order and Hal asked, "Do you know what shows are playing in town?"

The waiter carefully avoided recommending anything outside of the hotel. "I really don't...there are a few tickets available for Siegfried and Roy next week..."

"We aren't going to be here that long..."

"There are many venues of free entertainment throughout the hotel...jazz combos...comedians...magic acts...I'm sure you can find something you'll like...and then there is always the casino...poker...baccarat...roulette..."

"OK...I'm sure we'll find our way." Hal gave him their order and then turned to Mari. "Are you sure you don't want to take a spin or two at the roulette wheel?"

"No."

"Why? Don't you want to gamble?"

"I gamble all the time...life is a gamble...but I have a hard time throwing away my hard-earned money on something so tenuous. I have no moral issues with it...but I just get nothing out of it."

He studied her. "I pretty much feel the same way...but I have been known to take a flyer on the stock market."

She reached over and took his hand. "Right now, my biggest gamble is on you...and I'm betting everything I have on Hal Golan..."

"Well, that's a sure thing, Babe..." He smiled, but then saw the look of concern in her eyes. "...what's the matter? You don't still think that I'm not committed...do you?"

"No...no..." She looked down. "...it's my family...I have a hard time talking about them and I know I should..." She shook her head. "...they're not very nice people..."

"Come on, Babe...how bad could they be? Your mother...your father...they have got to want to know that you're getting married...that we plan to give them grandchildren...maybe they will want to come to the wedding..."

She flashed him a look that said "no" but did not say it. "My grandmother loved me...but she died years ago. And my oldest brother, Lars, loves me too. He was the one who told me I should leave...that there was nothing there for me...and that's it..."

Seeing the expression on her face, he gave the whole purpose of the trip another thought. "Look, Babe...if you want me to turn around and take us home...I will...no questions asked..."

She was slow to answer. "No...I think it is best that you take an honest look at where I came from...and then we can talk about it...and get it behind us..."

He turned her hand over and kissed it. "Agreed...now let's forget all this talk about your family...you have nothing to worry about...let's just have some fun! We're in Vegas, baby!"

She broke into a grin. "You've got a deal...what do you want to do?"

"Right now?"

"Yeah..."

An impish look crossed his face. "Right now I would love to bury my face in your cleavage...but that's just me..."

She made her Godfrey face and wagged her finger at him. "The gentleman and madam simply have no morals...no decorum whatsoever...all you have is a naked obsession. You have all of Las Vegas...an adult fantasy world...at your feet...and all the gentleman can think of is what's under madam's skirt. All madam can think of is what's in the gentleman's pants. Las Vegas is wasted on you. You may as well go to your room and screw!"

"Well, what do you want to do?"

She looked around, leaned forward, and whispered. "I think we should take Godfrey's advice." She fluttered her lashes at him.

***

The highway stretched out before them like a ribbon as the Camaro gobbled up the miles. After Las Vegas, and almost as a sign of Mari's reluctance to return to Minnesota, she planned a side trip to the Grand Canyon, then on to Salt Lake City and all the historic sites in southern Wyoming: Fort Bridger, Fort Laramie, Guernsey, and Register Cliffs. In South Dakota, they included Deadwood, Mount Rushmore, and the Crazy Horse Monument. After that, they made a beeline to Albert Lea and then on to the Carlson Farm.

The call that Mari had placed to her mother before leaving L.A. had been received with relative aplomb. No recriminations, no joyous reconciliation, not even a sign of parental relief was discernable. Acquiescing to a visit from her daughter, and her fiancé, was done out of a mixture of curiosity and familial duty, with no evident indication of affection. As the road signs showed an ever-diminishing distance to Albert Lea, Mari's apprehension grew. "Hal, I don't think we will be staying that long...when we get to Albert Lea let's just get a room at a motel to change clothes and clean up...but put our luggage back in the trunk..."

"We won't be staying with your family?"

"No...not at all. They will be expecting us for dinner...that's all. If that works out well...we can return the next day..."

Hal frowned. "They put those stipulations on your visit...?"

"No...I did."

"You did! Why?"

"Relationships are built on trust. I can't say I really know them anymore...but I doubt that they have changed...and I can't say that I trust them..."

"Mari...this is your mother you are talking about...you must be mistaken..." She looked at him, shook her head, and gave a rueful chuckle.

***

Following a two-lane country road, Mari finally pointed to a dirt road. "There it is...turn here."

Hal took a right and cautiously proceeded. He found the drive to be fairly hard and free of deep ruts, relieving his concern for the car's undercarriage. After a quarter mile, he came to a white farmhouse surrounded with trees; the proverbial red barn with a silo was nearby. Several outbuildings dotted the yard in an orderly fashion. The ground in front of the house was covered with neatly raked gravel. The place was as immaculate as the storybook pictures of McDonald's Farm and highly indicative of anal retentiveness. Nevertheless, Hal was impressed. "Your family homestead is charming..."

She stared ahead. "It would appear to be..."

"Babe...don't get in a mood...we'll just put our best foot forward and let them do the same."

The door opened and a middle-aged, spare woman stepped out. Considered pretty at one time, her refined features bore the effects of more than just time; a hard life and strict demeanor had taken their toll. She wore a dress that was suitable for church and receiving guests, dignified yet plain. Worn in a braided bun, her blonde hair was streaked with gray.

A man in an ill-fitting suit stepped out behind her. His hair was white, but for a man of his years he was remarkably well built, and he stood with an upright bearing. Even at a distance, Hal could see his eyes glowed a radiant hue of blue, a shade akin to Mari's. He had a good-looking, Nordic face made rugged by years of weather.

Unfastening his seatbelt, Hal prepared to step out of the car. "Put on your happy face, Babe..." He watched as she reached inside of herself to find a smile. "OK...let's go..." He sprang from the car, the picture of good cheer, and walked around to open the door for Mari. Together, they approached the porch.

Mari braved the icy stare of her parents, who seemed to greet her as the prodigal daughter. They regarded her trim, white suit, pearl stud earrings, touches of makeup, along with her loosely, tousled hair, as alien as though she had stepped from a spaceship. She returned the restraint with a formal greeting and the introduction of Hal. "Mom...Dad...this is my fiancé, Hal Golan..."

Hal first held out his hand to her mother who seemed unsure of what was expected before hesitantly offering her roughened hand. He took it with a slight bow and then grasped her father's hand. The firm grip, and heavy callouses, indicated a man who grappled to wrench a living from the earth. "I am so very honored to meet both of you."

"Pleased to meet you." They both mumbled in turn. Hal's quality suit, the flash car, and the extravagant ring on Mari's finger made them feel small and insignificant. They mistook his self-assurance as being brash and arrogant. Moreover, their inability to categorize his looks puzzled them. "Come inside and meet the rest of the family..."

Inside the simply furnished Carlson home stood three strapping men. Mari rushed into the arms of one of them. "Lars...I missed you..."

He hugged her and then held her at arm's length. "Who is this grand lady? What happened to my little Mari...?"

"I grew up..." She blinked back tears. She hugged her other two brothers. "I missed all of you..." She turned to Hal. "This is Lars...Anders...we call him Andy...and Rolf. Each of her brothers had light colored hair and blue eyes. They were lean, solid physical specimens, and all were attractive. Hal went down the line shaking each one's hand. She looked around the room with apprehension. Her California accent slipped into Minnesotan. "And where is Johan?"

Her mother relished the question, because she knew the real answer would contain elements of condemnation and retaliation. She deferred the moment of delivering the blow for when it would have the most impact. She presently evaded by simply stating, "He is not here."

Mari nodded and changed the subject. "The house smells good. What are you cooking?"

"I am making a sirloin tip roast marinated in vodka, pressgurka, creamed cabbage, onion and Jarlsberg pie, and for after we have berries and cream blotkake. It is almost ready...if you will help me in the kitchen, we will sit down in a half hour."

"Hal...that's a beast you're driving...what's under the hood?"

"It's just stock...but it packs a punch with an LS1 V-8 that has 330 horsepower. Some people think I'm crazy to have a five on the floor shift instead of an automatic in L.A....where you are in stop and go traffic for half your life. You end up shifting all the way to work and all the way back home…but when I do have an open road it makes it all worth it." He shrugged. "It's the one indulgence I allow myself."

"Do you mind if we have a look?" Lars asked.

"Not at all…come on." Hal fished the keys out of his pocket, went outside, and remotely unlocked the car. Reaching under the dash, he popped the hood and then went around the front to lift it. "This is a '98 Z28 SS and it is the first year to have an aluminum block which is much lighter than the iron block in the last Camaro I had…that was a '96. This has the LS1 V-8 and it has 350 pounds of torque at 3300 rpm." He went back inside the car and started it up. After the initial rumble the Camaro settled into a deep throaty purr. "There's a great stretch of road between L.A. and Las Vegas…not too much patrolling going on…where I took her up to a hundred and twenty. The speedometer goes up to one-fifty-five…but Mari was having a fit…so I slowed it down to cruise between ninety and a hundred…"

The Carlson brothers gazed at the engine with due respect. Then Andy asked Lars, "Should we show him Bertha?"

"Yeah…he's a man who would know what he's looking at…" Andy gestured with his head, "Come on to the pole barn."

Hal shut off the engine, closed up the car, and locked it with a beep and then followed the brothers. They went to a glorified shed and opened the door revealing a '55 Chevy Bel Air. It still had the original colors of India Ivory and Sea Mist Green that had not been restored. Hal's eyes opened wide. "Holy shit…!" He exclaimed. When they lifted the hood, he recognized a 454 big block engine with a high-rise manifold, four-barrel carburetor, and stainless-steel headers. "Aawwwww! Fuck me! She's beautiful, guys! You did this yourselves?"

"Yeah…over time. We got the block from a friend and rebuilt the engine ourselves. It used to be dad's car…his father got it new. Dad gave it to us about five or six years ago and we've been tinkering on it ever since. She can go some…"

"Go some?" Hal looked from one face to another. "Do you guys have any idea how much this car is worth?"

"You mean in money?"

Hal nodded, "Yeah!"

They looked at each other and shrugged. "No."

Hal walked around the car, looked inside, and gave them the news. "I'm no flippin' expert...but even I know that a '55 Chevy Bel Air...this well preserved is worth at least twenty to thirty grand...and souped-up like you've done...probably much more." He rubbed his hands together. "You gonna give me a listen?"

"Yeah."

Rolf got in the car and turned the key. The engine rocked the car as it roared to life; seeming as though it would take off on its own. They all grinned ear to ear. After asking them about the work they did, he threw up his hands. "If I wasn't wearing a suit...I would love to take a look at the suspension...is it the original?"

"No...we beefed it up some...but we still have all the original parts...engine and all."

"You mean you can put her back the way she was?"

"Yeah."

"That's epic!"

"You want to see what Bertha can do against your Camaro?" Andy posed the challenge.

Hal squinted. "You mean a drag race?"

They looked like they were as keen to take a dare as the running engine. "You betcha...!"

Hal shook his head. "Naw...Mari would have my head for it."

"You let her tell you what you can and can't do?"

Hal was matter of fact. "Yep...you're damned right I do...and I'm happy to let her have her way in anything I do."

"You let a woman tell you what to do?" Rolf was baffled.

"Gentlemen...your sister is the most beautiful woman in the world...inside and out." Hal put his hand to his chest. "I love her...and I'm the luckiest guy in the world that she loves me. If you take a look at her little finger...you will see me wrapped all around it and I'll give her anything she wants...I'm just damned glad she wants me..."

They looked at each other, confounded. "Looks like Mari has your balls in her pocketbook." Rolf observed.

Hal shrugged and smiled. "Isn't that the truth...and she can take them out and juggle them any time she wants." He knitted his brow. "Haven't any of you ever been in love?"

"Not like that." Rolf smirked.

Lars nodded his head. "Yeah...I have...a long time ago. She married someone else."

Hal sympathized. "Wow...that's tough...I'm sorry to hear that. What happened to break you up?"

Lars' mouth pulled to one side. "I acted like these jerks..." He pointed at his brothers with his thumb. "...like I didn't care about what she wanted. So, she married a guy who did."

There was a clanging in the distance. "That's dinner." Andy announced and they all headed toward the house.

Hal walked with Lars. "What was that noise...was that like a triangle thing?"

"Yeah."

"Aren't you going to lock up the car?"

"What for?"

Hal started to explain but changed his mind. "I guess I'm used to living in the city."

They washed their hands in an outside basin, sharing the water and the towel. Hal curbed his fastidious inclination and followed suit.

Stopping only to wipe their feet, they trudged into the house. From the living room you could see the table in the separate dining room, filled with platters and bowls piled high with farm fresh food. Mari rushed about wearing an apron and carried in even more. In Hal's mind this image of her could not compare to that of her on any given "table night." To honor him as their guest, Lars offered Hal his seat at the opposite end of the table from the family patriarch and sat next to Mari. She was placed at Hal's left. Andy sat next to Lars. Mari's mother, Greta, and Rolf sat on the opposite side. When all were seated, they bowed their heads in prayer.

Mari's father gave the usual invocation, that Mari could recite in her sleep, but with no special thanksgiving for the safe return of his daughter. When he was through, Lars spoke up. "I would like to add a prayer of my own. Dear Lord...I thank you for your benevolence in returning to me my beloved sister, Mari, and our new family member, Hal. I want to welcome him into our hearts and wish them every happiness as they go forward...together in life. Please shower them with your blessings and protect them...Amen."

Mari picked up her napkin and dabbed at tears. "Thank you, Lars. That was beautiful."

He patted her hand. "You did well, sis."

Hal reached over and shook his hand. "Thank you for your kindness."

At the other end of the table, Mari's mother and father exchanged eye contact as Lars usurped what should have been their position.

The bowls and platters were passed around and Mari dished up Hal's plate as well as her own. When everyone was served and all settled down, Mari's father, Kristoffer, stared across the table at Hal. "Well...young man, how did your trip go in getting here?"

"The way I like it...smooth with no problems...we enjoyed it very much..." Hal prepared for the longer discussion he knew was coming. "...we went to see the Grand Canyon, and someone recommended that we park at a viewing point before sunrise and watch the sun come up. We did, and the colors were amazing! The hues were constantly changing as the rising sun reflected off the canyon walls. It sounds simple...but it really is spectacular."

"What else did you do?"

"We spent a day in Las Vegas, but neither one of us gambles...and the shows were sold out...so we went on to the Grand Canyon...after that Salt Lake City. Mari has a history degree, so we went to Fort Bridger, Fort Laramie, Guernsey, and Register Cliffs. Then we dipped down into South Dakota, to see Deadwood, Mount Rushmore, and the Crazy Horse Monument...then we came straight here." Hal tried to read the man's eyes that were neither cold nor warm and he assumed her father was still trying to make up his mind about him. *What's the deal? His daughter walked out of his life seven years ago...and she is back for a visit...and HE is going to judge ME?*

"What type of work do you do?"

"I'm a contributing editor at Angel City Magazine..."

"What is that?"

"I write articles for the magazine..."

Carlson frowned. "When are you going to get a real job?"

Hal laughed. "That's what my father said." He decided to turn the tables on the old guy. "The type of work you do...farming...from the callouses on your hands I would say that was a real job. How many acres do you have?"

"Two hundred and eighty..."

"And you and your sons work it yourselves?"

"Yeah…and we hire help during harvest…"

"That sounds like back breaking work…but you make a big profit…right?"

"Some years do…some years don't. Depends on whether corn is up or down…or if the weather is favorable."

"Without mentioning actual figures…on average…about how much profit a year would a farm like this make?"

Lars wanted to keep the answer honest. "about seventy-five to eighty thousand a year…sometimes a hundred thousand in a really good year."

Hal frowned. "Wow…split four ways…that's only eighteen thousand, seven hundred and fifty to twenty thousand a year…twenty-five in a good year." He held out his hands. "…but your living expenses are included in the cost of doing business…so that probably reflects a lot larger amount than it appears to be."

"It don't get split four ways." Andy mumbled looking down at his plate.

"However it is handled, I have no comment…I was just considering how much labor it takes to produce a profit." Hal evaded what he saw as a sticky development.

"How much do you make?" Rolf posed the question they all wanted to know.

"Sixty K a year…but being a single male, I get taxed to death on that…and my insurance is through the roof…and taking into account my living expenses…I am left with about twenty thousand in bankable income." Hal deliberated. "So, it looks like we are pretty much even." He gave them that concession, knowing that they knew it was in no way even considering the labor put forth and the variables they faced.

"You never told me you made that much." Mari whispered.

"You never asked." He countered.

"I guess I never really cared." She smiled. "Do you want to know how much I make?"

"I already know…I got you your raise…"

"How sweet! For sure you're not marrying me for my money." She laughed.

"That's riii-iight!" He quipped.

She turned to her family. "Hal got the article of the year award."

210

"The what of the year?" Rolf asked.

"Article...he wrote the best article..."

"I can't take all the credit...Mari brought me the story. That's how we met." He beamed at her. "Mr. Carlson, you can be very proud of your daughter...because of her research...her investigating skills...a man who we believe was wrongly convicted will get another trial. She did great work..."

"We did great work...once I took the story to him...we worked side by side on it...he believed in me...and best of all...now he's my boss!"

Ma and Pa Carlson did not want to hear that, after leaving their sphere of influence, Mari achieved a modicum of success. They sat in stony silence.

"It sounds more like you are his boss!" Rolf interjected.

"What do you mean?" Mari knitted her brows.

"We wanted to race 'Bad Bertha' against his Camaro...and he said you wouldn't like that...and he wasn't going to do anything you didn't want him to do."

"He's right...I wouldn't like him taking unnecessary risks...I thought I had lost him once before...and I would never want to go through that again."

"What happened?" Lars asked.

"We were working on a story..." Hal started to tell the truth when Mari interrupted. "About the tunnels under Los Angeles...when this other reporter was working on a story that ended up getting him killed. It appeared that those who did not want to be exposed went after ALL the journalists on Angel City Magazine...they even tried to have Hal beat up...two guys jumped him, and he kicked their collective asses. Apparently, they did not know which reporter was on the story...but when they found out...they blew him up with a car bomb. I saw it on TV and thought it could be Hal...and I went crazy until I knew he was OK."

"That's how I lost my '96 Camaro...it was parked in the garage right next to Dirk's...the guy who was killed...and it was totaled." Hal put the finishing touches on the tale.

There was dead silence and then Mari's brothers started peppering them with questions until the abridged version of the story was told, leaving out what the article was about and that it had been Hal's project, not Dirk's. Mari concluded with, "So you see...if any of you put him in any danger...I'll have your heads for it...he gets enough of that on his job!"

"Hee-hee...I knew he wasn't chicken-shit!" Andy laughed. "He's letting our sis walk all over him...and he is getting his way by doing it!"

"Whatever..." Mari rolled her eyes.

Hal leaned over and whispered. "I told you things would go well..."

"Wait for it...Mom and Dad are not pleased that I'm happy...or that you are better off than they are...they're just waiting for the right moment...the right straw to grasp onto."

The brothers recounted their anecdotes of brawls, scrapes with the law, and narrow escapes. The name of Johan or John, as he was called, came up in passing. Mari saw her mother's eyes brighten. She whispered to Hal, "Here it comes..."

"Mari...you never asked me where John is..." Greta's tone was accusatory.

"Yes...I did...when I first got here. You said he wasn't here." Mari geared up for the onslaught. Out of the corner of her eye she could see Lars' jaw tighten.

"But you never asked why not..."

"I figured if you wanted me to know...you would tell me."

"I think that you...of all people...should know..." She paused for effect. "...he's dead...and it's all your fault."

The news did not hit Mari's heart or psyche the way Greta intended. The news came more as a relief than as a sorrow, but she did not accept that she was to blame. *She wants to find fault...but how? I wasn't even here.*

Before Mari could respond, Lars took her part. "I will have none of this! John is dead because John put himself behind bars...and he was killed there. He was your favorite and you want to blame everyone except for the person who was responsible for his death...he was...not me...not Dad...and certainly not Mari...so accept the fact that John had a screw loose...and he did himself in." He fumed and stared his mother into silence. She took the hem of her apron and wiped her eyes. "Don't sit there and play the martyr. I'll not have you put Mari on the cross again and sacrifice her to your twisted view of right and wrong." Lars looked around the table. Not even his father could reprimand him for speaking the truth.

The silence was awkward as each person retreated into unspoken ruminations. Mari's father, cleared his throat and then asked, "Mari...why did you leave us?"

Lars exploded. "How can you sit there and pretend you don't know. I'll tell you why she left...because I gave her every penny I had saved and told her to leave for her own sake. She was safer among strangers than she was with her own family. I watched every day as you and mom took out your frustration on a little girl...your daughter...as though she was to blame for anything. I finally put her on the bus and told her never to come back...that there was nothing good for her here. That's why she left...and I am glad to see she did much better for herself than she ever would have had she stayed here." He turned to Hal. "I like what you said back there about making her happy...you're a good Joe and I hope you will care for her always."

"So now it is you who gives the blessing to their marriage? Don't think that you are so big that you are now the father." Kristoffer glared.

"From how she turned out...it looks like I did a better job of helping her than you did...and I couldn't be prouder of her!" Lars defied him.

"ENOUGH!" Kristoffer exclaimed. "You forget yourself...it is my name on this house and on your birth certificate...and as your father I am the one who says what goes!" Under the barrage, Lars bowed his head and was silent now that he had his say.

Hal held onto Mari's hand as he watched the spectacle. In years past, Mari would have been reduced to tears, but now she watched her family dynamics with interest and could see through their facades. *They are frightened little people, nursing their petty grievances and cherished beliefs. Lars knew it a long time ago...that they never would have protected me. The only question I have is...why does he stay?*

Kristoffer addressed Hal. "As Mari's father...I want to know more about you before I give you my blessings. Do you come from a good family?"

"The best. As soon as we get back to L.A. I'm taking her to meet them. I know my mother will love her."

"Your family lives in the same town...and Mari hasn't met them yet?"

213

"Until Mari said she would marry me...I didn't want to get their hopes up." Hal dodged.

"Has the day been set...?"

"Not yet...I know my mother will want to help plan it." Mari shot him a look and he added, "That is if it is alright with Mari..."

"Where will it be held...what church?"

"It wouldn't necessarily be in a church...My mother would want it in her backyard...I'm thinking perhaps the beach...or wherever Mari wants it...but it wouldn't necessarily be a church...it could be a synagogue."

"A syna..syna...what?"

"A synagogue...it is a Jewish house of worship..."

"But Mari's a Christian...she's Lutheran..."

Mari chimed in. "That was a decision that you made for me when I was a child. Since I have grown up...and received an education...I have my own religious beliefs that do not necessarily include Christian dogma. For instance...I don't believe in virgin birth. If Christianity left out the magical hooey...and stuck to Christ's teachings...I would have no problem with it. But as it is...they have you recite the Nicene Creed where you swear to believe in things that I find...unrealistic."

All of her family was aghast, including Lars. Red-faced, Kristoffer pointed a finger at Hal. "Did you teach her this...blasphemy?"

"To be honest...we never discussed it much...because her beliefs are her personal beliefs." He held out his hands. "Under the Constitution...she's free to believe whatever she wants..."

In the southernmost county of Minnesota where the Carlsons had lived for several generations, and in the adjacent counties, the demographics did not include one single Jew. The Carlsons had no frame of reference, so Kristoffer fell back on the family's customary position and took offense. "This synagoggle thing...is that your religion."

"If you mean am I Jewish...yes...I am a secular Jew."

"A sec-lar Jew? What does that mean?"

"It means that I was born into a Jewish family...but I do not follow the Jewish faith. I would like for there to be a God...I hope there is a God...but I can't say I am sure there is a God."

"Does that mean you are not a Jew?"

214

"No...nobody ever gets kicked out of being a Jew..." Hal chuckled. "You're born a Jew...you die a Jew...because it is more than just a religion..."

Kristoffer crossed his arms and stared at Hal. "Are you willing to convert to Christianity?"

"Why?"

Rolf looked sideways at Hal. "Didn't the Jews kill Christ? Isn't it a blood curse on all Jews? Did the Jews kill Jesus Christ?"

"Such monumental ignorance!" Mari lamented.

Hal smirked. "That was two thousand years ago...I was born in 1969...I wasn't there...so I couldn't tell you. But it is rumored that it was the Romans who did the foul deed." Hal looked around the table. "Don't you know any Jewish people...friends...neighbors...?"

"No...but it sounds to me like Jews are irreligious."

"They are very religious...in fact your Jesus was a Jew...and you can't get more religious than that!"

"That's a lie!"

"Ask your minister! What's this all about? I never had to explain myself before...and it's getting a little tedious."

"What's getting tedious is having a Jew sit at my table...telling me he's going to marry my daughter."

"If that's the case then I'll be glad to leave your table...and your home...and take your daughter with me."

"You can go...but she's staying here!"

"That's where you are mistaken. She's my fiancée...she's over eighteen...and you have no say in the matter."

"She's not marrying a Jew...I would rather see her dead!"

Hal stood up and pulled Mari to her feet to stand behind him. He dug into his pocket and pulled out his keys. "Mari...go get in the car..."

"No...I'm not leaving you."

"Please...get in the car." He hissed between his teeth.

"I'm not going to leave you."

Kristoffer stood up and Rolf stood with him.

Lars stood but faced Kristoffer. Andy stood but backed up, flanking the two factions. Greta looked around at the brewing fray with a tight little smile.

Lars kept his eyes on his father but spoke to Hal. "I think you had better get Mari out of here, Hal...right now!" Hal nodded and took Mari by the shoulders and directed her to the door.

Kristoffer left the room. "Hurry, Hal...he's going for his gun..."

"Shit...!" At a full run Mari and Hal dashed for the car. Jumping inside Hal cranked the engine and it roared. Seeing the Carlsons pouring from the house he swerved the car into a donut, spraying them with gravel before taking off down the drive. Once he was on the road, he opened up the Camaro. "What a bunch of fucking lunatics!" Hal looked in his rearview mirror and saw "Bertha" turning onto the road. "Shit...shit...shit! Is your seatbelt fastened?"

"Yes."

"OK...because here they come!"

Mari turned to see the '55 Chevy gaining on them. "Oh my God!"

Hal stepped on the gas and the Camaro pulled away with ease. He looked at the gas gauge and saw he still had a comfortable three-fourths full. "How far is the state line?"

"Why don't we just go into Albert Lea?"

"Are you kidding me? They live here...we're from out of state. Any law enforcement is going to favor them over us. If we can get across the state line into Iowa...I think we would have a better chance if this gets to be more of a situation."

Mari kept an eye on the Chevy. "Can we go faster...they're coming on."

Hal pushed the Camaro harder and it flew in response. "We're doing a hundred and twenty...thirty...how far does this road go in a straight line?"

"Pretty far...I'll tell you when you have to slow to turn."

"Can you believe those assholes?"

"Yeah...I can..." She turned just in time to see a puff of smoke and then a white plume and the Chevy started to fall back. "Shit howdy...I think they blew their engine!"

Hal glanced in the rearview and saw the Chevy falling back in a haze of smoke. "Fucking Jew baiters..." He slowed to ninety, then to eighty, and then into a comfortable cruise. "...why didn't you tell me they were anti-Semitic?"

"I had no idea...there are no Jewish people in the whole county...the subject never came up! My guess is they never once gave it a thought until today…they were just looking for something…anything…as a reason to pick a fight. Especially after you told them how much you made…and intimated that my brothers were entitled to a fair share of the farm profits…I bet that will put the fat in the fire this evening!"

"Mari…how is it that you came from those people…and still turned out to be so wonderful? I think you were left on their doorstep!"

"I take it that you agree they're a pack of wolves."

"I would have a worse name for them than that!"

"Don't worry, Hal…you will never, ever have to see them again!"

***

"Pack a bag for the entire weekend, Babe...my mother will want us to stay with them for at least a couple of nights." Hal started throwing shirts and underwear on the bed to prepare to pack.

"What should I bring to wear?" Mari sorted through several potential dresses.

"She may want to take us out, or have guests in...so you will need a day dress or two...you know...one of your floaty-frilly numbers that you look so adorable in. Then you will need an evening dress or two...not a gown but a sophisticated dress...and a cocktail dress...oh, yeah...and a bathing suit...and odds and ends like jeans or shorts." He half frowned. "She will put us up in separate bedrooms...so no fancy lingerie...please."

"Oh, pooh!"

He put a shirt down, came around to her side of the bed, and wrapped his arms around her. He leaned his forehead against hers. "Don't worry...I'm not going to neglect you...but it will be a challenge to steal moments where we can be alone together." He looked supremely confident. "But, I'm inventive."

She kissed his nose. "You'd better be!"

He went back to packing. "My mother is going to love you...and I think you will love her too."

"What about your father?"

"Oh...he'll be in love too...with himself. I don't know what he will think...but that doesn't matter to me. My father and I have had a Jewish standoff for years...that's like a Mexican standoff only with yarmulkes instead of sombreros." He laughed.

"You've been in a great mood all day..."

"I guess I have..." He beamed. "...I can't wait to show you off!"

"Nothing like putting pressure on a girl!"

"We'll put in a half-day on Friday at work...and then we're off to my peeps. I promise you...you will have a wonderful time."

***

Mari watched with passive interest as Hal took one freeway after another to end up for a long stretch on the Santa Monica Freeway. "Your parents live near Terry?"

"Well...nearer than we do."

She went back to checking her makeup and hair. She wanted to look perfect. He took an off ramp she was unfamiliar with and headed north on Robertson Blvd. It seemed like a rather narrow, inconvenient street, but the farther north they traveled the more interesting the shops and restaurants became. At each stop he would gaze at her and then go back to the task of driving.

"Shouldn't we get some flowers or something for your mother?"

"No...that would be like taking coals to Newcastle."

"Coals to where?"

"Newcastle...it's a coal mining town in Britain...you don't need to take coal there."

"Oh." She looked around. "Hal...this looks like Beverly Hills..."

"It is...I just want to show you something..."

"Oh."

He turned onto Burton Way and again on Canon Dr. Driving north of Sunset, the street became Benedict Canyon. One fabulous mansion after another was set back from the street behind ornate fences and large, expansive lawns. Tall, thin palm trees lined the street. The traffic consisted of luxury cars driven by people made beautiful by their eminence, if not by plastic surgeons. It was a celebration of extravagance, the obscenity of avarice made magnificent, and the affirmation that too much was not enough.

He turned once again onto a street where the mansions were a shade more subtle, but still stunning. Driving for another block, he turned into a driveway. Mari saw a mansion with French traditional architecture. The landscaping was amazing. "Hal...what are you doing? You can't just drive up to one of these houses for a joke! The people who live here will be incensed and call the cops." He drove up the curved driveway to the front entrance and came to a stop. "For Christ's sake, Hal...if you don't get us out of here we are going to be in a LOT of trouble!" She scrunched down in her seat.

He smiled. "Don't worry...I know the people who live here."

She sat up slowly. "You...you...mean..." She waved a finger toward the house. "...this is where your...family lives?" He nodded. She squinted at him and started to take him seriously and then broke out laughing. "Come on, Hal...the joke is over...you had better get out of here before we get hit up for trespassing." The door opened and a pleasant looking, plump woman, with perfectly coiffed mixed gray hair, came out followed by her butler. "Oh shit...we're in it now!"

He got out of the car and the woman ran into his arms. "Hal...my bubeleh! It has been months since you came to see me."

"I know...I've been really busy." He kissed the top of her head. Leading her to the other side of the car he said, "There is someone I would like you to meet." He opened the door and gave Mari his hand to help her get out. "Mom...this is Mari Carlson...my fiancée. Mari...my mother, Vivian."

"Oh, my dear..." Vivian put her hands together. "...you are exquisite! My Hal says he loves you...and I can see why..." She started to tear up and hugged her. "Welcome...welcome my maideleh! I always wished for a daughter and now Hal brings you to me!"

"Thank you!" Mari hugged her back. From the corner of her eye she could see the butler grapple with the suitcases and carry them into the house. From over his mother's shoulder she gave Hal a fearful look as though she had never seen him before. *Oh my God...he's wealthy! This is fucking scary!*

"Come dear...you must be hungry...we have a little nosh for you...and we can talk." She kept her arm around Mari and guided her inside. Hal followed while wondering if it was too much to surprise her with all at once. He thought it would make her happy to know that she did not have to worry another day in her life. But, from the look on her face, he suspected she felt deceived.

The grandeur of the Golan mansion made Mari feel unnerved and insignificant. From the grand hall with a museum quality art gallery, to the lavishly furnished living room with classical music playing softly in the background, to the splendid dining room bedecked with exquisite silver, crystal, and porcelain, displayed in carved wood cabinetry, the eye was assaulted with symbols of overbearing opulence.

Mari was led to the dining room where a "little nosh" consisted of thin sliced Nova lox on a board, a bowl of cream cheese, mini bowls of shallots, capers, and dill, with several types of bagels in a basket along with schmears, on one side of a buffet. On the other side there were various types of hors d'oeuvres, cold cuts, deviled eggs, rolls, bread slices, condiments, and a basket of assorted muffins. The center held a masterpiece of a crystal caviar service with a mound of golden Osetra caviar surrounded by blinis, toast points, crème fraîche, lemon slices, chopped egg whites, and a separate dish of chopped egg yolks. Bottles of Veuve Cliquot Vintage Brut Champagne, orange juice, and white peach juice completed the feast. "Is she expecting the president to visit for a 'nosh'?" Mari whispered to Hal.

"No...just her son...and his beautiful intended."

The immense dining table was covered with lace trimmed linen and place settings for three at one end. Hal sat at the head of the table and the two women faced each other from opposite sides. "Your father had some pressing business to attend to...so he won't be here today..." Vivian mentioned in passing.

"Oh...you're breaking my heart..." Hal's sarcasm was laid bare.

"So...how was your trip?" Vivian went on to a more palatable subject.

"We had a great time." Hal skipped the unpleasantness with Mari's kin and stuck to the topic of sightseeing, regaling her with stories of their adventure. "We took lots of pictures...of Mari." He smiled. He suddenly remembered something and reached in his pocket. "Yesterday, I got this for you." He handed her a small square box.

"What is it?"

"Here...open it...it is a telephone you can carry with you. I got it set up for you already."

Her face broke into a smile. "I've seen these and thought I should get one...but I didn't know much about them..."

"It's a cell phone. Here...push this button. She pushed it and a noise came from Hal's pocket. He took out his cell phone and answered. "Ma...is that you?" he clowned.

"Ooohhh! This is wonderful. From how far away can I call you?"

"From wherever they have cell towers...for sure you can call from here to my house. Mari's number is in there too...and you can add phone numbers very easily. You just have to charge it before taking it with you."

"How do I call Mari?" Hal scrolled and punched up Mari's phone. "Mari...this is your new mother, Vivian."

"Hi, Vivian."

"Oh...you can call me ma...just like my Hal."

"OK, ma...what's new?"

"My son is getting married!"

"To anyone I know?" Mari laughed.

"She is a beautiful girl and she will be a stunning bride...much prettier than all the other brides of my friends' sons."

"Ma...Hal said that I would love you...and I think he is right." Her eyes clouded over from thinking of how different Vivian was from her own mother. "I have to go now...there are people waiting for me."

They both hung up and laughed.

***

Mari sat in the guest room that appeared to be at least half the size of their Silverlake apartment. The décor was traditional in a pale blue color scheme with splashes of pink, green, and beige mixed in. It had a fireplace and an oversized, lavish, pink marble bathroom. With the large vanity table and its multi-sided, lit mirrors, the room screamed femininity. Besides the California king-sized bed, there was a sitting area to one side of the fireplace and a desk and bookshelf area on the other side. She was overwhelmed.

There was a knock on the door and Hal quickly stepped inside. "Are you settling in OK?"

"Who are you...and what have you done with the man I'm engaged to?" She glared at him. "I fell in love with this wonderful guy...and I want to know where he is!"

"He's standing right here."

"Is he? All I see is some rich dude who has some tall explaining to do!"

"Is that what you think of me?"

"I don't know what to think...of you...and what can I possibly mean to you when you have all of this..." Her gesture took in the entirety of the house and the inherent fortune. "...what can I do for you that you couldn't have ten times...a hundred times better?" She started to cry. "I want Hal Golan back...I don't know who you are..."

"Babe, I'm right here. I'm still the same guy..."

"Why the deception? What are you playing at?"

"Let me explain." He sighed and knelt before her. "Look...I was about ten years old when I discovered two things...first, that I lived in a make-believe world...that had nothing to do with reality...and second, that I had a talent for writing. Deuce came to live with us...he was our maid's son and she lived in...and he went to my school. We learned a lot about life together. One of the things I learned was that I was not living a normal life and if I wanted to write about life...I had to live it. So, after I graduated from college...I bought the apartment building in Silverlake...and got a job."

"You own our apartment building?" Her brows went down.

"Yeah...I've been putting the rent you pay into a bank account for you." Reading the expression on her face, he added. "You made it a condition of your staying...and I wanted you to stay...I was desperate for you to stay...I loved you so much, Mari..."

"Why did you keep it a secret from me?"

"I keep it a secret from everybody, except Deuce. That way I can be respected for the work I do...that I earned my way...not paid my way. When we met, you were a colleague that I fell in love with...you did not love me..." He smiled. "...but then you did...and everything was magical. There were times that I wanted to tell you, but it didn't seem like it was that important to you. We were happy. I didn't want to upset the applecart. I didn't want to have the discussion we are having now. Do you understand? You loved me for me...just plain ol' Hal Golan. I really, really loved that. I really love you."

Mari listened and understood more than Hal knew. "Yes...I understand. We are happy...just you and me..." she relented. "...why spoil it with things that don't matter."

He pulled her to him and nuzzled her, brushing his lips against hers. "It's me, Babe...your Hal...and I will always want to be." He pulled her closer, kissed her, and felt her become one with him again. "You scared me for a moment there...I thought you wanted out..."

"Oh, no...never! It's just that all of this frightens me...it's beyond anything I could imagine."

"It's not mine anyway...all this belongs to my parents...so I'm still just your plain ol' Hal Golan..."

"Oh, Hal...who are you kidding...don't pretend you don't have a trust fund...like every other rich kid..."

"OK...I do...but that's about it...nothing else is mine..."

"Oh, boo fucking hoo!"

"One more thing...the jewelry I gave you...the jewels are not paste...they're real. Remind me to give you the insurance papers when we get home."

"And I've been wearing them all this time…everywhere?" Her eyes grew wide. "That's scary!"

"But…they look beautiful on you."

"Oh…for Christ's sake!"

***

Saturday was "girls' day out" for a day of shopping. Vivian took Mari window-shopping on Rodeo Drive. "I rarely buy anything here…you pay top dollar just to say you bought something on Rodeo Drive. There are places you can get the same name brands for half of what you would spend here."

"I didn't think that price would matter to you." Mari was puzzled.

Vivian lowered her sunglasses, staring at her over the tops. "No matter how much you have…nobody likes to get rooked."

Mari smiled. "I've got a lot to learn."

Changing their venue, they took Coldwater Canyon Drive to Studio City to an out of the way, nondescript shop. "This is where movie stars and VIP's sell their clothes, after a year, when they have to get a new wardrobe. Most of the clothes here were never worn or just once or twice. You can get designer clothes here for a pittance."

"Why do they have to sell their clothes after a year?"

"They have to keep up appearances. Usually…after fashion week…they clear out their closets to make way for the latest creations…and if they are famous…they are given gowns to promote the house that designed them."

"I have a Dyan Cannon reject! My friend Brian works in haute couture…he redesigned it for me."

"He's worth his weight in gold!" Vivian was impressed. "A woman with your looks…and now position…needs such a friend…"

"Position?"

"Yes…as Hal's wife. You will be under scrutiny…what you wear…where you go…who you're seen with…"

"But Hal isn't…'under scrutiny'…he goes to work, he comes home, and I fix dinner…no one cares…"

"My sweet girl…when he is with his family he is noticed…and now that he is marrying you…the beautiful woman that you are…he will come under a lot of scrutiny as well…the both of you will…"

"Oh."

"Here you can buy a wardrobe to look appropriate without spending a fortune on trivialities. Real money should be spent on things of importance…"

"Like what?"

"I don't know…I leave that to my husband…"

After an hour they emerged with several bags of designer clothing for Mari. Vivian suggested, "All this shopping has given me an appetite…I know a wonderful place where we can go…"

Zipping across town again, they ended up in a secluded patio restaurant bedecked with foliage that gave the illusion of privacy. Arriving near the end of the lunch hour, they soon had the place to themselves and they took their time chatting over lunch. "Today has been an eyeopener for me…I had no idea so much was involved in how to save money when you have money."

Vivian gazed at her with a sagacious look. "I have a million tips in that regard. How to save on caviar…when you are expected to serve a ton of it…where to buy furs…"

"I thought furs were out of fashion…cruelty to animals and all that…"

"Perhaps in L.A.…but not in Chicago…not in New York…and certainly not in Europe! You will need a decent fur, eventually, for when you go to colder climes like Aspen or St. Moritz."

"You know…I could never figure out why people poo-pooed wearing fur when they will wear leather shoes, leather jackets, and suede clothing…and will gladly eat a steak…it appears as though it's just the hair they object to.

"People are usually hypocrites." She eyed Mari. "Buying the best for less will become an art form to you soon enough."

"Ma…can I be absolutely honest with you? I can't thank you enough for taking me shopping and showing me the ropes…what I need to learn…but I find all of this rather disturbing."

"Disturbing…how?"

"Hal and I live very simply and we're happy. We don't spend a lot of money…in fact I feel pretty foolish now for all the times I got on him for spending too much money. What I mean is…all I really want is Hal. We just have a little apartment…and when I hear his car pull up when he comes home…I know it sounds silly…but it makes my heart jump. Wearing designer clothes for others…" Mari's eyebrows went up in supplication. "...I just want Hal's eyes to light up when he sees me. I know it must be hard for you to understand...but I didn't ask for any of this...and I find it sort of frightening. What really scares me is...I used to think that I was going out of my way to plan something special for him...you know...like to cook something he really likes...or plan a romantic evening..." She put her hands out. "...now, how can anything I do be special to him when he can have anything he wants a hundred times better?"

Vivian smiled brightly. "You love my son...don't you."

"More than anything."

"Then forget everything I told you today and just be yourself...because that is who he loves."

Mari was bewildered. "You don't mind then...if I don't exactly fit in?"

"In my book...you fit in fine just the way you are. Tell me...what attracted you to Hal?"

Mari's eyes grew distant. "Two things really got my attention. Even before I knew I loved him...it was his eyes...so dark...lively, penetrating, intelligent, and so very expressive. Now I can see where he got them. He definitely has your eyes..." Mari misted over. "...and then he does this incredible thing when he talks and he really wants you to listen to him...the first time he did it...I was startled at the complete intimacy of a simple act..." Mari reached across the table and took both of Vivian's hands. "...he took my hands like this and looked at me with those wonderful eyes as he explained what was important to him...and I immediately revered him...I felt the goodness in him...and each time he did it thereafter."

Vivian's eyes moistened. "I used to do that with him when he was a little boy...from the time he was a tot...I don't know when I stopped..."

"For him to do that meant everything to me...and now I just give him my hands when I need to talk to him..."

Vivian took Mari's hands and held them to her chest. "I don't know, or care, who you were born to...you are now my daughter...and I love you."

***

A number of French doors at the back of the Golan home opened to a wide veranda with outdoor dining and lounge furniture. From

226

there, stairs led down to the pool area, which was outsized and rectangular in shape. On one side was the pool house. On the other was a guesthouse. Either was inter-changeable. Beyond the pool was an expansive, well-manicured lawn surrounded by gorgeous flowerbeds. Hal, Mari, and Vivian sat under an umbrella at one of the tables by the pool, having a late Sunday morning coffee. Hal wore an open shirt over his blue swim trunks and Vivian was in a one-piece black bathing suit with a short robe. Mari was resplendent in her Polynesian bikini with the long sarong skirt.

Sauntering down the veranda steps, a fourth party made his way to the table. He was a barrel chested, middle-aged man with broad shoulders and a receding hairline. He wore red trunks and had a swagger to his step of exaggerated self-awareness. He kissed Vivian on the forehead before sitting down. "Sorry I'm late. I had to make a few calls...it's Monday morning in Taiwan. They start business at 3:00 a.m. and I wanted to lock up a few shares at opening bell. This must be the Mari I've heard so much about."

Hal glowed with pride. "Yes, there is no other...this is my Mari! Mari...this is my father Marvin."

She reached out and briefly took his hand. "Very happy to meet you."

He squinted his eyes. "You're quite a looker...not quite what I expected for Hal to marry." He glanced at Hal. "How did you convince her to take you on?"

"I finally worked up enough nerve to tell her I love her..." Hal took her hand. "...and she told me she loved me too...and the rest as they say...is history!"

"That's it?"

Mari shyly gazed at Hal. "Well there is more to it than that...we worked together for quite a while...Hal's my boss you know. I did try to tell him I love him...but I think he thought I was tipsy..."

"Where were you...in a bar?"

"Heavens no...usually I don't drink. We were at the opera...and I'm afraid that two Champagne Cocktails got me a little woozy...and I thought I told him then...but I must have muddled it...because he didn't know it for a long time."

"Well, Hal can be a bit dim-witted at times."

The smile faded from Mari's face and she looked at Hal who did not seem the least fazed, so she let it go and changed the subject. "Did you know that he won the Article of the Year Award?"

"Yeah...I did. Word drifted back to me."

Vivian turned to Marvin. "You never said anything to me..."

Hal smirked. "You never mentioned it to me either...a pat on the back would have been nice."

"It would only encourage you." Marvin scoffed. "You know how I feel about your line of work...waste of time. You'd be better off working with me...learning how to take over the company."

"I spent every summer from high school through college learning about the company. I did my time in Hell...just as you asked. It will be quite some time before you are ready to relinquish the reins...until then...I'll make my own way."

"Mari...can you talk some sense into his hard head?" Marvin deferred to her supposed influence.

"Sorry...contrary to popular opinion...I don't tell Hal what to do. He's my boss...he tells me. And whatever makes him happy...I'm all for it." She briefly paused to consider going one step further. "You're wrong about the work Hal does. It is extremely important...and he is the youngest and yet the best editor at Angel City. He is greatly respected."

"My dear...pushing a pencil from behind a desk is not important compared to what I do...and what my company does..."

Mari pulled her hand away from Hal and folded her hands together. She leaned slightly forward. "He does more than 'push a pencil' on his job. You have no idea how courageous he is...how brave. It takes guts to speak the truth in this world. You should be proud. Why do you belittle him?"

"How does that compare to making your world?"

"He is making his world...just in his way...not yours..."

"Oh, God...young love..."

"Mari...give it up. It's not worth it...believe me I tried." Hal interrupted.

"Marvin..." Vivian cautioned.

"Well look at him. He's not getting any younger. He's losing his hair and packing on the pounds. Playing at being a writer...doing work no one cares about. His work literally becomes yesterday's news..."

Marvin vented. "I'm surprised that this young girl was deluded into marrying him."

Mari's eyebrows dropped. "Mr. Golan...I don't know the person you are talking about...but let me introduce you to your son, Hal...because it is obvious to me that you have never met him. You don't even know who he is."

"Little lady...you've been around him for...what...about a year and you think you know what he's all about...do you?"

"I may not have been around him for as long as you have...but I did take the time to get to know him. Evidently, you have been around him for twenty-nine years...and never bothered."

"Who are you to tell me about my son?"

"I am sitting right here! I am his fiancée and I love him. I am not going to sit here and hear you...or anyone else...disparage him in my presence." Mari tapped her finger on the table. "I don't want to get off on the wrong foot. But that is an understanding we are going to have to come to. You sound to me like you are jealous of his talent...that you begrudge his independence...so you have to be a fault finder...a begrudger...and try to make Hal out to be some kind of chump because he doesn't jump when you snap your fingers."

"Doesn't that take the cake?! This girl who isn't smart enough to know when she's grabbed the brass ring...is so dumb as to tell me where to get off...in my own house..."

"I'm just as smart as you are...perhaps more...because I don't consider Hal a 'brass ring' in fact I'm finding your pushing your weight around...a bit tedious. I have a bachelor's degree in political science and a master's in history...that, I will bet, is a match to your degrees any day! And you have...?"

"Money!" Marvin grinned.

"Mari...there's no need to lie about your degrees...I don't care what he thinks." Hal had only heard her mention one degree in passing and she never connected a category to it.

"Lie about my degrees...I'm not lying!" She turned to Hal in surprise. "Why do you think I would lie? Didn't you look at my qualifications?"

"Not really...I just looked at your work."

"Then how can you sit there and say that I'm lying?" She screwed up her face. "Oh swell...really swell, Hal. You let this...this...*person* insult you...and then call me a liar." She got up. "I think I'll go for a swim and cool off." All eyes followed her as she flounced off to the deep end of the pool, took off her sarong, and dove in.

Hal immediately regretted stepping into a shit pile with her. "I never supposed that she had more than just a bachelor's."

"Well anybody can see the qualifications you were looking at, Hal. She's a fiery little bitch. What kennel did you find her in...?"

"Fuck you, dad!" Hal went and dove into the pool after Mari. He swam over to her and, after a few words, within minutes he kissed her.

Vivian looked on with relief. More than pissed, she admonished her husband. "Marvin, if you do anything to break them up...I will make you regret it for the rest of your life..."

Marvin snorted. "She's not a good match for him. She's not even Jewish."

"I don't care. He loves her...and as a matter of fact I love her, too. She is the daughter I always wanted. If you spoil this for Hal, I'll never forgive you."

"You saw how she talked to me."

"I saw how you deserved it. What did you think would happen talking about your son like that in front of her? I think she was right! I'm glad she has chutzpah...she will make him a good wife."

Marvin arched his eyebrow. "We'll see."

***

"Deuce...you should have seen her...she was like a tigress. She wouldn't let my father get away with his usual bullshit! He went into his study and sulked for the rest of the day!" Hal laughed. "Later, she apologized to my mother for causing a scene...but she couldn't just sit there and hear me being run down that way...and say nothing. To tell the truth...I think my mother loved it...she just passed it off."

Deuce grinned. "So, you guys got chased off the Carlson farm...Mari got mad at you for being rich...and she told your father off for being a prick. It sounds like meeting your respective in-laws went well. Maybe now you can keep your parents out of your business."

"There's only one thing that bothers me. When we got home, Mari insisted on showing me her degrees and she put on a big deal of searching for them and came up empty. She couldn't find them. She had her other important papers...but not her degrees."

"That could happen to anybody. With all that she's gone through...losing stuff isn't unusual. Besides...she couldn't have gotten her job without showing them something...or them verifying her application. All she has to do is to have the documents replaced by the university."

"Yeah...you're right. I told her it was no big thing...but now she's like a dog with a shoe. She's not letting it go."

"In a way you can't blame her. Never challenge a woman on her knowledge. She will move heaven and earth to prove she is right...and you are...what you are now and henceforth forever will be...wrong. But just go with it...Mari is a good woman and it is good to know that she will stand up for you. There's nothing like having a woman in your corner. As evil as Wanda is...she's not going to let anybody cross me...unless she's the one doing the crossing."

"Well...we have a return engagement in a couple of weeks. I think ma wanted to give everyone a chance to calm down...and then make peace. So, we will be back to spend another weekend."

"You're gonna do what? You're gonna give your father a chance to take another swipe at that little girl? Don't do it, man...let it rest for a while...a long while. See your mother at a restaurant...or have her over to your place...but don't take Mari back into that lion's den..."

"It's not as though she can't defend herself...or I should say defend me. It's not against her...it's against me."

"Oh no it ain't." Deuce narrowed his eyes at Hal. "First of all...she shouldn't have to defend anybody. Don't keep her in your father's face. In the second place, your father now has a reason for a vendetta against her...and he is not going to let it go that easy. He's going to come at her again...mark my words...you heard it here first!" Deuce sat back. "Take my advice...do not take her anywhere near your father until after the wedding...and marry her NOW!"

"But my mother wants to..."

Deuce cut him off. "You're not marrying your mother. Mari would marry you today...without the big wedding. If your mother wants a big wedding...she can still have it after a judge has married you...all you have to do is walk through the ceremony. I think you guys should have gotten married when you were in Vegas. I don't know, Hal...I just have a feeling you're blowing it...and you will never find a girl like Mari again."

***

"I'm not going to apologize to your father." Mari sat with her arms crossed in the passenger seat as Hal drove through Beverly Hills.

"No one is expecting you to apologize...just don't get into another argument with him. If he says anything off the wall...just ignore him." Hal explained.

"I meant what I said about coming to an understanding about how he talks about you in my presence..."

"Babe...just don't go there. He's not going to change, and it is not worth getting upset."

"So now you're defending him?"

"No...I'm not defending him...I'm just saying it is a waste of time towards no good end."

Mari frowned. "Maybe it is all a waste of time. He's right about one thing...it is his house...and I want nothing to do with him in his house. I would rather spend the evening being happy in my house."

"I would too...but my mother's heart has fixated on you...and she wants to be able to see her new maideleh and start planning our wedding."

"Oh, God...if it wasn't for your mother I wouldn't even go near Beverly Hills. OK, Hal...but keep your father away from me...you had better run interference."

***

When Hal and Mari arrived at the Golan home, Vivian was distressed. She came into the living room and drew Hal to one side. "Your father is up to something...I know it. He has been in his study all day and he has had a couple of strangers running in and talking for a couple of hours. One of them is still there. I can't tell what it is about...but he looks far too smug for it to be about anything good."

No sooner had she spoken than Hal was summoned to his father's study. He walked into Marvin's ornate, wood paneled office. Two stories of bookshelves lined half of the walls. Another wall held oil paintings and the one behind Marvin's desk had paneling that concealed a bar as well as a door to another room. Steeling himself for whatever was about to be thrown at him, Hal assumed a nonchalant air and sat in the easy chair in front of his father's elaborately carved desk. "You wanted to see me?"

"Yes." Marvin sat back in his leather, executive chair. "To get right to the point I want to talk to you about this girl you have chosen to marry..."

"Big surprise..."

"Look...I have nothing against her personally...and I can see why you are quite fond of her...but you neglected to do what a man in your position should always do before getting entangled with a woman...and that is to look into her background."

"Gee...do ya think?"

Marvin sat forward, looking Hal directly in the eye. "Luckily for you...I had the foresight to do it for you and within a week I was confronted by some very disturbing information about Mari."

"OK...let's have it."

"Brace yourself, son...it's not good..."

"Just say what you have to say..."

"From approximately 1990 to '91 or so to 1994 or '95 for a period of four to five years...she was an exotic dancer at Stony Malone's Gentlemen's Club owned by a man who goes by the name of Malone. These clubs have a very unsavory reputation for more than just

233

dancing." Marvin picked up a sheet of paper. "She danced under the name of Tupi…"

"You're lying!"

"Well…if you think I'm lying…let's ask Mari."

Hal stormed out of his father's study into the living room where Mari and Vivian were just sitting down to tea. He took Mari's arm and hustled her back to Marvin's study. "My father seems to think he has dug up some dirt on you…I want you to tell him he can stick it in his ear."

"What is it about?"

"He said you were some kind of dancer at a club."

"Hal…let me explain…"

He stopped in front of the study door. "Explain what?"

Her brows knitted, but she didn't say more. Twisting the knob on the study door, she burst into the room. "I understand you want to see me about my short-lived career as a dancer."

"Short-lived…I would say five years is considerable."

She leaned on his desk. "I came to L.A. when I was sixteen. I had no family here and I did not know a soul. The jobs I was able to get while finishing high school would not keep a roof over my head or food in my stomach. It wasn't long before it dawned on me that if I was going to survive on my own, I had to get a better education. At sixteen I got a job as a cocktail waitress…but that was not enough to support me and to pay for an education. So, I danced to pay my way through college. I was able to get accepted through a special program at USC and I was NOT going to pass on that opportunity because of some false sense of modesty…I wore a costume that showed no more than you would see on any Southern California beach…and I danced the Samba. I Samba'd my way to a bachelor's degree and a master's degree. Who handed you your education?"

"I have it on good authority that you danced naked on a brass pole…that is the only kind of exotic dancing that goes on at Stony Malone's. Furthermore…the girls that work there sell lap dances and worse. You are a naughty girl, Mari…or should I say Tupi…!" He pursed his lips.

"Sorry to disappoint you…but no nudity is allowed there. Besides, Malone respected that I was trying to better myself…and he never

234

tried to put me on a pole...also he knew that I would refuse...and I was underage."

A small smile tugged at Marvin's lips. "We'll see about that." He went to a door, opened it, and requested for the person inside to come in.

A tall, tan, lanky man stepped in. He had dark hair, combed straight back with wisps falling over his forehead, jet black eyes, and what would otherwise be a good-looking face was marred by a perpetual smirk. Mari recognized him immediately as the bartender at the Stony Malone's Gentlemen's Club. "Johnny...what are you doing here?"

"Hi, doll face...he wanted to know if I knew you." Johnny cocked his head toward Marvin.

"I'd like to say 'good to see you again'...but this guy..." Mari pointed her thumb at Marvin. "...is saying that I danced naked on the poles...and he is trying to make me out to be a slut."

"What? Stony Malone's is a titty bar...we serve alcohol...no full nudity allowed. You never danced the poles...you did this cute little number..." He held his hands out and shook them to show the moves she made. "...where you shook your booty...I loved it!"

"It's called a samba..."

"Yeah...that's right." He grinned.

"Did you ever see me give a lap dance or leave with a customer?"

"I never saw you...but, hey...I'm a busy guy and once the night gets going...I'm too busy to keep track of what you did. So, I don't know..."

She gave a frustrated click of her tongue and wrinkled her brow. "Tell Malone I will give him a call. I want to ask him if he will let me do my show just one more time. I need to show someone just what I did...and how I did it. Please tell him it's important to me."

"Sure...will do." He turned to Marvin. "Is there anything else?"

"No...you may go..."

"Wait..." Mari stopped him. "How much did he pay you?" She gestured at Marvin.

"Two hundred to finger you." Johnny's mouth pulled down in his customary smirk. "Looks like all he had to do is ask you."

Hal asked softly. "How do you know she never danced on the pole?"

"I was torn about that. I didn't know she was a minor. Frankly, I was hoping she would...you know with her figure and all...I really wanted to see her tits! I would have been so there if she had. But, on the other hand...she was one of the few decent girls who worked there...so I didn't want to see her reduced to that...and neither did Malone."

"What do you mean by 'reduced to that'?" Hal's eyes narrowed.

Johnny's face twisted. "It seems like something just cracks in some of them once they give up their pride...their self-esteem. They lose their spirit. Their eyes go dead as they go through their routines. Now some of them relish it...they lord it over the men in the audience that they have them by the balls and they know it. Look...they are on the poles for one reason only...to display the merchandise...they make their money off of tips...but the real money comes from lap dancing or table dancing for the V.I.P.'s. From there...it is a slippery slope into chippying for many of them. It's not good."

"What's chippying?" Hal wanted to know.

"You know...prostitution..."

"Why are you a part of it?" Hal's eyes fixed on Johnny.

"Hey...it's not me up there dancing...I just pour the drinks. They're over twenty-one..." He looked at Mari. "...except if they're not...and I don't know anything about that...and they can make those decisions for themselves."

An idea was forming in Marvin's head. "This Malone...does he frequently have under aged people working for him?"

Both Mari and Johnny turned and exclaimed in unison. "DON'T FUCK WITH MALONE!"

Johnny started backing out of the room. "Gotta bounce...don't ask or answer questions about Malone..." He gave Mari a little salute. "I'll tell Malone you'll give him a call...see ya around, doll face." And he was out the door.

Mari turned to face Hal. "There you have it. I will call Malone and arrange for you to see my act...what I did."

"You don't have to do that, Babe." Hal shook his head.

"Yes I do. I want you to see for yourself exactly what I did...no wild imaginings running amuck in your head...no suppositions or suspicions. I'm not saying the venue was pretty...because a bunch of howling guys is no picnic...but, at least for my act, it was not the picture of debauchery your father made it out to be. I want you to see it...I want you to know the truth of it...and then I am done with it and I never want to hear about it again!"

"Babe...it's no big deal." Hal frowned.

"Are you kidding me? He made it a big deal...he wanted it to come between us." She turned to Marvin. "You don't give two shits about your son's happiness do you? You don't care if you hurt him. You really are a piece of work."

"Look who's talking...the dancing queen."

"What I did was honest work...and I didn't hurt anyone."

Marvin slammed his fist on his desk. "Hal...you have a decision to make. You break it off with this slut right now...or I will disinherit you. I will give it all to my nephew..."

"WHAT THE FUCK!!"

"You heard me!"

The door opened and Vivian walked in. "And so did I, Marvin...I heard it all. Mari did nothing wrong...and I will not have you threaten our son!"

"You stay out of this!"

"If it wasn't for my father, you wouldn't have two cents to rub together. He tried the same thing with you when we got married...he tried to break us up...buy you off. You were smart enough to convince him that you actually loved me. So he acquiesced and made sure you had a respectable fortune...but that is all you have! This house and the lion's share of my father's money is mine...and will be Hal's no matter what he does. But if you think you are going to leave that pimply faced nephew of yours the money that was given to you by my father..."

Disgusted, Hal waved his hand. "Let him do what he wants to with it...he can shove it up his ass...I don't care..."

Rarely in a snit, Vivian was now on a roll. "I told you...I love this girl and you still tried to hurt her...you still tried to hurt my Hal...your son! Marvin, I have forgiven you much...I have forgiven you all...but THIS I will never allow!" She gestured for Mari and Hal to come to her. "Come my darlings...come with me..." She herded them out of the office into the living room.

"Ma...I'm sorry, but I just want to go home, I want to go home and just have Hal hold me. I can't stop shaking."

"I know, my maideleh. Now don't cry." She handed Mari over to Hal. "Take her home and tell her everything is going to be just fine. Pay no attention to your father. He will have no say in who I want for my daughter."

***

"Why didn't you tell me?" Hal took Mari straight to bed after they got home, poured her a small glass of Mogen-David to calm her, and climbed into bed with her. He held her close and stroked he hair. "You should have told me."

"I used to think perhaps I should...but after you reamed me over salsa dancing...and what you said about a brass pole...that really hurt...that cut so close to the bone because it wasn't easy keeping away from doing that...I was so desperately poor. The money Lars gave me lasted about five minutes in L.A. Lo-Lo and I looked out for each other...there were times I was all she and her son had...and then sometimes she was all I had. But Malone saw something in me...I don't know what...because he treated the other girls like shit...no matter how sad their story was...but he helped me."

"I'm so sorry, Babe...I didn't know..."

"It's just that when you asked me to marry you...I really thought I should tell you...but we both were so deliriously happy...and you said it wasn't important...and I truly don't think I did anything wrong...I didn't want to spoil everything...so I let it go..."

"As well you should. There was no need to drag all that up. Deuce warned me not to take you around my father until after we were married. I should have listened to him."

"Now that Marvin has dragged everything up...and poisoned the well...you're going to see exactly what I did...and only you can judge me."

"I don't think we should go there."

"I don't think we can avoid it."

***

Hal went down to research to carry the "Underground L.A." file to Mari. On the way he passed the Personnel Office and he paused, shook his head, and continued on. All eyes turned, as they usually did, as he approached Mari's cubicle, hoping for another morsel of gossip to chew on. He leaned over her shoulder and placed the file on her desk. Smelling her plumeria scent, he resisted the urge to bury his

238

nose in her hair. "What I think we need are a few more prohibition sites...you know, speakeasies...to bolster our story, even if they weren't underground. By the way, your interviews were fantastic."

She turned her face to him and mouthed, "I want to kiss you."

"Stop it." He whispered. "We're going to have to bring Godfrey to work."

On the way back to his office he stopped in front of Personnel again. He walked over to the door, hesitated, and then went in. The secretary was out, but Penny, who insisted on the title of Head of Human Resources, when nothing could sound less human, was in her office. Seeing him through her open door she fawned, "Mr. Golan...what brings you here to our little corner?"

"I want to see Mari's personnel file. I have a sticky assignment coming up and I want to make sure she's the right person for it."

Penny headed directly to the files. "I know she is quite good..." She opened a drawer and fingered through the files. "Here she is..." She handed the file to Hal.

He sat at the secretary's desk and thumbed through it. It showed her previous employment with Mallown Enterprises, Ltd. in a Four Plus Four program during her high school years and she continued with them full time until she came to work for Angel City Magazine.

There was a letter of recommendation from her supervisor there that was verified. She also had a letter of recommendation from a hardware store in some Podunk town in Minnesota. She filled in her education information listing her degrees, but there were no notes indicating any kind of verification. He searched the rest of the file for any kind of paper to denote that her education claims were vetted. "What happened to her education verification?"

"I processed her application myself...it must be there." Hal handed her the file and Penny nervously looked through it. "Barbara must have misfiled it because I know I did verify it...I must have."

"Don't worry...she has worked out just fine...and it is my decision anyway."

"I just don't understand what happened to it." Penny rifled through the file again. "I hope she will still be considered for the assignment. I will keep on looking."

"Don't bother. She's shown herself to be quite capable. I think I will give her the assignment anyway."

He returned to his office with his brow furrowed. *It doesn't matter. If it doesn't matter...why in the fuck did you check her file?* He closed his eyes. "It doesn't matter." He said out loud.

***

"I sure appreciate your picking me up. I ought to buy health insurance for that Benz of mine...it's beautiful...and it is a dream to drive...but when it needs to see a doctor...and of course it needs a specialist...uhm...the dollar signs mount up!" Deuce laughed. "I was looking forward to seeing Mari's show and I would have been sorry to miss it."

"Yeah sure." Hal responded. "It was on the way anyhow." Both Hal and Mari were strangely silent on the ride to West L.A. and Deuce sensed a storm was brewing. His efforts at lifting their mood went unnoticed.

When they arrived at Stony Malone's Gentlemen's Club, they dropped Mari off at the back door, and then Hal and Deuce went to a coffee shop to wait until it was close to the time for her to perform.

"Just keep me from blowing my top, Deuce. I hate this...but she insisted that I see what she did...and then never bring it up again."

"She's pretty brave to do this...but I think she's right. After tonight...you will have no questions...no doubts...about what it was all about. Please...just don't punch anybody out! And...no matter what...don't get mad at her. She's trusting you to understand."

"I can't believe my father went to the lengths of putting a private detective on her."

"I can...I told you not to put those two together in the same house...country...planet."

"But it makes no sense that he hates her so."

"It makes perfect sense...he's jealous of you...and she told him so. He's jealous of her too."

"What? She's going to be his daughter-in-law."

"Nonetheless...look at what you have! You have a hot looking woman...that would turn any man's head...she has a fierce love for you...and her only thought is to make you happy. Shit! I'm jealous of you! The only difference is that I'm happy for you. I just wish I had the same thing in my wife. But...your old man...he's pissed. You just keep doing better and better by not taking his advice." Deuce lowered his head. "Just because he's your father...don't think that he is not susceptible to human nature...he's a man just like the rest of us and he's capable of being just as turned on and jealous as the next guy."

***

Stony Malone's Gentlemen's Club was slightly more upscale in appearance than other clubs of its ilk. As soon as Mari walked through the back door she was immediately assaulted with arduous memories, and the recognition of how far she had come in life. She never thought that she would return for any reason and that the onerous episode would remain a part of her past, never to be thought of again. She carried a large suitcase that was lighter in weight than it appeared, containing only her costume. To her left was Gaby's office, the mother hen to the waitresses. Sticking her head through the door, she saw that Gaby was not there. Stepping into the large kitchen she saw the scruffy, skinny chef who had mixed gray stubble on a face prematurely wrinkled and tinged yellow from the cigarette that constantly hung from his lips. She wondered if he knew that the burned filet mignons, and those that accidently hit the deck, that he discarded, frequently ended up as meals for her and Lo-Lo when they waitressed there. Smiling, she now realized that his string of loud curses, when one got away from him, was a signal to the waitresses to look for it in the bin. Funny, she never knew his name.

Pushing through the double doors, an automatic "Coming through" came from her lips. There was a short hall that opened up into the club. Nothing had changed. In the middle of the room was a good sized, round stage with four equidistant poles. Steps on one side led to the top. Chairs were placed near the apron of the platform with rows of tables, across the aisle, staggered behind. Three quarters of the room were bounded with plush booths, some of which had poles installed on the tables. On the fourth wall was a long bar, lined with stools, with a sprawling mirror reflecting an unobstructed view of the stage. To one side was a stairway leading to V.I.P. rooms and private offices on the second floor. It also led to the entertainers' quarters.

It was early and three dancers gave lackluster performances in front of a sparse audience. Mari spotted Johnny behind the bar. He was in a dispute with a waitress that ended with him taking the mix gun and squirting her. Outraged, the girl called him a son of a bitch. He squirted her again and that settled the argument as she stomped away to clean up. "Hey...Johnny..." Mari waved.

He came over to the end of the bar and grinned at her. "So you're going on tonight?"

"Yeah. Still the fastest mix gun slinger? How come you were so mean to her? You were never that mean to me."

"You were never that stupid..."

"You're running low on limes...give me a knife and I'll cut up a couple of them for you."

He handed her the knife and limes. "So that's the guy you're going to marry? He's going to be here?"

"Yep and yep."

"You've got some balls bringing your guy here to see you work."

"Don't I just..."

"No guy wants to know the girl he is going to marry worked in a place like this. Aren't you afraid of losing him?"

"Yes...very much afraid...but I don't think I have much choice now that he knows."

"What do you mean?"

"I don't want him to doubt me...what I did...and what I didn't do. I don't want him to throw it in my face later...you know how things can work on your mind and make them out to be much worse than what actually happened. He is so special, Johnny...I know this will be tough on him and me...but I think he can deal with it...and if I'm wrong...I'm well and truly fucked...because I love him."

"Oh...I thought it was the money."

"No...I didn't know about the money then. Hey...thanks for being so supportive in not telling the truth." She said sarcastically. "You know I didn't sleep around, lap dance, or chippy!"

"How was I to know?"

"I didn't sleep with you, did I?"

"No."

"Well...there you go!" she lightly cuffed him.

He grinned. "Yeah...fuck me...like you would've..."

She pursed her lips. "Well that's a ringing endorsement...you could've mentioned it!"

"The man just paid me two hundred bucks...I couldn't totally cross him."

"Who looked you up in the first place?"

"A man named Gray...something Gray. Hold up...I have his card." He went to the cash register of the bar, looked in a drawer beneath it, took out a business card, and brought it back to her. "Here...you can have it. I have no need for it..."

"Thanks...it might come in handy." She tucked the card into her purse. "I have some Brazilian musicians coming, have them wait at a table until show time...and don't serve them alcohol until after we're through. Wish me luck!"

"Aw, doll face...you know I wish you the best...you're one of the good ones."

***

The stage was cleared of girls and the lights went out. In the darkness a loud whistle blew several times. Deep serdo drums started beating answered by high caixo drums and the sound repeated. Suddenly they were joined by a cadre of drums as the whistle and the squeak of a cuica kept time with the rhythm. Then they went into full samba mode as the lights went up and seven bare-chested, white, brown, and black percussionists, dressed in white pants and panama hats, marched in single file onto the stage. Lining up, their feet moved back and forth in unison with the beat. An unseen announcer's voice came over the loudspeaker. "Stony Malone's proudly presents the one you have been waiting for...direct from Rio...the fantasy girl...the fantastic TUUUPEEE!!"

Dressed in a costume of an outsized headdress of gold frosted feathers, a gold lamé beaded thong bikini, and gold high-heeled, jewel-studded boots, Mari bounced up the stairs and, to a howling audience, strode on stage. Parading across the stage, with a brilliant smile, she strutted up to one side, stopped, and did a mad samba turning to show her bare buttocks furiously shaking to the beat. Then she moved sideways to center stage, repeated the dance step, and did it again at the far side. The drummers shouted "Ayeee...Tupi!" She samba'd back across the stage turning as she went. There was a tassel hanging from the center back of her thong bikini. It swayed back and forth with each movement and then she stopped, and, making a round motion with her ass, she caused the tassel to twirl in a circle. One drummer let out a loud, "Brrrrrrrraaahhh!" Picking up the beat, she turned, held out her arms, and did a cross-step progression back to center stage. In alternating steps, bouncing back and forth, she did a shimmy, shaking her bosom toward the audience. With gyrating hips, she kept up the pace, breaking into and out of frenzied samba steps until the drummer signaled "Brrrrrrrraaahhh!"

The drums continued as the lights went dark and the pace slowed. When the lights came up again, they were a dim shade of blue and Mari was without her headdress. Starting from a reclining position on the platform, with her hair hanging free, Mari did a series of writhing, gyrating suggestive moves to a slow beat. Speaking in a Portuguese accent, the sultry tones of her voice coming over the sound system accompanied her exotic and graceful ballet.

"I am your fantasy,
You created me in your head,
I am the one imagery
You want for your bed.
I am a warm sensation,
I am not a reality,
I exist in your imagination
Where you feel my sensuality.
In the middle of the night,
I dance in your dreams,
Like a star so bright.
Nothing is as it seems.
You see me in the day
Where memories of me spin
Flashing in on your way
You still taste me in your sin.
Cha ta boom, cha ta boom, cha ta boom."

When the lights came back up, Mari continued her sensual dance near the edge of the stage where the men waved bills to give her. Lolling, rolling, and creeping like a cat from one man to another, she lightly touched the nose of one, air kissed an old guy on the cheek; with another particularly attractive man, she took the bill out of his hand and put it in his mouth and then took it back with her teeth. Smiling, she slipped it into her bosom. As she progressed around the platform some handed her money, while others tucked money into her bikini bottoms or her top straps, which she promptly took and stuffed into her top. Afterward, she took the nest egg, lifted one of the drummers' hats, deposited it inside, and then returned it to his head.

The beat picked up to a fast samba and the lights changed to a bright strobe light, freezing her movements into flashing images as she danced across the floor. As the lights changed back to normal, one of the percussionists came out to dance with Mari, yelling "Brrrrrrrraaahhh!" Tall and thin, he struck a pose, and tipped his panama hat. Mari turned with her back to him and danced a short samba, shaking her ass. He grabbed his heart and samba'd with his long legs in motion resembling eggbeaters. After they danced, he went back to playing the cuica and Mari announced the Stony Malone's Club dancers. Six girls in gold lamé string bikinis came on stage in a row, each announcing her name, while dancing to the drumming. Each one held two confetti poppers in her hands. Mari continued in her Portuguese accent. "This is my last night...I am going back to my beloved Rio. But I love you all and will never forget you." The rhythm picked up pace and Mari yelled "SAMBA" and the line of girls screamed and squealed as they danced in unison setting off the confetti poppers, spraying gold confetti in the air. As the glittering cloud drifted down, they all turned their backsides to the audience in one amazing display of shaking booties. "Brrrrrrrraaahhh!" They all shouted, turning so the audience could see them from all sides of the stage.

As the crowd went crazy, the girls all marched around and continued to dance as they waved and left the stage. Mari was the last to leave, waving, and throwing kisses.

The act got a standing ovation. The men stomped and shouted, demanding an encore and would not stop. Mari came out and danced a crazy samba, shaking her hair about, and, as she finished, she pranced out with the band following behind her.

***

On the drive home Deuce was jubilant. "Man oh man...what a show! Girl...I couldn't believe it was you out there. Where did you learn how to dance like that?"

"A Brazilian troupe was touring the country and when they got to California...one of the girls dropped out. I went to the audition to replace her. That was her costume I was wearing. I was a pretty good

246

dancer and the fact that I didn't know how to Samba didn't faze them. They liked my behind..."

"Big shocker!" Hal interjected.

"...so they taught me how to samba the way they do it in Brazil...the real way...not the Americanized, silly back and forth style. In Brazil their samba is danced just the way you saw it, in public, in celebrations...at Carnival time...everywhere! They celebrate a woman's derrière...they don't hide it."

"And that is how you did your act back in the day?" Deuce wanted her to make the point clear.

"Yes...my Brazilian guys came through for me tonight...every one of them. But I did change the last part when I brought all the girls on stage. I thought it would make a really big ending."

"It was the end of ends alright! All those pretty butts shaking...umm...umm...give a man heart failure" Deuce looked coy.

"I have one question for you. When you were showing your butt to hundreds of men...why were you so shy about the picture of you in your computer?" Hal's mind was racing.

"Because I cared very much about what you thought of me. Different time...different place...different standards. Your perception of me was very important...I trusted you. I didn't take the picture...I didn't put it in the computer...but in the off chance you would find it...I really didn't want you to think I was an awful person. Besides...like I said...I knew you wouldn't go all wacky doodle over it..."

"Yeah, I did!"

"Oh." She raised her eyebrows.

"Why did you trust me?" Hal pushed her further.

"I was in the lunchroom and there were four other girls there gossiping about the guys in the office. Of course...being the new girl...they didn't ask me to join them...but I could overhear their conversation. They talked about who they thought was the best looking...the worst...who was a dick...Dirk won that prize...and you were considered the nicest and the smartest. That is when I decided to give Cora my file on Mitchem. I was hoping that you would take a look at it with fresh eyes...and you did..."

"So you show your butt to hundreds of men...but you trusted me..."

"Hal...I think I always trusted you...long before you told me you loved me...and before I knew I was in love with you...the way you treated me...you made me feel safe...you made me feel protected. You cared about what I thought...what I felt. It was something I never had before. You made me feel...*cherished.*"

"Because I took care of you is why you love me?"

"No! What I am saying is that you stole my heart a piece at a time...until you had it all."

"Aw...that's the sweetest thing I ever heard." Deuce tried to cue Hal that he should back off and consider himself lucky.

"Did you have to take money from that guy's mouth?" Hal couldn't leave it alone.

Mari rolled her eyes. "I told you that I would show you what I used to do...and that is exactly what I did. I would pick out a clean, decent looking guy...and give him the kick of taking his money from his mouth...I never made contact when I did it. It was a Tupi move. That is who I was when I went on stage...Tupi. That is who I was tonight...it was all a show..."

"A damned good one if you asked me..." Deuce tried again. "What happened to the money?"

"I gave it to my Brazilian guys. We've all moved on in our lives and they have families and responsibilities...and they went way out of their way to be there for me tonight. So, I let them split it up."

"What was that 'I am your fantasy...created in your head' stuff?" Hal glanced at her.

"Oh...that. When I first started working at Stony Malone's, even as a waitress, one of the dancers told me that frequently the men were susceptible and fall in love with them...and they had to let them know that it was all a fantasy...none of it was real...you know...let them down easy. They wanted them to come back...but only for entertainment. So, when I started my act, I thought I should incorporate it to let the men who were watching me know that none of it was real. Funny...they seemed to enjoy the fact that Tupi was a fantasy they could play with in their heads..."

"Are you my fantasy?" Hal shot at her.

"Are you mine?" She shot back.

"Hey...children...what are you two going on about?" Deuce hoped he could get them to calm down. "Why are you sniping at each other...it was a great show...no harm no foul...and now it's over."

Hal sat in flinty silence the rest of the way. When he went to drop Deuce off at his house, Deuce asked him to get out of the car with him and come in for a moment. Once inside the door he turned to Hal. "I know that mood and I know that look...and, man you've got to seriously knock it off. Promise me that you are not going to go and get off on that little girl. If you get mad at her...you're just going to lose her. For your own sake...just don't say anything you'll regret." Deuce insisted, "She loves you, man...get over yourself!"

Hal looked away. "Yeah...yeah..."

"Promise?"

"OK...OK...I promise..."

***

After dropping Deuce off, Hal and Mari drove home in silence. She tried to penetrate his thoughts. "How did you like the show?"

Hal winced, but his voice was soft. "I'm trying to think. Do you mind if we don't talk right now?"

"Oh. I'm sorry." She turned her face to the window, lowered her seat back, and closed her eyes. *Did I just make the biggest mistake of my life?* She thought. She was tired, too tired to take on any of his issues, too tired to be apprehensive, and too tired to cry. She just waited.

When they arrived home, he carried her suitcase inside and then went to leave. "I gotta go. I'll be back when I get back."

She started to ask him where he was going but changed her mind. Her eyes narrowed. "Fine...you do what you gotta do. You take all the time you need to think...and so will I."

The last four words she said gave him a jolt and he did a double take before closing the door. Until then, he only thought of his judgment of her without thinking about her assessment of him. He did a quick step down the porch steps and got back into his car. Gunning the engine, he took off. After a few blocks he pulled over and parked. He put his head on the steering wheel.

The spectacle he had just witnessed kept going through his head. He wanted to hit something. *Why did she make me see that? What was there to gain from that?* It was two in the morning, but there was only one person he wanted to talk to. He took out his cell and pushed the button. The phone rang several times before it was picked up. "Mameleh...it's Hal. Can I come over and talk right now? I know...it's the middle of the night...but if I don't talk to someone...I'll go nuts."

By the time he got there the house was lit up and coffee steamed from a pot on the buffet. "What's wrong, my bubeleh?" She led him to the dining room. "Did you and Mari have words?"

"No...we didn't talk at all. I couldn't deal with...something. She had this idea that I should see her dance so that I would know just what she did..." He paced back and forth.

"I know...she told me. She asked me what I thought. I thought it was a good idea because she wanted to be honest with you...for you to know the truth..."

"You thought it was a good idea...do you have any idea what it was like??"

She fixed her eyes on him. "Will you settle down so I can look at you when we talk?" He took a chair. "Coffee?"

"I'll have anything stronger."

"No...you will listen. Marriage is not a game...it's not easy...and no matter who she is...your wife is not going to be perfect. One of the things that is most important is not to build a life on a string of lies...secrets from each other. The other is understanding...if she tells you her worst secret...and she lets you have it raw...the only thing that you must decide is does it affect your relationship now...and if it does not...then it doesn't matter. No one is perfect...but it seems to me that Mari did the best she could under the circumstances."

"I know her people are bat shit crazy...but she could have gone home rather than work in a place like that."

"Now who's bat shit crazy? Go back to people who were so bad that her own brother sacrificed his savings to get her away? Don't you think that they knew the situation better than you?" She took his hands in both of hers. "What was so bad about what she did?"

"All those...all those dirty, filthy guys yelling and howling at her every move...getting off to her...wishing they could fu..." He stopped mid-word.

"My tateleh..." She reached out and gently stroked his face and shushed the rising sobs in his chest. "You judge her too harshly. You love her and you can't stand for another man to look at her. Get over it. You just heard out loud what is going on in every man's head if she just walks down the street. God gave her the looks...the Devil gave men the thoughts. On the street it is silent...in the club the veneer is stripped off. If you blame her for it and you think badly of her for it...then look at me and think even worse."

"What are you talking about?"

"Mari was struggling...she had no education...no skills...no money. She used the only thing she had to offer...her beauty. No one touched her. She was on display like a sculpture...a movie...a painting...the sight of which gives pleasure." She searched his face. "I had no such excuses. I was very pretty when I was young..."

"I remember."

"I mean when I was a girl of fifteen...a very pretty girl. That is when you first discover a mystical power about yourself...that made boys stare. Being rich, I was given everything...especially the best education...and for that education I was sent to a school in a small town in upstate New York. It was a beautiful place with woods, a lake, pastures...and boys. Here is a secret that I tell you...that I have never told anyone else. I used to stare at myself in the mirror...undressed. I would turn to look at myself...curious about my own body. Then I found that I liked it when boys looked at me...and they would stumble and walk into things...and I thought it was funny.

"Once, I took it into my head to go out at night...cross into the woods and go down to the lake...and there I took off my nightgown to swim. I heard a noise...without turning around I knew that there were schoolboys watching me. I acted as if I did not know they were there, and I came out of the water and danced in the moonlight. The feeling was intoxicating...knowing they were staring...knowing they were transfixed by my beauty. I would move close to where I realized they were hiding...and then I would go where they could not see me. After a while I would put on my nightgown and run back to the dorm. The next day I could tell who was hiding in the bushes...by their red faces when they looked at me. Weather permitting...I did it once a week for almost a year...and then I got bored with it."

Hal smiled and dropped his head. "Ma...you were a tease! My mother the tease!"

"Yes...I'm afraid I inspired many wet dreams!" She laughed. "But it was different for Mari...she did not like what she did...and she did it out of necessity, but what she did was not dirty. Now you go home...and you tell her you understand...because there is one thing I know...right now her heart is breaking because you are not there."

***

Hal stuck the key in the door and opened and closed it as quietly as he could. He turned to find Mari still dressed and standing in the middle of the living room. She did not say a word, but she did not have to, her eyes told of the despair she was feeling.

Hal's brow was furrowed and his lips were tight as he slowly moved his head back and forth. He walked toward her and then around her. Her eyes followed him as she waited to take the brunt of his anger. He came to a stop in front of her. "Mari...I'm only going to ask you this once. Is there anything else in your past that I should know...anything at all?"

"No. Nothing of any consequence."

"What is your definition of 'consequence'?"

"What is yours? Do you want to know about past boyfriends? What? There's nothing else."

"Is there anything else that could come up that would bite us in the ass later?"

"No."

He paced around room in thought. He turned to her and started to say more, but then his face melted as he relented; he realized that he only had the choice of loving her. Putting his arms around her, he pulled her to him in a deep kiss and felt her relief as she responded. After covering his face with kisses and softly whispering to him, she settled her face into his neck. He picked her up and carried her to bed.

***

INTERLUDE

While Marvin was away on a business trip, Vivian took the opportunity to have Hal and Mari stay with her. She understood when Hal told her that he would not have Mari around his father until after they were married and thought it was a wise decision on his part. It was a week planned around simple pleasures. Mari showed Vivian how to make Norwegian Fyrstekake and Vivian was fascinated by the concept of cooking. It was a hobby she thought she might enjoy as much as she did growing prize roses. Both Hal and Mari taught Vivian the game of Scrabble. Vivian taught them both the ins and outs of a formal wedding. They sat down in the dining room while Vivian showed them the details given to her by the wedding planner. Each item was approved by Hal saying, "Whatever Mari wants," and Mari saying to Vivian, "Whatever you want." The only thing Mari insisted upon was that Brian would be in charge of her wedding dress. "He will do a wonderful job...in fact I should recommend him to your wedding planner. Once she sees what he will design for me...I know she will want to get his name."

"Is he the best? I want you to have the best." Vivian asked.

"I can vouch for him..." Hal conceded.

Mari added, "He's the only one I would trust for such an important day...and it would break his heart if he wasn't chosen to do this for me..."

Vivian nodded, "Then it's settled. Have you decided on May or June...that is when the garden is at its best for an outdoor wedding?"

"May." Mari responded and Hal obediently agreed.

Vivian marked it in her planning book and then looked up and smiled. "One other thing...I don't want to put pressure on you two..." She balled up her fists and lightly pounded the table. "...but I want grandchildren! Please tell me you are planning to have children..."

Hal grinned. "I promise you I will work on it diligently every day...and night!"

Mari hunched her shoulders and smiled. "If you insist, ma."

Vivian beamed and got back to her planner. "I will mark in here for next year to plan a baby shower!"

***

On the way home Mari commented, "Your mother is so excited about our wedding...I'm glad we went ahead and let her have her big wedding...it means a lot to her..."

"Yeah. She belongs to this women's social club...they do stuff...charities...social events...and just about all of their sons...at least the oldest ones...are already married. For years she has wanted to rub my wedding in their collective faces. Now...with my marrying you...oh my God...she's going to lord it over all of them that she has the most beautiful daughter-in-law...bar none!"

"Hal...I think she really loves me..."

"Oh, yeah...she does. Because, if she didn't...she would make Marvin look like a saint. If she thought that you didn't love me...she would fight you tooth and nail."

"Speaking of your father...I keep forgetting to give you his detective's business card. Johnny...you know...the bartender...he gave it to me. He thought I would want it."

"Yeah...I want that card! Be sure to give it to me when we get home and make sure that I put it in my desk. I'm all about retribution, Babe...and somehow...I don't know how...but that card may help me give him payback..."

"Hal...I just want to be with you...I don't want to hurt anybody..."

"You don't get it. What Marvin did was beyond the pale...I refuse to call him my father anymore...and payback is in order." He drove quietly for a while and turned off on the freeway exit to their home. When he came to a stoplight, he gazed at her and then looked away. "I know I didn't say it, Babe...but that show you put on was terrific...I just get blinded by what I feel for you. I just want to say that I'm sorry I was such a dick about it."

The light had changed, and a horn blasted for him to move it. Giving the driver behind him the L.A. salute, he drove on.

***

Tooling up Highway 99, Hal was taking Mari on a romantic getaway for Thanksgiving weekend. On Monday he announced that she should pack her bags so they could leave on Tuesday night and they would not be back to work until the next Tuesday morning. "I'm going to romance the hell out of you, Babe..."

"Where are we going?"

"It's a surprise..."

254

She frowned. "How will I know what to pack?"

"For the day...pack some jeans...casual stuff...maybe a dress or two because I love to show you off. For the night...you know what to pack...or bring nothing at all..."

"I see..." She skipped off to get her suitcases out of the closet.

They pulled into Fresno to overnight and the next morning they headed out on Highway 41 to the high country. After miles along the scenic road, they came to a tunnel. "OK, Babe...close your eyes..."

"Why?"

"Just close your eyes and keep them closed until I tell you to open them..."

"OK."

He drove through the tunnel and then parked. "Keep your eyes closed...I will get you out of the car." He went to the passenger side and opened the door. Helping her out of the car, he guided her to where he wanted her to stand in the "view" stop. "Now...open your eyes!"

A scene of magnificent beauty stretched out before her. She was so astonished and moved by the sight that tears welled up in her eyes. "Where am I?"

"Yosemite! That is El Capitan...He pointed to a granite cliff rising high above the valley floor. "Over there is Half Dome..." The spectacular, sheared off, granite monolith stood in the distance amongst other breathtaking granite cliffs and formations. The valley floor was still green, as were the pines, but fall colors were in full force among the oaks. The waterfalls were not as numerous as in the spring, but they still put on a show. Created by eons of glacial carving on granite, the stunning beauty evoked an emotional response that gave a sense that what you were privileged to see was holy; God was present.

"I have never seen such an exquisite place...even Yellowstone cannot compare." She cuddled up to him under his arm and stood in awe.

"I wanted you to see it all at once...spread out before you..."

"There's no better way."

"I already have a cabin for us...and dinner reservations at the Ahwahnee Hotel for Thanksgiving. After that, we can stay...or go to the gold country."

They drove down to the valley floor to give her a quick overview and then he took another road to a three-bedroom house that was modestly referred to as a cabin. A van was parked out front and Graham, Vivian's butler, was there to greet them. "Everything is prepared for you Mr. Golan." He off loaded their suitcases and carried them inside. He didn't quite know what to make of Mari. The elder Mr. Golan did not like her, Mrs. Golan did. While he never assumed it was his place to judge, he did not know what deference was due her, therefore he gave her a tactful nod.

Mari walked in and found a bouquet of roses awaiting her, chilled champagne, and place settings for two on a rustic table. Flames were dancing in the fireplace. "Did I do OK?" Hal smiled at her.

"Wonderful."

Graham asked, "At what hour shall I serve dinner?"

"I don't know about you…but I'm hungry right now." He looked at Mari.

"Me too."

"As soon as you can rustle something up…we're ready to eat."

"Then I'll get to 'rustling' right away." Graham disappeared into the kitchen.

They both went upstairs to find the bathroom to wash the day's travel off of them. "How long is Graham going to be here?" Mari asked.

"After we eat, he leaves. He should have stocked the refrigerator…so we will be on our own unless we decide for him to stay, and you want him to cook for us."

"Then he goes…I'll cook for us."

"Are you sure you don't mind?"

"I'd rather have you to myself."

He turned to find her dressed in a fetching little black dress. His mind imagined what she was wearing underneath. He gave a low whistle. "Come here."

"Oh, no. We eat first…and then you're next on the menu."

They sat down to a dinner of saddle of venison with lingonberry sauce. Graham showed Hal a bottle of red wine. "I selected a Bourgueil, a light to medium bodied Cabernet from the Loire Valley for your evening. I hope it meets with your approval." He uncorked the bottle and handed the cork to Hal and, after Hal sniffed it and nodded, he poured a soupçon of wine for Hal to taste while Mari looked on with fascination.

"That is a nice selection." Hal approved.

Graham went to pour Mari's glass first and she held up her hand. "None for me, thank you...I don't drink."

"Madam, may I suggest a glass of iced tea infused with red currants?"

"That sounds divine..."

Graham finished pouring Hal's glass and then made a decorous beeline for the kitchen.

Mari was mesmerized by Graham's waiting at the table in the European style, serving the side dishes with a deft handling of two serving spoons in one hand. The least crumb was unobtrusively whisked away with a small tool he carried in his pocket. "Godfrey could take a lesson from him." She whispered.

"Graham has been with us for years. I think I remember him smiling once when I was a kid."

"Wasn't it sort of creepy having someone always around the house...doing stuff for you and calling you mister all the time? It would kind of freak me out!"

"You don't have to have a butler if you don't want one...or you can have one if you want to. My mother always had one...and so she always will." He leaned forward and whispered, "I think he is in love with her."

"Oh...family scandal?"

"No...she doesn't have a clue...but I think he would die for her if it came to it. But his position dictates that he lives to serve her...and I guess that is enough for him."

"Well...I can hardly blame him. Your mother is adorable."

"Speaking of which...I want to ask you if you're willing to do something for her."

"Sure...anything..."

"She really...really wants a grandchild. Do you want to have a baby right away...I mean just as soon as we get married?"

"Do you?"

Hal's eyes lit up as a smile flickered across his face. "Yeah...I think I kinda do. I mean we already have been living like a married couple and going through the getting to know each other's quirks and stuff stage…I like your quirks…I would be over the moon if we had a kid."

Mari smiled. "I'll be right back." She went upstairs and returned with her container of pills. She looked at them for a moment and then handed them to him. She nodded her head. "Yes…Oh my God, Hal…I said yes! We're going to be parents, aren't we?"

They stared at each other for a minute and then Hal started laughing. "Yeah…we are, Babe!" He took the pill container, broke it open, and tossed the pills in the air. "We're gonna have a kid. What do you want to name her?"

"Vivian…of course!"

"And if it's a boy?"

"Hillel…"

"Are you shitting me?! I'm not doing that to my kid!" Hal put his hand to his forehead.

"What do you want to name him?"

Hal thought for a moment. "David…I think I would like to name him David."

"I like that too…and I hope he has your eyes." She leaned her cheek on her hand. "Now that I am off the pill, they say it takes three to four months, or longer, before I can get pregnant…but it is possible that I could get pregnant right away. What will that do to your mother's timetable for the wedding?"

"You know…I'm just so incredibly happy…I don't care…and I don't think she will either. She is just going to have to push up the date."

They finished dinner, quietly beaming at each other over their shared secret. Graham, puzzled by the small tablets on the table and floor, made quick and inconspicuous work of clearing them away. After he was told that he would not be needed, he took Hal and Mari into the kitchen, showed them the provisions he had stocked for the duration, and asked, "Is there anything else you wish to have?" Once they acknowledged that they were satisfied, he melted into the glow of the setting sun.

They moved to the couch in front of the fireplace and Hal stretched out putting his head in her lap. Dreamily, she gently scratched his head and drew lazy circles with her finger around his ear. Her fiddling with him sent flutters of pleasure through him. Turning, he put his arms around her and buried his face into her tummy. "Mari...it means so much to me that you want to have my baby. God, I love you...I can't believe this is real. I've never been so happy..."

"It's real. I want your baby more than anything."

Smelling her scent aroused his desire. He got up, pulled her to him, and while gazing into her face, they ascended the stairs.

***

Deciding to see the historical sites of the gold country, they packed supplies and took off north on Highway 49. "One hundred and fifty years later, the after-effects of hydraulic mining can still be seen." Mari read from the tourist guide. "The miners would guide or pump water into reservoirs on top of the mountains or cliffs and, under the force of gravity, funnel it into a large pipe descending through hoses with attached nozzles to aim the water. They had a guidance system that enabled one man to operate the hose. The weight of the water...from that height...created a powerful hydraulic jet that could tear at mountains and rocks. The runoff was guided through sluices with riffles to collect the gold." She looked up from the book. "How fucking ingenious...and how fucking disastrous for the environment. They got their gold...they got their payday now spent and gone...and we inherited the ruins they left...mounds of silt in a state park...Malakoff Diggins State Historic Park...a monument to man's greed."

After seeing the place where gold was discovered, Mari pointed out, "The guidebook says that John C. Fremont had lived in Bear Valley. They also have an old cemetery there...oh, God...I've got to see that! I love old cemeteries. Their historical value is so underrated." Her eyes sparkled. "Can we go there?"

"Sure, Babe...anywhere you want to go!" Hal grinned.

"Oh...and stop at the first major drugstore we come to."

The smile left his face. "Why?"

She fluttered her lashes and shyly looked at him. "I have to get some prenatal vitamins..." She hunched her shoulders with excitement. "I want to make sure that my body gives our baby everything it needs to be healthy."

At the next pullout he stopped the car. "Come here...come here." He leaned over the car console and drew her to him, with his fingers

259

in her hair. He caressed her face. "Babe...my beautiful...beautiful Babe..." He gently kissed her.

A car drove by and, seeing them, the driver honked his horn and shouted "whooo-hooo" out the window. They laughed and Hal started the car again and drove on to Bear Valley.

They arrived in town in the afternoon. There was nothing there but a few old abandoned buildings and a general store on the left side of the two-lane road and a fenced in pasture on the right. "Let's go into the store and ask if they know where the cemetery is."

They both went inside and inquired. There were three middle-aged men there. They all nodded, but one of them spoke up. "All you have to do is follow that path and it will take you right to it..."

"Which path?" Hal looked outside.

"The one that runs through the pasture...just open the gate...make sure you close it behind you...and follow it through to that clump of trees and you can't miss it..."

"But there's cattle on that end of the field..." Hal pointed to a herd in the distance. "...is it OK to go into the field with them there?"

"Sure...they won't bother you." The man reassured them.

"Thanks." Hal said as they left.

They crossed the road to the gate, opened it, entered, and carefully closed it. Following what looked like a well-worn footpath, they crossed the pasture into the small wooded area. There, overgrown with vines, bushes, and trees, forsaken by all, was a little cemetery of small to smaller-sized headstones. Climbing over dead branches and tangles of vines, Mari read from those inscriptions that were still visible. "Look at the dates, Hal. I don't see any later than the mid 1800's." She paused at a line of stones designated by the same last name. Her natural empathy brought tears to her eyes. "Hal...the children of this family were wiped out by an epidemic. Look at the date of death on the smallest headstones. They're all different dates...but within a couple of weeks of each other. And look...the parents lived through it." She wiped her face with her sleeve. "We have no idea how hard life was back then. An epidemic of scarlet fever, cholera, smallpox...whatever...would decimate a family...a town...and there was no help for it." She walked up to each tiny gravestone, five in all, and placed her hand on them, one by one, and then placed her hands on the parents' headstones. Hal thought she prayed for each one. After wandering through the cemetery, she stood there for a while with her gaze scanning the extent of what she could see, and then she was ready to leave.

Following the trail out of the woods, they came around the curve, looked down the path, and saw a great, black bull standing in the middle of the footpath, between them and the gate. "Oh, shit!" Mari exclaimed. "A fucking bull!"

"Well...they said the cattle wouldn't bother us."

Coming from the country, Mari knew better. "Hal...even you can't stop a bull!" She saw it lower its head and paw at the ground with one hoof. "Hal...that means only one thing...RUN!"

She took off in the direction of the shortest distance to the pasture fence. Hal was right behind her. When they got to the fence, he pushed one line of barbed wire down with his foot while lifting the one above it to make way for Mari to scramble through. She held the wires open for him to crawl though. On the other side, they found themselves in a sea of four o'clocks, picking up burrs that poked through their pants and socks. Chuckling at their narrow escape, they plucked the stickers from their clothing. "I'll bet those SOB's in the general store are laughing their asses off!" Hal smirked.

"Aw...don't begrudge them...out here it is probably the only entertainment they get!"

They got back in the car and drove off. Fidgeting in his seat, Hal lifted a butt cheek, felt around, and pulled off another burr. He let his window down and tossed it out. "Those fuckers...the tourist guides of Bear Valley..."

"Come on...you gotta admit it was funny." She barely contained a giggle.

"Yeah..." He laughed out loud. "...it kinda was!"

***

Within days, Mari's natural hormones, and pheromones, replaced those of the pill, giving off a more complex stimulus. The effect on Hal made him hotter than ever around her. Once they were home, he was even more amorous. He came up behind her, as she was stirring a simmering pot, and put his arms around her. "What's for dinner?"

"Nothing too complicated...chili...and a salad. If you want chili spaghetti...I'll put on another pot..."

261

"No...just make it as quickly as you can..." He ran a hand down her flat stomach, and he held her.

She knew what that meant, but she made him wait for it. "Hal...behave yourself...I'm cooking. We just did it this morning..."

"God...I don't know what's come over me. I want you all the time...during the day at work I can't stop thinking about you...I can't wait until we get home." He caressed her hip.

Demurely, her head tilted as her shoulder drew up. "You have been exuberant...but I know what you mean...I feel the same way...and I love it." She put the large spoon down, turned around, and put her arms around his neck.

"I didn't think it was possible, but I love you even more. Ever since we decided to have a kid...I've been delirious...and feeling so sure of us...our lives together. It is like a piece of me has always been missing and now I feel whole. It's hard to explain."

"Don't explain it. Show me!" She reached behind her and turned off the stove.

With his fingers in her scented hair, he gently kissed her. Mari noticed that ever since they decided to have a baby, he had been treating her with deference, gentleness, and reverence in their lovemaking. While it was a nice change, right now she wanted 'horny Hal" back, throwing her over his shoulder, caveman style.

She gently nipped him on the neck and then pushed him away. Slipping out of her dress, she picked it up off the floor, twirled it around a couple of times while backing away. When he moved toward her she threw the dress to him and skipped off into the living room. He loved that she would sometimes add play to her lovemaking, and he joined the game. "Mari...when I catch you...you're going to get it!" He took off his shirt and threw it on the floor.

"Oh, yeah? Well, I should hope so...but you've got to catch me first!" She laughed.

He unzipped his pants and stepped out of them. "Come on, Babe..."

She took off her bra and threw it to him. Cupping her breasts, she lightly bounced them. "Is this what you want?" She teased.

He grabbed at her. "You know what I want..."

Letting out a little shriek, she dodged away skipping to the other side of the coffee table. "No...tell me..."

He cornered her, or, she let him catch her. Using the fireman's carry, he tossed her over his shoulder, as she giggled, and took her to his lair. "You've been so bad...now you're going to get it." He tossed her on the bed and dove in after her. Pulling her to him, he kissed her long and insistently. The way he manhandled her was irresistible to her; rough enough to excite her, but never too much to hurt her. She reveled in the power of his body and how he could evoke incalculable pleasure. Erupting in paroxysms he finished, and then fell on the bed beside her, holding her and burying his face in her hair. "Did you say we're having chili tonight?"

"Yeah...chili with cheese and onions on top...or I can make chili spaghetti...but you must eat your salad first..."

"Just chili is fine...and I like your salads...and after dinner I want to love up on you again..."

"After dinner you'll probably fall asleep."

"Not this time. You have a way of getting me all stirred up...I can't get wanting you out of my head."

She turned over to face him. Caressing his ear, she gazed dreamily into his eyes and then gently kissed him. "I had better go finish dinner."

"Can it wait a while?"

"Sure...it can if you can...there's not much you can do to ruin a pot of chili."

"I just want to look at you...to be with you a little longer..."

"Ooooohh...I know where that's going. If I give you ten minutes...you'll take an hour." She smiled.

"Do you mind?"

"Naw...I won't even make you chase me this time." She nuzzled him.

***

Deuce looked up as Hal slipped into his chair at the table. "Hey...where you been? I haven't seen you in a couple of weeks."

"I've been romancing my girl..." Hal modestly lowered his eyes. "...she's the most wonderful thing to ever happen to me, Deuce. Mari's going to have my baby..."

Deuce broke out in a grin. "Mari's pregnant?"

"No...not yet...but she's going to be. We agreed that we would start trying right away. She stopped taking the pill. It will take around three to five months before she gets pregnant, but we both wanted a kid right away."

Deuce frowned. "You just may get one right away...Wanda missed a pill once and boom...my third boy was born!"

"That would be OK...we'll just move the wedding day up." Hal shrugged. "I just wanted to tell you that I have never been so happy in my life. Mari will soon be my wife...and we will have a kid on the way...and you will be Uncle Deuce."

"Terry...Uncle Terry! Mari is right...as the uncle to your kid...it has got to be more dignified. I'm Uncle Terry!"

***

YOU HEARTLESS BITCH

"I finally turned in 'L.A. Underground' and Vee said it was too bad I didn't submit it sooner. I probably would have won the article of the year award instead of Lance." Hal talked shop over late morning coffee. It was a leisurely Saturday morning and they were still in their robes.

Mari served him warm aebleskivers admonishing him not to eat more than two. "That means you will get it next year. Honestly, I think it is great that Lance got such a good start...and it is your doing in helping him find his footing."

"Yours too...the article you suggested took him on an entire journey of exploration into the Mexican culture and history in Los Angeles. The Pancho Villa thing that he wrote got him on a roll."

"It's not as though you haven't been preoccupied this year...and you can spare the accolades and give someone else a break."

"Maybe that's what Vee was hinting at...he wants me to pick up the pace. No matter what is going on in my life...he has a magazine to run. I get it." He secreted a third aebleskiver.

"Well, I don't. It is not as though you haven't devoted yourself to his magazine." From the corner of her eye, she saw him filch the aebleskiver and happily smiled to herself that they pleased him.

"The only criticism I have of Vee is that ever since that Nicholson Projects fiasco...he has been playing it safe. Nothing controversial...unless it is so far back in history that there are no feathers left to ruffle...like 'L.A. Underground' and Lance touching upon Chavez Ravine. I have to give it to him...he showed just the proper amount of outrage without succumbing to being maudlin. But Angel City is losing its cutting edge..."

"I had quite enough of its 'cutting edge' and controversies...thank you! I will not have you put yourself on the line like that again!"

"I was only on the line because the story got out before we could print it..."

"There will be no arguing with me on that subject! Your safety is all that matters to me..." She picked up the dishes, bent to lightly kiss him on the head, and carried them to the sink. "...I don't care if you write articles about needlepoint from now on."

He chuckled, "If Rosey Grier likes it...who am I to bitch? I might give it a try."

The telephone rang. "I'll get it." He trundled off into the living room while she rinsed the dishes and put them in the dishwasher. He was back in a few minutes. "I gotta go, Babe. Something is up with ma...she sounds upset and it has to do with Marvin. I'll try not to take too long."

"Do you want me to go with you?"

"No way...not until after we're married."

"Oh...wait." She ran off to the bedroom and came back with a small gift-wrapped box. "I made this for your mother. It's moisturizer and body lotion...I scented it rose. Be sure to kiss her for me."

***

When Hal arrived, the Golan house was visibly grieving. Graham's eyes were downcast as he wordlessly led Hal to Marvin's study. On the way, Hal saw his mother sitting in the living room crying her sorrow into a handkerchief. He put the gift on the credenza in the hall and detoured to talk to Vivian. "Tell him I will be there in a minute." The distress on Graham's face reflected the empathy he felt for Vivian, but he just nodded his understanding and continued down the hall. "Ma...what's going on?"

At the sight of Hal, Vivian let out a wail that ended muffled in her handkerchief, and then blurted out, "Oh...I am so sorry my bubeleh. How could I have been so wrong?" She went to her son and he put his arms around her as she cried on his chest.

His sense of doom grew as he tried to soothe her. "Wrong about what?"

"Talk to your father. I don't have the strength to talk." She demurred.

"Are you going to be alright?" He cupped her chin in his hand and lifted her face to his.

She looked away. "Nothing is going to be alright..." She waved him off and sent him down the hallway to Marvin.

As he entered the study, Hal noticed his father's facial tell that his mother frequently mentioned. While Marvin had his brows drawn up in what he hoped to be a sympathetic expression, he did indeed look smug and it gave him away. "Ma said you wanted to see me. It had better be good. The last time we talked you indicated that you no longer wanted me as your son...and I learned to live with

266

that...no...to be happy about that situation. So, now what do you want with me?"

"Son...I'm sorry if that was your take on what I said..." Marvin indicated for Hal to sit down. "...it certainly wasn't what I intended. You should know that I only had what is in your best interest at heart."

Hal sat down and leaned back in the chair. "So, what is in my best interest this time? I saw ma crying when I got here. Either someone has died...or this is about Mari. Either way...I'm not interested..."

"Don't be hasty son...yes...this is about Mari...but it is worse than even I could imagine." He tossed a legal sized file on the desk in front of Hal. "She has what is known as a rap sheet...that is a..."

"I know what a rap sheet is..." It flickered through Hal's mind that it was strange that his father was just now learning about a rap sheet instead of when he first had Mari investigated, but the thought soon faded as he opened the file and her arrest record for prostitution was revealed. The mug shot it contained clearly showed Mari's face. It was also noted that she was under investigation for fraud and check kiting. There were affidavits by men who testified that they had been a "mark" and had succumbed to her charms only to be conned out of their savings or left with debts that she ran up on their credit cards. The list of aliases she had used, Ava Johansson, Marissa Andersen, and Katarina Carlson were included. As Hal read each painful page, the blood rushed to his face, giving him a crimson glower. An involuntary whimper was torn from his chest as he reviewed the statements of the men who had known her. He realized that his nose was running before he felt the dampness on his cheeks and wiped his face with his jacket sleeve.

Before Hal could ask, Marvin said softly, "That's your copy...you can keep it...I have another. I also have something else, because I knew it would be hard for you to believe...but a woman who worked with her is here and I want you to talk to her. Her name is Vera...she works at Stony Malone's Gentlemen's Club and she knew Mari when she worked there."

Marvin hit the intercom on his phone. "Mr. Gray...please bring Vera in."

A man with dark, slicked back hair dressed in an expensive suit, that appeared outré in its attempt to cover his fat buns, came into the study. Everything about him was pudgy, his face, his body, his fingers, his lips, and even his greasy hair. He had a bottle-blonde woman by the arm who had seen better days. She looked roughly thirty-five and while her body was still holding up, her face was capitulating to the consequences of time, hard living, and the California sun, as she descended into floozyville. The clothing she wore, a black skirt and white blouse, showed her half-hearted attempt at decorum. Her brown eyes were furtive as she tried to assess her situation. Gray, none too gently, sat her in a chair opposite Hal's. "Go ahead and tell him what you know about Mari."

"What do you want to know?" Her eyes turned to Gray instead of Hal.

"What did she do at Stony Malone's?"

"She danced there."

"On the poles?"

"No. She did a little show twice a night on Thursday, Friday, and Saturday."

"Is that all?"

"No...she lap danced...and she did some chippying on the side."

"What do you mean by chippying?"

"You know...she had clients who liked her 'specialty' and she would...you know...have them pay her for it."

"Is there anything else she did?"

"That's all she did when I worked with her. After she left, I heard she would work 'marks' and had this one guy on the string that died...but she took up with a new one...that's all I know."

Hal's fingers dug into the leather armrests of his chair. "This 'specialty' you talked about...what was it?"

"You know...that 'thing' she did..."

As she spoke, Hal's hand went involuntarily to his ear. Vera watched his reaction. "Yeah...that's it...that thing."

The room fell silent. Every time Hal's eyes came to rest on the file in his hand his stomach quavered. He felt a trickle from his nose, wiped it again with his sleeve, and saw the blood red mark it left. He hoped he was dying and could exit this nightmare and the goblins that inhabited it, but it was only a nosebleed.

Marvin picked up the phone. "Get some towels in here. Hal has a nosebleed...I need to get him up to his room."

"No. I can take care of it myself." Hal got to his feet and went to the bathroom. He ran cold water on a towel, placed it on the back of his neck, and held his head back as he sat on the commode. Closing his eyes, he strived to think of nothing, to completely block out his mind, to try to delay the onslaught of his psyche that he knew would come. If he could just stave off the inevitable for a little while longer. *Don't think...don't think!* He told himself as jagged thoughts stabbed at the edges of his brain. Knowing that he did not want to give his father the satisfaction of having a breakdown in front him, he decided to go immediately. Walking out of the bathroom into the study, he picked up the file on his way out. "I'm leaving now."

"Son...don't you want to talk about it?"

"Talk about what? I think you said all there is to say...all of you did..." He looked at the faces around the room until his eyes landed on Gray. "Do you have a business card?"

Gray did carry them, but he pretended to fish in his pockets for one. "I'm sorry...I don't have any with me."

Hal nodded.

Marvin was not quite satisfied with Hal's reaction. He had anticipated milking a little more contrition from him. "But what are you going to do about Mari?"

"About who? Mari? I don't know a Mari."

***

The drive from Beverly Hills to Silverlake is long and complicated. Nothing in either area is "freeway close" with short distances to on and off ramps. The busy thoroughfares with interminable stoplights gave Hal the dose of reality he needed without the gross barbarity and cruelty he just endured. But as soon as he was on the freeway, he began to piece together the puzzle in a way that created an excuse, an out for Mari, but the opposite result kept occurring as his mind combed through the past. Nothing added up in her favor. *How did she find out that I was rich...that I was worth pursuing? I have kept that a secret from everybody...not even Vee knows. She's a research analyst...that is what she does for a living...asshole...find out things. That's why she brought that Mitchem project to me.* His heart wrenched with the realization. *And that..."don't look at my picture" bit...knowing goddamned good and well that I would and fall for what I saw. You poor stupid bastard...she had you eating out of her hand every inch of the way. Was it dumb fate that Zack beat her up...or was that planned...was he in on it? Where are her fucking degrees? Hey, I can believe that she got a degree in fucking...summa cum laude! She put herself right into my bed!* He mimicked her out loud. "Did I do it right?" Tears streamed down his cheeks. "Yeah...like you did a hundred other guys!"

Gradually his grief turned to anger and from anger to venom. *So I'm a "mark" and that's all I was to her. You have a surprise coming, Mari. I found you out!*

***

It was four o'clock by the time he arrived home. The table was in the living room with a note from Mari on it:

Sweet Dick,
Had to run out to the store. I will be back in a jiffy. There's a platter of fruit and cheese in the fridge to nibble on if you're hungry.
Love ya,
M.

He laid the file down over it.

Going into the kitchen, he found a Pyrex baking dish with halved Cornish game hens seasoned with Herbs de Provence and patted with butter waiting to go into the oven. There was a dull thud in his chest as he ached to share "table night" with her again. The idea of fucking her one last time, before finishing it with her, scurried through his mind, but he knew that if he did, he couldn't go through with what he had to do.

The sound of Mari's car pulling up to the curb brought him over to the living room window. He could see her emerge from the car with her silly, floppy petal hat on and her masses of curls flowing underneath. The pea jacket she wore with jeans and high-heeled boots showed off her legs and behind to an enchanting advantage. His breath came in quick, shallow gasps at the painful thought of parting with her. He watched as she lifted the wheeled cart filled with groceries out of the car, turned and struggled to get it up the steps, and then pulled it inside the outer door. Standing in flinty silence he heard the key turn in the door and saw her face brighten when she opened it. "Oh, good...you're home..." Lightly bussing him on the lips, she took off her jacket, and then rolled her cart to the kitchen. She called out as she offloaded the groceries. "...how did it go with your parents? Were you able to fix whatever their problem was?"

"Yes...it went fine."

She turned on the oven and slipped the game hens into it. "I was worried. I thought it was going to be another brouhaha." She appeared at the door smiling. "I'm making something different for you...I hope you like it."

Unsmiling, he beckoned to her. "Come here." Shaking, he took her in his arms and kissed her and ran his hands over the body he loved. She only took a fleeting moment to wonder why he was overcome with emotion before she was lost in the heat of his kiss. With trembling fingers, he lifted her sweater to stroke her breasts and then unfastened her jeans to slide his hand down her flat stomach to caress her mons veneris. Reaching around her, he rubbed her butt and gave it a firm squeeze. Holding her close, as he cradled her in his arms, he whispered in her ear, "Goodbye."

Her eyes were wide with confusion. "Goodbye? Where are you going?"

"Not me...you." He said quietly. He fastened her jeans and lowered her sweater. "Put on your coat and get your purse...I'm taking you somewhere."

"Oh." She bit her lip. "Should I turn off the oven?"

"Yes."

As she prepared to leave, she cautioned him. "I hope this doesn't take too long or dinner will be ruined."

"Don't worry about dinner...it will be just fine." He helped her with her jacket.

Once outside he took her arm and marched her quickly down the street toward the park around the reservoir. "Hal...slow down. I can't walk that fast..." He slowed to cross the street but grabbed her arm and picked up the pace again once they were in the park. "Hal...what's wrong with you? You're hurting me...I can't walk this fast!" He kept her on her feet as she stumbled along.

As the sun was going down, the park became deserted and Hal found a secluded spot to confront her. "Mari...it's over!"

"What?"

"We're over...done. How long did you think you could play me? Why did you ever pick me to be your mark?" His voice cracked. "Why did you ever make me love you...you heartless bitch!?!"

"What are you talking about? I don't understand!" Astonishment and fear came into her eyes. "How can you look at me like that...with such *contempt?*"

"Contempt is the least of what I feel for you!" He paced in front of her. "Everything, everything you said was a lie...everything you did was a lie!" He mimicked her, "...don't look at my picture...did I do it right..." He laughed. "...where did you get that one from? Worst of all you made me believe that you loved me! Just when did you find out I was rich and make up your mind that I would be an easy mark?"

"Hal I *do* love you...what is it that I did wrong? Why are you doing this to me? You're making a mockery of all the things we shared together!" she burst into tears. "Please...I beg you...don't do this to me. You're killing me!"

"Killing you? You can thank your lucky stars that I am not that kind of guy...because right now I could strangle you...you fucking bitch." He growled.

"No...no...you can't mean that! What have I done?" Holding her hands in supplication she went to him and then reached out to touch him.

He grabbed both of her wrists and held them in his grasp. "I told you I was only going to ask you *one* time if there was anything in your past. I guess it slipped your mind that you were...excuse me...*are* an alley cat!"

"Alley cat!" She twisted away from him.

"Or I guess you consider yourself a high-class feline that feeds on men's souls while you drain their bank accounts!"

"I never drained anything...I always worked..."

"Oh...you worked alright...and now I know your profession."

Pointing her finger in the direction of the apartment, her voice shook. 'What was that back there? Why did you hold me and kiss me...as though I meant something to you...and then say goodbye?"

A flicker of vulnerability passed behind his eyes. "I knew it would be the last time I would ever touch you..."

"And what about me...did I get to touch you knowing it would be the last time...before you turned into this *monster!?!* I TRUSTED YOU!

I LOVED YOU! God save me I still love you! What am I supposed to do with that?" Tears streamed. "Please, Hal just tell me what it is you want me to do…I'll do anything! I thought we were happy…weren't you happy? Did you ever really love me?"

"You have a nerve talking about love to me. That was just your goods in trade. There's nothing more, Mari…I mean it when I say it's *over!*"

The realization that this was his father's doing swept over her. "This isn't you talking! This is your father! What did he do to turn you against me…threaten to cut you out of his will again? It's all about money with you rich pricks! How much is enough, Hal? I didn't ask for your money…I didn't want any part of your money! All I wanted was you!" She stomped her foot and waved her hands. "And now you want to accuse me of doing something I never did. Is this the excuse you're making up…to sell me out…for what? What is your father offering you this time?"

"Brava…brava…what a tremendous little actress you are! Don't pretend that you weren't bought and sold a long time ago. The worst thing is that you did it to yourself! You really could have been something, Mari…instead of the backstabbing little whore that you are."

"I *am* something…I am educated, and I have a good job…"

That is a 'no' and a 'no' on both fronts, baby! I checked Personnel for your degrees…and somehow they were never verified…the notes just magically disappeared…"

"That's a lie!"

"As far as that good job goes…forget it! The most I will do for you is to verify that you worked for Angel City and two weeks' severance pay…but you will get no recommendation from me."

"Hal…please, please, PLEASE, don't do this to me…don't do this to us!" She started sobbing. "Whatever you are thinking…I promise you it's not true…it's all a lie. What can I do to prove it to you? Please…oh dear God, please…just give me the time to find out what happened…just a few days…that's all I ask."

"Mari…I am done. You can come back to the house one time to move out your things…"

"Nooooo…don't say that!" She cried.

His heart was hardened, and he was adamant. "Mari...I want you out of my *house*...and out of my *life!*"

"You're just going to leave me here?"

He shrugged. "Yeah. You're back in the street...a whore's commonplace hunting ground...you should do just fine." He turned his back on her and walked away, leaving her under darkening skies.

***

ALONE – SHE'S GONE

Still incensed with the outrage of a man taken in by deception, Hal strode away and briefly glimpsed Mari, with her hands covering her face, visibly weeping. Within the few minutes it took Hal to walk home from Silverlake Park, the sun had gone down and when he entered his house it was dark, cheerless, and quiet. No sound or delicious aromas emanated from the kitchen. No one was there with a smile or affection for him. The table that was the symbol of a scrumptious evening of food, fun, and sex, sat forlorn and out of place in the living room, as though oppressed by the file that lay upon it. Looking around, his utter loneliness came flooding in, astounding him.

He thought of Mari, left standing there in the park. *She looked so small in the middle of that wide expanse. What will she do and where will she go?* He looked out the window and saw that her car was still parked out front. *She shouldn't be in the park at this hour by herself. She deserved everything I said and more.* He tried to rationalize what he did to mollify his heart. *You can't leave her out there in the cold and dark! What were you thinking? Why hasn't she gotten into her car...drive to a friend's place...or get a room?* He knew he should go back to get her, but he resisted the urge to protect her. *The next thing you know she'll be back in my house...and with a short skip and a hop...back in my bed.* A wry smirk crossed his face as he tried to justify to himself a reason to take her in. *She did ask me for a few days. What good did she think that would do? You can't eradicate official records. Perhaps she thought she could worm her way back into my heart, given a few days. Goddamn it...she probably could.* He looked out the window again. *Look, asshole...you can't leave her out there. Go get her and make some decent arrangements for her until she can move into her own place.* He went back to the park to find her.

Starting where he left her, he searched the park to no avail. He took out his phone and called her. "Mari...it's me...pick up. Come on...pick up. I just want to take you in until we can get you settled. It's not safe for you out here."

Walking the jogging path, he hailed an approaching runner. "Have you seen a girl in a floppy hat with long blonde hair?"

"Yeah...about..." He jogged in place and looked at his watch. "...thirty-five minutes ago. She looked like she was crying. I started to ask why...but...you know...I didn't want to get involved."

"Where did you see her?"

"Farther down the path at the start of my run...I am just about at the end if you want to follow me."

Hating him for being so goddamned healthy, Hal jogged alongside him, refusing to lag behind. "How much farther?"

"See...straight ahead. She's not there...she must have left already. It's certain she didn't come this way. If I were you, I would keep on going in that direction."

"Thanks, pal...I'll do just that." He took out his phone again, punched up her number, and continued down the path. He heard it ringing several times, but it wasn't just over the phone; he thought he could hear Mari's ring tone. He hung up and called again, following the sound as it became louder. When he was sure he was right on top of it, he searched the area and saw the light flashing. The phone was on the ground beside the park bench. Picking it up, fear stabbed at his stomach. "Mari! Mari! Where are you?" He called out. Searching the entire park, he came up empty.

He went back home and got his car to cruise the entire neighborhood. She was not to be found. Retracing the area, he widened his search and found himself praying that he could find her. *Maybe she went back to our place..."our place"...as if you can still call it that. Perhaps she came back for her car.* He circled back to his apartment. Her car was still there. Parking, he went inside. There was no hint that she had returned. He went back to his car to drive around once more. Discouraged, he went home. As he turned into his driveway, he told himself, *she probably found some guy to help her out. She's resourceful...she will be just fine.* Somehow, that did not allay the panic that he felt, or the guilt.

Physically and emotionally exhausted, he realized that he had not eaten since morning. Opening the refrigerator, he found the fruit and cheese plate Mari had prepared for him. He took it out and stared at it. As usual, the fruit was arranged in a colorful pattern with melon slices cut into bite sized pieces surrounding a round of brie cheese. Blueberries were artfully scattered to please the eye as well as the palate and fresh pineapple triangles lined each side of the plate. A knot in his stomach rebounded and then pushed up through his chest as he let out an animal cry of grief.

Returning the plate to the refrigerator, he searched the cupboard for the bourbon he stored there, poured a slug, and went into the living room. Sitting down at the table that once represented joy; he tossed back the whisky in one shot and stared at the file wondering if he had just traded off his world of happiness for a goddamned police file. Instinctively, he knew the answer and he laid his head down on his folded arms and cried.

A decision, once made, necessitates justification, a confirmation of one's righteousness. The evidence of Mari's duplicity only existed in her police record, not in the life Hal shared with her. Yet he clung to the notion that his course of conduct was unassailable, regrettable as it may have been. He dragged himself to bed, knowing he had done the right thing.

***

Mid-morning light streamed brightly through Hal's bedroom window. Semi-somnolent, he did not find Mari snuggled under his arm as usual, so he turned over to spoon her sweet little butt. Finding her side of the bed empty, he smiled knowing that she had gotten up early to fix a "special" Sunday morning breakfast, as she would say. Missing was the aroma of freshly brewed coffee, the warm scent of baking biscuits, and the endearing clatter of dishes as she hummed her silly tunes. Realizing he was still fully clothed, he sat straight up with a start as everything came back to him. She was gone!

Jumping out of bed, he ran to the front window and, with growing dread, he saw her car had not moved. Taking out the telephone directory, he started looking up hospitals. *Don't be ridiculous...she's not in the hospital...she would have called...wouldn't she?* He went to the kitchen and took down a box of cornflakes, Mari's symbol of domestic displeasure, and dumped them in a bowl. As a rite of penitence, he ate them for breakfast.

Checking the car every half-hour, he staked it out from his living room. Trying to bolster his confidence, he turned on the TV and started watching the Miami Dolphins and San Diego Chargers game. *If she hears the television she will know I am home and knock on the door.* Remembering the things he said to her he got up and turned the set off. *If she knows I am home she will stay away from*

277

my door...that was the only choice I gave her. With shadows lengthening into late afternoon, he fortified himself with a re-read of her police record and a whisky. As night fell, he agonized; staring out at the damnable car he whispered, "Mari...where are you?"

***

Sitting in his office Hal picked up the phone and rang Mari's desk. She didn't pick up. After several tries, he rightly assumed that she was angry with him, but he dared not risk a scene by going to her cubicle. He decided to ring Cora. "Cora...Hal here. Have you seen Mari?"

"No...she hasn't come in."

He covered himself quickly. "Oh...that's right. I forgot I sent her to the library to search through the L.A. Times Archives. That's going to take a while. Sorry to bother you."

As Cora hung up, she wandered over to the next cubicle and leaned inside. "I think Mari and Hal are fighting again..." She snickered. "...he doesn't know where she is."

Steamed at himself for not having handled the situation better, it occurred to him that he had been bent on inflicting as much pain on Mari as he had felt at the devastating news. He should have waited until he calmed down, or given her the days she asked for, but his ripping the Band-Aid approach, quickly and decisively, was certainly effective in ending the relationship. But he still felt like a bastard.

He picked up the phone again and dialed Deuce. "Say hey...it's me. By any chance, has Mari called you?"

"What have you done now?" Deuce sounded impatient.

"We...we broke up...but I'm worried about her...I don't know where she is."

"Aw, Jesus Christ, Hal. I just caught my boy with marijuana. I've got to handle one child at a time. I'll see you tonight..."

"Can you come by my place?"

"Yeah...yeah...I'll see you around eight..."

"Thanks, man."

***

"What's this nonsense about you and Mari breaking up!?!" Deuce was annoyed as Hal opened the door. "Let's go to the garage, man...'cause this thing is going to get loud!"

278

Hal grabbed the file from the table and followed Deuce down the hall. "It wasn't my fault this time."

"We'll see about that! What's that funny smell?"

"What smell?"

"Shit if I know." They went out the back door and into the garage. Hal grabbed a couple of beers from the garage refrigerator and they both pulled up stools to the workbench. Hal slapped the file in front of Deuce. "What's this?"

"Mari's rap sheet. Read it all and then we will talk."

Deuce opened the file and his eyes widened as he was confronted with a mug shot of Mari and her arrest record. As he read it in minute detail, it elicited an "umm-umm" from time to time and an "aw, shit" as he came to the end and closed it. He didn't say a word but stared off into space thinking. Pointing at the file, he started to say something, but paused and thought again before saying, "What did you do when you read this?"

"I took her out of my house...down to the park...and told her it was over. Then I left her there."

"You did what? Why do I get the feeling it was a hell of a lot uglier than that?"

Hal looked down. "Because it was..."

"You tell me everything you said...and don't you leave nothin' out."

Hal confessed everything and, with Deuce being the only man to see his tears, he wept openly. At the end he shook his head, "Don't you see...I had no choice. I couldn't marry a woman who just saw me as a 'mark'...a meal ticket...her road to riches."

"Why not?"

"What?"

"Why not? That's how Wanda sees me. At some point in a marriage...when the bloom of love has faded and practicality kicks in...lots of women stay in a marriage as a means to an end for both them and their children." Deuce eyed Hal. "From what I could see you got the better end of that bargain. But, as usual...you fucked up!" He stared off into space.

"Fucked up...by not giving my life to a floozy?"

"She was no floozy. That girl loved you! I'd bet my life on it more than I would what's in that police record. Hal, even if she did everything her rap sheet said she did...can't you understand desperation? She came here at sixteen with nothing...and there are people in this town who would take advantage of that...teach her the ropes and turn her out." His eyes moistened.

"She could have gone back to Minnesota rather than take up a life like that."

"No..."

"She didn't have to become a whore."

"No..."

"What do you mean 'no'?"

Deuce took a huge breath, got up, and paced. He pointed at Hal. "Brother...buckle up...because I am about to tell you about yourself!" Deuce looked around and held out his hands to indicate the area where Hal lived. "You come into this neighborhood and you think you are living like the average Joe. You pat yourself on the back that you can make it without your folks' money. I'm not saying that I don't have respect for what you're doing...because I do...but you have NO idea what it is like to be the average Joe in that you have NEVER HAD TO RISK FAILURE! If things didn't work out for you...all you had to do was pack up and go home. Well for most of us average Joes and Janes...there is NO HOME TO GO BACK TO! Do you think my moms planned to be a maid and had a safety net when my father was killed in Vietnam? Before your family hired her and made accommodations for me...times was hard...and I'm not entirely sure she didn't go the same route as Mari! And if she did...God bless her for it! Do you think I had a safety net once I set out on my own? I was scared for most of those early years that I could fall short of providing for my wife and kid. If I got sick or lost my job...what would I do? And before you say...I could have come to you...how many people have rich friends that can carry them...and how many people would want that charity? I started moonlighting because I couldn't make my income stretch...and it turned out well for me as the start of my business. But, most people live in daily fear that they will slip through the cracks and not be able to provide for their families. Everything you have was handed to you...your home...your education...and through your education...your job. You had choices, man...you never had to worry about compromising your values...for food...for the basics of life. Now you tell me...what choices were handed to Mari?"

"She had a home to go to..."

Deuce's face twisted. "NO! NO SHE DIDN'T!"

"What do you mean?"

Deuce looked down and he spoke in a whisper. "She made me promise not to tell you. You both were so happy, and she didn't want to ruin it for you. She said she would tell you one day...but her brother..." Deuce choked out the words. "...her brother raped her...Yahn...or something like that. He trapped her in the barn...she didn't even know what was happening to her. All she knew was fear and the blinding, unbearable pain...she tried to fight him, but he was two years older than she was and much stronger...and it didn't end there until her oldest brother caught him in the act and pulled him off of her...and beat the dog-shit out of him. When her parents found out, all her mother did was to put her on the pill and blame her for seducing him...she was only a kid...she didn't know nothin' about seduction. Her father horse whipped him...and insisted that she watch...but that was just as horrifying for her. She took to hiding whenever she was alone. This Yahn attempted to rape another girl and was sent up for it. He was about to be released so her oldest brother sent her away." Deuce leveled his stare at Hal. "So, no...she could not go home."

"Goddamn!" Hal's stomach turned and he felt like the air had been knocked out of his chest. "That's what Lars meant when he talked about John. That's why she didn't tell me...she knew I would have killed him. Someone saved me the trouble...he's dead now...killed in prison before he was released. I guess she figured there was no point in telling me after she learned he was dead."

"Hal, kids run to L.A., from all over the country, every day...trying to escape bad situations at home...not to become movie stars. She told me that when she found you...for the first time in her life...she was happy...really happy. She more than loved you...she reveled in you, man...she reveled in you...and nobody can tell me any different."

"But, what about the file?" Hal was losing his grip on his perceived rectitude.

"I don't see it. I know what it says...but something's not right. When could she do all that? She was working and going to school...when did she get the time to do all that?"

"I checked her personnel file...they either couldn't or didn't verify her degrees."

"That doesn't ring true...there must be some mistake. She told me that while in college she had an affair with one of her professors. It was the first time that she learned that sex could be enjoyable. It ended when she found out that he had lied to her...he was married. That doesn't sound made up to me." Deuce scratched his head and shook it. "I'm not buying it, man...I'm not buying it. There is too much stuff that doesn't add up."

"I don't know how you can refute what is right there in black and white."

"Have you ever heard the term 'fitted up'?"

"No."

"It means like a frame up...when the evidence is made up to 'fit' a crime. I know you don't want to hear this...but, I think she is being fitted up...and if I'm right...you screwed up bad. I don't say I know how...but I am going to make it my business to find out. She is not what's in that file! You should have given her those days...and you are pretty much a shit for how you treated that little girl. I don't care how much your feelings were hurt...she didn't deserve that!" Deuce wiped his face. "You know...when she thought it was you who was killed in that car bombing...all she could say was she wanted to die...she would take her life." He paused. "Aw, shit, man...you can't find her anywhere?" His voice shook.

Suddenly getting his meaning, Hal looked alarmed. "You don't think..."

"I don't know!"

"We gotta find her!"

***

The next two days were spent covering a list of places to check. They started with her cell phone. There were only five numbers stored there, Hal's, Deuces', Lo-Lo's, Steven's, and Vivian's. Lo-Lo's phone was on voice mail. They did not leave a message. Steven's voice mail message had the lisping voice of Brian. "We've gone to Key West for the Christmas Holidays...so to all you bitches...eat your heart out. We have a big brute house sitting for us...I don't know if that is a warning or an invitation! Leave your message after the beep. Toodles!"

"Who the hell is that?" Deuce scoffed.

"Brian. He's really a lovely guy..." Hal shrugged.

Next they called all of the hospitals in the area, with no results. Hal balked when Deuce suggested trying the morgue. "I can't...I just can't..."

"You know it's a possibility..."

"I would rather not know..."

"You would leave her there?"

Hal clasped his hands in front of him and shook his head. "I can't...not now."

Deuce rubbed his forehead. "I'll look into it for you."

They spent the rest of the time racking their brains for any possibility. Deuce allowed, "I think that Lo-Lo has an idea where she is. I will follow up on that lead."

"I just remembered. She is scheduled to testify at the Mitchem trial next week...so am I. She's under subpoena...so she has to be there. I want to find her before that...just to make sure she's OK...but I'm sure I'll see her at court."

"You could have saved us a lot of trouble by just being a gentleman when you broke up." Deuce glared at him. "I'm not letting you off the hook for that! You could have spared her a few days."

"No I couldn't..." Hal's voice trembled. "If I did that...I could never have let her go..."

"Goddamn it...what's wrong with you? You know...before now I wasn't quite sure...but for the first time I am really certain that you did not kill Zack! A man don't kill for a woman and then just let her go!"

"I told you I didn't kill him..."

"I know what you said..."

"You actually thought I killed that guy and you're still my brother...who are you...Al Cowlings? Man...that makes you friend of the year...decade!" Hal was incredulous.

Deuce shrugged. "Some people have done worse."

Hal was beginning to regret more than just how he had handled things. "Deuce...do you really think there's a chance I was wrong?"

"More than a chance. No matter if you find her or not...or she takes your dumb ass back or not...one way or another, I'm going to prove it to you." Deuce sniffed the air. "What is that smell? You got mice problems or something?"

"No." Hal sniffed. "There is something that smells pretty gross, alright. What the fuck can it be?" He got up and followed the scent. It took him to the kitchen where the odor was stronger. "It's coming from here somewhere." They both looked around. "Is it your refrigerator drip pan...sometimes they get a bit foul?"

"No...I'm sure it's not that. Mari is pretty religious about keeping the refrigerator clean."

Deuce gave him another accusatory look for putting her out. He checked the cupboards and found them in good order. "Damn...Mari was neat. I wish Wanda kept house this good...and she don't work!" Deuce opened the oven and jumped back. "Jesus Christ! What's that you got in there!?!" The stench was overpowering and almost caused him to wretch.

Hal saw the putrid Cornish game hens that Mari had put in the oven for 'table night' four days ago. Holding a dishtowel over his nose he took them and ran out of the house to the trash can. He lifted the lid and threw them into the trash, dish and all. He stared after them and, somehow, he thought it was the perfect metaphor for what he had done. He took the beautiful things Mari did and turned them into garbage. He slammed the lid down.

***

The Criminal Courthouse had TV news vans and a gauntlet of reporters to run to gain entrance. Once inside, Hal went into the courtroom to let the defense attorney know he was there. He was asked to wait in the hallway until he was called. He took a seat on a bench in the hall and looked around. The other witnesses there looked his way and he nodded to acknowledge them, but he knew he was not to talk to them. His eyes swept the hall for Mari, but she had yet to appear. Clutching his briefcase, he stared off into space while his thoughts ran rampant.

He already had a tough morning and was emotionally overwrought. While dressing for court, he felt something in his pocket. He pulled out a crumpled piece of paper and Mari's panties. It was the poem he had written for her and her panties still held the scent of her perfume. He couldn't keep it together. He decided when he saw her at the courthouse today; he would beg her to come home. He no longer cared about her rap sheet or anything she had done in the past. He wanted her and their dream for a family back; nothing else mattered. Then he was called into the courtroom.

He was kept on the stand for three hours answering questions about how he and Mari determined that the evidence against Mitchem was in error and to explain the methods by which they checked the time frame. He made a special effort to hold the prosecution blameless for what he characterized as "human error" in calculating the chronology of Mitchem's activities in conjunction with the time of the crime. Taking his notes from his briefcase, he authenticated them to have them entered into evidence and then went on to testify how other activities around the witnesses that day confirmed their testimony as to the time of day they saw Mitchem. They verified that the delivery schedule of a Brinks truck, the train blocking the street as they delivered a boxcar, an ambulance call, and more, coincided with the times recalled by witnesses. When he was through, the court adjourned for lunch.

Out in the hallway again, he approached the defense attorney who shook his hand. "You did an excellent job on the stand. I can't thank you and Miss Carlson enough..."

"Miss Carlson? She's here? I didn't see her."

"Oh...she testified yesterday. She called my office to ask if she could be put on the stand yesterday. It presented no problem, so I rescheduled her. She was one of my best witnesses...and she knew how to dress for court to impress the jury...no makeup...her hair in a braided bun...and a demure suit with pearl earrings...she wowed them!"

"Yes...she is impressive."

"You know...I couldn't help noticing how very attractive she is even without makeup. Most women would die for a face like that! It makes you wonder why no man has snapped her up."

"I thought she was engaged."

"I didn't see a ring...not that I was looking or anything like that...I just found it curious." He held out his hand again. "Got to get going if I hope to have lunch. Drop by my office anytime and we'll have a drink." He shook Hal's hand once more and strode down the hall.

He had taken the shuttle bus to the courthouse but decided to walk back to Angel City's headquarters. Pulling out his cell phone, he called Deuce. "We can stop worrying about Mari...she is doing just fine. She testified in court yesterday."

"I'll drop by your house tonight...I want to go over some things with you."

"Sure...bring something for dinner. I'm a lousy cook."

His missed opportunity to talk to Mari ate at him. The police record meant less and less as it faded into the background. He needed her and he ached to see her. His presence on the street barely elicited a ripple of notice and his mind climbed higher in the sky to see himself as just one person out of the millions in Los Angeles, and higher still to see himself as a dust particle on the planet, insignificant and inconsequential except to the one person who saw him as her only delight. Thinking of how she would serve his food and then kiss and caress him as though he was something special for just sitting there, mortified him. Trying to vindicate his belief in the accuracy of her file, in order to overrule his doubts, he turned into the Salter Building and took the elevator to Angel City's offices.

As he stepped out of the elevator, he was assailed by Penny from Personnel. "Mr. Golan...Mr. Golan..." She waved a manila envelope at him. "I found Miss Carlson's papers...I hope it is not too late for her to get the assignment."

"Please come with me to my office." Hal walked ahead of her, dreading what he thought was in the envelope. Settling into his office, he sat at his desk. "What do we have here?" He said with a coolness that belied his heart.

"She gave me her degrees and grades...that is why I didn't need to verify them. I don't know how I did this...but I stuck her papers into my desk and forgot to return them to her. It must have been when I was going on vacation...and when I got back, I had forgotten all about them. I hope I didn't ruin her chances. When you see her, will you give them back to her for me...with my sincerest apologies."

"Well...as a matter of fact, she didn't get the assignment...I gave it to someone else. It would have meant a possible promotion for her...a difference in pay...but the other person was already in that position and eminently qualified. C'est la vie!" Hal couldn't resist twisting the knife in the stupid cow. *How could she be so cavalier with other people's important documents?* He took the envelope. "I'll give it to her as soon as I see her."

286

Closing the door behind Penny, he sat at his desk, opened the envelope, and slid out the diplomas and copies of her semester grades. It was all just as she said, but better. Her grade point average was higher than his and so was one of her degrees. There was something else stuck in the envelope that he shook out. It was her student ID card. He gazed at the picture of the young, unsophisticated girl in the picture and knew in his gut that her arrest record was fitted up.

***

The day had been long, and the traffic had made it even longer. Hal felt drained and wondered if he could even withstand Deuce's company tonight. But it was already arranged, and it wasn't as though he didn't have new information to share. He drove up Glendale Boulevard and stopped off at a market for a case of beer. Back on the road again, he never felt so sure that Deuce was right all along. Mari had the integrity to care about her court date when she could have half-assed it or begged off and just relied on his testimony to free Mitchem. He brooded, *she could have seen me...what difference would it have made to her if I was there?* Pulling into his driveway, he parked in the garage, and offloaded the beer into the fridge. Grabbing his briefcase off the passenger seat, he went through the backdoor into his apartment.

Once inside his eyes narrowed as he thought he could smell the light scent of plumerias. He called out. "Mari...Mari...Babe are you there?" He walked briskly into the living room and the heady scent was more pronounced. He looked around, but no one was there. Then his eyes landed on the table. Like a little shrine to the end of their betrothal, a neat stack of her jewelry box, keys, parking pass, computer, and an envelope, stood in the center of the table. She had been there on the very day when she knew he would be gone to testify. He ran to what was once her room and found her bedroom furniture and her clothes gone. The kitchen only held his meager utensils. The bathroom was devoid of her toiletries. He stumbled back into the living room and let out an anguished cry; his knees buckled, and he fell to the floor. He laid there as the darkness covered him creating a void where his mind could reject what it could not acknowledge. She had taken him at his word. It was irretrievably over.

287

A knock at the door roused him. Dragging himself up, he opened it to find Deuce there with a bag of KFC. "What you doin' in the dark? Turn some lights on so I can see."

Hal turned on the living room lights. "She was here. She picked the day when she knew I had to testify to get her stuff. All that is left of her is on that table." He gestured to the small stack of personal effects.

Deuce knew that this was going to be a long night of getting Hal's emotional state into a better place. The assorted articles looked as though Hal had not touched them. It was going to be grief city going through them with him. "Aw, shit. I was hoping you could talk to her. Let's go out to the garage and eat...we can come back to this later."

Hal nodded, grabbed his briefcase, and then followed Deuce out the back door and into the garage. Deuce was already setting out their boxed dinners, a bucket of extra chicken pieces and sides, as Hal put the briefcase on the bench. Augmenting the meal with a couple of beers, the two men sat down to eat. "What's in the briefcase?" Deuce asked with his mouth full.

"Mari's degrees. The old biddy in Personnel lost them and she just now found them. FUCK ME! I'll show them to you later. Her student ID is in there and as I looked at her picture from back then...there is no way she was the whore that the police records depict. You were right...there is something very wrong here...but I have yet to figure it out."

Deuce's sorrow for his friend grew. "We'll work this thing together...and get to the bottom of it. Right now...put it out of your mind and get some food into you."

They ate in silence, each knowing that when they did broach the subject, the heartache would be unbearable and lasting. When they finished their meal, they stalled over another beer. Deuce drained the last of his bottle and then spoke quietly. "Did you actually love her...or was your ego pumped by the fact that such a beautiful woman was in love with you?"

"How can you ask me that?"

"It just seems to me that there were so many times that you acted like a dipshit towards her like you wanted to alienate her. I just want to know...if you really love her before I bust my ass trying to clear her name. If you don't love her...why should I bother?"

"I can't tell you how deeply I love her. Right now, everything in my very soul is crying for her. When I find out what is going on...if she was fitted up...all hell is going to break loose!"

"Alright...show me those degrees and stuff." Hal took out the documents and showed them to Deuce. "Damn...she's smarter than the both of us put together."

"She's a crackerjack alright. Her work was excellent."

"Look...I have some ideas. I have yet to contact Lo-Lo and I was hoping Mari had an address book with her address in it...but that is not an option now. We only have the cell phone. The other thing is...Big has contacts in the police department and the district attorney's office. Perhaps we should take him the file and have him analyze it...check it out with some people in the know...and after we find out all there is behind this...then you can make an intelligent decision about what you want to do."

Hal agreed. "OK...where do we start?"

"I think we know where to start...and that is in your living room to see what she left you."

They cleaned up the workbench and carried the leftovers back into the house. Hal put his briefcase on his desk before turning his attention to what Mari had left on the forlorn little table. They both sat down. With a sinking heart Hal reached for the envelope. Opening it, he found Mari's engagement ring taped to the letter. His hands shook as he read:

My dearest Hal,

You will find on the table your house keys, the company car keys, and parking pass. I left you my computer because it has my notes on the Mitchem Project and other past and future projects and I hope you can put them to good use.

I have returned your jewelry and the rent money you put into my savings. I don't want to leave the impression that my motives for being with you were dishonorable. I could accept your gifts when I thought that you loved me, but I cannot accept them, in good conscience, knowing that you hate me.

With the greatest despair I return my engagement ring. I truly did love you and it will be some time, I know, before I can eradicate you from my heart. You made me believe in you and that all things were

possible in the beautiful dream you had for us. Now I am bereft of all happiness, confused, and dismayed. I do not know why you changed your heart or why you now hate me. I can only hope that you will learn someday that I have done nothing to harm you and that you will be able to remember me with fondness. Know that I love you still, but I will honor your wishes and seek a life without you.
Mari

When he was finished, he handed the letter to Deuce and then walked out into the kitchen. Deuce could hear the muffled sobs and it wrenched his heart. Reading the note, elegant and poignant in its brevity and simplicity, Deuce teared up.

***

"Penny...Mari quit. Here are her car keys and parking pass. I had the car parked in our area in the garage. I'll be packing up her things from her desk to take to her."

"Oh...my word..." Penny looked distressed. "...I hope she didn't quit because she didn't get that assignment."

"As a matter of fact...she did." Hal lied. He was not about to let Penny off the hook for being negligent with Mari's documents. It cost him an element of trust in Mari that did more damage than Penny would ever know. She was an easy target to share the blame, so he did not spare her.

Packing up Mari's cubicle was not an easy task. Under the glare of prying eyes, he filled a box with her personal belongings, finding pictures of himself flying a kite in Monterey, a posed portrait of him smiling, and a private one in her desk drawer of him sleeping. A plant had wilted and died in her absence. Tissues, a tube of lipstick, and a nail file completed her possessions. Along with the box, he transferred the files she was working on to his office. He stared at the desolate little stack in the corner of his office, all that was left of her existence there.

***

Big, or P.J. Biggerston as it read on his office door, was a senior partner at Biggerston, Bradley, and Cooper. After spending years as a prosecutor and witnessing the mishandling of the McMartin fiasco and the bungling of the Simpson case, he opened his own practice. Savvy to the games of both prosecutors and defense attorneys, he enjoyed a reputation in both factions as one to be reckoned with. As Hal and Deuce entered his office, Big's large brown eyes looked bigger than ever behind his horn-rimmed glasses. "Welcome...salutations...bienvenidos...wilkommen and bien venu..." He got up from behind his desk and guided his friends to the chairs in front of it. "I am so sorry...distressed...and perturbed that there was a bad turn of events for you and your lady. I hope I can render assistance...allay your grief...and be of some service."

Deuce looked around in amazement. "Damn...this is your office?!" He took in the baby grand piano in one corner, a giant screen TV, and a studio worthy sound system in another. West's California Reporter and Appellate Reports filled a bulwark of bookshelves. Wood paneling graced the walls, covered with degrees, certificates, and awards, and a Persian rug covered glistening hardwood floors. "What you doin' hangin' around Benny's? You can watch the game ten times better here."

"It reminds me of better times..."

"Better than this?!" Deuce found that incredible.

"All things are relative, my friend...besides, I would miss the atmosphere...the joviality...the camaraderie...the commonality...in other words...I would miss you guys." He sat behind his desk. "What can I do for you?"

"Three weeks ago, this file came into my hands and by every indication it is real. It is the rap sheet of the woman I'm in love with...and I broke off our engagement because of it. But now...I think there must be some mistake. I was wondering if you knew how to authenticate it...or find out if there is more to the story than just what is in that file. If what it says is true...and there is every reason to believe it is...were there extenuating circumstances for what she did." Hal handed the file to Big.

He opened the file and stared hard at the mug shot. Opening his desk drawer, he took out a magnifying glass and looked at it again.

"If I recall...you said your girl was petite...a shorty but well proportioned."

"Yes...I included a better picture of her so that you can see that she isn't the type of person she appears to be in the mug shot."

Big found the picture. "My God...this goddess fell in love with you?"

Hal shrugged. "So she said..."

Big picked up the magnifier once more and examined the mug shot. "How tall would you say your...what is her name?"

"Mari. She's this tall..." Hal stood up and held his hand at his upper chest level. "...but that's with high-heels. She always wore three-inch heels."

Big took out a tape measure, ran it out to Hal's hand, and marked down the result. "That would make her about five foot five with heels and five two without. Are you sure she was no taller?"

"Yeah...reasonably sure."

Big went back to his desk and held the magnifier. "Then this is not a picture of your Mari."

"What?"

"I want to check this file thoroughly...but I can tell you that there is something rotten in Denmark...definitely some sort of chicanery...flimflam...in other words bullshit!" He waved them over. "Come here and look at this mug shot. Look at the wall behind the girl where they have the measurements for height." He held the magnifying glass up to the picture. "How tall would you say that girl is?"

Hal and Deuce leaned over to look. Hal stood back. "How can that be? It shows her to be five seven to five eight."

"It's not her..." Big said with some authority. "This picture appears to be photoshopped."

"Photo what?"

"Photo-shopped...done with a computer...phonied up...Oswald with the rifle...a fake."

Hal closed his eyes and almost swooned. Both relief and grief swept over him. "It's not her...dear God...it's not her?" Still unsure, he took his seat. "What about the rest of the file?"

"I'll have the goods on that in a jiffy." Big picked up the phone and punched in a number. "Say hey...this is Big, and I need a favor fast.

Can you run a make on a..." He looked at the file. "...Mari Carlson? The first name is spelled M-A-R-I the last name C-A-R-L-S-O-N. Yeah...that's right." He also rattled off the list of aliases. "How soon can you let me know? That's good! I owe you one." Big put down the receiver. "He will get back to me within the hour. Meanwhile, do you mind if I have my secretary copy this file so I can work on it? There is a lot more that needs to be checked."

"Sure...go right ahead...I want to know everything about it." Surprisingly, Hal's anger, that had overridden his other emotions, led him to become calculating, mentally thrashing for a strategy, a scheme, a plan of retribution. He needed more information to put together the full picture of the hoax that had been played on him so he could plot out what was to be done. He was fast slipping into vengeance mode.

They waited for the anticipated phone call as the secretary took the file. "Do you feel comfortable telling me the events surrounding this file? I don't intend to pry more than I need to in order to do as you ask...but it may be helpful for me to know the particulars..." Big held out his hands. "...or not."

Deuce looked at Hal before he took it upon himself to speak. He did a double take at the expression on Hal's face that said World War III was about to commence. He was relaxed and cool, now that he knew the real deal, that he had been duped and by whom. Deuce could practically hear the wheels and gears in Hal's head as he devised how those responsible were going to pay. "What do you say, Hal?"

"Sure...why not...Big may have some useful tips I can use." He looked at Big. "I only regret I didn't come to you in the first place. My father gave me the file. He had dug up some information on Mari before...that mostly turned out to be true...but nothing I couldn't live with. So, when he gave me this file...I had every reason to trust that it was authentic. Based on the file and the statement of some woman...I broke off my engagement...told her it was over...and now I don't even know where Mari is."

"Oh...Jesus!" Big looked away as if he had committed a similar transgression. "OK, son...some mistakes are monumental and can't be overcome...and this may be one of them." He held his finger in the air. "But...most are not...or they can be fixed...or at least partially abated. Break it all down for me and let's see what we can do."

While Hal was explaining his plight in detail, the phone rang. Big picked it up and after a short conversation he hung up. "She has no record."

The prickly truth clawed up Hal's back in a distinct, cold chill. He let out a wail. "Oh God...what have I done...what have I done!?!" He leaned forward in his seat with his head in his hands. His shoulders shook as sobs ripped through him.

Before the end of the day, Hal learned that the arresting officer listed on Mari's record never existed at Rampart Division. The statements of the men who had been swindled were regarding women who were currently incarcerated or did not fit Mari's description.

Each new revelation twisted Hal's gut. *Mari was innocent...she was perfectly innocent, and I crushed her! Even if I find her, she will never take me back.* He writhed within. *But I have to find her if for no other reason than to let her know that she was right...I am a monster for doing what I did to her...the words sorrow and regret are too shallow for what I feel. Self-hatred is more accurate.*

As Deuce left with Hal, on the elevator ride to the first floor, on the walk through the parking lot, and on the ride to Hal's place, all he could think of was *he jumped the gun. He should have talked to me...or ANY BODY ELSE before hurting that little girl like that!* He started to tell him what he thought but realized from the pure torment on Hal's face that he already knew. He started to tell Hal *if you had controlled that jealous nature of yours that kept telling you that there was no way she could love a guy like you for yourself...and just accepted it for what it was; you wouldn't be in this fix.* Deuce also surmised that Hal was finally on to himself. Deuce thought of suggesting *you should have known that a sweet girl like Mari...who went out of her way to please you...was so into you...who was so guileless...could never have been a con...you should have married her when I told you to and forget your parents and everyone else* but he was sure that thought was already hammering in Hal's head. Deuce just shook his head and they rode on in silence. After a while he asked Hal, "Are you alright?"

"No...no...I guess I'll never be 'alright' again. I feel so low...disgusted...and sick at heart...what I have is what your peeps call the blues...that ache that just kills you...goes right through you...and tears out your heart."

"Naw...what you have, man, is 'supersized blues' when things are so big, so bad, and so ugly you can't stand it."

"That's what I got, alright...that's what I got..."

When they arrived at Hal's apartment, Deuce stopped before going to his car. "Big has a detective on it...he's going to find her, and you'll get your chance to beg and plead...like every other fucking fool on earth. You're going to be alright." From the look on Hal's face he wasn't so sure. "You want me to stay? I can stay with you for a little while."

Hal gave a dry chuckle. "No. You've got enough children to look after."

Deuce gave him a bear hug and clapped him on the back. "Knight's honor...we're going to fix this."

"Deuce...one last thing. I don't want this to get out. I don't want my father to know that I am on to him. He never thought that I would have that file checked out...and he was right. If it wasn't for your intuition...I would have gone through the rest of my life believing it. Until I can come up with something...I want him in the dark about this."

Deuce nodded. "You got it. I'll keep it under wraps."

Hal went inside and was greeted by the bleakness of his apartment. He went to the kitchen, slapped some baloney between two pieces of bread, and washed it down with a bottle of beer. He thought of ordering a pizza, but he was more tired than hungry and decided to just turn in for the night. He ventured into his bedroom. After that first night without Mari, he had shied away from his bed, and had taken to sleeping on his couch; he had not changed the sheets, and the bed was only partially made up. He took his pillow and tossed it in the middle of the bed. Picking up Mari's pillow, he was startled by the sight of her nightgown under it, where she had always put her nighties. He gently lifted it to his face and smelled her scent. Smoothing it out on the bed, he lay down beside it and gently stroked the silken texture. "I'm so sorry...I'm so sorry..." He whispered repeatedly as the pain deep inside of him erupted.

Clasping the gown to his chest he wept uncontrollably until he fell asleep.

***

Weeks went by with no further progress on finding Mari. Hal's grief and anxiety kept him from concentrating on a viable plan of retribution. Learning life's lesson, he did not want to act in haste, but decided to take his time until he could work out an effective scheme in detail. Realizing that Marvin's only pride was Arendt Medical, Inc., the family's company, he wondered how he could make it Marvin's undoing without destroying the company his great-grandfather built. There was no point unless Marvin's fortune was devastated as well. How could he do that without decimating his mother's interests? Unable to come up with answers, he turned his mind to another problem, how to cook a meatloaf.

It was mid-March before Deuce was able to reach Lo-Lo on the phone. Her voice was impatient when she snatched up the receiver. "Who is this who keeps calling and then hanging up?"

Deuce was tentative. "My name is Terry...I'm a friend of Mari's. I need to talk to Miss Loretta Johnson."

"I'm Loretta Johnson. Why didn't you leave a message on voicemail? I always do a lightweight screening of my calls."

"What I needed to talk to you about was...too sensitive a message to leave on the phone. Mari is missing...and we are trying to find her. I would like to talk to you in person to see if you can help us."

"Oh...no! Mari is missing? Of course I'll help you. Where do you want me to meet you?"

"Do you know where Musso & Frank Grill is?"

"Yes."

"We can talk there. Would tomorrow around eleven in the morning be alright with you?"

"Yes...how will I know you?"

"Mari showed me your picture...I'll know you."

"I'll be there."

***

An ebony colored woman, exotic in her beauty and regal in her carriage, strode into Musso & Frank Grill. Her hair was a symphony of braids plaited close to her scalp up to a topknot and then cascading down in a multitude of thin, bead-studded plaits hanging to just below her shoulders. Pausing, she looked around with an imperious air as though trumpets should announce her presence. Deuce got up and went to her. "Miss Loretta...I recognized you from the picture Mari showed me. I am so pleased to meet you."

Her eyes took note of him as he greeted her. She held out her hand as though he should kiss it. "Terry." He took her hand with a slight bow and let it linger in his before he let go. Guiding her to the booth where Hal waited, Deuce was intrigued.

Rising as she approached, Hal thanked her for coming as he sat back down. "I really appreciate your seeing us."

She slid into the booth and Deuce sat beside her. "I'm doing this for Mari. I'm only here because Mari said that Terry was a friend and a great guy. What happened? Why is she missing?" Her voice was sultry and smooth as velvet.

"That's what we're trying to find out. So, you don't have any idea where she can be?" Hal's voice was gentle as he tried not to show his distress.

"No. I just came back from vacation. I took my son back east to the Smithsonian Museum over the holidays. I know she must have tried to get in touch with me." Her voice showed a slight tremor of emotion. "Now I wish I had been home."

"Do you know any of her friends...boyfriends...or people who know her?"

"Only what she told me. I am her best friend...I don't think she has any other female friends. Women did not cotton to her."

"What about men friends?"

"You know how she looked...men were always coming on to her, but she wouldn't have any of them. I think she only had about three serious boyfriends in her life...I told her she should step up her game."

"Her game?"

"Yeah...she should get out and meet somebody instead of always being so studious."

"Who were her boyfriends?"

"Her first was a lying bastard by the name of Montfort. He was her political science professor. She thought...I don't know what she thought because I suspected he was married all along...but she was

297

naïve about that sort of thing. She was hurt when she found out...but I got her through it."

"Yeah?"

"I thought her next boyfriend had potential...nice looking guy...great job...but he turned out to be a turd. He lost his job...stole from her...beat her up...but he died in an accident..." Hal made a mental note that Mari didn't tell Lo-Lo everything, or she wasn't talking.

"Then she met this guy that she was nuts over...and he wouldn't even give her a tumble. It sounds crazy...she was living in his home...he took care of her...and he never once made a play for her. She thought something was wrong with her. She kept asking me for advice on how to get his attention. I told her to do what she did best...dance. That didn't work either. Then one day, out of the blue, bingo! And she was over the moon. She was set to marry him this May. I was going to be her maid of honor. That's the last I heard...I don't know what happened after that."

"I don't mean to prod into a sensitive area of her life, or yours, and I am not judgmental, but we have it on good authority that the both of you worked at Stony Malone's Gentlemen's Club as dancers."

Lo-Lo gave both of them a haughty stare. "Yeah...we did...what of it?"

"Did Mari do anything there or meet anyone who may have..."

"What are you asking? Just because she worked in that club...in that environment...doesn't mean she was dipped in shit. Mari was a good girl...and everyone knew it. Even Malone treated her different from the rest of us. She did her silly little dance twice a night for three nights a week...the rest of the time she went to school. Malone saw to it that she was paid, and she made tips...that's all she did."

"What was this Malone to her?"

"Her boss...he owns the place. Because he treated her with deference...some of the girls gossiped about her...you know...the same old shit...she must be sleeping with him. But I know she wasn't...she would have told me. She was a good girl...she wanted to be something, and she succeeded. We were all proud of her."

"What did you do at the club?" Deuce asked.

She gave Deuce a level gaze. "You know...men look with contempt on women who work in those clubs...lap dancing and chippying on

298

the side. But the way I look at it is if men acted the way men are supposed to...the way it says in the Bible...and took care of their daughters and their women...women wouldn't be out there working in those clubs. Men are the ones who should be held in contempt! I was young and seduced by a man who said he loved me. I didn't know any better and I fell hard for him. He was a goddamned musician. I got pregnant and had his baby...and he got gone! I had a son to take care of...and no skills. So, I am proud to say that I danced the poles...I lap danced and...yes...I chipped. I now own a prestigious beauty salon, my son is in a private school, and his college tuition is prepaid. When it comes to whores in Hollywood...it is only a matter of degree. Some of the biggest stars...both men and women...whored their way to the top. I did the best I could with a bad situation...and the son of a bitch that dropped me in it...nobody is calling him names or looking down their nose at him. So...yes...I did all of the above. But my son is not in the street gangbanging...and the statute of limitations has wiped my slate clean."

"Understood...and no disrespect intended." Deuce doffed the brim of his hat to her.

"Is there anything you can think of...anything at all? If she was in trouble...who would she turn to?"

Lo-Lo sat thinking. "First she would turn to me...but I was gone. She may have turned to her friend Steven..."

"No...he was in Key West for the holidays."

"Then that leaves Malone. She would never abuse the privilege...but if she was really hard up...I think she would turn to him."

"Can you put us in touch with Malone?"

"Yeah...I can. But, he's one serious dude. You can't go to him with any bullshit. Whatever you got to say...you better say it like it is...say it fast...and get out. If he's not inclined to help you...he's not going to do it...and if you push him...he'll push back hard. But if he says he will help...you got a rock-solid deal."

"I'm a serious dude too. I'm the guy Mari was going to marry..."

"You?!" She looked askance at him and almost laughed. "What you got...a diamond on the end of your dick?"

Deuce couldn't help breaking up. "According to Mari...yes he does!"

"Look...everything you said about men...is true. I blame myself for Mari disappearing and I have to let her know it was all a mistake."

She eyed him with suspicion. "What's this shit?"

Deuce interceded. "It wasn't his fault. I'll explain everything later...he's really a good guy."

She seemed mollified. "OK. I'll put you in touch with Malone. You come by my shop tomorrow after ten..." She dug in her purse and pulled out her business card and handed it to Deuce. "...I'll see what I can do."

***

"Man...that Lo-Lo is somethin'!" Deuce and Hal were on their way to see Big. "Mari was right about her hair...that look on her...umm-umm-umm!"

"Deuce...you're married..."

"Just window shopping...not buying...but I can look and dream!"

"Yeah...it's that looking and dreaming that will get you into trouble. I'm not saying that she isn't righteous...but a woman like that eats men for breakfast. I can't say I blame her...but I wouldn't want you to be her 'happy meal'!"

"Shit...just kill all my wet dreams..."

When they arrived at Big's office the look on his face did not portend good news. Ray, the detective, had his report in hand and it was not the success they had hoped for. "Gentlemen have a seat. Ordinarily...in the usual course of events...we would have found Mari by now. We have tracked her only so far...and then reached a dead end."

"What do you have?" Hal leaned forward clasping his hands.

"We have a court record showing that she became an emancipated minor at sixteen...the petition showing the reason for the court's ruling is under seal. She attended Hollywood High and then went to USC. She worked for Mallown Enterprises, Ltd....which is a front for several businesses...one of which is Stony Malone's Gentlemen's Club where she worked during her high school and college years. Her next employment was with Angel City Magazine of which you are aware. She used her credit card in Culver City at a U-Haul facility...and a few days later in San Francisco. We have no address on her yet...we are checking local post offices, and the DMV, but people don't usually change their driver's license that quickly...it's probably because going to the DMV is such a nightmare...but we'll stay on top of that. The last employer we have is Yarborough Publishing in San Francisco. However, she no longer works there...and that is where the trail ends. This is unusual because she has not used her credit card and we find nothing else under her name. Now...this is typical for when a woman gets married...then we can ordinarily pick her up through her marriage license...if she got married in the area...or the name change on her Social or on her credit card. However, she did something strange. She cancelled her credit card and her Social is still in her maiden name. She's gone dark on us."

"You've lost her?"

"Only temporarily. The marriage license thing may not work out, because California has a 'confidential marriage' law where no one can access the record of the marriage except for the married couple...or she just may have gotten married in Vegas or Reno. We have someone checking that out. There are other things we can do but it will be costly. We can send someone to snoop around Yarborough Publishing...and ideally get employment there...and pick up on any gossip..."

"What makes you so sure that she got married? That doesn't make sense..."

"We're *not* sure. It is just an angle that we usually work for women whose names drop out of sight...and then they typically reappear as married. I know that isn't a particularly pleasant aspect for you...but we must not overlook it. The other aspects are not pleasant either...jail...asylums...morgues...and they are all being checked. But a person who is living a normal life ordinarily leaves a trail that can be followed. If she gets another job under her maiden name...or applies for credit...we will have her. But to go this long without a job...or credit...means that someone is supporting her."

"I'll pay whatever is necessary to find her. Get someone on the inside at Yarborough. Maybe they will have her address in personnel...if they can snoop around." Hal took out his checkbook and started writing. "This should be enough to get you started. Send me your bill as you go along."

***

The Fabulous Lo-Lo Salon offered full beauty and spa services to a mixed clientele. All races and all genders, real or imagined, were welcome. Customers sipped wine while waiting or sitting under driers. A small buffet of snacks offered canapés, cheese, cold cuts, assorted fruit, rolls, and crackers. Lo-Lo's high-end patrons included wives of captains of industry and more than a few entertainers of note. Deuce and Hal asked for Lo-Lo at the reception desk. Impeccably trained, the receptionist welcomed them effusively, offered them a glass of wine, and indicated that they may partake of the buffet while they waited. Duly impressed, they sat in an inconspicuous corner.

Lo-Lo came down to the reception area and greeted them as though they were old friends, taking their hands in hers and giving each one the Hollywood air kiss. "Hal...Terry...I am so glad you came to see me." She did this more for the spectators in the waiting room as a show of goodwill for all. Looking around to see if there was anyone else in reception that she recognized that needed glad-handing, and seeing none, she continued with Hal and Deuce. "Please come back to my parlor..."

Wide-eyed, Hal and Deuce followed her though the maze of beautician stations, manicure stands, driers, and sinks, all with customers in various stages of hair or nail procedures. Beyond the salon were the spas. She took them to a stairway near the back entrance that led to her private quarters. "Sometimes I am here so late that I stay the night...so I have a little place where I can be comfortable." She unlocked a door and took them into a small, well-appointed parlor; her office was in an adjacent room. A bathroom and small private room were behind another door. "Please sit down...would you like a glass of wine?"

"Nothing for me. I have a long day ahead." Deuce held up his hand.

Hal shook his head, "No thanks." Impressed with what he had seen, he added, "This is very nice...and I must compliment you on your beauty salon...you have quite a going concern."

She poured herself a modest glass of white wine. "I'll bet the first thing that came to your mind was how many men did I have to fuck to get this place...?"

"No...not at all..." Hal lied.

"Well the answer is just one. He was a sweet old guy who got me started...and then let me buy him out...he's dead now...but I still take

302

flowers to his grave. When I am hard on the male gender...I don't mean all men...just most."

"I used to think I was the exception to that rule...I don't anymore..." Hal gestured toward Deuce. "...but he is...the best guy I know." She looked up at Deuce with a new light in her eyes and Hal immediately regretted what he said and tried to ameliorate it. "He's a great husband and father."

Her eyes briefly swept over Deuce. "Is he? That's good to know."

Deuce changed the subject. "Yesterday I forgot to ask you...how did you meet Mari?"

She smiled. "That was bittersweet. We both worked as waitresses at a pancake house. Not much money there...the old people who go there don't know the fifteen percent tipping rule. Anyway, Mari avoided me like the plague...hardly said two words and never came near me. I paid her no mind. Then one day she accidently bumped into me and she looked at me with such fear, I thought she was afraid I was mad at her. I told her it was alright...but she took off back to her station...and I went to mine. A week later she came to me before our shift started. She practically had tears in her eyes. She apologized to me for avoiding me and she said the craziest thing. She told me that where she came from there were no black people at all...and her parents had always told her that if you touch a black person your skin would turn black...and she believed it. She had panicked when she bumped into me...and all that week she waited for her skin to turn black. When it didn't, she realized it was a stupid lie...and she wanted to apologize for being so unfriendly to me. I never heard such a thing in my life...but she was so sweet and so contrite...I hugged her and told her it was alright...we were good. She looked so relieved I had to laugh...and then we both laughed. After that, we became the best of friends."

Hal confirmed her estimation of Mari's family. "I met her family. With the exception of her oldest brother, they all belong in the loony bin. We ended up running for our lives because I'm Jewish."

"Yeah...she told me about that." She laughed. "You know...you never told me what happened between you two. I know for Mari to get upset enough to leave you...it had to be pretty big. What happened?"

As both men explained the circumstance of Mari's leaving, Lo-Lo's hard, defensive shell cracked. Gone was her haughty, defiant bearing, replaced by the tender understanding of a woman's heart. While she was angered by what Hal did, she could see the anguish in his eyes when he talked about his guilt compounded by shame, and what Mari meant to him. She got up and pulled out a tissue, dabbed at her eyes, and stared out the window. "She's gone...she ain't never comin' back. You not only fucked yourself...but you took from me the best friend...the only friend I ever had." She turned to Hal. "She said that you had done so much for her and never asked for anything in return...then she fell for you and all she wanted to do was please you. She used to ask me about things she didn't know...because she wanted you to love her so much..." She broke down and Deuce went to her to comfort her.

When she composed herself, Hal made his case. "Now you see why I have to find her...will you get Malone to help us?"

"I'm doing this for Mari...she has got to know what went down...I don't hold out much hope for you, but it would be important to her." She took the phone from its stand and sat down. "Exactly what do you want me to tell him...?" She raised her finger. "...and no bullshit! He will know...and hold me responsible for taking your part."

"Tell him that Mari is missing and Hal Golan...Mari's ex-fiancé...is desperately trying to find her. It's important..."

"Honey...that ain't going to fly. He will tell you that it is not important to him...and you can fuck yourself." She took a sip of wine. "Think about it. If he is the one who helped her in the first place...he's not going to help you."

"What do you suggest?"

"No guarantees...but let me try." She dialed his private line and he picked up. "Malone...baby...this is Black Beauty."

"Hey, Beauty...why are you calling the Beast...you want to get up to a little something something...?"

"As interesting as that sounds...that's not why I'm calling..."

"What do you need?"

"There is someone who wants to meet you. His name is Hal Golan...Mari's fiancé...he has just cleared up a major...major...bad fuck up that she needs to know about. She's missing and he is trying to find her. He thinks you may be able to help him. He just wants to

304

explain the situation to you himself…on the off chance that you can get word to her."

"What's his name again?"

"Hal Golan…"

"What you are saying is that he fucked up with Mari…and now he wants to make up with her?"

"Something like that. He said it was important and after hearing what happened…I have to say I agree with him…"

There was a pause at the other end. "Tell him I said to go fuck himself."

"I told him that's what you would say…and you never disappoint."

"You can come by anytime…I miss your sweet ass."

"I'll be thinking on it. See you when I see you." She hung up. "Sorry guys…that was a 'no'."

Hal exhaled in a big sigh. "Thanks anyway for trying. This Malone is a real hard ass?"

"Iron clad."

Hal nodded. "He hasn't heard the last of me."

"Don't go fucking with him…you could get hurt…"

"He can't hurt me more than I already am." Hal got up. "We've got to go."

Deuce slowly got up and Lo-Lo put her hand out. "Can you stay for a while…I want to ask you something."

Deuce paused. "Well, he's my ride…so I have to go."

"I can drive you home…it would be my pleasure."

Deuce looked at Hal and then at Lo-Lo. "Hal…I'll catch you up later."

Hal smirked and shook his head. "OK…you're a grown man…it's your call." He turned on his heel and left.

Lo-Lo took Deuce a glass of wine and then went to a bejeweled little box and took out a joint. Lighting it she took a deep drag, held it, and slowly let out the smoke. "What I wanted to ask you is why they call you Deuce. Mari said your name is Terry." She passed him the joint and he took it.

Deuce took a puff and hissed as he inhaled. "Mari guessed right. I got that nickname when I was a kid…you know…the deuce is a wild card…she thought Terry was more suitable."

"Were you wild?"

Deuce laughed, "No...not by today's standards. I thought I was tough...and I was bigger than most kids my age...but I never got into trouble. I did learn how to fight though...that's just about a rite of passage growing up in L.A."

"What's with your friend...this Hal guy...I don't see how..."

"He's a good guy...the best. He was into Mari from the start. He just could not understand how someone as beautiful as she is...could go for a plain guy like him. Because of that he kept trippin' over his dick. After Zack beat her up he took her in...took care of her until she was well...then he arranged for her to stay with him as his roommate...gave her the run of his place. All the while he was scared to death that if he made a move on her that she would leave. He had no idea she loved him. I'm glad he heard it from you...because he never believed it from me. Even after it worked out between them...his father giving him that file played right into his paranoia...and coming from his father...he believed it to be true...every dirty lie." He took another hit and handed the joint back to her. "Now I'm scared about what he's going to do. I know that look...he's just trying to figure out a plan...and once he does...all hell is going to break loose."

"Let me know if there is anything else I can do to help."

"I'm sure we'll need your help before this is through."

"And what's your thing?"

"My thing...I'm just trying to get him through it..."

"No...what do you do? Who are you?"

Deuce shrugged. "I own a plumbing business...and I try to keep Hal out of trouble." She gazed at him, tilted her head, and quietly continued to contemplate him. "Girl...what you lookin' at me like that for?"

"I'm just trying to decide whether I want to go to bed with you or not."

He took a visible gulp and looked around. "Don't I have a say in it?"

"No...no you don't."

Deuce got up. "I think you should take me home now."

"Don't tell me you don't want me. Those soft brown eyes have been looking at me ever since you got here..."

His eyebrows went up and he gave her a smile that said she was right. He held out his hands with his palms up. "I'm not saying I don't want you...because it's true that I do." He bobbed his left hand. "But in this hand I got a wife, kids, a house, and a business..." He bounced his right hand like a scale. "...and you are in this hand. I'm not saying it isn't a close call...because it is..." He looked at her and sighed deeply. "But I got to choose the wife and kids."

She gave him a sideways glance. "Alright."

Deuce watched as she got up to get her coat. To him, she represented all that was missing in his life, passion, desire, a sense of living. For a moment he fought his impulses and then he gave way.

As they were walking toward the door, Deuce reached out and enfolded her in his arms. "Give me some of that sugar!"

From the moment he kissed her he knew that the balance between her and the wife and kids was going off-kilter.

***

CHANGES

After dozing off in front of the TV, an insistent knock at his door woke Hal up. As he stirred awake, he could hear Deuce's muffled voice. "Hal...it's me...let me in." When he opened the door, Deuce strode in and went straight to the phone and dialed his home. "Wanda, baby...I'm still here at Hal's. Don't wait up for me...it looks like he's going to need me to stay. Yeah...I'll be there in time to take them to practice. OK...love you. Bye.

"You got somethin' to eat?" Deuce went to the kitchen. "I'm so hungry I could eat a horse..."

"Just some old fucked up meatloaf I made...it's not too bad when you cover it with ketchup. It's frozen...and I have some frozen tater-tots..." Hal trailed along after him.

"Where's your microwave?"

"That was Mari's...I haven't had the heart to buy another one."

Deuce's eyes were wide. "I'm in some serious shit...man...and I need you to help me figure out what to do!"

"*You?!* You're in some kind of trouble? That's a role reversal!" Hal chuckled.

"It ain't funny! I'm actually scared."

Hal put the meatloaf and the tater-tots in the same frying pan, put them in the oven, and cranked it up to four hundred degrees. "OK...you got my full attention...what do you need?"

"A way out. That Lo-Lo...I slept with her...and Jesus...she changed my whole perspective. She did things that I never even heard of...she did things..."

"OK...so you slept with her...and the problem would be?"

"If Wanda ever finds out, she'll take me for everything I've got...the house, the kids, half my business...and because we have kids and she ain't never worked outside the home...and has no other skills...to maintain her in the style she has become accustomed to; the settlement on her will be horrendous. I'll be living in a trailer, like a pauper, and working just to keep her in luxury."

"Aren't you overreacting? You only slept with Lo-Lo once...and Wanda thinks you were with me. How is she going to find out?"

Deuce got a far-off stare in his eyes. "Because I don't intend to stop sleeping with her. Lo-Lo is like a drug...you got to have more. She don't just fuck you...for her fucking is just for starters...she plays on you…like your body is her instrument and she is the virtuoso. She takes her time and works you over. She knows all your pleasure points…she knows secret things…" His face twisted in puzzlement, wondering how to explain it. He held up his index finger and wiggled it. "…she gave me a digital probe and massaged something in there and I exploded like a teenager!"

"That's a thing? How did she do that?"

"Oh…it's a thing alright! I don't know how she did it! She went up my avenue "A" and rubbed somethin' in there and all of a sudden I launched like a rocket! I'm not kidding you…she made my teeth rattle!" Deuce was still reeling. "That woman has got my nose open…and I don't intend to fight it."

Hal tried to stifle a snicker. "God…please tell me she at least wore a rubber glove!"

Deuce resented his reverie being dampened by practicalities. "How should I know? My back was turned."

Hal shrugged. *"Goddamn!* I've never seen you like this…" He reached up into the cupboard and took down a bottle of bourbon. He poured a couple of shots and handed one to Deuce. "You've always been so cautious…a straight arrow…"

"I've never been like this!"

Hal thought, "You know…I've been looking into ways to fuck Marvin over…and I think that some of what I have learned can help you. We have got to plan every detail to the letter and then have Big take a look at it to make sure we're on solid ground."

"What are you thinking of?"

"For your situation…we play corporate musical chairs. We wrap up your company in a corporation with you as the CEO and me as the majority shareholder…not at first…but eventually. Wanda is going to have to sign off on it…but we will put it to her like this. You need the influx of cash to expand your business outside of South L.A. into the Westside and possibly the valley. I will provide the influx of cash by buying shares in the corporation. Tell her it is fifty-fifty…but I will have fifty-one percent giving me the controlling interest. With the prospect of doubling your income and protecting your assets, she will go along with it…and you will still be running the company. Then when everything is going along tickety-boo for a year or so…you ask me for a big loan for something that she would want…and agree to.

You put up half of your shares as collateral...and then default on the loan. Tell her it is OK because your old pal Hal would never collect on the shares...but I do! That will leave you with just twenty-four percent of the shares of which twelve would be hers. Now, I will be the bastard in this scenario...and it would be no fault of yours. Meanwhile, you have no more income showing than your CEO's salary...which could be whatever we make it."

"I want her to have the house. She is a good mother..."

"Let's talk to Big...I'm sure those things can be arranged. I have heard that there is such a thing as a fraudulent transfer...where the transfer of your assets can be reversed. So, you cannot divorce Wanda right away...this is going to take some time...at least a year or two...so we better start on it now. Meanwhile, you have to keep Lo-Lo on the down-lo. I can't cover for you all the time...so you are going to have to come up with something to justify your time away from home."

"I don't understand everything you just said...but it sounds good. You'll take care of me Hal?"

"Knight's honor...you know I will."

***

"Yes...this hypothetical could work." Big reviewed the outline Hal and Deuce had drawn up. "Justifying the loan would be difficult if it's for something frivolous."

"I was thinking it could be to put into a trust for my sons' education..."

"Better. I can see an irrevocable trust for your boys as being worthy and something your wife would agree to." Big looked at Deuce. "In this hypothetical...you must not be the one who initiates the dissolution of your marriage...let her be the one who does it. And one more thing...women are not as stupid as men think...they sense things. If you stop having normal sexual relations with your wife...she will become suspicious...possibly even have you followed. Your conduct must look above suspicion...any subterfuge you may engage in must have the quality of plausibility built into your actions."

Hal and Big looked at Deuce. He sat rubbing his chin and then he patted both hands on his legs. "Draw up the paperwork...I gotta do this."

Hal gently advised, "This part isn't going to hurt you...I'll never let it. But you think long and hard about divorcing Wanda...and what you're giving up...versus what you are getting."

"Like he said...I'm not going to divorce Wanda...this is a precaution in case she divorces me..."

"And your boys?"

"I'll always look after my boys...you know that!"

"OK...let's do this."

Big thumbed through his Rolodex. "I'm going to send you to someone else to handle your incorporation and he will be your agent of service of process. Do not tell him we sent you or reveal to him anything we talked about...it is best that we stay in the background."

***

After putting in a hard day's work, Deuce opened the door to the chaos that was his home. His youngest son ran up to him exclaiming "Daddy" and wrapped himself around Deuces leg to ride on it as Deuce walked into the house. His other two boys kept on wrestling on the floor. "Wanda...I'm home."

"Dinner is almost ready."

He pulled his youngest off of his leg and lifted him high in the air before kissing his cheek and putting him down. He went straight to the master bathroom to relieve himself and, as he stood in front of the toilet, he wondered if his being there made any difference to his family at all. True, he was the one who financed the outfit, but how much more was he to them than that? *If I wasn't here...would everything just go on as usual?* Flushing the toilet, he went to the basin to wash his hands and the day's grime off his face. Smelling his underarms, he took off his shirt and gave himself a going over with a washcloth.

Marrying at eighteen, his adult life started out as an endless struggle to keep his head above water. After achieving success, it was now an endless struggle to stay on top. The only respite he had was Monday night at Benny's to watch the game with Hal and Big, and the entertainment value of helping Hal figure out his life. Now, even that turned into a responsibility.

If he had to sum up Wanda in one word, it would be "selfish." Yes, she was a good mother, but being giving, loving, and affectionate toward him, it didn't exist. He tried to remember the last time they were crazy about each other, really into each other the way Hal and Mari were before everything blew up in their faces. She was extremely amorous when he was about to go to college and ended his dreams when she came up pregnant. Again, she was all over him when she thought that he was about to stray, and hence their second son. The third son, he was sure, was an accident. Of course, they had their moments, but they were not the stuff of deep desire and ardor. Even in Hal's present state of affairs, he truly envied him for the deep passion he felt for Mari.

It suddenly hit him; he had never loved Wanda, not for one day. What he felt toward her was obligation. Never had he experienced being knocked to his knees by a woman, as Hal was by Mari, until now. He wasn't sure if what he felt for Lo-Lo was love, but it certainly was a burning desire and a lot more than he had felt for any woman before. He was now thirty years old and, somehow, he felt he owed it to himself to break free of his chains and grab onto life.

Going into dinner he walked through his house that reflected everything he had been able to achieve. He felt reassured now that he knew he could preserve it against any eventuality. Sitting at the table, he said grace more to appease his wife than God and dug into a delicious dinner. He had to give it to Wanda, she could cook. "This is real good." He threw her a compliment.

Somewhat surprised she took it in stride. "Umm-hmm. I loaded up the freezer with those pork chops when they were on sale...and lots of other stuff preparing for that Y2K thing. We've been eatin' down on it ever since."

"I told you that wasn't real."

"Well, you couldn't tell that from all the notices we got from the utilities and the bank telling us how they were preparing for Y2K...and then...that they were ready for it. I just thought we should be ready...that's all..."

"What are we going to do with that generator you got?"

"We can use it for tailgating, camping, and stuff like that..."

"When did we ever tailgate or go camping?"

"Well...now we can."

"Suit yourself."

"Daddy...Junior said poop!" His five-year-old brightly smiled.

"Now don't go tellin' on your brother for something small like that...wait until he does something big before you try to get him into trouble with me."

His ten-year-old chimed in. "Junior didn't say poop...he said shit!"

Wanda jumped in. "How many times do I have to say...we don't use that kind of language in this house!"

Deuce let Wanda handle it while he quietly finished his dinner. After the children were excused from the table; he got himself a beer and sat back down with the expanse of table between him and his wife. "Wanda...we have to talk..."

She frowned. "What do we have to talk about?"

"It has to do with the business. I have been wanting to expand it for a long time now...and could never quite get just the right amount of money to do it...and to do it securely so that we don't let our reach exceed our grasp. I mentioned it to Hal...and he said that if we incorporated to protect ourselves from liability...he would be willing to buy shares in the company to give me the kind of cash that I need. Our shares would represent what we have now...his will expand us into the Westside...and I would run the company as usual."

"What does that have to do with me?"

"Half of everything I own is yours. I need for you to sign off on the deal so we can get started. This means we'll be rolling in it...I mean in the big time! Four...five years from now Deuce's plumbing will be a juggernaut!"

Wanda stared at him and blinked. "Alright...you know more about that than I do. Do you have the papers for me to sign?"

"Sure do." He took her into the office and showed her the papers on his desk and where to sign. She signed without question. "Now we are on our way!"

Later that night, when the kids were in bed, he slid into bed beside her. In her robe and slippers, she was eating from a bowl of popcorn while watching TV. He snuggled up to her and put his arm around her. After a few minutes he moved the bowl from her lap to the nightstand and pulled her to him.

"What are you doing? I'm trying to watch TV! Jerry Springer is on...and I want to see the paternity test results!"

Deuce reached for the bowl, put it back on her lap, and turned over to go to sleep.

Surrounded by darkness, Hal sat in his living room sipping bourbon, letting it run down his gullet and wash over his remorse. He was too dejected to turn on the TV or lamplights, even as the last vestiges of sunlight dimmed and the city lights appeared. Visions of Mari haunted him as he wore the memories of her like a second skin. *The taste of her, the feel of her touch, her smile, but more than that...those beautiful eyes looking at me...ME...with adoration...and I drove her away.* He knew he had to shake this depression that debilitated him, and kick start his brain into action, but for tonight, one last night, he would wallow in his pain.

As his mind sifted through all that had taken place, he was surprised to find that the nebulous cloud of ideas floating in the back of his mind, started to take shape and solidify. He knew he had to position himself to carry out any scheme and that meant making drastic changes to his life. With Mari gone, none of those changes were as difficult as they would have been before. He would have to capitulate to his father's will by joining the company. Without Mari, leaving Angel City Magazine was not a problematical proposition. Moving back into his parents' home and upgrading his car was now a practicality. Being encircled by everything that cried out for Mari trapped him into inaction. *Tomorrow my first order of business is to prepare myself to take back what is mine...my power...my self-esteem...and Mari.*

***

"Vee...I am tendering my resignation." Hal submitted an envelope containing a formal statement. "I have been very happy here, but I have to move on."

"For Christ's sake Hal...you're the best guy I've got! This is what comes from office romances...it's because Mari quit isn't it?"

"Yes and no. None of this is her fault...it was mine. I as much as fired her...and worse. It was all a mistake..."

"You fired her?"

"She thought I did...I didn't expect for her to leave just like that."

"Too bad...she was great at her job. We were going to throw a party for the both of you for freeing Mitchem, but she had left...I think that was the greatest story we ever did...you were quite a team and now you're both gone. What happened?"

314

"You just lost an employee...I lost my fiancée..."

"Aw...no. I'm really sorry, Hal." "

One day I'll tell you all about it...but right now it's too raw. All I can tell you now is that it was a mistake...and ask you to keep it to yourself. I have some work to do to straighten out what happened...and I don't even want a hint of this to get out."

"Sure...I'll stay mum. Why do I have the feeling that a story is in the offing?"

"Because it is. You might say that I am going undercover...and I think there is dirt that is safe to expose. I can't put my name to any of it...but you can rely on the story being accurate. All that I ask is that you publish it as soon as I get it to you."

"What's it about?"

"I don't even know yet...I just have a sixth sense that things are going to get real. I'm going to need a direct number for you...and your friendship."

"You've got both."

***

Hal and Vivian walked along the bizarre Ocean Front Walk, the promenade in Venice Beach, taking in the daily, aberrant show. Vivian was more intrigued than aghast, and she kept exclaiming, "I've never been here before! Why didn't I know about this place?" A man in Arab garb, on roller skates and playing a guitar, glided by, soon to be followed by two girls on roller blades in the briefest of bikinis. Musclemen by the side of the walk lifted weights while impromptu musicians poured out their latest compositions. Small booths and tables lined the walk where vendors hawked their wares to pedestrians. The carnival atmosphere was a constant to be ogled by sightseers from other parts of L.A. and from around the world.

"It is not exactly on your 'places to visit' list in finishing school." Hal smiled. "These are the people who thresh out their lives while they are young...some are absolute freaks and they remain so...happy to be oddities that harm no one. It is all what you used to call 'a happening' in the 60's with free expression of music, thought, dress, and even stages of undress." He bought snow cones and watched as Vivian daintily nibbled at hers and then got the hang of munching into the ice. "These are...or will become...the regular Joes and Janes that earn their daily bread by making our fortune. Some are more distinguished...accomplished...than others...but to think of them as the great unwashed is a mistake."

"I'm sorry to say...I never thought about them at all. Is that too terrible a thing for me to say?"

"No...it is an honest thing for you to say...and it is not your fault. You were never exposed to regular people...to get the chance to know them. I purposely adopted their lifestyle to see what I was made of, but as was pointed out to me, I never truly understood what they faced...the risk of loss...the risk of failure...until now. What I have suffered, is soul crushing. I know that others may have suffered worse things...but this is the worst that has ever happened to me."

"Oh...my bubeleh are you talking about Mari? She was one of my greatest regrets too...but she was no good for you."

"Ma...I brought you out here to ask you two things. The first is...can I move back home, into the guest house, until I can get my life together?"

"Of course...it is your home. Why not move into your old room?"

He chortled. "Yeah...you would love that...but, no. I have personal things I have accumulated that I need to have around me. The guest house will suit me just fine."

"The guest house it is, then. What else did you want to ask?"

"This is a highly personal question...but if you are to answer it, it is very important that you answer it truthfully. My very life could depend on it."

"Your *life?!*"

"I don't mean dying...but the direction in which it will go."

"Are you in some kind of trouble?"

"Yes and no...but before I tell you what this is about...I have to have your answer to this question."

"What is it? If it is that important...I will tell you the truth about anything you want to know."

"How much do you love Marvin?"

Vivian paused in thought before answering. "I don't want you to take this the wrong way. You are your own person... independent of who your father is...his sins are not imputed to you. They never were in my mind. The ugly truth is...I do not love your father at all...and I haven't for years. You are the only good thing to come out of our marriage. You needed a father...and any advantages that he could give you. After you were grown, I just never bothered to go through the public display of a divorce." Vivian looked into Hal's eyes for understanding. "He has had numerous affairs...and he presently has a mistress. I just ignore it and go on with my life and find my fulfillment elsewhere. It is not as though I have the necessity of remarrying."

"I take no joy in your being locked into a loveless marriage... but I have to admit that was the answer I was hoping for."

"You were hoping for? Why?"

He guided her to a bench that faced the ocean. They sat and watched people bobbing in the waves. "Ma...that is why I brought you out here to talk. We must not be overheard. Can I trust you with the most important secret of my life...whether you agree with me or not?"

"Hal...my bubeleh...you *are* my life...I will take your secret to the grave."

"I'm about to go to war with Marvin...to destroy him...the way he destroyed me. I want to take everything he has and leave him a beggar in disgrace!" After relating how Marvin fitted up Mari, he ended by saying, "I checked with the authorities and Mari had no record...the documents were forgeries. Because of it, I broke up with her in a pretty ugly way...and now Mari is missing. I can't find her. She was everything to me. Marvin must never find out that I had that file checked. I don't know how...but I am going to gain his confidence...and bring him down. But I don't want to hurt you in the process."

As he talked, Vivian's hand went to her mouth and her eyes moistened. "I knew something had to be wrong. I loved her and wanted her for my daughter. I knew what I sensed in her was right. Oh my God...what did you do to her, Hal?"

"It was pretty bad. She disappeared..." His voice trembled. "...and I never saw her again. I have a detective searching for her."

"How could he have done such a thing? You know, I wonder if he realized how deeply in love you were with Mari. I'm not even sure if he even knows what love is...if he ever really felt it. I don't think he ever loved anyone besides himself. He certainly doesn't love me, and he probably only saw you as an extension of himself...not as a son he should love. I don't think he even loves his mistress. He just wanted what he wanted, and love played no part in it."

"What kills me is that he manipulated me into being the one to inflict the blow to Mari. That hurts more than I can say."

Vivian wiped her eyes. "What can I do to help you?"

"I haven't figured it all out yet...but when I do I will let you know the plan. You may have to give me the run down on your finances to make sure you don't get hurt when I break him. Stay tuned for the next episode." He kissed her on the forehead. "Thanks ma...it's good to know that I have you in my corner in this fight."

"Whatever you plan to do...please make me a part of it. I told Marvin that if he ever did anything to hurt you, I would make him pay...and I intend to keep that promise."

***

"Dad...I'm ready to take my place at the company. I now realize that you can only depend on family. You kept me from making a bad mistake...and I thank you for it." Hal had rehearsed this line several times to keep from choking on it.

"Well...that's my boy! I'm glad you finally came around. Don't thank me...that's what fathers are for...to look out for the pitfalls. Whatever happened to that girl? Where is she living now?"

"I don't know. After we broke up, I lost track of her. Why do you ask?"

"She seemed like the type who would spread her filth around. I wouldn't want her to tell tales out of school about you...I think that kind of thing should be nipped in the bud."

"I'll see what I can find out. Meanwhile...when do I start work? What will my position be?"

"Let's get you in there tomorrow to start looking around...to see where you fit in. I want nothing less than a vice presidency for you...but of what department...that will be for you to decide. I've been waiting for this day a long...long time. Welcome aboard, son."

As Hal walked away from Marvin's study, a red flag waved in his head. Why did Marvin want to know where Mari lived? What did he intend to do to her? For the first time he was relieved she was no longer in L.A.

He got into his new BMW E46 3 and drove away. A week before, he reluctantly parted with his Camaro that was a constant reminder of better times. He incessantly envisioned Mari in the passenger seat in her white visor hat, pink ruffled blouse that showed her midriff and the white shorts that she wore on their trip across country. Recollections of her ready smile, her excitement at new discoveries, and the feel of the silken skin of her legs under his touch made parting with the car both difficult and necessary. After spending an hour in reverie, he turned the ignition key, listened to the rumble of the engine, and drove to the BMW dealer. He watched as his Camaro was driven away before he got into his new BMW and drove it off the showroom floor. The Bimmer was appropriate for his strategic position as a junior executive.

Now that he had settled all of his preparations, he was ready to consolidate a plan down to the last detail. First, he would build up his defenses and make them impregnable; then study the company from the inside to find out its vulnerabilities and research Marvin's finances for hidden weaknesses. Then he would be ready to make his move. The final coup de grâce should be a ruinous fatal blow.

***

PART TWO

MALONE

The name on the door was a one-word sobriquet, "Malone," as though that should suffice to elucidate. Before he was allowed to enter, Hal was subjected to a thorough search of his person, eliminating the possibility of a weapon or wire. When the door was opened, a man who appeared to be in his fifties was sitting at his desk. With dark hair, he was black Irish and wore the expression of an inscrutable Buddha. He gave Hal the once over with penetrating eyes. "Is he clean?"

"Yes." One of the men responded.

"I don't know..." Hal quipped. "...after the feeling up your guys gave me...from the way he cupped my balls...I feel pretty dirty that he didn't tell me to turn my head and cough!"

Malone stared at him without comment, gestured for Hal to sit, and waved away his henchmen. He folded his hands and leaned forward on his desk. "You're an annoying little prick. After three months of being repeatedly bounced out of here...I thought you would give up. What can I do for you, Mr. Golan?"

He started to say, *please...call me Hal*, but thought better of it...*this Malone IS a serious guy.* "It concerns a girl who used to work for you..."

"Would you like for me to have the bartender send up a drink for you?"

"Thank you...yes..."

"And you will have?"

"An Old Fashioned..."

Malone picked up the phone and called down for the drink. "They will bring it up shortly. You were saying..."

"Yes...I am trying to find Mari Carlson..."

"Go on..."

"I made a tragic mistake...deceitfully provoked by others...that adversely affected her...and I am trying to rectify a terrible wrong. I know it is just as important to her as it is to me, but I don't know where she is, and I was hoping you would be able to help me find her."

"You want my help." Malone sat back, studying Hal. "What makes you think that I can help you?"

"I was told that you might know where she is."

"How do I know she wants to be found?"

Hal winced. "After what happened, I am not sure she would want anything more to do with me...but I am positive she would want to know the truth about what was done to her."

There was a knock at the door and Malone called out "come." And a man entered with a small tray, served Hal his drink, and left. "That will be twenty-five dollars." Malone said with a deadpan face.

"Twenty-five dollars...for what?" He put down the drink.

"Mr. Golan...when you came in here you assumed I was your friend. I am not your friend and the drink is not on me." He frowned without malice. "The only reason I agreed to see you is that I was curious as to what kind of man you are. So far...I'm not impressed. You come in here with a joke on your lips...you ask for my help and you want a free drink...you are not a serious mensch as your people would say." Malone got up and walked to the corner of his desk and sat on it, staring down at Hal. "So, you want to know where Mari is. Give me a reason why I should tell you."

Hal knew he was in tall weeds with Malone, out of his league, and he wrestled with what to say next. "How much do you know about me?"

"More than you think."

"Look...I'm going to lay my cards on the table here...only because I'm desperate...and I think it is of major importance to her, as well. She has to know what went down...the truth. After that if she tells me to fuck off...I'll do whatever she wants. But the fact is...I fucked up...I fucked up bad...and I've got to make it right with her." Hal proceeded to confide in Malone the events that led up to Mari leaving.

"So, you're the one she put on that show for. After that show we had a spike in profits." He picked up the phone. "Do you want to talk to Vera about what she said?"

"No...I don't want it to get back to Marvin that I know what he did...besides, at this point I know that Vera lied."

"Smart. But I can't have my people talking about...our business. Johnny is still here because he is a damned good bartender...but he now knows that I'll rip him a new one if he talks out of turn again. Girls like Vera are a dime a dozen...and she is getting long in the tooth." He pushed buttons on the phone. "I want Vera transferred out of here..." He thought for a moment. "...to Wilmington." Out of the thirty-five clubs Malone owned across L.A. County, the one in Wilmington was the least desired by the girls. Boisterous and lowbrow, the work was harder for a lot less money.

Putting down the receiver, Malone returned to the subject at hand. "You know it was down to you that all this happened...your insecurities...your lack of self-confidence. Your father played you like a fiddle. When Mari said she loved you...I don't know why your first inclination was to doubt her. Beautiful girls fall in love with all kinds of guys...fat ones...skinny ones...good looking...ugly...you should see the parade of guys that drop these girls off...there is no explanation for it." Malone went back to his seat behind the desk digesting all he had heard. "I don't know why...but Mari evidently saw something in you worth marrying..." He clasped his hands together, thinking. "...and what did you do about your father?"

"Nothing yet...I have to come up with a plan..."

"I was seventeen when I kicked my father in the nuts and threw him out of his house and dared him to come back. From then on...I took care of my family. You will have to do the same thing...or you will never be a man. For me...it was the last time he beat my mother. In your case...you had what he wanted...and if he couldn't have her...neither could you. I shouldn't have to tell you that he didn't have your interest at heart. He took your woman from you...that's unforgivable."

"You're not the first person to tell me that." Hal grimaced. "Now I am going to have to figure out what I'm going to do about it."

"Look, kid...first of all, and most important, you have to develop a mental toughness. You have to sustain the ability to do the unthinkable. Once you have the cojones, then you've got to come at him where he is the most vulnerable...and take away from him what he values the most...destroy him...but never let him know that it was you who did it. Ingratiate yourself...play to his ego...and then render him impotent...figuratively cut off his balls. That will eat him up...it will kill him. My father didn't last more than two years after I kicked him out. You take your old man for everything he has...take him down."

Hal was silent for a moment, taking in Malone's shrewd advice, and then he nodded his understanding. Returning to his initial purpose, he asked, "Meanwhile, do you know where I can find Mari?"

"No…but she's fine…"

"How do you know that?"

"If she wasn't…she would call me."

"So you really don't know where she is?"

"No." Malone shook his head. "She asked me for help in finding her a decent job and a place to live in another town. I don't handle such things myself…so I put her in touch with a guy who knows a guy…"

"Mari said you helped her before…"

"Yeah…I got her the job at Angel City Magazine…"

"…and before that you gave her a job here to get her through school…"

"Mari worked for a corporation…she was never employed here…she was not old enough." Malone pointed his finger at Hal to make him understand.

"Of course…but my question is…why did you help her? What was she to you? You have beautiful women all around you…what made her special?"

A smile tugged at Malone's lips. "You think I was blinded by her beauty? When Mari first came here she was trying her best to look older than she was…too much makeup of the wrong kind. I grabbed her and took her over there…" He pointed to his private bathroom. "…and washed her face. I was none too gentle about it and I could tell she was frightened. Even so…she stood up to me. Not in the brash vulgar way of most of these girls…but with a pride and backbone that showed courage. She told me that all she needed was a job and a chance and that she was going to amount to something." Malone laughed and then became serious. "Have you ever seen a flower grow up through cement?"

"Yeah."

"That was little Mari…all I did was water her from time to time to help her thrive. She did not disappoint me. She finished her education…and from what I hear she was doing well on her job."

"She was. I was her boss." Hal stood up and prepared to leave. He took out his wallet. "Do you have a means of finding out where she is?"

"Put your money away. Of course I do. But unless she calls me…I'm not lifting a finger to find her. But I will do this…" He leaned forward. "I will help you to screw over your father. That's the first order of

324

business. Here's my private line...don't abuse it...call me if you need my help."

Hal went to leave but stopped and asked. "How much do you know about corporate law? My father is the CEO of a fairly substantial corporation. I was contemplating getting at him through his company...but I'm not exactly sure how."

Malone stared at him for a moment. "Come on back and sit down...I think we may be of assistance to each other."

***

Arendt Medical, Inc., the Golan family company, was started in 1920 by Vivian's paternal grandfather selling electrical and copper remedies for arthritis and other ailments. He then took on the challenge of making prosthetics for WWI veterans. Her father, Doren Arendt, taking the company in a different direction, expanded it based upon research and development, producing various medical supplies and applications. He took the company stock public, but retained controlling shares, and built it into a behemoth. After her father's death, Marvin Golan became CEO. While the company remained in the business of manufacturing and sales of medical equipment, there was a distinct emphasis on joint replacement devices. This is the history that Hal inherited when he walked through the doors of the family business.

The first meeting of officers and directors that Hal attended was dominated by his introduction to the company. He was treated with jovial contempt, a friendly handshake, a pat on the back, with the assumption that he knew nothing and had nothing to contribute. There was also a wariness regarding whose position would be jumped to give him a place of unearned ranking. There was almost a party atmosphere that did not settle down into the serious business of business. Marvin's leadership, or lack of it, allowed this farce to continue until Hal, under the guise of getting to know each man and the role of his responsibility, asked, "For my edification...could you go around the table and introduce yourselves and explain which departments you are responsible for?" He took his tablet and pen in hand.

It was an unexpected request, but they humored him. After the round of giving the requested information, Hal announced, "Within the next two weeks I will be calling your offices to make an appointment for a tour of your departments…I'm looking forward to meeting each of you on a more personal level."

The surprised looks were not hidden, but the resentment was. The first man to come up with an excuse said, "I would love to entertain you for an hour or two…but I will be on vacation."

"I am not expecting entertainment…what I am looking for is the skill and efficiency with which each department is run. I am sure your managers can demonstrate their skill and efficiency…and tell me just how much is due to your direction and knowledge." There was no second objection.

As Hal left the meeting he thought, *these mother fuckers are coasting on their laurels…if they ever had any. Are these Marvin's friends or did they earn their positions? Whatever they were…they are a bag full of bozos now!*

For the next two weeks, Hal poked around different departments. With his being the son of the CEO, at first the employees were reticent to talk to him, giving him short answers to long questions. Eventually, seeing that the questions he asked related to their concerns, they became more responsive and then downright honest. The problems they faced were usually from a lack of understanding between departments in coordinating their needs. The demands of one department made life difficult for another, frequently making for rocky relationships and slowing down production.

In manufacturing, he was struck by a mousy little man who had a perpetual frown. At first, he had an accusatory glare in his eye for Hal, which changed into a puzzled one as though he were wondering about Hal's true nature and his reason for inquiry. His demeanor changed into anxiousness as though he had something to say but was debating the wisdom of speaking. Hal approached him. "What is your name?"

"Mack."

"Mack…you look like a busy man. What is your job here?"

"I'm in charge of quality control."

"That's quite a responsibility. How long have you worked here?"

"Going on thirty-two years…I started when I was twenty-five…in the Parts Department. That was when Mr. Arendt, your grandfather, owned the business. He was quite a gentleman…I knew him personally. He came in every morning with a good word for everyone and during the day he would look in on each department. If you had a problem...you could bring it directly to him...whether it was related to the business or not." Mack paused. "I remember the day you were born. I've never seen a happier man. In a way...you sort of look like him. He was a friend to me. I went to his funeral...we all did. It was one of the saddest days of my life when he died." He paused again and then turned back to his work. "Now it's all different..."

"How is it different?"

"Impersonal...it's all money driven. No one cares about the next guy..."

"I'm glad I stopped to talk to you. I want you to know that I do care about the next guy. If you have any problems at all whether business related or personal...you can always come to me and we will solve whatever they may be together."

"Do you mean that?"

"I believe in my grandfather's philosophy...this company was built by you and others like you...we should look after one another." Hal pulled out his business card. "This is my direct line. Call me if you need anything." Hal sensed that Mack was sitting on a dark secret that stuck in his craw. With a little encouragement, perhaps he might tell him what was eating at him.

Within a month, Hal had answers. Mack placed a call to him in a panic. "Mr. Golan...they're laying me off!"

"They're what?" Hal sat up.

"They're laying me off and screwing with my pension..."

"Where are you?"

"I'm downstairs."

"Come up to my office right away!"

When Mack entered his office, he was shaking with both anger and fear. "Mr. Golan...I've been here for thirty-two years and they are just going to kick me to the curb like this? It's not just me...but all of the old timers...and they are taking our pensions. They offered me only thirty thousand to settle out my pension."

"Calm down..."

"Don't tell me to calm down...are you a part of this?"

"Most definitely NOT! I want to find out what is going on. Meanwhile, I want you to meet me at this address at this restaurant at seven tonight."

"I'm not running all over town to meet you. What for?"

"Your ass is in a sling right now and I am your only hope of getting it out! Meet me alone at seven on the dot...and I will give you a job...and your pension. Right now, this proposition is only for you. We will talk about anyone else."

Hal went to Marvin's office. He walked through a crowd of disgruntled workers being held at bay in reception. Walking past the secretary Hal burst into Marvin's office. He found a knot of executives huddled there. "The place is going crazy...what's going on?"

Marvin smiled at Hal's naïveté. "We are making some adjustments."

Hal stared at one of the executives seated at the front of the desk until the man got up and out of the chair, and he sat down. "What kind of adjustments?"

"The older...people...are costly. They are at the full extent of their pay grade for seniority...and in five to ten years we will be facing our pension obligations. If we lay them off now...we can get high school or college grads to do the same jobs for half to three quarters of their salaries...and we can settle our pension liabilities for pennies on the dollar. That's the bottom line."

"In other words, your bean counters have recommended that you throw grandma and grandpa to the wolves...sort of put them on an ice floe like Eskimos when they are no longer useful to you?"

"Not all...but most. Some are indispensable...but most are not."

Hal was disgusted, but he had to pick his battles. "May I suggest to you that you're probably in store for a slew of age discrimination suits?"

"We know. Not all of them will sue...but settling the lawsuits is cheaper in the long run than keeping them on."

"Touché." Hal acknowledged the point. He asked the executive whose seat he took to pour him a drink, since he had the misfortune to be standing by the liquor cart. Taking it, without thanks, he sipped it as he listened to what passed for accepted wisdom.

***

Mack came alone and was still looking harried. He spotted Hal at a table and came right over. "I can't stay long...my wife is distraught and in tears."

328

Following Malone's instructions, Hal conducted all of his backdoor business on "burner" cell phones. Accordingly, he reached inside his jacket and handed him a burner. "Mack you will stay for as long as I need you to stay. Call your wife and tell her everything is alright...because it is. You have a job...and I'll look after your pension. What I need from you is to know where the bones are buried in the company. Marvin may be my father...but it is my mother's interest that I care about preserving. From what I have seen thus far...there is much I need to be concerned about. You will work for me...confidentially...to help me find out what I need to know. I will meet your current income until you retire. If that meets with your approval...do we have a deal?"

"Why...why we sure do, Mr. Golan."

"Call your wife and tell her not to worry...but you won't be home for dinner...and keep the phone to call me whenever you need to. I'll give you another one like it when it runs out."

For the next hour and a half Mack did what he had longed to do, divulge the dirty laundry of Arendt Medical. "From 1994 through 1998 the Model ARH30 hip replacement device was defective. We started seeing the first trickle of lawsuits come in around 1997. They should have been recalled then because the failure rate was high. However, that would have involved a massive outlay for medical services and the surgeries involved. It was determined by the Accounting Department that it was cheaper to settle the lawsuits than to inform the public and recall that model. There are still thousands of them out there. Meanwhile, we are in the process of clearing out our inventory by exporting them to Mexico and Central America. This never would have happened with your grandfather. He was meticulous about quality materials in his products...that's why we still have a good name."

"How did that happen?"

"They cut costs. They used to contract with another company to manufacture joint devices. Then upstairs made what I considered to be some disastrous decisions to save money. They decided that we could manufacture the devices ourselves. Most of the problems were caused by lack of expertise, short cuts, and the choice of materials that required the skill our metallurgists did not have. Many of those problems could have been resolved by the use of better materials.

"While titanium is the best choice of metals, it is exceedingly expensive but, in my opinion, it is best suited for the purpose. The next best material is an alloy of cobalt, chromium, and molybdenum, which has been used in devices since at least the 1930's. It is highly wear and corrosion resistant and it is less costly. It is an excellent choice if the metallurgist knows his business...in the investment casting process. If he doesn't...intergranular corrosion can occur, which can be toxic to the host. In order to be more competitive, we switched to using the cobalt alloy when we decided to take on manufacturing our devices. Moreover, we learned...through what I understand was the result of a little industrial espionage...that one competing company was successfully researching a metal against metal joint replacement...utilizing the benefits of the hardness of cobalt alloys. We could claim that our R&D Department came up with it first by putting it out in our products first and we rushed it without proper testing. But, even with the minor degree of fretting or corrosion in the cobalt alloy, it soon became clear that it was a sufficient amount to cause toxicity. While it was thought that a minute amount of corrosion was harmless, it appears that some people are genetically predisposed to an allergic reaction to minute amounts of cobalt corrosion and others develop it over time. The resulting infection, necrosis, metal poisoning, hip pain, bone damage, etc. has been horrendous.

"Now, the other problem we have had is with the uncemented hip implants. The hip joint is what is referred to as a ball and socket joint. The socket portion...the acetabulum...is recessed into the pelvis and receives the ball portion at the head of the femur. During the surgery, the acetabulum is resurfaced and part of the implant is inserted and either cemented in place or is attached by osseointegration, or bone growth. In the opinion of some, the best attachment is for bone growth to take place to form a permanent attachment. With titanium the bone growth is rapid and complete over the entire surface. With the cobalt alloy, bone growth is spotty at best, attaching here and there in the best of conditions, but the body mostly covers the surface with a fibrous tissue. But that attachment is still substantial.

"However, one of the worst decisions made was to eliminate the expense of the acid bath toward the end of production. Although the device surface may look as though it is free of manufacturing debris at this point…only an acid bath ensures that all oils and debris are washed away. Without the acid bath, bone will not form an attachment if there is machine lubricant, or other debris, left on the device after it went through the machining process. More than a substantial number got away from us with that problem and now there are also lawsuits where slippage has occurred, and the hip joint has failed for that reason.

"By the time the complaints…lawsuits started coming in…we had thousands in distribution and thousands more already implanted into patients. Arendt has fought these suits by claiming surgeon error…but they have known for quite a while that the corrosion and the debris defects are out there."

Hal was both aghast and ecstatic. If Mack could prove what he was saying, he had what he needed. "Do you have proof of what you are claiming?"

"I sure do. After the spaghetti hit the fan, they put me into quality control. What they wanted was a rubber stamp. I made a report to the company about the defects in Model ARH30, how long that model had been produced, and I recommended a recall. I wanted to cover my ass. I know they got the report because I handed it in, I mailed it certified mail with a returned receipt, and I mailed it registered. I saw it in the company file…they knew about it alright."

"Do you have a copy of it…and the mailing receipts?"

"Sure do. Like I said…I wanted to cover my ass."

"I want to see everything you have on them."

"Oh…there's a lot more…not just the model we talked about."

"More defective products?"

"In the beginning…when we first took over manufacturing…they put a bunch of young kids in charge of inspection. They mismatched the screws to the holes…and the complaints started coming in that during surgery the screws fell out of the holes. We have had some sterilization problems at start up as well."

"Dear God! Is there anything else?"

"Yes…but more along the lines of failure to comply with FDA regulations. It is mandatory that we file MDR's with the FDA."

"What is that?"

331

"A report regarding defects in medical devices. But they didn't do it because they needed certification from the FDA in order to export the devices."

"You said you have proof in a report. Where do you have all this?"

"In my home..."

"OK...we have got to get it out of there and into a more secure place. Meanwhile, go ahead and take whatever they offer you to settle your pension...and look pissed off about it..."

"I *am* pissed off about it..."

"Call them a bag full of assholes or something...*after* they give you the money. We don't want them to suspect that you have a deal with me. Also, get the names and addresses of all of those who were laid off with you. They may have information that can be useful, as well. I want you to go on unemployment until they forget about you." Hal pulled out an envelope of cash. "Here is an advance until I can formally put you in my employment. When can I pick up your documents?"

"You can pick them up now." Mack shrugged. "I want my Maggie to meet you, anyway."

***

Hal used a burner to call Malone. "It's me. I was able to find what we needed sooner than I thought. I need to see you."

"How soon can you get here? I have a moment now."

"Ten or fifteen minutes."

"Good."

As Hal walked into Malone's office, he was in the middle of lunch. The smell of lamb curry and Moroccan couscous filled the air. "Sit...eat..."

A plate was dished for Hal and he gratefully grubbed down from the corner of the desk. "I've been at it all morning and haven't had a chance to eat..."

"What have you got for me...?"

"I think I have enough dirt to sink them...with a story in the news...and with a class action suit...an attorney I know suggested it...based on a hypothetical...he does not know what I plan, yet." Hal gave Malone a rundown of the information he had. "This sounds big to me."

Malone stopped eating. "It is big...damned big! Hold off on the class action suit for a while...and let them come to the realization that it would be beneficial to them to bring it on themselves. A constant barrage of individual lawsuits is more detrimental than a class action suit...because to settle a class action costs the company far less than individual suits."

"That's what I've been told. I think we should have our own guy come in with the class action suit...sort of like controlled opposition. But I am worried about the FDA. Will they revoke the export certificate...or shut down manufacturing?"

"By the time the FDA gets around to taking serious action...years will have gone by...and we will have free rein to do our business. They have a protocol they must follow that includes warning letters, et cetera. As long as we give them satisfactory answers...we can coast. Where you must take precaution is with insider trading...because exposure on that front can sink the entire project. Remember what I said about insider trading?"

"Yeah...but I think I can sufficiently distance myself from the information."

"You have the goods in a safe place?"

"Yes."

"Good. You will need a gun."

"A gun...what for?"

"Whenever you are a threat to a company that can cost them millions...possibly billions...and even bring down the whole enchilada...you should carry a piece. Subterfuge is not always enough. If there is a hint of your being behind this...your father most assuredly will have you killed." Malone picked up the phone and had one of his men sent in. "Manny is your gun clean?"

"Yeah, boss."

"Give Hal your gun...holster and all."

"But...boss..."

"You have another one at home, don't you?"

"Yeah..."

"Then give it to him...I'll find another one for you."

Both Hal and Manny removed their jackets. Manny took off the holster, with a .38 snub nose revolver, and handed it to Hal. After he fumbled with the straps, Manny helped him maneuver the holster into place and stuck the gun in it. "Are you sure this can't be seen?" Hal put on his jacket and flexed his shoulders.

"No...you're good."

"Why a revolver...that only has six shots?"

"Because each one will fire...it won't jam on you...but you better learn how to make each shot count if you ever have to pull it."

"I don't have a concealed weapon permit...and it is impossible to get one in L.A. County."

Malone sighed. "The gun you are wearing is not legal...not traceable. Just go about your daily life...but if you have to use it...wipe it clean and discard it...better yet just return it to me."

"I don't know Malone...if I get caught with it..."

"You are a rich, white male who lives in Beverly Hills. What cop is going to have the balls to frisk you? Get used to it cupcake...you are playing in the big leagues. With all you are proposing to do, it can get you just as much time as that gun. The only difference is...that gun can save your life."

"Touché!" Hal was learning to accede to greater wisdom.

***

Sitting in a rented car, Hal staked out the entry to Lo-Lo's apartment. He had arranged with Lo-Lo and Deuce to expect a visit from Marvin and just how to handle it. It had stuck in the back of his mind that Marvin had inexplicably inquired about where Mari was living. After hearing the opinions of two unrelated people, that Marvin was interested in Mari for himself, and learning that Marvin was a womanizer, as incongruous as it sounded; Hal decided to test the theory for himself.

Following up on the hunch, whenever Hal visited him in his study, he had started making notes in a pocket-sized tablet of Marvin's ramblings, as though they were pearls of wisdom. The gesture pleased Marvin and played to his ego. It also gave Hal the means of communicating Mari's supposed address to him. After clearing it with Lo-Lo, he jotted down her Hollywood address in his tablet as being where Mari lived. Then he set a trap.

"I am finding my way through the different departments. I had no idea there was so much to learn. Frankly, during the summers you had me spend there, I did the work by rote and didn't take much interest...now I wish I had."

"Don't worry son...you will pick it up soon enough. I like the way you handled yourself with Bullwinkle."

"Bullwinkle?"

"Yeah...that's what we call him...his face resembles a moose. It is never too soon to fight your way up the pecking order. Half of those guys are shaking in their boots thinking that you are going to replace them...the other half think you want to promote their department managers to their position."

"The second half may be right."

"Don't be too hasty to make enemies...until you have created allies."

"I'll keep that in mind...but Bullwinkle is on my short shit list...unless he proves to be indispensable."

"Now you're thinking."

"Oh...by the way...I happened to get an address on Mari. I ran into a friend of hers..." Hal pulled the tablet out of his pocket and looked at it for affect. "...she's living on Franklin...in an apartment complex in Hollywood..."

"Oh? I thought she left town..."

Marvin's slip was a dead giveaway that he had a detective searching for her too. "I don't know. If she did...I guess she must have come back. She's living with a roommate." He placed the tablet down on the front edge of Marvin's desk; it had the full address written down. "I have to use the gent's...I'll be right back..." He disappeared into Marvin's restroom and squeezed out a tinkle before flushing the toilet to cover the sound. He took his time washing his hands and toweling off before returning to the study. It was almost imperceptible, but the tablet looked like it had been moved. Marvin took the bait.

As Hal sat in the darkness, watching Lo-Lo's apartment, a familiar limousine pulled up, and finding no parking, the chauffeur double-parked. Marvin exited the limo carrying what appeared to be a florist's box for long stemmed roses. He entered the building.

When Marvin knocked on the door, he was stunned by the beautiful black girl who answered. He briefly considered a detour on a safari but decided to stick to his original prey. "I'm here to see Mari Carlson...is she at home?"

Lo-Lo asked, "Is she expecting you? She should be home soon."

"No...I'm Marvin Golan...Hal Golan's father..." His brows went up in a sympathetic affectation. "...I just heard that my son broke off their engagement and I am here to apologize for such rash behavior."

"Oh...she should be here any minute. Would you like to come in and wait?"

"Thank you. This is a nice place you have..."

"Yes...I decorated it myself. What's in the box?"

"Just a token of making amends. We got off on the wrong foot...Mari and I...and I hope she doesn't blame me for what my son did...I had no idea he would do such a thing. She is really a lovely girl and I feel very sorry for what happened."

"Yeah...it was pretty bad. She was broken up about it, but I think she found someone else. You know how that goes...on the rebound."

The telephone rang as prearranged. It was Hal on the other end. "Tell him I'm Mari and I will be out for the rest of the evening."

"Oh...so you're going to hang out? Uh-huh...uh-huh...OK... I'll see you when I see you." She hung up. "That was Mari..." Lo-Lo turned her head. "...looks like she is on a date and won't be home until the whenever. I'll tell her you came by...you can leave the present for her."

Marvin got up and handed her the box. "They're roses. Please put them in water for me. There is a card attached as well. Tell her I would like to apologize and discuss what happened...perhaps over dinner. I guess I'll be going."

Hal saw a dejected man get into the limo before it slimed its way down the street. There were no words for the hatred he felt. Only two words came to his mind. *No mercy...no mercy!*

***

Vivian gave Hal access to all the shares of stock held by the Golans in Arendt Medical, including Marvin's. Her faith in him was implicit. Hal loaned them to his "island corporation" and over the next six months it sold all of the shares at top dollar, in increments, so the trading would not bring attention. Then he called Vee at Angel City Magazine. "An irate little man by the name of Mack is going to drop off a box to you. He is going to say that he is bringing it to you because he wants to get back at my family through the magazine I work for. The article I wrote will be inside the box. Have someone else take credit for the byline and attribute the information to an anonymous source. All the documents verifying the facts are in the box. If you have any questions, be sure to ask the man while he is there...because he will be going on vacation for a while."

"How are you doing?"

"I'm doing great. After that article comes out...I'll be down there to raise hell with you for printing it. We can go for a drink after that so you can 'calm me down'. When is a good time for Mack to deliver it to you?"

"Tomorrow morning. Is that good for you?"

"Perfect. I'll see you within a day or so after the article runs."

"You've got it."

Next, he called Big. "The article will be out next month. Gear up for taking on individual lawsuits. Have the ads running within a couple of months. Are other attorneys working with you?"

"Everything is ready to go."

"After the article comes out...do you think you can pull strings with some friends to get it picked up by the evening news?"

"I'm already ahead of you on that. He's poised and ready for when the news breaks. He said he would run with it."

"I can't thank you enough, Big…"

"What do you mean? I can't thank you enough! I'm going to make a shitload off of these cases."

***

"I hate to disappoint you Dad, but I'm leaving the company. I have some moral qualms about how the company does business. I really found it hard to swallow how our senior employees were treated. Besides, I need to get away to finish my novel…I think I will go into the publishing business. But I learned a lot from you…I really did."

"Have you lost your mind? You're going to walk away from what I'm paying you…when all you have to do is to sit on your ass and do nothing?"

"Sit on my ass? There is a lot more that I don't like…and I raised it in the last meeting and was practically hooted down. The departments are not coordinated for a smooth operation. One hand does not know what the other is doing…causing costly delays and errors. You want to make money off the backs of your employees…people who have been loyal to this company…while ignoring the loss of earnings due to duplication of effort…delays and cancellations. Yes, you are making a huge profit…but it could be better still with just a little planning between departments, efficiency, and customer care."

"You've been here for less than a year…and you are going to tell me how to run this company?"

"No…I'm resigning." Hal pointed to the envelope on Marvin's desk. "That is my resignation on your desk. You run the company however you damn well please. I'm out of it."

"You'll come crawling back…"

"I doubt it."

***

Hal watched as his scheme played out. The story hit in Angel City Magazine about the defective hip implant devices sold by Arendt Medical, Inc. and was picked up by the evening news. Soon the financial papers picked it up. The stock plummeted. Ads soliciting clients, who were injured by implant devices, for potential legal action against the company, were all over the air. As the lawsuits

338

commenced, Mack gave his deposition and submitted his documents and the discovery process gave rise to more. The stock plummeted further. Soon the sales department complained that salesmen were leaving for greener pastures. They were fighting a fruitless battle in a war that was not of their making. They took their talents elsewhere. The drastic drop in sales precipitated an extreme drop in stock value.

Hal was the silent partner in a company formed by Malone. As finances became problematical for Arendt Medical, Hal got together with Malone to coordinate their next move.

It was nine in the morning when Hal arrived at Stony Malone's Gentlemen's Club. He entered through the back door and Manny was there to greet him. "Go to the front of the club. Malone is there having a..." He held up air quotes. "...'confab.'"

Hal laughed. "OK...a 'confab' is good." He went through the club, finding the stench of stale alcohol and tobacco predominating; he wondered where that smell goes in the evening when the club is full. Sitting at a separate table from the tight little group that sat with Malone, Hal waited until they were through discussing business.

"Dan...go and take Manny's place and send him here. I need him to sit in." Malone swapped the man at the back door as he usually did during briefings. Manny was soon seated, and the discussion continued.

As he waited, Hal spied a man approaching that he had not seen before. He had to be concerned about being seen in the company of Malone by people he did not know. His eyes narrowed on the man while the others appeared to be unaware of his presence.

Just off to the left of Hal, the man stopped. He reached in his jacket and pulled out a gun with a silencer and shouted, "MALONE!"

In a fraction of a second, Hal jumped up, placing himself between the gun and Malone. He pulled his revolver with his right hand while pushing the shooter's gun aside with his left, deflecting the bullet into the ceiling. As the shooter's gun went off, Hal blasted the man directly in the forehead, all in one swift movement. The would-be assassin instantly dropped.

It happened so fast; Hal was stunned by his act. He had instinctively reacted without thinking. Traumatized, he stood there and uttered. "I-I can't be seen here."

Malone's men sprang into action. Manny took the gun out of Hal's hand and wiped it clean. "Get the body out of here before he bleeds all over the carpet...and someone find the bullet and dig it out. You two...take Hal upstairs and put him in the shower and scrub him down...make sure you get his hands real good. Get him new clothes and burn the clothes he's wearing...that includes his shoes. Call 'clean up' to get rid of the body. And somebody find that bastard Dan! What was he doing...jacking off while this guy walked in?"

From the back door in the kitchen someone yelled, "We got another clean up here..." As they stumbled over Dan's dead body, they quickly worked to wrap him in a plastic trash bag as well.

Hal was in a fog as he was led upstairs. He robotically followed the directions of the men who took charge of him. Undressing and stepping into the shower, he washed himself from head to toe, and allowed them to take a scrub brush to his hands. He watched as they emptied his suit pockets and carried off his old clothes in a balled-up bundle. Dressing in hastily purchased sweats and running shoes, he redistributed his belongings and went downstairs.

Malone stood waiting at the bottom of the stairs. He stared at Hal for a full minute without speaking and then grabbed him by the shoulders. "You...you are now one of us forever. Wherever you go...whatever you do...all you have to do is call. One of us will be there for you. Now you have to go. This is all taken care of...the bodies will disappear. Find somewhere across town where you can be seen...make a few purchases...and call me in a week. I'll see you...and we'll get together to talk. Are you alright?"

"Just a little rattled...but I'll be OK."

"Do you want me to send Manny with you?"

"No...you're right. I have got to develop a mental toughness."

Like a homing pigeon, he went to Benny's and sat alone at his familiar table, thinking and drinking. Someone had the audacity to play the jukebox. The strains of "Still Got the Blues" filled the air and imprinted indelibly on Hal's mind. *It all started here...and now it has come to this. I just killed a man...and I don't regret it. Of course it was in defense of a life...but shouldn't I regret it? I regret a thousand times more what I said to Mari.* Listening to the lyrics pulled him into despair. *I wonder if I'll ever see her face again...touch her.* He laughed at himself. *As though she would ever let me touch her after what I did and said...even if I find her.* The musical riffs played upon his heart and scenes of his life with Mari drifted in his head. When the piece ended, he walked to the jukebox and took note of the title and artist, resolved to buy it, but he did not have the temerity to play it again, to the relief of others.

He called Deuce and found his voicemail on, something that never used to happen before he took up with Lo-Lo. He knew better than to call Big, because he was happily tied up with major cases that kept him busy for long hours. He resolved to stop feeling sorry for himself and focus on the task he had created, blowing up Marvin. Somehow, killing that man let him know that he had the power to do the unthinkable. For once in his life he was truly risking failure. If he succeeded, his personal fortune would be incalculable. If he failed, it meant years in prison. He straightened his back and adopted an inner hardness. *No one can say that I don't have the balls to risk failure now.*

***

EXECUTION OF THE PLAN

Malone's black Escalade pulled into Ferndell Park, an adjunct to Griffith Park. Malone got out and waved for Manny to drive up to the Observatory. He saw that Hal's BMW was already there and was glad he was on time. Entering the park, he strolled the pathways through tropical verdure and Sycamores, and crossed bridges over meandering streams, as he waited for Hal to catch up to him. Wearing his new sweat suit, Hal jogged through the park until he saw Malone and approached him to supposedly ask if he knew where the trail to the Griffith Observatory started. Malone pointed in the direction and offered, "I'll show you the way."

The park was crowded with Girl Scout cookouts, picnickers, and those out for a Saturday morning walk. Malone's voice was low key. "I am overwhelmed at what you did for me. I didn't know you had it in you."

"Neither did I. I guess I was never this pissed off at life before. I find that I am capable of all sorts of things."

"Sometimes that is what it takes to grow up...being that pissed off at life. That's what did it for me. But don't worry...I'll look after you now...you're like a son to me."

"Thanks...I'm in sore need of a father...mine keeps shitting on me."

"Yeah...what happened?"

"You were right...he wanted Mari all along. I set up a trap to test your theory...because someone else told me the same thing. Marvin asked if I knew where Mari lived and gave me a bullshit reason why he wanted to know. I set it up with a friend to use her address...and then I told him I found out Mari was living in Hollywood...he said he thought she had moved out of town. I never told either of my parents that she had left town. He must have a detective on her. I didn't give him the address but left a small tablet on his desk with the address written on it and then I left to go to the bathroom. When I got back...I saw he had looked at it. So...I staked out the address and sure enough he showed up. My friend told me he was definitely on the make." Hal looked at Malone. "I don't give a shit what we do to him now. I want to see him twist...I want to see him squirm...I want to see him have night sweats and horrors...I want to see his putrid soul poison his heart and watch him die. I have never hated and despised someone so much in my life."

"Welcome to the club...and the real world. You never expect that those who are supposed to love you will betray you. You go along in life...doing what you can for them...and then you get something that they want...or they resent you for some other reason...and the love and respect they should have for you, as family, goes out the window and all bets are off. I've seen it a million times in my own family...and others'."

They reached the head of the trail and embarked on it, trudging up the incline. Malone got down to business. "Our company is in place. We have a man who will be our representative to Marvin when he is desperate for cash and he can't get a loan anywhere else. Then we will make a deal and have him sign a loan...but then he will find out he has to earn the money. How soon before you can buy the company shares back?"

"My target is when it reaches five dollars a share or lower. That should be within a couple of days because right now it's down to seven...and the company's sales are nowhere. Marvin is thrashing around for money...or a takeover bid...which is unrealistic. When you approach him...I'll be surprised if he doesn't jump at the deal...but if he balks, I'll have my mother force his hand to take it. Meanwhile, since I already resigned, I'll be out of town taking a sabbatical to work on my novel...and I'll be totally out of the picture. I'll let you know when I have replaced the stocks."

"Good. We are up and running and can go in as soon as you are ready."

"About how long can we keep our little enterprise going before it has to disappear?"

"How long do you want to keep it going?"

"I don't know. How long is it safe to operate?"

"All the right people will be getting their cut...politicians, police, and we have some informants with the feds. They will tip us if there is something pending...or we can tip them if we want to shut it down with Marvin taking the fall. Personally, I don't like to stretch it out over a year...year and a half. People get testy...you know...working together...under pressure...or they get careless. I would say shut it down in about a year...unless everything is still running smoothly."

"How much will my cut be worth in that amount of time?"

"Millions...easy." Malone stopped on the trail. "Even after we shut this operation down...we pop up somewhere else. You don't have to do a thing kid...you'll get your cut."

"That's just it...when I find Mari...I will want out...and I want out clean."

Malone sighed. "I got to be honest with you. I'm not holding out on you...I don't know where Mari is...I checked with the people who found her the job with Yarborough Publishing. She only worked there for two or three months and then she left. But I suspect you already know that."

Hal's face fell. "Yeah...I do. You were my last hope of finding her."

"Look...I'm not giving you false hope here...people are found every day. When we find her...you can have out of the business any time you want."

"Tell me...can your people place someone else in Yarborough? My detective thinks that if we can get someone in there...we can nose around and find out what happened to her. I know it's a long shot...but it's the only one we've got."

"I'll look into it...but we have to wait until there is something available there and that is not always the case."

"Please do what you can."

Manny was waiting by the Escalade in the observatory parking lot. As Malone and Hal approached, Manny handed Hal an exercise satchel and then got into the driver's seat. Malone got into the car, dug into his pocket, and gave Hal a set of keys through the window. "Here are the keys to that Silver Mercedes over there. Go clean out your Bimmer and leave the keys under the seat. I'll have someone pick it up and by tonight it will be on a ship headed for Brazil. It was parked at the club's lot...someone may have seen it. The Mercedes already has your name on it...and the address it is registered to is your new house. Oh...and you have a new piece in the exercise bag."

"My new house?"

"Yeah. How old are you?"

"Twenty-nine...going on one hundred."

"Well...you are too old to be living with your mother. Besides...there are too many nosy nellies that you do not want snooping in your business. Got it?"

"Got it!" Hal nodded. "Thank you, Malone, for looking out for me."

Manny started the car and Malone waved, "The feeling is mutual." The window glided up and the car pulled out of the lot.

The silver CLK 430 Mercedes Benz Coupe glistened in the sunlight as Hal opened the door and slid into the seat. He was intoxicated by the new car smell as he tinkered with the various accessories on the dashboard. Peeking into the glove compartment he found the manual, and on the passenger seat he found a folder that gave him the location of his new home and preview pictures that looked like real estate ads. Gratified that he was still in Beverly Hills, he had to admit that it was a smart move for Malone to get him out of his mother's house and out of the purview of Marvin.

By the end of the day Arendt Medical stock was down to five dollars a share. Hal had to wait until the next day to buy, at a dollar fifty. The repurchased shares were returned to Vivian and Marvin never found out that Hal had made a fortune of forty-five million, five hundred and ninety-one thousand dollars by selling high and buying low. All during the crisis, Marvin thought he could reverse the downward spiral of Arendt and refused to fuel the panic by selling the family shares. Now the only way he could save the company, to get back on solid ground, was to find a white knight, or borrow against the company assets.

***

Constantly on the telephone in his desperation, Marvin contacted everyone who he thought was a friend. Surprisingly, he found that, in the face of adversity, most of his significant relationships were only superficial. It was as though they assumed that ruin was contagious and could be passed on through contact. Only one or two offered to "see what they could do" but wanted their names kept out of it. He found he had to abase himself for even that crumb of assistance. The company officers and directors, whose reputations he had elevated through the years, in spite of their lack of acumen, scurried to abandon ship like the vermin they were.

Across town, a man had taken up residence in a commonplace apartment and set about the business of bleaching his hair blond and applying blue contacts. His skin had the pallor of one who spent his professional life indoors, in executive suites and boardrooms. Manicured nails, a thousand-dollar suit, and a hand stitched leather briefcase completed the image. Smiling at the reflection of himself in a full-length mirror, he then whistled as he took out a phone, called for his ride, and set one suitcase beside the door. What appeared to be a cab picked him up, drove him to the Beverly Hills Hotel, and dropped him off. With an air that bespoke of privileged status, he sauntered to the desk. The clerk immediately greeted him and asked if he had reservations. "Yes." He answered. "Drummond...Mr. Gilbert Drummond..."

***

Gilbert Drummond, of Bartel Enterprises, entered Marvin's office and, although he offered his hand, he appeared to be appraising the man he was about to offer salvation. Drummond looked like a gent who was ordinarily given to good humor, but for the occasion he wore a somber expression to denote the grave circumstances. "Mr. Golan...I am sorry that we had to meet when you are facing such heavy concerns. But this is what we do...we turn around companies that are in the same or similar circumstances as yours."

Marvin attempted to cling to what little was left of his dignity. "I consented to see you out of the duty to correctly evaluate all of my extensive options. I have never heard of your company before...how did you hear about us? You said you were referred...by whom...?"

"Mr. Golan...you never heard of us before because we only go where we are needed...and we are discreet in matters of referrals...but it is probably the person you are thinking of." Drummond used his favorite ploy. "But if it is your assessment that you do not need the services we can render...I will be happy to share a cup of coffee with you to make my time worthwhile before taking the next flight to New York...where we might be of some assistance to a less fortunate company."

Properly chastened Marvin admitted, "We are having our difficulties and I am very interested in hearing your proposal. It may well be that you have the solutions we are..."

"Mr. Golan...let's not beat around the bush. I know your company needs help...and you know that you are going to accept our help because you have no other options left. I also know that you are going to check our credentials...and you will find them to your satisfaction. Now that we have that out of the way...let us discuss what you need. We are prepared to infuse Arendt Medical with enough liquidity to get it off the ground. We are also prepared to bring in enough new trade to replace what you have lost. But we must be adults about this...you may end in bankruptcy if our efforts come too late or your situation is too upside down to save."

Marvin was defeated. "I will need a couple of days to gather our account information..."

"No need...our proposal is that we will lend you eight point two million with your remaining assets as collateral..."

"You must be joking...we need at least twenty million to get us in the kind of shape to properly run our business."

Drummond sat back staring at Marvin, giving his assessment some thought. "OK...twelve million...and we put our key people in here to run a tight ship. You will have to make some adjustments...but I think we can make it work."

"But I said twenty..."

"I'm not hard of hearing, Mr. Golan...what I am is tenacious. You will live with twelve...and if you follow our directions...I will hold out the possibility of more. If we have an agreement...I'll have our attorneys draw up the paperwork. It should be ready by the end of the week. Meanwhile, I am staying at the Beverly Hills Hotel if you should need to reach me."

"That was brief...your spontaneity is surprising...shocking."

"Our alacrity is born out of prior research, Mr. Golan. By the time my company sends me out...they are already satisfied that we can do business with you. My only job is to let you know that we are here...and what we can do for you. No need to stretch it out or belabor the point." Drummond picked up his briefcase. "I will be in touch to let you know when we will be finalizing our agreement."

***

Marvin stared down at the contract lying on his desk. For some reason last minute qualms lingered. However, any misgivings were overcome because he had verified the legitimacy of Bartel Enterprises and its impeccable credentials. The money, such as it is, was a godsend. The new officers Drummond brought on board had fresh ideas and a vision for Arendt, and the new customers, mostly from Latin America, already placed orders. Marvin picked up his pen and signed the originals with a flourish.

Drummond collected his original of the contract and placed it in his briefcase. Then he produced a bottle of Paradis Cognac and poured a toast all around. "Here's to better days, my friends." He took out his cell and called a number. "Yes…bring them in and get them to work."

The spread on the buffet was lavish and, as the new officers filled their plates, one in particular, an attractive brunette, caught Marvin's eye. Distracted, he was drawn to her. "Today will certainly be one to remember." He smiled brightly, picked up a plate, and started filling it.

"Yes…it certainly will…" Her eyes were limpid.

"You are in charge of…?"

"Public Relations. It will be my job to restore the reputation of Arendt Medical."

Marvin could smell her perfume. The scent was heady. "May I sit with you a while and we can talk about…our plans?"

"It would be a delight."

Before midnight, Priscilla Baxter had Marvin in her bed, while concealed cameras snapped pictures in living color.

***

Marvin was never one to visit the various departments of the Arendt facilities. The managers kept things in line and humming. If there was a problem, it was up to the respective vice president to solve it. His style was to let the company function and to gather reports. Any problem that was so large that he had to get involved was usually handed off to a talented underling, or to Arendt's attorneys. There was a time, when he first came on board with the company, that he used to make the rounds with his father-in-law. Doren would go from department to department, sticking his nose into whatever was taking place. To Marvin it was boring and ludicrous to do a daily pilgrimage to see the same functions carried out over and over again, listening to the same exchanges of information. But it was what he bargained for when he married Vivian, and he only had to bide his time until he was CEO.

He met Vivian in 1967 when they both attended USC. Word spread across the nation that there would be a "happening" in San Francisco, the "Summer of Love." Heeding the call, they and their friends all loaded into Iggy's Beast, a psychedelic painted Volkswagen bus, and headed up the coast to converge on Haight-Ashbury. He was tall, dark, and with his longish, curly hair had the reputation of a super-

348

stud. Vivian caught Marvin's eye; she was a showstopper. The way she filled a sweater, her tight little butt, her long chestnut hair all brought his eyes into focus on her for the trip. All the way to San Francisco, he hardly spoke two words to her. But once they were there, celebrating in Golden Gate Park, he took her in his arms and danced with her the rest of the day on into the evening. Back at the pad where they crashed for the duration, they toked weed and lay down on the floor together, looking into each other's eyes until they were convinced that they were in love. The final day in 'Frisco, when everyone had taken off for their last look at the city; Marvin had Vivian to himself. They made love while "Light My Fire" blared in the background. She was the wildest lay he ever had. On the return trip to L.A. he held her in his arms and swore to himself that he would make her his wife. When he found out that she was an heiress, he fist pumped the air all the way to his next class.

Getting past Vivian's father was no easy task. The old bastard wanted to blow him out of the water, buy him off. But Marvin stuck it out, knowing that in the long run there was more money in the offing than he ever dared dream of. When the old guy softened to let Vivian have her way, he set up her fortune in separate trusts before they were married. Still, Marvin had to cater to Doren's every whim, under the glare of his displeasure. He walked carefully in the footsteps of the master. But, when Hal was born, all was forgiven. He was then accepted as Hal's father and as a part of the family. Doren made it his mission to turn Marvin into a success, to earn his own fortune.

After Doren died, and Marvin became CEO of Arendt Medical, he instituted a relaxed style and his own way of doing business; with the clock already wound, he just let it tick. Since analysis was not his strong suit; he took the advice of his accountants, not realizing that there was more to consider than just the bottom line. Unfortunately, old habits die hard and a relaxed style is not what is called for in a time of crisis, especially now that strangers are running the business. He did not attempt to find out just who had leaked the story about the defective devices. He just assumed it was the result of one, or more, of the attorneys on the pending lawsuits who spilled the beans. Even in the face of the unusually high turnover in warehouse personnel, he did not inquire as to why. Drummond had things well in hand and, as promised, sales were going up. As a smile played on Marvin's lips, he thought, *Meanwhile, Priscilla is fulfilling my fantasies.*

***

Forklifts ran through the warehouse in a frenzied atmosphere. In a partitioned part of the building, fifty cases were assembled for the hip implant devices being shipped. The blackened windows assured that all was done in secrecy. In the false bottom of each case were placed two tactical weapons of the Sa VZ 58 V or "kosa" as they are fondly called by the Czech military. Carefully concealing the weapons, a hip replacement implant device was tenderly placed over them, stabilized, and sealed. A total of one hundred VZ 58 semi-automatic-fully automatic rifles were prepared for shipment. Next, fifty VZ 61 Skorpion pistols, with the same sub-machine gun functions, were packaged under the shoulder implant devices. Two hundred VZ 58 banana clips, one hundred VZ 61 banana clips along with six thousand rounds of ammunition were secreted in knee and ankle joint replacement boxes.

The murky beginnings of these weapons started with legal purchases of "deactivated" guns that were sold as collectors' items, re-enactors' guns, and movie props that could only fire blanks. The exceedingly simplistic method of deactivating the weapons in the European country of origin made it an uncomplicated matter to activate the guns to their initial deadliness of semi-automatic and fully automatic capabilities. The worth of the weapons shipment and accoutrements came to just shy of a half a million dollars. Subtracting for all costs and adding the worth of the implant devices, the shipment value came to seven hundred and eighteen thousand, give or take a hundred dollars or so.

With the advent of NAFTA, the requirements of shipping sterilized equipment, under seal, within the regulations of Mexico, and with Arendt already exporting to that country, the shipments moved smoothly. Wire transfers were anonymously made through a company that changed the Peso, at the rate of exchange, into its own designated currency which was converted into dollars at the island destination bank account. Exports were made to other Latin American countries, most of which did not regulate their imports as tightly as Mexico. The pipeline to shift the guns from Europe had been established for quite some time. This new outlet was a great opportunity. In the weeks, months, and years to follow, the money flowed.

***

"OK, ma...now is the time to make your move." Hal placed a large manila envelope on the table. "Don't look at these...they are the kind of pictures that will justify your divorcing Marvin. I have a great attorney for you, and you have to move fast because things are going down."

"Don't look at them? Why not? I have wanted to see Marvin with his ass in a sling for a long time. I am going to thoroughly enjoy my divorce! And when it is final...you are taking me to Paris for dinner!" Vivian picked up the envelope and slipped out the pictures. "Goodness! Marvin is crawling all over that girl like...oh...I like this one with his butt in the air and his balls sagging down. I should frame it!"

Hal crooked his head and stared at his mother. "Ma...you are a marvel. I never gave you credit for being as strong as you are."

"I guess I never had a reason to be so angry before. Once I realized I no longer loved Marvin...it didn't matter to me very much what he did...how many women he had...and quite frankly, I feel sorry for his mistress because she does care." She sighed. "I guess I was never motivated before now. How soon can I see the attorney? I want to show him these pictures so we can all have a good laugh...and I can start my life all over again doing something I want to do...with no one to boss me."

"Don't show these to Marvin until after you have filed. I don't want him to know your plans yet. Be sure to have him move out of the house. When the shit hits the fan...I don't want him anywhere near you." Hal paused. "I love you...you are an amazing woman."

***

Graham listened to the fireworks going on in Marvin's study. He could not resist a smile as he heard Vivian finally give the turd his comeuppance. Taking pride in his ability to mask his extreme distaste for the senior Mr. Golan, he regarded it as the hallmark of his professionalism. Now, it appeared as though he would be free of that burden. Vivian, dear Vivian, was taking a stand.

"Marvin...your women...your mistresses...I have put up with everything all these many years. But now I am through with it! To have my nose rubbed in it...to be the laughingstock?! I will not stand for it! Our marriage is like cat shit in a box. I just kept covering it with kitty litter to cover the stench...but even that has its limits...and now it is time to empty the box! It is patently obvious, even to me, that nothing...nothing...ever meant anything to you at all. My father built you up and handed you your comfortable life on a platter. If it had not been for him...you wouldn't have attained the status and affluence that you have today."

"Vivian...you had the divorce papers served on me in MY OFFICE! How dare you disgrace and embarrass me in my place of business!"

"In your office is the only place where I knew I could find you! I can't keep track of your trollops' whereabouts...which hotel...which clandestine apartment..." She gave a wry laugh. "...and isn't it just like you to be more concerned that your ego was bruised than that your marriage has fallen apart. At least you're *consistent!*"

"Look...Vivian...I know I haven't been the perfect husband...but right now I am going through a thing. I don't need this right now..."

"Marvin...you haven't been a husband for over two decades! I have been 'going through a thing' all of those years. Well...I won't do it anymore. Every reason...every excuse...that I gave myself for staying in this marriage is gone...." She pointed to the divorce papers in his hand. "...those are your walking papers! I want you out of the house...NOW!!"

"Surely you will give me time to..."

"NO! You will not get another day out of me! Run to your mistress...she will take you in. Meanwhile, I will have Graham gather your things and send them to you. If you do not have your belongings out by the end of the month...I will sell them to cover storage costs. I am done here! Get out!"

Marvin vacillated not quite knowing what to do. He did not move, but his eyes showed a mixture of anger, fear, and uncertainty. Vivian casually strolled behind his desk and opened the top drawer. Even she was shocked at her bold behavior, but once she decided she had enough, there was no length she would not go to in order to enforce her words. She took out the pistol she knew she would find there and held it on him. "I said...GET OUT."

Bartel Enterprises did more than just firearms trafficking, they also engaged in money laundering. While they eschewed drugs, they did spread the joy in cleaning the proceeds for their better clients, as well as their own money. In circumstances where the wire service was not practical for firearms, business went on as usual without it. Utilizing their legitimate cash businesses, such as the gentlemen's clubs in Southern California, they cleaned fabulous amounts at fifteen percent. They saw no reason why Arendt Medical should not clean its fair share. The employees in the warehouse were already being paid in cash. Now, most suppliers were also paid in cash, out of the necessity to launder the money and because they would no longer extend credit. However, as the need was growing to handle more; personal involvement was required to hand carry currency out of the country.

***

Hal lay in the middle of the king-sized bed with his closed eyes rapidly moving in a deep sleep. His mouth moved in soft utterances between breaths. As his mind reached back into the past, he was lying next to Mari. "Mari...what do you see when you look at me?"

She turned over on her side to face him. "I see you..." She smiled. "...the man I want to snuggle."

"No...I mean what do I look like to you...what is it that you like about me?"

"Fishing for compliments...eh? OK...I like the way your eyebrows go up when you are surprised...or talk about something that's funny...and I like the way they go way down when you are serious." She made a face like his. "Your eyes...I love looking into your eyes when you make love to me. I love...the way you kiss." She stopped. "Why are you asking me all of this?"

"Because I don't get it...what is it that you see in me?"

"*You* don't get it? You don't have to 'get it.' I do...I get to 'get it'!" She held her hand to her chest. "I do get it and I love it..." She pushed him over on his back and her blonde curls tumbled over his chest, caressing him as she hugged him. "...and I love your body...there's so much of you. There's so much of you. There's so much of you. There's so much of...."

His eyes flickered awake. It was happening again. It seemed so real and then it was gone. "Oh God...oh God, Mari...if you are not coming back to me...please Babe... get out of my head."

He got up and paced inside his lavish room, in his spectacular house, and money was pouring into his coffers on the average of a quarter of a million a week. But there was only one thing he wanted to know. "Where are you Mari?"

***

PAYBACK

As the year 2000 was drawing to a close, Hal and Deuce sat at their table in Benny's. Hal was somewhat morose but showed concern for his friend. "Did Big get your boys' trusts set up alright?"

"Yeah...Wanda is real happy about it. You know...that their education, and a good start in life, is taken care of."

"Right around this time next year, I'll call in the loan. Mark it on your calendar and be sure to remind me. Try not to need it sooner."

"Yeah...Wanda and I are pretty good right now. She's real happy that I'm working so hard and staying out of her hair. She loves the TV commercials...gives her bragging rights."

"How are you and Lo-Lo getting on?"

"That girl is amazing. We're getting on just fine." Deuce peered at Hal. "Man...you look dogged. What's up?"

Hal finished his beer and set the glass down. "You know it was about this time last year that I told Mari to go fuck off. I told her to get out of my house and out of my life...and that is just what she did. God, Deuce...we were planning to ring in the new millennium together...and then my wonderful life took a nosedive. I rang in the New Year at your house, sitting in a corner, hoisting a glass of champagne to emptiness..." His mouth pulled down to one side. "...and I can't get her out of my head..."

"And you shouldn't. It's not over for you and Mari...you're going to find her...you have to find her." Deuce screwed up his face. "But that's old shit. What's really eating at you?"

Hal half laughed. "You don't want to know...and for once I am not going to tell you. Let's just say it has been an interesting year...and I am on target. You'll know what went down when the shit hits the fan...and even then you won't know the half of it. But I need to ask a favor of you. I want to set up an irrevocable trust for Mari. I do know her Social Security Number to identify her...and I want you to be co-trustee on it...and the executor of my will. If anything happens to me...I want to leave her everything I have."

"Jesus, Hal...what are you into?"

"Will you do it for me?"

"Of course...but what are you into?"

Hal shook his head. "Not going to tell you. But, do you remember when you told me that I never had to risk failure? Well...I am risking it big time now." He clasped Deuce's hand. "On knight's honor you can't breathe a word of what I am about to say."

Deuce nodded. "On knight's honor…"

"If I don't succeed…I'm going to prison…"

"What the fuck!?!"

"That's all I'm going to say, man…and that's all you need to know."

***

Marvin had heard rumblings about the employee turnover in the warehouse for months and politely ignored them in deference to his officers. But, with every employee that originally worked there being laid off, goaded into quitting, or fired outright, he finally worked up a concern. With the shock of Vivian filing for divorce, it finally dawned on him that perhaps he should look into matters more closely. He stood, straightened his tie, and now took the unfamiliar walk to the warehouse.

As Marvin pushed on the large swinging doors, he found that something was blocking them. Pressing them open a crack, he saw a forklift parked on the other side, barring entrance. *Who did such a damn fool thing?* He thought. Not having the warehouse number and extension on his speed dial, he had to call the desk to have his call put through to the manager. When someone finally picked up, Marvin demanded to know, "Who is this?"

"Who are you calling?"

"Goddamn who I'm calling…is this the warehouse…and who are you!?!"

"Who's this?"

"This is Marvin Golan, the CEO of this company…and if you do not have the doors to the warehouse cleared within two minutes…you are fired. DO YOU UNDERSTAND ME!?!"

"Yes, sir!" The man grabbed the shirt of the nearest worker, stopping him in his tracks. He held his hand over the mouthpiece of the phone and whispered. "Go find Mr. Drummond and bring him here immediately!"

After two minutes, Marvin started pounding on the door. At length, he heard the forklift start up and someone drove it away. As he entered, Drummond stood with arms crossed just inside the entrance. "What are you doing here Mr. Golan?"

"What am I doing here? This is the warehouse of my company...why shouldn't I be here? I came to look around to see why the employees here are so dissatisfied...why they are dismissed or leaving."

"You could have just asked me."

"Yes...I could have...but I opted to come down and have a look around..."

Drummond walked over to a rack and retrieved a guest hard hat and gave it to Marvin. "Then by all means...you shall have the tour." This was the make-or-break moment for Drummond that always came to each operation when they took over a legitimate business, when the chumps discover that they've been had. Depending on their proclivities, they would usually join in on the transgression, or they would balk. If they could not be convinced, they could meet with an unfortunate demise. However, in this case the mission was not to kill, but to have Marvin take the fall and go to prison. From what Drummond had observed, Marvin was the type to transgress, and he bet on it. "Please...follow me."

Within the next hour Drummond showed Marvin the key to the newfound success of Arendt Medical and why the implant devices had been flying off the shelves. With pride, he took him into the secret room where the weapon conversions took place. Only the most trusted, levelheaded men, with craftsman skills, ever entered here. They worked silently with no fanfare.

Then Drummond revealed the packing department and how the weapons were smuggled. He sat Marvin down in the warehouse office and explained how Arendt had been laundering money through its padded invoices, payroll, expenditures, and returned products, and that his loan had been 'zero-ed' out. Marvin was silent as he watched and listened. He realized that Arendt was only deriving profits from the sale of their implants, not the weapons; he wanted more. "And what's in this gun running for me?"

Even in Drummond's experience, it was unusual for a dupe to adapt so quickly without a little arm-twisting. "What's in it for you, Mr. Golan, is that your company will thrive...will be back on top...and you have no knowledge of anything untoward."

"Why shouldn't I have a cut to stay silent?"

Drummond stared at Marvin, ostensibly deep in thought. He calculated that the operation would close in just under a year. The amount he would give Marvin would be trivial. "How much do you want?"

"One hundred thousand." Marvin pulled a figure out of his ass.

Drummond was amazed that Marvin asked for so little after hearing the figures he had just tossed around. He correctly surmised that analysis and calculation were not Marvin's forte. "Agreed. It will be paid in monthly increments."

Marvin smiled and shook Drummond's hand. Returning to his office, he felt giddy with power. He had an edge that his competitors did not. He had Drummond.

***

Hal finished his novel, a sweeping history of a family in the westward movement of the United States. His research was impeccable, the story line, riveting. He decided to launch a publishing company and print it himself. Moreover, publishing on demand was just on the verge of coming into vogue. Baby boomers were now in their fifties and reminiscing on paper about their lives. Young talent wanted the instant gratification of seeing their musings in print. Following his instincts, he opened a subsidiary for on demand publishing. He then hired skilled marketeers and hard charging salesmen and set about making appearances in bookstores and television interviews.

Pamela Bates, aka Priscilla Baxter, was actually in the public relations business and did a good job for him. After a TV appearance they had dinner. "Your work has been outstanding. My book sales are rocketing."

"I'm glad you are pleased. We are focusing on you Mr. Golan...within a few months you should be in the Times Top Ten....and, of course, get Lady "O's" Book Club recommendation."

"It's all happening so fast...it's hard to believe."

"Why? You wrote an excellent book. With our backing...it is going to go all the way. I know what you are going to say. Lots of authors write excellent books that go nowhere. You are different...because you have special dispensation. That is not to take away from your talent...that is the reality of who makes it...and who doesn't. It is rare that an author is recognized purely on ability anymore. Cracking the top ten is genius combined with special approbations." She toyed with her glass, moving her fingers up and down the stem. "How long are you going to be in New York?"

"That depends on how many appearances you can arrange for me. I have return tickets for next week...but they can be changed."

"I think I can arrange two more appearances...but what I was about to suggest is that we see each other on an informal basis...to get to know each other."

"Why do you want to get to know me on an informal basis?"

"Come now...I'm sure you can think of a reason..."

"You mean..." He pointed a finger back and forth between them to convey his meaning.

Her eyes slowly swept over him. "Yeah...to see what develops..."

"Do you mind answering a question for me? You're a beautiful woman...what is there about me that you find attractive?"

"That's a first." She laughed. "Men are usually so into themselves that they can't understand if you refuse to give them a tumble."

"Please...I really want to know."

She gazed at him for a while and then responded. "What you have, Mr. Golan, is a certain vulnerability that is interesting...no...sexy...to women...irresistible in a way. You are a big man...very strong and masculine in appearance and yet there is a sweetness about you...a vulnerability. I'm sure that you have seen it work for you before now...many times. It is a quality that women find endearing."

"So it's a real thing?"

"Yes...why do you find it so surprising?"

"There was an exquisitely beautiful woman in my life...that I loved beyond all measure...I am still in love with her. She said she loved me...she swore she loved me...and she did everything to show love to me...but I could never understand how someone like her could fall in love with someone like me. At the first sign of...difficulties...I pushed her away. It wasn't her fault...and now she is gone. I could never understand what she saw...what you see...in me...until now."

"Wow...that speaks volumes...glad that I could be of help and save you the cost of a shrink." She smiled.

"Do you sleep with all your clients?"

"No…just the ones I like…or, if it's a job to set up those that I don't. I like you very much…I think we could enjoy each other's company. Then it is back to business…"

When Hal flew back to L.A. it was with a deeper appreciation for himself. Pamela set about her profession of making him a household name.

***

The telephone woke Hal and he wondered who could be calling at this hour of the morning. "Yeah?"

"Man…turn on the TV!" Deuce's voice signaled urgency. "They're flying planes into the World Trade Center!"

"Who is doing what?"

"THEY…whoever they are! We don't know…turn on the TV!"

Hal turned on the TV to see horrific images of New York with smoke pouring from the World Trade Center twin towers. "What the fuck happened?!"

"They'll show it again…but a plane flew right into one tower…and everyone thought it was an accident. Then another plane flew into the other tower…and now they are saying we are being attacked. People are jumping out of windows rather than being burned in the fires…this is the goddamndest thing I ever saw!"

"Let me get back to you…I want to see what's going on."

"OK…I don't know what to make of this shit!"

Hal watched as the atrocity unfolded. Disregarding their safety, heroic firemen rushed into the buildings to save lives. Amid the chaos and horror; the towers disintegrated into colossal billows of triturate, as people fled before the spreading, rolling dust storm of debris. On another flight, brave men took on the hijackers and died in the resulting plane crash that very likely saved the residents of the presumed target, the White House. The Pentagon was hit by yet another plane. He tried to call Pamela in New York, but the circuits were busy, and he doubted that anyone could get through. He sent her an email asking her to reassure him that she was all right. Then, as always, his thoughts turned to Mari. *She couldn't possibly be in New York…she doesn't know anyone there…she has no family there…as though she would want to see those clowns. You don't know…she could be anywhere. There is no chance she could be in New York.* But the thought still nagged at him.

Lupe, the maid, padded into the kitchen, tied an apron around her plump body and soon coffee was brewing. Hal went in, poured himself a cup, and turned on the TV there. They watched the tragedy together over breakfast. Hal thought he should give Malone a call. He went into the bedroom and dialed on the burner. "Yeah…this is me. Are we affected in any way by what we are seeing on TV?"

"I'm not sure. The only way to get a message through is by carrier pigeon. I have to wait until the telephones clear up. Then we have to meet to talk about it. Call me next Friday to arrange it."

"Let me know if you hear from Pamela."

"Pamela? Are you bangin' that broad?"

"Only briefly."

"Don't let Drum know…it will make him crazy."

"I had no idea she was his lady…she came on to me…"

"She's not…but don't tell him that. She came on to you? What have you got, kid…what kind of cologne do you use?"

"She said I had vulnerability…and I'm rather proud of it…"

"Vulnerable what? Whatever it is…we need to bottle it and sell it…because it is working overtime for you!" He laughed. "Gotta go." He hung up.

With terrible fascination, Hal watched the rest of the day and wondered what it meant for everyone. At first his outrage was palpable. But, if there was one thing he learned from Malone, it was that keeping a cool head is critical for clear thinking.

***

The view from the Santa Monica Palisades drew the eye in every direction. The greenery of the park, against the wide expanse of blue ocean dotted with sailboats, was picturesque. Hal waited in the park near the intersection of Montana and Ocean Avenues. He spotted Malone's Escalade and knew he would be along in a few minutes. He was hoping that all would continue as planned, but he sensed that the attack on the World Trade Center had brought about a change and for some reason he felt apprehensive. Malone came up the path holding a cigarette. He stopped and asked Hal for a light. Hal gave him a matchbook and Malone lit the cigarette, gave it back to him, and looked out over the railing as though engaged in idle conversation. "I was hoping we were near the end of our operation…but the east coast is sealed up tighter than a drum ever

361

since the attacks and they want us to pick up the slack. The thing that makes me nervous is that we have a smooth operation going here...and ordinarily I would not mind keeping it going a little longer...but under the circumstances, I think that shutting it down now would be the wise thing to do. When you have nervous nellies forcing your hand and overloading the pipeline...that is when things go wrong." He took a sincere drag off the cigarette and looked at it. "I forgot how good these damned things taste. I quit years ago." He took one more drag and flicked it over the cliffs into the sand below.

"Our plan was to tip off the ATF, have Marvin left with the goods, and close the doors by October...November at the latest. Are we still able to stick to that schedule?"

"That's the decision we have to make."

"Have you gotten any word about Pamela?"

"Yes...she's OK."

"That's a relief. I like her. She's intelligent. She knows who she is...she knows what she wants...and she makes no bones about it."

"Don't tell me you're going soft on her."

"Hell no!" Hal laughed. "You know me...I live with my obsession."

Malone nodded. "Still no luck?"

Hal shook his head, and then went back to the problem at hand. "I don't want to appear selfish here...but I would really like to shut this operation down...let Marvin slip in his own shit...and be done with it. They must have other outlets. How do you feel about it?"

"I agree. The only thing is the medical implants were such a great cover...they want to keep it going."

"What did they do before we came up with the implant scheme?"

"They have ingenious ways...but that was one of the best by far. Once the ATF knows about it...we will play hell using it again."

"Haven't they ever been able to use a ruse that they were caught using before? I was thinking that if they open a distributorship for the implants...we could sell them the implants and they can use them as before. I think that the reputation of a company would count for more than the product sold."

"I suppose...but that would take a lot of up-front money."

"Can we extend credit...and wait for the payoff?"

"Sounds pretty good...but I don't know if they will go for it after we have Arendt raided."

"After the raid...do you think that the ATF would suppose that we would be dumb enough to use implants again?"

"Like you said...we've used all kinds of things. They can't suspect every medical device manufacturer or distributor of smuggling." Malone rubbed his hands together. "We can make a counter proposal that they can open a distributorship...we will extend credit to buy the implants...and they can handle it all from...let's say...Texas...Arizona...whatever..."

"So that's a *go* on shutting us down?"

"Yeah...I think so. We'll just insist upon it."

"When do we do it?"

"How about Halloween?"

"Anyone ever tell you that you've got a macabre sense of humor?"

"Yeah..." He laughed. "...I even used a guy's head for a bowling ball...I slid him down the lane into the pins. It was a strike...and it broke up the crowd."

***

Drummond whipped out his burner and dialed. "Marvin...Drummond here. It's important that you meet me in the warehouse at nine p.m. sharp. We have some people arriving who will be there specifically to meet you and to do a walk through so they may expand our operation."

"Well...I had a prior engagement..."

"Cancel it! We need you there because the purchase of your products will be central to our plans and will more than double your sales. You are going to be the lynchpin on which this deal depends. You must be there."

"That sounds excellent...I will be there at nine sharp!"

Drummond hung up and dialed another number. "Hack...take out Bartel Enterprises, Gilbert Drummond, Priscilla Baxter...." He continued with the list of names and companies that needed to disappear from the computer files of several companies. His hair was now dyed dark again and his eyes were a soft chocolate brown. Carrying his suitcase, he got into his summoned cab and, as he was whisked away to LAX, he made another call to the warehouse. "OK...at five sharp...shut down the shop. Everyone must go. Leave the merchandise where it is. No...leave it where it is...we won't even miss it. There is a suitcase under the workbench...for God's sake...do NOT

363

touch it...it will explode!" Drummond hung up laughing to himself. The old "it will explode" line has always insured that the suitcase would remain untouched. Once at LAX, he went straight to the VIP Lounge and counted noses to make sure all of his people were there, and each had a carry-on bag. Like a mother hen, he marshaled them all into the plane. The plane taxied onto the runway, revved the jets to a scream, commenced its run and, building speed, it lifted off into the sky and disappeared.

***

The warehouse was brightly lit when Marvin arrived, but the usual hum of activity was gone. The night shift was not there. *Drummond probably let them go for the night since we are having guests.* Marvin told himself. He was slightly early because he did not want to be late, so he fiddled around waiting and found himself entering the conversion room. *That's odd that it's unlocked. Oh, it's probably because Drummond wants to show our operation when they get here.* He picked up a VZ 61 Skorpion and examined it, regretting that he never had the opportunity to shoot it. He pictured how his limousine liberal friends in Beverly Hills would react to seeing him shoot off a few rounds at a party. *They would shit their pants!* He chortled. He put the gun down and looked at his watch. *My watch must be fast...Drummond is never late.*

"ATF! ATF! ATF!" Men in dark vests with yellow lettering, designating ATF, burst into the warehouse swarming in from all sides. Their guns were drawn as they surrounded him, and then they quickly spread out to search the premises. "Secure all doors...!"

Fear bounded back and forth in Marvin's stomach as the shock of realization swept over him. "What's happening? Who are you? What does ATF mean?" Roughly handled, he was thrown to the floor and an officer pinned him there with a knee in his back.

"Hey...Harry...look what we have here!" An agent entered the conversion room and found a wealth of contraband. "Whooo-weee...lookee here!" One of the officers discovered the suitcase full of cash in small denominations. "Looks like he was ready to go somewhere."

Once Marvin was cuffed and lifted to his feet, he was shown a search warrant.

"But...you don't understand. I have nothing to do with this. It's all a mistake..." Marvin started sobbing. "...It's all a mistake..." Two large officers hooked their arms under his and carried him, with his toes dragging, to a waiting vehicle.

Outside, he could see lights flashing and that Arendt Medical was surrounded. Yellow tape was being crisscrossed over doors and across gate openings to the parking lot. With the exception of a bleary-eyed security guard, no one else was there. Search teams were brought in to secure the evidence. As Arendt Medical was being swarmed from top to bottom, Marvin cried, "I want an attorney...I want an attorney! I want an attorney..."

***

In a relatively seedy building on Sunset Boulevard, private detective, Matt Gray, loafed in his office staring at the pictures of him as a child actor, which adorned the room. His resentment of lost stardom, at an impressionable age, and then sinking into obscurity, still rankled him after decades of being out of the "business." Solace in his work as a private investigator was mainly derived from knowing the dirty little secrets, and the misery, of Hollywood's elite. The pleasure he derived from adding to their pain was enormous. The petty Golan affair was naught compared to murders swept under the rug, careers ruined in the path of embezzled funds, blackmail, and shakedowns. Sons, or daughters, being disillusioned, by fathers removing the scales from their eyes, or inventing unseemly notoriety, were fairly commonplace. The Golan case had been completely forgotten.

A squad of LAPD officers walked into his reception, brushed aside his secretary, and burst into his office. "Mr. Matthew Gray?"

"Who wants to know?"

An officer flashed his badge and ID. "Don't get cute, Gray...we have a search warrant for your office."

"A search warrant? What could you possibly be looking for?"

"Read the warrant...it is listed right there."

"You've got to be joking! You're looking for narcotics?"

"Oh...you can read and perceive. OK, guys...start taking this place apart."

More of a wrecking crew than a search party; the cops pulled out and overturned file drawers, desks, office supplies, a photo lab, a bathroom, and tore out ceilings and walls before going to the place where they were instructed to look. "The air conditioning vent...are you kidding me? How pedestrian of you." The officer made a face. "What have we got here? A kilo of smack...and two kilos of pot. Anything else? Some bags of ecstasy...priming the young crowd, Matt?"

"I never saw that shit before in my life!"

"For an actor...you think you would have come up with a better line. That's what they all say."

"Look...you gotta believe me..."

"No I don't...I just have to arrest you. It's a jury you are going to have to convince."

"I know people...if you dare to arrest me, I will have your badge. I know their secrets...they will do anything to get me out of a jam..."

"Oh...you want to threaten some big shots with what you know? I hate to break it to you, Sparky...but the last person who threatened to tell all they know...ended up extremely dead. So, if I were you...I would bite the bullet."

***

"Big...I need a recommendation for an attorney. What I want is one who has a great reputation...but really doesn't know his ass from first base." Hal called his friend.

"Oh...oh I see. You want him for your father. I saw that on the news last night. Yeah...I know just the guy...perfect for the job...none better...Jack Brady. Now there is a fuck up if there ever was one...a walking calamity...a legal jackass...costly...great reputation...but a fuck up, nonetheless. Don't tell him I recommended him to you. I tossed a dog turd into his briefcase and I don't know why...but out of a room full of attorneys he always suspected that it was me who did the dirty deed. Do I look like a dog turd wrangler to you?"

"Yeah...you look like a dog turd tosser to me...and I would highly recommend you to anyone who needs to have shit thrown!"

"Why thank you!!"

"Big...I love ya! Thanks for the referral."

***

Marvin sat by his attorney's side trying to assume a confident air. He had been advised that he could get immunity if he was able to assist in breaking up the firearms trafficking ring. Jack Brady, at six feet, four inches and over three hundred pounds, was imposing. His assertive voice added to that impression. But he did not have the thoroughness required of his profession which led to some major gaffes. "Mr. Golan wants immunity...he will then reveal who is behind this weapons trafficking scheme."

Unfortunately, before asking for immunity for his client, Brady did not verify if Marvin could substantiate his story. Nor did he get the proffer in writing. He wrote down the facts as alleged by Marvin, relied on his client telling the truth, and submitted his request for immunity.

The prosecutor cautioned Marvin. "You do understand that you must be perfectly candid in all particulars. If we find that you are not truthful in every material detail...your immunity will not be granted...or if granted will be revoked. Do you understand?"

"Yes...yes...I want to tell you everything because I feel that I have been tricked...left holding the bag." Marvin went on to explain what occurred in painstaking detail. He spelled out the crisis Arendt Medical was in, how Bartel Enterprises in the person of Gilbert Drummond stepped in to rescue the company, the use of the implants as cover to smuggle weapons, how he had inadvertently discovered the firearms trafficking, and how Drummond involved him in the operation. In other words, he spilled his guts.

The prosecutor listened intently, looked down at his file, and looked back at Marvin. "What about the money laundering?"

"Money laundering?"

"Yes...the simplest forensic auditing of your books shows that Arendt Medical laundered millions in the time frame you are referring to. Also...there is the matter of fraudulent wire transfers..."

"I know nothing about that." He lied.

"Mr. Golan...you are in deep doo-doo here. Your story is not credible. You wind us up with this fable...that you...the CEO of Arendt Medical...knew nothing of what was going on in your company." The prosecutor folded his file. "We will attempt to verify what you have told us...but your account of the illegal transactions of your company falls short of what we can prove."

It did not take long for the prosecution to debunk Marvin's story as fallacious. There was no Bartel Enterprises in existence, no Gilbert Drummond, no Priscilla Baxter, or any of the other names Marvin had conjured up. "Mr. Golan...it appears that nothing you have told us has any ring of truth to it. There is no Bartel Enterprises...and we cannot find any record of the people you referred us to. By your own admission you were the indispensable part...if not the kingpin...of an extensive arms trafficking ring. When you include money laundering and fraudulent transfers...you are looking at some heavy-duty time."

"But...but...I've told you everything I know!"

"And that is quite enough to get you convicted."

***

The year 2002 saw Marvin tried and convicted. With all the charges brought against him, he was sentenced to ten years in prison. The feds suspected that he had fiddled with Arendt stock, but the proof was tenuous and, with all the time he had accrued, they felt that justice had been served. They considered the matter closed. In addition to his sentence, the court deprived him of the ability to hold the position of CEO in any company and from holding Arendt stock. As the sentence was read, Hal and Vivian sat in the courtroom maintaining a glum aspect as they watched the proceedings. After court was adjourned, they made their way through the crowd of reporters muttering, "No comment."

Once they were ensconced in Vivian's home, Graham greeted them with champagne. He had correctly surmised that the two of them were not all that broken up about Marvin's predicament. "After such a trying day...I thought you could use some refreshment. You have my sincere sentiments for what you have had to put up with ..."

***

Even after dark, reporters milled around the outside of Vivian's home hoping for a glimpse of the family. Hal hired extra security to ensure that the most exuberant among them did not invade the mansion grounds. After giving the situation some well thought out analysis, he decided that there was no better time to gain public sympathy and to announce the future plans of Arendt Medical, Inc. The company's stock had revived under the guidance, and profiteering, of Bartel Enterprises. But it had been in steady decline since Marvin's arrest. If Hal could recapture the public's trust, he felt sure that he could put Arendt on solid footing once more. The gates to the Golan mansion opened and a security guard hailed the press. "The Golan family is ready to receive you...and to hold a press conference. Please show your press credentials and then follow me...and do not stray away from the area where you are permitted to go."

A stand of microphones and lights had been set up at the top of the veranda stairs a few steps from the massive front door. A space on the driveway had been cordoned off and filled with folding chairs to accommodate the media. A table of sandwiches and assorted snacks had been prepared to welcome them, along with a tub filled with ice-cold beverages. Grateful for sustenance after hours of staking out the entrance to the home, the reporters wolfed down the food and were happy to find a choice of beer in the midst of the proffered soft drinks. After giving them time to eat, Graham, dressed in shirtsleeves and slacks, came out on the porch, adjusted the sound system, and announced, "Ms. Vivian Golan and her son...Mr. Golan...will be making a statement to the press in about five minutes. You can ask ten questions...so you may want to decide amongst yourselves what to ask and who will pose the questions. If you have not yet had a chance to enjoy the buffet...may I suggest that you do so now." He turned and went back into the house.

When the door opened again, Hal, with a protective arm around Vivian, walked her to the podium and stood beside her as he gently positioned her in front of the microphone. Her face was drawn, and she carried a handkerchief. In a small voice she began to speak. "I want to thank all of you for being so patient with us during...what was for us a very difficult time. Up until now we only told you 'no comment' because we...we...were in shock. We could not believe the charges that were leveled against my hus...my ex-husband. It seemed impossible to us...and it wasn't until we heard the evidence presented in court...that we realized that it was inescapably true...what he did. My grandfather built Arendt Medical and my father grew it into a well-respected giant in the field. For eighty-two years Arendt has had an impeccable reputation in medical equipment...and overnight he destroyed..." She dabbed her eyes with the handkerchief and Hal went to her and pulled her away from the microphone and asked Graham to get a chair for her.

After Vivian was seated, Hal stepped up to the mike. "I want to thank you again for your understanding. Until now we had nothing to say because we didn't know *what* to say. We were traumatized. Now that we know the truth...we have had to cope with a number of things that we found unbearable. It was a terrible blow to find out about the illegal activities my father engaged in and quite frankly...as you may well understand...we are still reeling from his arrest and conviction. But, just as important...on a different level...is what has happened to our loyal employees...some who had been with us for decades...and our shareholders. My father ignored our moral obligation to our people. He also ignored our moral obligation to our customers. It was my great grandfather's and my grandfather's philosophy that our employees are the bedrock of Arendt Medical...and that they were to be respected and honored for their service and loyalty to the company. Also, they believed that putting a first rate, quality product on the market was the only way to ensure the necessary integrity that it takes to do business in the medical field. Our name and our reputation should supersede any other concern...so that our customers are able to trust...without reservation...in the products that we sell them. I am equally...and deeply...disappointed and dismayed that these laws of decency were violated as well.

"As you know...my father has been precluded from being CEO in any company and from holding shares in Arendt. He has signed his shares over to me. My mother has decided that she wants me to be the CEO of Arendt...to rebuild the ruins of the company into one her father would have been proud of. She is the majority shareholder, so I have been given my orders. To accomplish the task before me I will be contacting most of our former employees in an effort to re-hire them and restore their seniority and pension plans. I pledge to you...the public...that our products will be made from the best available materials...and will be the state of the art in quality. I have instructed our attorneys to consolidate the actions against Arendt for injuries...into a class action suit so that we may fairly and equitably compensate those who may have been injured. As we grow our company to its former prestige...our shareholders will reap the benefits that they have patiently awaited." Hal searched the faces of the reporters for their reaction. They looked predisposed to being sympathetic, but he cautioned himself against over confidence. "I will take your questions now."

One reporter stood and asked, "Has your relationship with your father been irreparably broken?"

Hal gave a big sigh. "No...out of a sense of duty...I will be visiting my father..." He screwed up his face. "...but it will be difficult. I must tell you that it will also be out of curiosity to ask him just what he was thinking." He stretched out his hands. "We don't pick our fathers. We can only ask them why."

***

Hal made the long drive to the federal penitentiary to relish the retribution Marvin was now enduring. What was unexpected was the sheer weight of despair the sight of a prison evokes, as seen from a distance, which only increases as you get closer. Due to the notoriety of Marvin's case, his social status, being a first offender, his age, and his attorney currying favor, he was being held in protective custody. Following the unsmiling guards' perfunctory instructions, Hal made his way to the visitors' room to await his turn. After what seemed like an interminable amount of time, he was then instructed to go to the indicated window and wait again. Marvin was directed to his seat by a guard and resignedly sat down. Gone was the robust Marvin, brash and full of confidence; he seemed to be ashen and old. Hal tried to look appalled, but it was just the manifestation he had been hoping for; he was a beaten, hoary man who had been stripped of all that he cared for. Hal picked up the receiver to talk. "How are you doing, dad? Are they treating you OK?"

Marvin waved his hand. "There is nothing OK in this place."

"Is there anything I can do for you?"

"No...as long as I have money...it will keep them off of me."

"Keep who off of you?"

"We've got some goons in here who think they are king of the jungle. I just don't want to be thrown into general population. How's my appeal going?"

"I have been so busy I haven't had the chance to call your attorney. Hasn't he come to see you?"

"Not in a while. Why hasn't your mother come to see me?"

"She divorced you, dad. She filed for divorce long before any of this happened. I don't think she wants to see you like this...and I don't think it would be good for her to see you in prison."

"I know we're divorced...but we were married for thirty-four years. You'd think that would count for something."

Hal thought, *you selfish, egotistical bastard...now you think your marriage should count for something...now that you can't bang every chick you can lay your hands on.* "I'll see what I can do. Is there anything I can get for you?"

"Yeah...stuff I can trade...candy, cigars, cigarettes...stuff like that..."

"OK. You know I am CEO of Arendt now. I moved into your offices...and I am selling off most of the junk in there. I don't need it. All I need is a good up to date computer system. Oh, and a lady friend of yours came by...she said she is...was your...companion?" Hal shrugged. "Anyway...it wasn't clear. She was looking for a handout...she said you would understand. I told her I had no idea who she was...and I was the person who has to understand...and I sent her packing."

"You sent her packing? Oh...Hal you fucked up. She meant a lot to me...she was my..."

"Yeah...ma said the same thing...she said she was your mistress and that I should have given her a couple of bucks. But how was I to know? Maybe she will come to visit you..."

"Vivian knew about her?"

"She said she has known for years...I guess ma is not as dumb as you thought she was..."

Marvin winced. "Son...try not to judge me too harshly..."

"I don't judge you at all...you're my father. I just want to know why you did what you did. I mean...gunrunning?"

Marvin took a deep breath. "Dealing in guns...it sounded like easy money. It was a way of getting Arendt back on top..."

"Did anyone else other than you...and the people you were dealing with...know about it?"

"No...all of the long-standing Arendt employees never knew...and over time they were driven out and replaced. It was real easy money...and a lot of it. The temptation was too great...I gave in to it. Everything seemed to be going along just fine...and then it exploded in my face."

Hal hoped that they were recording their conversation, for if they were, there went Marvin's appeal. It was a clear, uncoerced, confession that put the blame squarely on Marvin's shoulders and allayed any possible blame that could point to Hal. Marvin just exonerated him.

When visiting hours were over, Hal called Jack Brady. "Cut off his money and have him moved into general population...there is a tenner in it for you." Hal offered ten thousand.

"It will cost more than that. Try twenty."

"OK...but you decide how long you want to represent him. You keep fucking me over on costs...and *he* may decide he wants another attorney..."

"After what he is going to go through...he may decide that in any event...I'm just trying to make a living...and I have to pay off people too."

"OK...that's reasonable. Do what you gotta do."

***

Most of Arendt's former employees returned to the company, especially the old timers who were interested in the restoration of their pensions. The conference room was packed. Those that Hal designated to be the new officers and directors were seated at the long table. The rest crowded in to stand around the conference room for the meeting. Hal stood at the head of the table to address them. "I want to thank each and every one of you for returning to Arendt and for the loyalty you have shown to the company. We are at the starting line of a new beginning...and while the success of Arendt is not a sure thing...in your capable hands I have every faith that it will become what it used to be...what it was intended to be...a rock solid name in the industry.

"For those of you who have been with Arendt for ten years or more…I have restored your pensions. Let me draw your attention to the men and women seated at the table. These are the new officers and directors of Arendt…the very people who built this company and know how to meet the daily necessities of keeping it running. Mack…please stand…" He gestured for Mack to come forward. There was an outbreak of applause of general approbation. "…Mack will be my second in command. He is familiar with most of the operations of Arendt and will confer with those who will be in charge of each department. Mack…do you want to say a few words?"

"I just want to say that this is a great day. This is what we have been waiting for…a fair and decent man to take the reins of the company…and we are going to show him what we are made of…that we will turn Arendt around and build it the right way." Mack sat down to a round of applause.

Hal knew that Mack was the best man to help him run Arendt, but he was also an honest man, and there was nothing more dangerous to clandestine activities than an honest man. He would have to clean out all of the defective products with the appearance of propriety, while secretly making them available to Malone. He needed time. "As many of you know…we will be improving the quality of our products and that will call for some changes in suppliers and in manufacturing. Generally speaking, the company will be ready for startup in two weeks. During that time Mack will be busy preparing the production department with new equipment. The price of titanium has dropped to where it is now feasible for us to produce all of our replacement devices with titanium…the best in the business…" Hal played his ace card to win over their patience to wait out the two weeks. "Before I open the meeting to questions, I want you to know that by this time next year…if all goes well…I will issue stock in the company to each of you based on the number of years you have been with Arendt. You will have a stake in the company's success."

After the meeting was over Hal walked with Mack over to manufacturing, more to make sure he was out of the warehouse than the necessity of imparting instructions. "Mack…the supplier we want to do business with for our titanium will be calling on us tomorrow. Let him give us his full sales pitch and tell him we will let him know. Let him sweat it for a day or two…and then call him back and tell him we are interested...but we need a better price break. If he comes down in price...take the deal. If he doesn't...insist on a better price and give him time to talk to his people...then when he drops his drawers...and he will...take the deal."

"Well that hardly seems fair..."

"Actually, it is...they expect it and have already adjusted the price higher to accommodate haggling. It's done every day...and right now we need to get the best bargain we can...from all our suppliers."

"Oh...I see. Will do...and I'll call all of our suppliers to try to Je..." He cleaned up what he was going to say. "...to see if they will give us a break. Under our situation...they probably will..."

"That's the spirit..."

Once Mack was safely ensconced in manufacturing, Hal hotfooted it to the warehouse to supervise the disposal of the defective hip implants. Men on forklifts were still loading the inventory on pallets when a semi-truck pulled up to the dock. It was clearly marked "Disposal Services." Under the guise of taking the devices for recycling the metal, Hal was having them shipped to Malone's new distributorship in Arizona. The deal was off the cuff and off the books, with only a small amount showing for the purported recycling. He readied himself to follow the shipment to Arizona to take a look at the new operation. Hal and Malone were back in business.

***

Marvin limped over to the table and gingerly sat down. Now that he was in general population, he could have contact visits in the visiting room. "Son, what happened to my money? They said there was no money and I was thrown into general population." His voice wheezed as his eyes moistened. "I've been terribly abused."

"Dad...what happened?" Hal looked alarmed.

"I don't know. They said Brady never paid them...and they put me out there with those animals...and I can't...I can't..." He started to weep. "Don't leave me here, son. Get me out...get me out!"

"Aw geez, dad...didn't Brady come to see you? Didn't he pay everybody off?"

"Nooo." His voice shook. "Can't you do something? Can't you do something now?"

"I can try...what did they do to you?"

Marvin leaned over and muttered the indignities he endured. His tears came faster with each word. Spittle bubbled out of his mouth, and snot ran from his nose, as he blubbered out his tale of suffering.

"Nooooo...Oh my God! How can they let something like that go on? Where were the guards? Didn't anyone try to help you?"

"I cried out...I screamed...but nobody heard me."

"Did they get you medical attention?"

"No...they just laughed."

"I'll find out what's wrong with Brady today and why he hasn't taken better care of you."

Hal called Jack Brady after his visit with Marvin. "OK you can turn on the spigot again."

***

The phone could barely be heard above the noise of the shower. Stepping out of the shower and grabbing a towel, Hal dried his hands and face before picking up the burner.

"Yeah?"

"It's me...don't say any names..." Hal recognized Pamela's voice.

"OK...what's up?"

"One and two are walking into a trap. They are supposed to meet in Arizona tomorrow at nine at night...you know where...it's going to be bad..."

"Yeah...who are they meeting with and what's going down?"

"New York...and one and two...they're not going to leave the warehouse...I don't want you to be there with them..."

"Aw, shit! Do you know who has the job?"

"I've said too much already...I've got to go." She hung up.

Hal dialed Malone's direct line. There was no answer. He dialed the club's number. Johnny picked up. "Hey...I gotta talk to Malone...is he there?"

"Who is this...Super Jew?"

"Fuck you."

"OK...it's you. Malone's not here..."

"It is urgent that I talk to him...you got a number?"

"Do you think he would trust me with that? I got nothin'."

Hal hung up, deep in thought. *Malone is a big boy...he can take care of himself...he knows the risks that come with the game he's in. I'm a civilian...not a soldier...as they are always pointing out to*

376

me. Why should I go tearing off to his rescue? He wrestled with his conscience and rubbed his hands together as he paced. *Fuck! I'll be goddamned if I leave Malone twisting in the wind.* He slammed a fist into his other hand. *I got to go!*

He went to his closet and dug out a Skorpion he hid there and a box of banana clips. He got dressed in jeans and a turtleneck pull over. In the back of his closet he spied an old, khaki safari jacket with lots of pockets that he used to wear for photography excursions. He put it on. He called Deuce. "Hey buddy...I got a favor to ask...don't even say I'm calling you. You know that thing your father brought home from 'Nam?"

"What thing are you talking about?"

"You know we used to play with it when we were kids...it's a dud."

"Are you talking about that thing he brought home before he went back?"

"Yeah..."

"What you up to?"

"Nothing you need to worry your pretty little head about. It just might come in handy...for show and tell."

"Goddamn it...what have you done now?"

"I need it...are you going to bring it?"

"Yeah...I'll bring it...but I should shove it up your..."

"Thanks Deuce...get it to me as soon as you can...I need to get on the move pretty quick."

"You better believe I'm going to be there...and you've got some 'splainin' to do!"

Within a half hour, Deuce pulled up to Hal's door and carried a small paper bag with him. Before he could knock Hal opened the door. "You're a godsend..."

"I never heard of God asking for a grenade before. What's going on?"

"Look...it's just a dud...but it looks real and it just might come in handy to ferret out some bad dudes." Hal took the bag, looked inside, and packed it with the Skorpion.

"OK...who are these bad dudes? How deep are you in? I saw what happened to Marvin...that was you...wasn't it?"

Hal grinned. "It wasn't the Easter Bunny!"

"Are you in with these gun people?"

"Ask me no questions and I'll tell you no lies."

Deuce stared at him for a spell and then quietly asked, "Are you about to get yourself killed?"

The question brought Hal up short. The reality of actually dying never seemed real to him until Deuce gently pointed out what could happen. He took a deep breath. "I hope not."

"You are going to tell me what this is all about...and I'm going with you."

"No...you're not. I can't have you with me. This could get ugly..."

"If it is too dangerous for me to go with you...then it is too dangerous for you to go alone! You are going to tell me what kind of stupid donkey shit you got yourself into...I'm going with you...and I'm going to bring your dumb ass back home!"

***

"Hey lead foot...slow down to the speed limit. Have you forgotten that you are carrying dangerous cargo?" Deuce cautioned.

"Oh yeah...the guns."

"Fuck the guns...you got a black man in your car...in Arizona. This state rejected a holiday off from work rather than honor a black man...that's some deep hate. I wouldn't want you to get stopped by some cop here. Oh yeah...and we got those guns..." Deuce shifted in his seat. "I can't believe what all you got into. I admit that Marvin deserved everything he got..."

"What he did to me and Mari is a large part of it...but not all of it. Arendt was making heavy duty profits before I sank their ship...there was no need to shit on the senior employees for a few bucks more...he used them up for almost all of their productive lives and then tossed them out like so much garbage. I promoted them to run the show. Another damn fool thing was taking the manufacturing away from the contractor that put out a quality product for us...and after that they still cut corners...and that is what brought on the lawsuits. Then there is how he used up my mother's life without one concern for her feelings. He cheated on my mother with his mistress...and he cheated on his mistress with the next young thing that came along. I have never seen a more hedonistic bastard in my life. What he did was criminal...but you can't call it a crime. All I did was to expose him to his natural element, and he took to it like a duck to water. In fact...in a big way I have more respect for Malone and

378

friends...and that is why I've got to make sure that New York doesn't take them down."

"So, you killed this guy to save Malone's life? Now I'm thinking you killed that Zack as well."

"I didn't kill him!"

"Hey...just sayin' *respect!* You're tougher than I thought you were...all this shit you pulled off...I gotta say *respect!*"

"Now I have to figure out what we're going to do when we get there."

"What's the grenade for?"

"To flush them out if they hole up...one look at that...and they will shit their shorts and run. Then we can nail them. I just hope we're not too late."

***

The new distributorship was nothing more than a small showroom, a couple of offices and a large warehouse. It was located in what was supposed to be an industrial park, in the desert environs on the outskirts of Tucson, but after erecting the one building the developer ran out of funding and was more than happy to lease the place. It was close enough to town, not to appear antisocial, but far enough away from suspicious "nosy nellies."

When Malone went ahead with the raid on Arendt, his New York associates were disenchanted that their request had been dismissed. The proposition to take over the operation out of their own distributorship was even less appealing. They liked running the operation out of a legitimate business where their hands were invisible. They did not understand that they could be just as invisible and cut out the middleman expenses. They could fold their tents and disappear at any time. The lease was through a dummy corporation. In deciding how to alleviate their frustration, they chose to take over Malone's operation; the irony being that running their own distributorship was what Malone proposed for them to do in the first place. They sent Fat Man and Little Boy out to Arizona, something they did only when they decided to go nuclear.

Hal and Deuce pulled up to the warehouse at eight-thirty. Malone's Escalade was there, and another car Hal didn't recognize. He had given Deuce his holster with the thirty-eight snub nose and a box full of ammunition. He carried the Skorpion and the grenade; his pockets bulged with banana clips. "Shit...they both got here early..."

As they cautiously got out of the Mercedes, they heard gunfire. There was a ratta-tat-tat of a machine gun and several reports of a pistol. "You ain't going in there...!"

"I'm afraid I am."

"There's shootin' in there...how are you going to go in there?"

"Very carefully..."

"Son of a bitch...who do you think you are...the Mossad?"

"I wish I were...look, I'm scared enough...no more negativity..."

"Nega-fuckin'-tivity?! They are shootin' in there!!"

"I know...and I got to get Malone out..." Hal pulled out the Skorpion and headed for the door and stood to one side of it. Deuce shook his head and went after him. Trying the front door, Hal found it was unlocked. He twisted the knob and gently pushed it open. He quickly peeked inside the showroom and drew back. No one was there. Gunshots rang out again and he could tell they were coming from the warehouse. He dashed inside, followed by Deuce, and carefully advanced up the stairs to the warehouse catwalk. He eased himself out a few feet to see if he could locate the combatants. He could see that Malone and Manny were pinned down behind boxes with only pistols to defend their position. The New Yorkers had VZ-58's and were across the aisle about thirty feet away, protected by wall of stacked boxes. They would step out in an opening and give a burst of automatic gun fire before quickly retreating, hoping to draw return fire to deplete their rival's ammunition. Hal could see only two men, but they had superior firepower and he sensed that Malone and Manny were running low. If he shot from above, he would give away his position and take return fire with nothing to protect him. He saw an opening where he thought he could get to Malone's position without being seen. Creeping back off the catwalk, he signaled Deuce to go back down the stairs. Going through the showroom he opened the door to the warehouse and did a low crawl behind the boxes to get near Malone's position. There was another aisle where he would be visible. He waited for a burst of fire and then ran to Malone's nest. "Psssst...Malone...it's me, Hal..." He whispered. "Pssst...can you hear me."

"What the fuck...how did you get here?"

"A little bird told me you needed help...hold on...I got someone with me." There was a burst of fire and Hal returned fire to cover Deuce as he ran to his position. "Make an opening so we can come in."

Manny and Malone removed a few boxes behind them so Hal and Deuce could crawl in. Malone looked at Deuce. "Who's he?"

"My best friend...he knows that if you go down...I go down...he's righteous." He gave Malone and Manny a box of thirty-eights. "I saw the predicament you're in...from up there." He pointed to the catwalk. "We have a plan..." He took out the grenade. "This is a dud...but they don't know that. You, me, and Manny get set to take them out. Deuce will throw the grenade...he's got an arm you wouldn't believe. When it drops in on them...they will run like hell...and we'll get them!"

"That's your plan?"

"It's the only one we've got..."

Malone shrugged. "Let's go for it."

"Deuce...don't forget to pull the pin...it has to look real."

"I got it covered."

"Just lob it across the aisle...right over those boxes..."

Hal, Malone, and Manny moved into position. Deuce made a couple of practice motions and then he pulled the pin and hurled the grenade. They could hear it hit the cement floor between the cartons. A man from the other side blurted out, "What was that?" A huge explosion rocked the warehouse blowing boxes and body parts into the air and the four men ducked for cover. A gentle mist of blood and bits of tissue rained down on them as Hal and Deuce stared at each other in disbelief.

"JESUS CHRIST!! YOU SAID THAT WAS A DUD!! WE USED TO PLAY WITH THAT DAMNED THING AS KIDS!!!" Hal held his out his hands in astonishment.

"My mother said it was a dud...how was I to know?"

"Jesus Christ! Thank God we never pulled the pin!"

"My mother told us not to break it..."

Malone howled with laughter. "You two are the damndest rescuers..." He turned to Deuce. "What's your name, kid?"

"Deuce."

"No...what's your real name?"

"Terrence Farrell, the Second."

Malone thought it was a mismatched name for a big, black tough guy. "OK, Deuce, welcome to the club. If you ever need anything...you call me. Hal has the number."

"Am I in trouble? I just killed those two guys..."

"No...no trouble at all. You helped save our lives. Like I said...you're one of us now. We take care of our own..."

Manny took out his burner. "I'll call for clean up."

***

The year 2003 started without a hitch and continued to see Arendt recover its stature. A glowing report found its way into Angel City Magazine and was picked up by business periodicals. Hal followed Big's advice and consolidated Arendt's legal woes into a class action suit, which was advantageous to the company. Instead of handling the lawsuits on a one by one basis, which was the advice of the previous attorney, it was better for the company to have a class action suit against it where it could settle all liability at once for a comparative pittance. Instead of forking out jury verdicts of seven or eight million per plaintiff in individual cases, Arendt corralled its liability into a class action that it settled for approximately two hundred and fifty thousand or less per plaintiff. This move made for great public relations and, in limiting its liability, curried favor with investors.

Mack ran a tight ship. Following Doren Arendt's example, he checked in on each department daily to make sure everything was running smoothly. He addressed and solved problems quickly. It was a mystery to Hal why Marvin did not utilize the talent and knowledge of his senior employees by promoting them to run the company. There was very little left for Hal to do except to watch the company grow and have Mack train his replacement for when he retired.

Supplying the Arizona operation was similarly no problem. When New York could not take over the Arizona distributorship, they finally realized the efficacy of opening their own in Texas and finding another supplier. Fucking with Malone was too costly. Malone was a cautious and steady hand with a sixth sense for being low key and, since accounting was not within Mack's purview, Hal put in one of Malone's men who deftly kept all the accounts, paying special attention to the Arizona arrangement. The dealings were at arm's length like any other account, but Hal's weekly cut from gunrunning went on as usual.

***

Vivian noticed a subtle shift in her friends. Now that she was divorced, she took an interest in various activities. With more exercise, and a change in beauty salons, she had slimmed down and looked more glamorous than she had before. Gone was the matronly garb, exchanged for the appearance of an attractive, mature woman.

383

Her married girlfriends avoided her and shunted her over to the divorcée crowd. There she found old acquaintances she hadn't seen for years and had wondered what happened to them. "Dahling...once you are divorced and available again...wives do not want you around their husbands...you are a threat. I don't care how long you have been friends...they will snub you." One of her divorced socialites advised her.

She had no intentions of marrying again and was not even looking. Her lifestyle of doing what she pleased and answering to no one suited her. She worked for charities, joined clubs, and her life became a social whirl. Graham looked on in despair.

***

Hal went through his mail and found an envelope from his mother. He opened it and found an invitation to something called the "Nature's Friends Ball." He picked up the phone and called Vivian. "OK...what's this Nature's Friends Ball about...you're not trying to marry me off are you...introduce me to some slinky, scatterbrained, Beverly Hills misfit?"

"No...I am through with the marriage advice. Find your own headache." She chuckled. "I belong to Nature's Friends...an environmental club. They are holding their yearly charity ball to raise awareness about environmental issues. You will find my name listed on the left side of the invitation as being one of their important donors. So, I have to go...I just wanted you to go with me."

"I will on one condition...send an invite to Deuce and Wanda. When you drift off to socialize...I don't want to be stuck at a table with some vapid, boring, Botox bimbos..."

"I already sent them an invite...you can bring a date if you like...you don't have to go with me..."

"Naw...there is no one else I would rather take...and you have to save a dance for me."

***

The Beverly Hills Ballroom at the Beverly Hilton Hotel was buzzing with expectation as each new arrival was announced at the door. Hal arrived with Vivian on his arm and they were shown to their table. As expected, they were not there for ten minutes before Vivian rushed off to greet a bevy of matrons vying for the "who-looks-the-youngest" honor. Deuce appeared at the door, looking

384

every inch "Terrence Farrell, the Second" in his tuxedo. Wanda looked the best he had ever seen her, dressed in a cream and gold gown and an autumn haze mink. As soon as the Farrells were announced, he waved at them and they came over to be seated at the table. Hal gave Deuce a "man hug" and air kissed Wanda. "Wanda...you look beautiful as ever." She smiled at the compliment, glad to be amongst the crème de la crème. "Boy...I am glad to see you two here. I would be bored senseless without you."

"Why are you sittin' here all by yourself?"

"I came with my mother...and she did what she always does...she took off to hobnob with her friends."

Deuce nodded. "Well now you can hobnob with us. How are things going?"

Hal caught the look in Deuce's eyes that said, "is everything cool?" He returned a confident stare and said, "Couldn't be better. Business is good."

"Why are you asking people to sue your company?" Wanda frowned. "They are going to bleed you dry..."

"Actually...demanding a class action suit was a way of reducing our liability...and saving the company from bankruptcy. That way we can contain the damages."

Wanda never liked being told she was wrong. She just responded, "Umm, umm, umm."

Hal continued his line of thought. "We are thriving at Arendt...and within this year we will have recouped our losses and be back on track." He said loud enough for the next table to hear, word of mouth being the best advertising.

"Miss Loretta Johnson!" The doorman announced.

An aspect of terror passed over Deuce's eyes and Hal looked up in surprise. There, in all her magnificence, stood the fabulous Lo-Lo, dressed in a silver and black gown with silver beads in her hair. Hal excused himself and walked over to greet her. He put his arm around her shoulders and guided her to the bar. "Wonderful to see you again, Lo-Lo" He whispered. "Deuce is here with his wife...why are *you* here?"

"Vivian invited me..."

"My mother invited you? How does she know you?"

385

"She's a client at my salon...she had the same last name as you...and I asked if she knew you. She said you were her son...didn't she tell you?"

"Noooo. What are we going to do now? Shall I say you're my date?"

"No...just say that I am a friend of Mari's...and you haven't seen me in ages. You just took me over here to the bar to ask if I heard from her."

"Have you?"

"Damn it, Hal...you know I would have told you."

He hugged her. "Yeah...I do. Well...I guess there is no getting around it...let's go over there for introductions."

They walked arm in arm back to the table. Hal put his arm around her as if she was his sister. "Wanda...Terry...I want you to meet a friend of mine...Loretta Johnson. She was a friend of Mari's..."

Deuce took her hand and secretly squeezed it. "Nice to meet you."

Wanda did not offer her hand. "Yes...I remember you."

"You remember me?"

"Mari showed us a picture of you..."

"She did? Oh...how sweet. But, that's just like her, isn't it." Lo-Lo took a seat.

"Are you here with Hal?" Wanda intimated more with her expression.

"No...as it happens...his mother is a client at my salon, and she was kind enough to invite me. I guess she was hoping that I would meet you...and that we would all hit it off..."

"Oh...so *that's* how it is..." Her tone implied, *that's how it isn't.*

Lo-Lo gently called her out. "Mari used to be my best friend...and I still think of her that way. I consider Hal her property until she shows up and says he isn't. That she would say 'he isn't' is not likely..." She took Hal's hand and patted it. "He just came to me...about three years ago...to ask for my help in finding her...and we became friends."

A waiter wafted by and deposited four glasses of champagne in front of them and then drifted to the next table.

"Tell us about your salon...It must be one of the best for Vivian to go there." Deuce's soft brown eyes could not help caressing her.

"We pride ourselves in offering a full variety of beauty services...and we have an exclusive clientele. Right now, we are enjoying a wave of popularity and excitement...as we offer avant-garde methods and styles..."

Wanda looked away. "Uh-huh!"

Lo-Lo ignored her and asked Deuce, "Terry...what is your profession?" Her eyes regarded him with more fondness than that of strangers.

"I'm the CEO of a plumbing company...you may have seen my commercials. 'While your husband's watching football...we do it all.'"

"Oh, yes...I've seen that. So that's *you?* How charming..." Lo-Lo brightly smiled.

Wanda sensed an attraction between her husband and Lo-Lo that was not just one way. Deuce looked at Lo-Lo with a longing that she had not seen in years. Lo-Lo seemed to have the kind of affection for Deuce that doesn't develop instantly. Now she knew why "that woman" was here and it had nothing to do with Hal or his mother—and everything to do with her husband! "Deuce...will you help me find the lady's room?"

"Of course, dear."

Deuce accompanied Wanda out of the ballroom and into the hall. As they approached the women's restroom, Wanda went on the attack. "Where do you know that woman from?"

"What do you mean? I just met her."

"Bullshit...don't give me that! Where do you know her from? Did Mari introduce you?"

"Baby...I don't know what you're talking about. Why are you so upset?"

"I saw the way you looked at her..."

"Well, she's an attractive woman...I'm going to look..."

"Not like *that* you don't! I saw the way she looked at you and, on the surface, you ain't all that!" She pointed an accusatory finger. "You've been bangin' her... haven't you."

"Wanda...keep your voice down."

She looked around to see passersby staring at her and she stomped off into the restroom.

Deuce went back to the table. "Shit...she knows..."

"How could she know? We all heard what was said here tonight. Nobody slipped." Hal was baffled.

"It was from how we were looking at each other." He looked at Lo-Lo. "Sorry, darling...but when I look at you...I see everything I ever wanted."

Lo-lo looked contrite. "I thought I behaved myself. Now what?"

"I don't know." Hal tried to keep the lid on the situation. "Everyone...just remain calm. You denied it...right?"

"Yes."

"Then we will just keep on denying it."

When Wanda came back to the table her lips were pursed and her jaw tight. "So...you don't know my husband! Then how come you keep looking at him like he is devil's food cake?"

"I'm sorry...I don't understand..."

"What do you think I am...a fool?"

"I don't know you...but if you say so!"

"You flipping whore...you piece of shit!"

"Wanda...what's wrong with you!" Hal stepped in.

"This woman is having an affair with my husband...I know it!"

"How can you say that?"

Wanda was going full steam now and heads were turning. "Do you deny you're having an affair with him?"

"Yes...but I dare say that with a wife like you...I could probably have an affair with him if I wanted to."

Wanda threw her champagne into Lo-Lo's face. Lo-Lo retaliated in kind leaving Wanda's hairstyle dripping and her eyes blinking. Deuce grabbed Wanda and pushed her back down in her seat. Hal took out his pocket square and blotted Lo-Lo's face. "I think we have had quite enough for the evening...I'm taking you home, Lo-Lo. There is no need for you to stay and be treated this way."

"Yes..." She picked up her purse and then stopped to deliver what she felt was the ultimate social blow. "You will never know the luxury...the pure joy...to be had at my salon. You are blacklisted!" Lo-Lo swept from the room on Hal's arm.

Wanda sat there for a moment, steamed beyond belief. She got up, grabbed her purse and mink, and stormed from the ballroom. She walked quickly trying to catch up with Hal and Lo-Lo. Deuce followed behind, trying to deter her from doing further battle with her. "Baby...come on baby...just calm down. There's no reason for you to be fightin' with her."

"The hell there isn't! You saw what she did! That tramp threw champagne all over me…ruined my hair and dress…my evening…and she wants to ruin my marriage!"

"She's not ruining your marriage…I'm right here…"

Wanda caught up with Hal and Lo-Lo in the parking garage. She took off her shoe and threw it at Lo-Lo, hitting Hal in the back.

"What the fuck!" Hal turned to see Wanda taking off her other shoe and Deuce wrested it out of her hand.

Lo-Lo turned and started walking toward Wanda. "You want a piece of me bitch? Come on…come on…let's go!!"

"I want you to leave my husband alone!"

Lo-Lo's face twisted and she began to taunt Wanda. "Why? Why should I? I love the taste of Terry…I love the feel of him…I've licked him from head to toe and sucked on him like a big, long, caramel lollipop! Do you think he still wants your tired, old, dried up, sandpaper snatch when he can have this?" She ran both hands down the sides of her body to indicate her fine physique.

Wide-eyed, Hal raised his eyebrows and smirked at Deuce. Deuce returned the look by bobbing his head with an attitude of savoir-faire.

Wanda screamed and ran at her. Deuce caught her and picked her up, yelling and kicking, and carried her off. "Say goodnight, Wanda…"

***

The storm that rocked the Farrell household was unrelenting. Wanda was on the warpath and nothing was spared. Dishes crashed in the kitchen; pots were hurled across the room. Deuce hid the butcher block, full of knives, in the garage, and then went to the master bedroom to hide until she wore herself out. Grateful that the kids were spending the night with Wanda's mother, he poured himself a whiskey and tossed it back, waiting for its warmth to calm him. *Well…now it's here…all out in the open.* He briefly considered lying and saying that Lo-Lo was just trying to get her goat, but why? *You knew this day would come when she would find out…and that divorce would be inevitable. You may as well face it now…sooner than later!*

After about two hours things quieted down. He heard the whirring of the blender at the bar and knew that Wanda was making one of her alcohol ladened, overly sweet, confections, to be poured into a fancy glass and chewed as much as sipped. He girded his loins to face her. Entering the family room, he found her sitting on a bar stool sipping something green. He went behind the bar and refilled his glass. She looked at him with reddened eyes, "How long has it been going on?"

"About three years."

"Why?"

"Come on Wanda...we haven't had a marriage for years...if we ever had one. We only tolerate each other for the sake of the kids." He sat on the stool behind the bar and nursed his drink. "I can't think of a time when I actually loved you...I have always been duty bound to you. I got you pregnant...and all of a sudden at eighteen years of age I had a wife with a kid on the way. I had to give up college. Then you locked me up tight with another baby within a year's time. I never saw anything of life except working my ass off for a wife who barely cared about me."

"Are you saying that I trapped you on purpose?"

Deuce gave her a level stare. "I was going to college...leavin' you behind in high school. You kept crying that you thought I would find some other girl. Then all of a sudden you wanted to go to bed with me...to prove you loved me...or to give yourself to me before I went away...or some such romantic nonsense. I never complained about it because it took both of us...but yes...I think you trapped me on purpose." Wanda started to protest. "Don't bother denying it...the result was still the same. You got what you wanted."

"Was that so bad" She looked down. "You have three beautiful sons..."

"It wouldn't have been so bad if you had really loved me." He held his finger up. "But I never knew what true love was until I saw the passion that Hal felt for Mari...how it rocked him so deep inside that he couldn't see straight. I never got to feel that way about anyone...until I met Lo-Lo. Don't get me wrong...I love my sons completely...and I thought I could stick out this marriage for them...but I was wrong. I can't get Lo-Lo out from under my skin...and I don't intend to try."

"Are you telling me you want a divorce?"

"Yeah...I guess that is what I'm saying..."

"Was I really that bad of a wife?"

"I don't know…compared to what? I never had a chance to find out. It could be that love is overrated or underrated. All I know is that for the first time in my life I feel something that moves me…that excites me…I feel alive! I don't know if I will have regrets tomorrow…but I know that I would not have wanted to live my whole life without feeling what I feel today."

***

"What do you mean we only own twenty-four percent of Farrell's Plumbing?" Wanda fumed as they sat in her attorney's office.

"Just what I said…you and Deuce put up half of your shares as collateral for the loan I made to you." Hal explained. "It wasn't paid back, and I took the stock to repay the debt. Don't you remember signing those shares over to me? It was a couple of years ago. I sold them to recoup as much as I could of the loan. I still suffered a loss."

"How come I wasn't told about this?" Wanda eyed Hal suspiciously.

"You were…it's in the terms of the contract you signed."

Wanda turned to Deuce. "Is all he's sayin' true?"

"Yeah…the money didn't come in as expected to give myself a raise to pay the loan back…and still pay the expenditures to keep the company going. I didn't expect for him to call in the loan when it was due…but he had no choice in the matter when his father took Arendt Medical down."

"Why didn't you tell me?"

Deuce held out his hands. "Because I was hoping to buy the shares back when I could afford to. I just now found out he sold them. All we have left is twenty-four percent of the shares."

"What in the hell happened?" Wanda moaned. "Hal…you were supposed to be our friend. How could you take advantage of us like that?"

"I took advantage? When you asked for the loan, I made it in good faith…I even extended the time for repayment. How could I have known that my father was going to jeopardize Arendt Medical and throw a monkey wrench into the works? I needed the money back. I had to take the shares and sell them."

"You mother fucker…you can afford that and more…you could have waited!"

391

"Wanda...just like anyone else...I can only spend my disposable income. You borrowed a lot of money...three quarters of a mil. Even I can't just pull that out of my ass and say, 'let it ride.'"

Wanda's attorney cleared his throat. "Mrs. Farrell...I dare say that Mr. Golan has been more than fair. He acted as a friend and bent over backwards. The money was put into irrevocable trusts for your sons...and you still have the benefit of the purpose of the loan. Mr. Golan took quite a risk and took quite a loss in taking the shares and selling them...he did not get the value of the loan. He has been a good friend to you...I don't think you should insult him. Your community property is twelve percent of the shares. Now let's move on to the next item. The house?"

"She can have a life's estate in the house...and then it goes to my sons." Deuce conceded.

"Is that satisfactory to you, Mrs. Farrell?"

"Yes." Wanda was sullen, stared off into space, and wondered how she got screwed out of one fourth of her husband's company.

***

The conference room was packed, and the employees' lunchroom was filled to capacity as well. Hal had put a closed-circuit TV in the lunchroom where newsworthy announcements could be made to all personnel at once. Arendt Medical was now out of the woods and earning a profit. Hal had Marketing draw up a press release and had caterers come in to fuel the party with food and drink. Vivian and Graham drove over to join in the celebration. Hal took the microphone and made the announcement. "It has been a long hard struggle...but we have made it! Arendt is back on the map...and it is you...all of you who have put us back on top! Your hard work...your ingenuity...and your ceaseless loyalty has brought us back from the brink. Well done, everybody! Well done!" Each vice president took the mike in turn, singing the praises of their respective departments and setting future goals. Cheering employees could be heard from downstairs.

Hal strolled over to Vivian and Graham. "We did it, ma...we fought back, and we won!" He raised both fists in the air and sang a few bars of "Rocky."

She clasped her hands together. "You did it my bubeleh...you've made me so proud. I don't think my father could have done a better job!"

"I feel like I'm the 'king of the mountain.'"

Graham beamed at their happiness. "I'll go dish up a plate for Madam." He made his way through the crowd and lined up at the buffet.

Hal looked at his mother and teased her. "He's in love with you...you know."

"What? Oh...pish tosh!" Vivian pursed her lips. "You can't be serious."

"No...I'm not kidding. I think he always was. If anyone has suffered at the hands of Marvin as much as you have...it has been Graham watching what he did to you over the years."

"OK...this discussion is over..."

"Believe it or not...it's true." He pinched her cheek.

The conference room phone rang and kept ringing as the partyers ignored it. Finally, someone picked it up. "Hal...it's for you. They say it's important..."

Hal pushed his way through to the phone. "Golan here...who's calling?"

"This is Ray..."

"Who?"

"Your detective..."

"Yes...of course."

"I'm sorry to disturb you...but you said to call if there has been any progress. I can't say this is much...but we have been able to place someone on the inside at Yarborough Publishing."

"You have someone *inside?*"

"Yes...she just started. I don't know how successful she will be...so I don't want to hold out false hope. But, she's one of my best people...and if anyone can ferret out what happened to Mari...she can. I thought I should let you know."

"Oh yes! Thank you...thank you. Call me any time...day or night if you find out anything at all."

"Will do."

Hal hung up the phone. *They have someone inside.* The vision of Mari danced in his head and his stomach was flooded with butterflies. *We will find her...*

***

NEW YEAR'S EVE

New Year's Eve found Hal and Deuce sucking up beer in Benny's. Big had taken his missus to the sunny climes of the Caribbean to celebrate and Vivian took Graham with her on a tour of Europe to test Hal's theory of his unrequited love for her. Hal signaled for another round for both of them and studied his morose friend. "So, tell me...what happened with you and Lo-Lo?"

"When my divorce was final...I made the mistake of buying her a ring...and she asked me 'what is that for?' I got down on one knee and asked her to marry me...and she told me 'no' straight up! She said she wished I had never asked her...because she liked things the way they were. A man gettin' all serious about her was the last thing she wanted. She said she was never going to marry...and have some man rule the roost over her son...or have legal strings on her. Craziest thing...she called me a 'musician' like every other man. She faulted me for leavin' Wanda with all my kids. Evidently, she didn't feel the same way about me...the way I felt about her. I should have checked that out...instead of taking it for granted."

The waiter brought a pitcher of beer and two fresh mugs. "It's going to get busy in here...so I brought you a pitcher for the price of two beers, so you don't get neglected. Happy New Year."

"Thanks...we appreciate it." Hal turned back to Deuce. "My God, Deuce...I'm sorry, man. I thought you found the real deal in her. Can't you go back to how it was between you?"

"I tried...she said 'no.' She said she wouldn't be able to get it out of her mind that I was in love with her...and she didn't want to make the mistake of falling in love with me."

"Try not to blame her, Deuce...life has kicked her around pretty hard...made her scared of giving her heart away. You can still try to get back with her."

"Nope...she froze me out. She heard that call girls were getting forty grand a night in Monaco...and she flew over there to check it out. If it's true...she's thinking of getting back in the game while she's still young enough to make a go of it."

"Ahhh...she's just telling you that to get you to back off..."

"No...she was serious as a heart attack...I was the one who put her on the plane..."

"You put her on the plane? Jesus, Deuce...she's got you by the balls

395

to put her on the plane!"

"Yep...she does. Had the nerve to call me and said she needed a ride to the airport. I went and put all her luggage in the car...drove her there, and waved goodbye as she boarded the plane. I thought it would have a curative affect...but my heart flew off with her and hasn't come back."

"Who's running her salon?"

"Some pretty boy who's light in the loafers...you might say he is her protégé...and he took over managing the place before...she says she can trust him with her life."

"Goddamn! I guess you wish you never met her..."

"No. I'm damn glad I met her. I was in a rut...in a bad marriage...and I didn't have the good sense to get out of it on my own. Lo-Lo shook up my world and showed me that life was for living...not just existing...and she opened my eyes to what was possible. I'll always love her..." He shrugged. "...or maybe it was just the hot sex. Wanda never did me right in that department. Come to think of it...she was pretty selfish across the board. The only one I really miss is my youngest son...he made coming home worthwhile."

"So what are you going to do now?"

"Focus on my business...build the company up...pay you back that loan."

"Oh, fuck the loan. Wanda was right...I can afford to let it slide. I sold the Farrell stock to one of my companies...so you haven't lost a thing. One day...when they're old enough...just tell your boys that it was a gift from their Uncle Hal. I figure that, over the years, Wanda is going to tell them what a bastard I am...I hope it will be the antidote for her poisoning the well."

"Don't worry. I'll tell them the truth." Deuce poured another beer. "So what's up with you?"

"Same old, same old...business is going great...even better than expected. The other thing is going great guns, as well..." He smiled at the pun. "But the detective work on Mari is slow going. We have had a person on the inside for months now...and we got nothing. Evidently, Mari wasn't there long enough to work up a lot of gossip...which is unusual for Mari because she was a gossip magnet...women hated her. It could be because she was there...about four years ago and the employees have forgotten her at

Yarborough…it is as though she was never there. No one seems to remember her. Ray said he was going to try to get his girl into the personnel files…but it may take some time."

"Tell him to have his girl ask where they keep the file archives. Most companies don't keep their old files mixed in with the current ones. A huge company like Yarborough will probably archive their employee files to check against rehires…but it is really getting to the point where they may discard the old files…so Ray better have her get a move on."

"Awww…I hurt Mari so bad…for her to disappear like that without a word to anyone…not even to Lo-Lo…"

Deuce could see Hal's eyes moisten and tried to pull his buddy out of the doldrums. "Yeah…you'd think she would have at least told me to go kick your ass…"

"God knows I deserved it…"

"Ten…nine…eight…seven…six…five…four…three…two…one

(((((HAPPY NEW YEAR!!")))))

The crowd in the bar cheered. Some had dates they kissed for good luck. Others groaned at the thought of another goddamned year. Hal and Deuce clinked their glasses. "Here's to you…and to a better New Year…" Deuce toasted.

"I have a feeling that this is going to be the year…2004 is going to be the year I finally find her…"

Deuce chuckled. "You say that every year…"

"I know…but this time we made a step forward. I think we'll find her."

"From your mouth to God's ear…" He hoisted his glass and Hal did the same and then they fell silent, each lost in his own heartache.

***

Vivian found Graham to be an excellent travel companion. She wondered why she never thought of taking him on her travels before. By the time they got to Vienna, she treasured his company. He anticipated her every need before she gave it any thought. He was knowledgeable about cuisine, art, music, impeccable in his manners, and he was a wonderful dancer. But what was most surprising to

Vivian was that he had a good command of five languages. The one thing he did not do was to romance her. They were on a formal footing.

After all the years he had been her butler, she realized that she had never really looked at him before. Now that she studied his face, he wasn't half bad looking. His blue eyes were intelligent and crinkled with merriment when he laughed at her jokes. His smile was engaging. His features were regular and bordered on attractive but were perfect for a butler in not being too handsome. His once luxuriant, light brown hair was now thinning. Having met as young adults, they had reached middle age together and he knew her every habit, fault, and foible, and yet, he seemed to revere her.

They caught a whirlwind that spun them through Spain, France, and southern Germany that landed them in Austria three days before the New Year. Ensconced in a two-bedroom suite at the Sacher Hotel; they spent the next two days relishing the sights and sounds of glorious Vienna. But this evening was to be exceptional; they were going to celebrate the New Year at the Kaiser Ball.

After dressing herself for the evening, the woman in the mirror that looked back at Vivian, had been transformed. She almost looked as she did in her thirties. Luis, at Lo-Lo's, turned the gray streaks in her hair into highlights in her now auburn tresses and had cut her hair in a style that was impossible to muss. With a shake, every hair would fall back into place. Lo-Lo's face serum all but erased lines and gave her complexion a rosy glow. Tasteful shadowing and mascara tamed her dark, lively eyes into sultry orbs. Her new figure was womanly, with shapely curves, but no longer plump. She was attired in a peach tinted beige designer gown, with a sheer bateau neckline over a plunging bodice that flowed into a shimmering lace appliqued fitted body. The hem, embellished with more appliqued lace, was split in the back. She appraised herself with approval. Vivian was ready to ring in the New Year at the Hofburg Imperial Palace.

Graham knocked at her bedroom door and she opened it to find him flawlessly dressed in tails under his overcoat. He gazed at her for a second and then his eyes blinked as though he had thought of something else. "It is almost time for our carriage to arrive. It is very cold...you should wear a heavy coat..."

"I'm almost ready. Once I find my choker, I will need your help to fasten it." She looked around as he stepped into her room and saw the disarray of assorted clothing, shoes, and cosmetics and began to clear the mess. "Oh, leave that, Graham. Tonight you are my date...not my butler and I am Vivian...not Madam." She found her necklace and handed it to him and noted with some satisfaction that his ordinarily steady hands fumbled with the clasp before he could secure it. When he was through, she turned to him. "How do I look?"

"Never before have I seen Madam look so very...exquisite..." His voice was soft.

"Please call me Vivian."

"Yes...Vivian..." He went to her closet, selected a coat, and held it up with a questioning look.

"Yes...that matches perfectly." As he held it, she slipped it on and turned to the mirror. It was a full-length palomino blonde mink with a shoulder draping shawl collar. The color complemented her gown and the collar could be turned up against the weather as a loose-fitting hood. Graham held out his arm and escorted her through the hotel to their awaiting carriage. Vivian turned heads as they walked through the lobby and Graham could not help but thrust out his chest with pride that he was with her.

The fiaker, an open-air carriage, that waited was burgundy, pinstriped with gold; the horses were matched grays and the driver was dressed in a brown suit and tie, topped with a matching derby. Inside the carriage, in the chilly night air, Vivian reclaimed Graham's arm for coziness as she succumbed to the fantasy evening at a royal ball. The carriage ride to the Imperial Palace was of short duration, made longer once you passed through the archway to the Heldenplatz entrance and waited amongst the fiakers, interspersed with luxury cars, queued to pull up to the red carpet. Bathed in lights, the magnificent Imperial Place was built in a semicircle like two arms waiting to embrace.

The carriage rolled to a stop at the edge of the red carpet; Graham exited and turned to help Vivian. At her first tentative step, he smiled up at her and lifted her to the ground. "The carriage steps are awkward...you don't need to risk them. I'm here..."

After checking their coats in, they entered the Hofburg's expansive foyer to melt into the crowd of milling guests. While freely offered champagne flowed, they were entertained with classical chamber music. Both the people and the hall glittered as the well-to-do from around the world gathered in a veritable Tower of Babel, speaking in many languages, with English, the language of business, being the common denominator. Instinctively watching over Vivian, Graham put a protective arm around her. "Perhaps we can find a place that is less boisterous."

"Oh, no...I want to be amongst it all. I have spent my life being sheltered from the world. Now, I want to see what I have missed...I want to live it up!"

Above the foyer stretched the red-carpeted Grand Staircase. The lights dimmed in the foyer and beamed down on the magnificent flight of steps. Music swelled from the orchestra and the gala began with the Opening of the Grand Staircase. Ballet dancers from the Vienna State Opera, costumed in ivory and pink, streamed onto the steps and gave a whimsical performance, reminiscent of those that captured the fancies of emperors. Pianist, Pavel Singer, followed with selected pieces by Chopin and Singer's own compositions. At the end of the performance, the guests were invited to ascend the stairs to the Festsaal, the great festival hall, to dine.

Ascending the Grand Staircase with affected royal dignity, they were directed through a small hall that led to the Festsaal. Dwarfed by the immensity of the ballroom, with six sparkling chandeliers and frescoed ceilings, they looked for their table. Gleaming with stemware, all of the tables were set for eight, banquet style, and bordered with gold chairs. The orchestra seating was on a stage, in the front of the hall, awaiting the musicians. Above the stage was a giant clock garlanded with flowers with the year 2004 emblazoned in gold above it. Halfway up the ballroom floor, on the right side, they found their place and, being the first to arrive, they took the first seats across from each other at the edge of the dance floor. "Can you imagine the beautiful royal balls that took place here?" Vivian's eyes scanned the room.

"Actually, no. Not one royal ball was ever held here. The monarchy was abolished immediately after World War One...and the last Hapsburg left the palace in 1918. This ballroom was not completed until well after the Imperial reign."

"Oh...I had no idea..."

"Don't be disappointed. Right through there is the

Zeremoniensaal…for official ceremonies, court balls, and such. Napoleon asked for the hand of Mari Luise there…and it was also the throne room. So, if it is royal trappings you desire…it is all right here."

"I guess it is all fantasy…and that is what they are selling…the lure of feeling like a princess. How do you know all of this?"

"I made it a point to look it up when you told me our itinerary…" He was rewarded with her pleased smile. "…but what you are seeing is no fantasy…it was all too real at one time. The Hapsburgs were a powerful force in European and world history…and their palaces reflected such."

The hall was beginning to fill up as diners located their places. An American couple, with a distinct Texas drawl, found their way to the table. "Here we are, Jackie…" They chose to take the seats next to Vivian, sitting next to each other. "How ya'll doin'?" He nodded. "Let me introduce myself…I'm Fred…Fred Loomis. This is my wife, Jackie…and you are…?"

"Pleased to meet you. I am Graham Hollins and…"

"I am his date Vivian Golan…" Vivian interjected.

"Well…I guess they're putting Americans at the same table…it's not too hard for you to tell we're from Texas…where do you hail from?"

"Southern California…"

"Oh…we were just out there last summer…weren't we, honey…" He turned to his wife.

"Yes…and we saw so many movie stars' homes…we saw the homes of Lucille Ball, Jack Benny, Diane Keaton, and Jennifer Anniston and…"

"Yes…then you passed right by my house…" Vivian established her preeminent place in the pecking order.

"Your house?" Jackie's eyes grew wide. "Yes…they're neighbors or live close by…"

"Oh."

"Of course, Jack Benny and Lucille Ball passed away years ago…"

Another couple joined them who spoke German, but once they realized their party was American, the husband slipped easily into English. "We welcome you to Austria…are you enjoying your stay?"

"We are…but in a few days we will be moving on to Venice…"

"It is a wonderful time of year to go to Venice. You will escape the crowds..."

"Graham...what kind of business are you in? I'm in real estate. What's your profession?" Loomis was always on the lookout for important people to include in his network. Graham had the look of success about him, potentially a good connection. Loomis slipped his hand into his pocket to retrieve a business card.

Graham looked at Vivian and saw her give him a slight nod. "I am in the time-honored profession of being a butler."

Loomis' hand let go of the card and settled back on the table. He looked around wondering how he was placed at a table with a butler. "Did you say a butler?"

"Yes. I find what I do very rewarding. It has its perks and privileges...such as accompanying this gracious and beautiful lady to the ball." His eyes swept over Vivian.

"She is your employer?" Loomis' voice was beginning to imply more.

Vivian interjected, "He is my best friend...and the most intelligent...accomplished man I know..."

Jackie raised her eyebrows. "So...you go out with your butler as your beau?"

"Why not? He outshines most men...and I find snobbery very gauche. Don't you?" Vivian gave her a dismissive glance and turned away without waiting for an answer.

A quartet moved on stage and soon music was wafting through the air. An army of waiters appeared and started service. The first course was char, from Austria's Alpine lakes, generously topped with golden char roe, along with a savory vanilla cream sauce. Loomis started to take the wrong fork. Graham cleared his throat to get his attention. As he looked up, Graham indicated the mistake by lightly tapping the table with his finger below the correct fork before picking it up to eat. Red-faced, Loomis changed forks. Jackie, who had waited and watched the rest of the company, now followed suit with her utensils.

Vivian looked down at her filet of venison bathed in a peppercorn sauce and then looked wistfully at the char appetizer. "That looks really good. I shied away from it because vanilla sauce on fish sounded off-putting."

"It is a *savory* vanilla sauce. Here...have a bite..." He got up, cut off a small piece, scooped it onto the fork with a few roe eggs and a daub of vanilla cream and presented it to her. With his hand under the fork, he held it for her to taste.

"That is wonderful! Now I wish I had that instead." He whisked away her venison and exchanged it for his plate of char. "Oh...Graham...that is so sweet of you..."

"Tonight is your night...and I want it filled with magic for you..." He slightly bowed and went back to his chair. Vivian noted with aplomb that he savored using the fork that had touched her lips.

Jackie looked on wishing she had her own butler and made a mental note to demand one when she got back home.

Music filled the hall as dinner continued and more starters were served. Fresh cheese praline in a pistachio mantle with tomato cream and sausage soup were followed by a main course of beefsteaks in the Viennese style with foie gras, potato dumplings, and a bouquet of vegetables. The meal concluded with a panoply of desserts of vanilla foam and almond ladyfingers, crisp hazelnut feuilles with pomegranate cream mousse, praline with apple and cinnamon petits fours, and a selection of Viennese pastries and confections. Each dish was served with a superb, matched wine.

The full orchestra was seated, and the ball opening ceremony got underway with the customary introduction of the Elmayer School Debutantes, all dressed in white, with their dance partners. The entertainment was uninterrupted as a bevy of opera singers and ballet dancers gave impressive performances. Then the much-anticipated exclamation went up "LET'S WALTZ!"

Graham extended his hand to Vivian, "Remember what I taught you." He whispered and they both went whirling on the dance floor. He was a smooth dancer and he aided her with gentle pressure at her waist, indicating which direction to go. Next, he signaled the hand gestures to make as they both brought their right hands over between them and back again and then holding their hands together high above their heads for a few steps before he twirled her around and then went back to the basic waltz steps. The ballroom floor was soon packed, and they were limited in movement to a few square feet, but that did not dampen their spirits. Vivian felt at home in his strong, capable arms and he had all he could desire in holding her.

An intimacy flowed between them like a secret that was finally acknowledged.

At the countdown to midnight they held onto each other and the glasses of champagne they were given to toast the New Year. At the stroke of midnight, in the midst of the jubilant crowd, Graham looked down at Vivian's expectant face and kissed her. To her amazement, it was a real kiss, a lingering kiss, and a rather hot kiss. Then he held her close and whispered in her ear, "Happy New Year, my darling..." She could only stammer "Happy New Year," in return. The ringing of the Pummerin, the largest bell in Austria, could be heard from St. Stephen's Cathedral, drowning out the pounding in Vivian's chest. The traditional "Blue Danube Waltz" was played and on the jam-packed ballroom floor, no one had room to do more than hold on to each other and sway to the music. Clinking their glasses, they toasted the New Year and drained their champagne. Fireworks exploded in the night sky, as the cathedral bell continued to ring, and they went up to the Dachfoyer, a roof foyer with a gigantic window overlooking the city including Vienna's City Hall and St. Stephen's Cathedral, to see the fireworks display. There was yet room to stand at the window as others moved in to watch. Standing behind her, he wrapped his arms around her as the soaring, multi-colored lights put on a show above the city.

She leaned against his shoulder. "Have you ever seen such a night?"

He placed his cheek on the top of her head. "No...never..."

Loath to tear away from each other, even as the fireworks show began to wane, they stayed in the Dachfoyer basking in their newfound warmth. At length, she turned to face him, half expecting him to kiss her. He looked down at her, caressed her cheek, and then suggested they go back to watch the rest of the entertainment. Unrestricted in where they could wander in the palace, on their way back, they peeked into various rooms, halls, corners, and alcoves. "Goodness...you can get lost in this place. We should have dropped breadcrumbs to find our way back..."

"Absolutely not! I would be obliged to clean them up!" He laughed.

Finding their way to the Zeremoniensaal, filled with celebrants, they were stunned by the utter magnificence of the hall. Twenty-four round columns held up a barrel-vault cassette ceiling, lit up by twenty-six double chandeliers that at one time held thirteen thousand candles, now replaced by electric replicas. The opulence of the hall was staggering. Vivian spun around slowly, looking at the ceiling. "I never felt guilt before for all that I have...because that is all I have ever known...but when I see this vast accumulation of wealth, I wonder at whose expense...and at what human cost this was built."

"People make the quantitative determination of how much is too much...when the masses reach their limits...as they did in 1918...they tell their sovereign that enough is enough."

The entertainment was still continuing when they returned to the Festsaal and they took their seats and watched as singers, dancers, and comedy acts took their turn to mesmerize the audience. Then the master of ceremonies called for the Public Quadrille.

"Oh...let's dance the Quadrille!" She prodded.

"Are you sure? It is very energetic, not to mention confusing, and you cannot stop once you start...but if you think you are up to it...it will be my pleasure." He advised.

"Yes...let's do it!"

Three separate lines of couples ran the length of the ballroom floor. There was a caller who called out the steps, and the dancers executed simple steps made more intricate by the number of people, the fact that it was 2:30 a.m., the amount of alcohol consumed, and the many steps involved. The lines came together, bowed, put right hands together and turned in a circle, switched sides, came back again, changed partners and back again. Bumping into each other, forgetting steps, and scrambling to get to where they should be, complicated matters. Then each time the dance began again, it picked up tempo and had to be executed at a faster pace. Giggling, Vivian tried to keep up as Graham helped her through it. Spinning and bowing, stepping back and forth, until the crowd was giddy; they then had to try it again—much faster! When they were through; it all ended in couples dancing in a spirited, serpentine galop around the room.

By the time the ordeal ended they were both laughing. "You survived it very well." Graham gave her a short bow.

"No thanks to the guy across from me...I don't think he liked my toes very much...too exuberant!" Vivian looked down at the smudges on her shoes. "I hope the hotel can clean them. I'd like to wear them again this trip."

The orchestra struck up another waltz. "It is three in the morning...they will close at four...the dance floor is practically empty now. Would you like to dance another waltz or two with me before we go?"

"Yes...yes I would."

With scarcely forty couples on the ballroom floor, they seemed to have come to a tacit agreement to dance counterclockwise. "You are the most beautiful woman here. I want to show you to everyone." He lifted her high above him as he continued to dance. Instead of protesting, Vivian felt exhilarated. Stretching out both arms, she gloried in the moment. The other dancers stopped to watch. She was indeed the belle of the ball.

Graham and Vivian walked on In der Burg toward Michaelerplatz. Since it was more than a half hour wait in line for all sorts of transportation leaving the palace, they decided to walk the short distance to the hotel. She curled up against his arm as they strolled through the still decorated streets of Vienna. "I'm glad we decided to walk. It was madness to even try to get a scooter out of the Heldenplatz."

"I think I just wanted to prolong the time I have left to spend alone with you as your date." Graham seemed pensive.

"There will be other times. You don't think I am going to just stop going out with you after our holiday is over...do you?"

He stopped and turned to her. "Yes...because you must..."

"Didn't you enjoy this evening? I know you spent a lot of time looking after me...but I had the sense that you enjoyed it as much as I did." She looked down. "I even thought that you cared a great deal about being with me."

"Your intuition is right, Vivian. I do care for you more than you realize."

Her eyes searched his for meaning. "I don't understand."

"Ever since the first day I met you...I have loved you." He spoke softly.

"Why didn't you ever say anything?"

"It is not my place. I could never take advantage of you and compromise you in that way."

"How could you compromise me by being with me...by loving me?"

"You saw the Loomis's reaction at the notion that you would have the temerity to date your butler...something like that would have ruined your social standing...your reputation. A hundred years ago...you would have lived in a palace such as the one we just left...and it would have been my privilege to serve you then. But for me to presume to be more to you...to be the cause of your downfall...would be unconscionable."

"And what about me?" Vivian sighed. "I can't honestly tell you that I'm in love with you...I never thought about it before. I just know that I loved being with you tonight...and I would love to spend more time with you. Is that so very awful?"

"Yes...it is." He caressed her cheek. "But I would like to kiss you once more before our fairytale is over." She smiled and stood on tiptoes to kiss him as if he were her ardent lover. She could tell it rattled his cool demeanor. Then she took his arm once more and they walked on.

It occurred to Vivian that Graham was the snob, bolstering her status from below. The thought also dawned on her that the man who had been Marvin's butler lo these many years, was, in so many ways, far superior to the man he had served.

***

A cab pulled up in front of the Golan mansion and two weary travelers got out. Vivian was greeted by her maid while Graham saw to the luggage and tipped the driver. When she went inside, Vivian was not at all pleased to see that a meal was not prepared and waiting for them and little things seemed to be out of order. Graham was livid under his cool façade and went directly to the kitchen. Calling the servants together, he gave them a withering tirade. Thereafter, they scurried in all directions, as they went about the business of making the house ship shape.

"You have my apologies, madam. It appears to be a case of 'when the cat's away'...and such. Lunch will be ready shortly."

"Thank goodness. For a while there...I thought I was in the wrong house."

407

He started to leave and then he paused. "May I have a moment of your time?"

"Of course...what is it?"

"I just want to say...that the time I have spent with you on your holiday has been the most enjoyable...absolutely happiest time...I can remember. I want to sincerely thank you for thinking of me...and taking me with you." He stepped forward, bent down, and kissed her on the cheek, and with that, he turned and went back to being her butler again.

***

IT'S REALLY REAL?

Ray called with a progress report. He was almost giddy. "Mr. Golan...your suggestion that we check for archived files paid off. My girl was able to spend hours in Yarborough's basement without being noticed. It was the only place that had any sign of her. We found her file! With the information we now have...it will be only a matter of days or weeks before we find her."

"Days?"

"Or sometimes weeks...but now it's a sure thing!" Hal practically swooned. "Mr. Golan...are you there?"

"Yes...yes...that's wonderful news. I can't thank you enough. Please let me know the minute you find her."

"Will do."

In a daze, Hal hung up the phone. His heart thudded when he realized that he would see Mari again before long. Whirling with all sorts of thoughts, his mind leapt from one probability to another, evoking emotions that ran the gamut from joy to fear. *Will she hate me...could she still love me...has she forgotten me.* The odds were high that she was married. *Did she really love me if she married someone else so soon? What am I going to find? Ever since I crushed everything we had together, and literally put her out in the cold, she has no reason to care for me at all. What would an apology and a declaration of my love for her mean to her now?* He sat down with his head in his hands. He shook as a cry came from deep inside of him.

***

Hal threw an empty briefcase on the bed, opened it up, and then went through his boxes of Mari momentos to find things that might still matter to her. The poems he wrote for her, the jewelry she returned to him, pictures of their time together, his award for the Mitchem story, and her misplaced degrees all went inside the case. Pausing, he went back to the box and saw the cell phone she lost. It was the only proof he had that he went back to search for her. He tucked it in a corner of the case. Next he put in the items he had been longing to give her, an irrevocable trust, and his will naming her as beneficiary, and a hefty amount of Arendt Medical stock. He looked around; he was forgetting something. Then with a shuddering intake of air, he remembered. *That goddamned file.* He placed it on top and closed the briefcase.

He regarded himself in the mirror and squinted. *OK...I'm a little older...and a little heavier...but not by much. Mari never judged me by my looks, anyway. Still...I want to look good for her. I got to join a gym. What if she would want to come here? Why would she want to come here? You never know...I should get the place ready for her...just in case. What should I wear?* He stopped dead cold. *Now you are focused on superficial things...you will need to come up with a plan to make sure that things go your way. If she's married...you have to find a way to see her alone...without suspicion...you don't want to ruin her marriage if she's happy. The hell you don't! You'll want to run away with her to parts unknown...and love her for the rest of your life! Nothing is ever straightforward...there are always complications...so be ready for anything. What if she should tell me to go fuck off?* His brow furrowed as he tried to think of an excuse to still stay with her, but he could think of none. *Then I guess you will just have to be a gentleman about it and do what she wants and go fuck off.*

Four years ago, he never would have thought about how to manipulate things so that events would go his way; now, that manner of thinking came second nature to him. *I have to locate a new company somewhere near to where she lives...maybe in San Francisco...ready to handle any kind of business her husband may be in...and be prepared to offer him backing...or hire him. Then I can pull his strings like a marionette...perhaps control his every move.*

*** *** ***

"I need you in New York right away...you've made the Times Top Ten and everyone wants to interview you. Lady 'O' is considering you for her pick of the month for her book club...It's all happening..." The excitement in Pamela's voice crackled across three thousand miles.

"Bad timing, Pam. I can't leave right now. Something's come up." Hal demurred.

She was not used to being put off. Authors usually jump through the telephone at such news. "Bad timing...are you shitting me? You just hit the jackpot! I'm going to need you here for at least two weeks..."

"What do you do when someone is gravely ill or has a death in the family...and they just can't make it?"

He heard a deep breath as she fumed. "OK, Hal...I'll cover for you. But as soon as you can get away for an extended trip...you let me know."

"I will. I'm more excited than I sound, and I know this is down to your hard work. I thank you so much. Oh...and I want to thank you for that other thing too..." Hal referred to her tipping him off about the ambush in Arizona.

"I don't know what you're talking about..."

"I know."

Hal put down the telephone. He was being torn in different directions but chose to stay on track in preparation for finding Mari. He purchased a small corporation that had been around for years; not having gotten off the ground, it was just marking time. The name "Monarch" was generic, and it had a small bank account. He changed the headquarters to an upscale address and installed a CEO to set up offices. Then he waited.

***

Deuce's voice was near hysterical. Both laughing and crying, he bawled into the phone, "Hal...IT'S HER! WE FOUND HER!!"

"You found her? How did you find her? Where is she?"

"Not me...Ray found her. I'm at Big's office. He called me to come down to confirm for sure it was Mari before he called you. I just had to call you first, man. I'm so happy for you both!"

Hal's face crumbled with emotion and his voice shook. "So this is real...it's really real!?!"

"Yeah...we're coming over with the file so you can see it for yourself."

***

Deuce pulled his Mercedes S430 into the driveway. Big and Ray arrived with him and marched victoriously back to Hal's office. After they explained the particulars, and Big gave Hal his well-meaning admonitions, Hal sat quietly looking at Mari's picture and then spoke in a whisper. "How did you get this picture?"

"We took it from a distance. She never knew we took it." Ray responded. "We are very discreet in order not to disturb our subject."

"Do you have a picture of her husband?"

411

"Yes…it is further back in the file." Ray stepped forward and flipped through the file to Ed Baker's picture. His was an open, friendly face that wore what looked like a perpetual smile. His hair was mixed gray and his blue eyes seemed to hold a secret to his happiness. It was more than an appealing face; it was decidedly handsome.

"What do you know about her husband?"

Ray referred to his tablet. "He worked for Yarborough for thirty years. His last position there was as purchaser. Mari was hired to be his assistant. About two months after she was hired, they married, and he took an early retirement. He already had a small vineyard in Sonoma County…he built a house there and now produces grapes for a boutique winery."

"She married him after knowing him for only two months? He had to be hovering around fifty…"

Deuce chimed in, "Look…you hurt her pretty bad…after that…maybe all she was looking for was a father figure…someone to look after her. Don't you go blamin' her for nothin'."

"I'm not blaming her…I'm just puzzled."

Big advised, "All will be revealed in due time…wait for your answers…and deliberate on what you find. All the conjecture…speculation…suppositions…in the world…will not nearly approximate the truth. Be patient…and follow your heart in telling her what happened…what propelled you into the ignobility of your actions…and hope she understands."

Hal nodded and looked up at Ray. "I want you to find out all you can about Ed Baker's operations…what kind of grapes he grows…how much he produces…who he sells his grapes to…at what price…and who owns vineyards in his vicinity. I also want to know how many employees he has and his yearly gross…and if you can get it…his yearly profits."

"Yes, sir."

"Also…anything you can find out about his personal life…habits and attitudes…what kind of man he is."

Hal picked up the phone and called his idle CEO at Monarch. "Harry…I want you to call U.C. Davis and hire some students…or recent grads, to teach us something about viticulture…that's right, grape growing and wine making. Also find out all you can about the

412

grape market. Good...good. You have contacts? Even better. Get back to me in a day or so with what you have...and we will go from there."

Deuce's face grew dark. "What you plannin' to do to her husband? You ain't goin' to break up her marriage...are you?"

"Hell no...then she would really hate me..." He held out his hands. "...I mean, not unless she wanted me to. I just need a means of getting him out of the way for a while...on business...so I can talk to her alone." His three friends gave a sigh of relief.

The next three months were taken up with getting Monarch on track and locking up a couple of small grower's harvests at a higher price. The students' hours were staggered with their classes and it was arranged for them to get credit for the experience they gained. Word got out in Ed Baker's surrounding area and church that there was a new purchaser paying higher rates for quality grapes. It wasn't long before Ed and his closest friends were invited to tour the new facilities and hear the proposal for this fall's crop. Even if Ed rejected the deal, his absence for the day would have served its purpose. Then the offer would be made sweeter, and sweeter, until he accepted it where Hal, in the person of Harry, the CEO of Monarch, would have him permanently on the hook.

***

PART THREE

The 2004 Mercedes Benz CLK55 AMG drove slowly up the drive and around the circular approach to the traditional two-story house, which had been recently built. Hal paused, searching for any sign that Mari was there. Grabbing his briefcase from the passenger seat, he got out of the car. He stood there for a while looking around. The house was surrounded by a pleasant garden; the garage was detached with a car and two small farm utility vehicles parked in front. In the other direction, the drive continued past a vegetable garden, an apiary, a barn and to the vineyards off in the distance. The day was balmy, and the fresh scent of blossoms wafted in the air.

He strode up the steps to the distinctive glass and brass entry door. Finding no bell, he knocked. Inside he could hear light footsteps; a shadow crossed the curtain behind the glass, the door swung open, and there she stood. Even though he anticipated it, the moment still rocked him. The hurt that he felt swept over him and engulfed his heart. He was speechless as he took in the vision of her.

Mari had cut her hair to shoulder length and wore it tied back. The quality of the light in her eyes was different and reflected maturity, but she was otherwise unchanged. She wore a cable knit sweater, faded jeans, and wedge slip-on shoes. Without a hint of makeup, she was the picture of domesticity.

She saw a man that life had severely chastened but had matured in the process of fighting back. In the expensive suit he wore and with the luxury car in the drive that could only be his, he made no pretentions about his prosperity. She mouthed the word "Hal" with no sound.

"Mari...aren't you going to invite me in?" His voice was gentle.

She stood quietly for a moment and then said, "Yes...of course...why are you here?" She opened the door wider for him to come in but remained in the foyer. "I never thought I would see you again."

"You must have known that I would look for you."

"No...I didn't...you were quite adamant that you wanted nothing more to do with me...I..." She became cautious. "Why were you looking for me...do you know I'm married?"

"Yes...married or not...I had to see you to tell you it was all a mistake...a serious mistake...I just had to find you..."

"To tell me it was a mistake?"

"I'm saying this badly…I guess it's because I'm so very nervous…and there is a lot to relate…is there anywhere we can sit down?"

"Of course…where are my manners? Come on in…we can sit at the table…would you like some coffee?"

"Yeah…it was a long trip…I'd love some." He followed her into an expansive room. On the right was a full open kitchen with a large farm table. Sliding glass doors opened to a patio. Adjacent to the kitchen area was a divide, where the floor changed from wood to carpet, to designate a spacious living room. On the left side was the stairway to the second story. A long sofa faced a flat screen TV that hung on the wall next to the stairs. Wing back armchairs and a baby grand piano were at the far end of the room near a floor to ceiling fireplace with picture windows on each side. Through the windows there was a view of rolling hills covered with grapevines.

"I just made this pot a few minutes ago so the coffee is still fresh…" She turned to him. "One spoon sugar and cream?"

"You remembered…yes."

Mari carried two cups of coffee to the table and indicated where he was to sit by placing his coffee on one side and she sat on the opposite side. She noted that there was no ring on the third finger of his left hand. "You look good, Hal…has life been kind to you?"

"Yes and no…"

"Tell me about the 'yes' part." She tried to smile.

"I sold my book…" He nodded. "…and it's doing quite well…better than expected."

"I'd love to have a signed copy."

"For sure…and I have several other irons in the fire that have worked out for me…"

"And, the 'no' part?"

"That is what I am here to tell you about…"

She took a sip of her coffee and put it down in contemplation. "Why do I have the feeling that this is going to be painful to hear?"

"I had to let you know that I found out the truth of what happened between us."

She knitted her brows. "The truth…you could have just asked me…"

"It runs a lot deeper than that...you have no idea what was done...to us. Just hear me out." He lifted his briefcase. "May I put this on the table?"

She nodded and watched in silence as he opened it and took out a file.

"This is a file, on you, that Marvin gave to me. He said he had you investigated and that you had a police record for prostitution among other things...as well as complaints from men that you purportedly defrauded out of their life's savings. I had no reason to suspect that it wasn't real. It has everything in it that was shown to me about you...every lie. You will see that it looks very authentic...but it is not. Also, there was this woman...Vera...who said she knew you...and told me that I was your 'mark'...your intended victim." He handed the file to her. "And this is what my detectives...and Deuce...turned up to disprove everything in that file." He gave her the second file as a distraught expression passed over his face. In a voice so low it was almost inaudible he asked, "Mari...why didn't you talk to me..."

She looked up in surprise tinged with more than a little anger that came out as sarcasm. "I can't believe you think that I did not grovel enough."

"You know that's not what I meant...I mean why did you wait for the very day that you knew I would be in court...and couldn't be home...to move out? We could have talked..."

She avoided his eyes and stared away from him. "I couldn't withstand...your scorn..." She turned to him and her steady gaze met his. "You have no idea how devastating you can be...how frightening...when you are angry..." She drew a breath. "...and for some unknown reason...all of that anger was directed at me. You told me in no uncertain terms that you wanted me to go...and I had no choice in the matter. It took me years to get over it all...and to build a new life...why should I look at these now?" She indicated the files with a sweeping gesture.

"Please...it's important that you know what happened...and the people behind it...so you can realize that I didn't just lose my mind for no reason."

With exasperation, she picked up the first file and started to read, slowly turning the papers. Her face filled with dismay and confusion and then outrage as she took in the venom it contained. She walked over to an armchair by the window in the living room and continued to pore over it. Every now and then an involuntary gasp escaped from her.

Hal was baffled at her new demeanor. *Why isn't she crying? She used to cry over minor shit...and now she is toughing it out...seeing what's in that hideous file? What happened to her...?* Then the obvious answer hit him. *I happened to her!*

After twenty-five minutes of studying the file, she closed it and sat quietly, staring out the window. Hal picked up the other file and took it to her. "This one totally vindicates you."

"How could your father be so cruel...?"

"Mari...I am so sorry I played right into his hands...you have no idea how I regret what I did. Had you walked in the door a half hour later...even still believing all the vile things that were said about you...even if it was true...I still wanted you and I would have taken back everything I said...everything!"

She took the second file and read the private investigator's report, the statement of the LAPD detective confirming that she had no record, and Deuce's report, along with Lo-Lo's statement. All refuted the fraudulent information contained in the first file. "Tell Terry I love him...he was always a good friend to me..."

"Mari...come back to the table...there is more..." He held out his hand, but she did not take it. In silence, she went back to sit at the table. Hal followed and went back to his briefcase. He took out a manila envelope and handed it to her. "Here are your degrees...you had left them with Penny in personnel and she forgot to return them to you."

"So *now* you know I'm not a liar..." She purposely jabbed him.

"All of this information I was able to get within a month...what I couldn't do was to find you to bring you back. There is more...I made my father pay...pay for what he did...in the only way that mattered to him...I broke him. I took away everything he had...every dime...every ounce of pride...every last bit of respect...I broke him down to nothing because that is what he did to me when he caused me to lose you. Everything I have...all of my money, property, stock...I put in a trust for you...it's yours after I pass on."

"Money? What money? Money can't fix what he took away..."

"I know that just as well as you do...but money can keep you safe. The trust is irrevocable...I can only add to it...but I can't change it now. The papers are in the briefcase...I'm leaving it with you." She sat motionless. "There is only one thing I have left to do before I go..."

"What's that...?"

He hesitated, knowing that this was it. After this he would walk out the door with no excuse to see her again. His heart was in his throat. "Mari...with all my heart I want to ask...no...beg your forgiveness. I should have known...I should have trusted you...but even when I believed it was true...I should never have treated you the way I did. 'I'm sorry' is such a small, inadequate thing to say for such a great sin...but I do apologize with all my heart. Can you forgive me?"

She put her face in her hands, shaking her head side to side and then looked up at him. "Maybe one day I can...but today is not the day..."

He looked down. "I understand..."

"Do you? Do you really, Hal? I don't think you do. What did you expect? You didn't just break my heart...you tore it out by the roots...stomped all over it and wiped your feet on it. Now you want to come waltzing in here with proof that you should never have done it? What do you want from me?" She held out her hand gesturing in frustration. "What do you want me to be...nobler than I am? Do you want me to be the bigger person and tell you that makes it all better? Well, I can't be...it's just too much!"

"Babe...I wanted to take it all back...right after I said it. I went back to the park...I searched for you everywhere..." He pulled her cell phone out of the briefcase, "...all I could find of you was this."

"Where did you find it?"

"In the park by the bench." His eyes pleaded for understanding but found none. His voice cracked. "I searched for you for *four and a half years* to take it *all* back..."

Her hand went to her forehead and she leaned on it and closed her eyes for a moment. "Well...all of this comes too late to change anything...I'm sorry, Hal...you never got to take it back when it mattered."

"I can't say that I blame you for feeling the way you do...I guess I had better leave..." He reached into his pocket, retrieved a business card, and took out a pen to write on the back of it. "If you should ever need to get in touch with me…if you should need anything at all…here's where you can reach me. This number on the back is where I am staying now." He put the card on the table and walked to the door.

"You stop right there!"

He turned. "Yes?"

She got up and walked toward him. "I can't have you leave like this…" Standing before him, she struggled with what she wanted to say. "Hal…I don't want to sound like I'm not grateful that you know the truth…and I guess on some level it must matter…but I always knew that I had done nothing to cause…all of what happened between us." She bit her lip, wrestling with what she wanted to say next, and then looked up into his eyes. Her voice was just above a whisper. "Hal…I really…really did love you. I thought you should know that."

"I know…and I still love you…and I always will." He reached for her and took her in his arms, closed his eyes, and held her to him. Shaking with emotion, he whispered, "It feels so good to hold you again. Mari…I lost everything when I lost you. You have to believe me when I tell you how sorry I am. I love you so." He opened his eyes to see a small child staring at them. His heart pounded so hard that Mari felt it through his chest. It was a little boy with large dark eyes, and a shock of dark hair, that resembled Hal when he was a tot. There was no mistaking that the child was his. He slowly let Mari go, went to the boy, and stooped down. "Hello…my name is Hal…what is your name?"

"My name is David."

"You're a pretty big boy…how old are you?"

"I'll be this many on my birfday." He held up four fingers.

"When is your birthday?"

"In August."

"I'll be sure to buy you a present."

Mari picked him up. "You were supposed to be taking your nap."

"You forgot to tickle my tummy."

"Oh…mommy's sorry. Let's get you back upstairs and tuck you in."

Hal ached to hold the boy. "Mari…please…let me carry him up for you…please."

She looked at Hal's eyes and realized that he knew. "Yes...but that's all...you can't stay." She handed David to him.

"Come on little buckaroo...time to go beddy-bye. Hal will tuck you in...and even tickle your tummy." Following Mari's lead, he felt a thrill as he carried the boy upstairs to his room. He held him close to his chest and felt his little arms around his neck. Placing the child in his bed he said, "Tummy tickle!" and tickled David's tummy as the child squealed with delight. Stroking the boy's face, he said, "Sweet dreams...little one" and stayed until David drifted off. Kissing him on the head, he quietly left the room.

Hal tried to stay in control of his temper as Mari filed down the stairs after him. "When were you going to tell me, Mari?"

"Hal...you just showed up out of the blue...I needed to talk to my husband first..."

"About who the boy's father is?"

"He knows you're the father...he knows all about you. Do you think I would lie to him about that?"

"When were you going to tell me? I can't help but think that I was inches away from the door...and never knowing I had a son. How could you do that? What was there to talk about? Why didn't you tell me...why didn't you *tell me?* How big a price must I pay for my mistake?"

"I needed to talk to Ed first...he doesn't even know you're here. I couldn't just tell you that on my own without his knowing."

"No...no...why didn't you tell me that you were pregnant?"

"I didn't know until I was already in San Francisco. Even so...I wouldn't have told you...at least not for quite a while."

"Why?"

"You already accused me of trying to make you a mark...was I supposed to come back and tell you I'm pregnant and now you've got to marry me...just how well would that have been received!"

"I would have been thrilled..."

"Well...that news comes just a little too late. Until today...I had no way of knowing that. From our last conversation...all I could envision is that you would either ask me who the father was...or accuse me of trying to trap you...and I could not bear that, Hal...the last thing I had ringing in my ears was that you hated me...and I thought that you would probably tell me to go get an abortion."

"Why did you marry someone else...for God's sake Mari...couldn't you have given me a chance?"

"I *did* give you a chance...I tried to give us a chance. I begged you for a few days to find out what happened. Now that I know what happened I could have exposed it for the fraud it was within a couple of hours! Research was my specialty. All I had to do was go to the nearest police station...give them my ID and ask them to check my record. You talk about a chance...I didn't even know we had one..." She wrapped her arms around herself and started to pace. "I married Ed so that I would not have to get an abortion...I wanted my baby...David was all I had left of you...I *couldn't* kill your child. Ed made it possible for me to have him...and that's all of it!" She stopped pacing and stared at him. "I could only go by what I knew at the time. There was nothing that you said that would in any way make me think that you wanted any part of me...or our baby. The chance that you would care seemed so remote to me...telling you was not even a consideration. Hal, I was drowning, and Ed threw me a lifeline and I took it."

Tears moistened Hal's eyes and his voice shook. "I only know that you kept my son away from me. I didn't get to see him born...or his first steps...I missed all of it. But, not anymore...I won't let you keep my son from me...you can't do that to me. Mari...I've paid enough for what I did. How much more pain do you want to exact from me?" He started to say more but turned and left.

***

CUSTODY

Shaken by the experience of seeing Hal again, Mari walked to the kitchen table and sank into one of the chairs. Staring at the briefcase, she momentarily wondered what else it held, and then closed it. She could not take much more anguish today. Taking the briefcase, she went upstairs to her bedroom, hid it in the back of her closet, and sat down on her bed thinking of everything that had transpired. All the perceptions of her life's state of affairs had been overturned. She had not one inkling that Hal had given her a second thought after putting her out. Now, he said he still loved her. *How awful for him...how awful for me...I would have been better off not knowing the truth.* She thought.

Her life had settled into a regular, and comfortable, routine. She was content with a husband that loved her and a child she devoted her life to. She was not at all unhappy or riven with misgivings. She had cried her guts out until she finally came to grips with the fact that Hal did not love her and ultimately accepted it. After the years of longing, the sleepless nights, the endless desire for him was finally quenched; she was able to make an acceptable life for herself with Ed as her husband.

Now, her mind was topsy-turvy with suppressed memories bubbling to the surface. "What ifs" danced in her head. She was afraid of what else would come flying out of the briefcase that was akin to Pandora's Box. Torn, she got up and bravely walked toward the closet to retrieve it and then went back to sit on the bed again. *Don't be foolish...what are you afraid of?* She got up and resolutely got the briefcase out of its hiding place, opened it, and looked under the files and her degrees. She found Hal's award for the Mitchem article. She smiled, *he always said it belonged to me and now he gave it to me.* Much of what she discovered inside puzzled her. Legal papers, written in legalese, listing accounts and property, Hal's will, stock certificates, what appeared to be a lot of cash, a certificate of deposit, and a large manila envelope marked, "For Mari." She opened it and slipped out the papers. It was poetry he had written to her over the years. The first one grabbed her eye and her heart.

"If I lived one thousand lifetimes,
And searched the length and breadth of all,

'Tis but one beautiful face that I'll e'er recall,
'Tis but one who stirs my passion, and all I desire,
And sets my heart yearning, sets my soul on fire.
Mari, Mari, I found you at last...."

Deep in the pit of her stomach, her emotions tore at her to fight their way out. They roiled and pushed their way up in heaving sobs that made her finally cry out. "Oh my God, Hal...what have you done to me?"

***

As soon as Hal got to his hotel room, he got on the phone to Big. "Big...Big...you gotta help me." His voice sounded rattled and on the verge of tears.

"What happened? This was supposed to be the happiest day of your life! You didn't lose your temper, did you?"

"No...but I had every reason to. We talked...and we were getting on OK. She didn't forgive me...but I expected that...it was too much to ask for right away. She even let me hug her before I started to leave. But then...but then...I found out she had my kid and never told me. Oh, God, he's beautiful, Big...and smart. I got to hold him for a while. I've got to have custody of him, Big. He's mine...I'm his father. What can I do?" Hal snuffled.

Big could tell he was not emotionally ready to hear what he had to tell him. "Oh...shit! Slow down...we have to take this one step at a time. You are about to enter into the viper pit of family law...the most odious, ugly, vicious area of legal practice there is. I have worked criminal law all day...every day...for many years...you know...the guy did it or didn't do it...he's guilty or not guilty...cut and dried. But I have never seen anything as ugly and vicious as one day in family court. You have got to have a strong stomach for that shit."

"What are you telling me?"

"I'm telling you to come into the office and we will discuss what needs to be done."

"Do I have a chance to get custody of my son?"

"There's always a chance...we have to discuss what is involved in family court...that's all. Cheer up! You're a father! The other thing that means is...you're always going to have Mari in your life from now on."

"Yeah?"

"Yeah...it starts off with school plays, graduations, marriages, babies...and then there are holidays...Christmases or Chanukah...and more. For the rest of your life you and Mari are going to be thrown together...so keep that in mind when you go for custody...and don't let it get too ugly."

"OK...can I see you the day after tomorrow? I'm driving back."

"No...you are going to be too tired...and you have to be alert when we talk. Let's set it up for Friday...around two. That way if we run over...we can go into Saturday."

"OK...I'll be there."

"Oh...and by the way...congratulations...dad!"

Next, he dialed Deuce. "Hey, Uncle Terry...I'm a father..."

***

By the time Ed Baker got home, Mari was at the stove preparing dinner. While the files Hal brought were on the kitchen table, she had hidden the briefcase in her closet. After she dried her eyes and put on some makeup to eradicate the slight puffiness of her face, she busied herself making a complicated dish that required her to focus on the intricate recipe. When Ed walked into the kitchen, she smiled brightly and asked, "How did it go?"

"It went very well! You should have seen me in action! Your husband is one tough cookie. I negotiated a really sweet deal for this fall's harvest...especially when you consider that it was getting late in the day for getting a contract..." He walked over and kissed her on the cheek. David ran over and held out a toy truck to him. "Hey...David...what do you have there?" Ed picked him up.

"A twuck...I'm going to dwive a twuck!"

"What happened to being a fireman? Yesterday you wanted to be a fireman." Mari smiled.

"I'll be a fireman and dwive a firetwuck!"

"Ooohhh." Her eyes opened wide.

"Does that mean we get off easy and we don't have to pay for college?" Ed quipped.

"Hardly..." Mari chuckled. "So, everything went well?"

"Yes...we sold everything we can produce aaannnd they committed for next year at the same price! Our worries are

425

over...barring any unforeseen mishaps...we are going to turn a healthy profit. I told you God will look after us."

"We were doing well in any event." Mari reminded him.

"I know we were not necessarily going to be paupers...but when you put this kind of money, sweat, and love into your work it is a hard thing to come up small potatoes. Also...we would have had to tighten our belts and that is never any fun. Praise God...He has shone His light upon us."

Mari thought of the cash in the briefcase upstairs and realized what Hal meant. Knowing you have money was a definite stress reliever, although it would have been hard to explain where it came from. "By the way...I had an unexpected visitor today. Hal came to see me." The name struck Ed like a lightning bolt. He walked closer to her as she talked. "You see those files on the table? He brought them to me. After dinner...after you read to David...we need to talk. I know you've had a busy day, but this can't wait."

After David was in bed and all was quiet, Mari told Ed about Hal's visit and most, but not all, of what was said. He sat quietly, and patiently, listening until she was through. At the end, she blinked and looked away softly saying, "Well...that's one mystery solved. I never knew why he exploded that day...and I don't think I am better off for knowing." She looked back at Ed with more than a little trepidation in her eyes. "But now he knows about David. He didn't lose his temper...but he did...in so many words...threaten some kind of action. I think we need to consult a lawyer."

"Funny...I always knew this day would come. It never made sense to me that a man...who obviously loved you at one time...would throw a lady like you away. Evidently, he still cares because he never stopped searching for you. Mari...tell me now...is that going to be a problem between us? Do I have anything to worry about?"

"Of course not...and I don't think Hal intended it to be. He already knew I was married. After he gave me the br...files...I think he was just going to leave with the intention of never coming back. But then he saw David...and he knew instantly that David was his without my saying a word. He was blown away! He was very upset and asked me why I didn't tell him that I was pregnant. But...at the time...I couldn't even think of telling him. He either does not...or chooses not...to remember the things he said...because if he did...he never would have asked me that question."

Ed took her hand. "At the time I gently suggested that you should tell him...but perhaps it was too gently. Mari...I love you so much...maybe I was afraid that if you did, he would take you back and I would lose you. I was probably right on both counts...and perhaps it was selfish of me...but I just hope you don't regret the choices you made..."

"At the time...you were my only lifeline...there were no other choices." She briefly allowed herself to think of how it could have been with Hal had they known the truth then, had they married as planned, and had they known the joy of having their son together. He mistook her tears as tears of gratitude. "Now...I cannot imagine making any other choice." She lied.

***

All during the drive back to L.A., Hal thought his head would explode. Thoughts ran into each other and some ran for cover as bigger concerns overtook them. The past collided with the present and guilt vied with moral indignation for superiority. *Above it all sits Mari...Queen Mari...the love of my life...the bane of my existence. My raison d'être. So beautiful. So utterly exasperating. So wonderful. So smart. What was she supposed to do, asshole? You left her out there in the park in the cold and dark...what was there about that that told her you loved her? Look at it from her point of view. After everything that you did to her...everything you said...turning your back on her...why would you think she would come to you to make the happy announcement that she was going to have your baby?* He wanted to retch at what he had done.

Then the thoughts of David flooded his head. *My son...I have a son. He is incredible...a miracle. Mari wasn't supposed to be able to get pregnant for three or four months. Of course we knew that it was possible for her to get pregnant right away...but I never dreamed it would happen that fast.* Prior to leaving the hotel, he thought of calling Mari and asking if he could see David once more before he left for L.A. But, by that time her husband would be home and he had no idea what she may have told him, if anything. He heeded Big's advice about becoming the bull in the china shop. He barely had a rein on his temper as it was, although he realized that it really wasn't Mari he should be mad at. A million "ifs" marched through his head. *If only I had gone home and thrown the file in the trash and taken her in my arms instead. I would have gladly given her everything I have anyway.* He gave a wry chuckle. *You have given her everything…in your trust.* He paused and made a mental note to add David to the trust. Then it occurred to him that he had to clean up his life to make himself worthy of being David's father.

He had to call Malone and arrange a meeting. *I've got to get out of the business. It will be easier for Malone to let go if he had another supplier…or another method of smuggling.*

He needed to shore up his reputation as an author, someone David could be proud of. *I have to call Pamela. I could use a couple of weeks in New York to take my mind off of the mess I created. Yeah…it will be great to have people crawling up my ass telling me how wonderful I am…begging to eat up my shit! I could use the respite from being the jerk-off of the century.*

***

"You see this guy right here…he looks like a pretty normal guy…" Big was in the middle of introducing Hal to his family law attorney. "…but in reality…he is a cold-blooded shark…capable of tearing families limb from limb and having them at each other's throats for the slightest advantage and accusing one another of child abuse…to get custody…or using their children as pawns…bargaining chips…"

"Whoa…whoa…whoa! Big…that's no way to talk about your partner…" The man got up and, with a charming smile, offered Hal his hand. "My name is Dennis…Dennis Mayor…" Hal shook his hand.

"Don't let him fool you…his real name is Sotomayor…he lost his accent and he changed his name. He may look like a person…but he's a yellow-eyed, sharp toothed shark…and has nothing resembling a scruple."

Hal was taken aback. "Why are you recommending this gentleman if you have such a low opinion of him?"

"Because he's the best! I don't have a low opinion of him or his legal skills…I have a low opinion of the work he does…family law…I can't stomach it."

"Please…forgive my friend…he has his own way of looking at things. There is a need for attorneys to help families through the intricacies of withdrawing from unpleasant circumstances while maintaining as much as can be salvaged from broken dreams."

"Half of them are selfish bastards...and the other half are looking for revenge..." Big interjected. "...and the children watch in horror as their parents degenerate into petty, gun slinging, assholes!" He shook his finger in the air. "And, like I keep telling Sotomayor, here..."

"Mayor..."

"...more family law attorneys are shot and killed than in any other law practice. The emotions run high...but the average person's brain is set to *me...me...me!*"

Dennis coolly regarded Big. "If you are through with your tirade...I think we need to address the problem at hand." He turned to Hal while Big sat quietly behind his desk; the nattering that continued in his head reflected in his eyes. "Mr. Golan...I understand you just recently learned that you have a child...a son...and that you were cruelly deprived of the knowledge of his existence. You were never given the opportunity to become the father to this child that you would have wanted to be...because the woman involved withheld that information from you. Is that it...in essence?"

"Yes...but it is not quite a fair representation...you see I..."

"Mr. Golan...do you want *fair*...or do you want your son?"

Hal's brow furrowed. "I was hoping for both...I want to maintain a good relationship with his mother. I still have feelings for her."

"I'm sorry to hear that...because the reality is this...she is going to fight you like a tigress. She will come after you hammer and tong...and use every advantage against you...fair or unfair. I want you to understand what you are up against." Hal started to speak but Dennis held up his hand to allay him. "You see...just because you are the boy's father does not automatically entitle you to custody...nor does your wealth. What the court will look at is the welfare of the child above all else. If he is in a relatively safe and happy home...the court will be loath to disturb that setting. The most you can hope for is visitation rights. You cannot assert your right as the biological father as being stronger than the man who is legally the child's father. In California, the law recognizes the man who is married to the mother at the time of the child's birth as the legal father. The fact that you were never apprised of her pregnancy and the birth of your son...may play somewhat in your favor...but the court may exclude you for a time...if it feels that you may be a negative influence on the child, or the child's home. Now I want you to tell me every fact and circumstance that led up to the present situation."

With the exception of how he set up Marvin and his role in the gunrunning scheme, Hal explained how he had intended to marry Mari until his father had given him fraudulent information about her that led to the resulting consequences. "So, you see...I don't want Mari hurt in this affair. It wasn't her fault."

"Are you sure she didn't withhold the pregnancy from you as a means of getting back at you for hurting her?"

"No...she would never do that."

Dennis didn't pursue that line of questioning with his naïve client, but instead changed the subject. "It was all over the news that your father had 'difficulties' and that he is now in prison."

"Yes...he got the company into trouble...and then he got involved with the wrong kind of people...it was a total mess."

"Do you still see him?"

"Yes..." Hal shrugged. "...I'm the only one of the family who does. It is more out of a sense of duty...he is my father..."

"Even with what he did to you?"

For the first time Hal was caught in his bullshit. Why would a son go visit a father who had committed the worst sin possible against his son? Hal thought fast on his feet. "It was expedient for me not to go to war with him at the time I found out. He held the keys to the kingdom...to my inheritance and for my taking over the company one day. So, I never told him that I found out what he did to Mari. After the gunrunning shit hit the fan...and he was convicted, and I was made CEO...it seemed to be good publicity that a son would recognize his duty to his father...despite his breaking the law. As far as retribution goes...someone told me that God's law of justice shall prevail...and it certainly did in his case. He stepped on his own dick...big time."

Dennis sighed his relief. "I want you to visit him one last time to tell him that you will have nothing more to do with him...you can't visit or talk to him or appear to pardon what he did in any manner. You cannot have your character besmirched by anyone. Do it before we file."

"I have one last question. Do you think I should go to Mari and her husband to try to work it out...like joint custody...before we go to court?"

"I cannot advise that. The situation most likely will get out of hand...heated...tempers flare...recriminations fly back and forth. There is a need for the order and preeminence of the court to have control. We will be ready to file as soon as you take care of the business with your father."

"There are some other things I have to do before we go to court..."

"Like what?"

"I have to do a book tour...I made the top ten."

"Excellent! That will work in our favor!"

***

The clanking of cold steel on steel and the cheerless, drab gray cement and drab gray paint, made Hal thankful that he only had to visit Marvin one last time. This would be Hal's tour de force, the coup de grâce, the final deathblow to his relationship with Marvin and any pretext of love between them. He had rehearsed what he would say, as well as every facial expression, down to the last detail. He intended to relish this moment. Sitting at the table in the visitors' center, his face held a despondent expression. When Marvin sat down, Hal stared at him as though he were looking at a thing he did not recognize or understand. "Hello, Marvin."

"What...are you getting too big to call me dad anymore? You haven't been around to see me in a while, son."

"I've been busy, Marvin...lots of things came up..."

"What have you been up to?"

Hal shrugged one shoulder. "Running the company...it's doing very well. We're making a healthy profit now. We had the largest quarter ever."

"Yeah...I always knew you would take hold..."

"And, then there is this thing that came up...you're a grandpa..."

Marvin sat stunned for a second and then broke out in a grin. "You never told me you were seeing someone...or did you get married?"

"No...I didn't get married...but I was supposed to. You see...I ran into Mari the other week...she still looks great. She had a little boy with her that looked a lot like me...and I just found out I am a father...and I just found out she married someone else. We sat down and talked...like we should have four and a half years ago...and she asked me why I broke it off with her...or I should say threw her out. Eventually, I showed her the file you gave me...."

"Now look, son..."

"No...you look! She swore that what was in the file was a lie...so I took her to my attorney for verification. But instead, he refuted that file and proved that she had no record...never did! What she *did have* was my son! Now...do you want to tell me how in the hell *that* happened?"

"Look, son...I suppose you think that what I did was reprehensible...but I thought it was for your own good...for you to marry a girl like that was not good for you..."

"A girl like what? The one you faked?! What would you know about love and marriage? You had the best wife in the world, and you treated her like dirt. By the way...I think she has someone else in her life...and she looks happy!"

"Vivian...with someone else?"

"That's right. But getting back to your grandson...I want to let you know that you can't see him...Mari won't let you...I won't let you."

"I didn't expect you to bring him *here*...but don't you have a picture of him? What's his name?"

"When I said you can't see him...I meant *never ever see him!* I won't even give you his name...and because of you...he doesn't even have *my* last name."

"What about when he's older...you can't keep him from me."

"The hell I can't...he won't even know you exist."

"Son...you can't be that bitter...I'm the boy's grandfather..."

"Yes...I can be that bitter...and I am. You took the one person I love away from me...and now, because of you, I didn't even know I had a son until now. I could have had a wonderful wife and a family...the life I always wanted. Instead...I'm sitting here talking to a dried-up old fuck-stick about how he destroyed my life. Well...no more. I want you to take a long hard look at me, take a good long look...because you will *never* see me again!" Hal sat there for a minute watching Marvin hang his head, and then got up and left.

***

Dressed in a plaid shirt, jeans, a khaki vest overlaid with pockets, and a fisherman's khaki hat festooned with fishhooks, lures, and weights; Hal stood on the Santa Monica pier with a fishing rod praying that no fish would be foolish enough to bite. Beside him was a small ice chest, a tackle box, and a bucket of seawater. He checked his watch as the afternoon sun passed overhead. He looked at the dark green, murky water below, and hoped his proposal would meet with Malone's approval. Although Malone had promised to let him out of the business whenever he wanted out, Hal was savvy enough to know that when business is good, no one was going to let a key player go, without difficulty. There had to be something better in the works, making his absence advantageous.

Scanning the pier once more, he saw Malone half jogging toward him. He stopped near Hal to lean on the pier railing to catch his breath. "I can't for the life of me figure out why those health dicks want to run all the time."

Hal reached into the ice chest and retrieved a can of soda and handed it to him. "Here...take a break."

Malone stood next to Hal, opened the can of soda, and looked out over the ocean. "You needed to see me?"

"Yeah...I have two things I need to talk about. The first is that I found Mari..."

Malone broke out in a rare smile. "Well fuck me! Congratulations are in order..."

"Not so fast. She's married and has a kid...*my kid*...so now you're a grandpa too!"

Malone laughed. "Jesus...God gives with one hand and takes away with the other. So now what?"

"I want my kid...I've got to get out of the business and get out clean."

"That is going to be a problem right now..."

"I know. That brings me to the second thing I want to talk about. I have a proposition for you...one that lets me out clean...and means more business for you."

"I'm listening."

"You need a medical device supplier that 'understands' your needs. I need to distance Arendt from doing business with your company. Question...have you and New York kissed and made up yet?"

"No…but I know they want to. We are doing more business than they are simply because we have a better medical device product. They do get used by hospitals in the countries we ship to…and they do appreciate that they are not getting junk. I don't know what New York is shipping out of Texas…but it is not nearly as good. They are probably getting rid of the defective inventory for other device manufacturers. Here in the states companies are being sued left and right."

"Good…the better for what I am going to propose. What if you form one legitimate medical device company that supplies both Arizona and Texas? Arendt can supply such a company with its own product, in plain wrap, for it to re-package under its own label. That company can supply other *lawful* customers with a superior product while also shipping to Arizona and Texas, as well. You would have to have other customers to look authentic, because doing business with only two customers would raise suspicion. Arendt can supply your business at a discount, and you can sell at a competitive price to let's say…five or six small hospitals that specialize in joint replacement. Don't get too big or too hungry to draw attention to yourself…but just make a nice profit while you also supply Arizona and Texas. Now you could just supply Arizona…but if you cut Texas in on the deal…and they pay a decent price for the product…it adds to the legitimate company's profits. Meanwhile, Arendt has no idea who you are or who you sell your merchandise to. We just manufacture products for your label. I walk away clean…sort of…and you control your own supply. What do you think?"

Malone stood quietly thinking for a while. "We own a legitimate company…that sells to small hospitals…that also sells to Arizona and Texas…and as far as we know…Arizona and Texas are pure as the driven snow?"

"Yeah…Arendt will supply your company which is legit, and all Arendt gets is its profits from the medical devices…and you can have my cut of the operation. I can help you get set up."

"Naw…we can take care of that. You know what I think? I think you are a fuckin' genius! I don't know why I didn't think of that myself! As far as I'm concerned…it's a done deal. I think I'll let New York sweat it for a while."

"Why? I have to go to New York for a couple of weeks on a book tour. I can drop a hint with Pamela to suggest that they ought to talk with you…"

"Those mother fuckers tried to kill me."

"Don't I know it…I ended up on their menu too…but you always taught me not to think with my emotions. OK…OK…I do it anyway…but my point is that you will be losing profits by keeping them out…and that doesn't make sense if you plan to bring them in…in any event."

"But it's also not wise to make it too easy for them…they won't appreciate it."

"OK…I'll stay mum in New York. How soon can we get it up and running?"

"Give or take a month."

Hal reached into his pocket and pulled out an envelope. "This is what looks like a run of the mill credit application. I put a special number on it. Make it look legit…and send it to my attention. Be sure to put the amount of credit you want. I will approve it."

"I swear…the gods favored me the day they sent you to me. You are the son I always wanted."

"And you are the father I wish I had. Speaking of fathers…I just kicked Marvin to the curb!"

"You didn't let on…?"

"No…I told him I just ran into Mari…and now I know he fucked me…and adios!"

"And where is Mari in all of this…are you trying to get her back too?"

"I don't know. I only saw her once. She's married…I don't know how she feels about me. If I could I would make her mine in a flash…but I don't want to disrupt her life if she's happy. I was willing to walk away if she wanted me to…before I knew I had a son…but now everything has changed. I want my boy…I want her too if she wants me…but the boy is mine!" Hal turned to Malone and held out his hand, blinking back the moisture rising in his eyes. "One last thing…you have been more than a friend and a father to me. I can't thank you enough…there are no words. On advice of counsel…I won't be able to meet you again. I am trying to get joint custody of my son. I can't risk it."

Malone took his hand and patted it as he shook it. "Hal…you saved my life twice…there are no thank-yous needed between us…only a strong bond that will always be there. I know we can't meet…but if you need me…call me." Malone tossed the soda can in the trash, reluctant to leave. "OH! And in the year 2005…2006 at the latest; sell every last stick of real estate that you own…including your house. The bottom is going to drop out of real estate. Only keep what you plan to have for your future…and move your bank accounts to small local banks…keep nothing with the big boys. Things are about to get ugly!"

"What's going to happen?"

Malone spread his hands out and smiled and then turned to walk back up the pier. Hal was wistful as he watched him walk out of his life. He stayed for a while and then packed up his gear. When he got home, he made a list of his real estate assets and his U.S. bank accounts. He didn't know how Malone knew things; he just knew that he did.

***

Mari picked up the remote and flipped through the TV channels. It was the middle of the night and she couldn't sleep. As the channels paraded by, she ran into the very thing she was attempting to escape, the image of Hal. The show was a re-run of a talk show that was on earlier at eleven thirty. At three o'clock in the morning, with the house quiet and alone with her heartbeat, she watched and sensed his discomfort. The host was all smiles with a thin veneer of profundity barely covering his superficiality. "So, Golan, it appears that you have the reputation of a recluse…you were a hard 'get' for our show."

"I don't know if being a recluse is entirely true. I just can't imagine anyone wanting to inflict me on their audience."

"Your book debuted on the Times Top Ten at number nine…it has since climbed to number five."

"Yes…no one is more surprised than I am."

"Why is that?"

"It was my opinion that Americans, in general, are not that enthused about their own history. I did not know that my tome would have such a wide appeal. I was hoping that it would be entertaining enough for a wider audience...but I truly believed that it would attract a smaller readership. I am happy to say I was wrong."

"What inspired you to write 'The March Toward Manifest Destiny'?"

"As you know, I used to write for 'Angel City Magazine' a wonderful publication that focuses on all things L.A. From time to time they would do an historical piece that brought the broader history of the city down to the personal...the individuals affected. At that level there is an entirely different story in how history played out in people's lives. I wanted to explore history in the same manner for the country as a whole...and I found the perfect family in the Howards. While my book is fiction...the Howards are real...and I built a fictional story based upon their family's historical facts. They were truly amazing people."

"I understand you are pretty amazing yourself!"

"I can't imagine how."

"It was your story that helped to free an innocent man."

"Yes...I wrote it...but I cannot take sole credit for it. The pertinent facts that freed Mitchem were ferreted out by a wonderful research analyst, Mari Carlson, who brought the facts *she* discovered to me. Together, we investigated it further and I wrote the story...and received most of the accolades. But she is the one who put it together that the man was innocent."

"You are far too modest..."

"Not really...I am just that lucky."

"And so is Mitchem..." The host held up the book. "The book is called 'The March Toward Manifest Destiny' and is available in bookstores everywhere. It is a tremendous read about the greatness of our country...and the individuals who built it. Thank you for appearing on our show...we hope you will come back again."

"You can depend on it when I have another top seller." Hal shook the host's hand and the band played the show into commercial.

Mari turned off the TV and sat in the dark with salty tears streaming down her cheeks as she remembered the past. *On national television he gave me credit...just like he gave me his award...just like he gave me that briefcase. It's like he is trying to give me his whole life.* She squirmed in her seat. *He wants to be a father to David...that means he will be around me...all the time. I*

437

am Ed's wife...I can't be around Hal...I can't have him near me. I have to shut him out. The memory of how it felt to be held in his arms unsettled her.

***

Hal opened the envelope from Valiant Medical, Inc. and found the credit application he had given Malone. He picked up the phone. "Dennis...Hal Golan here. File for custody."

"Alright...but like I said...I don't think you can get full custody."

"I know...but when you are in negotiations...you always ask for more than you think you can get. Then when the other side argues that you should be reasonable...they will frequently offer you what you actually wanted. You go in swinging...you come out shaking hands."

"Not everything is a business deal, Hal. I hope you are right. Some judges frown on the party that looks too greedy..."

"Then get me the right judge."

***

MARI'S STORY

The knocking at the Bakers' door was loud and insistent. Annoyed, Mari put down the book she was reading and went to answer it. A brash looking fellow who appeared to be in his mid-thirties stood smiling at her when she opened the door. "Mari Baker?"

"Yes."

"You've been served." He handed her a manila envelope and when she did not take it, he dropped it at her feet and then left. She watched as his car drove away and then picked up the envelope and went inside.

Sitting at the kitchen table, she opened the envelope and saw that it was a petition for custody. Her hand went over her mouth as fear gripped her stomach. It had been so long since Hal's visit that she had convinced herself that he had second thoughts about a custody action. In August he did send David a collection of Disney animated features for his birthday, but nothing else transpired between them. While she and Ed consulted an attorney about the possibility of a custody suit, it somehow didn't seem real to her. Now that she was confronted with it, the words in the petition swam in tears and swirled about in unintelligible ink on paper.

When Ed came in for lunch, after checking on how the harvest was proceeding, he was surprised to find that his meal was not on the table and that Mari was upstairs. Instead, he found the petition and slowly sat down to read it. Unlike Mari, he had no doubt that Hal would pursue access to David in some manner, but he was shocked to see that he wanted full custody. *No, the man cannot be serious. If he consulted an attorney he would know what he is asking for is out of the question.*

He went upstairs to find Mari lying across the bed sniffling into a pillow. "Come on now...he can't get full custody. You heard what the attorney said. The court won't take David away from his home and his parents that love him."

"I know what he said...I just didn't believe that Hal would do this to us."

"Sometimes attorneys can talk people into doing things they otherwise wouldn't do."

"What really makes me afraid is that he is wealthy beyond belief...and money can buy you a lot of things that are out of reach for most people...like favoritism in the legal system. We don't have that kind of money."

"If it takes everything we get for the harvest, we're going to fight this. He's not going to get David."

***

The attorneys and their clients converged on the Law Offices of Hanlon & Hanlon. Dennis Mayor took on a local law firm as co-counsel so that he wouldn't get "home teamed" on the case. Small town courts frequently had a penchant for favoring the attorneys they were familiar with, rather than those from out of town. Also, the law firm would be convenient to the parties of the case. Hal leased a modest, inconspicuous house nearby in Santa Rosa where the only indication of his affluence was the Mercedes parked in the driveway.

The Bakers' attorney, Dean Fennerman, was a sole practitioner, who recognized he was up against heavy hitters, but relied on the fairness of the court to follow policy in all cases.

The Bakers were well known in the town, members of the church, and staunch pillars of society. While it was recognized by one or two well-educated people that David couldn't possibly be Ed's son, because two blue-eyed parents cannot produce a brown-eyed child, they were also sufficiently wise not to comment on the matter. Others were too polite to remark that David did not look like either of his parents. Some just assumed he was adopted. All agreed that the Bakers were far too nice to be the subject of idle gossip. They were good Christians. The custody battle could unleash a scandal if the case became public knowledge.

Hal arrived at the same time as the Bakers. He nodded to Mari and she turned her nose up and looked away. Dennis came up to him and distracted him from the snub. "Are you ready to go in?"

"Yeah...as ready as I'll ever be."

"Now remember...a deposition is under oath. If you have any concerns about any questions you can consult me before answering. You can even take a break if necessary."

"I'm good...let's go in."

"That couple that just walked in...is that them?"

"Yeah."

"She's the mother of your child?"

"Yeah."

"And you gave her the brush off?"

"Yeah."

Dennis tried not to look baffled as he showed his client into his co-counsel's office.

Mari was the first to be deposed. Having finished with the formalities, the questioning began in earnest. Dennis Mayor initiated the interrogation. After the subject matter of how she met Mr. Golan and how they developed a relationship was dispensed with, they moved on. "So, as I understand it...you were living with Mr. Golan in his apartment as his roommate in a platonic relationship?"

"Yes."

"When did the relationship become more than platonic?"

"I don't understand the question. Do you want to know the date...or when I developed feelings for Hal...or when we...?" She extended her hand.

"You may answer all three if you will."

"I can't attach any dates exactly. I know I fell in love with him long before he said anything about how he felt about me. He came in from jogging on a warm day. He was overheated and he fainted. It frightened me. After I got him cooled down with wet towels and put him in his bed...it just hit me how much I loved him and that I didn't ever want to be without him..." She thought of how that must have sounded to Ed. "...or so I thought at the time."

Dennis unconsciously raised his eyebrows. "And when did the relationship become intimate?"

"After he told me he loved me. I think that was sometime in October or November of 1997."

"Is it true that you were the one who initiated sexual relations?"

Mari was flustered by the boldness of the question. "Yes."

"So, the entire time you lived with Mr. Golan he never approached you sexually until you initiated it by getting into his bed." Mari looked to her attorney for help, but he seemed just as interested in the answer as Hal's attorney.

"Mr. Golan was a perfect gentleman. It was only after he told me he loved me and kissed me...that I thought...he meant it. It was the way he said it. It's hard to explain...but I was very drawn to him."

"It appears that I could use Mr. Golan's counsel..."

441

"Objection...there is no need for snide remarks..." Fennerman finally came to life.

"My apologies, Mrs. Baker." Mayor did not want to appear to insult the witness. "So, you admit that Mr. Golan is the biological father of your son, David?"

"Yes."

The questioning continued regarding the relationship between Mari and Hal and then Dennis dropped his bombshell. "I understand that you have a bachelor's degree in political science and a master's in history...is that correct...?"

"Yes."

"...and you went to USC?"

"Yes."

"Who paid for your college education?"

Mari sensed where the question was going and gritted her teeth. "I did."

"You did? Where did you get the money?"

"I earned it."

"How did you earn it...what type of work did you do?"

She looked at Hal. "How could you?"

"Mrs. Baker...were you an exotic dancer?"

"I was a dancer...but NOT an exotic dancer within the meaning of that term. I did traditional Brazilian dances."

"Didn't you dance at a gentlemen's club?"

"I was too young to dance at a gentlemen's club." She evaded the question.

Hal interrupted. "Can we take a break? I think we can all use a break for lunch...I know I can...and a bathroom break."

Dennis looked annoyed at his client. "Certainly...if you insist."

Hal found his way to the restroom and relieved himself. *Jesus...I didn't know he was going to use that against her like that! She must think that I am a real blue-ribbon turd.* After zipping up and flushing the urinal, he stood at the sink washing his hands and looked at himself in the mirror. His conscience ate at him. *Mari must think I'm a bastard. I've got to let her know I would never use her past to hurt her.* He went back into the hallway and saw Mari walking in his direction. When she was near enough, he tried to explain. "Mari...I didn't know he was going to do that..."

"We are both represented…I'm not supposed to talk to you…"

"Mari…please…"

"It's a good thing I'm not allowed to talk to you because I don't think you would like what I have to say…" She stormed off to the ladies' room.

***

At lunch Dennis tried to reason with Hal. "You have to use any dirt you have on her to make what you did look more reasonable. If she took off her clothes for money…it goes to the issue of her character…and it makes it all the more believable that you thought she had targeted you…and that she is not an appropriate parent for David."

"She didn't take off her clothes for money…she was *skimpily* clad…in a costume. I can't say she's a bad mother…she keeps a neat home…and from the little time I spent in her home she seems to be a loving mother."

"Mr. Golan…you can't win a war without ammunition."

Hal rubbed his forehead thinking how her dancing at the club could involve Malone. "Look…get off the dancer thing. I have more than one reason for that to be kept under wraps."

"You have another reason?"

"Yeah…I don't want David to know. Not that she did anything wrong…but it might get twisted."

"Mr. Golan…you're still in love with her."

"Yeah…but that doesn't mean she can keep my kid away from me."

***

When everyone returned from lunch the questioning resumed. Dennis looked at his yellow legal pad. "Now where were we…" The court reporter started to read back the testimony and Dennis snapped, "…it was a rhetorical question."

Mari steeled herself for more questions about the years she danced at Stony Malone's, but Dennis switched gears and went on to a new subject. She sensed that Hal was responsible for sparing her. She looked across the conference table at him with a flicker of gratitude in her eyes that he failed to see because he was staring down at his hands as he listened.

"Mrs. Baker…on the day that Mr. Golan asked you to leave…where were you?"

"In Silverlake Park..."

"Do you recall what was said...?"

"It was a very traumatic experience for me. I can't recall word for word...and I am sure that..." She made a circular motion with her hand. "...my mind blotted a lot of it out because it was just too painful...but basically it all ended with him telling me to get out of his house and out of his life."

"Is that all you remember?"

"No. He called me a heartless bitch...he said I had targeted him as a mark...he mocked just about everything we shared together...like I was trying to...like I was trying to..." She broke down and the attorneys in the room rushed for the Kleenex box they knew would be there.

"Mrs. Baker...do you want to take a break?"

Her voice was very small. "No...I want to get this over with." She dabbed her eyes and bravely went on.

Hal was in agony. He leaned over and whispered to Dennis. "I can tell you what I said...ask her where she went...why I couldn't find her."

"What happened after he told you he wanted you to leave?"

"He just turned and walked away and left me there. It was so unexpected...I was stunned. I think I was in shock...it wasn't real. I know I sat on a bench and just cried. I wanted to die...I just wanted to disappear. I was alone and some guy went jogging by and I didn't feel safe...I don't know why, but I crawled into some bushes near the rec center. Then it hit me like a ton of bricks...he was gone and was never coming back. I think I fainted. Have you ever seen a cartoon when at the end there is nothing but black shrinking into a circle and then it all goes totally black? That's what happened...that's exactly how it looked when I blacked out. I don't know how long I was there, but when I came to; I looked for my cell phone to see what time it was...and it was gone. Mr. Golan told me he found it near the bench where I had been sitting."

"When did he tell you that?"

"When he found out where I was living...and brought me the files."

"Oh...we don't want to get ahead of ourselves. What did you do after you came to...?"

"I walked until I found a store that was open...I told them my car broke down and asked if I could use their phone. I called my friends Steven and Brian and asked if I could stay with them. They told me to stay put and they came to pick me up. They took me home with them...and I stayed with them until I moved to San Francisco."

Hal got Dennis' attention and whispered to him. Dennis continued. "Your friends Steven and Brian...we have information that they were on vacation in Key West. Are you sure that you do not want to 'revise' your answer?"

"No...that is where I went...and they took me in..."

Hal couldn't contain himself. "But I called them, and they had a message on the recorder that they were on vacation in Key West...and they had some guy house sitting for them...or I would have looked for you there."

"Mr. Golan...please!" Dennis tried to control his client.

"No...that's where I went. I had no one else to turn to." Mari shot back.

"Who were you with...even Vee said that Steven and Brian were in Key West!?!" Hal demanded to know.

"Mr. Golan!"

Mari stood up, pounded her fist on the table. "I don't care what Vee said...that's where I was. God, Hal...when will you ever stop thinking that I lie to you...and under oath! Besides, you had just told me we were through! Why should it matter to you where I was? You didn't care then...why should it matter to you now!"

"Because I searched for you...right away I searched all over for you. For four and a half fucking years I searched for you!" He held out his hands. "I could have just found you with *Steven?*"

"You could have just asked me before you accused me! You could have told me what it was all about! You could have given me just one more day!" Frustrated and in tears, she left the conference room. Ed went out after her.

"Good going champ!" Dennis folded his file. "For the record, Mrs. Baker appears to be distraught and has left the room. We will continue this tomorrow or as soon as Mrs. Baker is able to finish her deposition."

***

When Mari and Ed got home, she thanked and paid the babysitter and went into the backyard to scoop her son up in her arms. "Mommy missed you all day." She kissed him and held him tight. "Have you been a good boy?"

"Yes...we made snickerdoodles!"

"I love snickerdoodles! Did you save some for me?"

"Sure...we made lots. You can have some too."

"Come on inside...daddy will want to see you."

They spent the rest of the day with their son and later had a quiet dinner. After David was tucked in for the night they went downstairs. Ed poured himself a glass of wine wondering how to begin. His thoughts had been churning all day with questions about what he had heard during the deposition. The more he thought about it, the more it narrowed down to one statement. "He still loves you...is that going to be a problem for you?"

"I know he does...he told me as much when he was here...and I was sending him on his way when David came downstairs and he saw him. I was hoping there would be a civilized way of working things out. I had no idea that a custody suit would be so barbaric. I know you must have questions about what was said..."

"No...you were honest with me about the things that are important. You told me at the time that you still loved him...but he was out of your life. I accepted that. What was important to me was that you and David were kept safe. Later you said that you had been able to move on and be a proper wife to me. It was one of the happiest days of my life. Do you love me, Mari?"

"Of course I do. How could I not? You've provided a loving home for me and my son...and you have been a wonderful husband to me."

"And how do you feel about Hal?"

"You've seen how exasperating he can be...and you know what he put me through. There is nothing left between us."

"Except David."

"Yes...except David."

***

"Mrs. Baker, I only have a few questions left for you." Dennis Mayor handed her a yellow pad. "Please write down the names, address, and telephone number of the people you stayed with after you left Mr. Golan's household."

"What do you need that for...why drag them into this?"

"They are witnesses. We would like to speak to them."

She jotted down the information and handed the tablet back to him. She looked at Hal. "There...you can ask them yourself...and then you can apologize to me *again* when you find out I'm telling you the truth!"

"Please, Mrs. Baker...restrain yourself to addressing me...and not Mr. Golan."

"Yes, sir."

"Did you know you were carrying Mr. Golan's child when you left Los Angeles?"

"No."

"Surely you must have had reason to think you might have been."

"If you mean...did I go off the pill...yes. I did it at Mr. Golan's request. Was it possible for me to be pregnant? Yes. Was it probable? No. I had been off of the pill for more or less a month. My gynecologist told me that it would be about three or four months before it was likely that I could get pregnant, but that it could be right away. Mr. Golan was aware of the possibilities just like I was. I'm not sure...but I don't think he would have put me out of his house...and left me on my own...had he known I was pregnant."

"Would you have left for San Francisco had you known?"

"I don't know...I was scrambling as fast as I could to find a means of taking care of myself."

"One question I forgot to ask you during our last session. You had a car at your disposal parked in front of Mr. Golan's home. Why didn't you use it?"

"Mr. Golan was not only my...fiancé...but like I said...he was also my boss. The car you are referring to was a company car. It did not belong to me. When he ended our relationship...he also fired me. I didn't think that I still had the right to use it."

"Oh, geez!" Hal softly whispered and put his head in his hand.

"Back to your pregnancy...how did you know you were pregnant?"

"I didn't until I started throwing up. I thought I had some sort of bug and went to the doctor. That is when I found out I was carrying Hal's child."

"Why didn't you tell him?"

"I know I don't remember all that he said to me...but the main thrust of what he said was that he thought I knew he was rich before I met him...and that was why I targeted him. I honestly didn't know anything about him except office gossip...and that was only that he was smart, talented, and a very nice person. That is the only reason that I went to him with the Mitchem case. I thought he would listen...and he did. I didn't know he was wealthy until after we were engaged. But he called me a whore and said I was after his money...and I had no idea what he was talking about...why he..." She put her hands to her face. "It was horrible...frightening. I didn't think he would accept me, or his child, back into his life. I couldn't bear it if he told me to get an abortion. There must be something about pregnancy that makes you delusional...I still loved him. I wanted to have his child...against all odds. I did not want an abortion. I felt that things would be better if I just went my own way without telling him."

"Is that why you married Mr. Baker?"

"Yes. I had a good job to support myself...but it would be only a matter of time before I could no longer work. Ed is a devout Christian...pro-life. He offered to protect me and my child. He wasn't married and he had no children. He wanted a family. He said he loved me from the start, and he proposed marriage. He was aware of Hal and my situation before we were married, and he accepted it for my sake. At the time he was a lifeline to save my baby...now he's my life."

"Do you have any reason to object to Mr. Golan having custody of David?"

Mari pursed her lips with disdain. "The very idea is ludicrous! My husband is the only father that David has ever known. Mr. Golan is a stranger to David. To suddenly take David from his home and thrust him into a strange environment is the most damaging thing you could do to a child! David is a happy, healthy little boy who is loved by both of his parents." With her eyes holding fear and anger, she looked at Hal. "I would die before being parted from my son. You would have to kill me to take him away from me."

Dennis paused to let Hal absorb Mari's response before continuing. "Would you object to Mr. Golan having joint custody of David?"

"Yes...I would fight him tooth and nail on that. David doesn't even know him. I don't even know him anymore or what kind of father he would be. Will he push David on someone else to care for him? What kind of atmosphere would David be exposed to? Would he be exposed to strange women coming and going? What qualifications does he have that makes him think he would be a good father? Does he have ANY idea what parenting entails? And the *big* question is...just what is he going to tell David about *who he* is? As far as David knows...and should only know at this point in his life...is that my husband is his father. Does Mr. Golan feel that at this late date he should disabuse David of that idea? Does he want to declare his fatherhood to a four-year-old? I THINK NOT!"

"Do you have any objection to Mr. Golan having visitation rights?"

"Yes...I object..."

"To *visitation?*" Both Dennis and Hal spoke in unison.

"I'm not going to have him take my child out of my home without both of his parents present...and I am not going to have him being a disruptive element in my family...in my home." Mari was more afraid of Hal's proximity to her than to her son. How would she fare with Hal being so near to her, in her life, and the unbidden thought of him in her bed?"

"But, why?" Hal pleaded.

Dennis echoed the question. "I think you should reconsider your objection."

Mari leaned forward, with her eyes wide with anger as she tapped the table with her index finger at every point she made. "I don't want him second guessing our parenting...I don't want him substituting his judgment for mine...or my husband's! I don't want him spoiling our son so that he will grow up to be a rich pr...a spoiled brat! And...I don't want him losing his temper!"

Hal whispered to Dennis. "Mr. Golan wants to know if you would allow his mother to visit David."

Mari folded her hands and closed her eyes and was silent for a moment. "Yes...yes I will allow Vivian to come see us and be a guest in our home for as long as she likes."

***

HAL'S STORY

As Hal sat down for his deposition, he was keenly aware that Mari was very much ahead with the impression she made. Dennis was right about using her "dancing" against her, but Hal could not bring himself to do it. He thought that perhaps he could make an issue of the fact she seduced him, but that was hardly a major point considering how beautiful she is. He decided to just play it straight and see where he landed. After the questions covered much of the same ground as those put to Mari, with him giving his point of view, they became more pointed. "Just when did you discover you had feelings for Mrs. Baker?"

"Please...Mari...that's the person I fell in love with...Mari Carlson." Hal frowned. "Mrs. Baker appears to be someone I'm not familiar with."

"OK...Mari Carlson?"

"I think I started having feelings for her the first night we worked together...of course I thought she would never look at me. But after we worked just about every night on the case, I fell in love with her. Not just because she's beautiful...but she's a wonderful person that is so adorable...she's funny...she's smart...she's caring...she's brave...she's more than I had ever hoped for. After the project was over, I ached to see her again...it was like a large part of my life was missing. When I finally worked up enough courage to call her and ask her to lunch...I found out that she missed me too. I was over the moon when she told me that."

"Did you give her any reason to believe that you were wealthy?"

"No."

"In fact, you lived rather simply...is that correct?"

"Yes."

"Why did you assume a frugal lifestyle?"

"My reasons were twofold. I wanted to prove to myself that I had the talent to make a living as a writer on my own merit...and I wanted to experience life in a way that I could realistically write about it. I was pretty young when I first learned that I was living in a bubble. I thought that I should break out of that mold. Very few people...outside of my family...were aware of my background."

"Did you do anything to foster the relationship between you and Mari Carlson?"

"After she was 'injured,' and I cared for her...my first concern was to get her well again. By then...I loved her so much...I was afraid that once she was well...she would move out. So, I convinced her to stay as my roommate. But I was petrified that if I made the slightest move to suggest that I wanted more than a friendship...she would be...displeased...distressed...and want to leave."

"Why did you think that?"

"Well...just look at her...she's more than gorgeous. I'm just a plain guy...nothing special to look at. I'm just glad our son got enough of her looks to modify mine. He's a great looking kid."

"Did you ever try to pursue her?"

"Yes."

"How?"

"I became unreasonably jealous when she had a date with Steven...and I asked her why she never went out on a date with me. Her answer was so simple...it was because I never asked her. Once I knew she would go out with me I planned a really special date...one that I knew she would like. I took her to the opera..." Gasps rippled through the conference room as the word "opera" was repeated.

"You took her to the *opera!?!*" Fennerman looked down. "That was a huge sacrifice on your part."

Dennis put his head in his hand. "You poor man."

Looking defensive, Hal answered, "I thought it would make her happy!"

"It did..." Mari whispered.

"How did things progress after that?"

"Not at all...I mean it probably would have gone really well...except I was jealous of her being close to Steven...and we had a spat about it. As it turned out I had nothing to worry about because Steven and Brian are partners." Hal strategically omitted the salsa dancing episode as being too evocative of what she did at Stony Malone's. "But, because of that rockiness...which was all my fault...she thought I wanted her to leave. In desperation I had to tell her that the last thing I wanted was for her to leave...that I loved her...and then I kissed her. I thought she returned my kiss, so I made a move on her, but then she asked me to stop...so I stopped and went to my room."

451

Mari leaned over and whispered something to Fennerman. "Yes...you can tell him."

"I only asked you to stop because my leg was caught against the coffee table...and I couldn't straighten it out...so when you bent me backward, it hurt..." She shrugged. "I really didn't mean for you to stop what you were doing." She gave a wry laugh. "I don't know why I should mention it except I was confused at the time. I didn't know why you left. I guess it's not important." She lowered her eyes.

"It's important to me." Hal whispered.

"What happened after that?" Hal held his hands open. "Well that's when she seduced me."

"How so?"

"After I calmed down, I wanted to know if she would still stay. So, I left my room and I could hear her in her room so I knocked on her door...and she said I could come in. When I opened the door, I saw her standing there...she was exquisite! She had changed into a gown that was not translucent...but I could tell that she had nothing on underneath because the soft fabric clung to every curve of her body. Her hair was long then...and it fell in curls over her shoulders and down her back. I thought my heart would leap out of my chest." Hal's eyes closed.

"Did you say anything to her?"

"Yes...I asked her if she was OK. She said yes...and something else...but I was so...you know...I guess I wasn't listening." Hal took a deep breath. "I had to go back to my room because I was afraid I would be all over her. So, I went to my room and went to bed. Needless to say, I couldn't sleep." He clasped his hands together. "Then she knocked at my door, came in, and told me that she loved me too. Then she got into my bed. I thought I was dreaming. I asked her if this was real...she told me yes...and then I made love to her."

"To be fair, Mr. Golan...did Mari 'seduce' you...or was she just being honest with you?"

Hal's eyebrows knitted and he looked at Mari. Her eyes were downcast. "I suppose it was both."

"Did you resent what she did?"

"No...not at the time...and not now. It's just that I blamed her for it when I believed the file was real."

"How long did your relationship last?"

"I would say over two years."

"Were you happy?"

"Yes...very happy."

"You were engaged?"

"Yes. We were to be married in May."

"What caused you to break it off with her?"

"My father told me he had Mari investigated and he found that she had a long arrest record for prostitution...and the statements of three men that she had fleeced out of money by claiming to love them...having a relationship with them...gaining access to their bank accounts...and then taking off with their money. He had what appeared to be an authentic copy of her purported rap sheet and the affidavits of the men who were defrauded. He also had the detective there who confirmed that he had obtained the file...and a floozy who said she knew Mari...and said that I was her mark."

"And you believed that information was true?"

"God help me...yes I did."

"Why?"

"My mother loves Mari...and she still does to this day. But my father didn't like her at all. Even so...I never dreamed that even *he* would stoop so low as to conjure up such a monumental, malevolent, and ugly lie as that. The file looked real...and I couldn't dispute an official record.

"Also...as a friend told me...that when someone tells you they love you...or if they are trying to con you...and they do things that are absolutely heaven to please you...it is difficult to tell if their actions are the truth or a lie...when they both look the same. Then I thought that the things Mari did to please me were just a part of her con.

"You see...there were times when I would think that there was no reason for her to love me...and I'm ashamed that it was easy to convince me that she knew I was rich from the start...rather than the fact that she found it in her heart to just simply love me."

"What did you do next?"

"I took the file and fumed all the way home. In my mind the most innocent, loving things she did turned into plots to deceive me...con me into loving her...to dazzle me with her beauty. Now...none of it makes any sense. She never asked me for a thing...and before she knew I had money to burn, one of our petty little disagreements was that she thought I spent too much on her. But I had that file...the so-called proof of her duplicity. As soon as I got home...I broke our engagement...and said a lot of ugly things that I'll regret for the rest of my life."

"Did you show her the file?"

"No. I wish I had. She was a research analyst. It would have been easy for her to disprove what was in that file...and we would be married today."

"Why didn't you show it to her?"

"I recently gave it to her...she can show it to you...it looks real. I thought it was beyond question. It even had a picture of her mug shot in it...it was photoshopped. I guess I didn't want to look at it again myself. I should have asked her about it...I should have done a million other things than what I did. You have no idea how much I hate myself for what I did."

"You said that you immediately searched for her. What did you do?"

"I thought about how small and helpless she looked when I walked away. I couldn't leave her there. I went back to the park. I saw that jogger she talked about...and he took me to where he last saw her. That's where I found her cell phone. I searched the park...I called out her name. I walked back home and got in my car and drove around looking for her. I called my friend to help look for her. We called hospitals...we called everywhere. When we didn't find her, we tried calling the numbers on her cell." He looked at Mari. "For God's sake...I called Steven and Brian...and they had a message on their voicemail that they were vacationing in Key West. I contacted Vee...and he also said they were in Key West. Had I known you were there...I would have gone there to take you back home. By that time...I didn't even care if it was true. I wanted you back." His eyes moistened. Looking away, he said softly, "I want to take a break."

"I just have a few more questions before we wrap this up...if you think you can persevere a little longer."

"Sure...go ahead and shoot."

"I understand that you took no action against your father for what he did...is that correct?"

"Yes. I was in no position to challenge him. He was in control of half of my inheritance. He was CEO of the family business and in total

454

control. If I was to be CEO one day...I would need his support. But it seems that God interceded on my behalf. He got himself into trouble and now I am CEO...and I own his shares of stock."

"Your father is in prison?"

"That's right. The kinds of difficulties that he brought on himself are not the kind that I would want my son to know about. I have no contact with him."

Mari could barely breathe. She remembered what Hal had said about making Marvin pay and she made an instant decision never to speak of it.

"Now you have had no contact with Mrs....Mari for over four years...since the day you left her in the park?"

"That's correct...except when I gave her the file."

"Is there anything you remember about the time when you loved her...?"

"I still love her."

"Strike that question."

"You still love Mrs. Baker?"

"Yes."

"If you were to gain access to your son...is there anything that you would do to become a disruptive force in her marriage?"

"No...absolutely not."

"Would you disrupt David's home?"

"Never."

"Would you countermand the Bakers' parenting?"

"I listened carefully to Mari's...Mrs. Baker's concerns...and I would never do anything that she thought would be detrimental to our son. But...one day it is inevitable that he will learn that I am his father. It will go a long way to make that day less traumatic for him if he at least gets to know me. I would do anything for David...and I would do anything for Mrs. Baker...except to be estranged from my son."

Mari consulted with Fennerman. "If you were to have access to your son...what would you tell him about who you are?"

"Anything Mrs. Baker tells me to say."

"I am going to call for a break right now, Mr. Golan...before I wrap this up." Fennerman motioned to the Bakers that he wanted to speak with them in private in his office.

***

455

"Mrs. Baker...are you adamant about keeping Mr. Golan out of David's life? It hardly seems fair to allow his mother to visit your son and then keep Mr. Golan away. We can put very strict rules on his visitation rights...at least at first while David is young...but I must admit that Mr. Golan has a point when he says it is inevitable that David will eventually find out who his father is and will resent being lied to. If you allow visitation...albeit restricted to your home and in your presence...David will become acclimated to Mr. Golan and you can better judge the type of parent he will be if David should ever choose to live with him. It happens sometimes that when children become teenagers...they become alienated from their parents...and may choose...as the court allows...to live with their other parent."

"You mean that David could choose to live with him instead of us?" Mari was incredulous.

"As remote a possibility as that may seem now...I have seen it happen more frequently than I would like to say. Mrs. Baker...the court would prefer that we come up with a reasonable agreement that the court can accept and just draw up the order. If we are still squabbling by the time this goes to court...you may not like the court's decision. In any event...I think we should end Mr. Golan's deposition on a softer...more agreeable note."

Ed looked at his wife. "Dear, just think of it from his point of view. He just found out he has a son. What did you think he would do? I know that I would do the same thing he is doing now. He just wants to be a part of his son's life..."

"No...no...he will take him from us...he has the money and power to do so."

Fennerman interjected. "Only the court can make that decision. At least let us go back in and try to make a nice, agreeable impression. Is there anything that you think he will remember with fondness from the time you spent together?"

"Aebleskivers..." At the puzzled look on Fennerman's face, she added, "...it's a Danish pastry sort of like donut holes...only bigger...you put syrup on them like a pancake...they're round, a little larger than golf balls. He used to love it when I made them for breakfast."

"Alright...we will end on an aebleskiver note...leave him with a good thought about you as we wrap up this session."

"We are just about through here." Fennerman made a show of flipping through the sheets of his yellow pad to review if there was any question he missed. Then he smiled. "Is there anything you remember with fondness about the time you spent together with Mari Carlson...?"

"Oh...there are so many things." A slight smile tugged at Hal's lips.

"Anything in particular that comes to mind?"

"There's something I just thought of. I loved washing her hair."

"Washing her hair? Mari thought you would say it was her aebleskivers."

"No...that is what she made for me the morning I broke our engagement. They are a rather sad memory for me now..." He turned his head and looked at Mari. "...but I always loved washing your hair."

***

457

ED'S STORY

The afternoon of the same day, right after Hal's deposition, the questioning in the custody suit resumed with Ed Baker as the deponent. After the preliminary questions Dennis Mayor continued. "Mr. Baker, how did you meet your wife?"

"She was hired at Yarborough Publishing to be my assistant."

"When was that?"

"About late January in 2000."

"So…you were her boss?"

"I don't think so…but she worked with me."

"So…it's like déjà vu all over again?"

"I don't know what you mean."

"Strike the question."

"When were you first attracted to the then Mari Carlson?"

"Immediately…when I met her. She was very sweet and well mannered…but I could tell she was troubled."

"How so?"

"She was kind of withdrawn. She mostly kept to herself and her eyes were…there's just no other way of saying it…she looked sad."

"At what point did you start a relationship with her."

"One day I had planned to work at home…but when I left the office that evening, I forgot my paperwork…so I went back. I found she was still there at her desk after hours…and it looked to me like she had been crying. Well, I'm not a nosy person…but it is my Christian duty to help the afflicted…so I asked her what was grieving her. She said it was a long story…so I took her to dinner."

Hal rolled his eyes. *Yeah…it is your Christian duty to help hot babes!*

"Is that when she told you about her pregnancy?"

"No…not at first. She told me about how her fiancé broke their engagement. Quite frankly…I was shocked that anyone would treat her like that…she is every inch a lady."

"Was anything else discussed?"

"Just that she was new to San Francisco and she did not know anyone. She did mention that she was still in love with her fiancé, but he didn't love her anymore…and she felt very lost."

"What happened then?"

"I took her home…she thanked me for dinner, and I left."

458

"Did she encourage your attention in any way?"

"No...but she didn't have to...she had my attention."

"Did the age difference bother you?"

"At the time I was forty-eight...I am now fifty-three. I think she did not object to a man who was more mature and understanding."

Hal took it as an insult. *Did he look at me? Did he just look at me?*

"When did she disclose to you that she was pregnant?"

"Well, in the next few weeks I got to know her better. If I couldn't get out of the office, she would bring me sandwiches for lunch...and we would sit and talk. Then sometime in late February she broke down and told me she was with child...her fiancé's child...and she didn't know what to do. After a while she wouldn't be able to work, and she wouldn't be able to support herself and the child. She was frantic...because she wanted the baby...and it seemed to her that she had no way out."

"Do you think she was trying to get you to marry her?"

"No...no...it wasn't like that. I was the only friend she had. She just needed to confide in someone about what she was up against. I told her I would pray on it and God will send us the answer."

"Did God send you the answer?"

"Yes...yes He did. You see...a long time ago...I had someone I was serious about. She was the kind of woman that was full of life and wanted adventure. Therefore, she was not keen on being saddled with children...her words, not mine. I was young and besotted with her and we planned to marry. At the time, I was ambivalent about children. So, I got a vasectomy to please her. It was a big mistake, because I found that I was more serious about her than she was about me.

"Later, I fell in love with a woman who wanted children...so I tried to have the vasectomy reversed. The doctor botched the job and it didn't work...and I was stuck with it...and the lady in question married someone else. Too late I realized that I did want children. Then here comes Mari into my life...that God sent to me to protect...and to protect her baby. That was how I looked at it. I loved her...and I figured that if she consented to marrying me...I would have the family I always wanted...and she would have the husband she needed."

"Didn't you think that the father should know?"

"Absolutely…that was the first thing I suggested to her when she told me. She said it was out of the question. She had no doubt that the father would think she was trying to play him for a fool…and ultimately reject her and the child…and she could not bear that. She said it was useless. Perhaps I should have insisted…but I figured she knew her situation better than I did. So, I backed off of that subject."

"What did she say when you proposed your…God's answer to her problem?"

"She told me she didn't love me, and she doubted that she could ever love me. I told her that I understood…but her child's life was more important to me. She told me that she wasn't sure she could be a proper wife to me…meaning marital relations. I told her we can pray on that…but it was up to her. It took over two long years before she was prepared to have marital relations…but we are on track now…"

"You're a patient man…"

"Truer words were never spoken! But when she said 'yes' to my proposal she told me that she had given up on love and she didn't think she could ever love anyone else ever again…but now she says she loves me. She said I made a warm, loving home for her and her son…and she loves me for that. I must say that we have been quite happy. David is the light of my life…and Mari is the most wonderful wife a man could hope for. I am truly blessed."

"When and where were you married?"

"We were married in March…2000…in Santa Barbara."

"We could not find a record of your marriage…and we checked Santa Barbara."

"In California…they have what is called a 'confidential marriage' where only the husband or the wife may obtain the marriage record. We thought that under the circumstances…that was best."

"Why did you leave San Francisco?"

"Before I met Mari, I had inherited land here near Guerneville…so I did what everyone else here did…over time I planted grapes. When we married, I had been at Yarborough for over thirty years…I started there when I was eighteen…so I decided to retire, sell my home in San Francisco, build one on my estate, and become a vintner. We moved here before David was born. I found it was easier to grow grapes than it was to make wine…so I sell my crop."

460

"After you married, Mrs. Baker never worked outside of the home?"

"That's right."

"Mr. Golan has testified that he is still in love with Mrs. Baker...your wife...what are your thoughts about that?"

"I feel very sorry for Mr. Golan. I think that he ruined what could have been a very happy life for him. If you are asking if I feel threatened that he still has feelings for Mari...the answer is no. I have discussed it with my wife, and she has assured me that there could be nothing more between them."

"Would you object to Mr. Golan having custody of David?"

"Absolutely! I would fight against that with every fiber of my being."

"Do you feel the same about joint custody?"

"To save you some time...I understand that Mr. Golan wants to be a part of David's life...but I must agree with my wife regarding what type of influence he would be on our son...and that David's level of understanding has not prepared him for being the solution to adult problems. I agree with her wholeheartedly."

"Then you feel that even visitation rights are out of the question?" Ed looked at Hal and then lowered his eyes. "Yes."

Hal muttered under his breath. "I thought it was your Christian duty to help the afflicted."

***

"You stayed with two homosexuals!" Ed's understanding had reached its limits. "When you said they were partners...I thought you meant in business...not an abomination in God's eyes. They are perverted people! My goodness, Mari...how could you even associate with such people?"

"They are two loving friends who didn't judge me...and I don't judge them. You lived in San Francisco...goodness, the rainbow is practically on the city seal...are you telling me you don't know any openly gay people? They're everywhere in L.A. They're consenting adults and that is all anyone should care about."

"Of course, I saw them...but I never went out of my way to develop a friendship with them."

"Who goes out of their way? Friendships happen when you meet people you like."

"Why would you go on a date with a...a..."

"I was single...and unattached...and my boss asked to meet his son...that's all. Steven was charming...and we hit it off very well...but we both realized that we could only be friends."

"So, you knew?"

"After about the first fifteen minutes of talking with him...yes." Mari threw up her hands. "Steven and Brian love each other, and they have been together longer than some heterosexual married couples...and much longer than my engagement." Mari could not resist commenting on the irony of it all.

"Well...they are not staying here...and they are not going to be around my son."

"Don't be daft. Mr. Mayor is putting them up at the Wayside Hotel...but they will come to dinner while they are here...I insist upon it...and you will treat them with respect!"

"You would have those sexual deviants around our son?"

"I would not only trust them with my son...I trusted them with my very life! I wanted to kill myself...and they saved me...they held on to me until I was able to face life without Hal...and regain my self-esteem and my will to live. You will be a gracious host to them and keep in mind that they are God's children."

"The Bible says that..."

"Jesus did not utter a word against gays...that was Saul, who changed his name to Paul...who knows why he needed an alias...and he got loaded on the road to Damascus and thought he saw an apparition...or something. Then he felt he could inflict his own biases on the church. Sorry, but I don't agree with a lot of what he said, and I should hope that after lo these millennia...we are more advanced than some sandal wearing, beard sporting, toga bedecked, misogynist!"

"MARI!"

"I'm sorry, Ed...but I don't believe the Bible should be taken literally where it doesn't make sense...or used as an excuse for hatred!" She stomped up the stairs.

"Mari?"

***

In the reception area of Hanlon & Hanlon, Steven, Brian, and Mari stood embracing in a tearful group hug. The reunion was bittersweet in that they had not heard from Mari since San Francisco swallowed her up. As is common in the mobile society of L.A., friends lose touch, lose each other, and life moves on. When Mari called them, they were ecstatic. When they heard the reason that she called, their joy was tempered by the gravity of the custody battle. "He wants you back after everything he did to you? The nerve of that man is unending." Brian clucked.

"No...he wants custody of our son...he knew I was married when he found me."

"Don't kid yourself, sweetie. He searched for you all those years..."

Steven's voice chimed in on the extension. "Oh, Brian...don't make more of it than it is."

"I'm not the one making more of it...*he* is." Brian pouted.

Steven was sympathetic. "You must be worried sick."

"Yes...I am. But our attorney said it was doubtful that he could get full custody."

"Well...whatever we can do to help." Steven comforted her.

"Both attorneys want to take your depositions...I hope it isn't too much of an imposition."

"Oh...to go to the wine country...on Hal's attorney's dime! I'm all over that! It comes at a good time. The fall shows are over, and I have

463

a respite until we start gearing up for spring." Brian put the best face on it.

"Oooohhh...the thought of the fall shows. I have been so out of it."

"Mari...have you lost your glam?" Brian scolded.

"I'm afraid so. I'm just a Hausfrau now."

"That does it...I'm bringing my beauty kit..."

"Brian...wait until you're asked..." Steven cautioned.

"No...I would love to have Brian spruce me up...I need a lot of sprucing."

"You got it sweetie...now...you didn't gain weight on me, did you?"

"No."

"Well...I'll see what I have...no promises..."

"You're a darling Brian...both of you are..." After hanging up, Mari felt better from hearing their voices and being reassured.

Now that they were there in person, it felt good to be in the warmth of their presence once more.

***

Hal walked into the reception area of Hanlon & Hanlon. He saw Steven and Brian waiting to be called for their depositions. He nodded to them. They squinted their eyes, pursed their lips, and looked away. Hal waved his hand in an arc, "Good day to you, too." and then went to the receptionist's desk. "I'm Mr. Golan..."

"Yes...we've been waiting for you. Please go right into the conference room."

Steven was the first to be called. His startling good looks were impressive, and it did not add up, in the minds of the attorneys, that Mari would choose Hal over him until they fully grasped the relationship between Steven and Brian. When he appeared at ease, the deposition began. "Mr. Vou...gee...how do you pronounce your name?"

"Vougiouklakis." Steven spelled it out for the court reporter.

"Thank you. We only have a few questions for you. I suppose we could have taken your deposition in Los Angeles...but it was more expedient to fly you here...so I hope you will enjoy your visit to the wine country."

"Yes...it is an unexpected treat."

"Well...let's get on with it." After the preliminary questions, Dennis asked, "How long have you known Mrs. Baker?"

"I think it was about seven years ago when we met."

"How did you meet?"

"On a blind date."

"Did a romantic relationship develop between you?"

"No...but we became fast friends."

"Mrs. Baker is an attractive woman...you had no interest in her?"

"She's a beautiful woman...but I was already in a relationship...so I had no romantic intentions. I went on the date to please my father."

"Your gender preference is not toward...the opposite sex."

"If you are asking if I am gay...that would be yes."

"Were you aware of Mrs. Baker's relationship with Mr. Golan?"

"No...not at first. When we met, I don't believe they were what you could call an 'item.' That came later. I know she became enamored with him."

"How did you know that?"

"She told me. She was heartsick that he didn't seem to care for her in the same way. Then she came to us...so very happy that things worked out for them. I never understood what went wrong...she seemed utterly happy."

"Sometime in 1999 did she have the occasion to stay with you?"

"Yes."

"When was that?"

"Sometime in late December...I remember it was just before Christmas..."

"Then you were not vacationing in Key West?"

Steven smiled. "No...that was something my partner made up to keep Hal from kicking down our door. He put it on our voicemail."

"Did you think that Mrs. Baker...Mari...did not want to see Mr. Golan?"

"I had no idea one way or the other...I just knew he had upset her terribly...the worst I've ever seen anyone distressed. I didn't know what had happened. I don't think she did either."

"Did you tell Mrs. Baker that you had that message on your phone?"

"Did I personally tell her?"

"Yes."

"No...I didn't...I didn't think of it at the time. We were too busy trying to get her well."

"Was she sick?"

"Was she ever! We thought she was suicidal…she cried for several days and wouldn't eat. We stayed with her night and day. Brian was simply heroic."

Dennis did not want to continue that line of questioning and he changed the subject.

"How long was she with you?"

"I don't remember…but it was like a couple or three weeks…until we helped her move from Hal's apartment…and then, after she found a job in San Francisco, we helped her move there."

"Did you remain in contact with her after you helped her move to San Francisco?" "

No…not very much…we just figured that she was trying to get her life together."

"So, at the time you knew where she lived?"

"We knew where she moved to…but after a couple of months…she fell off the radar."

"Did she ever tell you she was pregnant?"

"No. If she had…I think we would have gone to get her to bring her home with us to have her baby. The thought of her being all alone would have been very…disturbing to us."

***

Brian was called into the conference room to give his deposition. His pretty face was haughty as he took his place in the deponent's chair. "Please give your name."

"My name is Brian."

"What is your last name, Brian?"

"No last name…just Brian…you know like Cher…Fabio…I'm Brian."

"Is that your legal name?"

"Yes…I had it changed."

"I would like to see some identification of your name." Fennerman was perplexed.

Brian dug into his pants pocket and pulled out his wallet. Opening it to his license he passed it to Fennerman. "I know it is sooooo L.A.…but there you go, sweetie."

"Please…call me Mr. Fennerman." He handed it back. "I understand that you have known Mrs. Baker since 1997."

"Yes. We made custom moisturizers and lotions together. I still use her formulas." He smiled at Mari.

"What type of work do you do?"

"Oh...I do it all...swee...Mr. F. Without me the fashion industry would come crashing down! Hair...makeup...fashion...cracking the whip over those bulimic bitches to get them out on the runway on time...that's all me!"

"The entire fashion industry?"

"Yes...I like to think that there are a hundred little 'Brians' from Los Angeles to New York to Paris and Milan..." He moved his hands back and forth, fanning them open with each city he mentioned. "...working away to make the world more beautiful." Brian sat back and crossed his legs.

"I see." Fennerman didn't "see" at all but moved on. "Did Mrs. Baker have the occasion to stay with you in December of 1999?"

"Yes. Our dear, sweet Mari called us and said she had a big blow up with Hal...and asked if we could come and get her and if she could stay with us for a little while." He flickered a cold look at Hal. "Of course, we said yes. When we came for her...she looked awful. She had mud on her pants, and she had been crying. I couldn't imagine what that brute had done to her. I climbed into the back seat of the car with her and held her as she cried...all the way home."

"What happened next?"

"After we got home, I had her change into my pajamas and took her clothes and put them in the hamper to go to the dry cleaners. I made her some hot milk, with a little brandy in it...she can't drink too much...and then we asked her to tell us what happened. Well she poured out a horror story that was beyond belief." He stared at Hal with open hostility. "He called her a heartless bitch, he said he had nothing but contempt for her, he called her an alley cat, and a back-stabbing whore, he threw her out of his house with nowhere to go, and he fired her...so she had no means of taking care of herself." Brian's eyes overflowed. "He wouldn't even give her a few days to find out what he was so angry about...and then he turned his back on her and left her in the dark and the cold...and told her she was back on the street...a whore's hunting grounds! I had never heard anything so despicable and so cruel in my life!" He pointed a finger at Hal. "You took a sweet, innocent girl who loved you more than

467

anything and broke her down...made her a wreck...I had to hide the pills in the house because all she wanted to do was die! YOU MONSTER!"

"Mr. Brian...please confine yourself to the testimony."

"Well...I was the one who felt her pain and had to take it inside of me to try to lessen her agony from the poison he spewed at her." As angry tears flowed, he pointed his remarks at Hal again. "She cried until her eyes were so puffed up, they were mere slits! I had to take cold compresses to fix the ravages to her face...tea bags...cucumber slices! She wouldn't eat...I made a pot of my cream of chicken soup and got her to eat it a teaspoon at a time! She was beyond sick...she was done for! I didn't know if I could save her...bring her back...but I fought for her...and I kept her from going over the brink! I finally brought her back!" Brian tore several tissues from the proffered Kleenex box and buried his face into them, sobbing.

There was not a dry eye in the room. Ed had his arm around Mari as she cried on his shoulder. The court reporter sniffled as her fingers flew to catch every word. Dennis Mayor was angry with himself for allowing his client to insist on deposing the two witnesses and opening the floodgates of adverse testimony. Moreover, even he thought that Hal had been beastly to the lovely lady in question.

Hal got up, visibly shaken by what he had heard. "I have caused too much pain already." He slowly started in a low voice. "Mari...on my life...I believed what was in that damnable file and I thought I was talking to a hardened prostitute...not the girl I loved..." He began again. "You should not have had to take the brunt of..." He looked at Dennis. "I want to stop this...I want to stop this whole thing. I have caused too much pain...I can't go on with this."

Dennis needed to give his client time to reconsider. "I think we are all distraught. Let's take a long lunch and reconvene at..." He checked his watch. "...how about two-thirty?"

They all nodded and filed out of the room. Fennerman caught up with Brian. "You did an excellent job in there. It must have been difficult for you."

"No...it was just what that bastard deserved." Brian sniffed. "I have wanted to say that for years."

***

Dennis jabbed a fork into his steak and sawed the meat with his knife. "Hal, you have every chance of getting visitation rights to your son. Why give up now?"

"You heard Brian. My God, I had no idea what I put her through. It's unspeakable! I can't put her through this custody battle on top of everything else."

"Didn't you suffer as well? Didn't you pay the price for what you did? How much penitence should you pay? Do you have to give up your son too? We all make mistakes, Hal..."

"Yeah...well I made a doozy!"

"Large or small...we all have to learn to forgive ourselves."

"I can't forgive myself until she forgives me. I think the best thing I can do for her right now is to get out of her life and let her be happy."

"And what about your son...are you going to let her dictate that you have no right as a father? You see...most of the clients that I represent are pretty much selfish dicks or bitches. I don't see you as one of their ilk. You loved her...and you were duped. What you did was a mistake that any man could have made...that does not make you a bad guy...that just makes you human. You can't tell me that you haven't paid for it ever since...losing someone like her. She still loves you...you know."

"No...I killed that a long time ago."

"I have seen many, many couples in my line of work...and most of them hate each other's guts. Believe me...I have seen pure hatred. But a very few...like you and your Mari...still love each other...and usually my hunch about them is proven right by their remarrying after the divorce."

"How can you tell how she feels about me?"

"She wanted to let you know that you did make her happy with that opera stuff. She wanted to make it plain to you that she did not want to rebuff your advances when you tried to kiss her. Even now...it was important to her for you to know that she wanted you. And...that she can still get upset that you thought she was lying...or cry when she thinks about how she felt...still feels...when you broke your engagement. The only problems she still has with you are...one..." Dennis held a finger up. "...she is still hurt and angry...and two..." He held up a second finger. "...She has 'trust' issues with you...and I can see why. But that does not mean her heart has forgotten you...she still cares. By the time most women get pushed to the point of divorce...they don't give a flip about the bastard they're leaving."

Hal thought about it, took a sip of his coffee. "Is it true about the kid having a choice when he's older?"

"Yes...but how is he going to choose you when he doesn't even know you?"

"I can't stand to see her crying anymore. I'm tossing in the towel. I just want to tell her myself."

"I can't let you be alone with her without her husband's...."

"I don't have to be alone with her...I just want her to hear it from me."

"I'll arrange it."

***

When everyone reconvened in the conference room, Hal stood at the head of the table. "Mari...I want you to know that I am no longer going to pursue this custody case. I have caused you so much grief...and until these depositions...especially Brian's...I had no idea just how much...the extent of what I have put you through. I don't want to cause you another minute of sorrow. All of the questions that I have had, all these years, have been answered. I really had no intention of taking your son from you. I just wanted to be able to see my son...to watch him grow. I haven't earned the right to be his father...but I was hoping to. I will always love you...and I guess that living without you is a just sentence for what I did. I hope one day you can find it in your heart to forgive me." He turned to Ed. "I want to thank you, Ed, for being there to be...what I failed to be...the protector who shielded Mari and my son from the dangers that threatened them. I sincerely thank you. While it was not my intention...my actions placed them in a terrible situation. I shudder to think what could have happened to them if you had not stepped in to intervene. I promise you both...Mari and Ed...that you have nothing left to fear from me. I will leave you in peace to be happy once more." Hal sat down.

Dennis addressed Fennerman. "Mr. Golan has set up a fund to be used for David's college education and he will pay ten thousand dollars a month in child support to be used at Mari Baker's discretion. Do your clients have anything they wish to say?"

470

Fennerman looked at Mari. "Mrs. Baker...do you wish to address Mr. Golan?"

"I cannot accept his money." Mari exclaimed without thinking.

Dennis looked to Fennerman to enlighten his client.

"Mrs. Baker, the money is David's...not yours...you have no right to refuse it. Mr. Golan will be filing his claim of paternity with the court as is his right to do...his paternity of your son that you have already admitted to under oath...and his agreement to make said payments for the benefit of the child. Is there anything else you would like to say?"

Mari lowered her eyes. "No."

"I want to say something." Ed stood up. "It hardly seems fair...or Christian...that Mr. Golan will be deprived of seeing his child. I know what I said before...but I only know how I would feel if I were in his shoes. Mari showed me that file and I think I would have been fooled by it too. It was a cruel hoax. He has agreed not to be disruptive. I should think we would be able to come to some sort of arrangement where he can see his son...after all, his mother will be able to...why can't he?" He looked down at his wife's shocked face. "Mari...we must not be so hard hearted. We must have Christian charity."

Mari looked away. She had no real objections to Hal seeing his son. What she feared was having him close to her, in her house, and what it could mean to her marriage. She thought that she was over him and her life with him was behind her. But, from the first time she opened her door and saw him standing there; her feelings were stirred by him. At first, they were tinged with anger. Now they tussled in a free-for-all inside her. "Alright...we will come to some sort of arrangement." She heard herself say and hoped that she would not regret it.

***

MY SON

With an Old Fashioned in his hand, Hal sat alone in the kitchen of his house, nursed his drink, and thought of the unexpected outcome of his custody case that day. The Bakers agreed to visitation rights for one day a week, all holidays, and additional days as agreed to by all parties. The papers, acknowledging his paternity and support agreement, were signed and would be filed with the court the following day. It was now official; David was his son. *So, now what? You're the biological father...how do you become a dad? The real question is...how to be a dad without David knowing I'm his father?* He agreed to keep his paternity a secret until David was old enough to understand, but when would that be? He hadn't seen David since the day he discovered he had a child. Hal only knew that his heart was wrapped around his boy, but that was the beginning and end of his expertise. *I had better just follow Mari's lead...she knows what is best.*

His surroundings did not suit him. He wanted to be within thirty minutes from Mari and David, close enough to be on call, but not too close to smother the family. The house he settled for in Santa Rosa was close enough; but he leased it because it was expedient, not because he liked it. With his custody case settled, he had time to look for another place and he thought it was time to put his Beverly Hills house on the market, along with his other real estate, and only retain the Silverlake property. He made plans to rearrange his life. Could he remain CEO of Arendt from a distance? He had only one account that required his personal attention. Other than that, Mack could easily run the company. His constant presence was not required. He could buy or build a home nearby, so he could be there for David at a moment's notice. *Oh...and I should read up on parenting.*

The Bakers were gracious enough to extend an invitation for Vivian to stay with them for the weekend and to have Hal come to dinner while she was there. He picked up the phone and dialed. "Hi ma. Good news...I got visitation rights and Mari and her husband have invited you to stay with them for the coming weekend."

A squeal of delight came through the phone. "She asked for me to stay with her?"

"Yeah...she gave you visitation rights right off the bat...I had to fight for mine. For some strange reason, she didn't want me in David's life. It was her husband who changed her mind."

"That is strange indeed. Perhaps she will tell me why. Her husband was in your corner?"

"Yeah. He said it wasn't Christian to keep me away...thank God. Mari didn't even want me to pay any support. Can you imagine?"

"I find that hard to believe. It sounds as though she wants nothing to do with you...and once she loved you more than anything."

"I can't talk about it right now...it's too upsetting...but she has every reason not to love me. Marvin saw to that...and I played right into it."

"So did I, dear...so did I." Vivian sniffed. "I should have known better..."

"How soon can you fly here? They have direct flights from LAX to Santa Rosa."

"I will take off tomorrow...and I am bringing Graham. Can he stay with you?"

"Sure. I could use the company. Call me when you know the flight number and I'll pick you up and take you straight to Mari's. It will give me an excuse to see my son an extra day. Wait until you see him, ma. He's a great kid."

After he finished his call, he went to the refrigerator. Poking through Styrofoam containers of past meals, and finding nothing there that he cared to eat, he went out to the only restaurant in Santa Rosa that he knew served great steaks.

**

"It never made sense to me that Hal...did what he did..." Steven and Brian sat across from the Bakers at the best steak house in town. Now that Steven knew the whole story, he had a better understanding. "...he was always so jealous of you...maybe 'possessive' is the correct word...that I could never quite get my head around what happened. Knowing that he immediately searched for you shows me that he had a momentary lapse...a crisis of confidence."

"Oh...pooh! You are always so understanding. I'm not ready to forgive him." Brian grumbled. "But he was possessive alright. He kept mumbling under his breath that Raul was a dead man if he dropped

473

you..." Brian held his arms up to simulate Raul holding Mari over his head. "...I thought he was going to burst a blood vessel the entire evening."

"Yes...I know...we discussed it later. How long are you going to be in town?" Mari quickly asked, changing the subject.

"Why was someone holding you up high like that?" Ed made the same gesture as Brian.

"It was just an exhibition...a sort of ballet. Raul, a great artiste, held me over his head at the end."

"Oh." Ed went back to his appetizer plate.

Steven pinched Brian for talking too much. "We will be here for a day or two exploring the wine country...then it's back to L.A."

"I would love it if you could extend your stay through the weekend..." Marie cajoled. "...I could use the moral support."

Steven and Brian looked at each other and then nodded. "But tomorrow morning..." Brian added. "...before we go anywhere...I am going to give you the full treatment...facial...hair...and I brought a chic little number for you to wear. It's not all that...but it will set this little burg on fire!"

"I can hardly wait! It has been...a...while..." Mari looked up to see the hostess leading Hal into the dining area. "Look who's here..."

Ed looked up while Steven and Brian turned. Ed felt the obligation of being conciliatory. "It's Mr. Golan...perhaps we should invite him to sit with us."

"I don't know if that would be a good idea." Mari was still spent from the afternoon's ordeal.

"Dear...we must all learn to get along for David's sake. We may as well start now by offering Mr. Golan an olive branch."

"Alright...but just make sure he doesn't take the olive orchard."

Ed stood up in the hostess' path and stopped Hal with an extended hand. "Mr. Golan...it's a pleasant surprise to see you here. Would you like to join us at our table?"

Hal shook his hand but did not accept. Mari's glum expression told him he was not welcome. "Thank you...but I wouldn't want to intrude." The hostess looked back and forth between the two men for a clue as to what she should do.

"Nonsense...come and dine with us." Ed put on an affable face. He was actually sincere. All evening, as Mari entertained her guests, he had felt like the odd man out and wanted another party at the table.

"Perhaps I should dine alone tonight..." His eyes landed on Mari to indicate to Ed that she did not want him there. "...but my mother is flying in tomorrow so I will be seeing you this weekend. She is very excited about seeing Mari again and meeting her...David."

"Very well...we'll see you then." Ed sat back down, and Hal continued to his table. "Mari!" Ed whispered. "The man just agreed to pay over two million in child support for David over twenty-two years and we don't have to worry about college. The least you can do is to be polite!"

Brian's wide eyes fixed on Ed. "Did I hear that right? Two million!?! For that amount of money, I'd suck..."

Steven pinched him again. "Nobody wants to know what you would do, sweetie!"

Mari looked over her shoulder to see Hal sitting by himself, looking at a menu, and waiting for service. She closed her eyes for a moment and then decided to go to him. "I'll be right back."

She made a detour to the ladies' room to check how she looked. Adding a bit more lipstick and taming a few errant hairs, she wondered how she would survive the cards that life had dealt her. *Now is as good a time as any to start learning how to get through this.*

Hal smelled the scent of plumerias and looked up just as Mari sat down across from him. "I didn't think you wanted me at your table."

She started to feed him a platitude but decided that she should be honest. "You're right...I didn't. But it has been a long day for both of us and I felt as though I've been put through a wringer..." She half smiled. "...how about you?"

"Yeah...pretty much." He nodded.

"Our work is cut out for us because we're going to have to learn to put behind us all that happened in the past...and not to stumble over each other for David's sake. Do you think you can do that?"

"Can you?" His eyes searched hers.

"Hal, don't do that to me...I know I have to and so I will."

"I'm just trying to get my bearings in...in all of this...to find out what I'm supposed to do. I promise you...I will do my level best. I guess I should just follow your lead." His eyes wandered over her face. "Do you mind if I ask you a question?"

"Go ahead."

"Why did you want to keep me out of David's life? I know what you said...but..."

"This place is too public for me to answer that question. I will answer it at another time and place...between just the two of us."

"Do I get another question then?"

"Yes."

"Why did you cut your hair?"

She suppressed a laugh. "Hal...that much hair takes a lot of work...and so does a baby. After I had David, I didn't have the time to keep up with long hair...and it kept getting in the way. So, I cut it."

"Your hair looks great the way it is now...but I sort of liked it the way it was."

"Life changes things Hal...and not always for the better."

"Can I tell you something for one last time?"

"Sure."

"I love you, girl...and that will never change."

"Hal...don't..." She was shaken by his words and her eyes moistened. "...I can't tell you what you want to hear. I can never be what you want me to be..."

"Never is a long time." His dark eyes penetrated hers. "I can wait."

The waitress came to the table. "Are you ready to order?"

Mari gestured to the table across the walkway. "Mr. Golan will be dining at my table this evening. Please bring another place setting." As the waitress walked away, they both got up to move to Mari's table. "I guess we both need to practice being...reserved. I truly hope we can be just friends."

"OK, Mari...just friends. Whatever you say."

They moved to her table and Hal placed his order. Ed welcomed him. "I'm glad to see you changed your mind."

"Mari can be quite convincing." Hal gave him a polite smile. "Before I forget...I should have said this sooner, but it was a tiring day and I forgot my manners. Ed, I want to thank you from the bottom of my heart for being the better man in granting me the right to see David. It was truly big of you."

"It was no more than my Christian duty."

Hal turned to Brian. "Brian...I also want to thank you. I know you did not do it for me...you did it for Mari...to help her get through what must have been a nightmare. Steven said you were heroic, and I agree. If it hadn't been for you...none of us would be here tonight."

Brian's blue eyes emoted love for Steven. "You said I was heroic?"

"Yes...because you really were." Steven patted Brian's hand.

Brian looked down trying not to cry. "I love Mari. She's the sister I never had."

Steven looked surprised. "You have a sister..."

"That wicked stick figure that flies into town on her broom? I don't consider her my sister...she's just an accident of birth...and I do mean an accident...my mother wasn't very careful." Brian looked across the table at Mari. "You're my beautiful sister...and I won't have it any other way."

Ed turned to her. "How does it feel to have every man here in love with you?"

Hal was taken aback. Did he just say that...*did he actually say that? Did he look at me when he said that?* Then he unconsciously leaned forward to hear the answer.

"It...it...feels awful. It is quite a responsibility..." Her eyes first wandered over to Hal and then to Ed. "...I owe each of you a debt that I can never repay, and I love each and every one of you." She fell silent.

Brian thought to himself. *I knew it! She still loves Hal! Poor baby...she's stuck between a rock and a hard place...or is it a hard place and a hard place?*

Steven watched her struggle with her feelings. *If I were straight I would take her away from all of this.*

Ed's thoughts focused on Hal. *I know she felt gratitude for me...but she said those feelings turned to love. Why did she include Hal in what she just said?*

Hal held up his finger to signal the waitress and motioned for another round of drinks. *What did she mean by that? The only thing she owes me is a kick in the pants. As far as love goes she would be just fine if I dropped off the end of the earth...now she says she loves us all. I can never figure out what she is saying. I'm beginning to think that she does it on purpose...to keep me awake at night trying to make heads or tails of what she said. God it's easy for her to jerk me around.*

***

The Bakers' house was decorated with Christmas lights, shiny balls, and pine boughs. There was a nativity scene in the center of the round drive. Hal pulled up to the home in his silver Benz and as he took in the glorious sight, he much preferred the spring flowers. "Here we are, ma." He opened the door and the sound of Christmas carols floated over the crisp evening air. Graham got out on the other side and helped Vivian from the back seat.

Ed came bounding down the steps and warmly greeted them. "Merry Christmas! Welcome to our home."

"Happy Chanukah." Graham could not resist returning the faux pas.

Hal politely interposed. "Chanukah was over day before yesterday and Christmas is next week...so Merry-in-Between. Ed...this is my mother, Vivian. Ma, this is Ed Baker...Mari's husband."

"We are so glad to have you stay with us..." He took her hand. "...we have a full house tonight for dinner. Steven graciously volunteered to prepare a wonderful meal for us and Brian...well Brian...I don't know what he's doing...but he's working very hard at it." He laughed. "Come...let me help with the luggage and let's go inside. Mari is waiting for you."

Under the weight of Vivian's luggage, they lumbered their way up the front steps and into the house. The interior was overloaded with Christmas. Ersatz holly wound its way up the stair railings and festooned the room. A large snow flaked Christmas tree stood at the far-left corner of the living room. Cheery flames consumed pressed wood logs in the fireplace. On the piano, Hal saw that Mari had managed to work a menorah into the decoration scheme, probably under the guise of a generic candelabrum. Ed helped Graham carry the luggage to Vivian's room.

Radiant in an ivory cocktail dress, with a low-cut bodice spangled with gold bugle beads, Mari waited in the center of the living room holding David's hand. David was dressed in a suit and tie that seemed to mimic Hal's. Vivian stopped in her tracks, clasped her hands together, and stared. "Oh...my heart is so full!" She wanted to rush to David, but not wanting to frighten the child, she turned to Mari first.

"My dear girl...you have no idea how much I have missed you. You are even more beautiful than I remembered." She cupped Mari's face in both of her hands and kissed her on each cheek. "I thank God we can be together again." She looked down at David. "And who is this darling little man?"

"This is my son, David..." Mari bent over David, held him by the shoulders, and urged him forward with pride. "...David, this is Hal's mother..."

Vivian's face glowed with adoration. "You can call me Bubbe..."

"'Bubbe?' What's a bubbe?" David's questioning eyes turned to Mari.

Vivian responded. "It's a special name for an old lady who loves you."

"Oh." David held out his hand. "You can call me David."

Vivian sparkled with delight as she took his outstretched hand and shook it. "David."

Mari guided the boy in Hal's direction. "You remember Hal...don't you?"

David broke into a smile and shook Hal's hand vigorously. Then he cast a wary eye at Vivian. "Did your mother make you wear a suit and tie too?"

"No...not this time." Hal chuckled.

David held up his arms for Hal to pick him up; he lifted him into his arms and the joy that swept over Hal's face spoke volumes. Mari ran for her camera. "That will make a great picture." She spent the next few minutes capturing pictures of everyone there. "Brian...Steven...say cheese..."

Steven brought out a tray full of hors d'oeuvres and set them out on the coffee table. Brian followed serving cups of hot glögg. A cup of spiced fruit tea was served to David and Hal put him down to the table to have his cup with two small cookies. Ed and Graham came downstairs and Graham, dressed in his butler's suit and tie, wordlessly took his place behind Vivian who was seated at the corner of the sofa. All eyes gravitated to Graham. "You're the only one here that I haven't met." Brian ventured. "You are...?"

"Graham." He gave a curt bow. "I am madam's butler."

"Oh...a butler! How très intéressant!" Brian gushed. "I have never met a butler before! I have only seen them in movies!" Brian put both hands to his chest. "How did you become a butler?"

"I was trained in Britain and in France for over five years before I took up residence in the Golan household. When I started you actually had to work in each household position before being considered qualified to be a butler...then you had to train under the auspices of a head butler. Now, they have quickie courses that I do not think turn out true professionals. However, the profession is a continuing learning experience...there is always something new to learn. Also, it is one of loyalty to...and deep affection for...the family."

Vivian chimed in. "Graham is far too modest. He can speak five languages and knows the art and customs of those cultures. He is a connoisseur of wine and the culinary arts...and I know that I could not live without him. He is a blessing to me and a dear, dear friend."

"How beautiful! You have my admiration...Graham." Brian was sincere in his praise.

"What is your profession?" Graham asked.

"Fashion. Fashion is my life!"

"How trés intèressant." Graham nodded.

"Mari is wearing a little number that I created for Charli T...a well-known actress who does not want her name to get out. I purposely cut it fuller in the bust line so it wouldn't fit her...and of course I already had it beaded so I couldn't do alterations on it...so she rejected it and I gave it to Mari. Model it for me, Mari." Sucking her cheeks and mouth into the typical model pout, Mari strolled the living room in the classic fashion runway style pausing to turn and pose. Hal grabbed her camera and snapped away. "I also styled her hair in an upsweep to give her height and while she only needs a touch of makeup to add interest...I accented her lovely eyes to draw attention to her best feature and...stop pouting Mari...you look like Zoolander!" Mari broke into a laugh, did one more circuit around the room, and sat down. "I do work for many actresses, but I only received credit for it from one of them on the red carpet. I swear...I get in a purple rage when they name another designer that is famous...for my work. The one who said she was wearing 'Brian'...I think the interviewer thought she meant the man whose arm she was on. It's a tough world to work in...but I love it."

"You do indeed have my admiration." Graham bowed again.

"It is a nice dress...but I think the top is just a little too revealing." Ed remarked.

"That's the whole point of the dress. In Hollywood...if you've 'got it'...'flaunt it.' Mari definitely 'has it'...that is why I love dressing her. You would not believe how many stars have flawed figures that are difficult to work with...Mari is a dream."

Steven came to the edge of the kitchen. "Is the table ready...dinner is about to be served."

Brian rushed to check the place settings. "All done, sweetie."

The furrow in Graham's brow deepened as he looked over the table. "Brian...the table is a shamble. How many courses are there?"

Brian's eyes widened. "I don't know...but I will ask Steven."

Graham set about moving each place setting two inches from the edge of the table. Brian came back and reported. "The first course is a salad, the second pumpkin soup; the main course will be citrus and herb roasted pheasants with roasted endive and vegetables, and then a lemon sherbet to cleanse the palate. Later, there will be a choice of desserts."

"My...my...my! We definitely need more silv...flatware." He ventured into the kitchen. "Salad forks...soup spoons..." Graham kicked into gear to do the best he could, with the Bakers' limited dining implements, to bring the table up to madam's standards. Once the table had been improved, he set about helping with service. He looked at the design Steven had made on each salad plate on a bed of lettuce. A pâté flower with a red pimento center had long, thin cut scallions for the stem and leaves. A hard-boiled egg slice was the sun and chopped olives and scallion bits were the soil and grass blades. It was a charming rendering. "Very imaginative, Steven. Is it a clear oil and vinegar dressing you're using?"

"White wine vinegar, almond oil, a bit of sugar, and a pinch of salt and white pepper...with sesame crackers for the pâté..."

"Delightful."

Ed sat at the head of the table, while Mari sat at the other end. Vivian and Hal flanked David on one side and Steven, Brian, and Graham sat on the other side. Ed called for everyone to hold hands and bow their heads while he said grace. It was as much a speech to welcome those present as it was a thanksgiving for the meal.

Afterwards, Graham walked to the table with several dishes and started serving. Brian watched him and carefully followed suit at the other end. "Oooohs and aaaahs," greeted each dish as it was served. "What a nice little picture on the plate...it's almost a shame to eat it." Vivian remarked.

"Yes...I don't want to eat mine...I want to keep it." David protested.

"Go ahead and eat it...I can always make you another one." Steven smiled.

David watched as Hal took his knife and cut off a pâté petal and spread it on a cracker. He popped it into his mouth and chewed. "Yummm!" Hal broke a cracker in half and spread a small piece of pâté on it. "Here...you can taste mine if you like."

David took it and popped it into his mouth and imitated Hal. "Yummm." He pulled a piece of lettuce from his plate with his fingers and ate it.

"Tonight we are going to do something different. We are going to be elegant...do you know what that means?" Hal lifted his fork.

"No."

"It means fancy-schmancy..."

David laughed. "Noooo."

"Yes...it does. I promise you. Here...take your fork like this...and then jab a piece of lettuce like this...oh, that one is too big. I'm going to have to cut it..." Hal deftly showed how to cut with the knife. "...and now I can fit it into my mouth. Do you want to try it?" David picked up his fork with a fist grip. "Oh...no...you're choking Mr. Fork!" Hal put his hand to his throat and said in a tiny voice, "He's saying...help me...please help me!" David squealed with delight. "Here...relax your hand and hold it like this." David held his fork properly and jabbed a small piece of lettuce. "There you go...now you're elegant!"

Vivian surveyed the table and found it curious that no one from Ed's side of the family was there. "Are your parents still living, Ed?"

"Why, yes...and doing quite well for their age."

"Do you have any siblings?"

"I have two sisters."

"I was just wondering if you will be sharing the holidays with them...perhaps on Christmas."

"No..." Ed shook his head.

Mari intervened. "Ed's family has...you might say...shunned him...or I should say me. They think that I am 'different' and resent me for marrying him...they did not approve."

Ed found his voice and it was tinged with more than a little frustration. "My sisters took an immediate dislike to Mari...and my parents followed suit. They acted as though I...an adult man...had no right to make a decision for myself as to who I wanted to marry. They said the cruelest things about Mari...and I would not stand for it! So, we are estranged..."

Hal listened intently. "Are your sisters married?"

"Yes..."

"Oh...no wonder..." Hal wished he had done what Ed did when faced with familial jealousy. *His sisters probably took one look at Mari and wanted no part of her...around their husbands. It had nothing to do with anything Mari did. Dear God...I wish that I had taken that goddamned file and shoved it up Marvin's ass.* At that moment, he envied Ed's fortitude.

After dinner everyone gathered around the piano while Ed played Christmas carols. Although everyone sang, Steven's tenor voice soared above the rest. "Why don't you sing for us, Steven?" Mari requested.

"I will if Brian will play. Ed is wonderful, but Brian knows how to play the arrangements I know."

"By all means..." Ed relinquished the piano to Brian. "...I could use a break."

Brian sat down and ran the keyboard playing bits of Mozart, Bach, and pounding out pieces of Beethoven. "What do you want to sing, sweetie?"

"I don't know...you pick something."

Brian made the music ascend in a dramatic prelude to "Oh Holy Night." Steven's voice started out strong and clear and then grew in a powerful crescendo, effortlessly hitting high notes, and then softly fading into Brian's intermezzo. When Brian nodded, he began again soaring to a powerful ending. At first there was stunned silence and then wild clapping began as everyone stood up. Steven held his hands together, as if in prayer, when he bowed. As the applause died down, David walked up to Steven and tugged at his jacket. "Are you an angel?"

After coffee and desert Hal asked Ed, "Do you have an office or a den that I can use to go over some papers with Mari in private."

"In private?"

"Yes...some of the matters are personal...to me...and it pertains to how she wants things handled for David. I hope you understand."

"Yes...quite..." Ed clasped his hands. "...I don't have an office here in the house...it's about a half mile up the road in the equipment barn. You need a private room?"

"Yes...so we may talk freely."

"It's alright Ed...we can use one of the rooms upstairs." Mari interjected.

"Does it have a table where I can lay out some papers?"

"Yes...we have coffee in our room sometimes...the table should be large enough." She looked at Ed.

"That's fine by me. Do you have what you need with you?"

"The papers are in my car. I'll go get them." Hal went outside to retrieve a leather folder.

Ed looked perplexed. "Do you know what he wants?"

Mari shrugged. "It's news to me. Vivian?"

Vivian was happily holding David in her lap while the child laid his head on her bosom and slept. "My darling girl...Hal doesn't tell me anything. He comes and he goes...always in a hurry with business to attend to."

Ed felt awkward and looked to his wife. "You will tell me if it is anything... upsetting."

"Yes."

Vivian wagged her finger. "My boy is not like that. He respects Mari...he does not want to upset her. Of that I am sure."

Hal returned carrying the leather folder. Mari got up. "It's about time I put David to bed anyway. We may as well get to it."

***

Mari sat across the table from Hal in the master bedroom. David was snug in his bed and Vivian decided to retire for the night. The blurred conversation of the men downstairs could be faintly heard as Graham, Steven, and Brian waited for Hal to drive them back to Santa Rosa. Hal took out sheaves of paper and laid them out. "I want to go over these briefly so you can get an understanding of what they

484

are all about. I know I don't have the time or the expertise to go over them in depth...but the name and the address of the attorney who drew them up is on each page of the document...so if you need an in depth explanation just call him and he will fly up to see you and he will bill me for it. First, this adds David as a beneficiary to the trust I gave you...and the will that goes with it. I am the trustee and you are the successor trustee...and after that Deuce...Terry. In the event that I die...you and David are my only beneficiaries."

"What about Vivian?"

"My mother makes me look like a pauper. She has enough money to last her for ten lifetimes."

"What if you should want to marry?"

"Oh...I want to marry alright...but right now...that's impossible. Let me go on...I have set up another trust for you and another for David. You can draw on yours whenever you want to, and David may access his when he is twenty-five. There is ten million in each..."

"Why are you trying to impress me with your money?" Mari was guarded.

"I'm not trying to *impress* you...I'm trying to *protect* you."

"First you tell me that I was after your money...and now you are shoveling it at me? Why? Hal...I never wanted your money...I only wanted..."

"We don't have time to go down that road right now...any minute your husband is going to open that door and stick his head in, and our conversation will be over. I have too much to explain..."

"Why do you think that Ed will interrupt us?"

"Mari...you are sitting in a room with a bed a few feet away with a man who desperately wants to make love to you. If I were your husband...you wouldn't even be sitting here..."

"You haven't answered my question. Why are you giving me all of this money?"

"Mari...listen to me intently. Money is the great insulator from life's problems...and it is a very effective tool for any purpose you chose. It will protect you and David in ways you cannot imagine. My mother doesn't realize it because she has always had money...you don't realize it because you never did. But now you are rich...not fantastically...but well off. You may need to learn how to use it as a tool and I can teach you."

"If you think that all I ever wanted from you was money…you're wrong!"

"No…I don't think that…I didn't ever *really* think that…I don't know what came over me to ever think otherwise…!" Hal paused and held out his hands to her. "My God, Mari…you're doing it to me again. You're jerking me all around…back and forth, up and down like a yo-yo! You're the only person on earth who can do that to me."

"I jerk *you* around? Every time I talk to you it's like getting on an emotional roller coaster! I have to shut down every memory…everything I ever felt just to be in the same room with you…so get over yourself and answer my question. Why?"

He forced himself not to respond in kind. "Let me explain it to you this way. It breaks my heart that I can't even tell my son that I'm his father. I can't be with him every day to look after him. I can't be the husband to you that I wanted to be. I can't look after you or tell you how I feel. The only part of me that I have left to give you and my son is money…and that's the easiest thing to do because I have plenty of it. People wish their entire lives that they could have the wealth that I have. I wish I could have the life I had with you in our apartment again…I was truly happy."

"I was too." She whispered.

"I have more to tell you…and this you must never tell anyone. I have an envelope in the care of my attorney with your name on it…in case I should die. It is very important that you contact him, read the instructions, and follow them. That's all I can say for now."

"So…that's it? You just wave your magic wand and I'm rich?"

"Yeah…that's it"

"Jesus, Hal…that kind of power is scary…" She wondered who he was again. "I suppose I should thank you…but it's a bunch of papers…none of this seems to be real to me…"

"It's real alright. You can tell your husband…or not. I would suggest not. He may come to rely on what you have…and let this place go to shit. What you have here is a nice life. Just tell him that I arranged for David to come into some money after he finishes college…and that you will have to struggle along on what he makes."

"Hal…will you ever marry?"

"Yes…whenever you're ready."

"You know I can't…"

"Can't...won't...life is strange. Don't count me out."

"Is that why you gave me the money...so I can be independent...available?"

"No...that's not you. If that were the case...you would have fallen into my arms by now. No...you're thinking of David and how this will affect him...how I will affect him." Hal sighed. "Which brings me back to what I wanted to know...why didn't you want me in David's life?"

"Why did you want to take him away from me?" She countered.

Hal laughed. "That's easy to answer...pure negotiation tactics. In business negotiations you always ask for more than you think you can get. That way you have leeway to negotiate downward to what you actually want. My attorney warned me not to go that route...but you use what you are familiar with."

"Why did you stop fighting?"

"Because of you...because of what I put you through...and I was doing it to you again. I couldn't let it go on. Now it's your turn. Why didn't you want me in David's life?"

"Hal...I wasn't trying to be cruel...I was trying to protect my family. It wasn't David's life I was trying to shut you out of...it was mine. I have no problem with your seeing him...in fact I think you are good with him. I was just so afraid..."

"Of what?"

"Hal...you're like a tsunami...I mean look at what you just did! I don't know what to do with that kind of money. I can't tell Ed about it...it will emasculate him. What do I do?"

He shrugged. "Put the papers back in the folder and place it somewhere secure...like in the briefcase...wherever you hid it." He gave her a knowing look. "You never told him about that either...did you?"

"No. I found out the hard way that honesty is not always the best policy."

"What do you mean?"

"I should never have shown you exactly what I did at Stony Malone's. It made it easier for you to think the worst of me."

"No...you didn't have to hide anything from me..."

"Didn't I?" She gave him a level stare. "Well...anyway...I am truthful with him with just about everything...but not some things that don't matter that can only upset him. I just don't know what to do about this."

"You don't have to do anything...just go back to living your life...only now knowing that you are secure...nothing can harm you."

"I guess it is like you said...I'm in uncharted waters and I'm still trying to find my bearings, too..." She got up. "I guess I had better get back downstairs. Ed will wonder what is taking so long."

"So, I'm a roller coaster, huh? You used to like my 'E' ticket rides." He tilted his head toward the bed. "Are you sure you don't want another go?"

She tried not to laugh but chuckled in spite of herself. "Mr. Golan...you are amazing and incorrigible!"

"Hal...just plain Hal."

She looked at him incredulously. "There is nothing 'just plain' about you. You just gave me ten...million...dollars...American. Who does *that?!*"

Hal handed her the folder, got up, and smiled. "I do."

***

The last of the holiday guests had left the house, and Mari allowed Hal to take David to the airport to see his bubbe off. Mari had undressed and was about to step into the shower when she picked up her hair conditioner. The bottle was nearly empty. She held it upside down and shook it. She smacked it against the palm of her hand. The little conditioner that remained sagged down the side of the bottle but did not come out of the cap. *Damn it!* She left the bathroom and headed for the hallway closet where she kept her cosmetic crafting ingredients and stored her finished supply. She no sooner opened the door and stepped into the hallway when Hal came out of the guest bedroom carrying a piece of luggage. She made a small exclamation, "Shit!" and covered herself with both arms and retreated into her room. Shocked at the sight of her, he turned back into the guest room. "Hal...what are you doing here? I thought everyone had left." She hoarsely whispered from behind her cracked door.

"I had to come back for my mother's vanity case...she forgot it. Ed told me I could go in to get it before he took off." He responded from behind the opening in his door. The glimpse he had of her made him hunger to see more. *Fuck...what could it hurt?* He took a chance and stepped into the hallway. "Mari?"

"What?"

"Let me see you..."

"What!?! No!"

"Please...I promise...I won't touch you. I just want to look at you again. No one else is here. Please."

She was quiet for a moment and then, to his surprise, the door opened, and she appeared in the hall and stood there. There was a sharp intake of his breath that he exhaled slowly. His eyes caressed her from head to toe. Her body had hardly changed. "You're beautiful...you can't even tell you had a baby...you have no stretch marks."

"Yes...I do...right here..." She drew her hands down each side of her abdomen. "...they're faint...but I know they're there. My nipples are darker too." She touched her breast. She turned around slowly and then faced him again. "Seen enough?"

"Yes. Thank you." He whimpered.

She disappeared inside her room and he stared at the empty spot where she had stood. His heart was still pounding. *Why did she do that? Because you asked for it, asshole. She didn't have to do that! Maybe she wanted to remind you of what you threw away, asshole. Maybe she thought it was the least she could do for all the money you gave her. Yeah...sure...ten million for a peek...don't be stupid! She wanted you to see her...or she would have stayed in her room! You're her yo-yo alright...and you asked for this sleepless night, bub!* He went down the stairs and out to his car. He handed Graham the case through the window and then got behind the wheel.

"What happened? You look upset." Vivian could see he was rattled.

"Nothing..." He laughed at himself, "...everything...and nothing." and drove off.

***

LIFE IS A BEACH

Charts, floor plans, and diagrams covered a ping-pong sized worktable in the middle of Hal's living room. Notebooks of architecture, building materials, and interior design were stacked nearby. He pored over the gathered material hoping that the nebulous idea of the kind of house he wanted would take shape and materialize in his mind. His cell went off with the ringtone for Mari. He looked at his watch. It was eight-thirty. It was early even for her. "Hi kiddo. What's up?"

"Nothing much...just some shopping. I'll be in Santa Rosa today...I was wondering if you would like to see David while we're there."

"Sure. In need of a babysitter? I'll be happy to look after him."

"No. Nothing like that. He has asked a couple of times if it was your day to see him. I thought perhaps I could take care of some shopping and we could all go to lunch or something."

"That would be great. Besides, I wanted to get your opinion on a project I'm working on. Would you mind looking at some plans and stuff at my place."

"OK...if it's important to you. We can have lunch at your house. Do you want me to pick up some grub on the way?"

"Let me see what I have in the fridge." He opened the refrigerator to dubious fare. "Yeah...I guess you'd better pick something up. I haven't shopped in a while."

"What do you want me to bring?"

"Whatever you want to eat...except chicken...that's all I've had for a while. I could use a change of pace."

"Maybe I should do some serious shopping for you...so you can eat properly."

"No...I would only have to cook it and ruin whatever you get." He laughed.

"OK...I'll see you around ten-ish or eleven?"

"That sounds good."

After hanging up Hal raced to the bathroom, turned on the shower, and hopped around on one foot as he got out of his pants and clothes. *God...she wants to see me. No...she said David wanted to see me. God...I love my boy. I wonder what she wants. I've seen her lots over the holidays. Could it be she misses me? Don't be a jerkoff...why would she miss you? I should take care of myself, so*

490

I don't get too excited while she's here. He stepped into the shower and imagined how she looked, how she felt, her soft skin, and her mouth. After ejaculating he felt more relaxed and could shave without nicking his face up. *What to wear? Something casual...but not too casual. No...not jeans...you look like a day laborer in jeans. Slacks and a turtleneck pullover? Yeah...black slacks and black turtleneck. No...all that black might scare David. He'll think you're the boogieman. Shit!* He put on brown slacks with an ivory pullover, looked in the mirror, and threw up his hands. *I guess this will do.*

He raced around the house, picking up clutter and putting things away. He didn't have time to do a thorough job and wished he had brought his housekeeper with him to look after things rather than leave her to care for his house in Beverly Hills.

He heard Mari's 2001 Hyundai Elantra pull up in front of his house and watched as she got out of the car. He never tired of looking at her. She opened the rear door to take David out of the child's seat and, before he could come out of the house to assist her, she was coming up the walkway with David running to the door. As he came out of the house, David stumbled and fell and began to cry. Hal started to run to him, but she waved him off. She stooped down to look at David's skinned knee. "Oh...we have a boo-boo." She said calmly. "Now...what did I tell you? Be a brave boy and don't cry. If you count to ten it won't hurt so much anymore. One...two...three..." David counted with her. By the time they got to ten, he was dry-eyed and smiling once more. "Do you have some Bactine?"

"I think so. What was that...some kind of Jedi mind trick?"

"No...it is a grandma mind trick. She taught me that...so I wouldn't cry every time I skinned my knee. If you had picked him up, he would still be crying."

Hal stooped down. "Hey, buckaroo...did your horse throw you?" He lifted David up. "Let's go have a look at that. I have an old Indian magic potion to put on it...guaranteed to be made by old Indians."

"I'll be there in a minute. I have to get stuff out of the car." She went back to get two full reusable grocery bags.

Hal carried David to the bathroom and took out the Bactine. David cocked his head.

"That's not an old Indian poson...that's Bactine!"

"You think old Indians didn't make Bactine?"

"No...silly. My mommy did!"

"Ooooh!" Hal swabbed the medicine on his knee. "There. It will be all better in seven days. Or, perhaps a week."

They came back into the living room to find Mari holding the bags of groceries, staring down at the materials on the worktable. "Is this what you wanted me to look at?"

"Yeah. I was hoping you could apply some of your analytical skills to help me sort through that mess and come up with a plan for my new house."

"Your new house?"

"Yeah...I just purchased a house in Jenner. It is way too tiny...a one-bedroom mess...but it sits on five acres and has a view of the ocean you wouldn't believe. I am going to build my home there. It is about twenty-five miles from you...so if you or David ever need me for anything, I can be there in under a half hour."

"Wow...then you are going to stay up here."

"Yes...I want to see David as much as possible. That doesn't mean that I won't have to go down to L.A. from time to time...I do have a company to manage...but I will be living here. After all, with computers and such...I can run the company from anywhere in the world."

Mari nodded and then walked toward the kitchen. "That is why I wanted to see you." She put the bags on the table and started unpacking them. Hal sat at the table with David in his lap and watched as she unraveled the mysteries of the grocery bags. "I got fixings for hot roast beef sandwiches. I brought enough so you can make more for yourself later. I know you probably haven't eaten a green vegetable in days..."

"Weeks..."

She pursed her lips. "Weeks...I should have known. I got some things that are very easy to make or just heat up..." She opened his refrigerator. "...what's all this?" She started rummaging through his Styrofoam jungle. "How long has this stuff been in here?"

"I don't know."

"Jesus..." She looked at David and added, "...may He protect you. Hal, you can't eat this! Half of it has gone off and the other half is a lab experiment...it's growing stuff on it and turning colors." She started tossing out food that was beyond hope. "Here...dump your trash can before it stinks up the house!"

He sheepishly took the trash out the back door and David followed him with the same hangdog look. "Mommy makes me do stuff that I don't like, too." He commiserated.

"Your mommy is very smart...she knows things. I guess we better listen to her." Hal admitted.

Mari took David, sat him at the table, and gave him a coloring book and crayons. Then she busied herself preparing lunch. "Watch what I do so you can make it later." Working quickly, she mayonnaised five slices of white bread. "David won't eat more than a half sandwich...so this one gets one slice cut in half...with no horseradish. The other sandwiches get horseradish just on the top slice of bread." She held up a packet of beef gravy mix. "You follow the instructions on the back to make the gravy...I like to add a pinch of garlic powder, onion powder, and a tad more salt. I'm going to make two packets so you will have some left over already made. I got two pounds of sliced roast beef from the deli. I'll divide what we don't use into portions, put them into baggies and freeze them. When the gravy is done you just heat the sliced beef in the gravy...and it is ready to assemble. Put as much beef as you want on your sandwich...close the door on it with the top slice...and then pour the gravy over the top...and voilà...you're done." She took out more groceries. At the confused look on Hal's face she added, "You can call me, and I will tell you how to cook the vegetables."

He gave her a weak smile but stood and watched as she made lunch. Within twenty minutes she had it on the table and they sat down. "Now...that was easy...wasn't it?"

Giving her a noncommittal nod, he picked up his knife and fork, and dug in. "This is really good...and you made it so fast."

She cut David's sandwich into bite-sized pieces. "Sometimes you have to make a meal on the fly...that looks like you slaved over it. This one works out pretty well...although I should have served a vegetable with it. Somehow...I thought that you wouldn't mind if I didn't."

"You said you wanted to talk to me about something."

"Yes...when you started visiting David it was during the holidays...and Vivian was here until after New Year's...so you were there to see him more frequently than you would have on your regularly scheduled visits. David got used to seeing you a lot more than he does now." Her face showed concern. "Now he asks about you all the time. He wants to know why you don't come over to play with the train set you gave him. I keep telling him that you will come by on Saturday...but that means nothing to him..."

"I say 'God bless Hal.'" David's serious face turned up to him.

"Do you, little buckaroo?" Hal gave him a half smile and took a deep breath.

"And God bless my bubbe too."

Mari ran her hand over David's hair. "He thinks that if he includes you in his prayers at night...you'll be there the next morning..." She whispered.

"No..." David picked up a crayon and furiously scribbled in his coloring book. "...I say God bless Hal because he looks sad sometimes."

"You're worried about me?" Hal almost couldn't get the words out. David nodded and kept on coloring.

Mari took the crayon from David's hand and directed his attention back to his plate. "Ed and I have talked about it...and we wondered if it wouldn't be too inconvenient for you if you could come by twice a week to see him. I can't believe that he has taken to you so soon...and I don't know if it's a good thing for you to be there so often...but for now..."

"Aw, shit yeah, Mari. I'd love that."

"Shit yeah." David laughed.

Mari frowned and put her finger to her mouth, shook her head, and then laughed. "What days are best for you?"

"I'm open."

"Tuesdays or Wednesdays?"

"Sure. How about I call you first?"

"Great." Mari quietly ate her sandwich for a while. "Now, tell me about that house of yours."

"I would really like for you to see it so you will know what I'm up against. I don't know if I should incorporate the house that's there...or tear it all down and start over."

"Maybe we can all make a day of it and go see it. I know it's too cold for a picnic...are the utilities on?"

"I think so."

"Perhaps an indoor picnic?"

"Why not? I think you'll like the location. It's right on the beach so I'm going to try my hand at surf fishing."

"Surf fishing? Where did you get an idea like that?"

"From a wise old man...years ago."

"Can you imagine? He prays for me." Hal said softly as he watched his sleeping son and swallowed back his emotions. Mari had put David into Hal's bed for his nap. She motioned for Hal to follow her back into the living room and closed the door behind them.

"He has grown very attached to you...and he has Vivian wrapped around his finger. Please...try not to spoil him too much."

"I'm sure you will keep him level-headed. Thank you for giving me more days to be with him."

"Oh...I forgot to tell you. He also asks God to bless Cindy...a little girl in his Sunday school class."

"Let me guess...she has blonde curls and blue eyes..."

"Yes...how did you know?"

"Just a hunch." He smiled. "Here...let me show you what I have so far...for the house."

"How many people do you plan on having there?"

"Well...I have to have room for my housekeeper. Then there's you, Ed, David, my mother...and now she doesn't go anywhere without Graham...and I just might have all of you there at once...but most of the time I will live there by myself."

"Do you plan on having everyone stay with you, or farm them out to a motel or something?"

"Everyone I mentioned would stay in my home." Mari did the math on her fingers. "My God, Hal...that would call for five bedrooms plus the maid's quarters. Also, you need an office for you to conduct your business...and a quiet place for you to write. Four of those five bedrooms wouldn't be used for most of the year. Are you sure you want a house that big? You're talking about building a mansion."

"I don't know. I have to plan for the future. My mother may decide to come live with me. You and David may come...come over more than you think you will. Also, I have to think of the resale value...should you decide to sell it."

"Me…?"

"Yeah…you should be planning on outliving me…for sure David will. Why do you think that I want you to help plan it? It's for you…one way or the other."

"For Christ's sake, Hal…there you go again. Why do you do this to me? I don't ever want to think of your dy…"

"Look, Babe…I'm going to be known as the dearly departed one day. I hope you're not fixated on it…but you do have to plan ahead." Mari bit her lip and walked into the kitchen. She ran water into the sink and started putting the lunch dishes in to be rinsed. Hal followed her and saw her face cloud up. "Babe…I didn't mean to be so…depressing…"

"You're building your house for me…aren't you?"

"For you and David." He nodded.

She looked up at him as a tear crept over her lashes. "Stop it, Hal…just stop it."

"Stop what?"

"Giving me things…and calling me 'Babe' like you did when we were…"

He reached out caressing her face and she almost forgot herself to nuzzle his hand. "Don't you care for me at all, Mari? Is there nothing left inside of you…?"

She took his hand away. "Please don't do that." She whispered. "This house…is it for David?"

"Yes…yes it is."

"Then I will help plan it."

"Mari…" He stood there like a monolith. "I'm not going away."

"I don't want you to go away…"

"Well, what then?"

"I want to stop feeling guilty."

"Guilty? Guilty for what?"

"I don't know. This whole situation…like it's my fault…but I didn't do anything. Here you are all by yourself…living alone…and you don't know how to take care of yourself…and my son thinks you're the greatest thing since peanut butter…and you keep on giving me more and more stuff like I'm some empty shell that you can fill up with things to make me feel again."

"Mari...you tell me what I'm supposed to do, and I'll do it." His head dropped down. "Babe...you have no idea how it kills me that I once had everything that I ever wanted right here in my hand..." He held out his hand as though her heart was still in it. "...and even if it was by mistake...I should have known better...but I was the one who destroyed our happiness...our dreams...and I should have known better.

"Those beautiful eyes used to look at me with a light that showed you loved me...me of all people. Now they hold hurt and wariness and it kills me. But the fact that you are hurting too, tells me that on some level...you still care for me." He pointed a finger at her. "I know on some level you care for me. I have a trash barrel full of bad food that says you care for me. If you didn't give a shit...you wouldn't be here."

Another tear floated briefly on her lashes, spilled over, and then scurried down her cheek. She turned her head and brushed it off. "David wanted to see you."

"I love David with all my heart...he means everything to me. I thank God for him every day. But I also know that without him I wouldn't have had the excuse I need to see you...be near you. Now, I think that he is your excuse to see me. Be honest, Mari...you wanted to see me too." He paused looking her directly in the eye. She didn't answer. "That day when I first came to your house...I thought I would leave with no excuse to ever see you again. I was done for...I thought that was it...until I saw David. As mad as I was that you hadn't told me about him...I thanked God he was there to keep you connected to me. I know I must matter to you."

"Yes...you matter to me." She turned to the sink and resumed rinsing the dishes. "Come on and help me load the dishwasher...and then we'll go plan David's house...together."

***

In the middle of the night Mari got up, slipped on her robe, and came downstairs. She made a cup of hot milk and curled up in an armchair to read. She found herself reading the same sentence over and over again as her mind kept drifting away to the afternoon she spent with Hal and how he called her out. *Did I just use David as an excuse to see him?* Although it was true that David was anxious to see him, was she just as glad to spend time with him?

She thought of Ed softly snoring upstairs and how he insisted on her "wifely duty" to him before they went to bed. He wasn't crude about it; he cajoled her around her pretext of being tired after a long day. She did not mind his lovemaking, nor was she moved to passion by it. After a while she found him tepid, almost boring in the way he mixed religiosity with his physicality. On the occasions when she tried to "spice up" his routine, she found that he was not only shocked, but also more than a little frightened by heightened sexuality. Man on top, missionary position, was his forte; calculated variations, he was sure, were sinful. Frequently, just when she got to the point of enjoyment, he was finished. She had to prompt him into long drawn out foreplay for any hope of her achieving an orgasm. But he was oblivious and self-assured that he had always brought her to climax, even without her faking it. Sex with Ed was a hit or miss proposition which necessitated a great deal of concentration on her part.

Still, Ed was pleasant to be with, a gentle man trying to live up to his high ideals. He was hard working and kept his word. Decency, with a strong mix of Christianity, determined his actions. He was good to her and he loved David. Free to do whatever she wanted, within the confines of his idea of womanly decorum, she was content. Yet, she wondered if a hint of jealousy, of her spending the day with Hal, prompted him to demand attention from her. It was a thought that she immediately dismissed.

The inevitable comparison with Hal popped into her head. She didn't want to think about him; it was dangerous for her to think about him, but no amount of caution could drive the images from her head. She had done nothing to give him hope, nor was she alluring, or even flirtatious. But it ruffled her when, like today, he averred that she still loved him and that the house he was building would be hers. *Does he think that he can just buy me?* She did not view her newfound wealth the way he did. She was confused by his intentions. Perturbed, she did as he suggested; she ignored the money and did not inform her husband about it. It distressed her that she was still drawn to Hal. He was right; she had missed him, but never more so than tonight as she remembered the excitement of his touch. The memory of his making love to her caused a sharp intake of breath.

She knitted her brow at her involuntary reaction. *Yes...Hal, you still matter to me.*

***

"This is quite a place you have here." Ed carried the ice chest into Hal's new house. "The view is amazing. Mari tells me you're going to expand it."

"Or tear it down. I haven't decided yet." Hal put the box of picnic supplies on the table.

"You were right to tell us to get a sitter. This is no place for a four-year-old."

"Not yet it isn't...but it will be. He'll be a little older by then."

They both moved to the picture window and watched as Mari stood outside at the edge of the bluff. The sea surged past magnificent rock formations to crash on the generous sandy beach below. Ed gestured to her. "Mari said you were having her help with the plans."

"Yes...this will be David's one day. I thought she would like to have some input." Hal leaned over and put his hand to one side of his mouth. "Actually...she has better taste than I do. Don't tell her I said so."

"How are you two getting on these days?"

"Surprisingly well. Not that she is beyond turning Valkyrie on me now and then...and verbally jabbing me with her spear...she's still plenty mad at me...and I don't blame her...but most of the time we get along."

"She doesn't jab you in front of David...does she?"

"Oh, no...never. She's far too good a mother for that."

"Well, she's been a bit snippy with me too."

"I can't imagine that." Hal smiled inwardly but put on a sympathetic face. "She's just going through a tough time. These past few months haven't been easy on any of us."

"Tell me...if she hadn't been married when you found her...would you have asked her to marry you?" Ed asked out of the blue.

"To be perfectly honest...yes. But would she have is another question and I'm afraid the answer to that is...no. I screwed up bad, Ed...beyond redemption in her eyes. An even larger truth...between friends...if she ever left you...I would marry her in a New York minute. But she'll never do that...at least not for me."

"How do you know that? Did you ask her?"

"No...not in so many words...but she as much as told me so. You're one lucky bastard, Ed. You have everything I want...but can't have." Hal walked away from the window and did not see the smile on Ed's face, but he knew it was there. *That's right...get complacent. Don't you know I just put you on notice? If Mari ever gets over being angry with me...she's mine.*

Mari walked briskly to the house, ran up the steps, and went inside. "Brrrrr! It is cold out there...and not much warmer in here. Does the woodstove work?"

"Yes. I bought a cord of firewood. I'll get a fire going." Hal went outside.

Mari went to the table and started unpacking the box. "No wonder Hal wants to rebuild this place...the kitchen is abysmal." Ed went to her, wrapped his arms around her, and kissed her neck. "What brought all this on?"

"Something Hal said."

"What did he say? I'll have him say it more often."

"That you would never leave me."

"What the fuck?!" She pulled away. "Pardon my French...but why would he say something like that?"

"Because, I asked him."

"Why would you ask *him?* How about asking *me?* Why would you discuss me with *him* in the first place?" Mari took her surroundings into account and calmed down. "We planned a pleasant afternoon...and that is just what it will be. But I do plan on discussing this with you when we get home. The very idea!"

"It's nice to know."

"What...because *he* said so...give me a break." She put her hands on her hips. "If I ever get a wild hair to leave you, Ed...you'll be the first to know...not Hal Golan!" She went back to unpacking the box.

"Did I hear my name used in vain?" Hal carried in logs and filled the rack by the woodstove. *Don't tell me he was stupid enough to repeat what I said.*

"No...I was just wondering if you will like what I made for us." Mari feigned.

"I'm sure 'Hal Golan' will love what you made." He raised his brows and smiled to let her know he was on to her.

The stove and refrigerator were basic with little to recommend them. The cupboards were few and flimsy. Putting away the plates and utensils, Mari came across a couple of oil lamps and candles. "Looks like the previous people left something for you."

"No, I bought those too. I asked the real estate lady if the utilities were on. She said yes...but I should get some emergency lighting. Evidently, the power company isn't very reliable. Make a note that I need to get a generator." Hal easily fell back into the role of being her boss on the project.

"How soon do you want to eat?" She didn't mind that he thought he was in charge.

"Let's take a look at the place first." Ed was curious about value to money paid.

"Sure. I have a chart of the area that shows the lot. I know that it is five acres from the street to the bluff...I also own the beach frontage. We can walk down to the beach...but the stairway looks a bit old...I'm going to have to check it out. As soon as I get the fire started...we'll go have a look around."

The wind was streaked with a light drizzle as the weather worked up to a winter storm. With her parka hood up, Mari hiked beside the men who hunched down into their collars against the elements. Walking the perimeter of the lot, Hal pointed out prospective places to build. He wanted to keep as many trees as possible and add landscaping. "Do you see that rock outcropping over there? There are a few more like it on the grounds. I think I will turn them into rock gardens as points of interests. The one over there will be in view from the house. As for the house; Mari pointed out that the place will have to be pretty large to accommodate all of us. My housekeeper will probably need help."

"What about Jeeves? You know...the butler." Ed asked.

"Oh...Graham. He's family. He would be one of my guests."

"Will Terry be coming up?" Mari wondered out loud.

"You're damned right he is...perhaps Lo-Lo will come with him if he can get her to settle down."

"Terry and Lo-Lo? You never told me. Just when did that happen?"

"When we were looking for you. We called everyone on your cell...and when we asked for her help...she did everything she could." Hal laughed. "She swooped down on Deuce...broke up his

501

marriage...worked him over and then left for Monaco. She's baaaack...and now she's leading him around by his nose again. Somehow...I just don't see her settling down to be a wife with kids."

"She's my best friend ever, but you're right. Someday she will call him 'a musician' and leave him flat."

"She's already done that."

"And she took him back? That must be serious."

"I just stand on the sidelines and watch...and try to stay out of the way of flying champagne."

"Flying champagne?"

"Yeah...I'll tell you all about it sometime...and Wanda is still in the picture."

"Nooooh!"

"Who are these people you're talking about? They don't sound very nice." Ed was baffled.

"Oh...they're great!" Mari laughed.

"She's right. Best friends anyone could have." Hal concurred.

Ed looked off in the distance and saw the gray band of an approaching downpour. "We had better get back to the house."

Thunder clapped off in the distance and they scampered across the field to take shelter. The skies darkened and the deluge started in earnest once they were inside the house. Through the window they watched as the ocean churned. Pounding waves broke high upon the rocks as lightning flashed, intermittently illuminating the scene. "It's stunning...so very dramatic. I don't think I have ever seen the ocean like this before." Mari whispered.

"It's beautiful." Hal agreed.

"And frightening." Ed was overawed.

"Frightening?" Hal and Mari spoke in unison.

Ed stared straight out the window. "Yes...God is all powerful and He can be unsparing in his wrath."

Mari looked at Hal and shrugged. "We should turn on the lights...and I'll fix lunch."

A hearty beef bourguignon, with toasted French bread rubbed with garlic, paired with a rich Cabernet Sauvignon, brought elegance to the humble kitchen in which it was served. Mari poured herself a ginger ale.

"Mari...you never cease to amaze me! How do you do it?" Hal wolfed down another forkful.

"We must not forget to say grace!" Ed was mortified for them.

"Oh, yeah...sure." Hal put his fork down. "In my family we always say the Birkat Hamazon, the Jewish grace, after meals...but you go ahead...and after this wonderful lunch I'll give thanks for it."

Until now, Hal had sat through Christian prayers at dinners, and church services, showing respect, but not partaking. In this religious mix, in Hal's house, he thought it somewhat rude for Ed to foist his religious rituals on him as though it were a given. *He could have mumbled his personal mumbo-jumbo to himself before eating...or asked me to give a prayer in my religion. OK...I'm agnostic...but I can still work up a good Jewish shtick when I want to.*

Ed closed his eyes and folded his hands and said grace, while Mari and Hal sat patiently and looked at each other. "Bless o' Father this meal for our strength and to your praise. Come Lord Jesus be our guest and bless what you have provided for us. Amen."

"That was lovely, Ed." Mari affected reverence she did not feel.

They fell upon their meal with gusto with both men asking for seconds.

When everyone was finished, Hal started to say the Birkat Hamazon. "Barukh attah Adonai eloheynu melekh ha'olam hazzan et ha'olam kullo betuvo, beechen bechesed uvrachamim. Hu notein lechem lekholbasar ki le'olam chasdo. Uvtuvo haggadol tamid lo chaseid lanu ve'al yechsar lanu mazon le'olam va'ed, ba'avur shemo haggadol. Ki hu El zan umfarneis lakhol, umeitiv lakol umeikhin mazon lekhol b'riyotav, asher bara. Barukh attah hazzan et hakkol. Amein."

When he was finished, Mari beamed. "That was beautiful Hal...what does it mean?"

Ed fumed. When he found his voice, he immediately blasted it. "What type of heathen babble was that?"

"Heathen babble? Are you forgetting that Christianity was born out of Judaism? I don't speak babble...my prayer was in Hebrew...I learned it as a child."

"Well...I don't ever want you to recite that in front of David!"

"Ed!" Mari was shocked.

"I hadn't planned on reciting it in front of David...until now..."

"You plan on teaching David to be a Jew?"

"If you mean do I intend to teach him to believe in the Jewish religion...no. That is for him to decide when he is older. Do I intend to teach him that he is half-Jewish? Yes...when he is old enough to understand what that means. Will I refrain from speaking Hebrew in front of him? I don't speak Hebrew in my day-to-day life...and I have forgotten most of what I have learned. But I just might make the effort if it broadens my son's horizons. And...if I am forced to accept Christianity in my house...I see no reason why I cannot interject *my* faith."

"Your faith will not save my son's soul!" Ed shot back. "I have carefully nurtured him in the true faith for the benefit of his soul so that he can be saved in the name of Jesus Christ!"

"Fine...I have no problem with that. But since Jesus was a Jew...and He learned the Torah and the Jewish religion as a kid...and He turned out alright...I don't see how you can have a beef with it."

"I can't sit here and listen to this." Ed got up from the table and withdrew to the living room and took comfort in stirring the fire in the woodstove and tossing on another log.

"Oh, God, Hal...why did you do that?" Mari held her forehead. "I expected you to be smarter than that."

"You expected me to be smarter than Ed? That's a no brainer."

"Hal..."

"Well, what do you expect? I sit through all of his religious rituals without a word. I give due respect to all his praying and beliefs. I attended his church on Christmas Eve and I sing his Christmas carols...those jingles for Jesus...and he can't even give me my due in my own house? What kind of meshugener mamzre shit is that?"

"But you know how sensitive he is about his religion...and you are pretty much like me...you can take it or leave it...so why not just let him have his...*blankie.*" Mari could only think of the term her son used to call his security blanket.

"Is that why you pretend to believe it...?" Hal half smiled. "...to appease your husband in childlike behavior?"

"Hal...I was straight up honest with you in all things and just what did it get me?"

504

"My love, respect, my heart…little things like that…" Hal leaned forward. "You would think that he would snap to it that he was living with an illusion by now. He's really not that bright."

"Well, if you're so smart…how come I'm married to him and you're not?!"

"He didn't ask me?"

"Oh…you know what I meant!"

"You meant how come you're married to him and not to me?"

"Yeah…if you're so smart!"

"Will it save us both some time if I just consider myself told off?"

"Yeah!" she started to get up.

"Mari…are you still going to help me plan the house?"

She stood there for a while. "Of course." Then she leaned over and whispered in his ear. "Don't let this go to your head…but you were right."

***

I'M NOT GOING TO LOSE YOU AGAIN

The magnificence of the new Golan mansion was gentled by good taste to blend in with nature. While the exterior was finished, the interior had yet to be completed. Hal's master bedroom suite was more like business central. His office was right off the bedroom and was outfitted with flat screen TVs for conferencing. Another secluded room, filled with books and research tools, was just as large, and was set up for writing. An expansive Roman themed bathroom was designed for two, in contemplation of fulfilled dreams. From the vantage point of the bedroom the best view was to be found from the balconies or the picture windows. The "his" walk-in closet was partially full; the "her" closet was empty.

Sipping coffee on one of the balconies, Hal waited for Mari to arrive. Hearing her car approach, he made a mental note to get her a new car. He didn't like the little Korean four banger that she drove because it was small, and he thought that it wouldn't afford much protection in an accident. He thought the 2005 Audi A6 Sedan had much better safety test results and decided to get one for her. Descending the stairs at a clip, he went down to greet her. She looked adorable in her fitted parka with her hood up against the wind. "Hey, kiddo...what happened? You're on time."

"Ed is looking after David...so I didn't have to wait for a sitter." She opened the rear door. "I made some sandwiches. If the weather holds, we can eat on the beach when we break for lunch." She handed him a basket.

"Good idea. We don't have that much to do today..."

"That's what you said last time."

"Like you don't love the work. I know you, kiddo...you love applying your mind to projects and this is right up your alley."

"Alley?" Her brow wrinkled. "Not one of my favorite words..."

Hal took a deep breath. "Not one of mine either. Can we try 'bailiwick?'"

"Much better." She walked past him through the door and headed for the kitchen. Taking off her coat, she shook out her hair, and poured herself a cup of coffee. Carrying the cup with her she returned to the living room. Except for a couch in front of the fireplace, the raw room was devoid of furniture, giving a hollow echo to their footsteps.

"This is going to be gorgeous when it's done." She looked over the room visualizing it as it would appear.

"I have all your color schemes...the painters will be here tomorrow...and the carpet is scheduled for next week. I'm afraid that the furniture won't be here until next month...from back east."

"Good...it's all coming together."

"Did I tell you...I sold my house in Beverly Hills and got almost three times what I paid for this place...that includes the land and house."

"Vivian is moving here?"

"No...*my* house."

"You had a house in Beverly Hills? You never told me."

"I guess it wasn't worth mentioning. It wasn't much. But the price of houses in L.A. is going crazy...I'm selling everything I have down there...except for our apartment building...I'm keeping that."

Her eyes met his briefly with a mixture of nostalgia and regret. "I'm glad you didn't sell that. Did you rent out the apartment?"

"No."

She changed the subject. "What do you want to do with the bedrooms?"

"I have a lot of furniture coming up from L.A. and Santa Rosa...I figure we can work it all into the guest rooms. Until it gets here, and we get it all sorted out...there's no sense in planning color schemes. Lupe will be up here soon...thank God...she will be a great help. I gave her a vacation until we get organized. Like I said...there's not much to do today. I say we play hooky and take the day off. I got some new surf fishing rods...bait and tackle. Why don't we go try them out?"

Her eyes lit up. "You mean I get a day off?"

"Yeah...we both do."

She grabbed her parka and buttoned it against the elements. "I've wanted to see your beach for a long time. I'm glad we finally have the perfect day."

Soon they were trudging along the bluff towards the stairs that led down to the beach. Hal carried his fishing rods and tackle box and she carried the basket. The sun was out, and sea birds soared over the water, diving for an occasional meal. Mari's curly hair was tousled by the wind and her blue eyes glowed. For the first time since he found her again, she had a smile for him, and she looked happy. "A day without responsibility...how delicious." She laughed.

They headed down the stairs that zigzagged down the side of the bluff. "I guess you don't get many days off...with David and all...and you worked like ten people on this house. I can't thank you enough, Mari."

She stood on the steps and looked up at him. "I love working with you."

He almost stopped in his tracks as his heart thumped. *Did she just look at me the way she used to? Did her eyes light up when she looked at me?* He grinned. "Yeah...we always were a great team." They continued on.

She stopped and turned to him. "Hal..." Just then the outside of the step she was standing on gave way. She was thrown against the outer rail, cracking it. Teetering, she tried to regain her balance, but the step splintered. Shrieking, she dropped, breaking through the railing as the basket sailed down the side of the cliff, instantly followed by the clatter of fishing tackle. In mid-air she felt Hal grab her by the collar, pulling her back from the void.

"DON'T MOVE...DON'T MOVE...I'VE GOT YOU...I'M NOT GOING TO LOSE YOU, BABE!!" He yelled. As he pulled her up, the stairs shuddered. He tried backing up to the next higher step, but the step he was on partially collapsed and he ended up on his back. He tugged her up and over the top of him. In shock, she lay on him, shaking. "Mari...you have to climb over me and go back up the stairs." Whimpering with fear she shook her head "no." He tried again. "Listen to me. I'm not going to lose you again. I'll get us out of here. But you must do as I say and crawl over me and get back up the stairs." He lifted her and pushed her over him, and she started moving back the way they came. As she reached the solid portion of the stairway, he inched his way back until he could stand.

When they were both on solid ground, he picked her up and ran to the house. Once inside, he put her down and held her in a tight embrace as she clung to him, trembling. A cry tore from inside him. "My God...I thought I lost you! I can't lose you again...I can't." He buried his face in her hair, kissing her head, her wet cheeks, her mouth, as he cradled her in his arms.

He felt her go limp and he carried her to the couch. Running upstairs; he grabbed a pillow and blanket and returned to place the pillow under her head and to cover her. He sat on the floor beside the couch, stroking her hair and cheek. Her eyes fluttered open and she gazed at him with an intensity he hadn't seen before. She put her arms around his neck and pulled him to her. She pressed her cheek against his and whispered. "It's always been us...hasn't it? You and me...it has always been us. Everything has come between us...but we're still together...aren't we?" She tenderly kissed his lips and then placed her head on his shoulder and cried. "Do you think it would be alright if you laid down beside me and held me...nothing more?"

"Sure." He took off his jacket and tossed it on the floor and then helped her remove her parka. Climbing onto the couch he pulled the blanket over them and wrapped his arms around her. She put her head on his chest and clutched him, softly whimpering.

"Shhhhh...shhhhh." He gently rocked her.

"It happened again, Hal" She whispered.

"What happened?"

"My vision narrowed to a circle...and then black. I think I just fainted."

He ran his fingers through her hair and kissed her forehead. "That's understandable...you almost lost your life out there...which means we both would have died."

She turned her face up to his and held his dark eyes. Her fingers lightly touched his face, caressed his ear, and then she reached up to put her arms around his neck and pressed her cheek to his. "Thank you...thank you for saving my life. Thank you for David..."

"For David?" He looked at her with a half-smile. "I can truly say...my pleasure...I didn't do anything out of the ordinary."

"Hal...he is so much like you...he saved my life."

"Babe...if I could go back..."

"Shhhh." She put her fingertips over his lips. "No self-recriminations...not today..." With her hand cupping his face, she whispered, "and thank you for saying you still love me...it means more to me than you know..." She kissed him full on the mouth with a yearning for yesteryear. His breath quickened as he pulled her closer in his embrace. She was reticent to break through the barrier between them and buried her face in his chest. "I can't give you more.

I can't tear my family apart...David's home...I..." She started to weep once more.

"Don't...don't cry, Babe. We can talk tomorrow."

***

Hal's ringtone sounded. "Hi, Babe...I just called to see how you're doing."

"After you told Ed what happened yesterday...he insisted that I stay in bed today and he drove David in to school this morning. How are you?"

"I'm at the doctor's getting splinters pulled out of my ass..." He laughed.

"Oh...you didn't tell me you were hurt..."

"I wasn't about to let go of you for anything. It's not serious...in fact it's rather funny! Do you need for me to pick you up so you can get your car?"

"Thanks for driving me home last night..."

"You were in no shape to drive..."

"I guess Ed can drive me over to get my car."

"I really want...I really need to talk to you..."

She closed her eyes. "I know." She spoke softly.

"When can I see you?"

"Where are you going to be?"

"Can you come to Jenner?"

"No...David will be with me."

"I'll try to arrange to see you in Santa Rosa...within the next couple of days."

"Alright."

When she hung up, she wondered what she would tell Hal. Remembering every word she said to him in the intensity of heightened emotions, she wondered how she could backtrack to a neutral position. She meant everything she said, and more that she left unsaid, but she had lost her grip on herself and disclosed things she had never intended to reveal. Moreover, her display of her feelings for him made her blush. *If I hadn't been in shock...I never would have said what I did. Now what can I do? How can I take it all back?* As much as she wanted to be with him, an affair was out of the question. Divorce was out of the question. *Every fucking thing is out of the question!* She saw no way out.

510

***

Ed slowly drove by Hal's house. Mari's Elantra was parked in front. He did not pull into the driveway but parked some distance down the street. Surreptitiously, he walked along the property line through a stand of trees. Watching the house, he saw no indication of anyone at home. Going out into the open, he walked along the edge of the bluff to the top of the stairs that went to the beach. He walked down a few steps and saw the place where the incident happened that almost cost Mari her life. The collapsed steps, the broken railing, were just as described. Further down the cliff he saw the basket and the remnants of its contents, along with fishing gear, scattered on the rocks below. Satisfied that Hal and Mari had told him the truth, he made his way back to the car.

***

"I got David up very early this morning, and when I told him you would be taking us to Safari West, he couldn't contain himself. He thinks it's because of his Easter Vacation...he may want to be with you more this week." Mari strolled with Hal in the walking part of the wild animal preserve while David skipped happily ahead.

"How long can you stay in town today?"

"Ed got called away on business, in San Francisco...something about the contract for our grapes...so I pretty much have most of the day."

"Good. I want David to be tuckered out by the time we get to my house. I need to talk to you alone, Mari. My head has been spinning..."

"Mine too..."

Hal's phone went off. He looked at the message. "I have to deal with this." He walked a short distance away and placed a call. "I want you to keep him there until tomorrow...find a way...I don't care if you have to slash his tires. Keep him there." He walked back to Mari. "Some confusion at Arendt."

David was scampering too far ahead of them. "David!" Mari gestured for him to come to her.

"When do we get to see the giraffes?" David hopped with excitement.

Mari looked up at Hal. "When do we take the tour on the Safari trucks...or do we walk first?"

"I want to see the animals...I want to see the giraffe first." David pleaded.

"We are scheduled for ten o'clock. If he wants to see the giraffes first...we walk." Hal ruffled David's hair.

Mari smiled. "He had a stuffed giraffe as a baby...I think he still has it...hence his love of giraffes."

"Well, then...we should get to it." He picked up David and they headed for the walking tour. Hal's phone rang again. "It's Ed." He answered. "Hi, Ed. What's up? You can't get ahold of Mari? That's strange...she's right here. Hold on." He passed his phone to her.

"Hi, honey...I don't know...my phone is on."

Hal gestured for her to hand him her phone. "It says 'no service.'"

"It looks like I'm not getting any service here...Hal is...he has AT&T. He came by to take David to Safari West. He invited me to go with them. Are you on your way home? No? What happened? Tomorrow. Well that...OK...OK. I didn't plan to stay out too late. I thought you would be home by this evening. When will you be home? Call me when you know what hotel you'll be staying at. When you are ready to come home let me know and I'll have dinner ready for you. Ok...Ok. Me too." She hung up. "Ed's stuck in 'Frisco. He won't be back until tomorrow."

"Then I'll take you to dinner."

They took in the sights of exotic birds, cheetahs, and then David spotted the giraffes. He took off like a shot. "David!" Mari took off after him.

A sultry eyed giraffe, with long lashes, looked at David and ambled over to the fence. Gazing down at the boy it lowered its head to rest on his shoulder. David wrapped his arms around its neck and petted it. Hal snapped away with his camera. Mari approached slowly and the affectionate giraffe repeated the gesture by putting his head on Mari's shoulder. Hal zoomed in for the picture.

When the time came, they made their way to the Safari truck. First in the group to go on board, they opted to ride on top. Hal put his arm around Mari, held David secure in his lap and the truck rumbled and bucked along the rough road past zebras, gazelles, water buffalo, and Watusi long horn cattle, and of course more giraffes. At the first break, Mari herded her charges into the lower passenger level out of the sun, checked them for sunburn, and slathered them with sunscreen. The entire ride was two and a half hours with the tour guide illuminating his sightseers regarding the subject animals, as they bounced along the road.

Barely making it under the wire for the last lunch service, they were tempted by an array of choices. Mari scanned the menu. "I can't make up my mind...how about you taking the barbequed chicken and I'll take the pulled pork so we can share it?"

"OK..." Hal agreed. "...do you want mac n' cheese or basmati rice?"

They all said, "Mac n' cheese!"

"What about the appetizers?" Hal looked around the table.

"Fresh fruit for David...I know he'll eat that...why don't you have the cheese platter and I'll have the meatballs...and we can all share. Ooooh...and I want cornbread." Mari cooed.

"David, what do you want?"

"Did you see the giraffe? I love giraffes. I got to pet it!"

"Yes dear...but what do you want to eat?"

"I don't know."

"Do you want me to pick for you, buckaroo? That way it will be a surprise..." Hal smiled.

"Yeah."

"OK, Mari...point out what he will eat."

"He'll like the soup...if not, I'll give him my salad. You're having a salad too..."

Hal smirked, "Why..."

"To fake your body out...!" She gave him a level gaze. "...with something healthy."

"So...you're looking after me?"

"Somebody has to...I guess it's me."

"Well hi there, Mari...I thought that was you and David sitting over here. Where's Ed?" Ethan Brimley, a church member, ambled up to the table to greet her. "Betty over there thought it was you...fancy running into you here."

Mari gave Betty a diplomatic wave at the table across the room. "Ed had to go out of town on business. This is an old family friend from L.A....Hal Golan...he just moved up here and we are taking him for the grand tour. Hal...Ethan Brimley...he's a member of our church."

"Pleased to meet you." Both men nodded but did not shake hands. "Too bad Ed couldn't come with you."

"He was supposed to…but he got called away on short notice. Are you going to be in the Easter sunrise service this year?"

"Yes…in fact I'm in charge of the children's choir."

"Good." Mari held out her hand to cut off the conversation. "I'll see you at rehearsal then."

Ethan shook her hand while he took a good look at Hal, and then his eyes drifted to David. "Yes…I'll see you then." He wandered away and then sped back to his table.

"Shoot…now every move we make will be under scrutiny." Mari grumbled under her breath.

"Let's not let them put a damper on our day. We're not doing anything out of the ordinary…I mean it's not as though I'm going to pinch your butt or anything…"

"Hal said 'butt.'" David laughed.

***

After a long day at Safari West, and dining out, Hal returned to his home in Santa Rosa with Mari and David. The long-awaited moment to talk to Mari was finally at hand. Hal unfastened the child seat and carried David, who was sleeping soundly, into the house. Carrying his son straight away to his bedroom, he put him to bed. Shutting the door behind him, he went into the living room.

Mari stood in the center of the room, staring at him. They both started to speak. "You go first…" She said quietly.

"I haven't been able to sleep these past few days…because what you said has been going round and round in my head. You said it has always been us…and that's the way it has been for me too. It's always been you for me, Mari. Now that I know that it is the same for you…I can't play this game anymore. I want you…I want to spend my life with you. I don't want you to walk out of here and go back to him." He unconsciously wrung his hands. "The years are passing and I have no one…because there is no one but you. I want to have more children…I want to have a life. I want you for my wife…and I'll do anything you want to make that happen. I need an answer now. If you cannot tell me that it's me you want…then I have to try to move on in my life. I love you…that will never change. But I can't always want you…ache for you…and come up empty handed."

"Are you telling me goodbye?" Her voice quavered.

"No...no..." He went to her and took both her hands. "I'm asking you...I'm begging you...to choose me."

She took her hands away and sat down. "Do you have a drink?"

He was surprised but thought again. "No. No excuses...plain and sober...give it to me straight." Her eyes turned to him. His heart sank. *Oh shit...I know that look.*

"Hal...when I said what I said...I was scared shitless. You saved my life...and everything else in the world went away. There was just you and me...and a bunch of jumbled up emotions came to the surface and I said and did things that I shouldn't have." Her breath shuddered. "If I chose you and left Ed...you would never be able to trust me again...that I would be faithful to you. In fact, I have already betrayed Ed's trust...in just being here...just because..." she looked to him for understanding. "...there are times when I am drawn to be with you, and I would rather be here."

"Then *be* with me."

"But the world *didn't* go away, Hal. I'm right back in it...and I can't be irresponsible, selfish, and mean. Ed and I *are* a family unit...and we formed that unit around David. The home Ed provided is the only home David has known. You're asking me to tear that apart. You're asking me to tear my son's heart out...to tear Ed's heart out...and make them pay for a mistake in our past. I'm not always happy with Ed...but I am content...at least I was...and David...he is happy and secure."

"He's happy with me."

"Of course he is! You're the fun guy who comes over bi-weekly...you bring him things...you're focused on him...you explain things in a fun way...and play with him. You don't have the other job of a father...being the naysayer...being there in the middle of the night when he throws up...changing his linen when he wets the bed...telling him he's safe when he has a bad dream. Ed has done all that. I know he's not perfect...but he has done nothing to deserve my kicking him in the nuts and saying sayonara."

"You're saying you choose Ed...instead of me?"

"No...you don't get it. I choose David's happiness over you...his security..."

"You have more than enough to make him secure…I have seen to it that you have everything you need…"

"But not when I needed it!" She put her hands over her face. "Ed was there when there was no one else!"

Hal looked down. "Do you think there will ever be a time when we will be together?"

"I don't know." She shook her head.

"Mari…you love me…I know you do…"

"Oh…for Christ's sake, Hal. When I loved you…I loved you…I loved you…with all my heart…you thought I didn't! Now…when it would be the worst thing in the world for everyone…you keep telling me that I do. Your timing is awful. You don't want to know what I feel…it would be too painful for the both of us. May I have that drink now?" She needed a drink to alleviate the torment that she felt. She loved him and wanted him; but each time she had to tell him "no" she could see the suffering in his eyes, and it was like a knife in her heart.

"Only if you stay the night. I don't want you to be tipsy and alone with David."

"Deal."

He went to the kitchen. "Bourbon is all I have. I can mix an Old Fashioned for you."

"That's fine…I'll just have the one. Just so you know…this has been really hard for me…so many thoughts running through my head…trying to think of what's best for everybody."

He brought her drink and set it down on the coffee table. Holding her by her shoulders, he lifted her from the couch. "This is what's best for you." He embraced her, kissing her full on the mouth. Forgetting all decorum and misgivings, she put her arms around him, returning his ardor. He waited to hear the little sound she made that told him she was his. "You want me, don't you, Babe?" He breathed.

"Yes."

He kissed her again and felt her tremble. Thrusting his hand under her sweater, he gently kneaded her breast and she dissolved into him.

A little voice came from the hallway. "Mommy?" David stood there wide-eyed, staring at them both.

Mari pulled away and closed her eyes. The rude awakening let her know what she must do. She turned to her son. "Go back to bed, dear. Hal and I are talking."

"I want a glass of waddy."

"OK...go to bed and I'll bring you one." She went to the kitchen, filled a glass, and took it to her son. He took a couple of gulps and then handed it back. "Now you go back to sleep. I'll leave your water here in case you want more."

She returned to see Hal with his head in his hand.

"Is he OK?"

"That rips it, Hal. I can't be more than a friend to you. I almost made an awful mistake. I can't let things get so out of hand. Please drive us home." She went to the bedroom and gathered up her son. "Come on sweetheart. Hal is going to take us home."

They rode in silence in the car. She looked at Hal and saw not only hurt, but anger on his face. The agony and guilt she felt was not much better. She thought to herself how close she came to making a mistake. *A few minutes more and my son could have caught me in flagrante delicto with the man he looks up to.* A small, involuntary sob tore from her and she turned to look out the window, blinking back tears. *I wanted him so.*

After he drove them home, he returned to his empty house to find the drink he made on the table. Picking it up, he took a sip and sat deep in thought. *OK, Mari...if that's the way you want to play it...that's the way it will be. I'm done being your yo-yo.*

***

I'VE BEEN BAD

"Hi kiddo." Hal came through the patio to the sliding glass door. He could see Mari through the screen puttering in the kitchen.

"Come on in..." For some reason she looked agitated. "...I tried to call you, but I guess you had your phone off."

Hal took his phone out and turned it on. "Yeah. I turned it off while I was working this morning. I forgot to turn it back on. Why did you call me?"

"I tried to head you off. I don't think it is a good day for your visit."

"What did I do now?"

"Oh, Hal...you didn't do anything. It's just that we had a little fracas here and you're walking into the middle of it."

"What happened? Where's David?"

"David took an Easter basket and an offering envelope from the church. Ed spanked him and sent him to his room. He's been up there crying ever since."

"You said there was a 'fracas' over it. What happened there?"

"Well, Ed made him give back the basket and the envelope on the spot...and made him apologize. For his age...I thought that was enough. He was already crying. But as soon as we got home, Ed swatted him and sent him upstairs to his room. I didn't agree with that and said so. Now Ed's in the garden...sulking."

Hal turned and started for the stairs. Just then the front door opened, and Ed came in. "You can't see him today."

Hal kept walking up the stairs. "Who's going to stop me?"

As Hal walked down the hallway to David's room, he could hear Ed and Mari bickering downstairs and his son bawling in his room. *What a fucked-up mess!* He gently knocked on David's door and then opened it. "Hey little buckaroo...what's wrong?" David started crying louder and buried his face in his pillow. Hal sat on the edge of his bed. "Hey little guy...it can't be as bad as all that." He reached out and stroked his son's hair. "Come on...come on." He picked him up to sit with him and put his arm around him.

David's little tear stained face turned up at him. "I've been bad!"

"Oh...is that all? Haven't we all been bad at some time or another?" Hal made a sad face. "The trick is to learn from it...so we will know ahead of time when we are about to do something bad...and listen to what our conscience is telling us. Do you know where your conscience is?"

"Nooo." He sobbed.

"It lives right here in your tummy." Hal pointed to his stomach. "When we are about to do something bad...Mr. Conscience kicks up a fuss in your tummy and makes it knot up into a ball until it hurts. That's telling you 'Don't do it!'"

"Have you ever...been bad?" David still had spasms from crying.

Hal gave him a broad grin. "Have I ever! There are different types of bad. For some you can say I'm sorry...if you really mean it...and make up for it. I've done lots of those." Hal made a sorrowful face. "Then there are the really bad bads...that no matter how sorry you are...you can't take it back. You can say I'm sorry a hundred times...and you can't make it better. Then the knot in your stomach becomes a pain you have to live with."

"Have you ever done a bad bad?"

"Yes...one really big one...and I regret it to this day. Mr. Conscience kicks me in the tummy every day...and it hurts."

"I took an Easter basket that didn't belong to me...and something else."

"Did you feel a knot in your tummy?"

"Yes."

"Did you give back what you took?"

"Yes."

"Did you say you're sorry?"

"No...I apologized."

"Well that's just as good. Now this is important. Did you mean it?"

"I guess I did. Daddy made me give it back. I really wanted the chocolate bunny."

"But that would mean you would have that chocolate bunny...and the person whose basket you took wouldn't have one for Easter. You know your mother would have lots of bunnies for you. What if it was the only one a little girl or boy had. Wouldn't you feel bad for taking it?"

"Yes."

"Well there you go...that means you meant it." Hal picked him up, put him on his lap, and held him close. "Life is full of lessons like that…this is just the first of many. I'm glad to see you have a healthy conscience to help you know right from wrong."

"Did you ever do anything bad that you weren't sorry for doing?"

Hal looked down at his son and kissed the top of his head. "That would be a case of don't do what I have done…but…yes."

Hal held him until he fell asleep. He gently put him back to bed and kissed him. Going downstairs he met Mari in the kitchen. "He's asleep now. I want to ask you something."

"Thank God you calmed him down." Her eyes regarded him with appreciation.

"That's what I want to ask you. When I went up to see him…how long had he been crying?"

"Well over two hours…"

"When I went in to see him…it was like the little guy felt that he didn't have a friend in this world. He was devastated…like his heart was broken. I know I'm not supposed to interfere with your parenting…but when you can talk to the kid…do you have to spank him?"

"I wouldn't have…" She concurred with his assessment.

"What about Ed?"

"I'll talk to him."

"When David wakes up…can you just let it go?"

"I'll see to it."

He shuddered when he took a breath. "I guess I shouldn't stay for lunch." Hal compressed his lips and started to leave when his temper got the best of him. "Mari…if you think David needs a spanking…you do it…not Ed. You can tell that Jesus freak for me that if he ever lays a hand on my son again…I will do him the favor of crucifying him…and then stand back to see if he can be raised from the dead!" She raised her brows and nodded.

Mari set the table for two and was preparing a tray for David. Ed sat down for dinner. "What are you doing?"

"I'm taking dinner upstairs for David. I doubt that he feels like coming downstairs to eat."

"No you don't. I sent him to bed without supper."

"WHAT!?!"

"The child has to be punished."

"Fuck you, Ed! The 'child' has been punished enough...in fact too much. He's only five. Kids are going to make mistakes. They need guidance...not meanness."

"That's how my father punished me...and I turned out alright."

"Haven't you heard of people turning out 'alright' in spite of...not because of...their parents?"

"You're not taking him supper."

Mari turned with her face within a foot of his. Her voice was dangerously low. "This is where I draw the line...with my kid. If you don't have the sensibilities to understand the difference between correcting a child and brutalizing a child...then you will not punish my child. I'm not going to have him go hungry because you have issues."

"You said David was our child. Now he's just yours? Could it be that Hal's visit today has something to do with that?"

"Why do you have to drag Hal into it? This is me talking. But while I'm at it, let me make one thing clear. I pledged my marriage vows to you...and I have kept them...and I intend to keep them. You have provided a stable home for David and me...I have no intention of disrupting that. But if I ever feel that you hold the least bit of hostility toward David for being Hal's son...I will take steps to rectify the situation." She stepped away and then turned back. "And, don't ever tell Hal that he can't see David, again."

"And as your husband...I'm telling you...you can't see Hal outside of this house!"

"What?!"

"You heard me. You think that when you came home late that night I didn't know what you were up to?"

"For Christ's sake! I told you what happened. Why are you making Hal the issue? You are perfectly happy to take his money...and don't pretend it hasn't made life easier around here. What we spend on David goes a long way to help both of us...."

"You're the one in charge of that...and you put practically all of it in the bank."

"Except what I use for David...and that means we do not have to support him out of what we make."

"Can't you see...he has us fighting with each other? We never used to do that."

"All I can see is you're the one bitching about it...and you started this fight! Now I am going up and take David his dinner...and let him know I love him. You can sit here...mope if you want to...and think about what you said."

"You can't see Hal outside of this house!"

"Fine!"

"Wait." Ed capitulated. "I'll go with you."

They both entered David's room and found him in bed playing with a small toy car. "I brought dinner for you." Mari set the tray down and sat on the side of his bed. "I want you to know that mommy and daddy still love you..."

"I love you too!" David crawled toward Mari, hugged her, and kissed her on the lips.

"No...no...no. You don't kiss mommy like that."

"Where in tarnation did he learn that?" Ed exclaimed.

"Don't make a big deal of it, dear. He probably saw it on TV." Quickly heading off potential disaster, she interjected, "Here comes your dinner" as she sat him up in bed.

***

Hal pushed an empty cart up and down the grocery store aisles in his first attempt at serious shopping. He doubted that his mother ever shopped before, or that she ever cooked before. The Golans had domestics to do that for them. Until Mari came into his life, he had always gone to his favorite neighborhood restaurants to eat, thinking that was how normal people lived. Mari's ability to take raw materials and turn them into meals was a revelation to him.

The choices at the supermarket were overwhelming, enigmatic, and yet alluring. Every now and then he would stop, pick up a box or container with a picture he liked, and look it over. If the instructions looked understandable, he threw it into his basket and continued on his adventure. Certain things were self-explanatory. A can of tuna, a quart of milk, a dozen eggs, he grasped right away. But the mysteries of which brand, or what kind eluded him. *What's the difference between chunk tuna and albacore tuna...water packed or oil packed?* He got a can of each. *What kind of milk did Mari buy?* He tried to remember but was hit with an instant melancholia that he had to shake off. Strolling down the meat counter, he recognized porterhouse steaks, lamb chops, and chicken and tossed several packages in the basket; pausing at the pork chops, he looked over his shoulder and took two packs, as well. The sight of Cornish game hens depressed him further still.

Going into the produce department, he was even more at a loss. For the first time he recognized the wealth of knowledge and skill Mari had in her ability to discern, purchase, and prepare dishes that she made beautiful that tasted out of this world. He knew that lettuce and tomatoes were good for sandwiches and made a mental note to get some bread. Looking at the varieties, he picked what he thought she would get. Moving along he knew potatoes and carrots. *They make a good stew.* He remembered she would put one turnip into a stew. He saw the sign for turnips, but there were a couple of turnipy looking things on the shelf. *She would chop it up small and toss it in the pot...what did it look like? She said it was essential for flavor.* He went to reach for one and he heard a "ding" sound.

"Look out...you'll get your arm wet." He turned to see an attractive lady smiling at him. She pointed. "The sprayers are going to come on." Just then a fine mist of water sprayed out over the produce.

Hal pulled his arm back and laughed. "Oh...I didn't know about those...I'm rather new to shopping."

"Divorced?" She guessed.

"No...no." He started to tell her how he came to be on his own but realized that his story was too long and utterly ridiculous. "It's a long story. Can you tell me if those are turnips?"

"Those are rutabagas. The stack next to them are turnips."

"Oh. Is it better to get the large ones or the small ones?"

"That depends on what you are cooking."

"I'm making a stew."

"She raised her eyebrows and made a face. Not a lot of people like turnips in their stew...most prefer potatoes."

"Potatoes go in too...but the turnip has to go in first... according to my...friend." He didn't like referring to Mari as his "friend" but how could he explain his relationship to a stranger?

"Really...how does that work?"

He wrinkled his brow, trying to remember. "She chopped it up into tiny squares. Then I think she put it in right after she did something with the meat and put water...no...beef stock in...and she said the turnip cooks away leaving nothing but a delicious flavor."

"That sounds really good."

"It is, but I never really made it before."

"You said 'she'…is that your 'long story'?"

"Yeah…complicated and none too happy."

She looked at him for a second. "I'm Beth…" She held out her hand. "…and you are?"

"Hal." He appraised her for the first time. She had short auburn hair with light brown eyes almost the same color as her hair. Her breasts were small, but sufficient. Her hips and legs were a bit chunky, but her height saved them from being fat. She was not a perfect ten, but her face was pretty, made more so by her lively expression. He turned back toward the turnips.

She saw him briefly looking at her. "If it is going to cook into the beef stock…size doesn't matter. Pick any of them."

Hal reached up and picked out a big one and put it in his basket. "I'm not sure how it's going to turn out…"

"You know…you remind me of my husband. He knew a lot about a lot of things…but out of his element…he was as helpless as a baby." She smiled.

"You said 'knew'…you're wearing a ring…aren't you still married?"

"Thanks for noticing…but I'm widowed. He died about a year ago." She paused.

"I'm sorry to hear that…you seem like such a nice lady…I'm sorry that happened to you."

"Here…I'll help you with your shopping. What else did your 'long story' put into her stew?"

"Lots of things…carrots…mushrooms…and like you said potatoes…I think tomatoes…"

"There are some tables over by the deli. Why don't we go over there and have some coffee…and we can sort out your shopping…and you can tell me your long story…and I'll tell you mine."

He didn't tell her everything about himself, in fact next to nothing. He only told her the story of lovers who were torn apart by mistake and that she had married another. She didn't tell him everything about herself, either. She only told him of being a happy wife, whose children were now grown, and a husband she loved dearly, who died. Hal was thirty-six, she was forty-five. Two lonely people who happened to meet in the grocery produce section; by the end of the hour they exchanged phone numbers; by the end of the week she did a decent job of cooking his stew for him; by the end of the month he told her, "I don't love you...I can never love you."

She told him. "I know...I don't love you. I still love my husband. Neither of us can have the one we love. But I am fond of you...and I like being with you. Together...we can shut out the cold...the pain we feel."

"I can't have you near my home or my family...ever. I can't let you into my life...and I can't allow you to use up my time. I can only see you once a week."

"I don't want my children to know about you either."

"So, you can live with that?"

"I can live with that." She caressed his face.

Hal thought of all the nights he lay awake alone thinking of Mari with Ed. "Yeah...I can live with that too."

***

The clerk went back into the storeroom and brought out the two identical pictures Mari brought in to have framed. "This is really a darling picture."

"I took it a while ago on a picnic in the woods near my house. I took my camera with me to take nature shots...I was snapping away when a friend of mine came walking down the path holding hands with his little boy...they didn't see me snap it."

"It is so touching the way the son is looking up to his father...and the father is looking down at his son with all the love in the world. It almost brings tears to your eyes." The clerk held the picture up to look at it at arm's length.

"When I had it blown up...I had the photo processed to look like canvas, so it sort of looks like a painting..."

"I just love the frame you chose for it. The wood frame is perfect for the wooded scene."

"Yes...I got one for the grandmother...and of course one for my friend. They're Christmas presents."

When she got home, Mari laid the pictures on the bed to gift-wrap. Thinking that the sentiment of the picture was too personal to share at the mirthful opening of presents, she decided to send them both by mail. An accompanying note to Vivian was appropriate.

She took one of them and walked to the window to hold it up in the light. It captured a perfect moment in time. *This is the way it should have been...the way it was meant to be.* She thought of how happy they were when they decided to have David. They tossed her pills in the air in celebration. She laughed as tears streamed down her face. *I love you, Hal.*

***

PART FOUR

Malone sat quietly contemplating confidential financial reports and transcribing them into a code known only to him. The reports, written on rice paper, were then floated in a bowl of water to disintegrate. His private line rang. He answered, "It's me."

"Hey, dad...it's your prodigal son." Hal quipped.

"Good God! How the hell are you? It's been a while."

"Yeah. Business has been running that smoothly...nothing much to talk about."

"What do you need?"

"Nothing...I was just sitting here thinking about you...and I thought I would give you a call to let you know you're appreciated. You've done a lot for me."

Malone was silent for a moment. He was touched. In a low voice he muttered. "Now that you've crawled up my ass...what do you need?"

"Nothing...I got just about everything I want. Just called to say...hi..."

"Tell me...how are you and Mari getting on."

Hal chuckled. "You would ask me about my one failure..."

"Failure? You gotta be shittin' me. You haven't corralled that filly yet?"

"Nope. As Hillary told Bill...close but no cigar. She as much as told me she loves me...but she won't leave her husband. She feels she owes that dweeb...and perhaps she does. I just don't see why she thinks she should throw her life away on him."

"I take it you haven't given up."

"Well...yes and no. I'm still around...because of my son...but I don't make a play for her anymore. The ball is in her court. Meanwhile, I'm seeing someone else...nothing serious...but you know how it is."

"Yeah...I'm sorry to hear that."

"Other than that, I'm doing real well. I took your advice, sold my real estate, and made a fucking fortune. I built a new place up here...and business is good. My son is amazing...he's my life."

"And what's Mari doing now?"

"She's a housewife and mother...her husband, Ed, has a vineyard. He doesn't know it, but it's my company that buys his grapes."

"You can put him in the shitter then."

"No...I don't want to cause her any headaches. Ed would be a nice guy if he wasn't such a Jesus freak..."

"He owns a vineyard? Do I know this guy? He's up there in Napa...Ed...Ed...Oh...I forget his last name..." Malone feigned.

"Baker. No...he's in Sonoma...they have a place near Santa Rosa. It's a small vineyard...but a nice place. She said she's content...but she sure doesn't act like it."

Malone wrote down the information. "Women are the damnedest creatures...she wants you, doesn't she?"

"So she said..."

"When are you coming down here for a visit? I'd like to see you."

"I could be down there tomorrow. What do you need?"

"It's not that pressing...nothing but good news...if you could be here in the next couple of weeks...I'd appreciate it."

"Sure. You've got it. I'll call you when I get there."

"Good to hear your voice, son. See you then." Malone rang off. He punched another line.

"Manny...get your fat ass in here..."

"I love you too, boss!"

Manny came in with a quizzical look on his face. "What's up?"

"You know...Hal saved my life twice...and yours once. I think we should do something nice for him. I don't want him to know about it, because...you know...he's one of those guys. I mean he can play the game...be in the life...but he's not really a part of it. He's just a decent guy who wants to live his life with a wife and family. Mari is giving him fits. She won't leave her husband. Do you think we should do something about it?"

Manny grinned. "Do you want me to whack her old man?"

"No...nothing so tactless...besides he would probably be blamed for it. No...something with finesse...panache...something undetectable..."

Manny sat in thought. "Give me time and I might come up with something...but right now...I got nothing."

"I want you to send one of your guys up to Santa Rosa...to find out all he can about this guy." Malone handed Manny the paper with Ed's name on it. "He owns a vineyard near Santa Rosa and he's super religious. I know that in 2004 there was a custody suit...put your best guy on it."

Eleven o'clock on Sunday morning found Hal standing near Melrose and La Brea in Los Angeles, in front of Pink's hot dog stand. A homeless man approached him. He reached in his pocket and started to pull out a twenty when he recognized the man's voice and took a closer look to find it was Malone. "Shit! I didn't recognize you! You came to L.A. to be an actor, didn't you."

Malone laughed. "How did you know?"

"You enjoy playing the part too much."

"It gets me out of the house." Malone walked with Hal to the counter. At that hour on a Sunday, the famous long line of patrons hadn't materialized. "I'll have the Spicy Chicago Dog and an Orange Crush. What are you having, Hal?"

"I guess I'll have the Bacon Chili Cheese Dog...and the Holee Molee Fries for here...and the Double Bacon Chili Cheeseburger to go...oh...and some pink lemonade."

"So, you're unorthodox." Malone quipped.

"Yeah...you can blame it on Mari...she put pork in my meatloaf."

"I guess there's worse things."

The two men watched the man take charge of their order, build the burger and delectable dogs, and then they took their trays of food to the outside tables. Malone walked to the far end of the patio. No one else was there. "I always come here at this hour...no crowds to contend with...and if anyone is here...they think I'm homeless and they keep their distance. Who's the hamburger for?"

"Me...I'll have it later at home. My mother no longer objects to pork...so I'll have Graham heat it up." Hal sorted out his order. "What did you want to see me for?" He took a huge chomp out of his hot dog.

"The good news is that Valiant Medical is growing. Our legitimate business is up by almost twenty to twenty-three percent. The bad news is that Arendt is not keeping up with our demand for our special brand. We figure why should we give up all the new business...we want you to increase your output to us."

"Totally legit?"

"Totally."

"I'm going to need some time to hire more employees, expand that portion of the plant, get new equipment, and put on another shift. How soon do you need it?"

"I didn't want to bother you until I knew it wasn't a fluke...I could have used it yesterday, but as soon as you can get rolling."

"Done...I'll have to arrange to move down here for a while. I'll need a construction company...and someone to help oversee the project. Do you have someone who can qualify to be my right-hand man?"

"I'll see who I can come up with."

"They have to be clean."

Malone smiled. "Don't worry...they'll be so clean they'll squeak." He changed the subject. "By the way...the word on the cell block is that your father is sick...and has asked for compassionate leave."

"Marvin is dead to me. I'm surprised he's lived this long."

"I just wanted to let you know in case he asks your mother if he can stay with her. He has to involve someone on the outside in order to get out...and if he is asking for compassionate leave...that means he is probably very ill or terminal."

"I'll look into it. I have never seen my mother happier than when she divorced him...I don't want to have him dump his misery on her now."

"Good thinking...and if he is dying...don't be tempted to tell him at the end that it was you that fucked him. He could revive long enough to tell someone. Oh...and don't try to hasten his death by tampering with the medical equipment...it's not worth the few days you take from him to risk years in the joint. Just be content to sit back and watch him go."

Hal nodded. "Don't tell me you read minds too."

"Nope...I just know hatred. It can make you do foolish things."

***

Malone evaluated the young man sitting in his office. He was Manny's new guy, Dan, Jr. A legacy hire, he was the son of Dan, Malone's deceased soldier. Still in his twenties, he had the benefit of a college education, but was not long on experience. Blond and fairly nice looking, he could easily fit into social circles that were closed to the likes of Manny and Malone. *He is like the sole of new shoes...shiny and fresh...but slippery and not to be trusted until he has some wear.* Malone summed him up.

Manny also said he had the same misgivings about Dan. Generally speaking, he was satisfied with the kid, but he insisted on handing him relatively easy assignments where counting on him was not

531

crucial. Therefore, gathering information from public records, and snooping without drawing suspicion, was consistent with the kid's talents. "Dan put together a decent file on Ed Baker, boss. I'll let him tell you what he found." Manny nodded at Dan to start his presentation.

He picked up the file folder he developed on Ed and began his report. "Yes...to summarize...I found the address of Edward Thomas Baker in the tax assessor's office and I took up surveillance of him, his wife, Mari, and their son, David. There are pictures of each of them in the file. He is self-employed...personally supervising his vineyard. His five employees are all from the same family and they live on the estate. The Bakers live rather quiet, uneventful lives...with the main consistency being that they attend church every Sunday and he also regularly attends choir practice on Wednesdays. Of interest is that his break from his regular routine is the men's Christian fellowship activities. This usually involves retreats, seminars, and informal camping and fishing trips. These events are generally noted in the church monthly newsletter...except for the informal outings. Those are planned by the individuals involved. His vineyard is thriving, and he contracts to sell his crop every year with the same outfit...that pays him better than the going rate even though his crop is nothing out of the ordinary. He has some college education, he retired from Yarborough Publishing, and he has no military record and no arrest record. The court file of the custody suit is sealed, but I was able to obtain the name of the family attorney. Through his office I was able to get copies of the custody documents..."

"How did you do that?" Malone wanted to know how much exposure was involved.

"It wasn't difficult to get a very grateful receptionist to copy the file for me. She thinks I was a Treasury agent surreptitiously investigating Hillel Golan. She won't talk...because it would cost her more than her job."

"I see. Was it sex or money?" Malone laughed.

"Both." Dan didn't see the joke. "It appears that their son is not Edward Baker's child...but the son of one Hillel Golan, aka Hal Golan. The biological father, Golan, willingly settled child support for ten thousand a month...with the mother having sole control of those funds. Golan is the CEO of Arendt Medical...and the heir to the Arendt fortune. His residence is in Jenner, California...where he is located near the Baker family...presumably to be close to his son..."

"And the mother..." Manny added.

"OK...I've heard enough." Malone held out his hand for Dan to give him the file. "None of this information is to leave this room...ever. I will personally cut off the balls of anyone who talks about this...is that understood?"

"Yes, sir." Dan handed over the report.

"Now...what is our next step?" Manny looked to Malone.

Malone studied Dan. "Good job, Dan. You can go now." As Dan left the office and closed the door behind him, Malone furrowed his brow. "I get a strange vibe off that kid...I'm not that sure of him. He may have some of his father's genes...but I get the feeling he thinks he's better...smarter than us. I don't know."

"You seem to have put what I sensed into words. I was worried for a moment that you were going to trust him with what we're planning. I don't think he is ready for that." Manny concurred. "Have you come up with anything yet?"

"Yeah...I think so. I have a friend of a friend that knows a friend who worked with the CIA back in the day when the CIA was trying to whack Castro. The word on the street is that they developed a bio-weapon that could give a man cancer within days or weeks. They took a carcinogenic monkey virus SV-40 and irradiated it, causing it to mutate into a more aggressive cancer-causing form that kills within days. They took out Ruby by screwing with his immune system and then injecting him with the stuff. It was a rather crude formula back then because they had to x-ray him for forty-five minutes before giving him the needle. In the intervening forty years or so, what they have now is a lot more sophisticated...the SV-40 is combined with certain bacteria that predetermines what type of cancer it causes."

"Goddamn." Manny whispered.

"You never heard of this before?"

"Well I always figured that they gave Jack Ruby cancer...it was a little too convenient that he got it so fast and died...just before he was about to talk...but I had no idea how...that it was actually a thing."

"Well…it may take time to set up…but I think that is the way to go. No one…not even the doctor will have a clue…and there will be nothing that can lead back to us or anyone else." Malone opened the file. "All we have to do is to condense this file to pertain only to Ed Baker and take it to this friend of a friend…along with a shitload of money. The friend of a friend will see to it that the right person gets the file and makes the hit." Malone flipped the report open. "Awwwww. Did you see this picture of Hal's son? Damn if he isn't the cutest thing! He looks like Hal alright…"

"No…let me see. Hah! Look at that little guy!"

"Hal told me he was my grandson! That just makes me all the more determined to see that Hal and Mari get a chance to be together. Yeah…I can see why Hal has stuck it out all this time. That's his kid and no one else should come between him and his son." Malone took the picture and put it in his desk. "After you make a new file on just Ed Baker…burn the rest." He handed it to Manny. "You and Snuffy will be delivering the file."

***

"Glad to see you're back. Every day, David has asked me if you are back yet. How's Vivian?" Mari served Hal a cup of coffee and from his forlorn expression decided to add a small plate of cookies.

"She's doing great." He picked up his cup, took a sip, and put it down with a sigh. "Mari…I need to ask a big favor of you. I have to go to SoCal for a few months…and I'll be tied up there for a while." He looked up at her. "Is there any way that you can bring David down to see me?"

The concern she felt was not just for David, because she had come to look forward to his visits, as well. He had a knack with David that kept the child on an even keel, while she just needed to see him. She sat across the table from him. "How long will you be gone?" Her voice was soft.

"At least a couple of months…probably more. Business is good and Arendt has to expand, and I have to be there to oversee the project. I don't want to be away from my son that long."

She could see his eyes moisten and she looked away, blinking. "While he's in school, it is out of the question…but, maybe in the summer when school is out…something can be arranged."

"I need to see him, Mari…he's all that I have."

"Those conference screens that you have in your office...can you set one up in David's room?"

"That's a great idea! Yeah...I can do that while he's in school...and perhaps I can get away to come up here once in a while...but I would really love to have him during the summer..."

"How? You will be working all day...and as nice as Lupe is...I don't think she is someone I would want to take care of my son..."

"Lupe is staying here to look after the house...her grandson is coming up to look after her while I'm gone. Would you let him stay with my mother for the summer? You can come down there more often than I can come up here."

Mari thought for a while. She had never had David out of her care. Putting him to bed each night, waking him in the morning, David was her life as well. "I don't know, Hal. He's never been away from home."

"That screen works both ways...I can set up another one at ma's house for you to see him every day...and you know you can stay there anytime. Please..."

"Alright...I have to talk to Ed...but I think it will be alright." She saw relief sweep over his face. "Hal, I want you to know that I think you are a wonderful father to David. I know it is hard for you...with David not knowing...but you have made the best of a bad situation...and I always want you to be in his life...you are a large part of his life. He looks up to you. There are times when I think that for him...the sun walks in with you...and departs when you leave."

"When can we let him know?"

"He's too young."

"That's not what I asked...what age would be appropriate?"

"When he's older and can understand..."

"You don't know...do you..." Hal reached over and took her hand. "I don't want to get into a pissing contest with you... especially when you bent over backward for me to be with David...but I can't help but think that you find it difficult because you are afraid of how he would look at you...and me...for the big cock-up surrounding how he came into this world. I don't think he would judge us harshly." He could feel her hand tremble in his.

"You're right...that is a part of it...but not the most important part. I can't imagine the trauma he would feel if he learned that Ed was not his father."

"I will leave that to you...you know best. But, in my opinion...I think the kid could take that news in stride."

***

A strong, padded envelope addressed to David arrived in the mail. It was from Hal. Mari put it on the table for David to open when she picked him up from school. She turned it around and looked at the familiar handwriting. Gently drawing her index finger across the writing, as though it could bring her nearer to him, she realized how much she missed him. Every evening, an hour before David's bedtime, he would come onto the screen and talk to him about the day's events. It was a hallowed interaction between him and his son that Mari rarely entered into. Sometimes she listened, out of camera range, but other than helping to set up, she did not interfere unless Hal specifically asked for her to come on screen. She got up, grabbed her keys, and went to pick up her son.

David quickly opened the sliding glass doors and headed straight for the envelope. He struggled to tear it open. Mari came in behind him, got the scissors, and helped him cut it open. "Oh...look! There's a letter for you...and a DVD!" She handed him the letter. "Can you read it to me?"

"Dear David. As promised, I am sending you this DVD so you can see why I am here and why I am so busy. I hope you can...what's this word...?"

"Appreciate."

"Appreciate what I am doing. One day, when you are older you will know why it is so very im...por...tant...important to me, and to you, that I do this work. This DVD was made for you, but the company was so im...pressed with it that they are using it to share with our stock...holders. I hope you like it. Kiss your mother and give Ed a handshake for me. Love, Hal."

"You read that very well." Mari ruffled his hair.

"Can we see the DVD now?"

"Sure, pumpkin. We'll sit on the floor at the coffee table and watch it while we have a snack. Mari split a sandwich between them and sat down to watch.

The video opened with an aerial shot of Arendt Medical facilities. Mari was shocked. She had never seen the company before and was

536

overwhelmed by the size and number of buildings it comprised. The employee parking lot was comparable to that of a popular supermarket. A smiling Hal came on the screen, dressed in a suit and tie, casually leaning against his desk. "Hello...my name is Hal Golan, CEO of Arendt Medical, the foremost trusted name in medical devices. I am also the fourth generation to head this company. Arendt Medical is growing, and we are expanding our facilities to encompass that growth. I want to show David just what we do here. Follow me..."

The next scene was of Hal in a hard hat and casual dress walking through the building showing the mechanized facilities. "We have state of the art equipment...and yet there is detail that can only be handled by skilled personnel..." Women in lab coats, gloves, and caps worked with mysterious machines. He continued through the buildings, showing the polishing, packing, and the automated warehouse where the devices were inventoried and stored. "Now...all of that is old news. What we are excited about is the expansion of Arendt...and I must admit...to the kid in me...this is fun. Follow me..."

Next Hal is seen at a construction site. He walked up to a heavy equipment operator that was gouging out part of the parking area asphalt. "Hi there...tell me your name."

The man in the backhoe loader shook his hand. "I'm Clark."

"There is a little boy named David who wants to know about the work you're doing."

"Hi, David...I am using what is called a backhoe loader to excavate the site...preparing it so we can begin construction."

"Do you mind showing me how?"

"Not at all...hop in the cab and hold on." He showed Hal how to operate the gears and levers to run the backhoe. "First we have to put the stabilizers in place..." He worked one gear and the stabilizers came down on each side and stretched out to the ground, securely supporting the backhoe. "...next we break up the asphalt...just catch the edge with the bucket and pull off the asphalt in slabs..." He operated two other levers to deftly maneuver the backhoe. "...and dump the asphalt into the truck to haul it off to the dump..."

"Hence the name 'dump' truck..."

"Riiight..." Clark worked through the maneuver again. "That's all there is to it. Now you try it."

"I thought you would never ask." Hal jumped behind the controls, as was rehearsed, and worked the equipment like an expert. He looked like he was having the time of his life tearing up the parking lot and dropping the load into a dump truck. The camera work speeded up the action.

"What comes next?"

"The next part will take a couple of days...we have to excavate a lot of soil out of here to make room for the basement and foundation of the building. Don't worry...I have a few friends to help me." A parade of three more backhoe loaders came into the picture. With the action speeded up, a couple of days were compacted into a couple of minutes.

He spent the next part of the video going from place to place on the construction site, explaining various skills for David, working the task, and getting his hands dirty. "When this new part of our facility is finished, we are looking forward to a substantial increase in profits as outlined in our prospectus. Of course, there is much more to be done...new equipment...new personnel...and we get the satisfaction of knowing that we are contributing to the economy by providing new jobs." The next scene showed Hal back in his office, in a suit, but still wearing the hardhat. "So, David, as CEO you have to be able to wear more than one hat...and you have to have a lot of respect for the people who work for you. We hope you enjoyed our little tour of a big company that's getting bigger." He signed off with a salute.

At the end of the DVD both Mari and David sat staring. They had not touched their sandwiches. "Well...what do you think?" Mari ventured.

"He didn't tell me he could drive a backhoe loader...I want to learn how."

"Perhaps you can ask him about it tonight."

Over dinner David chattered away about Hal operating a backhoe and that Ed had to see the DVD. "OK...after dinner I'll have a look." But Ed put it off until after David went to bed. He relaxed with a glass of wine in the living room and Mari suggested that he watch the video. He sat through half of it and then shut it off, took it out of the machine, and put it back in its cover. Still in his hand he shook it while looking for a place to put it away. Exasperated he threw it across the room. "He's just trying to stick it to me!"

538

Mari scrambled to retrieve the DVD. "Ed! What's the matter with you?"

He's just trying to shove it up my ass how rich he is. His big company...he's a big-time CEO...trying to play the working man's game. What an asshole!"

"Asshole? That's not like you! That's not like the Ed I know!" She chided him. "Why are you surprised? You knew he was rich...just where did you think his money came from?"

"No...he's flaunting it..."

"He was just trying to show David why he couldn't be here."

"And you...what you could have had..."

"You don't want to go there Ed..." Her voice was suddenly low. "I could have chosen him...he asked me to choose him...and I said 'no.' I told him I would not break up our home. Now all he wants is to have David in his life. He knew that he would have to be gone for a long time...so while David is still in school...he did the best he could in setting up that screen for him. However, when school is out...I suggested that he can spend some time with Vivian...and Hal can see him at her house."

"I have no say in that?"

"Yes...you have 'say in that' as long as you can come up with a reasonable argument why David can't see his bubbe." She calmed down. "Look, Ed...one day David is going to be the major shareholder in Arendt Medical...and most likely CEO. He may as well learn about it now. So far...he's only impressed with the backhoe."

"And you?"

"I admit it was a bit of a shock. I had never seen the company before. I didn't know it was so large. When I fell in love with him, I thought he just had a good job..." At the sight of Ed's head jerking back, she added. "I never hid the fact from you that I was in love with him from the beginning...for Christ's sake Ed...grow up! I chose you!"

"You needn't blaspheme."

***

The tires of the jet screeched as they touched down at LAX. As the plane taxied to the terminal, Mari started gathering her carry-on bag and looked over at her son. "We're here, pumpkin...start getting ready."

The excitement David felt at his first time flying had worn off as the endless lines and waiting dulled his anticipation of the flight. By the time they had boarded and taken the up-and-down hour-long flight, he had had enough. "How soon before we get to Bubbe's?"

"We are closer now than we were before...but it will be a little bit longer because we have to get our bags and rent a car..."

"That's just the pits!" He squirmed against his seatbelt.

"You've got that right...so buck up and get ready to tough it out!"

He balled up his fists and flexed his arms in his "Hulk" pose. "Grrrrrr!"

Once through the airport and into the rental car, Mari was on the freeway on her way to Beverly Hills. Passing the Getty Museum, which was somewhere up on the bluff, she made a mental note to try to see it while she was in town. On the surface streets, the nostalgia for, and resentment of, Los Angeles hit her. Familiar places were now foreign, the bustle and energy was garish and blaring, impressive buildings were edifices of penile corporate power. She loved and hated L.A.

As she turned into the driveway of the Golan homestead, with its picture-perfect landscape, the memory of her first sight of the mansion, and the misgivings she felt at the time, came flooding back to her. She slowed the car to a crawl as she almost drowned in the emotion, but she forced her feelings down to a little corner of her psyche where they belonged. She was now Mrs. Baker and the mother of her son who wanted to spend the summer with his bubbe. The monster of the past was held at bay and she swallowed her anxiety. As she pulled in front of the door, she turned to David who had fallen asleep. She reached over and stroked his hair. "We're here, pumpkin."

Vivian and Graham rushed through the door to greet them. "There's my little David." She had him out of the car and into her arms before the child was fully awake. Mari had no sooner opened the trunk than Graham with the short greeting of, "Good to see you again,

Madam," whisked the luggage away into the house. She went over and hugged Vivian. "Oh...I am so glad to finally get here...flying is such a hassle these days...even David got airport fatigue."

"Mari, darling...thank you so much for bringing him to me...and letting me have him for the summer..."

"I don't know if you'll be thanking me after a week or so...he is such a bundle of energy...I always have to chase him down."

"It will be a joy!"

***

Mari had turned in early the previous night as she surrendered David to the ultimate happiness of being with Bubbe and Graham. Shafts of light streamed through the small opening in the drapes letting Mari know that it was morning. She had been awake and had reached the decision to leave the very next day. Vivian had warmly received her, showed her the love that she always held for her, and tried to make her feel welcome, but there was nothing here for her but the past. She didn't want to sightsee, not even the Getty. She wanted to go home. Tossing over again in her bed, she wished she hadn't been given the same guest room as before. The memory of Hal stealing into her room and slipping into her bed was both exciting and upsetting.

She turned over again. She heard the telephone ring and someone downstairs answer it. Checking her cell phone, she saw it was past nine o'clock. Reluctantly she threw back the covers and got up to face the day.

Taking a quick shower, dabbing some makeup on her face, and blow-drying her curls into submission, Mari dressed casually in a pullover sweater and jeans and then went downstairs in search of a cup of coffee. Finding the coffee pot on the sideboard, she poured the last cup and went to the window to see Vivian and Graham in the garden with David. She had him mesmerized by a patch of soil of his own to grow his garden. They caught sight of her and waved and she lifted her cup in response. Vivian took off her gardening gloves and headed for the house, leaving Graham to teach David the art of transplanting.

Vivian was flushed by the time she came into the house. "Oh, my little David is such a delight. He is so bright...you explain something once and he's got it...and so enthusiastic too." She looked at the near empty coffee pot. "Come to the kitchen, dear...this house is too large...I just rattle around in it...I find the kitchen is better. I'll make another pot of coffee and we can sit down, have a nosh, and chat...I haven't had a chance to chat with you for any length of time since you've been here. I want to know how you are doing...and all of that girl talk..."

Mari smiled and followed her. "There's not much to talk about on my end. Life is pretty simple around our house..." She took a seat at the kitchen table.

Vivian filled the coffee maker from a water cooler and started counting out scoops. At the questioning look from her housekeeper, she wrote a note that said, "Ve a ver una pelicula" and handed it to her. "I want you to go shopping...this is what I want you to buy...the money is in the vestibule by the telephone." Delighted to be paid to take the afternoon off, at the movies, she was out the door before Vivian finished counting out scoops into the coffee maker. "She is such a dear...I don't know what I would do without her." Vivian sat down at the table.

Mari shrugged. "I wouldn't know what I would do with her...I've never had a maid."

"Dear...this house is so unwieldy...if I ever want to have any free time at all...having housekeepers and a butler to run things is a necessity."

Mari nodded that she understood, but she really didn't.

"So how are things going with you?"

Mari shook her head. "The weather has not been playing along so far...we've had very bad conditions. We had twenty days of frost in April and it looks like the crop will be smaller this year. We're hoping for a good summer..."

"No dear...how are things with you..."

"Oh...pretty much the same..."

"You know...my Hal called this morning. He said he didn't know you would be staying here. He planned to take David to Disneyland and thought it would be nice if you would come along." Her hope faded at the expression on Mari's face.

"That is very generous of him...but I don't think it is a good idea..."

"Why not, dear? You both would be with David and you will have a lovely time...seeing him discover it for the first time."

"I don't think it would be a good idea for me to be with Hal without my husband…"

"Oooohh…" Vivian winced. "But…no one can say it was anything more than an innocent day with your son…" Seeing her discomfort at the subject she decided to drop it and dig deeper for how Mari felt. "Mari, can we talk…I mean woman to woman…a heart to heart talk?"

"I guess so…sure…as long as it stays just between us."

"Your husband…Ed…what is he like? I don't mean what he says or what he does…but what is he like on the inside…if you scratch the surface…what do you find?"

Mari sat in thought for a moment. "If you scratch Ed…you will find an archangel…"

"And if you scratched deeper?"

"You will find more archangel…he is uncomplicated…he's good…he's kind…dutiful…and loving in his own way…especially with David…he really loves David. Although sickeningly Christian…he at least tries to live his religion…"

"He does not sound like the type of man who would be very repressive."

"Ordinarily, he's not…but of late…" She made a face. "…he has been showing signs of jealousy. Therefore, I don't push it…"

"Jealousy? Of what?"

"It's really all in his head. But I guess it is the way David looks up to Hal. There is a natural attraction there. Of course, it's always an exciting time when Hal is with him."

"And you…is he jealous of you?"

"I've never given him a reason to be."

The coffee maker beeped, and Vivian got up to pour a cup. Reaching for a basket of muffins, she absentmindedly threw a question over her shoulder. "And my Hal…how do you see him?" She walked back to study Mari's expression, as she sat down.

"Do you mean if I scratch the surface of Hal?"

"Yes."

Her face brightened. "If you scratch the surface of Hal…hmmm…" She pondered for a moment. "…you will find pistachio ice cream…delicious…fun…and nutty!" Then she became serious and her blue eyes turned a darker shade and distant. She looked as though she was searching for words. "But if you go deeper…behind those wonderful dark eyes, there is a passion that is molten lava and earthquakes...it shakes you to your core...makes you feel desired...beloved...and before he is through you are completed...sated...and he leaves you breathless."

Vivian sat back and took a sip of her coffee to hide her amazement. *Is this what the poor girl has been hiding all of these years? They will never be done with each other.* "That is quite a description of my son."

"Vivian...your son is quite a man...and if he was in Ed's shoes...he would not like for me to go out with another man without him being there. It's not that he doesn't trust me...or at least I don't think it is..." She stopped. "Listen to me go on...I was talking about how it used to be...back then I was subsumed by him...unreservedly his. Of course, it's nothing like that now...I don't know what Hal is like now...I have no idea what I would find..." She was visibly upset.

"I didn't mean to upset you, dear..."

"No...I'm not upset..." She lied. Pausing, she wrestled with herself and then put her fingers to her lips removing her fingers between words. "Vivian...you are the only person I have that I can talk to honestly...and yet I did it again...I verbally ran away and hid in the bushes. It's not true that I don't know what Hal is like now." She clasped her hands and looked to her for understanding. "It's so hard because you're Hal's mother...but I feel very close to you...I love you as though you were my own. Yes, Hal made a mistake...but I feel as though I am compounding it. He has done everything to try to right what he did...he saved my life, for God's sake...and I can't give him what he wants...I am at a loss to know what I should do..."

"He saved your life?!"

Mari nodded "Yes."

Vivian was awe struck. "How?"

Mari told Vivian of the incident on the stairway down the cliff. "After we were safe, we were all over each other...I mean we didn't...we didn't...you know..." She looked down. "...but we came so close to dying it was like...why aren't we living? I was so emotional I said things to him I shouldn't have said...and it made him think that we could be together. The next time we saw each other...I don't know...I came to my senses and told him I couldn't leave Ed."

"Oh my *God!* Mari...are you sure you didn't make a mistake?"

"No...that's just it. I'm not sure. I am trying to do what everyone says you're supposed to do...but sometimes it doesn't feel right. That's why it is so difficult for me to be around Hal...and yet, when I don't see him...I...I..." She threw up her hands.

Vivian sat quietly while trying to mentally put herself in Mari's place. *What is it that keeps her from doing what she appears to desire?* She decided not to push the issue for now and changed the subject. "May I ask you another question?" She did not wait for her response. "My Hal...he said that you never forgave him...is that true?"

Mari knitted her brow. "That was years ago...it was hard at first. But now...of course I forgive him. What can it matter now?"

"It matters a great deal to him. Mari, I said I would talk from the heart. My son is so very unhappy, and he cannot come to terms with what he did...it would mean so much to him if you would at least tell him that you have forgiven him..."

"I will have to write to him...because I don't think I will be able to say it in person. That can get maudlin and messy."

"As you wish. When he comes back home...could you have your letter waiting for him?"

"Yes."

"Would you consider asking Ed if you can go to Disneyland?"

"Absolutely not. Vivian...it's not easy for me to be around Hal...I do what I must...but I can't do more."

"I understand, dear...I understand."

***

From her bedroom window, Mari could see Hal's Benz come up the driveway. She had changed her mind and was dressed to go to the Getty Museum. She thought she should stay in her room until after Hal picked up David and left. *Don't be such a coward...hiding in my room...and not even having the nerve to see my son off.* She thought. *I should at least go downstairs and kiss my son before he leaves.*

Everyone was downstairs finishing breakfast by the time Mari entered the dining room. "Good morning..." she brightly chirped and went to the sideboard to act as though she was selecting what she wanted to eat.

545

Hal stood off to one side. "Good morning, Mari...you look lovely...did you decide to spend the day with us after all?" Hal felt her gaze sweep over him and then she turned back to the buffet.

"No...I thought I would take in the museum..."

"Well that's just the pits!" David barked out. "You're not coming to Disneyland with us?" Frowning, he got out of his chair and went over to confront her. "Why won't you come to Disneyland with me?"

She looked down at her son and then up at Hal, standing a few feet behind him, and then back at her son. *Amazing...their expressions are almost identical.* "I thought you would want to spend the day...you know...just you two guys. Besides...with all the lines and all the rides...it would be hard for me..."

"You're always telling me that sometimes you have to tough things out...I tough things out for you all the time..."

Mari's mouth flew open as she looked at her little man. She broke out into a smile. "Well when you put it that way...all I can say is 'grrrrrr'...I'll tough it out..."

Hal looked up and away, barely able to conceal his pride. *That's my boy! That's my boy!*

***

"Main Street is a replica of how things were in the late nineteenth and early twentieth centuries. People were still using horse drawn wagons and carriages...but the reason cars looked so different back then is that they were fairly new inventions at the time...and the design was still based upon carriages. They had yet to learn about aerodynamics...that is just a big word for how air flows over a moving object...the sleeker the object the faster it can move through air. Electricity was new, motion pictures, the light bulb, the telephone...it was a world full of new possibilities..." Mari explained to David as they walked down the entrance to the rest of the park.

Hal listened intently. He had only seen Mari interact with David at her home, around the dinner table, or in the yard. He had never had such a personal view of their mother-son relationship. *She's a marvelous mother. No wonder the kid is so smart!*

While waiting in line for the Pirates of the Caribbean, Mari entertained them with the historical aspect. "The heyday of pirates was the seventeenth and eighteenth centuries. By that time...shipping the wealth extracted from the New World to

Europe...had been established...and the flow of traffic across the Atlantic was extensive. During those days...if you were not rich...life was very harsh, indeed. In order to live well...sometimes young men would take to the sea to make a dishonest living...by preying on ships...and capturing the goods they carried...called booty...or they would pillage towns and take everything. Ordinarily, they were hunted down and...if caught...hanged. However, some monarchs found their skills useful...and would give them special permission called 'letters of mark' to steal from their enemies. Now we romanticize their daring...their intrepidity...but for the most part...they weren't very nice."

She continued on with each ride, the exploration of Africa for the Jungle Ride, the American Indians, the importance of the river boats, until David finally asked, "How do you know so much about everything?"

She shot a look at Hal. "I have a master's degree in history." She smiled at her son. "And you will have a master's or a doctorate one day...it is inevitable..."

Taking a break after Frontierland, Hal decided the food was much better at the hotel, and they took the monorail to go to lunch. David was an observant child. He noticed how Hal was solicitous of Mari. He assisted her into every ride. He opened doors for her and now, at the restaurant, he held her chair. After she excused herself to go to the restroom, David leaned on his elbow and looked at Hal. "Why do you always open mommy's door...or hold out your hand for her to get off a ride...or pick her up out of the boats?"

"Because that is what a gentleman does when he is with a lady. He makes sure she doesn't fall and that she is comfortable. It shows her respect."

David wrinkled his nose. "Nobody else does it..."

"You will find that there are a lot of people who are not trained to have good manners...but some are...and that speaks volumes about them...it shows they care."

"Can I open doors for my mother and help her with rides? I respect her too...I love her. Did you know she is the prettiest mommy in my whole school?"

"I believe you...your mommy is beautiful."

"Do you love my mommy too?"

Hal was taken aback by the question. "Why do you ask me that...?"

"I don't know...sometimes I think you do. I think you wanted her to come with us today...like I did."

"David...there are all kinds of love...like I love you...I love my friends...I love my mother...and I love Mari."

David furrowed his brow. "I don't knoooow. There is a man over there who loves her too."

"How can you tell that?"

"When we came in, he stared at her like this..." David imitated the man gawking. "Sometimes I see you look at her like that too."

"OK...can you keep a secret?"

"Yeah."

"I love your mommy...but don't tell anybody..." Hal made a zipping motion across his lips. "...especially your mommy...she would be mad at me."

"OK." David whispered, "It's our secret."

Hal looked around the restaurant to see 'gawking man' and sure enough as Mari returned to the table his eyes hungered after her. *Goddamn my boy is smart!* He looked on with delight as David got up and held Mari's chair.

When the day was through, David slept in the back seat of the car with a hat of mouse ears on his head, surrounded by bags of toys, children's books, and goodies. Mari kicked off her shoes into the front passenger foot well and lowered the back of her seat. Hal guided the Benz up the Santa Ana Freeway. "Mari...I have to tell you something...our kid is even smarter than we know..."

"Shhhh...he may not be asleep..."

"He's tuckered out...he's asleep alright..." Hal adjusted the rearview mirror to take a look at the boy and saw he was sleeping soundly. He adjusted it back and continued. "He asked me if I love you...the kid has a sixth sense for bullshit...so I told him yes..."

"You told him 'yes'...how could you do that?" Her whisper was harsh.

"He acted like anyone who knew you should love you...he even thought the guy in the restaurant who stared at you...was in love with you...and I can't say he was wrong...he even said I looked at you the same way...and I will have to be more careful...but I can't say he was wrong."

Mari put her seat up, trying not to lose it. "Tell me everything...word for word what was said." Hal gave her a tight run down of David's conversation. "The kid is phenomenal..."

"I think you handled it the best way you could..."

"I'm glad you approve...I was worried I might have screwed up. You know...you are really a great mother...the best. I'm grateful to you."

"He's the best...the best kid in the world. I was looking at his little face this morning when he got up in my grille...I looked at him...and saw a younger version of you."

Hal laughed. "You should have seen *your* face..." He settled into his own thoughts for a while and then said, "Today was nice, Mari...it was a gift. This is how it should have been with us as a family...thank you for giving it to me. It gives me something to hold on to..."

Out of the corner of his eye he could see her staring at him intently. "Yes...this is how it should have been...with us as a family..." She said softly.

For miles they drove in silence. Impulsively, when he took the off-ramp at Robertson and turned north, he looked for a parking spot. Mari gave him a questioning look but said nothing. He parked on a side street and turned to her. "Mari, will you ever forgive me? I live with this turbulence...inside of me...a guilt that never leaves me...knowing what I did to you...and all the while you were perfectly innocent. Being fooled is no excuse...and I...I..."

She looked straight ahead. "I forgave you years ago...when I saw how you were with David...the depth of your heartbreak hit me. I opened that briefcase you left and re-read that damnable folder and asked myself what I would have done if someone I trusted gave me documented proof that you were...false in your intentions...unfaithful...or something similar. I like to think that I would have been smarter...better...that I would have had faith in you...or at least not break off our engagement unless I could independently verify the accusations.

"But I know I probably would have done the same thing. You see...I was always so jealous of your love...back then...I guess you would call it 'possessive'..." She looked down at her hands in her lap. "...I probably would have gone nuts if I believed you didn't love me...in fact I did go nuts when you told me you didn't love me." She turned to him with brimming eyes. "The thought entered my mind...I was convinced...that you made up a reason to get rid of me...so you wouldn't lose your father's inheritance...or you were tired of me...I didn't know what to think..."

"No, Mari...never..."

She looked down again. "At some point I realized that you did not do that to me...you did it to the woman in that file. Anyway, in my heart I forgave you long ago. I told your mother the other day and she said I should tell you. I was going to write you because I thought it would be too hard to say it..." She took a deep breath. "But now you know."

He swallowed hard, absorbing what she said, and stared through the windshield at nothing. "Mari...how much longer do we have to live this charade?"

"I'm far too tired to answer that question wisely."

He started the car. "Someday you are going to have to answer that question...if not for me...for yourself." Pulling out into the dark street, he took the long way to his mother's home.

***

"Where is Mari?" Hal had come to pick up David for a day at the beach and hoped he could persuade Mari to come with them. When she said she enjoyed their time together as a family; he wanted to share another day with her.

"She went back home."

"Did she say why?"

"Not really...she made up an excuse...but I think I can guess." Vivian paused for a moment. "Do not ever tell Mari that I betrayed her confidence...but I don't think she has ever gotten you out of her system..."

"Why do you think that?" he listened intently.

"It was something she said...oh my poor Mari...please forgive me for telling...she said you were like molten lava and earthquakes..."

"What is that? Now I'm like shake and bake? I never know what she's talking about..."

"No...it was the most passionate description I ever heard in my life." Vivian went on to repeat Mari's characterization of him. "Can you imagine...she went on to say you left her breathless. She did say that she was referring to how it used to be with you and that she did

550

not know what you are like now...but then she really came clean and poured her heart out. I won't say anything more than that she told me how you saved her life. Why didn't you tell me?"

"Everything turned out OK...so there was no need to worry you." He frowned. "What else did she say about that?"

"I'm not going to totally betray her confidence...but I will say this...I don't think she has forgotten...or could ever forget...what was between you. I am thinking that there is more between you...even more than she said. Imagine, molten lava and earthquakes..." She saw a smile creep over his face. "Don't look so smug...she is still determined to have nothing to do with you. Besides...she also described you as pistachio ice cream..."

"Did she also happen to mention a chimichanga?"

***

LOS AMIGOS

Dan walked into his old college hang out in Westwood. He was struck, and surprised, by how young the students were who congregated there. *I haven't been out of college that long...but now I feel like an old timer.* He looked around the noisy room and saw that his buddies, from his college days, had settled in at a far booth, chowing down on burgers and beer. He waved and walked toward them. "Hey...ameeegos!" He feigned a Spanish accent as they used to do, to show they were the "cool" college kids. "Como eeestaah? Que paassaah?"

"Hey...fuckin' Dan!" Two of the four guys there, got up to greet him, pounding him on the back and doing mock fisticuffs, before they sat down and made room for him. "How the hell are you? I couldn't believe it was you on the phone when you called." John grinned.

"Yeah. We haven't heard much from you since you graduated..."

Dan stretched out in his seat with an air of confidence. "You know how it is in L.A....I've been working hard...making lots of geetus...my job takes me all over the place. It does not leave time for much of a social life."

"You said you had an interesting proposition for us."

"Yeah...I heard you guys have had it pretty hard. None of you married the girl of your dreams. None of those wonderful jobs materialized when school was over. Now you are up to your necks in student loans...a debt you can't get rid of."

"You have job openings where you work?"

"No...but I do have all the pussy I can handle..." He gave them a knowing look and then he lowered his voice. "...even better...I have access to confidential information...that we could use to our advantage. We could make a couple of mil or more...easy...but it will take brass balls to do it."

"Why do I have the feeling that your proposition is not exactly on the up and up?" John muttered.

"Nothing that gets that kind of money is ever on the up and up...but, hey...*my* tuition is paid and I'm living large..." Dan rubbed his hands together. "...but if you're not interested..."

"Hey...I never said that..." John turned to the others. "...did I say that guys?"

"Naw...he never said that..."

"I brought this to you because you guys used to be awesome...we used to pull some pretty outrageous pranks...and got away with it...for no money...not a dollar sign in sight. We could have done some serious time if we had been caught. Compared to what we've done...this is easy."

"Yeah...like when we took that fat girl to the woods and lined up on her..."

"Shit...I think Mickey fell in love with her."

"Shut up!"

"Well...before I tell you my proposition...I have to know if you guys are up for it or not. It's not legal...but it is a one-shot deal. We get the money and get out..."

"What are you talking...a bank robbery?"

"Banks don't have the kind of money he's talking about."

"If it was a bank robbery...would you be up for it?"

The four guys looked at each other and then leaned in to look at Dan. "I would have to hear the plan...first." John spoke for the group.

"What if I told you that I had already staked out the bank...worked out the timing...and it was a guaranteed getaway?"

"How much time is involved if we get caught?"

"Considerable...but you're not going to get caught. There are no guards...there are no police...and as a matter of fact...there is no bank. There is just a secluded house...on a beach...owned by a man who is exceedingly rich...who has a little boy...and would pay millions to get him back. I have been keeping him under surveillance and right now he is in town...but the family routine is up in the air...and with LAPD and the FBI being what they are here...the odds are against us. But when he returns to his home in a tiny town in Sonoma County...it's a piece of cake. All we have to do is to pick up on the family routine for when the boy stays with him."

"Oh, fuck! Oh, fuck...you're talking a kidnaping! Oh...fuck me!"

"Stop your bellyaching. Most of those go off without a hitch. It's like taking candy from a baby. I would say he was good for at least five million...that's a million apiece...well worth the minimal risks involved."

"I don't know...I would have to hear your plan..."

"Bingo! Once you see what's involved...you would be fools not to jump at it."

A waitress came over to take his order. "What are you having?"

"A beer...a burger...and a side order of your sweet ass." He grabbed her bottom. She walked away, red-faced. "You see...nobody ever says anything or does anything...you can get away with almost anything...especially in the hayseed town I'm talking about. We have to go someplace private...where I can lay out my plans. If it's a slam dunk...are you on board?"

They all looked at each other, but they didn't say "no."

***

A PRIOR ENGAGEMENT

Enduring the late August heat wave, Mari dressed in white shorts with her blouse tied to bare her midriff. Standing at the kitchen counter, she was chopping carrots when there was a rap at the glass sliding doors and she looked up to see Hal waiting outside in the patio. "Come on in...it's open" she shouted.

"Hi, kiddo...is David here?"

"No...he went with Ed on a day trip...with the church you know..." Mari gave a resigned shrug of her shoulders. "...they won't be back until this evening."

"Oh...that's too bad. I was hoping to see him before I go to 'Frisco. I won't be able to attend Ed's Labor Day barbeque because I have a prior engagement."

"That's not like you...what are you doing?" She absently asked.

"I have a standing arrangement to meet a lady friend...that's sort of difficult to cancel..."

Mari's face instantly turned dark as she concentrated on chopping the carrots. "Oh...I didn't know...she must be important to you..."

"She's alright...she's a nice widow lady..."

"Does she love you?" She continued to look at the carrots, but her chopping became more deliberate.

"No...it's not like that. She doesn't love me, and I don't love her. We're just friends...convenient...accessible to each other... that's all." From the expression on her face, he added, "You didn't think I was living like a monk, did you?"

"I didn't think anything...I don't have the right to think anything..." Chop—chop—chop. "I don't have the right..." She whispered more for herself than for him.

"Aw, Mari...I shouldn't have said anything. I didn't know you would feel *that* way about it."

"I don't have the right to feel anything about it...but you are kidding yourself if you think she doesn't love you..."

"Look...she's still in love with her late husband..."

"...and as soon as she went to bed with you...she forgot all about her 'late husband' and fell hard for you. Remember who you're talking to...I should know..."

"What are you saying?"

"I'm saying that your whore is in love with you..."

"Are you…are you jealous? You shouldn't call her a whore."

"Maybe I am…no…I understand." Her voice gave an involuntary shudder. "It's just that you once showed me that perfect happiness can be achieved in life…and then you took it all away…and now this woman has what I once had." She bit her lip. "Oh…just go to hell."

He thought he could see tears and he walked over and took the knife out of her hand. Mari, I'm already in hell…don't you know that? I don't nearly have with her what we used to have…not even close. You were it for me. For years I've asked you to choose me…and you wouldn't…and now you're angry with me?"

"No…I'm not angry at you…I am angry at my life. I made a promise to Ed…I vowed to exchange the rest of my life for my son's life. At the time I had given up on happiness and my future looked very empty. All I wanted was to have my baby…and it seemed like a good solution…the only option I had. I never dreamed you would search for me and come back into my life." She stared straight ahead. "For years I have racked my brain to see if there was anything I could have done differently…" She shook her head. "…and now I'm trapped."

He drew closer. "You don't have to be…" She backed away. "Mari…why won't you let me near you?"

"Because every time I'm near you it makes it harder for me…frightening. I've tried everything…I've tried to make it stop…"

"Frightening? What are you afraid of…of me?"

"No…I can't say it…I can't say it out loud…" Her voice trembled.

"What? What is it? You can tell me…"

"I still love you, Hal. I don't know how to make it stop. There isn't a day that goes by…." She choked back tears and went to him, and wept openly on his chest.

"Oh, Babe…" He enfolded her. "I don't want you to ever make it stop." His lips found hers and she wildly responded. He lifted her to him and, turning, turning, turning, they moved past the divide into the living room descending to the floor. "I waited so long to hear you say you love me again." He hoarsely whispered. She touched his face and gazed into his eyes. "I never stopped loving you." She exhilarated under the physicality of him and urgently sought out his lips once more. Pulling up his shirt, her hands slipped underneath and ran over his bare back and he could feel her trembling. As he explored her silken skin, she moaned and writhed with pleasure beneath him;

his emotions soared as he felt himself overcome. He wanted her—right there and right then.

"Oh, no...I have to stop. I can't do this!" She pulled away from him.

"Mari...please don't stop me...God, Mari...please..."

"I have to...in another minute I would have been fucking you on the living room floor..."

"Wasn't that the idea?" He rolled over on his back in frustration.

"In my husband's house?"

"Why are you doing this to me?"

"I can't destroy everything David loves. I can't do this..." She sat up, put her arms over her stomach, and bent forward. "Oh God...what was I thinking...I'm sorry...I can't do this!"

He sat up, leaning his back on the couch, and stared up at the ceiling. "Not nearly as sorry as I am..." He put his hand to his forehead. "...what are you playing at, Mari...what are you doing this to me for?"

"Hal, I can't have an affair with you...these things always have a way of being found out...and it would destroy my marriage and David's home. I can't just think of me."

"Then why did you start this..."

"I...I wanted you so badly...I didn't think. I'm sorry I called your lady friend a whore...it seems that it is something we have in common. You have a special knack for making me your whore, as well."

"Are you blaming *me* for this...?" He held out his hand. "What did you think would happen when you cut off all possibility of our sharing a life together? I'm a man, Mari...not a saint."

"No...no...I'm sorry...I blame myself." She got up. "I behaved badly...I said things I shouldn't have said..."

He got up. His erection was still evident. "No shit!"

"Please don't be angry..."

"Oh...I'm pissed at you alright...but I just want to know one thing...did you mean what you said at all about still being in love with me?"

Under the glare of his justified rebuke, she turned her face away. "Yes." She whispered. "But that doesn't change anything."

He narrowed his eyes on her. "What did you want...to punish me?"

557

"Punish *you?*" Hot tears sprung to her eyes. "There are times when I think I would sell my soul to wake up in your arms once more...and I would gladly dance to the Devil's tune to make that happen...and that would be fine...if it was just me. But I will not trade one day of my son's happiness for it!"

He stared at her for a while and then pointed his finger at her. He started to say something and then changed his mind. "I gotta go."

***

"Deuce...I'm going nuts up here. Talk me down off the ceiling. I don't know what to fucking do!" Hal paced around his bedroom as he spoke to Deuce on the phone. "She was all over me...telling me that she still loved me...her hands were all over me...I was on the verge...I mean like...oh man...I was about to unzip...and then she freezes up on me!"

"Aw...she's just scared. She's been so tightly wrapped all these years to keep herself sane. Then you went and told her you had another woman...she just snapped...that's all. She doesn't want to risk her son's happiness over an affair...and that's all she sees that you have in store for her."

"I thought she wouldn't care about Beth. After all, she said she wouldn't leave Ed. She had to have figured it out..."

"No man...that's not the way women think...I bet on some level she thought you were cheatin' on her even though you haven't been together in years. It's not logical...it's purely emotional."

"Yeah...it did sort of sound like that..." Hal paused. "...doesn't she know that I would do anything for her...anything she wants...all she has to do is..."

"Ask? Hal...she ain't goin' to ask you for nothin'. What have you told her? What have you said to her in the last four years to make her believe that you want to do more than just bang her? If you haven't said anything...she took a big risk."

"She knows I want to marry her...spend my life with her. I gave her enough money to be independent. You would think that she would have left her husband...for me...but no. She said she wouldn't. I asked her to choose me...and she wouldn't do it. What do I do now?"

"Hell if I know. Did she give you a reason?"

"She says she thinks that David would be traumatized by the truth. But I don't think so. Now I think *she* is using it as an excuse not to face the truth…"

"You may be on to something there. Have you asked a specialist…some kind of child psychiatrist?"

"No."

"I think you ought to get an expert that she would listen to. That way she has to recognize what needs to be done…I agree with you that the kid can handle it. There again, she could be hiding behind that because she still loves you…even after what you did to her…it frightens her…and she's not quite ready to trust you. Why don't you try talking to her again? Let her know that neither of you can go on this way. Talk some sense to her."

"I don't think she'll see me alone anymore. Can you help me out…she'll talk to you…?"

"Who do you think I am…your 'Al Cowlings'?"

"Yeah."

"OK…if she agrees to see me…I'll fly up and talk with her…but you owe me big time."

***

Ed was gently snoring while Mari lay awake in bed beside him. She could not tear her mind away from the close call she had with Hal. Hungering for the feel of him, his touch, was almost more than she could bear. But her son was soundly and safely sleeping in his bed among his toys, pictures, and keepsakes and he was happy. The man beside her was responsible for his home and that happiness. She saw her future stretch out before her, long, bleak, uneventful, and passionless. Her spontaneous break out from her prison was for naught.

***

THE UNDETECTED

Labor Day was ordinarily a tedious bore for Mari. Ed insisted that they host a barbeque for his closest friends, all of whom were church members. The wives were mind-numbing chatterers, who would normally only tolerate her out of Christian charity. Flaunting their piety and engaging in the not so subtle game of competitive godliness, they usually condescended to proselytizing her, sensing that she was not sufficiently devout. Resenting her beauty, and the way she unwittingly grabbed their husbands' attention, they popularized the notion that she was unchristian, a pagan baby, not one of them. Still, they had to be polite, for Ed's sake; he was truly a man of the Lord.

Her only solace was in the González family, who lived and worked on the estate. They helped her host the barbeque, added to the festivities with games and music, and lent a hand in preparing the food. Their children played well with David, keeping the house filled with laughter. Moreover, their conversational topics were wide ranging and interesting. However, today she was grateful for the distraction of keeping busy, knowing that Hal was fucking some other woman. It drove her to tears in the few spare moments she was alone.

This year a new church member attended. He had transferred from back east to a company in Santa Rosa. A corpulent man, with a good-natured face and an easy smile, he had an enthusiasm for life that was infectious. His wife was prettier than one would expect, but she receded into the background of his ebullient personality. Ed had immediately taken a liking to him, inviting him to the barbeque. The new guy joked, "Don't worry about us having the same first names, Ed...my friends call me Fatso!"

"Isn't that a bit rude?" Ed was taken aback.

"Naahh! They were just calling it as they see it...just a bit of friendly ribbing...if they could find my ribs in here...hahaahhh...!" He laughed as he patted his sides. "...no sense in running from it...if I could run...so Fatso it is!"

"Well...if you don't mind, Fatso." Ed laughed with him. When the food was served, the praying began in earnest. As the long grace ended with an "Amen" someone continued to add his comparatively short-winded fillip to the prayer and an additional "Amen." Mari could not believe that yet another person had more to say and gave what she hoped was the final "Amen" and everyone paused to make sure that there was a consensus that the Lord was adequately thanked and praised and then broke the silence as they passed around the food in organized chaos.

"Harvest is going to be early this year...the Brix is already at twenty-one...that means that we harvest in ten days..." Ed pointed at Joel. "...that's plenty of time to go fishing next week!"

"Hey, Fatso...do you like to fish?" Joel sat across the table from Fatso. "We're planning a trip next weekend...just us guys. We thought you might want to come along."

"Fishing? I love to fish. I even learned to fly fish after I saw that movie...and now some consider me an expert. Yeah...something about fishing gets under your skin. Our Lord and Savior Jesus was a fisherman."

"Then you'll be coming with us?"

"Sure will. Where do we get together?"

"We all meet here at Ed's at four o'clock...Saturday morning. He lives closest to where we will be camping on the Russian River...then we camp out that night and then we are back here by Sunday night...

"We miss church services?"

"We hold our prayer meeting on Sunday afternoon...and Ed leads us in some hymns..."

"Where are we going...to a state park...a camp site...?"

"No...we have our favorite fishing hole...about a mile and a half from the road. We set up our tent and make a campfire at night. You will need a sleeping bag...and you will have to bring your own possibles..."

"Possibles?"

"Yeah...you know...besides your fishing tackle...your personal camping equipment..."

"Oh...right..."

"It's going to be great having you along..." Before Joel left the party, he drew Fatso aside. "It's OK to bring some beer...without the ladies present...we don't mind having a bottle or two around the campfire."

"Well, you are going to be glad you told me! I have a specialty beer...a custom-made brew that I brought with me from back east. I can't get any more of it…but, I couldn't think of a nicer bunch of guys to share it with. I'll bring it a long."

***

Hal came by on his usual mid-week visit. He carried a box with him and set it on the table. Mari was reserved, but she couldn't control her curiosity. "What's in the box?"

"Well…hello and how are you?" He mocked her lack of manners. "OK…I'll stop being a smart ass. It's something I got for David."

"You bought it in San Francisco?"

"As a matter of fact, I did." She gave him a forsaken look, as the corners of her mouth contracted into a pout but said nothing as she turned and busied herself in the kitchen. He felt like a heel for letting her assume the reason for his trip was to get laid, but it was the only way he got a reaction out of her. "Look…I know I messed up the last time I was here. It was all my fault…I should have just listened to you instead of taking advantage of you when you were vulnerable. I shouldn't have gotten angry with you because I wanted you too. You were right…there is more than just the two of us to consider. I will try to keep that in mind." He couldn't bring himself to say "I'm sorry" because he wasn't. He watched her as she moved about the kitchen, bending over to check the oven. *If you think I'm going to give up on you now that you said you love me…you're wrong!*

Now her look was accusatory. "So, what's in the box?"

"Fuck the box…Mari I can't get what happened out of my head…if you can see your way clear at the first opportunity…I need to talk to you alone."

"If you think I am going to be alone with you…you're crazy!"

He held out his hands. "You're alone with me now…"

"Ed just went to pick up David from school…he'll be back any minute."

"OK…look. I cancelled my appointment on Labor Day…but I did go to 'Frisco for another reason. I thought I could use some expert advice…and I want to talk to you about David."

Her look changed to defiant. "What about David?"

"I went to talk to an expert…in child development…and psychology…the best in the business. I went to talk about our situation to get an opinion. She wanted to at least get to see David in order to make an evaluation. She would want to see you as well, if

562

possible...and Ed too. I want to know if we are on the right track with David in not telling him who I am. He's going to know...sooner or later. I just want to know when the time is right. Do I have your permission to take him to see her?"

"No."

"No? Why not?"

"Do you think that you are just going to cut Ed out of his life?"

"I didn't say that...and no...I don't. I just want to know what age is appropriate to tell him I'm his father. Is it now...is it in his teens...for God's sake is it in his thirties?? I think you would say 'never.' This part of it is not about us...it's about David and what is right for him."

"What is this leading up to, Hal?"

"What do you mean by 'leading up to'? If nothing more comes of it...at least he will know he's my son...my heir...and I'm not some stranger that walked in off the street and took a liking to him."

The sliding door opened, and Ed walked in and he saw the expression on Mari's face. "What's going on here?"

David soon followed behind him. "Hal...I missed you!"

"Did you, buckaroo? I missed you too. But look...I got something special for you...for your room."

"That's a big box! What's in it?"

"Well let's open it and see." Hal took out the pen knife attached to his keys and slit the tape, opening the present.

"Oohhh...it's a sailing ship! Can I put it in water?" David hopped up and down with delight.

The replica was made of wood with cloth sails and strung with rigging. "No...I don't think so. This is just a model so you can see what the old ships looked like...and name the parts. There is a book to go with it. The ship is the USS Constitution and she is the oldest commissioned ship in the U.S. Navy. This book explains everything about it." Hal sat down and put David on his lap to read some of the information that came with the model. From the top to the bottom, Hal pointed out each feature of the ship and what it was for. "Look at this...there is a cut-a-way picture at the back of the book showing what the inside is like. Now close your eyes and imagine...being on the vast ocean with nothing to be seen but water in all directions...where your life depends on this splendid ship. You can feel the roll of the ship beneath your feet as you sail over the waves…and the wind blowing in your face that fills the sails. Can you see it?"

"Yes…"

"Do you see any dolphins?"

"Yes…now I do."

"Do you see a whale on the horizon?"

"Yes…yes…"

"Do you see an elephant?"

"Noooo…" David broke into laughter.

"Come on…let's take this to your room and we will find a place to put it." Hal carried the ship and they went up the stairs.

Watching Hal with David was always very affecting for Mari. She looked at Ed and could not help comparing him with Hal in her mind. Ed was a good, dutiful father to David, solid and reliable. But to her point of view, Hal was superb. *But would he always be there for me? And why is he trying to force the issue about telling David? Does he think that I will leave Ed if David knows? Or perhaps he's right…we should get the advice of an expert. He cancelled his assignation with that woman…he cancelled her…he cancelled her…*

As if he could read what she was thinking, Ed interrupted her thoughts. "What was going on when I came in? You looked rather defensive."

"Hal has this idea that I didn't exactly like at first but after thinking about it…he may be right."

"What idea is that?"

"He thinks we should get the advice of an expert regarding when we should inform David that Hal's his father…"

"WHAT?! That's rather presumptuous of him!"

"Ed…it's not that unreasonable…I was just assuming he was too young…I really don't know. He wasn't being presumptuous…he was asking for my permission."

"I'm against it! I think he has an ulterior motive…"

"And what could that be…that he wants his son to know he's his father? He is right about David finding out sooner or later…we should find out when he is ready to know."

"This has nothing to do with David! He figures that once David knows…you will no longer need me…"

"I did tell him that he could never cut you out of David's life...and he said that was not his intention. He just wants to know what is best for his son..."

"I forbid it!"

"I can hardly see how we can stop him...he does not need our permission to consult an expert. He wanted to include us. I guess that legally he has that right and can force the issue...I don't think he will do that...but he could get a court order..." She gave him a level gaze. "...and he could stop paying so much child support..."

Ed did love the money that rolled in each month. The relatively small expenditures that Mari made out of each payment did make a difference in their budget, but that did not mean that Hal could rule his roost. "I still forbid it!"

When Hal came downstairs, Ed approached him. "I'd like to speak to you alone...outside."

Hal gave him a lopsided smile. "Sure."

Mari frowned but did not interfere. She went to the window above the kitchen sink and opened it a crack so she could hear. Once outside the two men faced each other. "Hal...I want to make it clear to you that you are here at my sufferance."

"And how is your 'sufferance' any more or less different than it usually is?"

"It has come to my attention that you have taken advantage of my good nature in forcing your attention on my wife."

"I don't know what you're talking about...I never forced anything on Mari."

"I know everything...Mari told me..."

"I'm at a loss here...everything about what?"

"You know perfectly well...explain yourself..."

"Well if you know everything...there is nothing for me to tell. Look, pal...why don't you stop talking in circles and make your point?"

"You asked Mari to choose...and she chose me..."

"I told you about that long ago...is there anything new ticking you off?"

"Don't act as though you don't want her..."

"There's nothing new about that either...so what's your gripe, Ed? Why are you suddenly so lacking in confidence?" Hal spread his hands. "Perhaps problems in the bedroom...they say that happens to men your age...but I wouldn't know..." He taunted. "...don't keep me guessing, Ed...what is it that you know about?"

"You asshole!"

"There's nothing new about that either...come on Ed...you can do better than that. Are you mad about the DVD I sent David...and that Mari saw it? You shouldn't be. She already knows how very *big* my business is. She already knows that I have *preferred* stock...that I can *hold* for a very long time. Not to brag...but my business has a *long endurance* record that *outlasts* most businesses."

"You prick!"

"Oh...so you understood that's what I was referring to. Anything else you want to talk about?"

"Yeah...getting your visitation rights revoked."

"Ed...let me explain it to you this way. You're a fucking joke. You are a scared little man who hides behind religion because you are frightened by the world outside of your limited understanding. If you think you have the power to keep me from my son...keep me from Mari...you're kidding yourself. Mari is with you out of a sense of duty, gratitude, and guilt and you feed her insecurities to keep her by your side. You fill her head with that "cleave unto" in spite of hell shit! But Mari has her own decisions to make...I don't make them for her. You know, I used to think that I was nothing much...that I didn't deserve a woman as wonderful as Mari...and because of that I screwed up bad. Now, I can't say that I don't owe you...because I do. But I can tell you this...I am a better man than you are...especially for Mari. And that has *nothing* to do with how much money I have...it has *everything* to do with how much *ability* I have...and how much I love my son and Mari. So, don't you threaten me...because if I *ever* get the notion that you pose a danger to me...I will come at you with everything I've got." Hal's dark eyes pierced Ed. "I think we're done here." He went back into the house to spend the rest of his time with David.

Hal stayed for dinner just to piss Ed off, talking with David about the adventures of the tall ships on the high seas. The historical aspect was so interesting to Mari that she joined in; her enthusiasm was fueled by the knowledge that Hal cancelled on that woman. Ed sat at the head of his table but ruled over nothing but his glass of wine. When Hal went to leave, Mari whispered to him, "If you can get an appointment for David for this Saturday, and have him back home on Sunday, you may take him to San Francisco to see that child psychologist. Ed will be gone on a fishing trip...I won't tell him."

"Won't you come with me...please?"

"You know I can't, Hal..."

"Please...I want you to hear what she has to say so we will both know what we're doing. I'll make reservations for two rooms and I'll pick you up Saturday morning."

Mari closed her eyes, took a deep breath, and nodded. "OK...I'll go. But we just talk to the doctor and that's it." He lightly kissed her on the forehead and left.

***

The Russian River flows wild and free through one of the most scenic areas of California, periodically flooding the town of Guerneville. Sports and recreation are prolific along its course, drawing people from throughout the state, yet it was still possible to find secluded places in the forest where fish are plentiful, and God is near. Ed, Joel, Matthew, and Peter took Fatso to their secret spot where Smallmouth Bass called "Smallies," Bluegill, and Carp, abound. Taking the unpaved road to a fairly level, dirt parking area, they parked their caravan of cars and hiked the trail to the banks of the river where they bivouacked.

"What kind of rod you got there, Fatso?" Joel looked over to see what Fatso's equipment looked like.

"I figured we would be fishing from the bank...so I am going to use my six and a half footer...with a fifteen-hundred sized reel along with a thin diameter six-pound braid since the weather is warm. If that doesn't work, I'll switch to my seven-footer and thin diameter braid...around ten or fifteen pounds. It will get my jig to the bottom quicker and it increases my casts like a dream. I think I'll just use my old standby lure...the Gary Yamamoto Senko..." Fatso was cocksure of his fishing skills.

"Are you using barbless hook lures?"

"Barbless hooks...what the heck??" Fatso's double chin shook.

"This is a barbless hook river. If all you have are barbed hook lures...I'll help you cut off the barbs. After the end of October...you can't even use lures...just barbless hooks."

"Well, I'll be...how do you catch any fish?"

567

"Don't worry…they jump on your hook…" Joel laughed.

"Here we are." Ed called out to show Fatso their fishing spot. It had rock formations running from the bank to midway into the river.

Fatso waddled up to the bank and smiled. "No wonder you guys picked this spot. It's perfect…it has structures for the fish. Your biters are going to be on the current side of those rocks. I can't wait to get to it!"

They all unpacked their tackle and spread out far enough so as not to interfere with each other. They snipped Fatso's hooks and he demurred to having his better lures snipped. "I'll just go with hooks and Gary Yamamotos…" Before long, Fatso was catching Smallies every few minutes.

"What are you using there, Fatso?" Ed wondered at Fatso's success. He yanked out a few Yamamotos from his pocket. "Just these babies…"

"Do you have any to spare?" Matthew and Peter drew near.

"Sure…I got a crap load of them with me…here take some." He handed out what he had in his pocket to his friends. "I've got more…"

Their catch rate was phenomenal. They had more than enough for their fish fry and for bragging rights when they went home.

As the sun dipped lower in the sky, a campfire was built, and the fish fry began. "I think this is the best catch we've ever had! Look at all that food that pretty little wife of yours made. It looks like she didn't have much faith in your fishing skills." Fatso quipped.

Ed gave a good-natured smile that he did not feel. He had been morose since Hal gave him a dressing down. To make matters worse, Mari seemed to agree with him although she did not speak of the issue again. He felt as though he was losing his grip as Hal appeared to usurp his role as man of the house. Even when Hal was not there, his influence was everywhere in his household, from the new car he bought Mari because it was safer, to the spectacular toys he purchased for David that held the child's interest. Mari sought out Hal's decision-making over his and tried to justify it in his eyes by pouring out Hal's logic. *Yeah…that pretty little wife of mine…*

As the evening wore on, beer bottles materialized from the ice chests. "Fatso…where's that custom-made beer you were talking about?"

"I'm saving the best for last...once you taste this beer...it will be all you will be talking about for the rest of the week!" Fatso laughed.

They talked and joked around the fire, passing on gossip about church members, but carefully avoiding the stories concerning those present. As the hour grew late, Fatso brought out fancy labeled beer, opened the bottles, and passed them around. What no one saw was that the bottle he kept for himself had a cap of a different color. Whether they drank a little or the entire bottle, they soon would become tired and instinctively want to go to bed. They could still function and set out their sleeping bags, but one by one, they would retire, nonetheless, and soon be in a deep sleep. The feeling would be natural, one that they would remember in the morning without any strange sensation or suspicion. Once they were comfortably sleeping in their sleeping bags, it would make the next step of putting them under the influence of a general anesthesia easier, where they would lose all consciousness for a few hours. "Fatso...you were right. This beer is off the charts!"

"Glad you like it. They stopped making it...and I can't get any more. Something else I can't do anymore is see my toes..." They all laughed. Fatso yawned and stretched his arms out. "It's been a long day...starting out in the middle of the night. I'm ready to turn in." The suggestion had its affect as one after another; the men sought out their sleeping bags. "Ed...are you sleeping outside or in the tent?"

"I think I'll sleep outside...I want to fall asleep looking at the stars."

"Good idea, Ed...I guess I'll join you. It's better than being closed in with a bunch of men farting." Fatso laughed. He squeezed into his bag and gazed upward. "God's in his heaven and all's right with the world."

"Sometimes I feel so small...I wonder if He can see me. I wonder if everything I've ever done was for nothing. What was my existence all about? I give of myself and don't ask for much in return..."

Fatso sensed that Ed was troubled, but at this moment he did not want to feel empathy for the man, knowing what Ed was about to endure. He offered him a Christian platitude. "It sounds to me like you are troubled..." He said softly. "...remember...God sends us trials and tribulations to test our faith...and if we face them...God will give us the strength to overcome." He saw a tear run down the side of Ed's face. *Shit...this fucker really WANTS to go! OK...I am your angel of death...at your service!* "Just have faith in God and do what He asks of you...that's all you can do."

Ed turned his face to Fatso. "Thank you. You have helped me more than you know."

"God bless you, Ed."

Within an hour and a half, everyone was asleep. Fatso snapped on rubber gloves and took an aerosol can out of his backpack. He fitted it with an anesthetist's mask. He went into the tent and quietly administered the spray to the men. Then he came outside to Ed. He administered the spray, brought out a bright, directional lantern, and then pulled down Ed's pants in search of his femoral artery in the groin area. He prepared the injection.

***

"YOU WENT BEHIND MY BACK WHEN I EXPRESSLY FORBADE IT!" Ed was livid when Mari tried to tell him about her visit to the psychologist. She did not tell him that Hal took her and David or that they overnighted in San Francisco, because there was nothing untoward to tell. The small talk during the trip centered on David's interests and she barely looked at Hal the entire time. She kept her distance, she was aloof, and she was just appropriately congenial. After she had taken David to school on Monday, she broached the subject and the usually mild-mannered Ed exploded.

"You forbade me to *tell* David...not to talk with the doctor. I am an adult, Ed. Where do you get off forbidding me to use my own judgment?"

"That's just it...it is not *your* judgment...but *his.*"

"You act as though I can't think on my own! It may have been his idea...but I decided it was a good one and acted on it. Don't you even want to know what the psychologist said?"

"No...no I don't! She probably said whatever he paid her to say."

"Look he paid double her fee...because it was on a Saturday...but he wanted an honest opinion...and she will write up a report for us...but I think an honest opinion is what she will give."

"And if you don't agree with it?"

"I'll cross that bridge if I come to it...but I know that if I disagree...it had better be for valid reasons...not selfish ones."

"What do you mean by 'selfish'?"

"Hal once asked me if the reason I didn't want to tell David was that I would be ashamed of what he would think of me. For the first time I had to look at myself and answer that question...not to Hal...but to me. Right now, I am leaning toward doing whatever the psychologist suggests."

"And what if I don't agree?"

"Ed...why wouldn't you?"

He sat down and spoke in a soft voice. "Because once David knows that Hal is his father...and with you being his mother...who am I? I'm nobody. The closer you get to Hal...the three of you...the further you will draw away from me. It's inevitable. I see the three of you together...and I'm odd man out. He sees it...he knows it...and somewhere, down deep, I think you do too. That is why he wants David to know. It will make it easier for you to leave me."

Mari walked over and stood beside him. "You actually believe that?"

"Yes! I see your eyes when you look at him, Mari...they glow with a light you never had for me. You say you love me...and I believe you do...but not with the same passion you have for him. I didn't want to admit it to myself...but there it is...you know it's true."

"Ed...I am not going to leave you. I told you that. What I *didn't* tell you is...I am not with you because I depend upon your support. With the exception of what I spend on David...we live on no more than your income..."

"I know...as soon as you leave me for him you will have all the money you could hope for..."

"No...I am *already* independently wealthy. Do you remember at our first dinner together before Christmas, when Hal wanted to talk to me alone in private? He gave me ten million dollars...with no strings attached...not to him or anyone...no conditions. He said that money would always protect me, and he wanted me safe. If I were going to leave you...I could have done so years ago."

"He just gave you that kind of money...for nothing...he can do that?"

"Yes...and the same amount again for David, for when he graduates from college. The money sits in an account...I never touched it. But I can have it...or any part of it...any time I want."

"Why didn't you tell me?"

"I thought it would come between us. You see…when he asked me to choose…I think he wanted me to have a real freedom of choice…and I chose you. I think it hurt him, because he knows that I still love him…and I know that telling you this may hurt you. But you are my husband, Ed, and the only father David has ever known. I'm not going to leave you…not now…and not when David learns that Hal is his father."

Ed flung his arms around her, burying his face in her stomach. He wept openly. "Oh…Mari…Mari…I've been so foolish. I was so worried that you would leave me. My dear sweet Mari…I love you. You can tell David…I won't interfere."

She stroked his hair to reassure him. "Shhhh, shhhh. I'm here…don't cry." Her brow furrowed as she realized that she had just slammed the door on her prison cell, but she could not desert the man who stood by her when she had no one.

***

The motel had been deserted for a number of years, old fashioned, out of the way, and abandoned as a financial disaster. A money pit, where patronage was sparse, it could not compete with the modern chains conveniently located in the area. What was once the manager's quarters came to life as five men took over the facility. Dan, and his band of educated ne'er-do-wells, used the place as their headquarters to plot their scheme, and as their hideout for carrying it out. Fifty miles, or so, from their intended target, Dan brought his crew to Sonoma County to familiarize them with the location and strategy. "OK…pay attention guys. We have to get this down because we only have one shot at getting it right. This is our target in Jenner. He lives alone there with his maid. Periodically, he has company for a few days or visitors for the afternoon. Lately his routine has been sporadic…nothing regular that can be pinned down and relied upon. I believe that is because he has had some sort of disruption in his life. This is the man who is the father…" Dan showed them a picture of Hal. "…this is the mother…" He showed another picture.

"Shit…we should kidnap her instead!"

"Get serious dude…she's married, and her old man doesn't have that kind of money…" Dan did not want to lose control of his men. He showed them a picture of David, saying, "…this is the boy…we grab him!" Dan spread out a map. "We are here…and the house is here."

He drew his finger down the proposed route. "This is a longer route...but less traveled. We can disappear on it in several places."

"How will we know when the time is right?"

"The disruption in his life appears to be temporary. After you guys get to know the territory...and what to do...you go back down to L.A. and wait. John and I will keep watch on him until we know his routine is a lock. I'll send for you to come up...then it's a go!"

***

AN OLD FRIEND

"Ed…I want to go to 'Frisco for a couple of days…on Wednesday. An old friend called to say they would be there on a business trip and they would love to see me. I figure I don't want to make that drive twice in one day…so I will overnight there…and probably do some shopping too. Estefana said she would look after David with the rest of her kids while I'm gone."

Ed had been mollified ever since Mari reassured him that she was his loyal wife. He no longer questioned her plans, her motives, or her whereabouts. "Alright, honey…just call me when you get there. Do you know where you're staying?"

"Not yet. I'll make reservations today and write everything down for you."

"Who are you seeing?"

Mari started to tell him the truth, but at the last moment revised it. "Loretta and her husband…they are going to be there for some sort of convention…"

"Be sure to give them my regards…and tell them they are welcome to visit us here if they ever come up our way." He paused and then added, "I may be out of the house…so call me on my cell."

"Oh? Where are you going?"

"Just to take care of some business…nothing important…"

***

Mari quickly stepped across the courtyard at Ghirardelli Square. "Terry!" she waved as he got up from a table to greet her.

"Well Miss Thing…aren't you a sight for sore eyes!" Deuce beamed, "All dressed up in your Sunday go to meetin'!" He gave her a bear hug and helped her to her seat.

"That's no joke…this is literally one of my Sunday go to meeting outfits. My husband insists that we go every Sunday…and sometimes during the week." She rolled her eyes.

"So, you married a 'good Christian'…did you?"

"Yes. Ed…he's the best…but sometimes that Christian stuff can get overbearing. Enough of that…how've you been? You look good…like life has been treating you really well."

"Can't complain…no one would listen if I did…business is good. You know your friend Lo-Lo turned me inside out…broke up my home...cost me a bunch in the divorce...but she was worth every penny!"

"You and Lo-Lo? I hadn't heard." She feigned so she could hear the story from him. "What happened?"

"Oh...you know...I wasn't getting on that well with Wanda. At the time we had sort of drawn a truce...and that is how we got along. She took care of the kids...and I took care of the business. But once she got a look at Lo-Lo...and how Lo-Lo looked at me...well the fight was on and it led straight to a divorce."

"I'm sorry to hear that."

"Oh...it's nobody's fault. I was steering a leaky ship for a long time...and it just finally went under. Soon after the divorce, Lo-Lo took off to Monaco! She came back for a while...but she's gone again. She lives like a queen over there. More power to her..."

"Awwww. Did she call you a musician?"

"Yeah...how did you know?"

Mari smiled. "That's her way of blaming the man for the breakup. The first man who ever did her wrong...really wrong...was a musician...I think he played the saxophone...jazz...her son's father. Ever since, when she breaks up...the man was 'a musician.' Why did you two break up?"

"She got mad at me for divorcing Wanda and...mostly for leaving my kids. She was fine as long as I was married. But when Wanda found out about us and pitched a bitch...I lost them both. I didn't mind Wanda divorcing me though...she never did love me. I remember telling Hal at the time, when we were still married, that I wished my wife loved me half as much as you loved him..."

Mari looked down at her hands and then back up to meet his gaze, "Well it looks like that ship sank too."

"Look...this is ol' Terry here...why are you talkin' smack, girl?" He gave her a knowing look. "You know down deep you love his bad ass."

"Is this why you asked me to see you...to talk about Hal?" She squinted at him. "Oooohh...he asked you to...didn't he. He told you what happened, didn't he?"

"OK...OK...I'm not going to pretend I don't know...but I would have come up to see you anyway...to see how you're doing and all that...but yeah...he did ask me." His face held a troubled expression. "You know he's goin' crazy, don't you? You've gotta put that boy out of his misery." He paused and then began again in a low voice, "Yeah...he told me what went down...and he doesn't know what to do with himself. He wants to talk with you...but he thinks you won't see him. He needs to understand what happened that day and why..." He took her hand to let her know he empathized with her.

Mari spoke so softly it was like she breathed the words. "I can't explain what happened to myself...or anybody else...I just became overwhelmed...all those years of acting as though I didn't care. Somehow I knew if I actually said it...said it out loud...especially to tell Hal that I loved him...I would have to face it...face it really hard..." She looked away from his eyes. "You know he has another woman..."

"No he doesn't. He has someone he fucks...the guy's just trying to get through life...without you. Now you've got him all tangled up again. He'd give anything...anything at all to be with you...but you just wouldn't have it...up until now. What's changed?"

"Jesus...Terry...nothing's changed. I wake up each morning...and I see my husband there. Don't get me wrong...I do love him...but I'm not *in love* with him...do you know what I mean...the difference?"

"Yeah...I think I do..." He nodded. "I'm not saying this because Hal is like my brother...I'm sayin' it because it's true...he's the better guy for you, honey. Neither one of you is going to be happy without the other...and he's got the money to make it happen for you."

"It's never been about money. Right now, it's about a little boy's perception. I do see Hal when it's about David...but I just don't talk about us when I do. We are trying to straighten things out so that my son can know that Hal is his father...but I don't know. My son has all this shit swirling about him...where the so-called adults have fucked it all up and made a mess of things. If I could figure a decent way out...I would." She looked to him for commiseration. "I didn't mean to string Hal along...I didn't mean to give him false hope...I didn't mean to be...unkind...and yes...I am *in love* with him...but I can't break up my family."

"Mari...kids are tough...they grow up...they get smarter...and they get wiser. As long as their parents...or the people around them...show them love they'll be OK and for some...better than OK..."

"What I did with Hal was unforgivable. I don't know how to shut off what I feel. He's trying to make a life for himself with someone else...and I..."

"I don't think you understand, Mari. He's not going away. He doesn't want nobody else. What he wants is you and his son...and the longer you go on with Ed...the harder it's going to be. Will you at least talk to him? Let him explain himself to you...it's only fair...this is his life too. Will you see him?"

"I don't know. It was just as hard for me to get over what happened...and I don't want to start that up again. That's why I refuse to talk with him about it anymore. For days it tore me up inside to know that he was with that woman. All Labor Day when I knew he was with her...we had a party that day...but whenever I was alone, I couldn't stop crying. Later on, he told me he canceled his day with her...but where do I get off being upset over that? He has a right. I have to learn to be stronger than that." She shook her head. "I don't know what the right thing to do is anymore."

"Just talk to him...listen to what he has to say. There is no sense in the both of you going through life in pain. Life is too short...and you will look back with regret if you don't give him a chance."

The sympathy his eyes held for both of them made her relent. "I don't suppose it would hurt to hear him out...after all, David is his son." She took a deep breath and steeled herself. "Alright. When does he want to see me?"

"How about I take you to him right now?"

***

Dim sunlight shone through the myriad pieces of clear leaded glass that made up the graceful, arching, nineteenth century ceiling of the Garden Court Restaurant. It extended over the marble walls of the exquisite room inside the historic Palace Hotel. Palms were interspersed about the room and upholstered armchairs afforded luxurious comfort around each table. In his attempt at seclusion in the wide expanse of the room, Hal sat at a far table rehearsing in his mind what he would say, assuming that Deuce was able to convince Mari to see him. Dressed in a suit to impress her, he felt as though the outcome of his life depended on what he said today. Two tables away, he saw one gentleman's head turn in the direction of the door. Then he alerted the man sitting across from him who also turned in his seat to look. Hal gave a wry smile as he realized, without looking, that Mari had arrived.

The beige suit Mari was wearing seemed to glow in the half-light of the restaurant, giving her an otherworldly aura. Her matching hat was cocked and decorated with a twisted scarf of fall colors that complemented the colors of her blouse. Her fitted jacket showed off her waist and the mid-length skirt with an off-center split revealed the calf of one leg as she walked. The affect hit Hal with a thump of his heart as he watched her approach. Deuce followed her to his table. Hal stood up. "Thanks for seeing me here, Mari...I know it wasn't easy for you."

She just nodded her acknowledgment and followed his gesture to sit in the armchair across from him. To her surprise, Deuce did not sit down. He took Hal's outstretched hand in an upward clasp and said, "Good luck, bro." He turned to Mari. "I have to catch an early flight...but I'll be back to see you. Now you get this thing worked out. I love you both, madly." He smiled and then turned and was gone.

"I didn't know Terry wouldn't stay." Mari anxiously looked after Deuce as he walked away.

"He thought it was better if we had a chance to talk alone." He accurately surmised that she would be more receptive if it was Deuce's idea and not his.

"Hal...I want to apologize. I didn't mean to..."

He slightly raised his hand to stop her. "There is no need for apologies...it just happened and I'm glad it did because we needed to have this talk for a long time...I just didn't know..." He didn't finish his thought. He clasped his hands in front of him. "Mari...it is mostly all my fault...but whatever has gone down between us is because we were not honest with each other...about how we felt after our circumstances became so out of control...and we didn't know how to get back...or if it was even possible to get back...what we once had. Now, we are pinned down by the conditions we created. I don't want to make the mistake of thinking our situation is hopeless...when all we have to do is to grab our chance at happiness, while we still can.

"I am asking you to help me understand how you see us...where do you see us going...and I will listen...just please be honest. Then I will tell you how I see things if that is alright with you." He waited for her to talk and waited.

Finally, she started to say something and then stopped. She looked down at the table, avoiding his eyes, and spoke in a whisper. "There are two ways I see things...the one is what I always wished for...and the other is how I think it is going to be."

"Yes?"

"What I wish for is not what is going to be...not for a long time...if ever. What I see for us is that I need to let go of you so you can...begin again...to live your life...because I don't see a way out for me." She took a breath. "Besides David...there is Ed...and he has done *nothing* to deserve my abandoning him. And what do I tell David? All I see as *my* future is to go on as before...but that does not mean you have to pay. Do I love you, Hal? Yes...more than I have the right to tell you. Do I want to trap you? No. I think you should give up hope that we will ever be together...because I just don't see how." She placed her hands on the table to show she was finished.

Hal's voice was gentle. "Mari...you can't make that decision for me...or expect me to accept your version of how it is going to be for us. You see...I don't live in hope. I live in determination...and if I didn't have enough determination before you told me that you love me...I certainly do now. I am not going to force you into anything you don't want...it will have to come from you...but I am determined that you *will* be my wife." At the astonishment in her eyes, he leaned forward to press his point. "Just how long do you think you can keep Ed living in a fool's paradise...with a wife that cannot love him in the way he deserves? Shouldn't he be free to find someone who does?"

"But what about David?"

"I received the psychologist's report, but I have been talking to more than one to get a second...and third opinion. They are all of the opinion that David should have been told about me a long time ago...when I first learned that he was my son. Children of that age are more receptive and adapt more readily...that is not to exclude Ed at that time...but just to tell David that I was his father. Now it will be more difficult...but just as necessary...because the older he gets...the more traumatic the truth will be. It is not so much the truth of the matter that hurts the child...but the fact that he has been lied to by those he trusted. I can identify with that analysis."

"I don't understand...you're saying that he would not be affected by finding out that Ed is not his father?"

"Not if it is handled right. Ed is the father who raised him thus far...and I am his biological father. There is no need for long explanations at this point...but there is a need for the truth."

"I have to think that one through..."

"I'll send you the report and the names of the child psychologists I have talked to so they may advise you. But, Babe...the years are ticking by with us apart...you are mine...I sensed it before, and now I know it." He reached across the table and took her hand. She didn't pull away. "Babe...please do us both a favor...would you spend the rest of the day with me? Just give me a day to show you that it could work between us." He gambled that he could parlay a day into a lifetime.

"I don't know..."

"Let me take you to dinner...let me take you dancing...let me show you some of the town. Don't you feel a little quiver of excitement?" He cajoled.

"I feel more than a little excitement...I'm overwhelmed. I should go back to my room and think..."

"There's plenty of time for that. Besides you don't want to disappoint Godfrey by not eating at his posh restaurant! Be my date for the day...I promise you won't regret it...

" He saw the sparkle come back into her eyes. "Oh...that would be so nice. I haven't gone out anywhere in years." She wrinkled her nose at him. "OK...you're on. Do I need to change what I'm wearing?"

"No...you look beautiful."

***

The world seemed to spin faster on its axis as time flew by at a quicker pace. After a day of taking in the bay tour by boat, and walking Fisherman's Wharf, when evening fell, he took her to dine at Acquerello Restaurant. The ambiance was not only beautiful, it was decidedly romantic. Mari could feel the clock hands race and realized that she needed more time—more time to spend with him. She felt like she was teetering between two worlds, the one she was living in, and the other with Hal. *Can we go back to the way it was between us? At what cost?* She caught him studying her face and wondered if her eyes gave away what she was feeling.

"This restaurant came highly recommended. You wouldn't believe the hoops I had to jump through to get dinner reservations for us...even for a weeknight...I hope you enjoy the food here." He gave her a gentle reminder to enjoy herself, rather than being pensive.

She instantly brightened. "I know I will...and I am enjoying being with you. I even have to admit that it was funny having the wind blow my hat off into the water with both of us trying to grab it."

"I was sorry to see it go...you looked adorable in it. You just looked a little sad right now and I was wondering why."

"I don't know...it's just that time is passing so fast. I wish it would slow down a bit. I sort of want to hold on to today..."

He started to remind her that she could hold on to it forever, but even to him it sounded too pushy. He just agreed. "I feel the same way."

The waiter approached to serve them an amuse bouche. "I know there are a lot of wonderful dishes to choose from...but may I suggest a dish that is on the tasting menu...even if you chose the pre fixe menu...we are able to serve it to you. Our ridged pasta with foie gras, black truffle, and Marsala is one of our premier dishes...not to be missed. So, if you desire to have that as one of your courses, we will be happy to oblige you even if you select the pre fixe menu."

Hal looked at Mari and she nodded back at him. "Yes, we will be sure to order that dish."

As the waiter walked away, Mari whispered, "Godfrey lives! Viva Godfrey!"

"What I wouldn't give to have him scold us once more..." His face clouded over as he seemed to retreat inside himself. Understanding his intense emotion that she shared, she reached across the table and took his hand. Touched by her response, he clasped her hand and held it.

Hal ordered the five-course meal and Mari ordered three courses. Soon they were laughing and sharing the gastronomic experience.

Leaving Acquerello, the cab ride was of short duration to the Mark Hopkins Hotel, less than a mile. When they arrived, Hal tipped the driver a twenty to make the fare worth his while. Taking the elevator straight to the nineteenth floor to the Top of the Mark, they were soon sitting at a table with a view of the city lights and San Francisco Bay. A small combo with a brilliant piano player performed dance music for the midweek crowd, which was more subdued than the boisterous weekend patrons. Ordering their drinks, Hal waited at the table while Mari excused herself to find the ladies' room. He was all too aware that the evening was drawing to a close with no indication from Mari that she was at least considering his way of seeing things. Had he struck out? Was this it for them with nothing more? He couldn't allow himself to think that everything he ever wanted was lost to him. *No...never...I know she's mine.*

Mari looked at herself in the mirror as she refreshed her makeup. *What will I do? After tonight, there can be nothing more between us.* The thought was crushing. She returned to the table with a smile. "You remembered what I drink."

"I remember everything, Mari...every detail about you." He changed the subject. "The music is pretty nice. Would you like to dance with me?"

"Of course."

Dancing at the Top of the Mark, they moved together at a slow tempo as the band played "Misty Roses." The piano player had a decent voice and he crooned the lyrics that touched Hal. "Mari...we've got to try. We had too much together, and we can have it all back again. Please don't throw us away. Let me hold you and dance through life with you..."

Mari looked up at Hal studying his features. *Is this going to be for the rest of my life...or never again?* She asked herself. *Is he right that we could finally be together with our son?* He looked down into her eyes and misread her and thought to kiss her. She gently avoided his kiss by placing her cheek on his, but it was still too emotive for her. As the piece ended, the band took a break and they went back to their table. When they sat down Mari was wistful and slowly took both of Hal's hands in hers. "Hal...can I ask you a serious question?"

"You haven't taken my hands like this in...it's gotta be almost nine years. You can ask me anything you want...you can ask me for anything you want..."

"If we had never parted...tell me what you think it would have been like for us."

"Oh...that's an easy one. We would have let my mother have the joy of planning our wedding...and it would have been a big one..."

"I wanted a small wedding with just you...and a few of our friends..."

"We would have bought a modest house in a normal neighborhood...I don't want my kids to grow up to be privileged pricks...and I would insist on a picket fence...we would have had three kids by now...we would have been very happy...I would have seen to that...and I would love you forever...the last part happened anyway."

"And now...what do you think it would be like if we tried to be together."

"That's a tough one...because we would have to face some very difficult challenges...but attainable goals. First...you would have to tell Ed that you want a divorce. Then we would have to get professional help on how to tell David that he is my son. I should think he would still want a connection to Ed and that would be good. We would let my mother plan our wedding...you have no idea how long she has wanted to do that..."

"OK...she would plan it..."

"*Will* plan it...I don't know if you want more children now...but whatever you want...and I'll buy you whatever you want...house...wherever you want it...car...jewelry...you name it..."

"I don't want a lot of things, Hal...I just want you..." She sat up at a thought. "...and I want to help you research your books!"

Hal smiled. "Does that mean you will...?"

"No...no...well...I don't know...I guess I want something to dream about. Do you really think...?"

"That's all I've been trying to tell you, Mari...now you have to make your own choices."

The rest of the evening they talked very little with both lost in their own thoughts. They danced through the next set, holding onto one another. She felt the movement of his body next to hers and his hot breath on her cheek. Mari reached up to bring his ear close to her lips. "Hal...take me with you." She breathed.

"Sure...where do you want to go, Babe?"

"Anywhere you go."

***

The door flew open to his hotel room. They were no sooner through it when Mari and Hal were in each other's arms and he kicked the door shut with his foot. Panting, they undressed each other, tossing away their clothes, grasping and caressing, with

583

muffled sounds through their hungry kisses. Desperate in their desire for each other they careened toward the bed. Once there, they made love until dawn.

***

It was after dark when Hal pulled up behind Mari's car in the turnout on the road to her house. He got out of his car, walked to hers, and got into the passenger seat. Neither one of them said a word for a moment, and then he prompted her. "OK, Babe...do you remember what you are going to say?"

"Yes...but I just promised him I wouldn't leave him. That is going to make it very hard."

"Yeah...but I can't believe that after you told him you loved me...he could still be so selfish as to guilt-trip you into staying. He even admitted that he could see that you loved me..." Hal shook his head. "Mari...as much as I love you...if I thought that you did not love me...I could never try to hold on to you that way." He saw her stare straight ahead. "I want to come in with you...you don't know how he's going to react."

"No. That will make things worse."

"OK...but I'll be right here. Call me if you need me and I'll be there in under a minute. Be sure to unlock the door." He was agitated. "I don't like this. I want to go in with you. After you tell him, come home with me...I don't want to leave you alone with him. Are you sure David is all right where he is?"

"Yes...he is staying with the González family. He's happy as can be with all their kids. I called Estefana and let her know to keep him for another night. Let me handle this, Hal. I'll be fine."

"OK...but I'm right here. Be sure to call me after you tell him." He went back to his car to wait.

Driving up to her house, Mari could see that the kitchen light was on. The rest of the house was dark. She pulled into the parking area in front of the garage and entered by the side sliding door. Ed was sitting at the table, sipping a glass of wine and it was obvious he was waiting for her. "Ed...I'm sorry I got back later than expected. Did you find the shepherd's pie in the freezer? Did you eat dinner?"

"No. Estefana called to say she was keeping David over..."

"Yes. When I realized that I would be home after dark...I asked her to keep him there. Why didn't you eat?"

"Mari, sit down...I have something to tell you."

"What is it, Ed?" She sat down wondering if there was any possible way he found out about her being with Hal. She was hoping for a clean break without recriminations.

"I have some bad news and I want you to know that we don't have much time together."

She stared. "We don't have much time together?"

"I'm very ill...I have fourth stage prostate cancer. I went to the doctor yesterday...he says it's terminal."

"Oh, God!" She burst into tears. "Ed...you had to sit here alone all this time. Why didn't you call and tell me to come back right away? Oh, dear God...there's nothing that can be done? We can get treatments...."

"Dear, he told me that I could have surgery...chemo...and such. But, at my stage...it's not going to save me...it will just make the end more wretched. They can keep me comfortable until the end...that's all they can do...and that is what he recommends."

"That's horrible!"

"No...I've accepted it. It was good for me to be here alone. I could think and look over my life...and the one thing I'm sure of is the best thing I ever did was to marry you and help bring David into this world. God gave me a gift in you, and I am eternally grateful."

"I don't know what to do. I've got to call Hal...he'll know what to do."

"Yes...call him. I need to tell him as well."

Mari dialed Hal. "Hal...oh my God, Hal...something came up and I need to see you right away. Can you be here in thirty minutes?"

"I'm here...I'll be there right now."

"No...no...I'm fine...can you get here from your house in thirty minutes or so?"

"You didn't tell him, did you."

"No...something came up and we need to see you."

"Is David OK?"

"Yes...but we need to see you."

"I take it you want it to look like I'm driving from my house?"

"That's right...will you be here?"

"OK...I'll wait for thirty minutes and then I'm coming in."

"Oh...thank you...thank you. I'll leave the side door open. Just come on in."

"What kind of meshugass..." Hal looked at his watch. *Why didn't she just tell him? What can be more important than that? Why did she say we?* The minutes dragged on with him anxiously checking his watch. When it hit the twenty-minute mark, he rationalized that if he had been at home when he received her call...he would have broken the speed record to get here. He started the car. When he got there, he could see Mari was crying and Ed was trying to console her. "What happened?"

"Oh, Hal! Ed...tell him..." Mari wiped her eyes.

"We just got some very bad news. I have terminal cancer..."

"Oh...shit! Ed...I'm so sorry. I know of some of the best oncologists that could see you...are you sure?"

"The doctor said that it isn't worth treating me...it's too far along."

"But you looked fine...it happened so fast. I'm truly sorry, Ed."

"Mari is very upset. Will you look after her?"

"Of course."

"She will need a lot of help to get through this...can you be there for her...for David?"

"You can count on it. What kind of care will you need?"

"They're going to recommend a hospice."

"No, Ed...you will want your family with you...you're staying with me at my home...I have room enough for everyone there. Mari and David can live there with you. I'll have a room set up for you and a nurse on duty to look after you. Anything you could need will be there."

Ed looked up at Hal. "Thank you. I never expected so much..."

Hal gave Ed a cheerless smile. "...of course, I'm going to take care of you."

Ed got up. "I'm tired. I guess I'll turn in."

Hal and Mari watched him ascend the stairs and listened for the bedroom door to open and close. "Oh, God, Hal...what a nightmare! I can't thank you enough for giving him the comfort of your home...for helping him through this." Her face dissolved into tears. "This is my fault..."

"Your fault? How?"

"I should never have..."

Hal took her by the arm and guided her out of earshot into the laundry room. "How is this your fault?"

"I broke my promise to him…I betrayed him…"

"And what does that have to do with cancer? Mari…he already had terminal cancer when you left the house on Wednesday morning…before you chose me…"

"I don't know…it just seems like he's paying for what I did. I *never* wished him dead. Did you?"

"No…no. There was a time or two I may have thought it…but I never, ever wished him dead…"

"You thought of it? My God, Hal…"

"Look…he's the one with the hotline to God…not me. Why are you blaming us for what happened to him? I know you didn't go to San Francisco with the intention of being with me. He was already terminal yesterday when you left…you're not making sense, Mari." He held her as she sobbed into his chest. "None of this is your fault or mine…we just love each other and finally acted on it. He was already sick…and it has nothing to do with us. All we can do is help him as much as we can. But we can't blame ourselves for something we had no control over."

"I just feel so awful…"

"So do I, Babe…so do I." Hal was surprised that he really meant it. For as much as he wished that the impediment of Ed was gone, he never really imagined that he would be completely out of their lives. *And how will we tell David that Ed is dying?*

***

The dawn came cold and gray, making Hal aware that he had sat up all night while holding Mari as she cried herself to sleep. He looked down at her face, kissed her, and then laid her down on the couch with a throw pillow under her head. He poured himself a glass of wine and walked to one of the picture windows to watch the sun come up over the autumn colored leaves of the vineyard. He wondered how long Ed would last. *Will he make it through the holidays? We should tell David as soon as possible that I am his father so that he won't relate that in his mind with Ed's dying. I have to at least show Mari that report…who am I kidding….she's in no shape to handle anything…neither is Ed. I think that what Ed was trying to tell me is that he wants me to take over. Alright…I'm here.*

Mari stirred and then sat straight up as last night's events came back to her. She saw Hal at the window. "You're up already."

"Yeah, Babe...I couldn't sleep. Too much going on in my head." He went to her and crouched down to talk to her. "You have to pull yourself together...for David. Try to act as normal as possible. Don't tell him yet. I'll take care of it. I'll take care of everything...you don't have to worry about another thing."

"David...what will we tell David?"

"Just go get him and bring him home as usual. Don't tell him anything...I'll talk to him."

"Are you sure?"

He took both of her hands. "Mari, as far as I'm concerned...you are my wife from this moment on. I'll take over running things. I think that was what Ed was asking me to do when he said to look after you. You go up and change...and I'll make breakfast..."

"You can make breakfast?"

Hal smiled. "I had to learn how. I can fry bacon...scramble eggs...and toast is not too much of a challenge. Just show me where everything is."

Mari went to the kitchen and set out the food. "I'm tempted to stay and watch...but I have to get ready..."

"Yeah...and after we eat, I have to go home and pick up some things. Is Ed well enough to come down?"

"I'll check on him." She went upstairs.

He could hear the shower running and her footsteps upstairs as he got breakfast underway. For years he had been stalled, stymied in place, always marking time to get what he wanted. Now everything was moving fast, all obstacles swept away. He was in the captain's chair and he had to set the ship's course.

As Mari came downstairs with Ed, breakfast was ready to put on the table. "I know this is not as good as what you are used to...but it is better than a cold breakfast and a kick in the pants."

"It looks good, Hal...better than I could do." Ed appreciated the effort.

They sat down and ate in silence speaking only in fits and starts. Hal could see the strain on both of their faces, and he was sure it was reflected on his own. "Ed...I want to know...what do you need for me to do around the estate."

He stared at Hal and his eyes moistened. "Everything...everything..." He put his hands over his face and began to weep. "I'm afraid I will not be able to do much for very long."

"You've got it, Ed...you've got it. Right now, I promise you...I will see to everything...and you will have the best care that I can give you. I'm here for you."

"Hal...I...I..." "Shhhh...don't say anything. I know. You've already paid it forward, Ed."

***

Hal went home to pack and to make some calls. "Lupe..."

She peeked her head out of the kitchen. "Yes?"

"We're going to have company. Make sure the guest rooms are ready...with flowers, et cetera...you know the drill. One of the rooms will have to accommodate a cancer patient. Make sure it's the guest room with the best ocean view. We have to make him as comfortable as possible."

He peeled off three hundred dollars. "Here...go shopping and lay in more groceries."

"Yes, Meester Hal."

He made a call to Arendt to check in with Mack and then called Deuce. "I don't have much time to talk...but I wanted to call to thank you..."

"How did it go?"

"She's mine, man...she's mine."

"Alriiight! I knew this would happen!"

"There is so much more to tell you, but I don't have time right now. I gotta go...love you bro."

He called a nurse registry to have someone in place by Monday. "I'm paying double...so I want the best you have."

"We can send you one of our best people..."

"I said I want *the* very best..."

"Well the very best...she's on another case..."

"Are they paying double your rates?"

"No."

"Then get her off the other case and on to mine...and have her here by Monday."

"Yes...we can do that..."

He wrapped up business for the morning, tossed some papers into his briefcase, and then looked at the psychologist's report on his desk. He started not to take it because he already had in mind what he wanted to do and did not need further affirmation. *They've been pussyfooting around this for too long as it is.* But on reflection he threw it in his briefcase, anyway.

Walking out the door, he called his construction company. "Can you throw up a picket fence around my place by Friday? I'm going to have a youngster here and I don't want him running over the cliff...nothing fancy...just something to keep him inside the grounds. You can have someone out tomorrow? Good."

He drove the road to the Baker Estate and gathered his thoughts. *By the end of business today...David is going to know I'm his father.*

He pulled up to the house in the late afternoon. David ran out to greet him. He knelt on one knee as the boy ran into his arms. "Hey, little buckaroo...how's it going?"

"I think mommy is mad at daddy because she's not speaking to him and he's in his room."

He stood up and got his suitcase out of the trunk. "Oh? Well maybe I can fix that. I'm going to be staying with you for a couple of days...and then you and your mommy and daddy will be coming to stay with me."

"Why?"

"It's a long story. But, don't get me started...I'll talk your ear off..." He entered through the kitchen and found Mari dutifully cooking dinner.

"Thank God you're back. I'm a wreck." She held up the coffee pot. "Shall I make you a cup?"

"No...I haven't been to sleep yet and I was hoping to get a couple of hours of shut-eye before dinner. Will you wake me?"

"You look like you could use it. Yes...I'll come up and get you. Go on up...you know the way."

"Before I go...I brought the report with me...do you want to see it?"

"No...I already made up my mind. Whatever you think is best...that is what we will do."

"Then I think we should sit down with David after dinner."

David looked back and forth between the two of them. "Sit down with me...why"

"We have some good news for you." Mari kissed his nose.

David cocked his head with a quizzical look. "Are you going to have a baby?"

Mari briefly looked at Hal, made a face, and crossed her eyes. "I don't think so. Why do you ask?"

"Because every time Gregorio's parents want to talk to *him*...they're going to have another baby."

"This is about something else, buckaroo..." Hal smiled. "Would you like to have a brother or sister?"

David thought for a moment. "Yeeeaah...a little sister."

"What about a little brother?" Mari smiled.

"No...he'll want to play with my toys."

"Oh...so you don't want to share?" She frowned.

"No I don't...most kids don't take care of their toys...they break them."

"Good point." Hal moved toward the stairs. "But, that's a talk for another day."

Hal moved down the hall towards his room and heard Ed call out to him. He peered into the room. "Hey, Ed...did you get any sleep?"

"Not much...the pills they gave me don't work that well."

"I'll get you set up so you don't feel a thing...I ordered a nurse for you...she starts Monday. I hope to be ready by then and move all of you out there." Hal sat on the side of the bed. "Do you feel well enough to come downstairs? Mari and I are going to tell David tonight that I'm his father...and I could use your moral support."

"Tonight?"

"Yes...after dinner...I want to tell him before we have to let him know that you are sick...while you are still looking fit. It would be better if we can all be there and make it sound like it's a happy occasion...you know...good news."

"Yes...I'll be there."

"Is there anything I can get for you?"

"Not even you can buy my way out of this..."

"Yeah...I do have my limitations." Hal shrugged. "I'll come back for you when dinner is ready."

He went into the guest room and deposited his suitcase in the closet. Now that he could let go, he found that he was wearier than he thought. He went to turn back the covers on the bed and found an envelope on the pillow with his name on it in Mari's writing. He opened it and read:

If I lived one thousand lifetimes,
And searched the length and breadth of all,
'Tis but one manly face that I'll e'er recall
'Tis but one who stirs my passion, and all I desire
And sets my heart yearning, sets my soul on fire.

Hillel, Hillel, I have you at last,
My journey across eons is now through
All my desperate dreams are fulfilled by you
After my ship was tossed on a stormy ocean
The treasure I seek is your love and devotion.

Hillel, Hillel you live in my dreams,
When I know how much you care
And feel the heat of the kiss we share
The words to speak of my love for you
Are written in the sky and the morning dew.

Hillel, Hillel always in my thoughts
The very thought of you gives me a rush
With visions of you that make me blush
The heat of your body melts my existence
Into one with yours without resistance.

Hillel, Hillel I'll love you forever
Our lives should be for always entwined.
If we live where benevolence has shined
With our love to shelter us from the cold
Together hand in hand I wish to grow old.

He clasped his hand over his mouth as all his desires spiraled to the sky. He couldn't hold back the tears and he held the paper to his chest. *My beautiful Babe!* He folded the paper, put it back in the envelope, and slipped it into the briefcase. Taking off his shoes, he laid down on top of the covers. With the week's events swirling in his head, he finally fell into a deep sleep.

Feeling a gentle caress on his face, the fog of slumber lifted, and he saw Mari sitting beside him. "I let you sleep an extra hour. You needed it."

He reached up and pulled her to him. "I got your message...you have no idea how much it meant." He whispered.

"Yes I do...it meant everything to me when you gave it to me. I could never have written anything half as wonderful...so I borrowed it." He sought out her lips and rolled over her. "We don't have time...they're at the table waiting for you."

"You go ahead. I'll splash some cold water on my face and be right down."

Hal took the steps in double time as he came down for dinner. "Something smells wonderful."

"I didn't feel that creative today...so I fell back on confetti spaghetti...with all kinds of colorful veggies in the sauce." She set out a salad, garlic bread, and Chianti wine to complete the meal. She shared apple juice with David.

Hal started to say he remembered her spaghetti but thought better of it. He waited patiently as Ed said a longer grace than usual and then digging in, he realized he hadn't eaten since breakfast and he had to slow himself from wolfing down his food. "I really hope there's more of this."

"You know me...I always make more...there is enough for seconds and leftovers." Mari reassured him.

"I hear your harvest went well this year."

"Yes...we had about a twenty percent loss...but the quality was superior. What we lost in quantity...we made up in quality...it looks like it is going to be a spectacular wine...if all indications are right. The price is up so we will be OK."

"One day you are going to have to show me how you do it...coax the grapes into being something special."

"How about tomorrow...we can bring David too..." He turned to David. "...how do you feel about skipping school tomorrow?"

"Hurray!"

The dinner went on with everyone chattering cheerfully as though their lives had not changed forever. The charade for David proved irresistible and after a while was no longer an act. The after-dinner conversation shifted into the living room. Hal moved the wingback chairs to the other side of the coffee table in front of the couch so they could all sit facing each other. He sat Ed in one chair and took the other for himself. Mari sat with David on the couch. Hal started first. "David, my little buckaroo...I have wanted to tell you something for a long time, but I had to wait until you were a big boy...so you could understand. You know that Ed here has been your father for a long time..."

David squirmed and stood up. "But he's not my father...you are..."

Hal's eyebrows went up. "Why, yes...yes I am. Who told you that I was your father? Where did you learn that?"

"At church. I heard Mr. Brimley say that there was no way that Ed Baker was my father. He said that he met my father when he saw us at Safari West. Mr. Brimley said I look just like you."

"Well...Mr. Brimley sounds like he is a nosy busybody...and for sure a gossip. I would have put it more delicately...but Mr. Brimley's guess was right. I'm so very proud to be your father."

"How come you never told me? How come you pretended that Ed was my father?"

"Oh...that was no pretext. Mr. Brimley was wrong about Ed not being your father. Ed was married to your mother when you were born...and under California law...legally that made him your father...and he has been a good father to you for all of your life." Hal smiled and held out his arms for David to come to him and sit on his lap. "But I am your biological father...that means it is my blood that flows through your veins...my DNA..."

"How did that happen?"

Hal laughed. "That is a much longer discussion for another day...but I used to know your mommy a long time ago...and then I lost her. I looked everywhere for her for a long time. But Ed found her and married her. I didn't know she was carrying you...my child...until I found her again. We thought you were too young to understand a complicated story...so we waited to tell you. But evidently...you already knew our happy news."

"Can I call you dad now?"

"Yes...you can call both of us 'dad' now." Hal looked at his watch. "Well, it's way past your bedtime and we have a big day tomorrow. Ed is going to show us how to grow the best grapes ever." He took David by the hand and led him upstairs. "Come on...I'll read you a story about a horse...it's a big book...so we will read just the first chapter tonight."

"OK, dad." David smiled. "I'm so glad I have two dads...most kids only have one."

Hal looked across the room at Mari and nodded. "It feels so good to finally hear you call me 'dad' after I waited so long. My boy..." He picked him up and carried him the rest of the way in his arms.

***

Joel, Matthew, and Peter craned their necks to take in the architecture and interior design of Hal's home. From the floor to the twelve-foot high ceiling, double-paned, glass windows gave the effect of bringing the outdoors into the living room and formal dining room. East of the living room, through the double doors, was a family room with a glorified soda fountain, dedicated to David's interests. That room held a platform for David's train set with a miniature village. Off to one side, between the living room and the dining room, a grand staircase ascended to the second floor where the master bedroom suite, offices, library, and guest rooms, were located. The kitchen, not needing a spectacular view, was on the east side of the dining room. It was outfitted with an equally huge, Sub-Zero refrigerator and freezer, complemented by a matching, stainless steel, six-burner, double oven, gas range. A large farmhouse style table did double duty for food preparation and informal dining. A walk-in pantry was off of the laundry room, as was another door that Hal always kept locked.

Hal showed Ed's openmouthed guests around the first floor of the house. "Mari actually designed the house, inside and out. Her taste is impeccable. Of course we had an architect draw up the plans that incorporated her ideas. The only thing I can take credit for is the location and financing."

"Hal is far too modest. We worked on the place together...a lot of his ideas went into it." Mari added.

"Very nice...very nice indeed." Their modest remarks belied the stunned look on their faces, as well as their intent to gallop back to the church with new gossip. Mari led them upstairs to Ed's guest room suite. Mrs. Baumgartner, a middle aged, buxom nurse plumped up pillows behind Ed to help him sit up. Appearing very small in the vast bed, he received his guests. The notice of his cancer had been given in the church newsletter importuning their members to put Ed in their prayer circle. "Well...we miss you, Ed. How are you getting on?"

"Good to see you guys...I'm doing better than expected, now that you're here. Where is Fatso? I owe him a debt of gratitude for giving me a brighter outlook."

"He was transferred back east to his old job. The new guy they hired to take his place didn't work out...and he had to go right away.

He was deeply saddened when he heard about your having cancer...and wished he could have had the time to see you...but he said his job was done here and he had to go. Good guy...I for one am going to miss him."

"He truly is a man of the Lord...a good-hearted soul." Ed nodded and the rest concurred.

"The view from your room is magnificent...God's paintbrush. Hal has a nice home here. How much does a house like this cost?"

"I don't know...but according to him, not nearly as much as his house in Beverly Hills. It was his great luck that he sold all his Southern California real estate at the height of the bubble just before he moved here...he wasn't hurt by the crash."

"How are you and Mari related to Hal? How did you meet him?"

"Hal is David's biological father. He was Mari's boss when she lived in Southern California and they were engaged at one time. When he learned about David, he moved up here to be near his son. We are a family now. Hal has given me the benefit of his home so that my family can be with me in my last days. He is a good man." Now that Ed knew that the gossip about David had been circulating in the church, he saw no further need for hiding the truth.

"I never would have guessed!" Joel lied. He had heard the scandalous gossip. At first, he was shocked to hear the truth, from Ed's mouth, but somehow, in the way Ed explained it, the taint of immorality disappeared.

"God sends our family to us in many ways." Ed waxed philosophical. "I am blessed that He sent Mari and David to me...and then Hal."

Matthew took out his Bible and began reading it in a soft voice. The effect of it was soothing and it comforted Ed. Then they sang hymns, a capella, their voices blending in harmony.

When they left, they reassured Ed, "We'll keep you in our prayers, Ed...and we will come back to see you." They never came back.

***

Late at night, Hal walked past Ed's room; he was on his way to the kitchen after a night of writing. The door was open, so he popped his head in. Ed was asleep and gently snoring. Then he saw Mrs. Baumgartner do something odd. She was drawing a liquid out of a bottle labeled "alcohol" with a hypodermic needle and transferring it into the morphine ampoules.

"What are you doing?"

Startled, she turned around. "I didn't expect that anyone would be up at this hour."

"What are you doing?"

"Oh...this. I am making sure he will rest comfortably and will be able to sleep. This is not alcohol in this bottle...it is heroin." She stated it with such aplomb, it was as if she had said saline. "I use it on my patients...in very small doses...to help them deal with the pain along with the morphine...the combination seems to have a pleasing effect to give them a kind of euphoria so that they do not suffer at all. As they build up tolerance to it...I increase the heroin and decrease the morphine."

"Is that legal?"

"No...but it *is* moral. As a painkiller, heroin combined with morphine is far superior to morphine alone and is used in many countries. It is called 'diamorphine' and it is used extensively in Britain...but it is illegal in this country." She turned to Hal looking straight into his eyes. "It keeps him from screaming in pain...and it keeps you from hearing those screams for years after he is dead. You asked for the very best nurse. This is the reason I come highly recommended. My patients are terminal...they die as the cancer progresses...I do nothing to hasten that...but I do ease their way into heaven."

Hal did not ask how she got the illicit drug, or anything else. He did not want to question her further. "Thank you, Mrs. Baumgartner. I didn't see a thing."

"You can call me Bummy." She actually smiled.

***

Hal added a mechanized chair to make it easier for Ed to traverse the stairs. They all gathered in the family room to put on their engineer hats and run the miniature railroad. A spirited debate decided which train to run, the passenger or the freight, and what cars to add on, the lumber, cattle, flat cars or what-have-you. The freight train usually won over the passenger; the various types of cars kept changing over the afternoon. The laughter was contagious and even the stoic nurse, Mrs. Baumgartner, was seen to chuckle.

"We need to add people...and luggage carts to our station. That's why we never use the passenger train...we don't have anyone to go anywhere..." Mari pointed out.

"We only have one depot...where are they going?" Hal bantered.

"Like most people in life...in circles..." She countered.

"What are we going to name our town?" Ed asked. "If we are going to have people, we have to name their hometown."

"We can have another depot for them to go to...with another name." Mari suggested.

"The platform has to be expanded so we can build a city. That way they can go from a small town to the city." Hal thought for a minute. "That means we have to add roads and mechanized cars...and a river and bridges...of course the city has to have skyscrapers..."

Mari rolled her eyes. "Ever the visionary! The next thing you know this *house* will become a part of our imaginary world."

"What makes you think it's not?" Hal lifted his hands and made a face like a controlling monster about to attack the city and emitted the typical monster laugh. "Whooooaaaaaahhhhh!"

David was having a great time watching the adults act like children. Some things were a curiosity to him, and he asked what they were used for. "What do the flat cars carry?" David always turned to Hal for answers.

"Sometimes new cars to take to dealers...sometimes fully loaded trucks to piggyback on trains between big cities...I have seen heavy operating equipment...pipes...shipping containers...just about anything."

"What should we put on *our* flat cars?" David looked around the platform for appropriate goods.

"That's a good question...we're going to have to get something we like."

Lupe appeared in the doorway. "Dinner will be ready in fifteen minutes." She announced and then disappeared back into the kitchen.

Still wearing their hats, the children, both big and little, tore themselves away from the train set and trailed out into the dining room. They always tried to dine at the hour when they could watch the sun go down.

At the insistence of Mari, individual salads were already on the table. After Ed gave the blessing, they all dug in and continued the railroad debate. "Since the train is electric...the cars should be too...and the boats on the river..." Hal's enthusiasm knew no bounds.

"Boats? Who said anything about boats? Are we going to have boats?" Mari looked around the table.

Hal shrugged. "Why not? If we're going to have cars on the road...why not boats on the river? David...what do you think? Do you think we should have boats?"

"Yeeaahhh!"

"Well...there you have it from our chief engineer..."

"I make Meester Hal's favorite dinner..." Lupe started bringing in the entrée. "I make chicken fried steak, chili rellenos, and mash potatoes."

Mari put her head in her hand. "Well, at least there's some green in there somewhere."

When her plate was set before her, Mrs. Baumgartner stared at it, with uncertainty. Hal saw her hesitation. "Try it Bummy...I think you'll like it."

"That's what gives me pause...I'm afraid that your dietary heresies are growing on me."

The anarchical, but delicious, fare became a new favorite around the table. Too full to go back to railroading, everyone sat around the table making small talk. Ed began to fidget with a pinched look on his face. Hal sensed he was in pain. "Ed...do you need for Bummy to give you a little something?"

"Yes...I think I do..."

Bummy got up to take Ed upstairs and Hal called her aside. "Load him up as much as you can...I don't want him to be in pain..." He whispered. "...then bring him back down to spend more time with us." Bummy gave a nod that she understood, and then took Ed upstairs.

When they returned, apple crumble with whipped cream was being served. Ed was a little euphoric when he returned, but pain free. He passed on his dessert and while the others were eating, he started to sing. "On a hill far away stood an old rugged cross..." Being accustomed to singing in a group, he only sang the bass harmony of the hymn. Bummy joined in with a passable soprano. To Mari's amazement, Hal started to sing as well. "Where did you learn that?" She whispered.

Hal leaned toward her. "Are you kidding...do you know how many unconstitutional prayers and hymns were performed in my school? In this country you are bombarded with Christianity everywhere. I figure if it makes Ed happy...what's the harm?"

When it was David's bedtime, Hal took him upstairs to read the next chapter of "The Black Stallion" before he went to sleep. When Hal came back down, everyone was still at the table, eschewing TV, or other banal distractions, and focused on being together with Ed.

The peace of the Golan household was suddenly shattered by multiple penetrating projectiles crashing through the plate glass windows. Hal pulled Mari to the floor and shielded her with his body. "What the fuck is going on?" White smoke emanated from the projectiles clouding everyone's vision. "LUPE...BUMMY...QUICK...FOLLOW ME!" Hal carried a shrieking Mari through the kitchen door, followed by Lupe and Bummy. The kitchen being clear of smoke; he hustled his charges to the pantry. "Stay here...I'll be right back."

"Hal...David...GET DAVID!" Mari screamed in terror.

"I'll get him...no one's going to hurt my boy. No matter what you hear...you stay right here. I'll be back for you..."

He went to the door beside the pantry and punched in the code. From behind the door he retrieved a Skorpion, his safari jacket, and two Taurus 24/7 .45 OSS pistols. "Bummy, you're in charge. You do what you have to...to keep Mari and Lupe in here...don't let them leave. He handed Bummy one of the pistols. "Do you know how to use this?"

"Aber natürlich...but of course!" Bummy's expression reassured Hal that she could handle herself in a crisis.

He put on his jacket and slung the Skorpion over his shoulder. "Well then, get ready...if anyone tries to get in here that you don't know...SHOOT THEM!"

"Sofort...you can depend on me!"

Hal ventured back into the dining room. It was filled with smoke all the way through to the living room. Figures dressed in black were barely visible in the fog. Ed was still calmly seated at one corner of the table. Thinking that the intruders would not be able to find their way in the dark, Hal slipped back to the electrical control panel and switched off the main circuit breaker leaving the house in total blackness.

Ed was confused by finding himself in the dark. *Did I just die? Where is the bright light and the face of the Lord?* In his rich basso he started singing the harmony of "Nearer my God to Thee."

Crawling across the kitchen floor, Hal made his way back to the dining room. He heard voices yelling. "UPSTAIRS...GO GET THE KID!" From upstairs David, who was awakened by the crash of broken glass, was crying out in fear. "DADDY! DADDY! WHERE ARE YOU?"

"DAVID! RUN AND HIDE!" Hal moved; his location was given away when he yelled.

One of the kidnappers shouted from upstairs, "I'VE GOT HIM!"

Hal ran back to the circuit breaker and switched the lights back on. Ed looked around him. *Maybe I'm not dead. It was just a power outage. Oh fudgsicles, now I have to reset all the clocks. No...Hal has to reset them!* He became aware of the fog surrounding him once more, as well as the barely visible men in black ski masks. *Are those the Devil's minions?*

One of the men came downstairs holding David under one arm. "I found him wandering in the hallway bawling for his daddy." The boy kicked and wriggled until he saw a bare spot between the sleeve and the glove of the kidnapper. He sank his teeth into his wrist. The man yelped and put the boy down and then passed him over to Dan. "Here...you take the little bastard!"

Hal walked upright into the dining room; not knowing where David was, he did not dare use the Skorpion that was still over his shoulder—but he was holding the .45. "WHOEVER THE FUCK YOU ARE...THINGS ARE ABOUT TO GET GODDAMN REAL IN HERE. WHO HAS MY KID?!"

Dan stepped out of the clearing mist, holding David and a revolver. "We do, Golan, and you can have him back for five million dollars. I suggest you drop your gun..."

Hal scowled and kept the gun in his hand. "Five million? Why didn't you ask for ten? I mean if you are going to die...it may as well be for ten rather than five! Let me tell you how this is going to go down. You let go of my boy and leave...and in spite of wrecking my

603

house...I'll let you live. But if you try to take my boy...you're dead...GOT IT?!"

"You seem to think you are in control here. I'm the one who has your kid...and you are the one who has to pay to get him back..."

"Wrong. You've got nothing. You can't kill me because I am the only man who can get the money. You can't kill my son...because he is not only your bargaining chip...he is your shield. If he goes you have nothing but my bullet in your head...or the needle. Right now, you are willing to gamble that you can get out of here with my son and your life. I'm here to tell you...you will get neither. I promise you...I will kill you." He looked at David. "Don't be afraid, son. When I tell you to run...you run like hell and hide..."

Seconds ticked by in silence. It was a standoff with nobody moving. Then Dan sneered, looked over his shoulder, and motioned with his gun to one of his men. "Tie him up."

The man moved toward Hal and Hal shot him, blowing him backwards. "I'M SHOT! The man screamed and two of his cohorts caught him and dragged him away toward the opening in the blown-out glass window. DAN! GET THE KID AND LET'S GET OUT OF HERE!"

Using David as a shield, they backed away and out the window. Dan gave a parting shot at Ed, wounding him. *I think I may have been shot...but it was like a tap...it didn't hurt. Why didn't it hurt?* He thought for a moment. *Good ol' Bummy...she won't let me hurt.*

"Are you OK, Ed?"

"I think so. I may have been shot...but I'm good. Are we at war, Hal? Did they take David?"

"Yeah...and we're going after them."

Having received his marching orders, Ed stood up. "We are God's sword of vengeance!" He started tramping forward as he sang, "Onward Christian soldiers...marching as to war...with the cross of Jesus...going on before..."

Hal dashed through the opening in the window after them, with the ski-masked men clearly visible in the ground's floodlights. Dan was still backing away across the lawn with his hand holding David fast to him. The others were running, slowed by their wounded accomplice, but the distance was far enough away from David for Hal to risk shooting at them. He cranked off a couple of rounds and they took cover behind lawn furniture, returning fire. They called over a walkie-talkie for their wheelman to drive through the fence into the yard to pick them up. "We're under fire...you have to come in and get us."

John revved the off-road GMC and crashed straight through the fence. He spotted his men and drove behind the lawn furniture, but still in the line of fire, to retrieve them. Scrambling to get under the cover of the vehicle, they sent a barrage of fire at Hal to cover them as they dove into the car. "Go! Go! Go!" one of them urged.

"Shit...I've been hit!" Hal, spun to the ground by the slug, briefly looked at his shoulder and then brought the Skorpion around into position. As the GMC headed straight for him; he unexpectedly stood up and sprayed the it with automatic fire. With bullets hitting the driver, the man slumped over the steering wheel, sending the car out of control and veering toward the edge of the bluff at full speed. It hit a natural outcropping of rocks that turned it over on its side. Skidding on the lawn, through the picket fence, unable to stop, it went over the side. The screams were audible as it plunged to the rocks below and then hit with an explosion that rocked the ground and lit up the night sky.

Hal turned his attention to the man they called Dan, who had been deserted by his partners. He saw Ed marching toward Dan who leveled the revolver at him. "STOP! STOP RIGHT THERE!" Dan shouted at Ed.

Ed kept on coming and was strangely singing, "At the sign of triumph Satan's host doth flee...on, then, Christian soldiers on to victory...Hell's foundations quiver at the shout of praise; brothers lift your voices...loud your anthems raise..."

Dan fired a shot...and then another...and another. Ed kept marching toward him. He fired twice more and then the revolver went click, click, click, as he tried to fire again. As Dan took out a speed loader to reload, Ed fell upon him with his hands at his throat. Hal shouted as loud as he could, DAVID! RUN...RUN LIKE HELL...RUN!" David scrambled free and ran for all he was worth.

***

THE UPSHOT OF IT IS...

It seemed as though every sheriff's unit in Sonoma County was parked around Hal's home, their lights flashing red, white, and blue. Investigators and crime scene analysts roamed the grounds and inside the house. Neighbors stood behind the perimeter of yellow tape gawking at the two dead bodies that could be seen and hearing of those that had perished in a car at the base of the cliff. Sheriff Connors stood at the precipice and looked down at the still burning wreck. "Jesus! That Golan fella must have fought like ten devils to take out all of these fuckers."

"They were trying to kidnap his kid." Deputy Moore shook his head. "If it had been me...and some assholes tried to take my kids...I would have torn them up too. But it's not too often that you see a civilian with that kind of guts...especially a rich one."

"Let's go in and talk to him." They walked to the house, noting the tempered glass broken by the invaders. The spent smoke projectiles lay in place where they landed in the midst of scattered shards. The smell of smoke still hung in the air. A photographer was taking pictures and they tried to avoid disturbing the crime scene. Nevertheless, glass rubble crunched under their feet as they approached.

In the middle of the dining room, Hal sat with his shirt off while paramedics tended to his shoulder. He held David on his lap with his other arm, as Bummy and Lupe looked on. "You were lucky to have a nurse on the scene...you could have lost a lot more blood than you did. It looks like it was a through and through...the bullet did not break any bones...you're going to be fine..." The paramedic assured him. "Are you sure you don't want to go to the hospital?"

"No...I have my nurse here...she's the best. I have my family to look after."

"OK. Be sure to see your doctor in the morning...he will still have to keep an eye on you." Hal nodded, and the emergency medical staff packed up their equipment and left.

Hal looked up as the sheriff waited. "You are?"

"Sheriff Art Connors and this is my deputy, Carson Moore. It looks like you had quite a time out here. World War Three would be my guess."

"Yeah...pretty close to it."

"We understand that the intruders tried to kidnap your boy...and you fought them off..."

"Me and Ed Baker...he's the man in the robe and pajamas..." Hal took a deep breath. "He was killed by one of the kidnapers...who is lying next to him..."

"I hate to bother you, Mr. Golan, but we have a few questions about what went on out here."

"Yes...I understand. Would it be possible for me to come to the station to make a statement? My son is still in shock...and Mrs. Baker is upstairs under sedation. She was hysterical with everything that happened...and she just learned that she lost her husband."

"Sure thing. My people will be out here for a couple of hours. Be sure to ask them if you need anything. Why don't you give me a call when you go into town to have that shoulder looked at? We'll schedule an interview for you..."

***

The house at the beach was boarded up and Hal moved everyone back to the Baker Estate. He called Malone. "I had some serious trouble here and I could use your help."

"What the fuck happened?"

"Some assholes tried to kidnap my son...and they killed Mari's husband."

"Jesus Christ!" Malone sat up. "Give it to me...who did this?"

"Ed and I killed the bastards...they didn't get my boy...but I have no idea who's behind it. I need some bodyguards to protect my family until we can get down to L.A."

"You're coming down here?"

"Yeah...right after Ed's funeral..."

"I want to see you when you get here. How many men do you need?"

"I don't know...five maybe six to work in shifts."

"You got it! They will leave tonight."

"Thanks Malone. Oh...and I will need another bug...mine was confiscated. I told them that it was the kidnappers'."

"I'll send that...and some more toys. Don't worry, kid...I've got ya."

He called Deuce and laid out the kidnaping incident to him in detail. Outraged, Deuce was ready. "I'm on my way up there with some brothers..."

"No need…our friend has his people on the way. I'll see you in a couple of weeks when we move down there. My house is tore up and Mari's house is…too small and too many memories."

"Ummm, ummm, ummm! I never thought her old man would go out like that!"

"Me neither. No one up here knew who I was or what I was worth. It never occurred to me that I needed security…not in this peaceful little burg. There are other people up here who have money…why me?"

"That's a question you need to answer right away."

"I never thought I would say this…but we were safer in L.A."

"I got to say this…you are one bad-assed mother fucker…balls of steel, man, you've got balls of steel…"

"You bet I do when it comes to my kid!"

***

As Hal drove the road to Santa Rosa, he was haunted by the shoot out and the way Ed died. *He was supposed to have a peaceful, painless death…not a violent one.* The visions of Ed's death played in his mind.

Hal held Ed as he was dying. "Do you think that God will forgive me for what I just did?"

"Forgive you for what? You didn't do anything wrong. Ed…you saved our son…"

"Our son…I love that kid. You know, Mari and David…they mean everything to me. You take care of her, Hal…never leave her again. That's what she's afraid of or she would have left me a long time ago for you…"

"No…no…she wouldn't leave you…"

"I know what she said…but you always had her heart. You were right…I am a joke…"

"No…you're not a joke! You're a hero! A better man than I am…"

Ed smiled and then started to cough as his lungs filled with blood. "Do you hear that, Hal? Do you hear the music? It's so beautiful. Listen…it's beautiful…I want to go there…" He went into spasms and then lay still, his open eyes staring at the night sky.

When Hal arrived at the sheriff's station, he was shown to an interview room. The sheriff did not send a subordinate but came down himself to greet him. "This is just a formality, Mr. Golan. Did you have your shoulder looked at?"

"Yes...just before I came here. It appears that I was pretty damned lucky."

"You can say that again. The one perpetrator, that we could identify, had a minor record...for weed...nothing serious...he was from Los Angeles. The others were burned beyond recognition and we are hoping to identify them through dental records...they were probably amateurs, but how they knew to target you is mystery."

"I've been trying to figure that out myself. I was hoping that you would have a line on that."

"Well I would love to tell you that it will come to light...but sometimes these things never do. My advice to you is to take precautions until you find out...if you ever do."

"I've hired security. I would like to get the names of the kidnappers...and have a PI take a crack at it."

"I'll give you a copy of what we have...and I'll let you know as more info comes in."

Connors switched on the video cam. "Just tell me in your own words what happened."

Hal related the incident in detail with a couple of minor changes. "I shot once inside the house...but I don't know if I hit anybody or not...but that is when they started backing off out through the window. Once outside...I shot the kidnapper who was holding that Tommy gun..."

"It's a Skorpion...Czechoslovakian make..."

"Oh. Well...when he was hit, he dropped it on the ground. The others dragged him away and I continued to fire, and I picked up that gun. They returned fire...that is when I was hit. Then someone drove through the fence...and they were able to get into the car. That's when the driver headed straight for me and I let loose with the Tommy...whatever kind of gun that is...the car went out of control and over the side..." Hal paused in reflection. "...it was after that I saw Ed struggling with the kidnapper who had my son...that son of a bitch shot Ed several times until he was out of bullets, but Ed kept coming at him with his bare hands...Ed tried to choke him...but the man struggled away and started reloading. I shouted for my boy to run...and run he did. Then the man reloaded, and Ed struggled for the gun and they fell to the ground...a shot was fired and then Ed got the gun and shot him...point-blank...right between the eyes. I never knew Ed had it in him! But seeing his son in danger must have done something to him..."

"I thought you said the boy was *your* son..."

"He is...and Ed's. I am David's biological father...Ed is his legal father. David loved the both of us and we love him. It's a long story...but it worked well for us because we were a family. Ed was at my home because he had terminal cancer. My home was large enough so all of us could be with him during his last days...and I hired a nurse so he could have the best of care. We were a family..." Hal's face darkened. "I can't get over how he died...so violent and ugly. It wasn't supposed to be that way..."

"That is quite something, Mr. Golan. Is there anything else you want to add?"

"Yes...the upshot of it is...Ed is a hero and he should be remembered that way."

Connors sidled up to his deputy as he watched Hal leave the station. "I think he is a very courageous man...what do you think?"

Deputy Moore had been watching the interview on camera. "His statement matches up with the forensics. I think the case is closed."

***

The small church was packed to overflowing. Ed Baker's schoolmates, co-workers from the Bay Area, family, and friends gathered for the funeral service. With attendance spurred on by the media reporting on the sensational kidnaping attempt, the crowd overflowed into the Fellowship Hall where it could be seen on closed circuit TV.

After the minister finished with his part of the service, Hal took to the pulpit to speak of Ed's heroism. When he concluded, Mari delivered her eulogy for Ed in a quavering voice. "I was once asked about Ed's character...that if you scratched beneath the surface, what would you find? My answer was quickly given and facile. I said, 'an archangel.' I didn't have to think about it twice...he lived it every day. There are those of you who remember Ed as a co-worker at Yarborough Publishing, where he dedicated thirty years of his life...not only to the company...but to his colleagues to whom he extended the warmth of his heart...being a friend in joy and being a friend to those in need.

"My fondest memories of him will always be seeing him among his treasured vines. It was almost as though each row was a home for that family of vines. As he moved from one to another, he labored...as hard as his workers...making sure that his charges, his beloved grapes...that were given to his care by the Lord...were cared for by loving hands. From pruning, to suckering, to phase drop, to netting...veraison and harvest it was Ed's hands and guidance that brought forth each year's crop. He loved the González family as his brethren who labored in the Lord's work.

"Some of you may know that when I met Ed; I was beset by an erroneous set of circumstances and misfortune. I found myself alone and with child. What was to me an insurmountable dilemma...was to Ed his calling to fight for a child's right to life. As a result, Ed always thought that God had sent me to him so that he could have a family. I must agree. When David's biological father learned he had a son...it was Ed who included him into his family. For some of us, living a Christian life...free of challenges...is easy. But God deigned to challenge Ed through tests that many would fail. I think he surpassed God's expectations to the last...sacrificing his life to save the son he loved." Hal helped her from the pulpit to be seated in the front pew.

The long funeral procession trailed through Santa Rosa to the Santa Rosa Memorial Cemetery. Hal stood with one arm around Mari and his other hand resting on his son's shoulder and watched as the coffin was lowered into the ground. He couldn't help but wonder how different it all could have been if he had just granted Mari a few days. That one mistake, made within seconds in one day of his life, cost everyone so much. While he did not want to admit it, because it bordered on the superstitious, he somehow felt that Mari was right; Ed's death was connected to their regaining their happiness in some mystical sense. Was he a sacrificial lamb? He shook the thought from his mind and held David and Mari closer to him.

Traveling the road back, struggling to get to the point where he started, was not a round trip. Striving to rectify his wrong constantly took him to unknown destinations, as he ventured inside his soul, in the world, and into the driving forces of others. What started that day, with ill-considered words, began an odyssey that had been long, arduous, and fraught with trials by fire. The realization of everything he had lost and everything he had won overpowered Hal.

***

Hal parked at a supermarket, got a basket, and walked inside. Continuing on, he left the basket in one of the aisles and exited out the back door. He waited and looked impatiently around. One of Malone's taxis drove into the parking lot to pick him up. The drive to Stony Malone's took several freeways in a circuitous route, ending at the back door of the gentlemen's club. He saw Johnny setting up and gave him the L.A. salute.

Johnny replied in kind with the addition of the catcall "Hey...if it isn't Super Jew!"

Hal called out, "You better believe it, baby!" as he grabbed his crotch.

The men on Malone's door were new and they frisked him, like in the old days, before showing Hal into Malone's office. "He was carrying this, boss." The man held up Hal's snub nose .38.

Malone sat at his desk. "Give it back to him...what are you guys doing? This is Hal! Go get him a drink...an Old Fashioned. How the hell are you doing kid...it's good to see you."

Hal holstered his gun. He noticed that Manny was sitting at the end of Malone's desk, but did not get up to greet him. *There is something going on...Malone wanted to meet me here...and Manny has a bug up his ass about something.* Hal held out his hands. "Manny? Don't you love me anymore?"

"Yeah...sure." Manny was ambiguous.

The rebuff was palpable, and Hal was going to get to the bottom of it. "OK guys...what's up? All of a sudden I got BO or something? What's the deal?"

"Naahh. One of Manny's soldiers is missing...and he thinks it may have something to do with you...and that fiasco you had up at your place."

"What the fuck? How can it have anything to do with me...?"

"Just sit down and listen. What I am going to say is probably going to piss you off...but we did what we did with the best of intentions...and we think it is connected to what happened at your place somehow."

Hal sat down and stared at Malone and then his eyes wandered to Manny. "What happened at my place? I love you guys...I trust you...how can anything like kidnapping my kid be connected to you?"

Malone looked at Manny. "That's what I said." Malone held out his hands. "But now, I think it just might be."

Hal's face hardened. "Go on."

"You know...you did a lot for us, kid...went out of your way...saved our lives..."

Manny snorted and Hal called him out. "I didn't see you wave me and Deuce off when you were pinned down in Arizona...I didn't hear you say, 'no thanks guys, we got this.' We drove hundreds of miles just to make sure your dumb ass was safe. I'm not expecting you to kiss my ass...but not being acknowledged by you...?" Hal shook his head.

"Everybody calm down...and be civil. It's nothing we can't work out." Malone looked like he was running out of patience with Manny. "Look, kid...what happened was this...I wanted to do something nice for you...after what you did for us...saving our lives..." Malone shot Manny a look. "...and you made it possible for Valiant Medical to be one of the fastest rising companies in the country. I wanted to see you happy...and I knew there was only one thing in life you wanted. Mari! So, I thought about it to see if there was anything that I could do to make her turn to you...and there was. The only obstacle in your way appeared to be her husband...sooooo...we thought about what we could do to eliminate him in a way that could not be connected to you...so we called a friend...who contacted someone...who gave him...a dose of cancer..."

Hal jumped to his feet. "WHAT THE FUCK! Are you telling me that Ed got cancer because of something you did? Is that even possible? How...why...?"

"Sit down, kid. Yes...it is possible...but that is not the most interesting part when it comes to the kidnapping. You see...in order for us to get to Ed...we had to send someone up there to snoop around...find out all about him...because giving a guy cancer is not like giving him a case of the clap...you have to know his every move...and the inside guy has to know when he has an opportune situation. We had to send this soldier to investigate Ed...learn his routine..." Malone glared at Manny. "...that was *all* he was supposed to do! But in doing his job...he ran across information on you...he banged the law office receptionist and got a copy of your custody file. Up to this point...that's all we know. But that guy is missing..."

Hal's voice went very low. "Would his name happen to be Dan?"

Manny stiffened and there was a charged pause. Malone continued. "Yes...yes it would."

Hal took a folded manila envelope out of his suit pocket and tossed it on the desk in front of Malone. "That's the police report on the kidnapping...there is an autopsy picture of the one kidnapper that was still photogenic. The rest were burnt to a crisp...they are still trying to identify them through dental records. The gang with him called him 'Dan' and he appeared to be the leader."

Malone took out the papers, looked at the picture, and tossed it in front of Manny. "That's him all right. Did you know him...or know anything about him?"

"They had ski masks on...I didn't even know what he looked like until I saw that autopsy picture. The cops said he was from L.A. I was going to ask you guys to look into it for me."

Manny quietly inquired. "His mother is going to want to know how he died. Did you kill him?"

Hal's lips tightened and his voice was ominously low. "He died because he invaded my house and tried to take my kid. He needlessly shot Ed...and took my kid out of my house! This is how it went down." He gave the full description of the incident to the very end. "Ed put the gun right up to his head and pulled the trigger. Ed didn't die from the cancer you gave him...he died a hero." Hal sat back and pointed a finger at Manny. "When I walked in here you cut your eyes at me and had an attitude like your guy's coming up missing had something to do with me. I am pissed! Your guy is dead because YOU couldn't control him...he went *rogue* on your ass...and now you are thrashing about looking for someone to blame. Well, HE is to blame...he's dead because he couldn't follow instructions!"

"Oh...I think it runs deeper than that...doesn't it, Manny." Malone pushed the intercom button. "Snuffy...get in here."

A tall affable man walked in. "Yeah, boss?"

"How often did Dan fail to report in?"

Snuffy looked puzzled. "He still hasn't reported in."

"I'm talking about since he first got back from Santa Rosa."

Snuffy gave a somewhat disapproving frown. "Dan was always skimpy on reporting...he would go for days at a time...sometimes a whole week. Manny knows about it...he said it was OK."

"Manny..." Malone looked annoyed. "...you've been doinking Dan's mother."

"No I haven't boss..."

"It wasn't a question...it was a statement of fact. Why would you tell me a dooky? You've either been letting her kid run wild...or you put him up to it..." Malone watched Manny squirm. "...which is it?"

"Boss...you don't believe that I would..."

"You know...I always wondered who killed Dan, Sr. at the back door that day...and now I know it was you. Back when Dan was killed...someone tried to deliver a DVD to me, the recorded surveillance of the back of this place by the cops. Luckily, one of my guys on the force was assigned to the stakeout...so he took it and tried to have it delivered to me. Somehow it went missing. If it had not been for Hal asking me to look into the kidnapping...I never would have found out about it. When I checked my source for Hal...he asked me why I never got back to him about the DVD. He just now learned that I had not received it. At my request, he traced the delivery and found it was ultimately put into your hands instead of mine. How did that happen? It showed that you were the one who shot Dan just before the gunman came in. You were the logical choice to take my place if something tragic happened to me. But Hal got in the way and ruined your scheme...and you were just biding your time. It has always been Hal that foiled your plans. I mean when you don't acknowledge when a man has saved your life...what could be more important? Was the warehouse shootout your setup too?"

"How can you say that? They were shooting at me, too..." Manny countered.

"Were they? Because of Hal...we never got down to the brass tacks of who they were actually going to kill once they got the drop on us." Malone's brows knitted. "I know you resented my favoritism for Hal...and that I look upon him like a son. So, while you were waiting for your next opportunity...for your next chance to get at me...you thought you could go behind my back and kidnap his son...my *grandson!*"

"Boss...NO...it's not like that." Manny's eyes grew wide.

"No? Tell me...what was it like."

"Dan did this on his own. I knew nothing about it..."

"Are you telling me that one of your men went rogue and you knew nothing about it? In my book...that is just as bad." Malone pulled a .44 Magnum from his desk drawer and, without hesitation, blasted him. "Snuffy go call for cleanup...and while you are at it...have my offices remodeled...and close the door behind you."

"Jesus Malone...it was Manny behind the kidnapping?" Hal stared down at Manny's lifeless body. "That *everything* was Manny all a long?"

"Of course...a soldier doesn't go rogue without his boss's blessing. Manny had to have known and been a part of it. I guess he saw an opportunity to take you for some money...and he guessed correctly that I would never have sanctioned it. It was Manny who went rogue and had a takeover deal with New York. I only found out about the rest the other day when I went to see my contact inside the police force...after you called. If it hadn't been for you...I wouldn't have found out about the other stuff."

Hal was relieved. "Now that I know who was behind it and this was just a one off...a rogue operation...I'm breathing a lot easier."

"So, you killed Dan's whole crew they sent after your kid. Remind me not to fuck with you!" He laughed. Then he leaned forward on his elbows quietly contemplating Hal. "You know...in my estimation...Mari's husband didn't strike me as the type to shoot a man. He always sounded so milquetoast to me." Malone gave Hal a shrewd look. "OK...Manny's gone now and we're alone...you can't bullshit a bullshitter. You killed Dan...didn't you."

Hal sat back only half surprised at Malone's perception. In his mind's eye he replayed the video of that night at the beach house.

Dan fired a shot–and then another–and another. Ed kept marching toward him. He fired twice more and then the revolver went click, click, click, as he tried to fire again. As Dan took out a speed loader to reload the revolver, Ed fell upon him with his hands at his throat. Hal shouted as loud as he could, "DAVID! RUN...RUN LIKE HELL...RUN!" David scrambled free and ran for all he was worth toward the house.

Hal ran to Ed who was still choking Dan into unconsciousness. "Ed...Ed...you've got to grab the gun. Ed took the gun. Hal could see that Dan had loaded the gun and the cartridges were in place, but the cylinder was open. While Ed held the gun, Hal lifted Dan's hand and used it to slam the loaded cylinder into place. "Ed, point the gun at his head and pull the trigger…"

"I can't…Hal…I'm dying…my immortal soul."

"Then point the gun out toward the ocean and shoot it." Ed did as he was told. Hal took Ed's hand, still clasping the revolver, and guided it back to point at Dan's head. Just then Dan's eyes flickered open to see the two men, both of David's fathers, looming over him. Hal bared his teeth. "I keep my promises, mother fucker." With his finger over Ed's, Hal pulled the trigger leaving a smoking hole in the ski mask.

"Come on, kid, you can tell me. You killed Dan, didn't you?"

Hal smiled at Malone. "You're goddamned right I did!"

***

EPILOGUE

Hal, Deuce, and Big sat at their table in Benny's bar. Big drank his coffee while Deuce and Hal shared a pitcher of beer. "Goddamn! That's one hell of a fuckin' story. Remind me not to let you play outside until you grow up! Man, I can't let you out of my sight!" Deuce stared wide-eyed at Hal. "I'm glad to see that you and Mari got together again..."

"Yeah. My mother hasn't stopped grinning since she started planning our wedding. I had to tell her to hurry it up...because Mari's pregnant."

"You mean I not only get to be best man...I'm going to be the Godfather too!"

"Yeah...San Francisco did the trick! I can't thank you enough."

"San Francisco? What happened in San Francisco? I left my heart in San Franciscooo...oooh ...oooh" Big sang and then turned from Hal to Deuce.

"I flew up to talk some sense to Mari because she trusted me...and talked her into seeing Hal. I don't know what he said to her...but our boy here talked her into bed...and bingo...just like that she's pregnant." Deuce gave himself a congratulatory smile. "I knew it...I knew it all along. She never got over you!"

"How are you and Lo-Lo getting along...or dare I ask...inquire or probe?" Big wrinkled his brow.

"We ain't a 'we' anymore. She came back from Monaco for a while to see me. She told me I was the best man she had ever known...and that she may even love me...but she's marrying some Swiss chocolatier...a billionaire...ain't that ironic...she's bitter-sweet chocolate alright."

"After she broke up your marriage?" Big was incredulous.

"She really didn't break up my marriage. I did that to myself...and I'm glad I did. I'm back with Wanda now..."

"Nooooo!" Hal and Big said in unison.

"Yeah. She asked me to come over...you know to look after the boys...some shit they did...and she said I should stay the night. I could use the guest room. She came into the room..."

Wanda carried two cups of hot milk into the guest room. "I could hear you were still awake, so I made you a cup of hot milk with

618

brandy in it to help you sleep."

"That's nice of you, Wanda...thank you..." Deuce took the cup. She started to leave when he stopped her. "Why don't you sit down with me while you drink your cup?"

"Alright." She sat on the other side of the king-sized bed. "You know it's funny...how much nicer we are to each other now that we are divorced."

"Yeah...I guess I started out thinking of you more as a responsibility than a wife...you know with you being pregnant and all." His brow furrowed. "Tell me, Wanda...did you ever love me?"

She gave a short chuckle. "Now you ask." She rolled her eyes. "Yeah...I loved you, Deuce...you know...the way only a young girl can love...totally. I was so innocent. You said you thought I trapped you. I had a long time to think about us after we split up...and I don't think that I really set out to trap you...it's just that all I could see, then, was that you were leaving me, and I did so desperately love you. I never had no real idea about pregnancy...that if I let you make love to me that I could get pregnant. It was never a real thing...that it could actually happen...I just wanted to be with you...that's all I was thinking about." Her eyes grew distant. "And then when I found out I was going to have a baby...oh Lord...I was scared and happy at the same time.

"Then everything was a blur...it seemed that the pregnancy and the baby drove you away from me while you were working all the time. The responsibility of the baby...day and night...you were gone at work...I was alone with the baby...all of that drove romantic notions right out of my head...and then bam...I was pregnant again. Then I just cried...diapers...baby bottles...endless laundry...no one to talk to...I lost friends...and everybody thought I should be happy. Tedium, boredom, and crying babies were my constant companions...and you...you were so engrossed in trying to make a living that I don't think you even saw me...and I know I lost sight of you. You were right. By the time we divorced...we were strangers."

"I never knew it was like that for you...I never, ever thought about it. I did think that you should just be happy..."

"Well...the boys are getting bigger now...and they really do need their father...I just..."

Deuce stretched out his arm to her. "Come here and sit with me."

619

She moved over to sit next to him, and he put his arm around her. "I'm sorry I didn't see what was happening with you. You must have felt very lonely...I thought you just didn't care..."

"At some point...I guess I did fall out of love with you and I did take you for granted. It really shook me when I saw you with that woman. It should have woke me up...but I was just too angry...to ask myself the hard questions...I felt betrayed. I thought you would have married her by now. What happened?"

"She flew off to Monaco and found herself a billionaire."

Wanda laughed. "No Shit?"

"No shit...he's a chocolatier and I guess he wanted a big chocolate doll for his collection."

"You know that salon of hers...it is the 'in' place to go. Everybody talks about it. Now I'm kind of sorry that I threw champagne at her."

"I'm not. It was the most emotional and caring thing you had done for me in years." He gave her shoulder a squeeze. "Let's not talk about her...she's gone now and she's happy...let's try to be happy too."

"Do you think we can be?"

"We can try."

"I was about to ask you if you could move back here...you can have this room...the boys need you...they want their daddy a lot these days..."

"You really want me here?"

"I wouldn't mind."

"Alright."

"So, I moved back home and within a week...Wanda comes tippin' down the hall to my bedroom...and crawls in my bed. The next thing you know...she's fuckin' me like a mad woman! She ain't never fucked me like that before in her life! All these years she's been holdin' back. Now...she just let loose! And she brings me little things...and she rubs my back...I'm the king of my castle." Deuce smiled.

"When are you going to remarry?" Hal asked.

"I'm not going to marry that woman! I like things fine just the way they are. You guys already got me clear of her financially. I'm not going to mess that up. She gave me a BJ the other day and I didn't even have to ask for it. We get along fine...and the boys are happy.

Shit...she even bakes me cookies."

"Do you think she loves you?" Hal studied his friend.

Deuce raised both of his shoulders and his mouth twisted in a wry smile. "I don't know. She hasn't said anything to me about it. I guess we're just used to each other. But I'm glad she told me that at first she did...when we were still in our teens...I never knew that."

***

Due to his serious illness, the prison gave Marvin compassionate leave and he was to be sent to Vivian's home, over Graham's objections. "Madam, my dear Vivian...I overstep my bounds...I cannot allow you to be subjected to that man's vulgarities again. I implore you; do not take him into your care."

"You called me 'Vivian.'"

"Please forgive me...I am distraught beyond my limits. I care very deeply what happens to you. I could barely tolerate seeing how he treated you when you were his wife. Now that you are free of him...it would be unforgivable for me to stand by and say nothing."

She walked toward him. "You called me 'my dear Vivian.'" She stood before him. "Could it be that you have stepped away from being my butler again? That you are once again seeing me as a woman...your woman?"

"It is not my place as your butler to say so."

"Could it be your place as a man?" The look of utter helplessness and hopelessness crossed Graham's face. She could see he wanted to act as a man but was locked in his position as her professional servant. She stood on tiptoe and kissed him on the lips. His reaction was immediate as he enfolded her in an embrace and fervently returned her kiss leaving Vivian breathless. "Oh my...we're going to have to do something about this." She gave their state of affairs a short-lived deliberation. "Graham...go up to my room. I will be up shortly so we may discuss this further."

By the time Vivian emerged from her room, much had been settled. Graham was to call her "Vivian," he was to visit her room every night, and he was put in charge of what was to be done with Marvin. Graham saw to it that Marvin was sent elsewhere.

***

"Mr. Golan, what your father has is acute liver failure. This was caused primarily by Hepatitis B in combination with Hepatitis D

621

and probably more strains of hepatitis. Unfortunately, the disease is rampant among prison populations. Moreover, for a number of reasons...especially your father's age, he does not qualify for a liver transplant under the King's College Criteria. He is terminal and will die within a few days or weeks."

Hal tried to keep a forlorn expression on his face, when the only reason he came to see his father was for a sweet moment of revenge. "I understand."

The doctor showed Hal, and his little family, into Marvin's room and then left. Hal, Mari, and David stared down at Marvin who lay in a hospital bed near death. Marvin gazed up at them. "Hal..."

Not one word did Hal say. He took Mari into his arms and kissed her. He picked up David and showed him to Marvin and then set David back down again. Then he gave Marvin a big grin. Lifting both hands in the air he showed him the middle finger on each hand and shook them up and down. Then he gathered his little family and left.

***

Vivian's fall garden was augmented with flowers from Hawaii. Mari was every inch the stunning bride that Vivian had dreamt of and she did not miss the opportunity to flaunt her new daughter-in-law in her friends' faces. Deuce stood by Hal's side as best man and Lo-Lo flew back from Monaco to be Mari's matron of honor. David was the ring bearer. Mari's gown, a Brian creation, was ivory satin overlaid with lace and pearls. Under the chuppah Hal and Mari were wed. At the end of the wedding, Hal stomped the ceremonial glass and crushed it. Vivian wept throughout.

Steven and Brian held hands as Brian openly wept. They both longed for the day when they could celebrate their committed relationship in marriage. "I knew that in spite of everything...they would be married one day. He made an awful mistake that broke his heart as well as hers...but he never let her go. That is so beautiful." Brian blew his nose into his handkerchief and sighed while tears of happiness flowed.

Big showed up with a beautiful woman who, despite her age, still retained the spirit of youth. "Lily...this is the couple I told you about.

I am proud to say I was instrumental in their getting together and finding happiness."

She regarded him with adoration. "My darling...you spread happiness everywhere you go. You just can't help yourself..." She puckered her lips to receive the kiss that she knew he would give her. "Romance is your métier..."

On the way to the wedding reception, Hal noticed a blind man sitting on the groom's side, whose caretaker looked strangely like Snuffy. As he passed them Hal whispered, "Glad to see you could make it."

The reception started out with Deuce giving a toast to the couple. "Let us raise our glasses to Hal and Mari. To Hal, my brother, my friend, and my knight in honor...I love you bro...and I prayed this day would come. You always thought that Mari was too good for you...more beauty than you had the right to touch...more love than you deserved...more goodness than you could fathom. And you were right...she is too good for you...but thank your lucky stars she doesn't see it that way. She thinks you're perfect! Mari...please take good care of this lug...he loves you more than you can know...but he needs to be looked after...housebroken..." He reached for an open box. "Here is a strong leash...a wild animal whip...a pair of handcuffs; I know those will come in handy..." He lifted out a black bra. "...how'd that get in there...?" he tossed it back. "Seriously...Mari, he only has one heart and that belongs to you. He only has one mind and that is yours as well. Hal you fought hard to get back the girl you lost...you never gave up...you are a man above men, a mensch." He held up his glass. "Respect, bro!" All the guests repeated, "Respect."

As the reception went on, it was time for the bride and groom to have the first dance. With the orchestra playing, Steven stepped to the microphone and in his superb tenor voice sang "All I ask of you." As Hal and Mari danced to the song; the lyrics poignantly reflected their struggle and a longing for their new life together. "Hal...you are everything to me. I will love you forever...for all my life." Mari kissed him behind his ear.

As the best man and matron of honor joined them, Deuce whispered to Lo-Lo, "I didn't know you were going to be here."

"I knew *you* would be..."

"Is your husband here with you?"

"No." She looked up at Deuce with languid eyes. When their dance was over, they disappeared.

The traditional customs were honored at the reception; the crowd picked up the couple in their chairs and lifted them above their heads. They danced the Hora around the ballroom to "Hava Nagila" in celebration. Next came the tossing of the garter, the tossing of the bouquet until Hal couldn't take any more. He tossed Mari over his shoulder and ran upstairs. "Get dressed...I'm taking you out of here."

Mari changed into the best "Brian" dress of her trousseau, and kissing Vivian and David goodbye, they were off amid a hail of rice to the decorated car. Puffed with pride in his wife, Hal opened the door for Mari, assisting her inside. He closed the door, gave a salute to his guests, and jumped into the driver's seat. Revving the engine, they were off. Once alone inside the car, they broke out laughing. "You know...I didn't think I wanted a big wedding...but I must say I loved it."

"Yeah...I think the one who loved it the most was ma...she happily wept through it all."

"Did you see David's face...he was so proud. It was like everything had been set right in his world. You know...I think he wanted you to be his father all along...he loves you so. Now, I think this makes it official for him."

"It is official...we are a family." Hal pulled over and took out a blindfold. "Here...I want you to put this on...where I'm taking you is a surprise."

"Oh...come on..." she protested.

"No...really...it will ruin the surprise if you look."

"OK." She tied it over her eyes.

"No peeking."

"Honest...I can't see a thing."

He took off driving for miles and like a five-year-old Mari kept asking him, "Are we there, yet?"

When they arrived at their destination, Hal lifted her out of the car and carried her into what she sensed was indoors. She could smell flowers—plumeria. He took off her blindfold and she found herself in their old apartment. Plumerias were everywhere. The beloved table was in the living room already set for two. Dinner was already prepared and the champagne chilled.

"I thought we could have 'table night' once more."

***